THREE *NEW YORK TIMES* BESTSELLING AUTHORS

LINDA LAEL MILLER

BARBARA DELINSKY

TESS GERRITSEN

Heatwave

Three Complete Novels

HARLEQUIN-83402 $9.99 U.S./$11.99 CAN.

ISBN 0-373-83402-0

9 780373 834020

50999

Praise for these
New York Times
bestselling authors

Linda Lael Miller

Named the "Most Outstanding
Writer of Sensual Romance."
—*Romantic Times Magazine*

"Her characters come alive and walk right off
the pages and into your heart."
—*Rendezvous*

Barbara Delinsky

"When you care to read the very best,
the name of Barbara Delinsky should come
immediately to mind."
—*Rave Reviews*

"One of this generation's most gifted writers of
contemporary women's fiction."
—*Affaire de Coeur*

Tess Gerritsen

"Tess Gerritsen brings us action, adventure
and compelling romance."
—*Romantic Times Magazine*

"Gerritsen's romances are thrillers from
beginning to end."
—*Portland Press Herald*

New York Times bestselling author **Linda Lael Miller** started writing at age ten and has made a name for herself in both contemporary and historical romance. Her bold and innovative style has made her a favorite among readers. Named by *Romantic Times Magazine* "The Most Outstanding Writer of Sensual Romance," Linda Lael Miller never disappoints.

Barbara Delinsky was born and raised in suburban Boston. She worked as a researcher, photographer and reporter before turning to writing full-time in 1980. With more than fifty novels to her credit, she is truly one of the shining stars of contemporary romance fiction! This *New York Times* bestselling author has received numerous awards and honors, and her books have appeared on many bestseller lists. With over 12 million copies of Barbara's books in print worldwide, her appeal is definitely universal.

When **Tess Gerritsen** was a third-year medical resident, one of her patients presented her with a bag of romance novels. By the second chapter of the first book she was hooked. She has been reading and writing romances ever since—and using her medical knowledge to add to her intricate and dramatic stories. A *New York Times* bestselling author, she is also writing mainstream medical thrillers with much success.

LINDA LAEL MILLER
BARBARA DELINSKY
TESS GERRITSEN

Heatwave

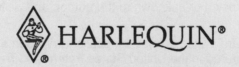

HARLEQUIN®

TORONTO • NEW YORK • LONDON
AMSTERDAM • PARIS • SYDNEY • HAMBURG
STOCKHOLM • ATHENS • TOKYO • MILAN • MADRID
PRAGUE • WARSAW • BUDAPEST • AUCKLAND

HARLEQUIN BOOKS
225 Duncan Mill Road, Don Mills,
Ontario, Canada M3B 3K9

ISBN 0-373-83402-0

HEATWAVE

Copyright © 1998 by Harlequin Books S.A.

PART OF THE BARGAIN
Copyright © 1985 by Linda Lael Miller

THE DREAM UNFOLDS
Copyright © 1990 by Barbara Delinsky

UNDER THE KNIFE
Copyright © 1990 by Terry Gerritsen

CONTENTS

PART OF THE BARGAIN

Linda Lael Miller

For Laura Mast
Thank you for believing and being proud.

Chapter 1

The landing gear made an unsettling *ka-thump* sound as it snapped back into place under the small private airplane. Libby Kincaid swallowed her misgivings and tried not to look at the stony, impassive face of the pilot. If he didn't say anything, she wouldn't have to say anything either, and they might get through the short flight to the Circle Bar B ranch without engaging in one of their world-class shouting matches.

It was a pity, Libby thought, that at the ages of thirty-one and thirty-three, respectively, she and Jess still could not communicate on an adult level.

Pondering this, Libby looked down at the ground below and was dizzied by its passing as they swept over the small airport at Kalispell, Montana, and banked eastward, toward the Flathead River. Trees so green that they had a blue cast carpeted the majestic mountains rimming the valley.

Womanhood being what it is, Libby couldn't resist watching Jess Barlow surreptitiously out of the corner of her eye. He was like a lean, powerful mountain lion waiting to pounce, even though he kept his attention strictly on the controls and the thin air traffic sharing the big Montana sky that spring morning. His eyes were hidden behind a pair of mirrored sunglasses, but Libby knew that they would be dark with the animosity that had marked their relationship for years.

She looked away again, trying to concentrate on the river, which coursed beneath them like a dusty-jade ribbon woven into the fabric of a giant tapestry. Behind those mirrored glasses, Libby knew Jess's eyes were the exact same shade of green as that untamed waterway below.

"So," he said suddenly, gruffly, "New York wasn't all the two-hour TV movies make it out to be."

Libby sighed, closed her eyes in a bid for patience and then opened them again. She wasn't going to miss one bit of that fabulous view—not when her heart had been hungering for it for several bittersweet years.

Besides, Jess had been to New York dozens of times on corporation business. Who did he think he was fooling?

"New York was all right," she said, in the most inflamatory tone she could manage. *Except that Jonathan died,* chided a tiny, ruthless voice in her mind. *Except for that nasty divorce from Aaron.* "Nothing to write home about," she added aloud, realizing her blunder too late.

"So your dad noticed," drawled Jess in an undertone that would have been savage if it hadn't been so carefully modulated. "Every day, when the mail came, he fell on it like it was manna from heaven. He never stopped hoping—I'll give him that."

"Dad knows I hate to write letters," she retorted defensively. But Jess had made his mark, all the same—Libby felt real pain, picturing her father flipping eagerly through the mail and trying to hide his disappointment when there was nothing from his only daughter.

"Funny—that's not what Stace tells me."

Libby bridled at this remark, but she kept her composure. Jess was trying to trap her into making some foolish statement about his older brother, no doubt, one that he could twist out of shape and hold over her head. She raised her chin and choked back the indignant diatribe aching in her throat.

The mirrored sunglasses glinted in the sun as Jess turned to look at her. His powerful shoulders were taut beneath the blue cotton fabric of his workshirt, and his jawline was formidably hard.

"Leave Cathy and Stace alone, Libby," he warned with blunt savagery. "They've had a lot of problems lately, and if you do anything to make the situation worse, I'll see that you regret it. Do I make myself clear?"

Libby would have done almost anything to escape his scrutiny just then, short of thrusting open the door of that small four-passenger Cessna and jumping out, but her choices were undeniably limited. Trembling just a little, she turned away and fixed her attention on the ground again.

Dear heaven, did Jess really think that she would interfere in Cathy's marriage—or any other, for that matter? Cathy was her *cousin*—they'd been raised like sisters!

With a sigh, Libby faced the fact that there was every chance that Jess and a lot of other people would believe she had been involved with Stacey Barlowe. There had, after all, been that exchange of letters, and Stace had even visited her a few times, in the thick of her traumatic divorce, though in actuality he had been in the city on business.

"Libby?" prodded Jess sharply, when the silence grew too long to suit him.

"I'm not planning to vamp your brother!" she snapped. "Could we just drop this, please?"

To her relief and surprise, Jess turned his concentration on piloting the plane. His suntanned jaw worked with suppressed annoyance, but he didn't speak again.

The timbered land below began to give way to occasional patches of prairie—cattle country. Soon they would be landing on the small airstrip serving the prosperous 150,000-acre Circle Bar B, owned by Jess's father and overseen, for the most part, by Libby's.

Libby had grown up on the Circle Bar B, just as Jess had, and her mother, like his, was buried there. Even though she couldn't call the ranch home in the legal sense of the word, it was *still* home to her, and she had every right to go there—especially now, when she needed its beauty and peace and practical routines so desperately.

The airplane began to descend, jolting Libby out of her reflective state. Beside her, Jess guided the craft skillfully toward the paved landing strip stretched out before them.

The landing gear came down with a sharp snap, and Libby drew in her breath in preparation. The wheels of the plane screeched and grabbed as they made contact with the asphalt, and then the Cessna was rolling smoothly along the ground.

When it came to a full stop, Libby wrenched at her seat belt, anxious to put as much distance as possible between herself and Jess Barlowe. But his hand closed over her left wrist in a steel-hard grasp. "Remember, Lib—these people aren't the sophisticated if-it-feels-good-do-it types you're used to. No games."

Games. *Games?* Hot color surged into Libby's face and pounded there in rhythm with the furious beat of her heart. "Let go of me, you bastard!" she breathed.

If anything, Jess's grip tightened. "I'll be watching you," he warned, and then he flung Libby's wrist from his hand and turned away to push open the door on his side and leap nimbly to the ground.

Libby was still tugging impotently at the handle on her own door when her father strode over, climbed deftly onto the wing and opened it for her. She felt such a surge of love and relief at the sight of him that she cried out softly and flung herself into his arms, nearly sending both of them tumbling to the hard ground.

Ken Kincaid hadn't changed in the years since Libby had seen him last—he was still the same handsome, rangy cowboy that she remembered so well, though his hair, while as thick as ever, was iron-gray now, and the limp he'd acquired in a long-ago rodeo accident was more pronounced.

Once they were clear of the plane, he held his daughter at arm's length, laughed gruffly, and then pulled her close again. Over his shoulder she saw Jess drag her suitcases and portable drawing board out of the Cessna's luggage compartment and fling them unceremoniously into the back of a mud-speckled station wagon.

Nothing if not perceptive, Ken Kincaid turned slightly, assessed Senator Cleave Barlowe's second son, and grinned. There was mischief in his bright blue eyes when he faced Libby again. "Rough trip?"

Libby's throat tightened unaccountably, and she wished she could explain *how* rough. She was still stung by Jess's insulting opinion of her morality, but how could she tell her father that? "You know that it's always rough going where Jess and I are concerned," she said.

Her father's brows lifted speculatively as Jess got behind the wheel of the station wagon and sped away without so much as a curt nod or a halfhearted so-long. "You two'd better watch out," he mused. "If you ever stop butting heads, you might find out you like each other."

"Now, that," replied Libby with dispatch, "is a horrid thought if I've ever heard one. Tell me, Dad—how have you been?"

He draped one wiry arm over her shoulders and guided her in the direction of a late-model pickup truck. The door on the driver's side was emblazoned with the words "CIRCLE BAR B RANCH," and Yosemite Sam glared from both the mud flaps shielding the rear tires. "Never mind how I've been, dumplin'. How've *you* been?"

Libby felt some of the tension drain from her as her father opened the door on the passenger side of the truck and helped her inside. She longed to shed her expensive tailored linen suit for jeans and a T-shirt, and— oh, heaven—her sneakers would be a welcome change from the high heels she was wearing. "I'll be okay," she said in tones that were a bit too energetically cheerful.

Ken climbed behind the wheel and tossed one searching, worried look in his daughter's direction. "Cathy's waiting over at the house, to help you settle in and all that. I was hoping we could talk..."

Libby reached out and patted her father's work-worn hand, resting now on the gearshift knob. "We can talk tonight. Anyway, we've got lots of time."

Ken started the truck's powerful engine, but his wise blue eyes had not strayed from his daughter's face. "You'll stay here awhile, then?" he asked hopefully.

Libby nodded, but she suddenly found that she had to look away. "As long as you'll let me, Dad."

The truck was moving now, jolting and rattling over the rough ranch roads with a pleasantly familiar vigor. "I expected you before this," he said. "Lib..."

She turned an imploring look on him. "Later, Dad—okay? Could we please talk about the heavy stuff later?"

Ken swept off his old cowboy hat and ran a practiced arm across his forehead. "Later it is, dumplin'." Graciously he changed the subject. "Been reading your comic strip in the funny papers, and it seems like every kid in town's wearing one of those T-shirts you designed."

Libby smiled; her career as a syndicated cartoonist was certainly safe conversational ground. And it had all started right here, on this ranch, when she'd sent away the coupon printed on a matchbook and begun taking art lessons by mail. After that, she'd won a scholarship to a prestigious college, graduated, and made her mark, not in portraits or commercial design, as some of her friends had, but in cartooning. Her character, Liberated Lizzie, a cave-girl with modern ideas, had created something of a sensation and was now featured not only in the Sunday newspapers but also on T-shirts, greeting cards, coffee mugs and calendars. There was a deal pending with a poster company, and Libby's bank balance was fat with the advance payment for a projected book.

She would have to work hard to fulfill her obligations—there was the weekly cartoon strip to do, of course, and the panels for the book had to be sketched in. She hoped that between these tasks and the endless allure of the Circle Bar B, she might be able to turn her thoughts from Jonathan and the mess she'd made of her personal life.

"Career-wise, I'm doing fine," Libby said aloud, as much to herself as to her father. "I don't suppose I could use the sunporch for a studio?"

Ken laughed. "Cathy's been working for a month to get it ready, and I had some of the boys put in a skylight. All you've got to do is set up your gear."

Impulsively Libby leaned over and kissed her father's beard-stubbled cheek. "I love you!"

"Good," he retorted. "A husband you can dump—a daddy you're pretty well stuck with."

The word "husband" jarred Libby a little, bringing an unwelcome image of Aaron into her mind as it did, and she didn't speak again until the house came into sight.

Originally the main ranch house, the structure set aside for the general foreman was an enormous, drafty place with plenty of Victorian scrollwork, gabled windows and porches. It overlooked a sizable spring-fed pond and boasted its own sheltering copse of evergreens and cottonwood trees.

The truck lurched a little as Ken brought it to a stop in the gravel driveway, and through the windshield Libby could see glimmering patches of the silver-blue sparkle that was the pond. She longed to hurry there now, kick off her shoes on the grassy bank and ruin her stockings wading in the cold, clear water.

But her father was getting out of the truck, and Cathy Barlowe, Libby's cousin and cherished friend, was dashing down the driveway, her pretty face alight with greeting.

Libby laughed and stood waiting beside the pickup truck, her arms out wide.

After an energetic hug had been exchanged, Cathy drew back in Libby's arms and lifted a graceful hand to sign the words: "I've missed you so much!"

"And I've missed you," Libby signed back, though she spoke the words aloud, too.

Cathy's green eyes sparkled. "You haven't forgotten how to sign!" she enthused, bringing both hands into play now. She had been deaf since childhood, but she communicated so skillfully that Libby often forgot that they weren't conversing verbally. "Have you been practicing?"

She had. Signing had been a game for her and Jonathan to play during the long, difficult hours she'd spent at his hospital bedside. Libby nodded and tears of love and pride gathered in her dark blue eyes as she surveyed her cousin—physically, she and Cathy bore no resemblance to each other at all.

Cathy was petite, her eyes wide, mischievous emeralds, her hair a glistening profusion of copper and chestnut and gold that reached almost to her waist. Libby was of medium height, and her silver-blond hair fell just short of her shoulders.

"I'll be back later," Ken said quietly, signing the words as he spoke so that Cathy could understand too. "You two have plenty to say to each other, it looks like."

Cathy nodded and smiled, but there was something sad trembling behind the joy in her green eyes, something that made Libby want to scurry back to the truck and beg to be driven back to the airstrip. From there she could fly to Kalispell and catch a connecting flight to Denver and then New York....

Good Lord—surely Jess hadn't been so heartless as to share his ridiculous suspicions with Cathy!

The interior of the house was cool and airy, and Libby followed along behind Cathy, her thoughts and feelings in an incomprehensible tangle. She was glad to be home, no doubt about it. She'd yearned for the quiet sanity of this place almost from the moment of leaving it.

On the other hand, she wasn't certain that she'd been wise to come back. Jess obviously intended to make her feel less than welcome, and although she had certainly never been intimately involved with Stacey Barlowe, Cathy's husband, sometimes her feelings toward him weren't all that clearly defined.

Unlike his younger brother, Stace was a warm, outgoing person, and through the shattering events of the past year and a half, he had been a tender and steadfast friend. Adrift in waters of confusion and grief, Libby had told Stacey things that she had never breathed to another living soul, and it was true that, as Jess had so bitterly pointed out, she had written to the man when she couldn't bring herself to contact her own father.

But she wasn't in love with Stace, Libby told herself firmly. She had always looked up to him, that was all—like an older brother. Maybe she'd become a little too dependent on him in the bargain, but that didn't mean she cared for him in a romantic way, did it?

She sighed, and Cathy turned to look at her pensively, almost as though she had heard the sound. That was impossible, of course, but Cathy was as perceptive as anyone Libby had ever known, and she often *felt* sounds.

"Glad to be home?" the deaf woman inquired, gesturing gently.

Libby didn't miss the tremor in her cousin's hands, but she forced a weary smile to her face and nodded in answer to the question.

Suddenly Cathy's eyes were sparkling again, and she caught Libby's hand in her own and tugged her through an archway and into the glassed-in sunporch that overlooked the pond.

Libby drew in a swift, delighted breath. There was indeed a skylight in the roof—a big one. A drawing table had been set up in the best light the room offered, along with a lamp for night work, and there were flowering plants hanging from the exposed beams in the ceiling. The old wicker furniture that had been stored in the attic for as long as Libby could remember had been painted a dazzling white and bedecked with gay floral-print cushions. Small rugs in complementary shades of pink and green had been scattered about randomly, and there was even a shelving unit built into the wall behind the art table.

"Wow!" cried Libby, overwhelmed, her arms spread out wide in a gesture of wonder. "Cathy, you missed your calling! You should have been an interior decorator."

Though Libby hadn't signed the words, her cousin had read them from her lips. Cathy's green eyes shifted quickly from Libby's face, and she lowered her head. "Instead of what?" she motioned sadly. "Instead of Stacey's wife?"

Libby felt as though she'd been slapped, but she recovered quickly enough to catch one hand under Cathy's chin and force her head up. "Exactly what do you mean by that?" she demanded, and she was never certain afterward whether she had signed the words, shouted them, or simply thought them.

Cathy shrugged in a miserable attempt at nonchalance, and one tear slid down her cheek. "He went to see you in New York," she challenged, her hands moving quickly now, almost angrily. "You wrote him letters!"

"Cathy, it wasn't what you think—"

"Wasn't it?"

Libby was furious and wounded, and she stomped one foot in frustration. "Of course it wasn't! Do you really think I would do a thing like that? Do you think Stacey would? He *loves* you!" *And so does Jess,* she lamented in silence, without knowing why that should matter.

Stubbornly Cathy averted her eyes again and shoved her hands into the pockets of her lightweight cotton jacket—a sure signal that as far as she was concerned, the conversation was over.

In desperation, Libby reached out and caught her cousin's shoulders in her hands, only to be swiftly rebuffed by an eloquent shrug. She watched, stricken to silence, as Cathy turned and hurried out of the sunporch-

turned-studio and into the kitchen beyond. Just a moment later the back
door slammed with a finality that made Libby ache through and through

She ducked her head and bit her lower lip to keep the tears back. That,
too, was something she had learned during Jonathan's final confinement
in a children's hospital.

Just then, Jess Barlowe filled the studio doorway. Libby was aware of
him in all her strained senses.

He set down her suitcases and drawing board with an unsympathetic
thump. "I see you're spreading joy and good cheer as usual," he drawled
in acid tones. "What, pray tell, was *that* all about?"

Libby was infuriated, and she glared at him, her hands resting on her
trim rounded hips. "As if you didn't know, you heartless bastard! How
could you be so mean...so thoughtless..."

The fiery green eyes raked Libby's travel-rumpled form with scorn.
Ignoring her aborted question, he offered one of his own. "Did you think
your affair with my brother was a secret, princess?"

Libby was fairly choking on her rage and her pain. "What affair, dammit?" she shouted. "We didn't *have* an affair!"

"That isn't what Stacey says," replied Jess with impervious savagery.

Libby felt the high color that had been pounding in her face seep away.
"What?"

"Stace is wildly in love with you, to hear him tell it. You need him
and he needs you, and to hell with minor stumbling blocks like his wife!"

Libby's knees weakened and she groped blindly for the stool at her art
table and then sank onto it. "My God..."

Jess's jawline was tight with brutal annoyance. "Spare me the theatrics,
princess—I know why you came back here. Dammit, *don't you have a
soul?"*

Libby's throat worked painfully, but her mind simply refused to form
words for her to utter.

Jess crossed the room like a mountain panther, terrifying in his grace
and prowess, and caught both her wrists in a furious, inescapable grasp.
With his other hand he captured Libby's chin.

"Listen to me, you predatory little witch, and listen well," he hissed,
his jade eyes hard, his flesh pale beneath his deep rancher's tan. "Cathy
is good and decent and she loves my brother, though I can't for the life
of me think why she condescends to do so. And I'll be *damned* if I'll
stand by and watch you and Stacey turn her inside out! Do you understand
me?"

Tears of helpless fury and outraged honor burned like fire in Libby's
eyes, but she could neither speak nor move. She could only stare into the
frightening face looming only inches from her own. It was a devil's face.

When Jess's tightening grasp on her chin made it clear that he would
have an answer of some sort, no matter what, Libby managed a small,
frantic nod.

Apparently satisfied, Jess released her with such suddenness that she nearly lost her balance and slipped off the stool.

Then he whirled away from her, his broad back taut, one powerful hand running through his obsidian hair in a typical gesture of frustration. "Damn you for ever coming back here," he said in a voice no less vicious for its softness.

"No problem," Libby said with great effort. "I'll leave."

Jess turned toward her again, this time with an ominous leisure, and his eyes scalded Libby's face, the hollow of her throat, the firm roundness of her high breasts. "It's too late," he said.

Still dazed, Libby sank back against the edge of the drawing table, sighed and covered her eyes with one hand. "Okay," she began with hard-won, shaky reason, "why is that?"

Jess had stalked to the windows; his back was a barrier between them again, and he was looking out at the pond. Libby longed to sprout claws and tear him to quivering shreds.

"Stacey has the bit in his teeth," he said at length, his voice low, speculative. "Wherever you went, he'd follow."

Since Libby didn't believe that Stacey had declared himself to be in love with her, she didn't believe that there was any danger of his following her away from the Circle Bar B, either. "You're crazy," she said.

Jess faced her quickly, some scathing retort brewing in his eyes, but whatever he had meant to say was lost as Ken strode into the room and demanded, "What the hell's going on in here? I just found Cathy running up the road in tears!"

"Ask your daughter!" Jess bit out. "Thanks to her, Cathy has just gotten *started* shedding tears!"

Libby could bear no more; she was like a wild creature goaded to madness, and she flung herself bodily at Jess Barlowe, just as she had in her childhood, fists flying. She would have attacked him gladly if her father hadn't caught hold of her around the waist and forcibly restrained her.

Jess raked her with one last contemptuous look and moved calmly in the direction of the door. "You ought to tame that little spitfire, Ken," he commented in passing. "One of these days she's going to hurt somebody."

Libby trembled in her father's hold, stung by his double meaning, and gave one senseless shriek of fury. This brought a mocking chuckle from a disappearing Jess and caused Ken to turn her firmly to face him.

"Good Lord, Libby, what's the *matter* with you?"

Libby drew a deep, steadying breath and tried to quiet the raging ten-year-old within her, the child that Jess had always been able to infuriate. "I hate Jess Barlow," she said flatly. "I hate him."

"Why?" Ken broke in, and he didn't look angry anymore. Just honestly puzzled.

"If you knew what he's been saying about me—"

"If it's the same as what Stacey's been mouthing off about, I reckon I do."

Libby stepped back, stunned. "What?"

Ken Kincaid sighed, and suddenly all his fifty-two years showed clearly in his face. "Stacey and Cathy have been having trouble the last year or so. Now he's telling everybody who'll listen that it's over between him and Cathy and he wants you."

"I don't believe it! I—"

"I wanted to warn you, Lib, but you'd been through so much, between losing the boy and then falling out with your husband after that. I thought you needed to be home, but I knew you wouldn't come near the place if you had any idea what was going on."

Libby's chin trembled, and she searched her father's honest, weathered face anxiously. "I...I haven't been fooling around with C-Cathy's husband, Dad."

He smiled gently. "I know that, Lib—knew it all along. Just never mind Jess and all the rest of them—if you don't run away, this thing'll blow over."

Libby swallowed, thinking of Cathy and the pain she had to be feeling. The betrayal. "I can't stay here if Cathy is going to be hurt."

Ken touched her cheek with a work-worn finger. "Cathy doesn't really believe the rumors, Libby—think about it. Why would she work so hard to fix a studio up for you if she did? Why would she be waiting here to see you again?"

"But she was crying just now, Dad! And she as much as accused me of carrying on with her husband!"

"She's been hurt by what's been said, and Stacey's been acting like a spoiled kid. Honey, Cathy's just testing the waters, trying to find out where you stand. You can't leave her now, because except for Stace, there's nobody she needs more."

Despite the fact that all her instincts warned her to put the Circle Bar B behind her as soon as humanly possible, Libby saw the sense in her father's words. As incredible as it seemed, Cathy would need her—if for nothing else than to lay those wretched rumors to rest once and for all.

"These things Stacey's been saying—surely he didn't unload them on Cathy?"

Ken sighed. "I don't think he'd be that low, Libby. But you know how it is with Cathy, how she always knows the score."

Libby shook her head distractedly. "Somebody told her, Dad—and I think I know who it was."

There was disbelief in Ken's discerning blue eyes, and in his voice, too. "*Jess?* Now, wait a minute..."

Jess.

Libby couldn't remember a time when she had gotten along well with him, but she'd been sure that he cared deeply for Cathy. Hadn't he been the one to insist that Stace and Libby learn signing, as he had, so that everyone could talk to the frightened, confused little girl who couldn't hear? Hadn't he gifted Cathy with cherished bullfrogs and clumsily made valentines and even taken her to the high-school prom?

How could Jess, of all people, be the one to hurt Cathy, when he knew as well as anyone how badly she'd been hurt by her handicap and the rejection of her own parents? How?

Libby had no answer for any of these questions. She knew only that she had separate scores to settle with both the Barlowe brothers.

And settle them she would.

Chapter 2

Libby sat at the end of the rickety swimming dock, bare feet dangling, shoulders slumped, her gaze fixed on the shimmering waters of the pond. The lines of her long, slender legs were accentuated, rather than disguised, by the old blue jeans she wore. A white eyelet suntop sheltered shapely breasts and a trim stomach and left the rest of her upper body bare.

Jess Barlow studied her in silence, feeling things that were at wide variance with his personal opinion of the woman. He was certain that he hated Libby, but something inside him wanted, nonetheless, to touch her, to comfort her, to know the scent and texture of her skin.

A reluctant grin tilted one corner of his mouth. One tug at the top of that white eyelet and...

Jess caught his skittering thoughts, marshaled them back into stern order. As innocent and vulnerable as Libby Kincaid looked at the moment, she was a viper, willing to betray her own cousin to get what she wanted.

Jess imagined Libby naked, her glorious breasts free and welcoming. But the man in his mental scenario was not himself—it was Stacey. The thought lay sour in Jess's mind.

"Did you come to apologize, by any chance?"

The question so startled Jess that he flinched; he had not noticed that Libby had turned around and seen him, so caught up had he been in the vision of her giving herself to his brother.

He scowled, as much to recover his wits as to oppose her. It was and always had been his nature to oppose Libby Kincaid, the way electricity opposes water, and it annoyed him that, for all his travels and his education, he didn't know why.

"Why would I want to do that?" he shot back, more ruffled by her presence than he ever would have admitted.

"Maybe because you were a complete ass," she replied in tones as sunny as the big sky stretched out above them.

Jess lifted his hands to his hips and stood fast against whatever it was that was pulling him toward her. *I want to make love to you,* he thought, and the truth of that ground in his spirit as well as in his loins.

There was pain in Libby's navy-blue eyes, as well as a cautious mischief. "Well?" she prodded.

Jess found that while he could keep himself from going to her, he could not turn away. Maybe her net reached farther than he'd thought. Maybe, like Stacey and that idiot in New York, he was already caught in it.

"I'm not here to apologize," he said coldly.

"Then why?" she asked with chiming sweetness.

He wondered if she knew what that shoulderless blouse of hers was doing to him. Damn. He hadn't been this tongue-tied since the night of his fifteenth birthday, when Ginny Hillerman had announced that she would show him hers if he would show her his.

Libby's eyes were laughing at him. "Jess?"

"Is your dad here?" he threw out in gruff desperation.

One shapely, gossamer eyebrow arched. "You know perfectly well that he isn't. If Dad were home, his pickup truck would be parked in the driveway."

Against his will, Jess grinned. His taut shoulders rose in a shrug. The shadows of cottonwood leaves moved on the old wooden dock, forming a mystical path—a path that led to Libby Kincaid.

She patted the sun-warmed wood beside her. "Come and sit down."

Before Jess could stop himself, he was striding along that small wharf, sinking down to sit beside Libby and dangle his booted feet over the sparkling water. He was never entirely certain what sorcery made him ask what he did.

"What happened to your marriage, Libby?"

The pain he had glimpsed before leapt in her eyes and then faded away again, subdued. "Are you trying to start another fight?"

Jerry shook his head. "No," he answered quietly, "I really want to know."

She looked away from him, gnawing at her lower lip with her front teeth. All around them were ranch sounds—birds conferring in the trees, leaves rustling in the wind, the clear pond water lapping at the mossy pilings of the dock. But no sound came from Libby.

On an impulse, Jess touched her mouth with the tip of one index finger. Water and electricity—the analogy came back to him with a numbing jolt.

"Stop that," he barked, to cover his reactions.

Libby ceased chewing at her lip and stared at him with wide eyes.

Again he saw the shadow of that nameless, shifting ache inside her. "Stop what?" she wanted to know.

Stop making me want to hold you, he thought. *Stop making me want to tuck your hair back behind your ears and tell you that everything will be all right.* "Stop biting your lip!" he snapped aloud.

"I'm sorry!" Libby snapped back, her eyes shooting indigo sparks.

Jess sighed and again spoke involuntarily. "Why did you leave your husband, Libby?"

The question jarred them both: Libby paled a little and tried to scramble to her feet; Jess caught her elbow in one hand and pulled her down again.

"Was it because of Stacey?"

She was livid. "No!"

"Someone else?"

Tears sprang up in Libby's dark lashes and made then spiky. She wrenched free of his hand but made no move to rise again and run away. "Sure!" she gasped. "'If it feels good, do it'—that's my motto! By God, I *live* by those words!"

"Shut up," Jess said in a gentle voice.

Incredibly, she fell against him, wept into the shoulder of his blue cotton workshirt. And it was not a delicate, calculating sort of weeping— it was a noisy grief.

Jess drew her close and held her, broken on the shoals of what she was feeling even though he did not know its name. "I'm sorry," he said hoarsely.

Libby trembled beneath his arm and wailed like a wounded calf. The sound solidified into a word usually reserved for stubborn horses and income-tax audits.

Jess laughed and, for a reason he would never understand, kissed her forehead. "I love it when you flatter me," he teased.

Miraculously, Libby laughed too. But when she tilted her head back to look up at him, and he saw the tear streaks on her beautiful, defiant face, something within him, something that had always been disjointed, was wrenched painfully back into place.

He bent his head and touched his lips to hers, gently, in question. She stiffened, but then, at the cautious bidding of his tongue, her lips parted slightly and her body relaxed against his.

Jess pressed Libby backward until she lay prone on the shifting dock, the kiss unbroken. As she responded to that kiss, it seemed that the sparkling water-light of the pond danced around them both in huge, shimmering chips, that they were floating inside some cosmic prism.

His hand went to the full roundness of her left breast. Beneath his palm and the thin layer of white eyelet, he felt the nipple grow taut in that singular invitation to passion.

Through the back of his shirt, Jess was warmed by the heat of the spring sun and the tender weight of Libby's hands. He left her mouth to trail soft kisses over her chin, along the sweet, scented lines of her neck.

All the while, he expected her to stiffen again, to thrust him away with her hands and some indignant—and no doubt colorful—outburst. Instead, she was pliant and yielding beneath him.

Enthralled, he dared more and drew downward on the uppermost ruffle of her suntop. Still she did not protest.

Libby arched her back and a low, whimpering sound came from her throat as Jess bared her to the soft spring breeze and the fire of his gaze.

Her breasts were heavy golden-white globes, and their pale rose crests stiffened as Jess perused them. When he offered a whisper-soft kiss to one, Libby moaned and the other peak pouted prettily at his choice. He went to it, soothed it to fury with his tongue.

Libby gave a soft, lusty cry, shuddered and caught her hands in his hair, drawing him closer. He needed more of her and positioned his body accordingly, careful not to let his full weight come to bear. Then, for a few dizzying moments, he took suckle at the straining fount of her breast.

Recovering himself partially, Jess pulled her hands from his hair, gripped them at the wrists, pressed them down above her head in gentle restraint.

Her succulent breasts bore his assessment proudly, rising and falling with the meter of her breathing.

Jess forced himself to meet Libby's eyes. "This is me," he reminded her gruffly. "Jess."

"I know," she whispered, making no move to free her imprisoned hands.

Jess lowered his head, tormented one delectable nipple by drawing at it with his lips. "This is real, Libby," he said, circling the morsel with just the tip of his tongue now. "It's important that you realize that."

"I do...oh, God...Jess, *Jess.*"

Reluctantly he left the feast to search her face with disbelieving eyes. "Don't you want me to stop?"

A delicate shade of rose sifted over her high cheekbones. Her hands still stretched above her, her eyes closed, she shook her head.

Jess went back to the breasts that so bewitched him, nipped at their peaks with gentle teeth. "Do you...know how many...times I've wanted...to do this?"

The answer was a soft, strangled cry.

He limited himself to one nipple, worked its surrendering peak into a sweet fervor with his lips and his tongue. "So...many...times. My God, Libby...you're so beautiful..."

Her words were as halting as his had been. "What's happening to us? We h-hate each other."

Jess laughed and began kissing his way softly down over her rib cage, her smooth, firm stomach. The snap on her jeans gave way easily—and was echoed by the sound of car doors slamming in the area of the house.

Instantly the spell was broken. Color surged into Libby's face and she bolted upright, nearly thrusting Jess off the end of the dock in her efforts to wrench on the discarded suntop and close the fastening of her jeans.

"Broad daylight..." she muttered distractedly, talking more to herself than to Jess.

"Lib!" yelled a jovial masculine voice, approaching fast. "Libby?"

Stacey. The voice belonged to Stacey.

Sudden fierce anger surged, white-hot, through Jess's aching, bedazzled system. Standing up, not caring that his thwarted passion still strained against his jeans, visible to anyone who might take the trouble to look, he glared down at Libby and rasped, "I guess reinforcements have arrived."

She gave a primitive, protesting little cry and shot to her feet, her ink-blue eyes flashing with anger and hurt. Before Jess could brace himself, her hands came to his chest like small battering rams and pushed him easily off the end of the dock.

The jolting cold of that spring-fed pond was welcome balm to Jess's passion-heated flesh, if not his pride. When he surfaced and grasped the end of the dock in both hands, he knew there would be no physical evidence that he and Libby had been doing anything other than fighting.

Libby ached with embarrassment as Stacey and Senator Barlowe made their way down over the slight hillside that separated the backyard from the pond.

The older man cast one mischievously baleful look at his younger son, who was lifting himself indignantly onto the dock, and chuckled, "I see things are the same as always," he said.

Libby managed a shaky smile. *Not quite,* she thought, her body remembering the delicious dance Jess's hard frame had choreographed for it. "Hello, Senator," she said, rising on tiptoe to kiss his cheek.

"Welcome home," he replied with gruff affection. Then his wise eyes shifted past her to rest again on Jess. "It's a little cold yet for a swim, isn't it, son?"

Jess's hair hung in dripping ebony strands around his face, and his eyes were jade-green flares, avoiding his father to scald Libby's lips, her throat, her still-pulsing breasts. "We'll finish our...discussion later," he said.

Libby's blood boiled up over her stomach and her breasts to glow in her face. "I wouldn't count on that!"

"I would," Jess replied with a smile that was at once tender and evil. And then, without so much as a word to his father and brother, he walked away.

"What the hell did he mean by that?" barked Stacey, red in the face.

The look Libby gave the boyishly handsome, caramel-eyed man beside her was hardly friendly. "You've got some tall explaining to do, Stacey Barlowe," she said.

The senator, a tall, attractive man with hair as gray as Ken's, cleared his throat in the way of those who have practiced diplomacy long and well. "I believe I'll go up to the house and see if Ken's got any beer on hand," he said. A moment later he was off, following Jess's soggy path.

Libby straightened her shoulders and calmly slapped Stacey across the face. "How dare you?" she raged, her words strangled in her effort to modulate them.

Stacey reddened again, ran one hand through his fashionably cut wheat-colored hair. He turned, as if to follow his father. "I could use a beer myself," he said in distracted, evasive tones.

"Oh, no you don't!" Libby cried, grasping his arm and holding on. The rich leather of his jacket was smooth under her hand. "Don't you *dare* walk away from me, Stacey—not until you explain why you've been lying about me!"

"I haven't been lying!" he protested, his hands on his hips now, his expensively clad body blocking the base of the dock as he faced her.

"You have! You've been telling everyone that I...that we..."

"That we've been doing what you and my brother were doing a few minutes ago?"

If Stacey had shoved Libby into the water, she couldn't have been more shocked. A furious retort rose to the back of her throat but would go no further.

Stacey's tarnished-gold eyes flashed. "Jess was making love to you, wasn't he?"

"What if he was?" managed Libby after a painful struggle with her vocal cords. "It certainly wouldn't be any of your business, would it?"

"Yes, it would. I love you, Libby."

"You love *Cathy!*"

Stacey shook his head. "No. Not anymore."

"Don't say that," Libby pleaded, suddenly deflated. "Oh, Stacey, don't. Don't do this..."

His hands came to her shoulders, fierce and strong. The topaz fever in his eyes made Libby wonder if he was sane. "I love you, Libby Kincaid," he vowed softly but ferociously, "and I mean to have you."

Libby retreated a step, stunned, shaking her head. The reality of this situation was so different from what she had imagined it would be. In her thoughts, Stacey had laughed when she confronted him, ruffled her hair in that familiar brotherly way of old, and said that it was all a mistake. That he loved Cathy, wanted Cathy, and couldn't anyone around here take a joke?

But here he was declaring himself in a way that was unsettlingly serious.

Libby took another step backward. "Stacey, I need to be here, where my dad is. Where things are familiar and comfortable. Please...don't force me to leave."

Stacey smiled. "There is no point in leaving, Lib. If you do, I'll be right behind you."

She shivered. "You've lost your mind!"

But Stacey looked entirely sane as he shook his handsome head and wedged his hands into the pockets of his jacket. "Just my heart," he said. "Corny, isn't it?"

"It's worse than corny. Stacey, you're unbalanced or something. You're fantasizing. There was never anything between us—"

"No?" The word was crooned.

"No! You need help."

His face had all the innocence of an altar boy's. "If I'm insane, darlin', it's something you could cure."

Libby resisted an urge to slap him again. She wanted to race into the house, but he was still barring her way, so that she could not leave the dock without brushing against him. "Stay away from me, Stacey," she said as he advanced toward her. "I mean it—stay away from me!"

"I can't, Libby."

The sincerity in his voice was chilling; for the first time in all the years she'd known Stacey Barlowe, Libby was afraid of him. Discretion kept her from screaming, but just barely.

Stacey paled, as though he'd read her thoughts. "Don't look at me like that, Libby—I wouldn't hurt you under any circumstances. And I'm not crazy."

She lifted her chin. "Let me by, Stacey. I want to go into the house."

He tilted his head back, sighed, met her eyes again. "I've frightened you, and I'm sorry. I didn't mean to do that."

Libby couldn't speak. Despite his rational, settling words, she was sick with the knowledge that he meant to pursue her.

"You must know," he said softly, "how good it could be for us. You needed me in New York, Libby, and now I need you."

The third voice, from the base of the hillside, was to Libby as a life preserver to a drowning person. "Let her pass, Stacey."

Libby looked up quickly to see Jess, unlikely rescuer that he was. His hair was towel-rumpled and his jeans clung to muscular thighs—thighs that only minutes ago had pressed against her own in a demand as old as time. His manner was calm as he buttoned a shirt, probably borrowed from Ken, over his broad chest.

Stacey shrugged affably and walked past his brother without a word of argument.

Watching him go, Libby went weak with relief. A lump rose in her throat as she forced herself to meet Jess's gaze. "You were right," she muttered miserably. "You were *right.*"

Jess was watching her much the way a mountain cat would watch a cornered rabbit. For the briefest moment there was a look of tenderness in the green eyes, but then his expression turned hard and a muscle flexed in his jaw. "I trust the welcome-home party has been scheduled for later—after Cathy has been tucked into her bed, for instance?"

Libby gaped at him, appalled. Had he interceded only to torment her himself?

Jess's eyes were contemptuous as they swept over her. "What's the matter, Lib? Couldn't you bring yourself to tell your married lover that the welcoming had already been taken care of?"

Rage went through Libby's body like an electric current surging into a wire. "You don't seriously think that I would...that I was—"

"You even managed to be alone with him. Tell me, Lib—how did you get rid of my father?"

"G-get rid..." Libby stopped, tears of shock and mortification aching in her throat and burning behind her eyes. She drew a deep, audible breath, trying to assemble herself, to think clearly.

But the whole world seemed to be tilting and swirling like some out-of-control carnival ride. When Libby closed her eyes against the sensation, she swayed dangerously and would probably have fallen if Jess hadn't reached her in a few strides and caught her shoulders in his hands.

"Libby..." he said, and there was anger in the sound, but there was a hollow quality, too—one that Libby couldn't find a name for.

Her knees were trembling. Too much, it was all too much. Jonathan's death, the ugly divorce, the trouble that Stacey had caused with his misplaced affections—all of those things weighed on her, but none were so crushing as the blatant contempt of this man. It was apparent to Libby now that the lovemaking they had almost shared, so new and beautiful to her, had been some sort of cruel joke to Jess.

"How could you?" she choked out. "Oh, Jess, how could you?"

His face was grim, seeming to float in a shimmering mist. Instead of answering, Jess lifted Libby into his arms and carried her up the little hill toward the house.

She didn't remember reaching the back door.

"What the devil happened on that dock today, Jess?" Cleave Barlowe demanded, hands grasping the edge of his desk.

His younger son stood at the mahogany bar, his shoulders stiff, his attention carefully fixed on the glass of straight Scotch he meant to consume. "Why don't you ask Stacey?"

"Goddammit, I'm asking *you!*" barked Cleave. "Ken's mad as hell, and I don't blame him—that girl of his was shattered!"

Girl. The word caught in Jess's beleaguered mind. He remembered the way Libby had responded to him, meeting his passion with her own, welcoming the greed he'd shown at her breasts. Had it not been for the arrival of his father and brother, he would have possessed her completely within minutes. "She's no 'girl,'" he said, still aching to bury himself in the depths of her.

The senator swore roundly. "What did you say to her, Jess?" he pressed, once the spate of unpoliticianly profanity had passed.

Jess lowered his head. He'd meant the things he'd said to Libby, and he couldn't, in all honesty, have taken them back. But he knew some of what she'd been through in New York, her trysts with Stacey notwithstanding, and he was ashamed of the way he'd goaded her. She had come home to heal—the look in her eyes had told him that much—and instead of respecting that, he had made things more difficult for her.

Never one to be thwarted by silence, no matter how eloquent, Senator Barlowe persisted. "Dammit, Jess, I might expect this kind of thing from Stacey, but I thought you had more sense! You were harassing Libby about these blasted rumors your brother has been spreading, weren't you?"

Jess sighed, set aside the drink he had yet to take a sip from, and faced his angry father. "Yes," he said.

"Why?"

Stubbornly, Jess refused to answer. He took an interest in the imposing oak desk where his father sat, the heavy draperies that kept out the sun, the carved ivory of the fireplace.

"All right, mulehead," Cleave muttered furiously, "don't talk! Don't explain! And don't go near Ken Kincaid's daughter again, damn you. That man's the best foreman I've ever had and if he gets riled and quits because of you, Jess, you and I are going to come to time!"

Jess almost smiled, though he didn't quite dare. Not too many years before the phrase "come to time," when used by his father, had presaged a session in the woodshed. He wondered what it meant now that he was thirty-three years old, a member of the Montana State Bar Association, and a full partner in the family corporation. "I care about Cathy," he said evenly. "What was I supposed to do—stand by and watch Libby and Stace grind her up into emotional hamburger?"

Cleave gave a heavy sigh and sank into the richly upholstered swivel chair behind his desk. "I love Cathy too," he said at length, "but Stacey's behind this whole mess, not Libby. Dammit, that woman has been through hell from what Ken says—she was married to a man who slept in every bed but his own, and she had to watch her nine-year-old stepson die by inches. Now she comes home looking for a little peace, and what does she get? Trouble!"

Jess lowered his head, turned away—ostensibly to take up his glass of Scotch. He'd known about the bad marriage—Ken had cussed the day Aaron Strand was born often enough—but he hadn't heard about the little boy. *My God, he hadn't known about the boy.*

"Maybe Strand couldn't sleep in his own bed," he said, urged on by some ugliness that had surfaced inside him since Libby's return. "Maybe Stacey was already in it."

"Enough!" boomed the senator in a voice that had made presidents tremble in their shoes. "I like Libby and I'm not going to listen to any more of this, either from you or from your brother! Do I make myself clear?"

"Abundantly clear," replied Jess, realizing that the Scotch was in his hand now and feeling honor-bound to take at least one gulp of the stuff. The taste was reminiscent of scorched rubber, but since the liquor seemed to quiet the raging demons in his mind, he finished the drink and poured another.

He fully intended to get drunk. It was something he hadn't done since high school, but it suddenly seemed appealing. Maybe he would stop hardening every time he thought of Libby, stop craving her.

Too, after the things he'd said to her that afternoon by the pond, he didn't want to remain sober any longer than necessary. "What did you mean," he ventured, after downing his fourth drink, "when you said Libby had to watch her stepson die?"

Papers rustled at the big desk behind him. "Stacey says the child had leukemia."

Jess poured another drink and closed his eyes. *Oh, Libby,* he thought, *I'm sorry. My God, I'm sorry.* "I guess Stacey would know," he said aloud, with bitterness.

There was a short, thunderous silence. Jess expected his father to explode into one of his famous tirades, was genuinely surprised when the man sighed instead. Still, his words dropped on Jess's mind like a bomb.

"The firewater isn't going to change the fact that you love Libby Kincaid, Jess," he said reasonably. "Making her life and your own miserable isn't going to change it either."

Love Libby Kincaid? Impossible. The strange needs possessing him now were rooted in his libido, not his heart. Once he'd had her—and have her he would, or go crazy—her hold on him would be broken. "I've never loved a woman in my life," he said.

"Fool. You've loved one woman—Libby—since you were seven years old. Exactly seven years old, in fact."

Jess turned, studying his father quizzically. "What the hell are you talking about?"

"Your seventh birthday," recalled Cleave, his eyes far away. "Your mother and I gave you a pony. First time you saw Libby Kincaid, you were out of that saddle and helping her into it."

The memory burst, full-blown, into Jess's mind. A pinto pony. The new foreman arriving. The little girl with dark blue eyes and hair the color of winter moonlight.

He'd spent the whole afternoon squiring Libby around the yard, content to walk while she rode.

"What do you suppose Ken would say if I went over there and asked to see his daughter?" Jess asked.

"I imagine he'd shoot you, after today."

"I imagine he would. But I think I'll risk it."

"You've made enough trouble for one day," argued Cleave, taking obvious note of his son's inebriated state. "Libby needs time, Jess. She needs to be close to Ken. If you're smart, you'll leave her alone until she has a chance to get her emotional bearings again."

Jess didn't want his father to be right, not in this instance, anyway, but he knew that he was. Much as he wanted to go to Libby and try to make things right, the fact was that he was the last person in the world she needed or wanted to see.

"Better?"

Libby smiled at Ken as she came into the kitchen, freshly showered and wrapped in the cozy, familiar chenille robe she'd found in the back of her closet. "Lots better," she answered softly.

Her father was standing at the kitchen stove stirring something in the blackened cast-iron skillet.

Libby scuffled to the table and sat down. It was good to be home, so good. Why hadn't she come sooner? "Whatever you're cooking there smells good," she said.

Ken beamed. In his jeans and his western shirt, he looked out of place at that stove. He should, Libby decided fancifully, have been crouching at some campfire on the range, stirring beans in a blue enamel pot. "This here's my world-famous red-devil sauce," he grinned, "for which I am known and respected."

Libby laughed, and tears of homecoming filled her eyes. She went to her father and hugged him, needing to be a little girl again, just for a moment.

Chapter 3

Libby nearly choked on her first taste of Ken's taco sauce. "Did you say you were known and respected for this stuff, or known and feared?"

Ken chuckled roguishly at her tear-polished eyes and flaming face. "My calling it 'red devil' should have been a clue, dumplin'."

Libby muttered an exclamation and perversely took another bite from her bulging taco. "From now on," she said, chewing, "I'll do the cooking around this spread."

Her father laughed again and tapped one temple with a calloused index finger, his pale blue eyes twinkling.

"You deliberately tricked me!" cried Libby.

He grinned and shrugged. "Code of the West, sweetheart. Grouse about the chow, and presto—you're the cook!"

"Actually," ventured Libby with cultivated innocence, "this sauce isn't too bad."

"Too late," laughed Ken. "You already broke the code."

Libby lowered her taco to her plate and lifted both hands in a gesture of concession. "All right, all right—but have a little pity on me, will you? I've been living among dudes!"

"That's no excuse."

Libby shrugged and took up her taco again. "I tried. Have you been doing your own cooking and cleaning all this time?"

Ken shook his head and sat back in his chair, his thumbs hooked behind his belt buckle. "Nope. The Barlowes' housekeeper sends her crew down here once in a while."

"What about the food?"

"I eat with the boys most of the time, over at the cook shack." He rose, went to fill two mugs from the coffeepot on the stove. When he turned around again, his face was serious. "Libby, what happened today? What upset you like that?"

Libby averted her eyes. "I don't know," she lied lamely.

"Dammit, you *do* know. You fainted, Libby. When Jess carried you in here, I—"

"I know," Libby broke in gently. "You were scared. I'm sorry."

Carefully, as though he feared he might drop them, Ken set the cups of steaming coffee on the table. "What happened?" he persisted as he sat down in his chair again.

Libby swallowed hard, but the lump that had risen in her throat wouldn't go down. Knowing that this conversation couldn't be avoided forever, she managed to reply, "It's complicated. Basically, it comes down to the fact that Stacey's been telling those lies."

"And?"

"And Jess believes him. He said...he said some things to me and...well, it must have created some kind of emotional overload. I just gave out."

Ken turned his mug idly between his thumb and index finger, causing the liquid to spill over and make a coffee stain on the tablecloth. "Tell me about Jonathan, Libby," he said in a low, gentle voice.

The tears that sprang into Libby's eyes were not related to the tang of her father's red-devil taco sauce. "He died," she choked miserably.

"I know that. You called me the night it happened, remember? I guess what I'm really asking you is why you didn't want me to fly back there and help you sort things out."

Libby lowered her head. Jonathan hadn't been her son, he'd been Aaron's, by a previous marriage. But the loss of the child was a raw void within her, even though months had passed. "I didn't want you to get a firsthand look at my marriage," she admitted with great difficulty—and the shame she couldn't seem to shake.

"Why not, Libby?"

The sound Libby made might have been either a laugh or a sob. "Because it was terrible," she answered.

"From the first?"

She forced herself to meet her father's steady gaze, knew that he had guessed a lot about her marriage from her rare phone calls and even rarer letters. "Almost," she replied sadly.

"Tell me."

Libby didn't want to think about Aaron, let alone talk about him to this man who wouldn't understand so many things. "He had...he had lovers."

Ken didn't seem surprised. Had he guessed that, too? "Go on."

"I can't!"

"Yes, you can. If it's too much for you right now, I won't press you. But the sooner you talk this out, Libby, the better off you're going to be."

She realized that her hands were clenched in her lap and tried to relax them. There was still a white mark on her finger where Aaron's ostentatious wedding ring had been. "He didn't care," she mourned in a soft, distracted whisper. "He honestly didn't care..."

"About you?"

"About Jonathan. Dad, he didn't care about his own son!"

"How so, sweetheart?"

Libby dashed away tears with the back of one hand. "Th-things were bad between Aaron and me b-before we found out that Jonathan was sick. After the doctors told us, it was a lot worse."

"I don't follow you, Libby."

"Dad, Aaron wouldn't have anything to do with Jonathan from the moment we knew he was dying. He wasn't there for any of the tests and he never once came to visit at the hospital. Dad, that little boy cried for his father, and Aaron wouldn't come to him!"

"Did you talk to Aaron?"

Remembered frustration made Libby's cheeks pound with color. "I *pleaded* with him, Dad. All he'd say was, 'I can't handle this.'"

"It would be a hell of a thing to deal with, Lib. Maybe you're being too hard on the man."

"Too hard? *Too hard?* Jonathan was terrified, Dad, and he was in pain—constant pain. All he asked was that his own father be strong for him!"

"What about the boy's mother? Did she come to the hospital?"

"Ellen died when Jonathan was a baby."

Ken sighed, framing a question he was obviously reluctant to ask. "Did you ever love Aaron Strand, Libby?"

Libby remembered the early infatuation, the excitement that had never deepened into real love and had quickly been quelled by the realities of marriage to a man who was fundamentally self-centered. She tried, but she couldn't even recall her ex-husband's face clearly—all she could see in her mind was a pair of jade-green eyes, dark hair. Jess. "No," she finally said. "I thought I did when I married him, though."

Ken stood up suddenly, took the coffeepot from its back burner on the stove, refilled both their cups. "I don't like asking you this, but—"

"No, Dad," Libby broke in firmly, anticipating the question all too well, "I don't love Stacey!"

"You're sure about that?"

The truth was that Libby *hadn't* been sure, not entirely. But that illadvised episode with Jess at the end of the swimming dock had brought everything into clear perspective. Just remembering how willingly she had submitted to him made her throb with embarrassment. "I'm sure," she said.

Ken's strong hand came across the table to close over hers. "You're home now," he reminded her, "and things are going to get better, Libby. I promise you that."

Libby sniffled inelegantly. "Know something, cowboy? I love you very much."

"Bet you say that to all your fathers," Ken quipped. "You planning to work on your comic strip tomorrow?"

The change of subject was welcome. "I'm six or eight weeks ahead of schedule on that, and the mechanicals for the book aren't due till fall. I think I'll go riding instead, if I can get Cathy to go with me."

"What's a 'mechanical'?"

Libby smiled, feeling sheltered by the love of this strong and steady man facing her. "It's the finished drawing that I turn in, along with the instructions for the colorist."

"You don't do the colors?" Ken seemed surprised at that, knowing, as he did, her love for vivid shades and subtle hues alike.

"No, I just do the panels and the lettering." It was good to talk about work, to think about work. Disdainful as he had been about her career, it was the one thing Aaron had not been able to spoil for her.

Nobody's fool, Ken drew her out on the subject as much as he could, and she found herself chattering on and on about cartooning and even her secret hope to branch out into portraits one day.

They talked, father and daughter, far into the night.

"You deserve this," Jess Barlowe said to his reflection in the bathroom mirror. A first-class hangover pounded in his head and roiled in his stomach, and his face looked drawn, as though he'd been hibernating like one of the bears that sometimes troubled the range stock.

Grimly he began to shave, and as he wielded his disposable razor, he wondered if Libby was awake yet. Should he stop at Ken's and talk to her before going on to the main house to spend a day with the corporation accountants?

Jess wanted to go to Libby, to tell her that he was sorry for baiting her, to try to get their complex relationship—if it *was* a relationship— onto some kind of sane ground. However, all his instincts told him that his father had been right the day before: Libby needed time.

His thoughts strayed to Libby's stepson. What would it be like to sit by a hospital bed, day after day, watching a child suffer and not being able to help?

Jess shuddered. It was hard to imagine the horror of something like that. At least Libby had had her husband to share the nightmare.

He frowned as he nicked his chin with the razor, blotted the small wound with tissue paper. If Libby had had her husband during that impossible time, why had she needed Stacey?

Stacey. Now, there was someone he could talk to. Granted, Jess had not been on the best of terms with his older brother of late, but the man had a firsthand knowledge of what was happening inside Libby Kincaid, and that was reason enough to approach him.

Feeling better for having a plan, Jess finished his ablutions and got dressed. Normally he spent his days on the range with Ken and the ranch hands, but today, because of his meeting with the accountants, he forwent his customary blue jeans and cotton workshirt for a tailored three-piece suit. He was still struggling with his tie as he made his way down the broad redwood steps that led from the loftlike second floor of his house to the living room.

Here there was a massive fireplace of white limestone, taking up the whole of one wall. The floors were polished oak and boasted a number of brightly colored Indian rugs. Two easy chairs and a deep sofa faced the hearth, and Jess's cluttered desk looked out over the ranchland and the glacial mountains beyond.

Striding toward the front door, in exasperation he gave up his efforts to get the tie right. He was glad he didn't have Stacey's job; not for him the dull task of overseeing the family's nationwide chain of steak-house franchises.

He smiled. Stacey liked playing the dude, doing television commercials, traveling all over the country.

And taking Libby Kincaid to bed.

Jess stalked across the front lawn to the carport and climbed behind the wheel of the station wagon he'd driven since law school. One of these times, he was going to have to get another car—something with a little flash, like Stacey's Ferrari.

Stacey, Stacey. He hadn't even seen his brother yet, and already he was sick of him.

The station wagon's engine made a grinding sound and then huffed to life. Jess patted the dusty dashboard affectionately and grinned. A car was a car was a car, he reflected as he backed the notorious wreck out of his driveway. The function of a car was to transport people, not impress them.

Five minutes later, Jess's station wagon chortled to an asthmatic stop beside his brother's ice-blue Ferrari. He looked up at the modernistic two-story house that had been the senator's wedding gift to Stacey and Cathy and wondered if Libby would be impressed by the place.

He scowled as he made his way up the curving white-stone walk. What the hell did he care if Libby was impressed?

Irritated, he jabbed one finger at the special doorbell that would turn on a series of blinking lights inside the house. The system had been his own idea, meant to make life easier for Cathy.

His sister-in-law came to the door and smiled at him somewhat wanly, speaking with her hands. "Good morning."

Jess nodded, smiled. The haunted look in the depths of Cathy's eyes made him angry all over again. "Is Stacey here?" he signed, stepping into the house.

Cathy caught his hand in her own and led him through the cavernous living room and the formal dining room beyond. Stacey was in the kitchen, looking more at home in a three-piece suit than Jess ever had.

"You," Stacey said tonelessly, setting down the English muffin he'd been slathering with honey.

Cathy offered coffee and left the room when it was politely declined. Distractedly Jess reflected on the fact that her life had to be boring as hell, centering on Stacey the way it did.

"I want to talk to you," Jess said, scraping back a chrome-and-plastic chair to sit down at the table.

Stacey arched one eyebrow. "I hope it's quick—I'm leaving for the airport in a few minutes. I've got some business to take care of in Kansas City."

Jess was impatient. "What kind of man is Libby's ex-husband?" he asked.

Stacey took up his coffee. "Why do you want to know?"

"I just do. Do I have to have him checked out, or are you going to tell me?"

"He's a bastard," said Stacey, not quite meeting his brother's eyes.

"Rich?"

"Oh, yes. His family is old-money."

"What does he do?"

"Do?"

"Yeah. Does he work, or does he just stand around being rich?"

"He runs the family advertising agency; I think he has a lot of control over their other financial interests too."

Jess sensed that Stacey was hedging, wondered why. "Any bad habits?"

Stacey was gazing at the toaster now, in a fixed way, as though he expected something alarming to pop out of it. "The man has his share of vices."

Annoyed now, Jess got up, helped himself to the cup of coffee he had refused earlier, sat down again. "Pulling porcupine quills out of a dog's nose would be easier than getting answers out of you. When you say he has vices, do you mean women?"

Stacey swallowed, looked away. "To put it mildly," he said.

Jess settled back in his chair. "What the hell do you mean by that?"

"I mean that he not only liked to run around with other women, he liked to flaunt the fact. The worse he could make Libby feel about herself, the happier he was."

"Jesus," Jess breathed. "What else?" he pressed, sensing, from Stacey's expression, that there was more.

"He was impotent with Libby."

"Why did she stay? Why in God's name did she stay?" Jess mused distractedly, as much to himself as to his brother.

A cautious but smug light flickered in Stacey's topaz eyes. "She had me," he said evenly. "Besides, Jonathan was sick by that time and she felt she had to stay in the marriage for his sake."

The spacious sun-filled kitchen seemed to buckle and shift around Jess. "Why didn't she tell Ken, at least?"

"What would have been the point in that, Jess? He couldn't have made the boy well again or transformed Aaron Strand into a devoted husband."

The things Libby must have endured—the shame, the loneliness, the humiliation and grief, washed over Jess in a dismal, crushing wave. No wonder she had reached out to Stacey the way she had. No wonder. "Thanks," he said gruffly, standing up to leave.

"Jess?"

He paused in the kitchen doorway, his hands clasping the woodwork, his shoulders aching with tension. "What?"

"Don't worry about Libby. I'll take care of her."

Jess felt a despairing sort of anger course through him. "What about Cathy?" he asked, without turning around. "Who is going to take care of her?"

"You've always—"

Jess whirled suddenly, staring at his brother, almost hating him. "I've always *what?*"

"Cared for her." Stacey shrugged, looking only mildly unsettled. "Protected her..."

"Are you suggesting that I sweep up the pieces after you shatter her?" demanded Jess in a dangerous rasp.

Stacey only shrugged again.

Because he feared that he would do his brother lasting harm if he stayed another moment, Jess stormed out of the house. Cathy, dressed in old jeans, boots and a cotton blouse, was waiting beside the station wagon. The pallor in her face told Jess that she knew much more about the state of her marriage than he would have hoped.

Her hands trembled a little as she spoke with them. "I'm scared, Jess."

He drew her into his arms, held her. "I know, baby," he said, even though he knew she couldn't hear him or see his lips. "I know."

Libby opened her eyes, yawned and stretched. The smells of sunshine and fresh air swept into her bedroom through the open window, ruffling pink eyelet curtains and reminding her that she was home again. She tossed back the covers on the bed she had once shared with Cathy and got up, sleepily making her way into the bathroom and starting the water for a shower.

As she took off her short cotton nightshirt, she looked down at herself and remembered the raging sensations Jess Barlowe had ignited in her the day before. She had been stupid and self-indulgent to let that happen, but after several years of celibacy, she supposed it was natural that her passions had been stirred so easily—especially by a man like Jess.

As Libby showered, she felt renewed. Aaron's flagrant infidelities had been painful for her, and they had seriously damaged her self-esteem in the bargain.

Now, even though she had made a fool of herself by being wanton with a man who could barely tolerate her, many of Libby's doubts about herself as a woman had been eased, if not routed. She was not as useless and undesirable as Aaron had made her feel. She had caused Jess Barlowe to want her, hadn't she?

Big deal, she told the image in her mirror as she brushed her teeth. *How do you know Jess wasn't out to prove that his original opinion of you was on target?*

Deflated by this very real possibility, Libby combed her hair, applied the customary lip gloss and light touch of mascara and went back to her room to dress. From her suitcases she selected a short-sleeved turquoise pullover shirt and a pair of trim jeans. Remembering her intention to find Cathy and persuade her to go riding, she ferreted through her closet until she found the worn boots she'd left behind before moving to New York, pulling them on over a pair of thick socks.

Looking down at those disreputable old boots, Libby imagined the scorn they would engender in Aaron's jet-set crowd and laughed. Problems or no problems, Jess or no Jess, it was good to be home.

Not surprisingly, the kitchen was empty. Ken had probably left the house before dawn, but there was coffee on the stove and fruit in the refrigerator, so Libby helped herself to a pear and sat down to eat.

The telephone rang just as she was finishing her second cup of coffee, and Libby answered cheerfully, thinking that the caller would be Ken or the housekeeper at the main house, relaying some message for Cathy.

She was back at the table, the receiver pressed to her ear, before Aaron spoke.

"When are you coming home?"

"Home?" echoed Libby stupidly, off-balance, unable to believe that he'd actually asked such a question. "I *am* home, Aaron."

"Enough," he replied. "You've made your point, exhibited your righteous indignation. Now you've got to get back here because I need you."

Libby wanted to hang up, but it seemed a very long way from her chair to the wall, where the rest of the telephone was. "Aaron, we are divorced," she reminded him calmly, "and I am never coming back."

"You have to," he answered, without missing a beat. "It's crucial."

"Why? What happened to all your...friends?"

Aaron sighed. "You remember Betty, don't you? Miss November? Well, Betty and I had a small disagreement, as it happens, and she went to my family. I am, shall we say, exposed as something less than an ideal spouse.

"In any case, my grandmother believes that a man who cannot run his family—she was in Paris when we divorced, darling—cannot run a company, either. I have six months to bring you back into the fold and start an heir, or the whole shooting match goes to my cousin.''

Libby was too stunned to speak or even move; she simply stood in the middle of her father's kitchen, trying to absorb what Aaron was saying.

"That," Aaron went on blithely, "is where you come in, sweetheart. You come back, we smile a lot and make a baby, my grandmother's ruffled feathers are smoothed. It's as simple as that."

Sickness boiled into Libby's throat. "I don't believe this!" she whispered.

"You don't believe what, darling? That I can make a baby? May I point out that I sired Jonathan, of whom you were so cloyingly fond?"

Libby swallowed. "Get Miss November pregnant," she managed to suggest. And then she added distractedly, more to herself than Aaron, "I think I'm going to be sick."

"Don't tell me that I've been beaten to the proverbial draw," Aaron remarked in that brutally smooth, caustic way of his. "Did the steak-house king already do the deed?"

"You are disgusting!"

"Yes, but very practical. If I don't hand my grandmother an heir, whether it's mine or the issue of that softheaded cowboy, I stand to lose millions of dollars."

Libby managed to stand up. A few steps, just a few, and she could hang up the telephone, shut out Aaron's voice and his ugly suggestions. "Do you really think that I would turn any child of mine over to someone like you?"

"There is a child, then," he retorted smoothly.

"No!" Five steps to the wall, six at most.

"Be reasonable, sweetness. We're discussing an empire here. If you don't come back and attend to your wifely duties, I'll have to visit that godforsaken ranch and try to persuade you."

"I am not your wife!" screamed Libby. One step. One step and a reach.

"Dear heart, I don't find the idea any more appealing than you do, but there isn't any other way, is there? My grandmother likes you—sees you as sturdy peasant stock—and she wants the baby to be yours."

At last. The wall was close and Libby slammed the receiver into place. Then, dazed, she stumbled back to her chair and fell into it, lowering her head to her arms. She cried hard, for herself, for Jonathan.

"Libby?"

It was the last voice she would have wanted to hear, except for Aaron's. "Go away, Stacey!" she hissed.

Instead of complying, Stacey laid a gentle hand on her shoulder. "What happened, Libby?" he asked softly. "Who was that on the phone?"

Fresh horror washed over Libby at the things Aaron had requested, mixed with anger and revulsion. God, how self-centered and insensitive that man was! And what gall he had, suggesting that she return to that disaster of a marriage, like some unquestioning brood mare, to produce a baby on order!

She gave a shuddering cry and motioned Stacey away with a frantic motion of her arm.

He only drew her up out of the chair and turned her so that he could hold her. She hadn't the strength to resist the intimacy and, in her half-hysterical state, he seemed to be the old Stacey, the strong big brother.

Stacey's hand came to the back of her head, tangling in her freshly washed hair, pressing her to his shoulder. "Tell me what happened," he urged, just as he had when Libby was a child with a skinned knee or a bee sting.

From habit, she allowed herself to be comforted. For so long there had been no one to confide in except Stacey, and it seemed natural to lean on him now. "Aaron...Aaron called. He wanted me to have his...his baby!"

Before Stacey could respond to that, the door separating the kitchen from the living room swung open. Instinctively Libby drew back from the man who held her.

Jess towered in the doorway, pale, his gaze scorching Libby's flushed, tear-streaked face. "You know," he began in a voice that was no less terrible for being soft, "I almost believed you. I almost had myself convinced that you were above anything this shabby."

"Wait—you don't understand..."

Jess smiled a slow, vicious smile—a smile that took in his startled brother as well as Libby. "Don't I? Oh, princess, I wish I didn't." The searing jade gaze sliced menacingly to Stacey's face. "And it seems I'm going to be an uncle. Tell me, brother—what does that make Cathy?"

To Libby's horror, Stacey said nothing to refute what was obviously a gross misunderstanding. He simply pulled her back into his arms, and her struggle was virtually imperceptible because of his strength.

"Let me go!" she pleaded, frantic.

Stacey released her, but only grudgingly. "I've got a plane to catch," he said.

Libby was incredulous. "Tell him! Tell Jess that he's wrong," she cried, reaching out for Stacey's arm, trying to detain him.

But Stacey simply pulled free and left by the back door.

There was a long, pulsing silence, during which both Libby and Jess seemed to be frozen. He was the first to thaw.

"I know you were hurt, Libby," he said. "Badly hurt. But that didn't give you the right to do something like this to Cathy."

It infuriated Libby that this man's good opinion was so important to her, but it was, and there was no changing that. "Jess, I didn't do anything to Cathy. Please listen to me."

He folded his strong arms and rested against the door jamb with an ease that Libby knew was totally feigned. "I'm listening," he said, and the words had a flippant note.

Libby ignored fresh anger. "I am not expecting Stacey's baby, and this wasn't a romantic tryst. I don't even know why he came here. I was on the phone with Aaron and he—"

A muscle in Jess's neck corded, relaxed again. "I hope you're not going to tell me that your former husband made you pregnant, Libby. That seems unlikely."

Frustration pounded in Libby's temples and tightened the already constricted muscles in her throat. "I am not pregnant!" she choked out. "And if you are going to eavesdrop, Jess Barlowe, you could at least pay attention! Aaron wanted me to come back to New York and have his baby so that he would have an heir to present to his grandmother!"

"You didn't agree to that?"

"Of course I didn't agree! What kind of monster do you think I am?"

Jess shrugged with a nonchalance that was belied by the leaping green fire in his eyes. "I don't know, princess, but rest assured—I intend to find out."

"I have a better idea!" Libby flared. "Why don't you just leave me the hell alone?"

"In theory that's brilliant," he fired back, "but there is one problem: I want you."

Involuntarily Libby remembered the kisses and caresses exchanged by the pond the day before, relived them. Hot color poured into her face. "Am I supposed to be honored?"

"No," Jess replied flatly, "you're supposed to be kept so busy that you won't have time to screw up Cathy's life any more than you already have."

If Libby could have moved, she would have rushed across that room and slapped Jess Barlowe senseless. Since she couldn't get her muscles to respond to the orders of her mind, she was forced to watch in stricken silence as he gave her a smoldering assessment with his eyes, executed a half salute and left the house.

Chapter 4

When the telephone rang again, immediately after Jess's exit from the kitchen, Libby was almost afraid to answer it. It would be like Aaron to persist, to use pressure to get what he wanted.

On the other hand, the call might be from someone else, and it could be important.

"Hello?" Libby dared, with resolve.

"Ms. Kincaid?" asked a cheerful feminine voice. "This is Marion Bradshaw, and I'm calling for Mrs. Barlowe. She'd like you to meet her at the main house if you can, and she says to dress for riding."

Libby looked down at her jeans and boots and smiled. In one way, at least, she and Cathy were still on the same wavelength. "Please tell her that I'll be there as soon as I can."

There was a brief pause at the other end of the line, followed by, "Mrs. Barlowe wants me to ask if you have a car down there. If not, she'll come and pick you up in a few minutes."

Though there was no car at her disposal, Libby declined the offer. The walk to the main ranch house would give her a chance to think, to prepare herself to face her cousin again.

As Libby started out, striding along the winding tree-lined road, she ached to think that she and Cathy had come to this. Fresh anger at Stacey quickened her step.

For a moment she was mad at Cathy too. How could she believe such a thing, after all they'd been through together? How?

Firmly Libby brought her ire under control. *You don't get mad at a handicapped person,* she scolded herself.

The sun was already high and hot in the domelike sky, and Libby smiled. It was warm for spring, and wasn't it nice to look up and see clouds and mountaintops instead of tall buildings and smog?

Finally the main house came into view. It was a rambling structure of red brick, and its many windows glistened in the bright sunshine. A porch with marble steps led up to the double doors, and one of them swung open even as Libby reached out to ring the bell.

Mrs. Bradshaw, the housekeeper, stepped out and enfolded Libby in a delighted hug. A slender middle-aged woman with soft brown hair, Marion Bradshaw was as much a part of the Circle Bar B as Senator Barlowe himself. "Welcome home," she said warmly.

Libby smiled and returned the hug. "Thank you, Marion," she replied. "Is Cathy ready to go riding?"

"She's gone ahead to the stables—she'd like you to join her there."

Libby turned to go back down the steps but was stopped by the housekeeper. "Libby?"

She faced Marion, again, feeling wary.

"I don't believe it of you," said Mrs. Bradshaw firmly.

Libby was embarrassed, but there was no point in trying to pretend that she didn't get the woman's meaning. Probably everyone on the ranch was speculating about her supposed involvement with Stacey Barlowe. "Thank you."

"You stay right here on this ranch, Libby Kincaid," Marion Bradshaw rushed on, her own face flushed now. "Don't let Stacey or anybody else run you off."

That morning's unfortunate scene in Ken's kitchen was an indication of how difficult it would be to take the housekeeper's advice. Life on the Circle Bar B could become untenable if both Stacey and Jess didn't back off.

"I'll try," she said softly before stepping down off the porch and making her way around the side of that imposing but gracious house.

Prudently, the stables had been built a good distance away. During the walk, Libby wondered if she shouldn't leave the ranch after all. True, she needed to be there, but Jonathan's death had taught her that sometimes a person had to put her own desires aside for the good of other people.

But would leaving help, in the final analysis? Suppose Stacey did follow her, as he'd threatened to do? What would that do to Cathy?

The stables, like the house, were constructed of red brick. As Libby approached them, she saw Cathy leading two horses out into the sun—a dancing palomino gelding and the considerably less prepossessing pinto mare that had always been Libby's to ride.

Libby hesitated; it had been a long, long time since she'd ridden a horse, and the look in Cathy's eyes was cool. Distant. It was almost as though Libby were a troublesome stranger rather than her cousin and confidante.

As if to break the spell, Cathy lifted one foot to the stirrup of the Palomino's saddle and swung onto its back. Though she gave no sign of greeting, her eyes bade Libby to follow suit.

The elderly pinto was gracious while Libby struggled into the saddle and took the reins in slightly shaky hands. A moment later they were off across the open pastureland behind the stables, Cathy confident in the lead.

Libby jostled and jolted in the now unfamiliar saddle, and she felt a fleeting annoyance with Cathy for setting the brisk pace that she did. Again she berated herself for being angry with someone who couldn't hear.

Cathy rode faster and faster, stopping only when she reached the trees that trimmed the base of a wooded hill. There she turned in the saddle and flung a look back at the disgruntled Libby.

"You're out of practice," she said clearly, though her voice had the slurred meter of those who have not heard another person speak in years.

Libby, red-faced and damp with perspiration, was not surprised that Cathy had spoken aloud. She had learned to talk before the childhood illness that had made her deaf, and when she could be certain that no one else would overhear, she often spoke. It was a secret the two women kept religiously.

"Thanks a lot!" snapped Libby.

Deftly Cathy swung one trim blue-jeaned leg over the neck of her golden gelding and slid to the ground. The fancy bridle jingled musically as the animal bent its great head to graze on the spring grass. "We've got to talk, Libby"

Libby jumped from the pinto's back and the action engendered a piercing ache in the balls of her feet. "You've got that right!" she flared, forgetting for the moment her earlier resolve to respect Cathy's affliction. "Were you trying to get me killed?"

Watching Libby's lips, Cathy grinned. "Killed?" she echoed in her slow, toneless voice. "You're my cousin. That's important, isn't it? That we're cousins, I mean?"

Libby sighed. "Of course it's important."

"It implies a certain loyalty, don't you think?"

Libby braced herself. She'd known this confrontation was coming, of course, but that didn't mean she wanted it or was ready for it. "Yes," she said somewhat lamely.

"Are you having an affair with my husband?"

"No!"

"Do you want to?"

"What the hell kind of person do you think I am, Cathy?" shouted Libby, losing all restraint, flinging her arms out wide and startling the horses, who nickered and danced and tossed their heads.

"I'm trying to find that out," said Cathy in measured and droning words. Not once since the conversation began had her eyes left Libby's mouth.

"You already know," retorted her cousin.

For the first time, Cathy looked ashamed. But there was uncertainty in her expression, too, along with a great deal of pain. "It's no secret that Stacey wants you, Libby. I've been holding my breath ever since you decided to come back, waiting for him to leave me."

"Whatever problems you and Stacey have, Cathy, I didn't start them."

"What about all his visits to New York?"

Libby's shoulders slumped, and she allowed herself to sink to the fragrant spring-scented ground, where she sat cross-legged, her head down. With her hands she said, "You knew about the divorce, and about Jonathan. Stacey was only trying to help me through—we weren't lovers."

The lush grass moved as Cathy sat down too, facing Libby. There were tears shining in her large green eyes, and her lower lip trembled. Nervously she plied a blade of grass between her fingers.

"I'm sorry about your little boy," she said aloud.

Libby reached out, calmer now, and squeezed Cathy's hands with her own. "Thanks."

A lonely, haunted look rose in Cathy's eyes. "Stacey wanted us to have a baby," she confided.

"Why didn't you?"

Sudden color stained Cathy's lovely cheeks. "I'm deaf!" she cried defensively.

Libby released her cousin's hands to sign, "So what? Lots of deaf people have babies."

"Not me!" Cathy signaled back with spirited despair. "I wouldn't know when it cried!"

Libby spoke slowly, her hands falling back to her lap. "Cathy, there are solutions for that sort of problem. There are trained dogs, electronic devices—"

"Trained dogs!" scoffed Cathy, but there was more anguish in her face than anger. "What kind of woman needs a dog to help her raise her own baby?"

"A deaf woman," Libby answered firmly. "Besides, if you don't want a dog around, you could hire a nurse."

"No!"

Libby was taken aback. "Why not?" she signed after a few moments.

Cathy clearly had no intention of answering. She bolted to her feet and was back in the palomino's saddle before Libby could even rise from the ground.

After that, they rode without communicating at all. Knowing that things were far from settled between herself and her cousin, Libby tried to concentrate on the scenery. A shadow moved across the sun, however, and a feeling of impending disaster unfolded inside her.

Jess glared at the screen of the small computer his father placed so much store in and resisted a caveman urge to strike its side with his fist.

"Here," purred a soft feminine voice, and Monica Summers, the senator's curvaceous assistant, reached down to tap the keyboard in a few strategic places.

Instantly the profit-and-loss statement Jess had been trying to call up was prominently displayed on the screen.

"How did you do that?"

Monica smiled her sultry smile and pulled up a chair to sit down beside Jess. "It's a simple matter of command," she said, and somehow the words sounded wildly suggestive.

Jess's collar seemed to tighten around his throat, but he grinned, appreciating Monica's lithe, inviting body, her profusion of gleaming brown hair, her impudent mouth and soft gray eyes. Her visits to the ranch were usually brief, but the senator's term of office was almost over, and he planned to write a long book—with which Monica was slated to help. Until that project was completed, she would be around a lot.

The fact that the senior senator did not intend to campaign for reelection didn't seem to faze her—it was common knowledge that she had a campaign of her own in mind.

Monica had made it clear, time and time again, that she was available to Jess for more than an occasional dinner date and subsequent sexual skirmish. And before Libby's return, Jess had seriously considered settling down with Monica.

He didn't love her, but she was undeniably beautiful, and the promises she made with her skillfully made-up eyes were not idle ones. In addition to that, they had a lot of ordinary things in common—similar political views, a love of the outdoors, like tastes in music and books.

Now, even with Monica sitting so close to him, her perfume calling up some rather heated memories, Jess Barlowe was patently unmoved.

A shower of anger sifted through him. He *wanted* to be moved, dammit—he wanted everything to be the way it was before Libby's return. Return? It was an invasion! He thought about the little hellion day and night, whether he wanted to or not.

"What's wrong, Jess?" Monica asked softly, perceptively, her hand resting on his shoulder. "It's more than just this computer, isn't it?"

He looked away. The sensible thing to do would be to take Monica by the hand, lead her off somewhere private and make slow, ferocious love to her. Maybe that would exorcise Libby Kincaid from his mind.

He remembered passion-weighted breasts, bared to him on a swimming dock, remembered their nipples blossoming sweetly in his mouth. Libby's breasts.

"Jess?"

He forced himself to look at Monica again. "I'm sorry," he said. "Did you say something?"

Mischief danced in her charcoal eyes. "Yes. I offered you my body."

He laughed.

Instead of laughing herself, Monica gave him a gentle, discerning look. "Mrs. Bradshaw tells me that Libby Kincaid is back," she said. "Could it be that I have some competition?"

Jess cleared his throat and diplomatically fixed his attention on the computer screen. "Show me how you made this monster cough up that profit-and-loss statement," he hedged.

"Jess." The voice was cool, insistent.

He made himself meet Monica's eyes again. "I don't know what I feel for Libby," he confessed. "She makes me mad as hell, but..."

"But," said Monica with rueful amusement, "you want her very badly, don't you?"

There was no denying that, but neither could Jess bring himself to openly admit to the curious needs that had been plaguing him since the moment he'd seen Libby again at the small airport in Kalispell.

Monica's right index finger traced the outline of his jaw, tenderly. Sensuously. "We've never agreed to be faithful to each other, Jess," she said in the silky voice that had once enthralled him. "There aren't any strings tying you to me. But that doesn't mean that I'm going to step back and let Libby Kincaid have a clear field. I want you myself."

Jess was saved from answering by the sudden appearance of his father in the study doorway.

"Oh, Monica—there you are," Cleave Barlowe said warmly. "Ready to start working on that speech now? We have to have it ready before we fly back to Washington, remember."

Gray eyes swept Jess's face in parting. "More than ready," she replied, and then she was out of her chair and walking across the study to join her employer.

Jess gave the computer an unloving look and switched it off, taking perverse pleasure in the way the little green words and numbers on the screen dissolved. "State of the art," he mocked, and then stood up and strode out of the room.

The accountants would be angry, once they returned from their coffee break, but he didn't give a damn. If he didn't do something physical, he was going to go crazy.

Back at the stables, Libby surrendered her horse to a ranch hand with relief. Already the muscles in her thighs were aching dully from the ride; by morning they would be in savage little knots.

Cathy, who probably rode almost every day, looked breezy and refreshed, and from her manner no one would have suspected that she harbored any ill feelings toward Libby. "Let's take a swim," she signed, "and then we can have lunch."

Libby would have preferred to soak in the hot tub, but her pride wouldn't allow her to say so. Unless a limp betrayed her, she wasn't going to let Cathy know how sore a simple horseback ride had left her.

"I don't have a swimming suit," she said, somewhat hopefully.

"That's okay," Cathy replied with swift hands. "It's an indoor pool, remember?"

"I hope you're not suggesting that we swim naked," Libby argued aloud.

Cathy's eyes danced. "Why not?" she signed impishly. "No one would see us."

"Are you kidding?" Libby retorted, waving one arm toward the long, wide driveway. "Look at all these cars! There are *people* in that house!"

"Are you so modest?" queried Cathy, one eyebrow arched.

"Yes!" replied Libby, ignoring the subtle sarcasm.

"Then we'll go back to your house and swim in the pond, like we used to."

Libby recalled the blatant way she'd offered herself to Jess Barlowe in that place and winced inwardly. The peaceful solace of that pond had probably been altered forever, and it was going to be some time before she could go there comfortably again. "It's spring, Cathy, not summer. We'd catch pneumonia! Besides, I think it's going to rain."

Cathy shrugged. "All right, all right. I'll borrow a car and we'll drive over and get your swimming suit, then come back here."

"Fine," Libby agreed with a sigh.

She was to regret the decision almost immediately. When she and Cathy reached the house they had both grown up in, there was a florist's truck parked out front.

On the porch stood an affable young man, a long, narrow box in his hands. "Hi, Libby," he said.

Libby recognized Phil Reynolds, who had been her classmate in high school. *Go away, Phil,* she thought, even as she smiled and greeted him.

Cathy's attention was riveted on the silver box he carried, and there was a worried expression on her face.

Phil approached, beaming. "I didn't even know you were back until we got this order this morning. Aren't you coming into town at all? We got a new high school..."

Simmonsville, a dried-up little community just beyond the south border of the Circle Bar B, hadn't even entered Libby's thoughts until she'd seen Phil Reynolds. She ignored his question and stared at the box he held out to her as if it might contain something squirmy and vile.

"Wh-who sent these?" she managed, all too conscious of the suspicious way Cathy was looking at her.

"See for yourself," Phil said brightly, and then he got back into his truck and left.

Libby took the card from beneath the red ribbon that bound the box and opened it with trembling fingers. The flowers couldn't be from Stacey, please God, they couldn't!

The card was typewritten. *Don't be stubborn, sweetness,* the message read. *Regards, Aaron.*

For a moment Libby was too relieved to be angry. "Aaron," she repeated. Then she lifted the lid from the box and saw the dozen pink rosebuds inside.

For one crazy moment she was back in Jonathan's hospital room. There had been roses there, too—along with mums and violets and carnations. Aaron and his family had sent costly bouquets and elaborate toys, but not one of them had come to visit.

Libby heard the echo of Jonathan's purposefully cheerful voice. *Daddy must be busy,* he'd said.

With a cry of fury and pain, Libby flung the roses away, and they scattered over the walk in a profusion of long-stemmed delicacy. The silver box lay with them, catching the waning sunlight.

Cathy knelt and began gathering up the discarded flowers, placing them gently back in their carton. Once or twice she glanced up at Libby's livid face in bewilderment, but she asked no questions and made no comments.

Libby turned away and bounded into the house. By the time she had found a swimming suit and come back downstairs again, Cathy was arranging the rosebuds in a cut-glass vase at the kitchen sink.

She met Libby's angry gaze and held up one hand to stay the inevitable outburst. "They're beautiful, Libby," she said in a barely audible voice. "You can't throw away something that's beautiful."

"Watch me!" snapped Libby.

Cathy stepped between her cousin and the lush bouquet. "Libby, at least let me give them to Mrs. Bradshaw," she pleaded aloud. "Please?"

Glumly Libby nodded. She supposed she should be grateful that the roses hadn't been sent by Stacey in a fit of ardor, and they *were* too lovely to waste, even if she herself couldn't bear the sight of them.

Libby remembered the words on Aaron's card as she and Cathy drove back to the main house. *Don't be stubborn.* A tremor of dread flitted up and down her spine.

Aaron hadn't been serious when he'd threatened to come to the ranch and "persuade" her to return to New York with him, had he? She shivered.

Surely even Aaron wouldn't have the gall to do that, she tried to reassure herself. After all, he had never come to the apartment she'd taken after Jonathan's death, never so much as called. Even when the divorce had been granted, he had avoided her by sending his lawyer to court alone.

No. Aaron wouldn't actually come to the Circle Bar B. He might call, he might even send more flowers, just to antagonize her, but he wouldn't come in person. Despite his dismissal of Stacey as a "softheaded cowboy," he was afraid of him.

Cathy was drawing the car to a stop in front of the main house by the time Libby was able to recover herself. To allay the concern in her cousin's eyes, she carried the vase of pink roses into the kitchen and presented them to Mrs. Bradshaw, who was puzzled but clearly pleased.

Inside the gigantic, elegantly tiled room that housed the swimming pool and the spacious hot tub, Libby eyed the latter with longing. Thus, it was a moment before she realized that the pool was already occupied.

Jess was doing a furious racing crawl from one side of the deep end to the other, his tanned, muscular arms cutting through the blue water with a force that said he was trying to work out some fierce inner conflict. Watching him admiringly from the poolside, her slender legs dangling into the water, was a pretty dark-haired woman with beautiful gray eyes.

The woman greeted Cathy with an easy gesture of her hands, though her eyes were fixed on Libby, seeming to assess her in a thorough, if offhand, fashion.

"I'm Monica Summers," she said, as Jess, apparently oblivious of everything other than the furious course he was following through the water, executed an impressive somersault turn at the poolside and raced back the other way.

Monica Summers. The name was familiar to Libby, and so, vaguely, was the perfect fashion-model face.

Of course. Monica was Senator Barlowe's chief assistant. Libby had never actually met the woman, but she had seen her on television newscasts and Ken had mentioned her in passing, on occasion, over long-distance telephone.

"Hello," Libby said. "I'm—"

The gray eyes sparkled. "I know," Monica broke in smoothly. "You're Libby Kincaid. I enjoy your cartoons very much."

Libby felt about as sophisticated, compared to this woman, as a Girl Scout selling cookies door-to-door. And Monica's subtle emphasis on the word "cartoons" had made her feel defensive.

All the same, Libby thanked her and forced herself not to watch Jess's magnificent body moving through the bright blue water of the pool. It didn't bother her that Jess and Monica had been alone in this strangely sensual setting. It didn't.

Cathy had moved away, anxious for her swim.

"I'm sorry if we interrupted something," Libby said, and hated herself instantly for betraying her interest.

Monica smiled. Clearly she had not been in swimming herself, for her expensive black swimsuit was dry, and so was her long, lush hair. Her makeup, of course, was perfect. "There are always interruptions," she said, and then she turned away to take up her adoring-spectator position again, her gaze following the play of the powerful muscles in Jess's naked back.

My thighs are too fat, mourned Libby, in petulant despair. She took a seat on a lounge far removed from Jess and his lovely friend and tried to pretend an interest in Cathy's graceful backstroke.

Was Jess intimate with Monica Summers? It certainly seemed so, and Libby couldn't understand, for the life of her, why she was so brutally surprised by the knowledge. After all, Jess was a handsome, healthy man, well beyond the age of handholding and fantasies-from-afar. Had she really ever believed that he had just been existing on this ranch in some sort of suspended animation?

Cathy roused her from her dismal reflection by flinging a stream of water at her with both hands. Instantly Libby was drenched and stung to an annoyance out of all proportion to the offense. Surprising even herself, she stomped over to the hot tub, flipped the switch that would make the water bubble and churn, and after hurling one scorching look at her unrepenting cousin, slid into the enormous tile-lined tub.

The heat and motion of the water were welcome balm to Libby's muscles, if not to her spirit. She had no right to care who Jess Barlowe slept with, no right at all. It wasn't as though she had ever had any claim on his affections.

Settling herself on a submerged bench, Libby tilted her head back, closed her eyes, and tried to pretend that she was alone in that massive room with its sloping glass roof, lush plants and lounges.

The fact that she was sexually attracted to Jess Barlowe was undeniable, but it was just a physical phenomenon, certainly. It would pass.

All she had to do to accelerate the process was allow herself to remember how very demeaning Aaron's lovemaking had been. And remember she did.

After Libby had caught her husband with the first of his lovers, she had moved out of his bedroom permanently, remaining in his house only because Jonathan, still at home then, had needed her so much.

Before her brutal awakening, however, she had tried hard to make the rapidly failing marriage work. Even then, bedtime had been a horror.

Libby's skin prickled as she recalled the way Aaron would ignore her for long weeks and then pounce on her with a vicious and alarming sort of determination, tearing her clothes, sometimes bruising her.

In retrospect, Libby realized that Aaron must have been trying to prove something to himself concerning his identity as a man, but at the time she had known only that sex, much touted in books and movies, was something to be feared.

Not once had Libby achieved any sort of satisfaction with Aaron—she had only endured. Now, painfully conscious of the blatantly masculine, near-naked cowboy swimming in the pool nearby, Libby wondered if lovemaking would be different with Jess.

The way that her body had blossomed beneath his seemed adequate proof that it would be different indeed, but there was always the possibility that she would be disappointed in the ultimate act. Probably she had been aroused only because Jess had taken the time to offer her at least a taste of pleasure. Aaron had never done that, never shown any sensitivity at all.

Shutting out all sight and sound, Libby mentally decried her lack of experience. If only she'd been with even one man besides Aaron, she would have had some frame of reference, some inkling of whether or not the soaring releases she'd read about really existed.

The knowledge that so many people thought she had been carrying on a torrid affair with Stacey brought a wry smile to her lips. If only they knew.

"What are you smiling about?"

The voice jolted Libby back to the here and now with a thump. Jess had joined her in the hot tub at some point; indeed, he was standing only inches away.

Startled, Libby stared at him for a moment, then looked wildly around for Cathy and the elegant Ms. Summers.

"They went in to have lunch," Jess informed her, his eyes twinkling. Beads of water sparkled in the dark down that matted his muscular chest, and his hair had been towel-rubbed into an appealing disarray.

"I'll join them," said Libby in a frantic whisper, but the simple mechanics of turning away and climbing out of the hot tub eluded her.

Smelling pleasantly of chlorine, Jess came nearer. "Don't go," he said softly. "Lunch will wait."

Anger at Cathy surged through Libby. Why had she gone off and left her here?

Jess seemed to read the question in her face, and it made him laugh. The sound was soft—sensuously, wholly male. Overhead, spring thunder crashed in a gray sky.

Libby trembled, pressing back against the edge of the hot tub with such force that her shoulder blades ached. "Stay away from me," she breathed.

"Not on your life," he answered, and then he was so near that she could feel the hard length of his thighs against her own. The soft dark hair on his chest tickled her bare shoulders and the suddenly alive flesh above her swimsuit top. "I intend to finish what we started yesterday beside the pond."

Libby gasped as his moist lips came down to taste hers, to tame and finally part them for a tender invasion. Her hands went up, of their own accord, to rest on his hips.

He was naked. The discovery rocked Libby, made her try to twist away from him, but his kiss deepened and subdued her struggles. With his hands, he lifted her legs, draped them around the rock-hard hips she had just explored.

The imposing, heated length of his desire, now pressed intimately against her, was powerful proof that he meant to take her.

Chapter 5

Libby felt as though her body had dissolved, become part of the warm, bubbling water filling the hot tub. When Jess drew back from his soft conquering of her mouth, his hands rose gently to draw down the modest top of her swimsuit, revealing the pulsing fullness of her breasts to his gaze.

It was not in Libby to protest: she was transfixed, caught up in primal responses that had no relation to good sense or even sanity. She let her head fall back, saw through the transparent ceiling that gray clouds had darkened the sky, promising a storm that wouldn't begin to rival the one brewing inside Libby herself.

Jess bent his head, nipped at one exposed, aching nipple with cautious teeth.

Libby drew in a sharp breath as a shaft of searing pleasure went through her, so powerful that she was nearly convulsed by it. A soft moan escaped her, and she tilted her head even further back, so that her breasts were still more vulnerable to the plundering of his mouth.

Inside Libby's swirling mind, a steady voice chanted a litany of logic: she was behaving in a wanton way—Jess didn't really care for her, he was only trying to prove that he could conquer her whenever he desired—this place was not private, and there was a very real danger that someone would walk in at any moment and see what was happening.

Thunder reverberated in the sky, shaking heaven and earth. And none of the arguments Libby's reason was offering had any effect on her rising need to join herself with this impossible, overbearing man feasting so brazenly on her breast.

With an unerring hand, Jess found the crux of her passion, and through the fabric of her swimsuit he stroked it to a wanting Libby had never experienced before. Then, still greedy at the nipple he was attending, he deftly worked aside the bit of cloth separating Libby's womanhood from total exposure.

She gasped as he caught the hidden nubbin between his fingers and began, rhythmically, to soothe it. Or was he tormenting it? Libby didn't know, didn't care.

Jess left her breast to nibble at her earlobe, chuckled hoarsely when the tender invasion of his fingers elicited a throaty cry of welcome.

"Go with it, Libby," he whispered. "Let it carry you high...higher..."

Libby was already soaring, sightless, mindless, conscious only of the fiery marauding of his fingers and the strange force inside her that was building toward something she had only imagined before. "Oh," she gasped as he worked this new and fierce magic. "Oh, Jess..."

Mercilessly he intensified her pleasure by whispering outrageously erotic promises, by pressing her legs wide of each other with one knee, by caressing her breast with his other hand.

A savage trembling began deep within Libby, causing her breath to quicken to a soft, lusty whine.

"Meet it, Libby," Jess urged. "Rise to meet it."

Suddenly Libby's entire being buckled in some ancient, inescapable response. The thunder in the distant skies covered her final cry of release, and she convulsed again and again, helpless in the throes of her body's savage victory.

When at last the ferocious clenching and unclenching had ceased, Libby's reason gradually returned. Forcing wide eyes to Jess's face, she saw no demand there, no mockery or revulsion. Instead, he was grinning at her, as pleased as if he'd been sated himself.

Wild embarrassment surged through Libby in the wake of her passion. She tried to avert her face, but Jess caught her chin in his hand and made her look at him.

"Don't," he said gruffly. "Don't look that way. It wasn't wrong, Libby."

His ability to read her thoughts so easily was as unsettling as the knowledge that she'd just allowed this man unconscionable liberties in a hot tub. "I suppose you think...I suppose you want..."

Jess withdrew his conquering hand, tugged her swimsuit back into place. "I think you're beautiful," he supplied, "and I want you—that's true. But for now, watching you respond like that was enough."

Libby blushed again. She was still confused by the power of her release, and she had expected Jess to demand his own satisfaction. She was stunned that he could give such fierce fulfillment and ask nothing for himself.

"You've never been with any man besides your husband, have you, Libby?"

The outrageous bluntness of that question solidified Libby's jellylike muscles, and she reached furiously for one of the towels Mrs. Bradshaw had set nearby on a low shelf. "I've been with a thousand men!" she snapped in a harsh whisper. "Why, one word from any man, and I let him...I let him..."

Jess grinned again. "You've never had a climax before," he observed.

How could he guess a thing like that? It was uncanny. Libby knew that the hot color in her face belied her sharp answer. "Of course I have! I've been married—did you think I was celibate?"

The rapid-fire hysteria of her words only served to amuse Jess, it seemed. "We both know, Libby Kincaid, that you are, for all practical intents and purposes, a virgin. You may have lain beneath that ex-husband of yours and wished to God that he would leave you alone, but until a few minutes ago you had never even guessed what it means to be a woman."

Libby wouldn't have thought it possible to be as murderously angry as she was at that moment. "Why, you arrogant, *insufferable*..."

He caught her hand at the wrist before it could make the intended contact with his face. "You haven't seen anything yet, princess," he vowed with gentle force. "When I take you to bed—and I assure you that I will—I'll prove that everything I've said is true."

While Libby herself was outraged, her traitorous body yearned to lie in his bed, bend to his will. Having reached the edges of passion, it wanted to go beyond, into the molten core. "You egotistical bastard!" Libby hissed, breaking away from him to lift herself out of the hot tub and land on its edge with an inelegant, squishy plop, "You act as if you'd invented sex!"

"As far as you're concerned, little virgin, I did. But have no fear—I intend to deflower you at the first opportunity."

Libby stood up, wrapped her shaky, nerveless form in a towel the size of a bedsheet. "Go to hell!"

Jess rose out of the water, not the least bit self-conscious of his nakedness. The magnitude of his desire for her was all too obvious.

"The next few hours will be just that," he said, reaching for a towel of his own. Naturally, the one he selected barely covered him.

Speechless, Libby imagined the thrust of his manhood, imagined her back arching to receive him, imagined a savage renewal of the passion she had felt only minutes before.

Jess gave her an amused sidelong glance, as though he knew what she was thinking, and intoned, "Don't worry, princess. I'll court you if that's what you want. But I'll have you, too. And thoroughly."

Having made this incredible vow, he calmly walked out of the room, leaving Libby alone with a clamoring flock of strange emotions and unmet needs.

The moment Jess was gone, she stumbled to the nearest lounge chair and sank onto it, her knees too weak to support her. *Well, Kincaid,* she reflected wryly, *now you know. Satisfied?*

Libby winced at the last word. Though she might have wished otherwise, given the identity of the man involved, she was just that.

With carefully maintained dignity, Jess Barlowe strode into the shower
room adjoining the pool and wrenched on one spigot. As he stepped under
the biting, sleetlike spray, he gritted his teeth.

Gradually his body stopped screaming and the stubborn evidence of
his passion faded. With relief, Jess dived out of the shower stall and
grabbed a fresh towel.

A hoarse chuckle escaped him as he dried himself with brisk motions.
Good God, if he didn't have Libby Kincaid soon, he was going to die of
pneumonia. A man could stand only so many plunges into icy ponds,
only so many cold showers.

A spare set of clothes—jeans and a white pullover shirt—awaited Jess
in a cupboard. He donned them quickly, casting one disdainful look at
the three-piece suit he had shed earlier. His circulation restored, to some
degree at least, he toweled his hair and then combed it with the splayed
fingers of his left hand.

A sweet anguish swept through him as he remembered the magic he
had glimpsed in Libby's beautiful face during that moment of full surrender. *My father was right,* Jess thought as he pulled on socks and old,
comfortable boots. *I love you, Libby Kincaid. I love you.*

Jess was not surprised to find that Libby wasn't with Cathy and Monica
in the kitchen—she had probably made some excuse to get out of joining
them for lunch and gone off to gather her thoughts. God knew, she had
to be every bit as undone and confused as he was.

Mostly to avoid the sad speculation in Monica's eyes, Jess glanced
toward the kitchen windows. They were already sheeted with rain.

A crash of thunder jolted him out of the strange inertia that had possessed him. He glanced at Cathy, saw an impish light dancing in her eyes.

"You can catch her if you hurry," she signed, cocking her head to
one side and grinning at him.

Did she know what had happened in the hot tub? Some of the heat
lingering in Jess's loins rose to his face as he bolted out of the room and
through the rest of the house.

The station wagon, an eyesore among the other cars parked in front of
the house, patently refused to start. Annoyed, Jess "borrowed" Monica's
sleek green Porsche without a moment's hesitation, and his aggravation
grew as he left the driveway and pulled out onto the main road.

What the hell did Libby think she was doing, walking in this rain?
And why had Cathy let her go?

He found Libby near the mailboxes, slogging despondently along,
soaked to the skin.

"Get in!" he barked, furious in his concern.

Libby lifted her chin and kept walking. Her turquoise shirt was plastered to her chest, revealing the outlines of her bra, and her hair hung in dripping tendrils.

"Now!" Jess roared through the window he had rolled down halfway.

She stopped, faced him with indigo fury sparking in her eyes. "Why?" she yelled over the combined roars of the deluge and Monica's car engine. "Is it time to teach me what it means to be a woman?"

"How the hell would I know what it means to be a woman?" he shouted back. "Get in this car!"

Libby told him to do something that was anatomically impossible and then went splashing off down the road again, ignoring the driving rain.

Rasping a swearword, Jess slipped the Porsche out of gear and wrenched the emergency brake into place. Then he shoved open the door and bounded through the downpour to catch up with Libby, grasp her by the shoulders and whirl her around to face him.

"If you don't get your backside into that car *right now*," he bellowed, "I swear to God I'll *throw* you in!"

She assessed the Porsche. "Monica's car?"

Furious, Jess nodded. Christ, it was raining so hard that his clothes were already saturated and she was standing there talking details!

An evil smile curved Libby's lips and she stalked toward the automobile, purposely stepping in every mud puddle along the way. Jess could have sworn that she enjoyed sinking, sopping wet, onto the heretofore spotless suede seat.

"Home, James," she said smugly, folding her arms and grinding her mud-caked boots into the lush carpeting on the floorboard.

Jess had no intention of taking Libby to Ken's place, but he said nothing. Envisioning her lying in some hospital bed, wasted away by a case of rain-induced pneumonia, he ground the car savagely back into gear and gunned the engine.

When they didn't take the road Libby expected, the smug look faded from her face and she stared at Jess with wide, wary eyes. "Wait a minute...".

Jess flung an impudent grin at her and saluted with one hand. "Yes?" he drawled, deliberately baiting her.

"Where are we going?"

"My place," he answered, still angry. "It's the classic situation, isn't it? I'll insist you get out of those wet clothes, then I'll toss you one of my bathrobes and pour brandy for us both. After that, lady, I'll make mad love to you."

Libby paled, though there was a defiant light in her eyes. "On a fur rug in front of your fireplace, no doubt!"

"No doubt," Jess snapped, wondering why he found it impossible to deal with this woman in a sane and reasonable way. It would be so much simpler just to tell her straight out that he loved her, that he needed her.

But he couldn't quite bring himself to do that, not just yet, and he was still mad as hell that she would walk in the pouring rain like that.

"Suppose I tell you that I don't want you to 'make mad love' to me, as you so crudely put it? Suppose I tell you that I won't give in to you until the first Tuesday after doomsday, if then, brandy and fur rugs notwithstanding?"

"The way you didn't give in in the hot tub?" he gibed, scowling.

Libby blushed. "That was different!"

"How so?"

"You...you *cornered* me, that's how."

His next words were out of his mouth before he could call them back. "I know about your ex-husband, Libby."

She winced, fixed her attention on the overworked windshield wipers. "What does he have to do with anything?"

Jess shifted to a lower gear as he reached the road leading to his house and turned onto it. "Stacey told me about the women."

The high color drained from Libby's face and she would not look at him. She appeared ready, in fact, to thrust open the door on her side of the car and leap out. "I don't want to talk about this," she said after an interval long enough to bring them to Jess's driveway.

"Why not, Libby?" he asked, and his voice was gentle, if a bit gruff.

One tear rolled over the wet sheen on her defiant rain-polished face, and Libby's chin jutted out in a way that was familiar to him, at once maddening and appealing. "Why do you want to talk about Aaron?" she countered in low, ragged tones. "So you can sit there and feel superior?"

"You know better."

She glared at him, her bruised heart in her eyes, and Jess ached for her. She'd been through so much, and he wished that he could have taken that visible, pounding pain from inside her and borne it himself.

"I don't know better, Jess," she said quietly. "We haven't exactly been kindred spirits, you and I. For all I know, you just want to torture me. To throw all my mistakes in my face and watch me squirm."

Jess's hands tightened on the steering wheel. It took great effort to reach down and shut off the Porsche's engine. "It's cold out here," he said evenly, "and we're both wet to the skin. Let's go inside."

"You won't take me home?" Her voice was small.

He sighed. "Do you want me to?"

Libby considered, lowered her head. "No," she said after a long time.

The inside of Jess's house was spacious and uncluttered. There were skylights in the ceiling and the second floor appeared to be a loft of some sort. Lifting her eyes to the railing above, Libby imagined that his bed was just beyond it and blushed.

Jess seemed to be ignoring her; he was busy with newspaper and kindling at the hearth. She watched the play of the muscles in his back in weary fascination, longing to feel them beneath her hands.

The knowledge that she loved Jess Barlowe, budding in her subconscious mind since her arrival in Montana, suddenly burst into full flower. But was the feeling really new?

If Libby were to be honest with herself—and she tried to be, always—she had to admit that the chances were good that she had loved Jess for a very long time.

He turned, rose from his crouching position, a small fire blazing and crackling behind him. "How do you like my house?" he asked with a half smile.

Between her newly recognized feelings for this man and the way his jade eyes seemed to see through all her reserve to the hurt and confusion hidden beneath, Libby felt very vulnerable. Trusting in an old trick that had always worked in the past, she looked around in search of something to be angry about.

The skylights, the loft, the view of the mountains from the windows beyond his desk—all of it was appealing. Masculine. Quietly romantic.

"Perfect quarters for a wealthy and irresponsible playboy," she threw out in desperation.

Jess stiffened momentarily, but then an easy grin creased his face. "I think that was a shot, but I'm not going to fire back, Libby, so you might as well relax."

Relax? Was the man insane? Half an hour before, he had blithely brought her to climax in a hot tub, for God's sake, and now they were alone, the condition of their clothes necessitating that they risk further intimacies by stripping them off, taking showers. If they couldn't fight, what *were* they going to do?

Before Libby could think of anything to say in reply, Jess gestured toward the broad redwood stairs leading up to the loft. "The bathroom is up there," he said. "Take a shower. You'll find a robe hanging on the inside of the door." With that, he turned away to crouch before the fire again and add wood.

Because she was cold and there seemed to be no other options, Libby climbed the stairs. It wasn't until she reached the loft that her teeth began to chatter.

There she saw Jess's wide unmade bed. It was banked by a line of floor-to-ceiling windows, giving the impression that the room was open to the outdoors, and the wrinkled sheets probably still bore that subtle, clean scent that was Jess's alone...

Libby took herself in hand, wrenched her attention away from the bed. There was a glass-fronted wood-burning stove in one corner of the large room, and a long bookshelf on the other side was crammed with everything from paperback mysteries to volumes on veterinary medicine.

Libby made her way into the adjoining bathroom and kicked off her muddy boots, peeled away her jeans and shirt, her sodden underwear and socks. Goosebumps leapt out all over her body, and they weren't entirely related to the chill.

The bathtub was enormous, and like the bed, it was framed by tall uncurtained windows. Bathing here would be like bathing in the high limbs of a tree, so sweeping was the view of mountains and grassland beyond the glass.

Trembling a little, Libby knelt to turn on the polished brass spigots and fill the deep tub. The water felt good against her chilled flesh, and she was submerged to her chin before she remembered that she had meant to take a quick shower, not a lingering, dreamy bath.

Libby couldn't help drawing a psychological parallel between this tub and the larger one at the main house, where she had made such a fool of herself. Was there some mysterious significance in the fact that she'd chosen the bathtub over the double-wide shower stall on the other side of the room?

Now you're really getting crazy, Kincaid, she said to herself, settling back to soak.

Somewhere in the house, a telephone rang, was swiftly answered.

Libby relaxed in the big tub and tried to still her roiling thoughts and emotions. She would not consider what might happen later. For now, she wanted to be comforted, pampered. Deliciously warm.

She heard the click of boot heels on the stairs, though, and sat bolt upright in the water. A sense of sweet alarm raced through her system. Jess wouldn't come in, actually *come in,* would he?

Of course he would! Why would a bathroom door stop a man who would make such brazen advances in a hot tub?

With frantic eyes Libby sought the towel shelf. It was entirely too far away, and so was the heavy blue-and-white velour robe hanging on the inside of the door. She sank into the bathwater until it tickled her lower lip, squeezed her eyes shut and waited.

"Lib?"

"Wh-what?" she managed. He was just beyond that heavy wooden panel, and Libby found herself hoping...

Hoping what? That Jess would walk in, or that he would stay out? She honestly didn't know.

"That was Ken on the phone," Jess answered, making no effort to open the door. "I told him you were here and that I'd bring you home after the rain lets up."

Libby reddened, there in the privacy of that unique bathroom, imagining the thoughts that were probably going through her father's mind. "Wh-what did he say?"

Jess chuckled, and the sound was low, rich. "Let me put it this way: I don't think he's going to rush over here and defend your virtue."

Libby was at once pleased and disappointed. Wasn't a father *supposed* to protect his daughter from persuasive lechers like Jess Barlowe?

"Oh," she said, her voice sounding foolish and uncertain. "D-do you want me to hurry? S-so you can take a shower, I mean?"

"Take your time," he said offhandedly. "There's another bathroom downstairs—I can shower there."

Having imparted this conversely comforting and disenchanting information, Jess began opening and closing drawers. Seconds later, Libby again heard his footsteps on the stairs.

Despite the fact that she would have preferred to lounge in that wonderful bathtub for the rest of the day, Libby shot out of the water and raced to the towel bar. This was her chance to get dried off and dressed in something before Jess could incite her to further scandalous behavior.

She was wrapped in his blue-and-white bathrobe, the belt securely tied, and cuddled under a knitted afghan by the time Jess joined her in the living room, looking reprehensibly handsome in fresh jeans and a green turtleneck sweater. His hair, like her own, was still damp, and there was a smile in his eyes, probably inspired by the way she was trying to burrow deeper into her corner of the couch.

"There isn't any brandy after all," he said with a helpless gesture of his hands. "Will you settle for chicken soup?"

Libby would have agreed to anything that would get Jess out of that room, even for a few minutes, and he would have to go to the kitchen for soup, wouldn't he? Unable to speak, she nodded.

She tried to concentrate on the leaping flames in the fireplace, but she could hear the soft thump of cupboard doors, the running of tapwater, the singular whir of a microwave oven. The sharp *ting* of the appliance's timer bell made her flinch.

Too soon, Jess returned, carrying two mugs full of steaming soup. He extended one to Libby and, to her eternal gratitude, settled in a chair nearby instead of on the couch beside her.

Outside, the rain came down in torrents, making a musical, pelting sound on the skylights, sliding down the windows in sheets. The fire snapped and threw out sparks, as if to mock the storm that could not reach it.

Jess took a sip of the hot soup and grinned. "This doesn't exactly fit the scenario I outlined in the car," he said, lifting his cup.

"You got everything else right," Libby quipped, referring to the bath she'd taken and the fact that she was wearing his robe. Instantly she realized how badly she'd slipped, but it was too late to call back her words, and the ironic arch of Jess's brow and the smile on his lips indicated that he wasn't going to let the comment pass.

"Everything?" he teased. "There isn't any fur rug, either."

Libby's cheekbones burned. Unable to say anything, she lowered her eyes and watched the tiny noodles colliding in her mug of soup.

"I'm sorry," Jess said softly.

She swallowed hard and met his eyes. He did look contrite, and there was nothing threatening in his manner. Because of that, Libby dared to ask, "Do you really mean to...tó make love to me?"

"Only if you want me to," he replied. "You must know that I wouldn't force you, Libby."

She sensed that he meant this and relaxed a little. Sooner or later, she was going to have to accept the fact that all men didn't behave in the callous and hurtful way that Aaron had. "You believe me now—don't you? About Stacey, I mean?"

If that off-the-wall question had surprised or nettled Jess, he gave no indication of it. He simply nodded.

Some crazy bravery, carrying her forward like a reckless tide, made Libby put aside her carefully built reserve and blurt out, "Do you think I'm a fool, Jess?"

Jess gaped at her, the mug of soup forgotten in his hands. "A fool?"

Libby lowered her eyes. "I mean...well...because of Aaron."

"Why should I think anything like that?"

Thunder exploded in the world outside the small cocoonlike one that held only Libby and Jess. "He was...he..."

"He was with other women," supplied Jess quietly. Gently.

Libby nodded, managed to look up.

"And you stayed with him." He was setting down the mug, drawing nearer. Finally he crouched before her on his haunches and took the cup from her hands to set it aside. "You couldn't leave Jonathan, Libby. I understand that. Besides, why should the fact that you stuck with the marriage have any bearing on my attitude toward you?"

"I just thought..."

"What?" prodded Jess when her sentence fell away. "What did you think, Libby?"

Tears clogged her throat. "I thought that I couldn't be very desirable if my o-own husband couldn't...wouldn't..."

Jess gave a ragged sigh. "My God, Libby, you don't think that Aaron was unfaithful because of some lack in you?"

That was exactly what she'd thought, on a subliminal level at least. Another woman, a stronger, more experienced, more alluring woman, might have been able to keep her husband happy, make him want her.

Jess's hands came to Libby's shoulders, gentle and insistent. "Lib, talk to me."

"Just how terrific could I be?" she erupted suddenly, in the anguish that would be hidden no longer. "Just how desirable? My husband needed other women because he couldn't bring himself to make love to me!"

Jess drew her close, held her as the sobs she had restrained at last broke free. "That wasn't your fault, Libby," he breathed, his hand in her hair now, soothing and strong. "Oh, sweetheart, it wasn't your fault."

"Of course it was!" she wailed into the soft green knit of his sweater, the hard strength of the shoulder beneath. "If I'd been better...if I'd known how..."

"Shhh. Baby, don't. Don't do this to yourself."

Once freed, Libby's emotions seemed impossible to check. They ran as deep and wild as any river, swirling in senseless currents and eddies, causing her pride to founder.

Jess caught her trembling hands in his, squeezed them reassuringly. "Listen to me, princess," he said. "These doubts that you're having about yourself are understandable, under the circumstances, but they're not valid. You are desirable." He paused, searched her face with tender, reproving eyes. "I can swear to that."

Libby still felt broken, and she hadn't forgotten the terrible things Aaron had said to her during their marriage—that she was cold and unresponsive, that he hadn't been impotent before he'd married her. Time and time again he had held up Jonathan as proof that he had been virile with his first wife, taken cruel pleasure in pointing out that none of his many girlfriends found him wanting.

Wrenching herself back to the less traumatic present, Libby blurted out, "Make love to me, Jess. Let me prove to myself—"

"No," he said with cold, flat finality. And then he released her hands, stood up and turned away as if in disgust.

Chapter 6

"I thought you wanted me," Libby said in a small, broken voice.

Jess's broad back stiffened, and he did not turn around to face her. "I do."

"Then, why...?"

He went to the fireplace, took up a poker, stoked the blazing logs within to burn faster, hotter. "When I make love to you, Libby, it won't be because either one of us wants to prove anything."

Libby lowered her head, ashamed. As if to scold her, the wind and rain lashed at the windows and the lightning flashed, filling the room with its eerie blue-gold light. She began to cry again, this time softly, wretchedly.

And Jess came to her, lifted her easily into his arms. Without a word, he carried her up the stairs, across the storm-shadowed loft room to the bed. After pulling back the covers with one hand, he lowered her to the sheets. "Rest," he said, tucking the blankets around her.

Libby gaped at him, amazed and stricken. She couldn't help thinking that he wouldn't have tucked Monica Summers into bed this way, kissed *her* forehead as though she were some overwrought child needing a nap.

"I don't want to rest," Libby said, insulted. And her hands moved to pull the covers down.

Jess stopped her by clasping her wrists. A muscle knotted in his jaw, and his jade-green eyes flashed, their light as elemental as that of the electrical storm outside. "Don't Libby. Don't tempt me."

She *had* been tempting him—if he hadn't stopped her when he did, she would have opened the robe, wantonly displayed her breasts. Now, she was mortally embarrassed. What on earth was making her act this way?

"I'm sorry," she whispered. "I don't know what's the matter with me."

Jess sat down on the edge of the bed, his magnificent face etched in shadows, his expression unreadable. "Do we have to go into that again, princess? Nothing is wrong with you."

"But—"

Jess laid one index finger to her lips to silence her. "It would be wrong if we made love now, Libby—don't you see that? Afterward, you'd be telling yourself what a creep I was for taking advantage of you when you were so vulnerable."

His logic was unassailable. To lighten the mood, Libby summoned up a shaky grin. "Some playboy you are. Chicken soup. Patience. Have you no passion?"

He laughed. "More than I know what to do with," he said, standing up, walking away from the bed. At the top of the stairs he paused. "Am I crazy?"

Libby didn't answer. Smiling, she snuggled down under the covers—she was just a bit tired—and placidly watched the natural light show beyond the windows. Maybe later there would be fireworks of another sort.

Downstairs, Jess resisted a fundamental urge to beat his head against the wall. Libby Kincaid was up there in his bed, for God's sake, warm and lush and wanting him.

He ached to go back up the stairs and finish what they'd begun that morning in the hot tub. He couldn't, of course, because Libby was in no condition, emotionally, for that kind of heavy scene. If he did the wrong thing, said the wrong thing, she could break, and the pieces might not fit together again.

In a fit of neatness, Jess gathered up the cups of cold chicken soup and carried them into the kitchen. There he dumped their contents into the sink, rinsed them, and stacked them neatly in the dishwasher.

The task was done too quickly. What could he do? He didn't like the idea of leaving Libby alone, but he didn't dare go near her again, either. The scent of her, the soft disarray of her hair, the way her breasts seemed to draw at his mouth and the palms of his hands—all those things combined to make his grasp on reason tenuous.

Jess groaned, lifted his eyes to the ceiling and wondered if he was going to have to endure another ice-cold shower. The telephone rang, startling him, and he reached for it quickly. Libby might already be asleep, and he didn't want her to be disturbed.

"Hello?"

"Jess?" Monica's voice was calm, but there was an undercurrent of cold fury. "Did you take my car?"

He sighed, leaning back against the kitchen counter. "Yeah. Sorry. I should have called you before this, but—"

"But you were busy."

Jess flinched. Exactly what could he say to that? "Monica—"

"Never mind, Jess." She sighed the words. "I didn't have any right to say that. And if you helped yourself to my car, you must have had a good reason."

Why the hell did she have to be so reasonable? Why didn't Monica yell at him or something, so that he could get mad in good conscience and stop feeling like such an idiot? "I'm afraid the seats are a little muddy," he said.

"Muddy? Oh, yes—the rain. Was Libby okay?"

Again Jess's gaze lifted to the ceiling. Libby was not okay, thanks to him and Stacey and her charming ex-husband. But then, Monica was just making polite conversation, not asking for an in-depth account of Libby's emotional state. "She was drenched."

"So you brought her there, got her out of her wet clothes, built a fire—"

The anger Jess had wished for was suddenly there. "Monica."

She drew in a sharp breath. "All right, all right—I'm sorry. I take it our dinner date is off?"

"Yeah," Jess answered, turning the phone cord between his fingers. "I guess it is."

Monica was nothing if not persistent—probably that quality accounted for her impressive success in political circles. "Tomorrow night?"

Jess sighed. "I don't know."

There was a short, uncomfortable silence. "We'll talk later," Monica finally said brightly. "Listen, is it okay if I send somebody over there to get my car?"

"I'll bring it to you," Jess said. It was, after stealing it, the least he could do. He'd check first, to make sure that Libby really was sleeping, and with luck, he could be back before she woke up.

"Thanks," sang Monica in parting.

Jess hung up the phone and climbed the stairs, pausing at the edge of the bedroom. He dared go no further, wanting that rumple-haired little hellion the way he did. "Libby?"

When there was no answer, Jess turned and went back down the stairs again, almost grateful that he had somewhere to go, something to do.

Monica hid her annoyance well as she inspected the muddy splotches on her car's upholstery. Overhead, the incessant rain pummeled the garage roof.

"I'm sorry," Jess said. It seemed that he was always apologizing for one thing or another lately. "My station wagon wouldn't start, and I was in a hurry..."

Monica allowed a flicker of anger to show in her gray eyes. "Right. When there is a damsel to be rescued, a knight has to grab the first available charger."

Having no answer for that, Jess shrugged. "I'll have your car cleaned," he offered when the silence grew too long, and then he turned to walk back out of the garage and down the driveway to his own car, which refused to start.

He got out and slammed the door. "Damn!" he bellowed, kicking yet another dent into the fender.

"Problems?"

Jess hadn't been aware of Ken until that moment, hadn't noticed the familiar truck parked nearby. "It would take all day to list them," he replied ruefully.

Ken grinned a typical sideways grin, and his blue eyes twinkled. He seemed oblivious of the rain pouring off the brim of his ancient hat and soaking through his denim jacket and jeans. "I think maybe my daughter might be at the top of the list. Is she all right?"

"She's..." Jess faltered, suddenly feeling like a high-school kid. "She's sleeping."

Ken laughed. "Must have been real hard to say that," he observed, "me being her daddy and all."

"It isn't...I didn't..."

Again Ken laughed. "Maybe you should," he said.

Jess was shocked—so shocked that he was speechless.

"Take my truck if you need it," Ken offered calmly, his hand coming to rest on Jess's shoulder. "I'll get a ride home from somebody here. And, Jess?"

"What?"

"Don't hurt Libby. She's had enough trouble and grief as it is."

"I know that," Jess replied, as the rain plastered his hair to his neck and forehead and made his clothes cling to his flesh in sodden, clammy patches. "I swear I won't hurt her."

"That's good enough for me," replied Libby's father, and then he pried the truck keys out of his pocket and tossed them to Jess.

"Ken..."

The foreman paused, looking back, his eyes wise and patient. How the hell was Jess going to ask this man what he had to ask, for Libby's sake?

"Spit it out, son," Ken urged. "I'm getting wet."

"Clothes—she was...Libby was caught in the rain, and she needs dry clothes."

Ken chuckled and shrugged his shoulders. "Stop at our place and get some of her things then," he said indulgently.

Jess was suddenly as confused by this man as he was by his daughter. What the hell was Ken doing, standing there taking this whole thing so calmly? Didn't it bother him, knowing what might happen when Jess got back to that house?

"See ya," said Ken in parting.

Completely confused, Jess got into Ken's truck and drove away. It wasn't until he'd gotten a set of dry clothes for Libby and reached his own house again that he understood. Ken trusted him.

Jess let his forehead rest on the truck's steering wheel and groaned. He couldn't stand another cold shower, dammit. He just couldn't.

But Ken trusted him. Libby was lying upstairs in his bed, and even if she was, by some miracle, ready to handle what was destined to happen, Jess couldn't make love to her. To do so would be to betray a man who had, in so many ways, been as much a father to him as Cleave Barlowe had.

The problem was that Jess couldn't think of Libby as a sister.

Jess sat glumly at the little table in the kitchen, making patterns in his omelet with a fork. Tiring of that, he flung Libby a beleaguered look and sneezed.

She felt a surge of tenderness. "Aren't you hungry?"

He shook his head. "Libby..."

It took all of her forbearance not to stand up, round the table, and touch Jess's forehead to see if he had a fever. "What?" she prompted softly.

"I think I should take you home."

Libby was hurt, but she smiled brightly. "Well, it *has* stopped raining," she reasoned.

"And I've got your dad's truck," added Jess.

"Um-hmm. Thanks for stopping and getting my clothes, by the way."

Outside, the wind howled and the night was dark. Jess gave the jeans and loose pink sweater he had picked up for Libby a distracted look and sneezed again. "You're welcome."

"And you, my friend, are sick."

Jess shook his head, went to the counter to pour coffee from the coffeemaker there. "Want some?" he asked, lifting the glass pot.

Libby declined. "Were you taking another shower when I got up?" she ventured cautiously. The peace between them, for all its sweet glow, was still new and fragile.

Libby would have sworn that he winced, and his face was unreadable. "I'm a clean person," he said, averting his eyes.

Libby bit the inside of her lower lip, suddenly possessed by an untimely urge to laugh. Jess had been shivering when he came out of that bathroom and unexpectedly encountered his newly awakened houseguest.

"Right," she said.

Jess sneezed again, violently. Somehow, the sound unchained Libby's amusement and she shrieked with laughter.

"What is so goddamn funny?" Jess demanded, setting his coffee cup down with an irritated thump and scowling.

"N-nothing," cried Libby.

Suddenly Jess was laughing too. He pulled Libby out of her chair and into his arms, and she deliberately pressed herself close to him, delighting in the evidence of his desire, in the scent and substance and strength of him.

She almost said that she loved him.

"You wanted my body!" she accused instead, teasing.

Jess groaned and tilted his head back, ostensibly to study the ceiling. Libby saw a muscle leap beneath his chin and wanted to kiss it, but she refrained.

"You were taking a cold shower, weren't you, Jess?"

"Yes," he admitted with a martyrly sigh. "Woman, if I die of pneumonia, it will be your fault."

"On the contrary. I've done everything but throw myself at your feet, mister, and you haven't wanted any part of me."

"Wrong." Jess grinned wickedly, touching the tip of her breast with an index finger. "I want this part..." The finger trailed away, following an erotic path. "And this part..."

It took all of Libby's courage to say the words again, after his brisk rejection earlier. "Make love to me, Jess."

"My God, Libby—"

She silenced him by laying two fingers to his lips. Remembering the words he had flung at her in the Cessna the day of her arrival, she said saucily, "If it feels good, do it."

Jess gave her a mock scowl, but his arms were around her now, holding her against him. "You were a very mean little kid," he muttered, "and now you're a mean adult. Do you know what you're doing to me, Kincaid?"

Libby moved her hips slightly, delighting in the contact and the guttural groan the motion brought from Jess. "I have some vague idea, yes."

"Your father trusts me."

"My father!" Libby stared up at him, amazed. "Is that what you've been worried about? What my father will think?"

Jess shrugged, and his eyes moved away from hers. Clearly he was embarrassed. "Yes."

Libby laughed, though she was not amused. "You're not serious!"

His eyes came back to meet hers and the expression in their green depths was nothing if not serious. "Ken is my best friend," he said.

"Shall I call him up and ask for permission? Better yet, I could drive over there and get a note!"

The taunts caused Jess to draw back a little, though their thighs and hips were still touching, still piping primitive messages one to the other. "Very funny!" he snapped, and a muscle bunched in his neck, went smooth again.

Libby was quietly furious. "You're right—it isn't funny. This is my body, Jess—mine. I'm thirty-one years old and I make my own living and I *damned well* don't need my daddy's permission to go to bed with a man!"

The green eyes were twinkling with mischief. "That's a healthy attitude if I've ever heard one," he broke in. "However, before we go up
those stairs, there is one more thing I want to know. Are you using me,
Libby?"

"Using you?"

"Yes. Do I really mean something to you, or would any man do?"

Libby felt as though she'd just grabbed hold of a high-voltage wire;
in a few spinning seconds she was hurled from pain to rage to humiliation.

Jess held her firmly. "I see the question wasn't received in the spirit
in which it was intended," he said, his eyes serious now, searching her
burning, defiant face. "What I meant to ask was, are we going to be
making love, Libby, or just proving that you can go the whole route and
respond accordingly?"

Libby met his gaze bravely, though inside she was still shaken and
angry. "Why would I go to all this trouble, Jess, if I didn't want you?
After all, I could have just stopped someone on the street and said, 'Excuse me, sir, but would you mind making love to me? I'd like to find
out if I'm frigid or not.'"

Jess sighed heavily, but his hands were sliding up under the back of
Libby's pink sweater, gently kneading the firm flesh there. The only sign
that her sarcasm had rankled him was the almost imperceptible leaping
of the pulsepoint beneath his right ear.

"I guess I'm having a little trouble understanding your sudden change
of heart, Libby. For years you've hated my guts. Now, after confiding
that your ex-husband put you through some kind of emotional wringer
and left you feeling about as attractive as a sink drain, you want to share
my bed."

Libby closed her eyes. The motion of his hands on her back was hyp-
notic, making it hard for her to breathe, let alone think. When she felt
the catch of her bra give way, she shivered.

She should tell him that she loved him, that maybe, despite outward
appearances, she'd always loved him, but she didn't dare. This was a man
who had thought the worst of her at every turn, who had never missed a
chance to get under her skin. Allowing him inside the fortress where her
innermost emotions were stored could prove disastrous.

His hands came slowly around from her back to the aching roundness
of her breasts, sliding easily, brazenly under the loosened bra.

"Answer me, Libby," he drawled, his voice a sleepy rumble.

She was dazed; his fingers came to play a searing symphony at her
nipples, plying them, drawing at them. "I...I want you. I'm not trying
to p-prove anything."

"Let me look at you, Libby."

Libby pulled the pink sweater off over her head, stood perfectly still
as Jess dispensed with her bra and then stepped back a little way to admire
her.

He outlined one blushing nipple with the tip of his finger, progressed to wreak the same havoc on the other. Then, with strong hands, he lifted Libby up onto a counter, so that her breasts were on a level with his face.

She gasped as he took languid, tentative suckle at one peak, then trailed a path with the tip of his tongue to the other, conquering it with lazy ease.

She was desperate now. "Make love to me," she whispered again in broken tones.

"Make love to me, *Jess*," he prompted, nibbling now, driving her half-wild with the need of him.

Libby swallowed hard, closed her eyes. His teeth were scraping gently at her nipple now, rousing it to obedience. "Make love to me, Jess," she repeated breathlessly.

He withdrew his mouth, cupping her in his hands, letting his thumbs do the work his lips and teeth had done before. "Open your eyes," he commanded in a hoarse rumble. "Look at me, Libby."

Dazed, her very soul spinning within her, Libby obeyed.

"Tell me," he insisted raggedly, "that you're not seeing Stacey or your misguided ex-husband. Tell me that you see *me*, Libby."

"I do, Jess."

He lifted her off the counter and into his arms, and his mouth came down on hers, cautious at first, then almost harshly demanding. Libby was electrified by the kiss, by the searching fierceness of his tongue, by the moan of need that came from somewhere deep inside him. Finally he ended the kiss, and his eyes were smiling into hers.

Feeling strangely giddy, Libby laughed. "Is this the part where you make love to me?"

"This is it," he replied, and then they were moving through the house toward the stairs. Lightning crackled and flashed above the skylights, while thunder struck a booming accompaniment.

"The earth is moving already," said Libby into the Jess-scented wool of his sweater.

Jess took the stairs two at a time. "Just wait," he replied.

In the bedroom, which was lit only by the lightning that was sundering the night sky, he set Libby on her feet. For a moment they just stood still, looking at each other. Libby felt as though she had become a part of the terrible storm that was pounding at the tall windows, and she grasped Jess's arms so that she wouldn't be blown away to the mountaintops or flung beyond the angry clouds.

"Touch me, Libby," Jess said, and somehow, even over the renewed rage of the storm, she heard him.

Cautiously she slid her hands beneath his sweater, splaying her fingers so that she could feel as much of him as possible. His chest was hard and broad and softly furred, and he groaned as she found masculine nipples and explored them.

Libby moved her hands down over his rib cage to the sides of his waist, up his warm, granite-muscled back. *I love you,* she thought, and then she bit her lower lip lest she actually say the words.

At some unspoken urging from Jess, she caught his sweater in bunched fists and drew it up over his head. Silver-blue lightning scored the sky and danced on the planes of his bare chest, his magnificent face.

Libby was drawn to him, tasting one masculine nipple with a cautious tongue, suckling the other. He moaned and tangled his fingers in her hair, pressing her close, and she knew that he was experiencing the same keen pleasure she had known.

Presently he caught her shoulders in his hands and held her at arm's length, boldly admiring her bare breasts. "Beautiful," he rasped. "So beautiful."

Libby had long been ashamed of her body, thinking it inadequate. Now, in this moment of storm and fury, she was proud of every curve and hollow, every pore and freckle. She removed her jeans and panties with graceful motions.

Jess's reaction was a low, rumbling groan, followed by a gasp of admiration. He stood still, a western Adonis, as she undid his jeans, felt the hollows of his narrow hips, the firmness of his buttocks. Within seconds he was as naked as Libby.

She caught his hands in her own, drew him toward the bed. But instead of reclining with her there, he knelt at the side, positioned Libby so that her hips rested on the edge of the mattress.

His hands moved over every part of her—her breasts, her shoulders, her flat, smooth stomach, the insides of her trembling thighs.

"Jess..."

"Shh, it's all right."

"But..." Libby's back arched and a spasm of delight racked her as he touched the curls sheltering the core of her passion, first with his fingers, then with his lips. "Oh...wait...oh, Jess, no..."

"Yes," he said, his breath warm against her. And then he parted her and took her fully into his mouth, following the instinctive rising and falling of her hips, chuckling at the soft cry she gave.

A violent shudder went through Libby's already throbbing body, and her knees moved wide of each other, shaking, made of no solid substance.

Frantic, she found his head, tangled her fingers in his hair. "Stop," she whimpered, even as she held him fast.

Jess chuckled again and then went right on consuming her, his hands catching under her knees, lifting them higher, pressing them farther apart.

Libby was writhing now, her breath harsh and burning, her vision blurred. The storm came inside the room and swept her up, up, up, beyond the splitting skies. She cried out in wonder as she collided with the moon and bounced off, to be enfolded by a waiting sun.

When she came back inside herself, Jess was beside her on the bed, soothing her with soft words, stroking away the tears that had somehow gathered on her face.

"I've never read..." she whispered stupidly. "I didn't know..."

Jess was drawing her up, so that she lay full on the bed, naked and sated at his side. "Look it up," he teased, kissing her briefly, tenderly. "I think it would be under O."

Libby laughed, and the sound was a warm, soft contrast to the tumult of the storm. "What an ego!"

With an index finger, Jess traced her lips, her chin, the moist length of her neck. Small novas flashed and flared within her as her pulsing senses began to make new demands.

When his mouth came to her breast again, Libby arched her back and whimpered. "Jess...Jess..."

He circled the straining nipple with a warm tongue. "What, babe?"

No coherent words would come to Libby's beleaguered mind. "I don't know," she managed finally. "I don't know!"

"I do," Jess answered, and then he suckled in earnest.

Powerless under the tyranny of her own body, Libby gave herself up to sensation. It seemed that no part of her was left untouched, unconquered, or unworshiped.

When at last Jess poised himself above her, strong and fully a man, his face reflected the flashing lightning that seemed to seek them both.

"I'm Jess," he warned again in a husky whisper that betrayed his own fierce need.

Libby drew him to her with quick, fevered hands. "I know," she gasped, and then she repeated his name like some crazy litany, whispering it first, sobbing it when he thrust his searing magnificence inside her.

He moved slowly at first, and the finely sculptured planes of his face showed the cost of his restraint, the conflicting force of his need. "Libby," he pleaded. "Oh, God...Libby..."

She thrust her hips upward in an instinctive, unplanned motion that shattered Jess's containment and caused his great muscular body to convulse once and then assert its dominance in a way that was at once fierce and tender. It seemed that he sought some treasure within her, so deeply did he delve, some shimmering thing that he would perish without.

His groans rose above the sound of thunder, and as his pace accelerated and his passion was unleashed, Libby moved in rhythm with him, one with him, his.

Their bodies moved faster, agile in their quest, each glistening with the sheen of sweet exertion, each straining toward the sun that, this time, would consume them both.

The tumult flung them high, tore them asunder, fused them together again. Libby sobbed in the hot glory of her release and heard an answering cry from Jess.

They clung together, struggling for breath, for a long time after the slow, treacherous descent had been made. Twice, on the way, Libby's body had paused to greedily claim what had been denied it before.

She was flushed, reckless in her triumph. "I did it," she exalted, her hands moving on the slackened muscles in Jess's back. "I did it...I responded..."

Instantly she felt those muscles go taut, and Jess's head shot up from its resting place in the curve where her neck and shoulder met.

"What?"

Libby stiffened, knowing now, too late, how grave her mistake had been. "I mean, *we* did it..." she stumbled lamely.

But Jess was wrenching himself away from her, searching for his clothes, pulling them on. "Congratulations!" he yelled.

Libby sat up, confused, wildly afraid. Dear God, was he going to walk out now? Was he going to hate her for a few thoughtless words?

"Jess, wait!" she pleaded, clutching the sheet to her chest. "Please!"

"For what, Libby?" he snapped from the top of the stairs. "Exhibit B? Is there something else you want to prove?"

"Jess!"

But he was storming down the stairs, silent in his rage, bent on escaping her.

"Jess!" Libby cried out again in fear, tears pouring down her face, her hands aching where they grasped the covers.

The only answer was the slamming of the front door.

Chapter 7

Ken Kincaid looked up from the cards in his hand as the lights flickered, went out, came on again. Damn, this was a hell of a storm—if the rain didn't let up soon, the creeks would overflow and they'd have range calves drowning right and left.

Across the table, Cleave Barlowe laid down his own hand of cards. "Quite a storm, eh?" he asked companionably. "Jess bring your truck back yet?"

"I don't need it," said Ken, still feeling uneasy.

Lightning creased the sky beyond the kitchen window, and thunder shook the old house on its sturdy foundations. Cleave grinned. "He's with Libby, then?"

"Yup," said Ken, smiling himself.

"Think they know the sky's turning itself inside out?"

There was an easing in Ken; he laughed outright. "Doubt it," he replied, looking at his cards again.

For a while the two men played the two-handed poker they had enjoyed for years, but it did seem that luck wasn't running with either one of them. Finally they gave up the effort and Cleave went home.

With his old friend gone, Ken felt apprehensive again. He went around the house making sure all the windows were closed against the rain, and wondered why one storm should bother him that way, when he'd seen a thousand and never found them anything more than a nuisance.

He was about to shut off the lamp in the front room when he saw the headlights of his own truck swing into the driveway. Seconds later, there was an anxious knock at the door.

"Jess?" Ken marveled, staring at the haggard, rain-drenched man standing on the front porch. "What the hell...?"

Jess looked as though he'd just taken a first-rate gut punch. "Could I come in?"

"That's a stupid question," retorted Ken, stepping back to admit his unexpected and obviously distraught visitor. "Is Libby okay?"

Jess's haunted eyes wouldn't quite link up with Ken's. "She's fine," he said, his hands wedged into the pockets of his jeans, his hair and sweater dripping rainwater.

Ken arched an eyebrow. "What'd you do, anyway—ride on the running board of that truck and steer from outside?"

Jess didn't answer; he didn't seem to realize that he was wet to the skin. There was a distracted look about him that made Ken ache inside.

In silence Ken led the way into the kitchen, poured a dose of straight whiskey into a mug, added strong coffee.

"You look like you've been dragged backward through a knothole," he observed when Jess was settled at the table. "What happened?"

Jess closed his hands around the mug. "I'm in love with your daughter," he said after a long time.

Ken sat down, allowed himself a cautious grin. "If you drove over here in this rain just to tell me that, friend, you got wet for nothing."

"You knew?" Jess seemed honestly surprised.

"Everybody knew. Except maybe you and Libby."

Jess downed the coffee and the potent whiskey almost in a single gulp. There was a struggle going on in his face, as though he might be fighting hard to hold himself together.

Ken rose to put more coffee into Jess's mug, along with a lot more whiskey. If ever a man needed a drink, this one did.

"Maybe you'd better put on some dry clothes," the older man ventured.

Jess only shook his head.

Ken sat back in his chair and waited. When Jess was ready to talk, he would. There was, Ken had learned, no sense in pushing before that point was reached.

"Libby's beautiful, you know," Jess remarked presently, as he started on his third drink.

Ken smiled. "Yeah. I've noticed."

Simple and ordinary though they were, the words triggered some kind of emotional reaction in Jess, broke down the barriers he had been maintaining so carefully. His face crumbled, he lowered his head to his arms, and he cried. The sobs were deep and dry and ragged.

Hurting because Jess hurt, Ken waited.

Soon enough, his patience was rewarded. Jess began to talk, brokenly at first, and then with stone-cold reason.

Ken didn't react openly to anything he said; much of what Jess told him about Libby's marriage to Aaron Strand came as no real surprise. He was wounded, all the same, for his daughter and for the devastated young man sitting across the table from him.

The level of whiskey in Ken's bottle went down as the hour grew later.

Finally, when Jess was so drunk that his words started getting all tangled up with each other, Ken half led, half carried him up the stairs to Libby's room.

In the hallway, he paused, reflecting. Life was a hell of a thing, he decided. Here was Jess, sleeping fitfully in Libby's bed, all alone. And just up the hill, chances were, Libby was tossing and turning in Jess's bed, just as lonely.

Not for the first time, Ken Kincaid felt a profound desire to get them both by the hair and knock their heads together.

Libby cried until far into the night and then, exhausted, she slept. When she awakened, shocked to find herself in Jess Barlowe's bed, she saw that the world beyond the windows had been washed to a clean sparkle.

The world inside her seemed tawdry by comparison.

Her face feeling achy and swollen, Libby got out of bed, stumbled across the room to the bathroom. Jess was nowhere in the house; she would have sensed it if he were.

As Libby filled the tub with hot water, she wondered whether she was relieved that he wasn't close by, or disappointed. A little of both, she concluded as she slid into her bath and sat there in miserable reverie.

Facing Jess now would have been quite beyond her. Why, why had she said such a foolish thing, when she might have known how Jess would react? On the other hand, why had *he* made such a big deal out of a relatively innocuous remark?

More confused than ever, Libby finished her bath and climbed out to dry herself with a towel. In short order she was dressed and her hair was combed. Because she had no toothbrush—Jess had forgotten that when he picked up her things—she had to be content with rinsing her mouth.

Downstairs, Libby stood staring at the telephone, willing herself to call her father and confess that she needed a ride home. Pride wouldn't allow that, however, and she had made up her mind to walk the distance when she heard a familiar engine outside, the slam of a truck door.

Jess was back, she thought wildly. Where had he been all night? With Monica? What would she say to him?

The questions were pointless, for when Libby forced herself to go to the front door and open it, she saw her father striding up the walk, not Jess.

Fresh embarrassment stained Libby's cheeks, though there was no condemnation in Ken's weathered face, no anger in his understanding eyes. "Ride home?" he said.

Unable to speak, Libby only nodded.

"Pretty bad night?" he ventured in his concise way when they were both settled in the truck and driving away.

"Dismal," replied Libby, fixing her eyes on the red Hereford cattle grazing in the green, rain-washed distance.

"Jess isn't in very good shape either," commented Ken after an interval.

Libby's eyes were instantly trained on her father's profile. "You've seen him?"

"Seen him?" Ken laughed gruffly. "I poured him into bed at three this morning."

"He was drunk?" Libby was amazed.

"He had a nip or two."

"How is he now?"

Ken glanced at her, turned his eyes back to the rutted, winding country road ahead. "Jess is hurting," he said, and there was a finality in his tone that kept Libby from asking so much as one more question.

Jess is hurting. What the devil did that mean? Was he hung over? Had the night been as miserable for him as it had been for her?

Presently the truck came to a stop in front of the big Victorian house that had been "home" to Libby for as long as she could remember. Ken made no move to shut off the engine, and she got out without saying good-bye. For all her brave words of the night before, about not needing her father's approval, she felt estranged from him now, subdued.

After forcing down a glass of orange juice and a slice of toast in the kitchen, Libby went into the studio Cathy and her father had improvised for her and did her best to work. Even during the worst days in New York, she had been able to find solace in the mechanics of drawing her cartoon strip, forgetting her own troubles to create comical dilemmas for Liberated Lizzie.

Today was different.

The panels Libby sketched were awkward, requiring too many erasures, and even if she had been able to get the drawings right, she couldn't have come up with a funny thought for the life of her.

At midmorning, Libby decided that her career was over and paced from one end of the studio to the other, haunted by thoughts of the night before.

Jess had made it clear, in his kitchen, that he didn't want to make love just to let Libby prove that she was "normal." And what had she done? She'd *gloated.*

Shame ached in Libby's cheeks as she walked. *I did it,* she'd crowed, as though she were Edison and the first electric light had just been lit. God, how could she have been so stupid? So insensitive?

"You did have a little help, you know," she scolded herself out loud. And then she covered her face with both hands and cried. It had been partly Jess's fault, that scene—he had definitely overreacted, and on top of that, he had been unreasonable. He had stormed out without giving Libby a chance to make things right.

Still, it was all too easy to imagine how he'd felt. Used. And the truth was that, without intending to, Libby had used him.

Small, strong hands were suddenly pulling Libby's hands away from her face. Through the blur, she saw Cathy watching her, puzzled and sad.

"What's wrong?" her cousin asked. "Please, Libby, tell me what's wrong."

"Everything!" wailed Libby, who was beyond trying to maintain her dignity now.

Gently Cathy drew her close, hugged her. For a moment they were two motherless little girls again, clinging to each other because there were some pains that even Ken, with his gruff, unswerving devotion, couldn't ease.

The embrace was comforting, and after a minute or two Libby recovered enough to step back and offer Cathy a shaky smile. "I've missed you so much, Cathy," she said.

"Don't get sloppy," teased Cathy, using her face to give the toneless words expression.

Libby laughed. "What are you doing today, besides being one of the idle rich?"

Cathy tilted her head to one side. "Did you really stay with Jess last night?" she asked with swift hands.

"Aren't we blunt today?" Libby shot back, both speaking and signing. "I suppose the whole ranch is talking about it!"

Cathy nodded.

"Damn!"

"Then it's true!" exalted Cathy aloud, her eyes sparkling.

Some of Libby's earlier remorse drained away, pushed aside by feelings of anger and betrayal. "Has Jess been bragging?" she demanded, her hands on her hips, her indignation warm and thick in her throat.

"He isn't the type to do that," Cathy answered in slow, carefully formed words, "and you know it."

Libby wasn't so certain—Jess had been very angry, and his pride had been stung. Besides, the only other person who had known was Ken, and he was notoriously tight-lipped when it came to other people's business. "Who told you?" she persisted, narrowing her eyes.

"Nobody had to," Cathy answered aloud. "I was down at the stables, saddling Banjo, and one of the range crews was there—ten or twelve men, I guess. Anyway, there was a fight out front—Jess punched out one of the cowboys."

Libby could only gape.

Cathy gave the story a stirring finale. "I think Jess would have killed that guy if Ken hadn't hauled him off."

Libby found her voice. "Was Jess hurt? Cathy, did you see if he was hurt?"

Cathy grinned at her cousin's undisguised concern. "Not a scratch. He got into an argument with Ken and left."

Libby felt a strong need to find her father and ask him exactly what had happened, but she knew that the effort would be wasted. Even if she could find Ken, which was unlikely considering the size of the ranch and all the places he could be, he wouldn't explain.

Cathy was studying the messy piece of drawing paper affixed to the art board. "You're not going to work?" she signed.

"I gave up," Libby confessed. "I couldn't keep my mind on it."

"After a night with Jess Barlowe, who could?"

Libby suddenly felt challenged, defensive. She even thought that, perhaps, there was more to the deep closeness between Jess and Cathy than she had guessed. "What do you know about spending the night with Jess?" she snapped before she could stop herself.

Cathy rolled her beautiful green eyes. "*Nothing.* For better or worse, and mostly it's been better, I'm married to Jess's brother—remember?"

Libby swallowed, feeling foolish. "Where is Stacey, anyway?" she asked, more to make conversation than because she wanted to know.

The question brought a shadow of sadness to Cathy's face. "He's away on one of his business trips."

Libby sat down on her art stool, folded her hands. "Maybe you should have gone with him, Cathy. You used to do that a lot, didn't you? Maybe if you two could be alone...talk..."

The air suddenly crackled with Cathy's anger and hurt. "*He* talks!" she raged aloud. "I just move my hands!"

Libby spoke softly, gently. "You could talk to Stacey, Cathy—really talk, the way you do with me."

"No."

"Why not?"

"I know I sound like a record playing on the wrong speed, that's why!"

"Even if that were so, would it matter?" signed Libby, frowning. "Stacey knew you were deaf before he married you, for heaven's sake."

Cathy's head went down. "He must have felt sorry for me or something."

Instantly Libby was off her stool, gripping Cathy's shoulders in firm, angry hands. "He loves you!"

Tears misted the emerald-green eyes and Cathy's lower lip trembled. "No doubt that's why he intends to divorce me and marry you, Libby."

"No," insisted Libby, giving her cousin a slight shake. "No, that isn't true. I think Stacey is confused, Cathy. Upset. Maybe it's this thing about your not wanting to have a baby. Or maybe he feels that you don't need him, you're so independent."

"Independent? Don't look now, Libby Kincaid, but *you're* the independent one! You have a career...you can hear—"

"Will you stop feeling sorry for yourself, dammit!" Libby almost screamed. "I'm so tired of hearing how you suffer! For God's sake, stop whining and fight for the man you love!"

Cathy broke free of Libby's grasp, furious, tears pouring down her face. "It's too late!" she cried. "You're here now, and it's too late!"

Libby sighed, stepped back, stricken by her own outburst and by Cathy's, too. "You're forgetting one thing," she reasoned quietly. "I'm not in love with Stacey. And it would take two of us to start anything, wouldn't it?"

Cathy went to the windows and stared out at the pond, her chin high. Knowing that her cousin needed this interval to restore her dignity and assemble her thoughts, Libby did not approach her.

Finally Cathy sniffled and turned back to offer a shaky smile. "I didn't come over here to fight with you," she said clearly. "I'm going to Kalispell, and I wanted to know if you would like to come with me."

Libby agreed readily, and after changing her clothes and leaving a quick note for Ken, she joined Cathy in the shiny blue Ferrari.

The ride to Kalispell was a fairly long one, and by the time Cathy and Libby reached the small city, they had reestablished their old, easy relationship.

They spent the day shopping, had lunch in a rustic steak house bearing the Circle Bar B brand, and then started home again.

"Are you really going to give that to Jess?" Cathy asked, her eyes twinkling when she cast a look at the bag in Libby's lap.

"I may lose my courage." Libby frowned, wondering what had possessed her to buy a T-shirt with such an outlandish saying printed on it. She supposed she'd hoped that the gesture would penetrate the barrier between herself and Jess, enabling them to talk.

"Take my advice," said Cathy, guiding the powerful car off the highway and onto the road that led to the heart of the ranch. "Give him the shirt."

"Maybe," said Libby, looking off into the sweeping, endless blue sky. A small airplane was making a graceful descent toward the Circle Bar B landing strip.

"Who do you suppose that is?" Libby asked, catching Cathy's attention with a touch on her arm.

The question was a mistake. Cathy, who had not, of course, heard the plane's engine, scanned the sky and saw it. "Why don't we find out?"

Libby scrunched down in her seat, sorry that she had pointed out the airplane now. Suppose Stacey was aboard, returning from his business trip, and there was another uncomfortable scene at the airstrip? Suppose it was Jess, and he either yelled at Libby or, worse yet, pretended that she wasn't there?

"I'd rather go home," she muttered.

But Cathy's course was set, and the Ferrari bumped and jostled over the road to the landing strip as though it were a pickup truck.

The plane came to a smooth stop as Cathy parked at one side of the road and got out of the car, shading her eyes with one hand, watching. Libby remained in her seat.

She had, it seemed, imagined only part of the possible scenario. The pilot was Jess, and his passenger was a wan, tight-lipped Stacey.

"Oh, God," said Libby, sinking even further into the car seat. She would have kept her face hidden in her hand forever, probably, if it hadn't been for the crisp, insistent tap at her window.

Having no other choice, she rolled the glass down and squinted into Jess Barlowe's unreadable, hard-lined face. "Come with me," he said flatly.

Libby looked through the Ferrari's windshield, saw Stacey and Cathy standing nearby, a disturbing distance between them. Cathy was glaring angrily into Stacey's face, and Stacey was casting determined looks in Libby's direction.

"They need some time alone," Jess said, his eyes linking fiercely, warningly, with Libby's as he opened the car door for her.

Anxious not to make an obviously unpleasant situation any worse, Libby gathered up her bags and her purse and got out of the car, following along behind Jess's long strides. The station wagon, which she hadn't noticed before, was parked close by.

Without looking back at Stacey and Cathy, Libby slid gratefully into the dusty front seat and closed her eyes. Not until the car was moving did she open them, and even then she couldn't quite bring herself to look at the man behind the wheel.

"That was touching," he said in a vicious rasp.

Libby stiffened in the seat, staring at Jess's rock-hard profile now. "What did you say?"

The powerful shoulders moved in an annoying shrug. "Your wanting to meet Stacey on his triumphant return."

It took Libby a moment to absorb what he was implying. When she had, she slammed him with the paper bag that contained the T-shirt she'd bought for him in Kalispell and hissed, "You bastard! I didn't know Stacey was going to be on that plane, and if I had, I certainly wouldn't have been there at all!"

"Sure," he drawled, and even though he was grinning and looking straight ahead at the road, there was contempt in his tone and a muscle pulsing at the base of his jaw.

Libby felt tears of frustration rise in her eyes. "I thought you believed me," she said.

"I thought I did too," Jess retorted with acid amusement. "But that was before you showed up at the landing strip at such an opportune moment."

"It was Cathy's idea to meet the plane!"

"Right."

The paper bag crackled as Libby lifted it, prepared to swing.

"Do that again and I'll stop this car and raise blisters on your backside," Jess warned, without so much as looking in her direction.

Libby lowered the bag back to her lap, swallowed miserably, and turned her attention to the road. She did not believe Jess's threat for one moment, but she felt childish for trying to hit him with the bag. "Cathy told me there was a fight at the stables this morning," she dared after a long time. "What happened?"

Another shrug, as insolent as the first, preceded his reply. "One of Ken's men said something I didn't like."

"Like what?"

"Like didn't it bother me to sleep with my brother's mistress."

Libby winced, sorry for pressing the point. "Oh, God," she said, and she was suddenly so tired, so broken, and so frustrated that she couldn't hold back her tears anymore. She covered her face with both hands and turned her head as far away from Jess as she could, but the effort was useless.

Jess stopped the station wagon at the side of the road, turned Libby easily toward him. Through a blur, she saw the Ferrari race past.

"Let go of me!"

Jess not only didn't let go, he pulled her close. "I'm sorry," he muttered into her hair. "God, Libby, I don't know what comes over me, what makes me say things to hurt you."

"Garden-variety hatred!" sniffled Libby, who was already forgiving him even though it was against her better judgment.

He chuckled. "No. I couldn't ever hate you, Libby."

She looked up at him, confused and hopeful. Before she could think of anything to say, however, there was a loud *pop* from beneath the hood of the station wagon, followed by a sizzle and clouds of steam.

"Goddammit!" rasped Jess.

Libby laughed, drunk on the scent of him, the closeness of him, the crazy paradox of him. "This crate doesn't exactly fit your image, you know," she taunted. "Why don't you get yourself a decent car?"

He turned from glowering at the hood of the station wagon to smile down into her face. "If I do, Kincaid, will you let me make love to you in the back seat?"

She shoved at his immovable chest with both hands, laughing again. "No, no, a thousand times no!"

Jess nibbled at her jawline, at the lobe of her ear, chuckled huskily as she tensed. "How many times no?"

"Maybe," said Libby.

Just when she thought she would surely go crazy, Jess drew back from his brazen pursuits and smiled lazily. "It is time I got a new car," he conceded, with an evil light glistening in his jade eyes. "Will you come to Kalispell and help me pick it out, Libby?"

A thrill skittered through Libby's body and flamed in her face. "I was just there," she protested, clutching at straws.

"It shouldn't..."—Jess bent, nipped at the side of her neck with gentle teeth—"take long. A couple of days at the most."

"A couple of days!"

"And nights." Jess's lips were scorching their way across the tender hollow of her throat. "Think about it, Lib. Just you and me. No Stacey. No Cathy. No problems."

Libby shivered as a knowledgeable hand closed over one of her breasts, urging, reawakening. "No p-problems?" she echoed.

Jess undid the top button of her blouse.

Libby's breath caught in her throat; she felt heat billowing up inside her, foaming out, just as it was foaming out of the station wagon's radiator. "Wh-where would we s-stay?"

Another button came undone.

Jess chuckled, his mouth on Libby's collarbone now, tasting it, doing nothing to cool the heat that was pounding within her. "How about"— the third button gave way, and Libby's bra was displaced by a gentle hand—"one of those motels...with the...vibrating beds?"

"Tacky," gasped Libby, and her eyes closed languidly and her head fell back as Jess stroked the nipple he'd just found to pebble-hard response.

"My condo, then," he said, and his lips were sliding down from her collarbone, soft, soft, over the upper rounding of her bare breast.

Libby gasped and arched her back as his lips claimed the distended, hurting peak. "Jess...oh, God...this is a p-public road!"

"Umm," Jess said, lapping at her now with the tip of his tongue. "Will you go with me, Libby?"

Wild need went through her as he stroked the insides of her thighs, forcing her blue-jeaned legs apart. And all the while he plied her nipple into a panic of need. "Yes!" she gasped finally.

Jess undid the snap of her jeans, slid his hand inside, beneath the scanty lace of her panties.

"Damn you," Libby whispered hoarsely, "s-stop that! I said I'd go—"

He told her what else she was about to do. And one glorious, soul-scoring minute later, she did.

Red in the face, still breathing heavily, Libby closed her jeans, tugged her bra back into place, buttoned her blouse. God, what if someone had come along and seen her letting Jess...letting him play with her like that?

All during the ride home, she mentally rehearsed the blistering diatribe he deserved to hear. He could just go to Kalispell by *himself,* she would tell him. If he thought for one damned minute that he was going to take her to his condo and make love to her, he was sadly mistaken, she would say.

"Be ready in half an hour," Jess told her at her father's front door.

"Okay," Libby replied.

After landing the Cessna in Kalispell and making arrangements to rent a car, which turned out to be a temperamental cousin to Jess's station wagon, they drove through the small city to an isolated tree-dense property beyond. There were at least a million stars in the sky, and as the modest car rattled over a narrow wooden bridge spanning a creek, Libby couldn't help giving in a little to the romance of it all.

Beyond the bridge, there were more trees—towering ponderosa pines, whispering, shiny-leaved birches. They stopped in the driveway of a condominium that stood apart from several others. Jess got out of the car, came around to open Libby's door for her.

"Let's get rid of the suitcases and go out for something to eat," he said.

Libby's stomach rumbled inelegantly, and Jess laughed as he caught her hand in his and drew her up the darkened walk to the front door of the condominium. "That shoots my plans for a little fun before dinner," he teased.

"There's always after," replied Libby, lifting her chin.

Chapter 8

The inside of the condominium was amazingly like Jess's house on the ranch. There was a loft, for instance, this one accessible by both stairs and, of all things, a built-in ladder. Too, the general layout of the rooms was much the same.

The exceptions were that the floors were carpeted rather than bare oak, and the entire roof was made of heavy glass. *When we make love here, I'll be able to look up and see the stars,* Libby mused.

"Like it?" Jess asked, setting the suitcases down and watching her with discerning, mirthful green eyes.

Libby was uncomfortable again, doubting the wisdom of coming here now that she was faced with the realities of the situation. "Is this where you bring all your conquests?"

Jess smiled, shrugged.

"Well?" prodded Libby, annoyed because he hadn't even had the common decency to offer a denial.

He sat down on the stone ledge fronting the fireplace, wrapped his hands around one knee. "The place does happen to be something of a love nest, as a matter of fact."

Libby was stung. Dammit, how unchivalrous could one man be? "Oh," she said loftily.

"It's my father's place," Jess said, clearly delighting in her obvious curiosity and the look of relief she couldn't quite hide.

"Your father's?"

Jess grinned. "He entertains his mistress here, from time to time. In his position, he has to be discreet."

Libby was gaping now, trying to imagine the sedate, dignified Senator Barlowe cavorting with a woman beneath slanted glass roofs, climbing ladders to star-dappled lofts.

Jess's amused gaze had strayed to the ladder. "It probably puts him in mind of the good old days—climbing into the hayloft, and all that."

Libby blushed. She was still quite disturbed by that ladder, among other things. "You did ask the senator's permission to come here, didn't you?"

Jess seemed to know that she had visions of Cleave Barlowe carrying some laughing woman over the threshold and finding the place already occupied. "Yes," he assured her in a teasing tone, rising and coming toward her. "I said, 'Mind if I take Libby to your condo, dear old dad, and take her to bed?' And he said—"

"Jess!" Libby howled, in protest.

He laughed, caught her elbows in his hands, kissed her playfully, his lips sampling hers, tugging at them in soft entreaty. "My father is in Washington," he said. "Stop worrying."

Libby pulled back, her face hot, her mind spinning. "I'm hungry!"

"Umm," replied Jess, "so am I."

Why did she feel like a sixteen-year-old on the verge of big trouble? "Please...let's go now."

Jess sighed.

They went, but they were back, arms burdened with cartons of Chinese food, in less than half an hour.

While Jess set the boxes out on the coffee table, Libby went to the kitchen for plates and silverware. Scribbled on a blackboard near the sink, she saw the surprising words: "Thanks, Ken. See you next week. B."

A soft chuckle simmered up into Libby's throat and emerged as a giggle. Could it be that her father, her serious, hardworking father, had a ladyfriend who visited him here in this romantic hideaway? Tilting her head to one side, she considered, grinned again. "Naaaah!"

But Libby's grin wouldn't fade as she carried plates, forks, spoons and paper napkins back into the living room.

"What's so funny?" Jess asked, trying to hide the hunk of sweet-and-sour chicken he had just purloined from one of the steaming cartons.

"Nothing," said Libby, catching his hand and raising it to his mouth. Sheepishly he popped the tidbit of chicken onto his tongue and chewed.

"You lie," Jess replied, "but I'm too hungry to press the point."

While they ate, Libby tried to envision what sort of woman her father would be drawn to—tall, short? Quiet, talkative?

"You're mulling over more than the chow mein," accused Jess presently in a good-natured voice. "Tell me, what's going on in that gifted little head?"

Libby shrugged. "Romance."

He grinned. "That's what I like to hear."

But Libby was thinking seriously, following her thoughts through new channels. In all the years since her mother's death, just before Cathy had come to live on the ranch, she had never imagined Ken Kincaid caring about another woman. "It isn't as though he's old," she muttered, "or unattractive."

Jess set down his plate with a mockingly forceful thump. "That does it. Who are you talking about, Kincaid?" he demanded archly, his wonderful mouth twitching in the effort to suppress a grin.

She perused him with lofty disdain. "Am I correct in assuming that you are jealous?"

"Jealous as hell," came the immediate and not-so-jovial response.

Libby laughed, laid a hand on his knee. "If you must know, I was thinking about my father. I've always kept him in this neat little cubicle in my mind, marked 'Dad.' If you can believe it, it has just now occurred to me that he's a man, with a life, and maybe even a love, of his own."

Mirth danced in Jess's jade eyes, but if he knew anything about Ken's personal life, he clearly wasn't going to speak of it. "Pass the eggroll," he said diplomatically.

When the meal was over, Libby's reflections began to shift to matters nearer the situation at hand.

"I don't know what I'm doing here," she said pensively as she and Jess cleared the coffee table and started toward the kitchen with the debris. "I must be out of my mind."

Jess dropped the cartons and the crumpled napkins into the trash compactor. "Thanks a lot," he said, watching her attentively as she rinsed the plates and silverware and put them into the dishwasher.

Wearing tailored gray slacks and a lightweight teal-blue sweater, he was devastatingly attractive. Still, the look Libby gave him was a serious, questioning one. "What is it with us, Jess? What makes us behave the way we do? One minute, we're yelling at each other, or not speaking at all, and the next we're alone in a place like this."

"Chemistry?"

Libby laughed ruefully. "More like voodoo. So what kind of car are you planning to buy?"

Jess drew her to him; his fingertips were butterfly-light on the small of her back. "Car?" he echoed, as though the word were foreign.

There was a soft, quivering ache in one corner of Libby's heart. Why couldn't things always be like this between them? Why did they have to wrangle so fiercely before achieving this quiet accord? "Stop teasing me," she said softly. "We did come here to buy a car, you know."

Jess's hands pulled her blouse up and out of her slacks, made slow-moving, sensuous circles on her bare back. "Yes," he said in a throaty rumble. "A car. But there are lots of different kinds of cars, aren't there, Libby? And a decision like this can't be made in haste."

Libby closed her eyes, almost hypnotized by the slow, languid meter of his words, the depth of his voice. "N-no," she agreed.

"Definitely not," he said, his mouth almost upon hers. "It could take two—or three—days to decide."

"Ummm," agreed Libby, slipping deeper and deeper under his spell.

Jess had pressed her back against a counter, and his body formed an impassable barricade, leaning, hard and fragrant, into hers. He was tracing the length of her neck with soft, searing lips, tasting the hollow beneath her ear.

Finally he kissed her, first with tenderness, then with fervor, his tongue seeking and being granted sweet entry. This preliminary joining made Libby's whole entity pulse with an awareness of the primitive differences between his body and her own. Where she was soft and yielding, he was fiercely hard. Her nipples pouted into tiny peaks, crying out for his attention.

Seeming to sense that, Jess unbuttoned her blouse with deft, brazen fingers that felt warm against her skin. He opened the front catch on her bra, admired the pink-tipped lushness that seemed to grow richer and rounder under his gaze.

Idly he bent to kiss one peak into ferocious submission, and Libby groaned, her head falling back. Etched against the clear roof, she saw the long needles of ponderosa pines splintering the spring moonlight into shards of silver.

After almost a minute of pleasure so keen that Libby was certain she couldn't bear it, Jess turned to the other breast, kissing, suckling, nipping softly with his teeth. And all the while, he worked the opposite nipple skillfully with his fingers, putting it through delicious paces.

Libby was almost mindless by the time she felt the snap and zipper of her jeans give way, and her hands were still tangled in his dark hair as he knelt. Down came the jeans, her panties with them.

She could manage no more than a throaty gasp as his hands stroked the smooth skin of her thighs, the V of curls at their junction. She felt his breath there, warm, promising to cherish.

Libby trembled as he sought entrance with a questioning kiss, unveiled her with fingers that would not await permission.

As his tongue first touched the tenderness that had been hidden, his hands came to Libby's hips, pressing her down onto this fiery, inescapable glory. Only when she pleaded did he tug her fully into his mouth and partake of her.

Jess enjoyed Libby at his leisure, demanding her essence, showing no mercy even when she cried out and shuddered upon him in a final, soaring triumph. When her own chants of passion had ceased, she was conscious of his.

Jess still knelt before her, his every touch saying that he was worshiping, but there was sweet mastery in his manner, too. After one kiss of farewell, he gently drew her jeans and panties back into place and stood.

Libby stared at him, amazed at his power over her. He smiled at her wonder, though there was a spark of that same emotion deep in his eyes, and then lifted her off her feet and into his arms.

Say "I love you," Libby thought with prayerful fervor.

"I need you," he said instead.

And, for the moment, it was enough.

Stars peeked through the endlessly varied patterns the fallen pine needles made on the glass roof, as if to see and assess the glory that glowed
beneath. Libby preened under their celestial jealousy and cuddled closer
to Jess's hard, sheet-entangled frame.

"Why didn't you ever marry, Jess?" she asked, tracing a soft path
across his chest with her fingers.

The mattress shifted as he moved to put one arm around Libby and
draw her nearer still. "I don't know. It always seemed that marriage could
wait."

"Didn't you even come close?"

Jess sighed, his fingers moving idly in her hair. "A couple of times I
seriously considered it, yes. I guess it bothered me, subliminally, that I
was looking these women over as though they were livestock or something. This one would have beautiful children, that one would like living
on the ranch—that sort of thing."

"I see."

Jess stiffened slightly beneath the patterns she was making in the soft
swirls of hair on his chest, and she felt the question coming long before
he uttered it.

"What attracted you to Aaron Strand?"

Libby had been pondering that mystery herself, ever since her marriage
to Aaron had begun to dissolve. Now, suddenly, she was certain that she
understood. Weak though he might be, Aaron Strand was tall, dark-
haired, broad in the shoulders. He had given the impression of strength
and self-assurance, qualities that any woman would find appealing.

"I guess I thought he was strong, like Dad," she said, because she
couldn't quite amend the sentence to a full truth and admit that she had
probably superimposed Jess's image over Aaron's in the first place.

"Ummm," said Jess noncommittally.

"Of course, he is actually very weak."

Jess offered no comment.

"I guess my mistake," Libby went on quietly, "was in seeing myself
through Aaron's eyes. He made me feel so worthless..."

"Maybe that made him feel better about himself."

"Maybe. But I still hate him, Jess—isn't that awful? I still hate him
for leaving Jonathan in the lurch like that, especially."

"It isn't awful, it's human. It appears that you and Jonathan needed
more than he had to give. Unconsciously, you probably measured him
against Ken, and whatever else he is, your dad is a hard act to follow,
Libby."

"Yes," said Libby, but she was thinking: *I didn't measure Aaron against Dad. God help me, Jess, I measured him against you.*

Jess turned over in a graceful, rolling motion, so that he was above her, his head and shoulders blocking out the light of the stars. "Enough heavy talk, woman. I came here to—"

"Buy a car?" broke in Libby, her tone teasing and full of love.

He nuzzled his face between her warm, welcoming breasts. "My God," he said, his voice muffled by her satin flesh, "what an innocent you are, Libby Kincaid!" One of his hands came down, gentle and mischievous, to squeeze her bottom. "Nice upholstery."

Libby gasped and arched her back as his mouth slid up over the rounding of her breast to claim its peak. "Not much mileage," she choked out.

Jess laughed against the nipple he was tormenting so methodically. "A definite plus." His hand moved between her thighs to assert an ancient mastery, and his breath quickened at Libby's immediate response. "Starts easily," he muttered, sipping at her nipple now, tugging it into an obedient little point.

Libby was beyond the game now, rising and falling on the velvet swells of need he was stirring within her. "I...Oh, God, Jess...what are you...ooooh!"

Somehow, Jess managed to turn on the bedside lamp without interrupting the searing pace his right hand was setting for Libby's body. "You are a goddess," he said.

The fevered dance continued, even though Libby willed herself to lie still. Damn him, he was watching her, taking pleasure from the unbridled response she could not help giving. Her heart raced with exertion, blood boiled in every vein, and Jess's lazy smile was lost in a silver haze.

She sobbed out his name, groping for his shoulders with her hands, holding on. Then, shuddering violently, she tumbled into some chasm where there was no sound but the beat of her own heart.

"You like doing that, don't you?" she snapped when she could see again, breathe again.

"Yes," replied Jess without hesitation.

Libby scrambled into a sitting position, blue eyes shooting flames. "Bastard," she said.

He met her gaze placidly. "What's the matter with you?"

Libby wasn't quite sure of the answer to that question. "It just...it just bothers me that you were...you were looking at me," she faltered, covering her still-pulsing breasts with the bedclothes.

With a deliberate motion of his hands, Jess removed the covers again, and Libby's traitorous nipples puckered in response to his brazen perusal. "Why?" he asked.

Libby's cheeks ached with color, and she lowered her eyes. Instantly Jess caught her chin in a gentle grasp, made her look at him again.

"Sweetheart, you're not ashamed, are you?"

Libby couldn't reply, she was so confused.

His hand slid, soothing, from Libby's chin to the side of her face. "You were giving yourself to me, Libby, trusting me. Is there shame in that?"

She realized that there wasn't, not the way she loved this brazen, tender, outlandish man. If only she dared to tell him verbally what her body already had.

He kissed her softly, sensing her need for greater reassurance. "Exquisite," he said. "Even ordinarily, you are exquisite. But when you let me love you, you go beyond that. You move me on a level where I've never even been touched before."

Say it now, Libby urged silently, *say you love me.*

But she had to be satisfied with what he had already said, for it was immediately clear that there would be no poetic avowals of devotion forthcoming. He'd said she was exquisite, that she moved him, but he'd made no declaration.

For this reason, there was a measure of sadness in the lovemaking that followed.

Long after Jess slept, exhausted, beside her, Libby lay awake, aching. She wanted, needed more from Jess than his readily admitted lust. So much more.

And yet, if a commitment were offered, would Libby want to accept it? Weren't there already too many conflicts complicating their lives? Though she tried to shut out the memory, Libby couldn't forget that Jess had believed her capable of carrying on with his brother and hurting her cousin and dearest friend in the process. Nor could she forget the wedge that had been driven between them the first time they'd made love, when she'd slipped and uttered words that had made him feel as though she'd used him to prove herself as a woman.

Of course, they had come together again, despite these things, but that was of no comfort to Libby. If they were to achieve any real closeness, more than just their bodies would have to be in accord.

After several hours, Libby fell into a fitful, dream-ridden sleep. When morning came, casting bright sunlight through the expanse of glass overhead, she was alone in the tousled bed.

"Lib!"

She went to the edge of the loft, peering down over the side. "What?" she retorted, petulant in the face of Jess's freshly showered, bright-and-shiny good cheer.

He waved a cooking spatula with a flourish. "One egg or two?"

"Drop dead," she replied flatly, frowning at the ladder.

Jess laughed. "Watch it. You'll get my hopes up with such tender words."

"What's this damned ladder for, anyway?"

"Are you this grouchy every morning?" he countered.

"Only when I've engaged in illicit sex the night before!" Libby snapped, scowling. "I believe I asked you about the ladder?"

"It's for climbing up and down." Jess shrugged.

Libby's head throbbed, and her eyes felt puffy and sore. "Given time, I probably could have figured out that much!"

Jess chuckled and shook his head, as if in sympathy.

Libby grasped the top of the peculiar ladder in question and gave it a vigorous shake. It was immovable. Her puzzlement made her feel even more irritable and, for no consciously conceived reason, she put out her tongue at Jess Barlowe and whirled away from the edge of the loft, out of his view.

His laughter rang out as she stumbled into the bathroom and turned on the water in the shower stall.

Once she had showered and brushed her teeth, Libby began to feel semihuman. With this came contrition for the snappish way she had greeted Jess minutes before. It wasn't his fault, after all, that he was so nauseatingly happy in the mornings.

Grinning a mischievous grin, Libby rummaged through the suitcase she had so hastily packed and found the T-shirt she had bought for Jess the day before, when she'd come to Kalispell with Cathy. She pulled the garment on over her head and, in a flash of daring, swung over the loft to climb down the ladder.

Her reward was a low, appreciative whistle.

"Now I know why that ladder was built," Jess said. "The view from down here is great."

Libby was embarrassed; she'd thought Jess was in the kitchen and thus unable to see her novel descent from the loft. Reaching the floor, she whirled, her face crimson, to glare at him.

Jess read the legend printed on the front of the T-shirt, which was so big that it reached almost to her knees, and laughed explosively. "'If it feels good, do it'?" he marveled.

Libby's glare simply would not stay in place, no matter how hard she tried to sustain it. Her mouth twitched and a chuckle escaped her and then she was laughing as hard as Jess was.

Given the situation, his words came as a shock.

"Libby, will you marry me?"

She stared at him, bewildered, afraid to hope. "What?"

The jade eyes were gentle now, still glistening with residual laughter. "Don't make me repeat it, princess."

"I think the eggs are burning," said Libby in tones made wooden by surprise.

"Wrong. I've already eaten mine, and yours are congealing on your plate. What's your answer, Kincaid?"

Libby's throat ached; something about the size of her heart was caught in it. "I...what..."

"I thought you only talked in broken sentences at the height of passion. Are you really as surprised as all that?"

"Yes!" croaked Libby after a struggle.

The broad shoulders, accentuated rather than hidden by a soft yellow sweater, moved in a shrug. "It seemed like a good solution to me."

"A solution? To what?"

"All our separate and combined problems," answered Jess airily. Persuasively. "Think about it, Lib. Stacey couldn't very well hassle you anymore, could he? And you could stay on the ranch."

Despite the companionable delivery, Jess's words made Libby's soul ache. "Those are solutions for me. What problems would marriage solve for you?"

"We're good in bed," he offered, shattering Libby with what he seemed to mean as a compliment.

"It takes more than that!"

"Does it?"

Libby was speechless, though a voice inside her kept screaming silly, sentimental things. *What about love? What about babies and leftover meatloaf and filing joint tax returns?*

"You dad would be happy," Jess added, and he couldn't have hurt Libby more if he'd raised his hand and slapped her.

"My dad? My *dad?*"

Jess turned away, seemingly unaware of the effect his convoluted proposal was having on Libby. He looked like exactly what he was: a trained, skillful attorney pleading a weak case. "You want children, don't you? And I know you like living on the ranch."

Libby broke in coldly. "I guess I meet all the qualifications. I do want children. I do like living on the Circle Bar B. So why don't you just hogtie me and brand me a Barlowe?"

Every muscle in Jess's body seemed to tense, but he did not turn around to face her. "There is one other reason," he offered.

For all her fury and hurt, hope sang through Libby's system like the wind unleashed on a wide prairie. "What's that?"

He drew a deep breath, his hands clasped behind him, courtroom style. "There would be no chance, for now at least, of Cathy being hurt."

Cathy. Libby's knees weakened; she groped for the sofa behind her, fell into it. Good God, was his devotion to Cathy so deep that he would marry the woman he considered a threat to her happiness, just to protect her?

"I am so damned tired of hearing about Cathy," she said evenly, tugging the end of the T-shirt down over her knees for something to do.

Now Jess turned, looked at her with unreadable eyes.

Even though Libby felt the guilt she always did whenever she was even mildly annoyed with Cathy, she stood her ground. "A person doesn't have to be handicapped to hurt, you know,'' she said in a small and rather uncertain voice.

Jess folded his arms and the sunlight streaming in through the glass ceiling glittered in his dark hair. "I know that," he said softly. "And we're all handicapped in some way, aren't we?"

She couldn't tell whether he was reprimanding her or offering an olive branch. Huddling on the couch, feeling foolish in the T-shirt she had put on as a joke, Libby knotted her hands together in her lap. "I suppose that remark was intended as a barb."

Jess came to sit beside her on the couch, careful not to touch her. "Libby, it wasn't. I'm tired of exchanging verbal shots with you—that was fine when we had to ride the same school bus every day, but we're adults now. Let's try to act as such."

Libby looked into Jess's face and was thunderstruck by how much she cared for him, needed him. And yet, even a week before, she would have said she despised Jess and meant it. All that rancor they'd borne each other—had it really been passion instead?

"I don't understand any of this."

Jess took one of her hands into both of his. "Do you want to marry me or not?"

Both fear and joy rose within Libby. In order to look inward at her own feelings, she was forced to look away from him. She did love Jess, there was absolutely no doubt of that, and she wanted, above all things, to be his wife. She wanted children and, at thirty-one, she often had the feeling that time was getting short. Dammit, why couldn't he say he loved her?

"Would you be faithful to me, Jess?"

He touched her cheek, turning her face without apparent effort, so that she was again looking into those bewitching green eyes. "I would never betray you."

Aaron had said those words too. Aaron had been so very good with words.

But this was Jess, Libby reminded herself. Jess, not Aaron. "I couldn't give up my career," she said. "It's a crazy business, Jess, and sometimes there are long stretches of time when I don't do much of anything. Other times, I have to work ten- or twelve-hour days to meet a deadline."

Jess did not seem to be dissuaded.

Libby drew a deep breath. "Of course, I'd go on being known as Libby Kincaid. I never took Aaron's name and I don't see any sense in taking yours—should I agree to marry you, that is."

He seemed amused, but she had definitely touched a sore spot. That became immediately obvious. "Wait a minute, lady. Professionally, you can be known by any name you want. Privately, however, you'll be Libby Barlowe."

Libby was secretly pleased, but because she was angry and hurt that he didn't love her, she lifted her chin and snapped, "You have to have that Circle Bar B brand on everything you consider yours, don't you?"

"You are not a thing, Libby," he replied rationally, "but I want at least that much of a commitment. Call it male ego if you must, but I want my wife to be Mrs. Barlowe."

Libby swallowed. "Fair enough," she said.

Jess sat back on the sofa, folded his arms again. "I'm waiting," he said, and the mischievous glint was back in his eyes.

"For what?"

"An answer to my original question."

Fool, fool! Don't you ever learn, Libby Kincaid? Don't you ever learn? Libby quieted the voice in her mind and lifted her chin. Life was short, and unpredictable in the bargain. Maybe Jess would learn to love her the way she loved him. Wasn't that kind of happiness worth a risk?

"I'll marry you," she said.

Jess kissed her with an exuberance that soon turned to desire.

Jess frowned at the sleek showroom sports car, his tongue making one cheek protrude. "What do you think?" he asked.

Libby assessed the car again. "It isn't you."

He grinned, ignoring the salesman's quiet disappointment. "You're right."

Neither, of course, had the last ten cars they had looked at been "him." The sports cars seemed to cramp his long legs, while the big luxury vehicles were too showy.

"How about a truck?" Libby suggested.

"Do you know how many trucks there are on the ranch?" he countered. "Besides, some yokel would probably paint on the family logo when I wasn't looking."

Libby deliberately widened her eyes. "That would be truly terrible!"

He made a face at her, but when he spoke, his words were delivered in a touchingly serious way. "We could get another station wagon and fill the backseat with kids and dogs."

Libby smiled at the image. "A grungy sort of heaven," she mused.

Jess laughed. "And of course there would be lots of room to make love."

The salesman cleared his throat and discreetly walked away.

Chapter 9

"I think you shocked that salesman," observed Libby, snapping the seat belt into place as Jess settled behind the wheel of their rental car.

Jess shrugged. "By wanting a station wagon?" he teased.

"By wanting *me* in the station wagon," clarified Libby.

Jess turned the key in the ignition and shifted gears. "He's lucky I didn't list all the other places I'd like to have you. The hood, for instance. And then there's the roof..."

Libby colored richly as they pulled into the slow traffic. "Jess!"

He frowned speculatively. "And, of course, on the ladder at the condo."

"The ladder?"

Jess flung her a brazen grin. "Yeah. About halfway up."

"Don't you think about anything but sex?"

"I seem to have developed a fixation, Kincaid—just since you came back, of course."

She couldn't help smiling. "Of course."

Nothing more was said until they'd driven through the quiet, well-kept streets to the courthouse. Jess parked the car and turned to Libby with a comical leer. "Are you up to a blood test and a little small-town bureaucracy, Kincaid?"

Libby felt a wild, twisting thrill in the pit of her stomach. A marriage license. He wanted to get a marriage license. In three short days, she could be bound to Jess Barlowe for life. At least, she *hoped* it would be for life.

After drawing a deep breath, Libby unsnapped her seat belt and got out of the car.

Twenty minutes later, the ordeal was over. The fact that the wedding itself wouldn't take nearly as long struck Libby as an irony.

On the sidewalk, Jess caught her elbow in one hand and helped her back into the car. While he must have noticed that she was preoccupied, he was chivalrous enough not to say so.

"Stop at that supermarket!" Libby blurted when they'd been driving for some minutes.

Jess gave her a quizzical look. "Supermarket?"

"Yes. They sell food there, among other necessary items."

Jess frowned. "Why can't we just eat in restaurants? There are several good ones—"

"Restaurants?" Libby cried with mock disdain. "How can I prove what a great catch I am if I don't cook something for you?"

Jess's right hand left the steering wheel to slide languorously up and down Libby's linen-skirted thigh. "Relax, sweetheart," he said in a rather good imitation of Humphrey Bogart. "I already know you're good in the kitchen."

The obvious reference to last night's episode in that room unsettled Libby. "You delight in saying outrageous things, don't you?" she snapped.

"I delight in *doing* outrageous things."

"You'll get no argument on that score, fella," she retorted acidly.

The car came to a stop in front of the supermarket, which was in the center of a small shopping mall. Libby noticed that Jess's gaze strayed to a jewelry store down the way.

"I'll meet you inside," he said, and then he was gone.

Though Libby told herself that she was being silly and sentimental, she was pleased to think that Jess might be shopping for a ring.

The giddy, romantic feeling faded when she selected a shopping cart inside the supermarket, however. She was wallowing in gushy dreams, behaving like a seventeen-year-old virgin. Of *course* Jess would buy a ring, but only because it would be expected of him.

Glumly Libby went about selecting items from a mental grocery list she had been composing since she'd checked the refrigerator and cupboards at the condominium and found them all but empty.

Taking refuge in practical matters, she frowned at a display of cabbage and wondered how much food to buy. Jess hadn't said how long they would be staying in Kalispell, beyond the time it would take to find the car he wanted.

Shrugging slightly, Libby decided to buy provisions for three days. Because that was the required waiting period for a marriage license, they would probably be in town at least that long.

She looked down at her slacks and brightly colored peasant blouse. The wedding ceremony was going to be an informal one, obviously, but she would still need a new dress, and she wanted to buy a wedding band for Jess, too.

She pushed her cart along the produce aisle, woodenly selecting bean sprouts, fresh broccoli, onions. Her first wedding had been a quiet one, too, devoid of lace and flowers and music, and something within her mourned those things.

They hadn't even discussed a honeymoon, and what kind of ceremony would this be, without Ken, without Cathy, without Senator Barlowe and Marion Bradshaw, the housekeeper?

A box seemed to float up out of the cart, but Libby soon saw that it was clasped in a strong sun-browned hand.

"I hate cereals that crunch," Jess said, and his eyes seemed to be looking inside Libby, seeing the dull ache she would rather have kept hidden. "What's wrong, love?"

Libby fought back the sudden silly tears that ached in her throat and throbbed behind her eyes. "Nothing," she lied.

Jess was not fooled. "You want Ken to come to the wedding," he guessed.

Libby lowered her head slightly. "He was hurt when Aaron and I got married without even telling him first," she said.

There was a short silence before a housewife, tagged by two pre-schoolers, gave Libby's cart a surreptitious bump with her own, tacitly demanding access to the cereal display. Libby wrestled her groceries out of the way and looked up at Jess, waiting for his response.

He smiled, touched her cheek. "Tell you what. We'll call the ranch and let everybody know we're getting married. That way, if they want to be there, they can. And if you want frills and flash, princess, we can have a formal wedding later."

The idea of a second wedding, complete with the trimmings, appealed to Libby's romantic soul. She smiled at the thought. "You would do that? You would go through it all over again, just for show?"

"Not for show, princess. For you."

The housewife made an appreciative sound and Libby started a little, having completely forgotten their surroundings.

Jess laughed and the subject was dropped. They walked up one aisle and down another, dropping the occasional pertinent item into the cart, arguing good-naturedly about who would do the cooking after they were married.

The telephone was ringing as Libby unlocked the front door of the condo, so she left Jess to carry in their bags of groceries and ran to answer it, expecting to hear Ken's voice, or Marion Bradshaw's, relaying some message from Cathy.

A cruel wave of *déjà vu* washed over her when she heard Aaron's smooth, confident greeting. "Hello, Libby."

"What do you want?" Libby rasped, too stunned to hang up. How on earth had he gotten that number?

"I told you before, dear heart," said Aaron smoothly. "I want a child."

Libby was conscious of Jess standing at her elbow, the shopping bags clasped in his arms. "You're insane!" she cried into the receiver.

"Maybe so, but not insane enough to let my grandmother hand over an empire to someone else. She has doubts, you know, about my dependability."

"I wonder why!"

"Don't be sarcastic, sugarplum. My request isn't really all that unreasonable, considering all I stand to lose."

"It is unreasonable, Aaron! In fact, it's sick!" At this point Libby slammed down the receiver with a vengeance. She was trembling so hard that Jess hastily shunted the grocery bags onto a side table and took her into his arms.

"What was that all about?" he asked when Libby had recovered herself a little.

"He's horrible," Libby answered, distracted and very much afraid. "Oh, Jess, he's a monster—"

"What did he say?" Jess pressed quietly.

"Aaron wants me to have his baby! Jess, he actually had the gall to ask me to come back, just so he can produce an heir and please his grandmother!"

Jess's hand was entangled in her hair now, comforting her. "It's all right, Lib. Everything will be all right."

Then why am I so damned scared? Libby asked herself, but she put on a brave face for Jess and even managed a smile. "Let's call my dad," she said.

Jess nodded, kissed her forehead. And then he took up the grocery bags again and carried them into the kitchen while Libby dialed her father's telephone number.

There was no answer, which was not surprising, considering that it was still early. Ken would be working, and because of the wide range of his responsibilities, he could be anywhere on the 150,000 acres that made up the Circle Bar B.

Sounds from the kitchen indicated that Jess was putting the food away, and Libby wandered in, needing to be near him.

"No answer?" he asked, tossing a package of frozen egg rolls into the refrigerator-freezer.

"No answer," confirmed Libby. "I should have known, I guess."

Jess turned, gave her a gentle grin. "You did know, Libby. But you needed to touch base just then, and going through the motions was better than nothing."

"When did you get so smart?"

"Last Tuesday, I think," he answered ponderously. "Know something? You look a little tired. Why don't you climb up that ladder that bugs you so much and take a nap?"

Libby arched one eyebrow. "While you do what?"

His answer was somewhat disappointing. "While I go back to town for a few hours," he said. "I have some things to do."

"Like what?"

He grinned. "Like picking up some travel brochures, so we can decide where to take our honeymoon."

Libby felt a rush of pleasure despite the weariness she was suddenly very aware of. Had it been there all along, or was she tired simply because this subtle hypnotist had suggested it to her? "Does it matter where we honeymoon?"

"Not really," Jess replied, coming disturbingly close, kissing Libby's forehead. "But I like having you all to myself. I can't help thinking that the farther we get from home right now, the better off we're going to be."

A tremor of fear brushed against Libby's heart, but it was quickly stilled when Jess caught her right earlobe between gentle teeth and then told her in bluntly erotic terms what he had wanted to do to her on the supermarket checkout counter.

When he'd finished, Libby was wildly aroused and, at the same time, resigned to the fact that when she crawled into that sun-washed bed up in the loft, she would be alone. "Rat," she said.

Jess swatted her backside playfully. "Later," he promised, and then calmly left the condo to attend to his errands.

Libby went obediently up to the bedroom, using the stairs rather than the ladder, and yawned as she stripped down to her lacy camisole and tap pants. She shouldn't be having a nap now, she told herself, when she had things of her own to do—choosing Jess's ring, for one thing, and buying a special dress, for another....

She was asleep only seconds after slipping beneath the covers.

Libby stirred, indulged in a deliciously lazy stretch. Someone was trailing soft, warm kisses across her collarbone—or was she dreaming? Just in case she was, she did not open her eyes.

Cool air washed over her breasts as the camisole was gently displaced. "Ummm," she said.

"Good dream?" asked Jess, moistening one pulsing nipple to crisp attention with his tongue.

"Oooooh," answered Libby, arching her back slightly, her eyes still closed, her head pressed into the silken pillow in eager, soft surrender. "Very good."

Jess left that nipple to subject its twin to a tender plundering that caused Libby to moan with delight. Her hips writhed slightly, calling to their powerful counterpart.

Jess heard their silent plea, slid the satiny tap pants down, down, away. "You're so warm, Libby," he said in a ragged whisper. "So soft and delicious." The camisole was unlaced, laid aside reverently, like the wrapping on some splendid gift. Kisses rained down on Libby's sleep-warmed, swollen breasts, her stomach, her thighs.

At last she opened her eyes, saw Jess's wondrous nakedness through a haze of sweet, sleepy need. As he ventured nearer and nearer to the silk-sheltered sanction of her womanhood, she instinctively reached up to clasp the brass railings on the headboard of the bed, anchoring herself to earth.

Jess parted the soft veil, admired its secret with a throaty exclamation of desire and a searing kiss.

A plea was wrenched from Libby, and she tightened her grasp on the headboard.

For a few mind-sundering minutes Jess enjoyed the swelling morsel with his tongue. "More?" he asked, teasing her, knowing that she was already half-mad with the need of him.

"More," she whimpered as his fingers strayed to the pebblelike peaks of her breasts, plying them, sending an exquisite lacelike net of passion knitting its way through her body.

Another tormenting flick of his tongue. "Sweet," he said. And then he lifted Libby's legs, placing one over each of his shoulders, making her totally, beautifully vulnerable to him.

She cried out in senseless delirium as he took his pleasure, and she was certain that she would have been flung beyond the dark sky if not for her desperate grasp on the headboard.

Even after the highest peak had been scaled, Libby's sated body convulsed again and again, caught in the throes of other, smaller releases.

Still dazed, Libby felt Jess's length stretch out upon her, seeking that sweetest and most intimate solace. In a burst of tender rebellion, she thrust him off and demanded loving revenge.

Soon enough, it was Jess who grasped the gleaming brass railings lest he soar away, Jess who chanted a desperate litany.

Wickedly, Libby took her time, savoring him, taking outrageous liberties with him. Finally she conquered him, and his cry of joyous surrender filled her with love almost beyond bearing.

His breathing still ragged, his face full of wonder, Jess drew Libby down, so that she lay beside him. With his hands he explored her, igniting tiny silver fires in every curve and hollow of her body.

This time, when he came to her, she welcomed him with a ferocious thrust of her hips, alternately setting the pace and following Jess's lead. When the pinnacle was reached, each was lost in the echoing, triumphant cry of the other, and bits of a broken rainbow showered down around them.

Sitting Indian-style on the living-room sofa, Libby twisted the telephone cord between her fingers and waited for her father's response to her announcement.

It was a soft chuckle.

"You aren't the least bit surprised!" Libby accused, marveling.

"I figured anybody that fought and jawed as much as you two did had to end up hitched," replied Ken Kincaid in his colorful way. "Did you let Cleave know yet?"

"Jess will, in a few minutes. Will you tell Cathy for me, please?"

Ken promised that he would.

Libby swallowed hard, gave Jess a warning glare as he moved to slide an exploring hand inside the top of her bathrobe. "Aren't you going to say that we're rushing into this or something like that? Some people will think it's too soon—"

"It was damned near too late," quipped Ken. "What time is the ceremony again?"

There were tears in Libby's eyes, though she had never been happier. "Two o'clock on Friday, at the courthouse."

"I'll be there, dumplin'. Be happy."

The whole room was distorted into a joyous blur. "I will, Dad. I love you."

"I love you, too," he answered with an ease that was typical of him. "Take care and I'll see you Friday."

"Right," said Libby, sniffling as she gently replaced the receiver.

Jess chuckled, touched her chin. "Tears? I'm insulted."

Libby made a face and shoved the telephone into his lap. "Call your father," she said.

Jess settled back in the sofa as he dialed the number of the senator's house in Washington, balancing the telephone on one blue-jeaned knee. While he tried to talk to his father in normal tones, Libby ran impudent fingertips over his bare chest, twining dark hair into tight curls, making hard buttons of deliciously vulnerable nipples.

With a mock-glare and a motion of his free arm, Jess tried to field her blatant advances. She simply knelt astraddle of his lap and had her way with him, her fingers tracing a path of fire around his mouth, along his neck, over his nipples.

Jess caught the errant hand in a desperate hold, only to be immediately assaulted by the other. Mischief flashed in his jade eyes, followed by an I'll-get-you-for-this look. "See you then," he said to his father, his voice a little deeper than usual and very carefully modulated. There was a pause, and then he added, "Oh, don't worry, I will. In about five seconds, I'm going to lay Libby on the coffee table and kiss her in all the best places. Yes, sir, by the time I get through with her, she'll be—"

Falling into the trap, Libby colored, snatched the receiver out of Jess's hand and pressed it to her ear. The line was, of course, dead.

Jess laughed as she assessed him murderously. "You deserved that," he said.

Libby moved to struggle off his lap, still crimson in the face, her heart pounding with embarrassment. But Jess's hands were strong on her upper arms, holding her in place.

"Oh, no you don't, princess. You're not getting out of this so easily."

"What—"

Jess smiled languidly, still holding her fast with one hand, undoing his jeans with the other. "You let this horse out of the barn, lady. Now you're going to ride it."

Libby gasped as she felt him prod her, hard and insistent, and fierce needs surged through her even as she raged at the affront. She was powerless, both physically and emotionally, to break away from him.

Just barely inside her, Jess reached out and calmly untied her bathrobe, baring her breasts, her stomach, her captured hips. His green eyes glittered as he stroked each satiny expanse in turn, allowing Libby more and more of him until she was fully his.

Seemingly unmoved himself, Jess took wicked delight in Libby's capture and began guiding her soft, trim hips up and down, endlessly up and down, upon him. All the while, he used soft words to lead her through flurries of silver snow to the tumultuous release beyond.

When her vision cleared, Libby saw that Jess had been caught in his own treachery. She watched in love and wonder as he gave himself up to raging sensation—his head fell back, his throat worked, his eyes were sightless.

Gruffly Jess pleaded with Libby, and she accelerated the up-and-down motion of her hips until he shuddered violently beneath her, stiffened and growled her name.

"Mess with me, will you?" she mocked, grinning down at him.

Jess began to laugh, between rasping breaths. When his mirth had subsided and he didn't have to drag air into his lungs, he caressed her with his eyes. In fact, it was almost as though he'd said he loved her.

Libby was still incredibly moved by the sweet spectacle she had seen played out in his face as he submitted to her, and she understood then why he so loved to watch her respond while pleasuring her.

Jess reached up, touched away the tear that tickled on her cheek. It would have been a perfect time for those three special words she so wanted to hear, but he did not say them.

Hurt and disappointed, Libby wrenched her bathrobe closed and tried to rise from his lap, only to be easily thwarted. Jess's hands opened the robe again, his eyes perused her and then came back to her face, silently daring her to hide any part of her body or soul from him.

With an insolent finger he brushed the pink buttons at the tips of her full breasts, smiled as they instantly obeyed him. Apparently satisfied with their pert allegiance, Jess moved on to trace patterns of fire on Libby's stomach, the rounding of her hips, the sensitive hollow at the base of her throat.

Jess seemed determined to prove that he could subdue Libby at will, and he only smiled at the startled gasp she gave when it became apparent that all his prowess had returned in full and glorious force.

He slid her robe off her shoulders then and removed it entirely. They were still joined, and Libby shivered as he toyed idly with her breasts, weighing them in his hands, pressing them together, thumbing their aching tips until they performed for him.

Presently Jess left his sumptuous playthings to tamper elsewhere, wreaking still more havoc, eliciting little anxious cries from a bedazzled Libby.

"What do you want, princess?" he asked in a voice of liquid steel.

Libby was wild upon him, her hands clutching desperately at his shoulders, her knees wide. "I want to be...under you. Oh, Jess...under you..."

In a swift and graceful motion, he turned her, was upon her. The movement unleashed the passion Jess had been able to contain until then, and he began to move over her and within her, his thrusts deep and powerful, his words ragged and incoherent.

As their very souls collided and then fused together, imitating their bodies, it was impossible to tell who had prevailed over whom.

Libby awakened first, entangled with Jess, amazed that they could have slept the whole night on that narrow couch.

A smile lifted one corner of her mouth as she kissed Jess's temple tenderly and then disengaged herself, careful not to disturb him. Heaven knew, he had a right to be tired.

Twenty minutes later, when Libby returned from her shower, dressed in sandals, white slacks and a lightweight yellow sweater, Jess was still sleeping. She could empathize, for her own slumber had been fathomless.

"I love you," she said, and then she went to the kitchen and wrote a quick note on the blackboard there, explaining that she had gone shopping and would be back within a few hours.

Getting into the rented car, which was parked in the gravel driveway near the front door, Libby spotted a cluster of colorful travel brochures fanned out on the opposite seat. Each one touted a different paradise: Acapulco, the Bahamas, Maui.

As Libby slid the key into the ignition and started the car, she grinned. She had it on good authority that paradise was only a few yards away, on the couch where Jess lay sleeping.

The day was a rich mixture of blue and green, set off by the fierce green of pine trees and the riotous blooms of crocuses and daffodils in quiet front yards. Downtown, Libby found a parking place immediately, locked the car and hurried on about her business.

Her first stop was a jewelry store, and while she had anticipated a great quandary, the decision of which wedding band to buy for Jess proved an easy one. Her eyes were immediately drawn to one particular ring, forged of silver, inset with polished chips of turquoise.

Once the jeweler had assured her the band could be resized if it didn't fit Jess's finger, Libby bought it.

In an art-supply store she purchased a sketching pad and a gum eraser and some charcoal pencils. Sweet as this interlude with Jess had been, Libby missed her work and her fingers itched to draw. Too, there were all sorts of new ideas for the comic strip bubbling in her mind.

From the art store, Libby pressed on to a good-sized department store. None of the dresses there quite struck her fancy, and she moved on to one boutique and then another.

Finally, in a small and wickedly expensive shop, she found that special dress, that dress of dresses, the one she would wear when she married Jess Barlowe.

It was a clingy creation of burgundy silk, showing off her figure, bringing a glow of color to her cheeks. There were no ruffles of lace or fancy buttons—only a narrow belt made of the same fabric as the dress itself. It was the last word in elegant simplicity, that garment, and Libby adored it.

Carrying the dress box and the heavy bag of art supplies, she hurried back to the car and locked her purchases inside. It was only a little after ten, and Libby wanted to find shoes that would match her dress.

The shoes proved very elusive, and only after almost an hour of searching did she find a pair that would do. Tired of shopping and anxious to see Jess again, Libby started home.

Some intuitive feeling made her uneasy as she drove toward the elegant condominium hidden in the tall trees. After crossing the wooden bridge and making the last turn, she knew why—Stacey's ice-blue Ferrari was parked in the driveway.

Don't be silly, Libby reprimanded herself, but she still felt alarmed. What if Stacey had come to try to talk her out of marrying Jess? What if Cathy was with him, and there was an unpleasant scene?

Determined not to let her imagination get the upper hand, Libby gathered up her loot from the shopping trip and got out of the car. As she approached the house, she caught sight of a familiar face at the window and was surprised all over again. Monica! What on earth was she doing here? Hadn't she left for Washington, D.C., with the senator?

Now Libby really hesitated. She remembered the proprietary looks the woman had given Jess as he swam that day in the pool at the main ranch house. Looks that had implied intimacy.

Libby sighed. So what if Jess and Monica had slept together? She could hardly have expected a man like him to live like a monk, and it wasn't as if Libby hadn't had a prior relationship herself, however unsatisfactory.

Despite the cool sanity of this logic, it hurt to imagine Jess making love with Monica—or with any other woman, for that matter.

Libby grappled with her purchases at the front door, reached for the knob. Before she could clasp it, the door opened.

Jess was standing there, shirtless, wearing jeans, his hair and suntanned chest still damp from a recent shower. Instead of greeting Libby with a smile, let alone a kiss, he scowled at her and stepped back almost grudgingly, as though he had considered refusing her entrance.

Bewildered and hurt, Libby resisted a primal instinct urging her to flee and walked in.

Monica had left the window and was now seated comfortably on the couch, her shapely legs crossed at the knee, a cocktail in her hand.

Libby took in the woman's sleek designer suit and felt shabby by comparison in her casual attire. "Hello, Monica."

"Libby," replied Monica with a polite nod.

The formalities dispensed with, Libby flung a hesitant look at Jess. Why was he glaring at her like that, as though he wanted to do her bodily harm? Why was his jawline so tight, and why was it that he clenched the towel draped around his neck in white-knuckled hands?

Before Libby could voice any of her questions, Stacey came out of the kitchen, raked her with guileless caramel eyes and smiled.

"Hello," he said, as though his very presence, under the circumstances, was not an outrage.

Libby only stared at him. She was very conscious of Jess, seething somewhere on the periphery of her vision, and of Monica, taking in the whole scene with detached amusement.

Suddenly Stacey was coming toward Libby, speaking words she couldn't seem to hear. Then he had the outright gall to kiss her, and Libby's inertia was broken.

She drew back her hand and slapped him, her dress box, purse and bag of art supplies falling to the floor.

Stacey reached out for her, caught her waist in his hands. She squirmed and flung one appealing look in Jess's direction.

Though he looked anything but chivalrous, he did intercede. "Leave Libby alone, Stacey."

Stacey paled. "I've left Cathy," he said, as though that settled everything. "Libby, we can be together now!"

Libby stumbled backward, stunned. Only when she came up against the hard barrier of Jess's soap-scented body did she stop. Wild relief went through her as he enclosed her in a steel-like protective embrace.

"Get out," he said flatly, addressing his brother.

Stacey hesitated, but then he reddened and left the condo in a huff, pulling Monica Summers behind him.

Chapter 10

Furious and shaken, Libby turned to glare at Jess. It was all too clear what had happened—Stacey had been telling more of his outrageous lies and Jess had believed them.

For a few moments he stubbornly returned her angry regard, but then he spread his hands in a gesture of concession and said, "I'm sorry."

Libby was trembling now, but she stooped to pick up her dress box, and the art-store bag. She couldn't look at Jess or he would see the tears that had clouded her eyes. "After all we've done and planned, how could you, Jess? How could you believe Stacey?"

He was near, very near—Libby was conscious of him in every sense. He moved to touch her, instantly stopped himself. "I said I was sorry."

Libby forgot that she'd meant to hide her tears and looked him full in the face. Her voice shook with anger when she spoke. "Sometimes being sorry isn't enough, Jess!" She carried the things she'd bought across the room, tossed them onto the couch. "Is this what our marriage is going to be like? Are we going to do just fine as long as we aren't around Stacey?"

Jess was standing behind her; his hands came to rest on her shoulders. "What can I say, Libby? I was jealous. That may not be right, but it's human."

Perhaps because she wanted so desperately to believe that everything would turn out all right, that a marriage to this wonderful, contradictory man would succeed, Libby set aside her doubts and turned to face Jess. The depth of her love for this erstwhile enemy still staggered her. "What did Stacey tell you?"

Jess drew in an audible breath, and for a moment there was a tightness in his jaw. Then he sighed and said, "He was sharing the glorious details of your supposed affair. And he had a remarkable grasp on what you like in bed, Libby."

The words were wounding, but Libby was strong. "Did it ever occur to you that maybe all women like essentially the same things?"

Jess didn't answer, but Libby could see that she had made her mark, and she rushed on.

"Exactly what was Monica's part in all this?" she demanded hotly. "Was she here to moderate your sexual discussion? Why the hell isn't she in Washington, where she belongs?"

Jess shrugged, obviously puzzled. "I'm not sure why she was here."

"I am! Once you were diverted from your disastrous course—marrying me—she was going to take you by the hand and lead you home!"

One side of Jess's mouth lifted in a grin. "I'm not the only one who is prone to jealousy, it appears."

"You were involved with her, weren't you?"

"Yes."

The bluntness of the answer took Libby unawares, but only for a moment. After all, had Jess said no, she would have known he was lying and that would have been devastating. "Did you love Monica?"

"No. If I had, I would have married her."

The possible portent of those words buoyed Libby's flagging spirits. "Passion wouldn't be enough?" she ventured.

"To base a marriage on? Never. Now, let's see what you bought today."

Let's see what you bought today. Libby's frustration knew no bounds, but she was damned if she was going to pry those three longed-for words out of him—she'd fished enough as it was. "I bought a wedding dress, for your information. And you're not going to see it until tomorrow, so don't pester me about it."

He laughed. "I like a woman who is loyal to her superstitions. What else did you purchase, milady?"

Libby's sense of financial independence, nurtured during the insecure days with Aaron, chafed under the question. "I didn't use your money, so what do you care?" she snapped.

Jess arched one eyebrow. "Another touchy subject rears its ugly head. I was merely curious, my love—I didn't ask for a meeting with your accountant."

Feeling foolish, Libby made a great project of opening the art-store bag and spreading its contents out on the couch.

Jess was grinning as he assessed the array of pencils, the large sketchbook. "Have I been boring you, princess?"

Libby pulled a face at him. "You could be called many things, Jess Barlowe, but you are definitely not boring."

"Thank you—I think. Shall we brave the car dealers of Kalispell again, or are you going to be busy?" The question was guileless, indicating that Jess would have understood if she wanted to stay and block out some of the ideas that had come to her.

After Aaron, who had viewed her cartooning as a childish hobby, Jess's attitude was a luxury. "I think I'd rather go with you," she said with a teasing smile. "If I don't you might come home with some motorized horror that has horns on its hood."

"Your faith in my good taste is positively underwhelming," he replied, walking toward the ladder, climbing its rungs to the loft in search of a shirt.

"You were right!" Libby called after him. "The view from down here is marvelous!"

During that foray into the jungle of car salesmen and gasoline-fed beasts, Libby spent most of her time in the passenger seat of Jess's rented car, sketching. Instead of drawing Liberated Lizzie, her cartoon character, however, she found herself reproducing Jess's image.

She imagined him looking out over the stunning view of prairies and mountains at home and drew him in profile, the wind ruffling his hair, a pensive look to his eyes and the set of his face. Another sketch showed him laughing, and still another, hidden away in the middle of the drawing pad, not meant for anyone else to see, mirrored the way Jess looked when he wanted her.

To field the responses the drawing evoked in her, Libby quickly sketched Cathy's portrait, and then Ken's. After that, strictly from memory, she drew a picture of Jonathan, full face, as he'd looked before his illness, then, on the same piece of paper, in a profile that revealed the full ravages of his disease.

She supposed it was morbid, including this aspect of the child, but to leave out his pain would have meant leaving out his courage, and Jonathan deserved better.

Touching his charcoal image with gentle, remembering fingers, Libby heard the echo of his voice in her mind. *Naturally I'm brave,* he'd told her once, at the end of a particularly difficult day. *I'm a Jedi knight, like Luke Skywalker.*

Smiling through a mist of tears, Libby added another touch to the sketch—a tiny figure of Jonathan, well and strong, wielding a light saber in valiant defense of the Rebel Alliance.

"That's terrific," observed a gentle voice.

Libby looked up quickly, surprised that she hadn't heard Jess get into the car, hadn't sensed his presence somehow. Because she couldn't speak just yet, she bit her lower lip and nodded an acknowledgment of the compliment.

"Could I take a closer look? Please?"

Libby extended the notebook and it was a gesture of trust, for these sketches were different from the panels for her comic strip. They were large pieces of her soul.

Jess was pensive as he examined the portraits of himself, Cathy, Ken. But the study of Jonathan was clearly his favorite, and he returned to it at intervals, taking in each line, each bit of shading, each unspoken cry of grief.

Finally, with a tenderness that made Libby love him even more than she had before, Jess handed the sketchbook back to her. "You are remarkably talented," he said, and then he had the good grace to look away while Libby recomposed herself.

"D-did you find a car you like?" she asked finally.

Jess smiled at her. "Actually, yes. That's why I came back—to get you."

"Me? Why?"

"Well, I don't want to buy the thing without your checking it out first. Suppose you hated it?"

It amazed Libby that such a thing mattered to him. She set the sketchbook carefully in the back seat and opened her car door to get out. "Lead on," she said, and the clean spring breeze braced her as it touched her face.

The vehicle in question was neither car nor truck, but a Land Rover. It was perfectly suited to the kind of life Jess led, and Libby approved of it with enthusiasm.

The deal was made, much to the relief of a salesman they had been plaguing, on and off, since the day before.

After some discussion, it was decided that they would keep the rental car until after the wedding, in case Libby needed it. Over a luncheon of steak and salad, which did much to settle her shaky nerves, Jess suggested that they start shopping all over again, for a second car.

Practical as it was, the thought exhausted Libby.

"You'll need transportation," Jess argued.

"I don't think I could face all those plaid sport jackets and test drives again," Libby replied with a sigh.

Jess laughed. "But you would like to have a car, wouldn't you?"

Libby shrugged. In New York, she had depended on taxis for transportation, but the ranch was different, of course. "I suppose."

"Aren't you choosy about the make, model—all that?"

"Wheels are wheels," she answered with another shrug.

"Hmmmm," Jess said speculatively, and then the subject was changed. "What about our honeymoon? Any place in particular you'd like to go?"

"Your couch," Libby said, shocked at her own audacity.

Again Jess laughed. "That is patently unimaginative."

"Hardly, considering the things we did there," Libby replied, immediately lifting a hand to her mouth. What was wrong with her? Why was she suddenly spouting these outlandish remarks?

Jess bent forward, conjured up a comical leer. "I wish we were on the ranch," he said in a low voice. "I'd take you somewhere private and make violent love to you."

Libby felt a familiar heat simmering inside her, melting through her pelvis. "Jess."

He drew some bills from his wallet, tossed them onto the table. "Let's get out of here while I can still walk," he muttered.

Libby laughed. "I think it's a good thing we're driving separate cars today," she teased, though secretly she was just as anxious for privacy as Jess was.

He groaned. "One more word, lady, and I'll spread you out on this table."

Libby's heart thudded at the bold suggestion and pumped color over her breasts and into her face. She tried to look indignant, but the fact was that she had been aroused by the remark and Jess knew it—his grin was proof of that.

As they left the restaurant, he bent close to her and described the fantasy in vivid detail, sparing nothing. And later, on the table in the condo's kitchen, he turned it into a wildly satisfying reality.

That afternoon, Libby took another nap. Due to the episode just past, her dreams were deliciously erotic.

As he had before, Jess awakened her with strategic kisses. "Hi," he said when she opened her eyes.

She touched his hair, noted that he was wearing his brown leather jacket. "You've been out." She yawned.

Jess kissed the tip of her nose. "I have indeed. Bought you a present or two, as a matter of fact."

The glee in Jess's eyes made Libby's heart twist in a spasm of tenderness; whatever he'd purchased, he was very pleased with. She slipped languid arms around his neck. "I like presents," she said.

Jess drew back, tugged her camisole down so that her breasts were bared to him. Almost idly he kissed each dusty-rose peak and then covered them again. "Sorry," he muttered, his mouth a fraction of an inch from hers. "I couldn't resist."

That strange, magical heat was surging from Libby's just-greeted breasts to her middle, down into her thighs and even her knees. She felt as though every muscle and bone in her body had melted. "You m-mentioned presents?"

He chuckled, kissed her softly, groaned under his breath. "I was momentarily distracted. Get out of bed, princess. Said presents await."

"Can't you just...bring them here?"

"Hardly." Jess withdrew from the bed to stand at its side and wrench back the covers. His green eyes smoldered as he took in the sleep-pinkened glow of her curves, and he bent to swat her satin-covered backside. "Get up," he repeated.

Libby obeyed, curious about the gifts but disappointed that Jess hadn't joined her in the bed, too. She found a floaty cotton caftan and slipped it on over her camisole and tap pants.

Jess looked at her, made a low growling sound in his throat, and caught her hand in his. "Come on, before I give in to my baser instincts," he said, pulling her down the stairs.

Libby looked around curiously as he dragged her across the living room but saw nothing out of the ordinary.

Jess opened the front door, pulled her outside. There, beside his maroon Land Rover, sat a sleek yellow Corvette with a huge rosette of silver ribbon affixed to its windshield.

Libby gaped at the car, her eyes wide.

"Like it?" Jess asked softly, his mouth close to her ear.

"Like it?" Libby bounded toward the car, heedless of her bare feet. "I love it!"

Jess followed, opened the door on the driver's side so that Libby could slide behind the wheel. When she did that, she got a second surprise. Taped to the gearshift knob was a ring of white gold, and the diamond setting formed the Circle Bar B brand.

"I'll hog-tie you later," Jess said.

Libby's hand trembled as she reached for the ring; it blurred and shifted before her eyes as she looked at it. "Oh, Jess."

"Listen, if you hate it..."

Libby ripped away the strip of tape, slid the ring onto her finger. "Hate it? Sacrilege! It's the most beautiful thing I've ever seen."

"Does it fit?"

The ring was a little loose, but Libby wasn't ready to part with it, not even to let a jeweler size it. "No," she said, overwhelmed, "but I don't care."

Gently Jess lifted her chin with his hand, bent to sample her mouth with his. Beneath the hastily donned caftan and her camisole, Libby's nipples hardened in pert response.

"There's only one drawback to this car," Jess breathed, his lips teasing Libby's, shaping them. "It would be impossible to make love in it."

Libby laughed and pretended to shove him. "Scoundrel!"

"You don't know the half of it," he replied hoarsely, drawing Libby out of the beautiful car and back inside the house.

There she gravitated toward the front windows, where she could alternately admire her new car and watch the late-afternoon sun catch in the very special ring on her finger. Standing behind her, Jess wrapped his arms around her waist and held her close, bending to nip at her earlobe.

"Thank you, Jess," Libby said.

He laughed, and his breath moved in Libby's hair and sent warm tingles through her body. "No need for thanks. I'll nibble on your ears anytime."

"You know what I meant!"

His hands had risen to close over her breasts, fully possessing them. "What? What did you mean?" he teased in a throaty whisper.

Libby could barely breathe. "The car...the ring..."

Letting his hands slip from her breasts to her elbows, Jess ushered Libby over to face the mirror above the fireplace. As she watched his reflection in wonder, he undid the caftan's few buttons and slid it slowly down over her shoulders. Then he drew the camisole up over her head and tossed it away.

Libby saw a pink glow rise over her breasts to shine in her face, saw the passion sparking in her dark blue eyes, saw Jess's hands brush upward over her rib cage toward her breasts. The novelty of watching her own reactions to the sensations he was stirring inside her was erotic.

She groaned as she saw—and felt—masculine fingers rise to her waiting nipples and pluck then gently to attention.

"See?" Jess whispered at her ear. "See how beautiful you are, Libby? Especially when I'm loving you."

Libby had never thought of herself as beautiful, but now, looking at her image in the mirror, seeing how passion darkened her eyes to indigo and painted her cheeks with its own special apricot shade, she felt ravishing.

She tilted her head back against the hard breadth of Jess's shoulder, moaned as he softly plundered her nipples.

He spoke with a gruff, choked sort of sternness. "Don't close your eyes, Libby. Watch. You're beautiful—so beautiful—and I want you to know it."

It was hard for Libby not to close her eyes and give herself up to the incredible sensations that were raging through her, but she managed it even as Jess came from behind her to bend his head and take suckle at one breast.

Watching him do this, watching the heightened color in her own face, gave a new intensity to the searing needs that were like storm winds within Libby. Her eyes were fires of ink-blue, and there was a proud, even regal lift to her chin as she watched herself pleasing the man she loved.

Jess drank deeply of one breast, turned to the other. It was an earthy communion between one man and one woman, each one giving and taking.

Presently Jess's mouth slid down over Libby's slightly damp stomach, and then he was kneeling, no longer visible in the magic mirror. "Don't close your eyes," he repeated, and Libby felt her satiny tap pants sliding slowly down over her hips, her knees, her ankles.

The wide-eyed sprite in the mirror gasped, and Libby was forced to brace herself with both hands against the mantel piece, just to keep from falling. Her breathing quickened to a rasp as Jess ran skilled hands over her bare bottom, her thighs, the backs of her knees. He heightened her pleasure by telling her precisely what he meant to do.

And then he did it.

Libby's release was a maelstrom of soft sobs that finally melded together into one lusty cry of pleasure. Jess was right, she thought, in the midst of all this and during the silvery descent that followed: she *was* beautiful.

Standing again, Jess lifted Libby up into his arms. Still feeling like some wanton Gypsy princess, she let her head fall back and gloried in the liberties his mouth took with the breasts that were thrust into easy reach.

Libby was conscious of an other-worldly floating sensation as she and Jess glided downward, together, to the floor.

Rain pattered and danced on the glass ceiling above the bed, a dismal heralding of what promised to be the happiest day of Libby Kincaid's life.

Jess slept beside her, beautifully naked, his breathing deep and even. If he hadn't actually spoken of his love, he had shown it in a dozen ways. So why did the pit of Libby's stomach jiggle, as though something awful was about to happen?

The insistent ringing of the doorbell brought Jess up from his stomach, push-up style, grumbling. His dark hair hopelessly rumpled, his eyes glazed, he stumbled around the bedroom until he found his robe and managed to struggle into it.

Libby laughed at him as he started down the stairs. "So much for being happy in the mornings, Barlowe," she taunted.

His answer was a terse word that Libby couldn't quite make out.

She heard the door open downstairs, heard Senator Barlowe's deep laugh and exuberant greeting. The sounds eased the feeling of dread that had plagued Libby earlier, and she got out of bed and hurried to the bathroom for a shower.

Periodically, as Libby shampooed her hair and washed, she laughed. Having his father arrive unexpectedly from Washington, probably with Ken and Cathy soon to follow, would certainly throw cold water on any plans the groom might have had for prenuptial frolicking.

When Libby went downstairs, her hair blown dry, her makeup in place, she was delighted to see that Cathy was with the senator. They were both, in fact, seated comfortably on the couch, drinking coffee.

"Where's Dad?" Libby asked when hugs and kisses had been exchanged.

Cleave Barlowe, with his elegant, old-fashioned manners, waited for Libby to sit down before returning to his own seat near Cathy. "He'll be here in time for the ceremony," he said. "When we left the ranch, he was heading out with that bear patrol of his."

Libby frowned and fussed with her crisp pink sundress, feeling uneasy again. Jess had gone upstairs, and she could hear the water running in the shower. "Bear patrol?"

"We've lost a few calves to a rogue grizzly," Cleave said easily, as though such a thing were an everyday occurrence. "Ken and half a dozen of his best men have been tracking him, but they haven't had any luck so far."

Cathy, sitting at her father-in-law's elbow, seemed to sense her cousin's apprehension and signed that she wanted a better look at Libby's ring.

The tactic worked, but as Libby offered her hand, she at last looked into Cathy's face and saw the ravages of her marital problems. There were dark smudges under the green eyes, and a hollow ache pulsed inside them.

Libby reprimanded herself for being so caught up in her own tumultuous romance with Jess as to forget that during his visit the day before, Stacey had said he'd left Cathy. It shamed Libby that she hadn't thought more about her cousin, made it a point to find out how she was.

"Are you all right?" she signed, knowing that Cathy was always more comfortable with this form of communication than with lip reading.

Cathy's responding smile was real, if wan. She nodded and with mischievous interest assessed the ring Jess had had specially designed.

Cleave demanded a look at this piece of jewelry that was causing such an "all-fired" stir and laughed with appreciation when he saw his own brand in the setting.

Cathy lifted her hands. "I want to see your dress."

After Jess had come downstairs, dressed in jeans and the scandalous T-shirt Libby had given him, the two women went up to look at the new burgundy dress.

The haunted look was back in Cathy's eyes as she approved the garment. "I can hardly believe you're marrying Jess," she said in the halting, hesitant voice she would allow only Libby to hear.

Libby sat down on the rumpled bed beside her cousin. "That should settle any doubts you might have had about my relationship with Stacey," she said gently.

Cathy's pain was a visible spasm in her face. "He's living at the main house now," she confessed. "Libby, Stacey says he wants a divorce."

Libby's anger with Stacey was equal only to her sympathy for his wife. "I'm sure he doesn't mean any of the things he's been saying, Cathy. If only you would talk to him..."

The emerald eyes flashed. "So Stacey could laugh at me, Libby? No, thanks!"

Libby drew a deep breath. "I can't help thinking that this problem stems from a lack of communication and trust," she persisted, careful to face toward her cousin. "Stacey loves you. I know he does."

"How can you be so sure?" whispered Cathy. "How, Libby? Marriages end every day of the week."

"No one knows that better than I do. But some things are a matter of instinct, and mine tells me that Stacey is doing this to make you notice him, Cathy. And maybe because you won't risk having a baby."

"Having a baby would be pretty stupid, wouldn't it? Even if I wanted to take the risk, as you call it. After all, my husband moved out of our house!"

"I'm not saying that you should rush back to the ranch and get yourself pregnant, Cathy. But couldn't you just talk to Stacey, the way you talk to me?"

"I told you—I'd be embarrassed!"

"Embarrassed! You are married to the man, Cathy—you share his bed! How can you be embarrassed to let him hear your voice?"

Cathy knotted her fingers together in her lap and lowered her head. From downstairs Libby could hear Jess and the senator talking quietly about the vote Cleave had cast before coming back to Montana for the wedding.

Finally Cathy looked up again. "I couldn't talk to anyone but you, Libby. I don't even talk to Jess or Ken."

"That's your own fault," Libby said, still angry. "Have you kept your silence all this time—all during the years I've been away?"

Cathy shook her head. "I ride up into the foothills sometimes and talk to the wind and the trees, for practice. Do you think that's silly?"

"No, and stop being so afraid that someone is going to think you're silly, dammit! So what if they do? What do you suppose people thought about me when I stayed with a man who had girlfriends?"

Cathy's mouth fell open. "Girlfriends?"

"Yes," snapped Libby, stung by the memory. "And don't tell my dad. He'd faint."

"I doubt it," replied Cathy. "But it must have hurt terribly. I'm so sorry, Libby."

"And I'm sorry if I was harsh with you," Libby answered. "I just want you to be happy, Cathy—that's all. Will you promise me that you'll talk to Stacey? Please?"

"I...I'll try."

Libby hugged her cousin. "That's good enough for me."

There was again a flash of delight in Cathy's eyes, indicating an imminent change of subject. "Is that car outside yours?"

Libby's answer was a nod. "Isn't it beautiful?"

"Will you take me for a ride in it? When the wedding is over and you're home on the ranch?"

"You know I will. We'll be the terror of the back roads—legends in our own time!"

Cathy laughed. "Legends? We'll be memories if we aren't careful."

Libby rose from her seat on the bed, taking up the pretty burgundy dress, slipping it carefully onto a hanger, hanging it in the back of the closet.

When that was done, the two women went downstairs together. By this time Jess and his father were embroiled in one of their famous political arguments.

Feeling uneasy again, Libby went to the telephone with as much nonchalance as she could and dialed Ken's number. There was no answer, of course—she had been almost certain that there wouldn't be—but the effort itself comforted her a little.

"Try the main house," Jess suggested softly from just behind her.

Libby glanced back at him, touched by his perception. Consoled by it. "How is it," she teased in a whisper, "that you managed to look elegant in jeans and a T-shirt that says 'If it feels good, do it'?"

Jess laughed and went back to his father and Cathy.

Libby called the main house and got a somewhat flustered Marion Bradshaw. "Hello!" barked the woman.

"Mrs. Bradshaw, this is Libby. Have you seen my father this morning?"

There was a long sigh, as though the woman was relieved to learn that the caller was not someone else. "No, dear, I haven't. He and the crew are out looking for that darned bear. Don't you worry, though—Ken told me he'd be in town for your wedding in plenty of time."

Libby knew that her father's word was good. If he said he'd be there, he would, come hell or high water. Still, something in Mrs. Bradshaw's manner was disturbing. "Is something the matter, Marion?"

Another sigh, this one full of chagrin. "Libby, one of the maids told me that a Mr. Aaron Strand called here, asking where you could be reached. Without so much as a by-your-leave, that woman came right out and told him you were in Kalispell and gave him the number. I'm so sorry."

So that was how Aaron had known where to call. Libby sighed. "It's all right, Marion—it wasn't your fault."

"I feel responsible all the same," said the woman firmly, "but I'll kick myself on my own time. I just wanted to let you know what happened. Did Miss Cathy and the senator get there all right?"

Libby smiled. "Yes, they're here. Any messages?"

"No, but I'd like a word with Jess, if it's all right."

Libby turned and gestured to the man in question. He came to the phone, took the receiver, greeted Marion Bradshaw warmly. Their conversation was a brief one, and when Jess hung up, he was laughing.

"What's so funny?" the senator wanted to know.

Jess slid an arm around Libby and gave her a quick squeeze. "Dare I say it in front of the creator of Liberated Lizzie, cartoon cave-woman? I just got Marion's blessing—she says I branded the right heifer."

Chapter 11

Libby stood at a window overlooking the courthouse parking lot, peering through the gray drizzle, anxiously scanning each vehicle that pulled in.

"He'll be here," Cathy assured her, joining Libby at the rain-sheeted window.

Libby sighed. She knew that Ken would come if he possibly could, but the rain would make the roads hazardous, and there was the matter of that rogue grizzly bear. "I hope so," she said.

Cathy stood back a little to admire the flowing silken lines of Libby's dress. "You look wonderful. Here—let's see if the flowers match."

"Flowers?" Libby hadn't thought about flowers, hadn't thought about much at all, beyond contemplating the wondrous event about to take place. Her reason said that it was insanity to marry again, especially to marry Jess Barlowe, but her heart sang a very different song.

Cathy beamed and indicated a cardboard box sitting on a nearby table.

At last Libby left her post at the window, bemused. "But I didn't..."

Cathy was already removing a cellophane-wrapped corsage, several boutonnieres, an enormous bouquet made up of burgundy rosebuds, baby's breath, and white carnations. "This is yours, of course."

Libby reached out for her bridal bouquet, pleased and very surprised. "Did you order these, Cathy?"

"No," replied Cathy, "but I did nudge Jess in the florist's direction, after seeing what color your dress was."

Moved that such a detail had been taken into consideration, Libby hugged her cousin. "Thank you."

"Thank Jess. He's the one that browbeat the florist into filling a last-minute order." Cathy found a corsage labeled with her name. "Pin this on, will you?"

Libby happily complied. There were boutonnieres for Jess and the senator and Ken, too, and she turned this last one wistfully in her hands. It was almost time for the ceremony to begin—where was her father?

A light tap at the door made Libby's heart do a jittery flip. "Yes?"

"It's me," Jess said in a low, teasing voice. "Are the flowers in there?"

Cathy gathered up the boutonnieres, white carnations wrapped in clear, crackly paper, made her way to the door. Opening it just far enough to reach through, she held out the requested flowers.

Jess chuckled but made no move to step past the barrier and see his bride before the designated moment. "Five minutes, Libby," he said, and then she heard him walking away, his heels clicking on the marble courthouse floor.

Libby went back to the window, spotted a familiar truck racing into the parking lot, lurching to a stop. Two men in rain slickers got out and hurried toward the building.

Ken had arrived, and at last Libby was prepared to join Jess in Judge Henderson's office down the hall. She saw that august room through a haze of happiness, noticing a desk, a flag, a portrait of George Washington. In front of the rain-beaded windows, with their heavy, threadbare velvet draperies, stood Jess and his father.

Everyone seemed to move in slow motion. The judge took his place, and Jess, looking quietly magnificent in a tailored three-piece suit of dark blue, took his. His eyes caressed Libby, even from that distance, and somehow drew her toward him. At his side stood the senator, clearly tired from his unexpected cross-country trip, but proud and pleased, too.

Like a person strolling through a sweet dream, Libby let Jess draw her to him. At her side was Cathy, standing up very straight, her green eyes glistening with joyous tears.

Libby's sense of her father's presence was so strong that she did not need to look back and confirm it with her eyes. She tucked her arm through Jess's and the ceremony began.

When all the familiar words had been said, Jess bent toward Libby and kissed her tenderly. The haze lifted and the bride and groom turned, arm in arm, to face their few but much-loved guests.

Instead of congratulations, they met the pain-filled stares of two cowboys dressed in muddy jeans, sodden shirts and raincoats.

Suddenly frantic, Libby scanned the small chamber for her father's face. She'd been so sure that he was there; he had seemed near enough to touch.

"Where—" she began, but her question was broken off because Jess left her side to stride toward the emissaries from the ranch, the senator close behind him.

"The bear..." said one of them in answer to Jess's clipped question. "We had him cornered and"—the cowboy's Adam's apple moved up and down in his throat—"and he was a mean one, Mr. Barlowe. Meaner'n the devil's kid brother."

Libby knew what was coming and the worn courthouse carpeting seemed to buckle and shift beneath her high-heeled burgundy sandals. Had it not been for Cathy, who gripped her elbow and maneuvered her into a nearby chair, she would have fallen.

"Just tell us what happened!" Jess rasped.

"The bear worked Ken over pretty good," the second cowboy confessed.

Libby gave a strangled cry and felt Cathy's arm slide around her shoulders.

"Is Ken dead?" demanded Cleave Barlowe, and as far as Libby was concerned, the whole universe hinged on the answer to that question.

"No, sir—we got Mr. Kincaid to the hospital fast as we could. But...but."

"But what?" hissed Jess.

"The bear got away, Mr. Barlowe."

Jess came slowly toward Libby, or at least it seemed so to her. As he crouched before her chair and took her chilled hands into his, his words were gentle. "Are you all right?"

Libby was too frightened and sick to speak, but she did manage a nod. Jess helped her to her feet, supported her as they left the room.

She was conscious of the cowboys, behind her, babbling an account of the incident with the bear to Senator Barlowe, of Cathy's quiet sobs, of Jess's steel arm around her waist. The trip to the hospital, made in the senator's limousine, seemed hellishly long.

At the hospital's admissions desk, they were told by a harried, soft-voiced nurse that there was no news yet and directed to the nearest waiting room.

Stacey was there, and Cathy ran to him. He embraced her without hesitation, crooning to her, smoothing her hair with one hand.

"Ken?" barked the senator, his eyes anxious on his elder son's pale face.

"He's in surgery," replied Stacey. And though he still held Cathy, his gaze shifted, full of pain and disbelief, to Libby. "It's bad," he said.

Libby shuddered, more afraid than she'd ever been in her life, her arms and legs useless. Jess was holding her up—Jess and some instinct that had lain dormant within her since Jonathan's death. "Were you there when it happened, Stacey?" she asked dully.

Stacey was rocking Cathy gently in his arms, his chin propped in her hair. "Yes," he replied.

Suddenly rage surged through Libby—a senseless, shrieking tornado of rage. "You had guns!" she screamed. "I know you had guns! Why didn't you stop the bear? Why didn't you kill it?"

Jess's arm tightened around her. "Libby—"

Stacey broke in calmly, his voice full of compassion even in the face of Libby's verbal attack. "There was too much chance that Ken would be hit," he answered. "We hollered and fired shots in the air and that finally scared the grizzly off." There was a hollow look in Stacey's eyes as they moved to his father's face and then Jess's, looking for the same understanding he had just given to Libby.

"What about the bear?" the senator wanted to know.

Stacey averted his eyes for a moment. "He got away," he breathed, confirming what one of the cowboys had said earlier at the courthouse. "Jenkins got him in the hind flank, but he got away. Ran like a racehorse, that son of a bitch. Anyway, we were more concerned with Ken at the moment."

The senator nodded, but Jess tensed beside Libby, his gaze fierce. "You sent men after the grizzly, didn't you?"

Stacey looked pained and his hold on Cathy tightened as her sobs ebbed to terrified little sniffles. "I...I didn't think—"

"You didn't think?" growled Jess. "Goddammit, Stacey, now we've got a wounded bear on the loose—"

The senator interceded. "I'll call the ranch and make sure the grizzly is tracked down," he said reasonably. "Stacey got Ken to the hospital, Jess, and that was the most important thing."

An uncomfortable silence settled over the waiting room then. The senator went to the window to stand, hands clasped behind his back, looking out. The cowboys went back to the ranch, and Stacey and Jess maneuvered their stricken wives into chairs.

The sounds and smells peculiar to a hospital were a torment to Libby, who had endured the worst minutes, hours, days, and weeks of her life in just such a place. She had lost Jonathan in an institution like this one—would she lose Ken, too?

"I can't stand it," she whispered, breaking the awful silence.

Jess took her chin in his hand, his eyes locking with hers, sharing badly needed strength. "Whatever happens, Libby, we'll deal with it together."

Libby shivered violently, looked at Jess's tailored suit, her own dress, the formal garb of Cathy and the senator. Only Stacey, in his muddy jeans, boots, shirt and sodden denim jacket, seemed dressed for the horrible occasion. The rest of the party was at ludicrous variance with the situation.

My father may be dying, she thought in quiet hysteria, *and we're wearing flowers.* The smell of her bouquet suddenly sickened Libby, bringing back memories of Jonathan's funeral, and she flung it away. It slid under a couch upholstered in green plastic and cowered there against the wall.

Jess's grip tightened on her hand, but no one made a comment.

Presently the senator wandered out, returning some minutes later with cups of vending-machine coffee balanced on a small tray. "Ken is my best friend," he announced in befuddled tones to the group in general.

The words brought a startling cry of grief from Cathy, who had been huddled in her chair until that moment, behind a curtain of tangled, rain-dampened hair. "I won't let him die!" she shrieked, to the openmouthed amazement of everyone except Libby.

Stacey, draped over the arm and back of Cathy's chair, stared down at her, his throat working. "Cathy?" he choked out.

Because Cathy was not looking at him, could not see her name on his lips, she did not answer. Her small hands flew to cover her face and she wept for the man who had loved her as his own child, raised her as his own, been her strength as well as Libby's.

"She can't hear you," Libby said woodenly.

"But she talked!" gasped Jess.

Libby lifted one shoulder in a broken shrug. "Cathy has been talking for years. To me, anyway."

"Good God," breathed the senator, his gaze sweeping over his shattered daughter-in-law. "Why didn't she speak to any of us?"

Libby was sorry for Stacey, reading the pain in his face, the shock. Of course, it was a blow to him to realize that his own wife had kept such a secret for so long.

"Cathy was afraid," Libby explained quietly. "She is very self-conscious about the way her voice sounds to hearing people."

"That's ridiculous!" barked Stacey, looking angry now, paler than before. He bolted away from Cathy's chair to stand at the windows, his back to the room. "For God's sake, I'm her husband!"

"Some of us had a few doubts about that," remarked Jess in an acid undertone.

Stacey whirled, full of fury, but the senator stepped between his two sons before the situation could get out of hand. "This is no time for arguments," he said evenly but firmly. "Libby and Cathy don't need it, and neither do I."

Both brothers receded, Stacey lowering his head a little, Jess averting a gaze that was still bright with anger. Libby watched a muscle leap in her husband's jaw and stifled a crazy urge to touch it with her finger, to still it.

"Was Dad conscious when you brought him here?" she asked of Stacey in a voice too calm and rational to be her own.

Stacey nodded, remembering. "He said that bear was almost as tough as a Mexican he fought once, down in Juarez."

The tears Libby had not been able to cry before suddenly came to the surface, and Jess held her until they passed. "Ken is strong," he reminded her. "Have faith in him."

Libby tried to believe the best, but the fact remained that Ken Kincaid was a mortal man, strong or not. And he'd been mauled viciously by a bear. Even if he survived, he might be crippled.

It seemed that Jess was reading her mind, as he so often did. His hand

came up to stroke away her tears, smooth her hair back from her face.
"Don't borrow trouble," he said gently. "We've got enough now."

Trying to follow this advice, Libby deliberately reviewed pleasant
memories: Ken cursing a tangle of Christmas-tree lights; Ken sitting
proudly in the audience while Cathy and Libby accepted their high school
diplomas; Ken trying, and somehow managing, to be both mother and
father.

More than two hours went by before a doctor appeared in the waiting
room doorway, still wearing a surgical cap, his mask hanging from his
neck. "Are you people here for Ken Kincaid?" he asked, and the simple
words had the electrifying effect of a cattle prod on everyone there.

Both Libby and Cathy stiffened in their chairs, unable to speak. It was
Jess who answered the doctor's question.

"Mr. Kincaid was severely injured," the surgeon said, "but we think
he'll be all right, if he rests."

Libby was all but convulsed by relief. "I'm his daughter," she managed to say finally. "Do you think I could see him, just for a few
minutes?"

The middle-aged physician smiled reluctantly. "He'll be in Recovery
for some time," he said. "Perhaps it would be better if you visited your
father tomorrow."

Libby was steadfast. It didn't matter that Ken was still under anesthetic;
if she could touch his hand or speak to him, he would know that she was
near. Another vigil had taught her the value of that. "I must see him,"
she insisted.

"She won't leave you alone until you say yes," Jess put in, his arm
tight around Libby's shoulders.

Before the doctor could answer, Cathy was gripping Libby's hands,
searching her cousin's face. "Libby?" she pleaded desperately.
"Libby?"

It was clear that Cathy hadn't discerned the verdict on Ken's condition,
and Libby's heart ached for her cousin as she freed her hands, quickly
motioned the reassurances needed.

When that was done, Libby turned back to the doctor. "My cousin
will want to see my father too."

"Now, just a minute..."

Stubbornly Libby lifted her chin.

Three hours later, Ken Kincaid was moved from the recovery room to
a bed in the intensive-care unit. As soon as he had been settled there,
Cathy and Libby were allowed into his room.

Ken was unconscious, and there were tubes going into his nostrils, an
IV needle in one of his hands. His chest and right shoulder were heavily
bandaged, and there were stitches running from his right temple to his
neck in a crooked, gruesome line.

"Oh, God," whimpered Cathy.

Libby caught her cousin's arm firmly in her hand and faced her. "Don't you *dare* fall apart in here, Cathy Barlowe," she ordered. "He would sense how upset you are, and that would be bad for him."

Cathy trembled, but she squared her shoulders, drew a deep breath and then nodded. "We'll be strong," she said.

Libby went to the bedside, barely able to reach her father for all the equipment that was monitoring and sustaining him. "I hear you beat up on a bear," she whispered.

There was no sign that Ken had heard her, of course, but Libby knew that humor reached this man as nothing else could, and she went on talking, berating him softly for cruelty to animals, informing him that the next time he wanted to waltz, he ought to choose a partner that didn't have fur.

Before an insistent nurse came to collect Ken's visitors, both Libby and Cathy planted tender kisses on his forehead.

Stacey, Jess and Cleave were waiting anxiously when they reached the waiting room again.

"He's going to live," Libby said, and then the room danced and her knees buckled and everything went dark.

She awakened to find herself on a table in one of the hospital examining rooms, Jess holding her hand.

"Thanks for scaring the hell out of me," he said softly, a relieved grin tilting one corner of his mouth. "I needed that."

"Sorry," Libby managed, touching the wilting boutonniere that was still pinned to the lapel of his suit jacket. "Some wedding day, huh, handsome?"

"That's the wild west for you. We like excitement out here. How do you feel, princess?"

Libby tried to sit up, but the room began to swirl, so she fell back down. "I'm okay," she insisted. "Or I will be in a few minutes. How is Cathy?"

Jess smiled, kissed her forehead. "Cathy reacted a little differently to the good news than you did."

Libby frowned, still worried. "How do you mean?"

"After she'd been assured that you had fainted and not dropped dead of a coronary, she lit into Stacey like a whirlwind. It seems that my timid little sister-in-law is through being mute—once and for all."

Libby's eyes rounded. "You mean she was yelling at him?"

"Was she ever. When they left, he was yelling back."

Despite everything, Libby smiled. "In this case, I think a good loud argument might be just what the doctor ordered."

"I agree. But the condo will probably be a war zone by the time we get there."

Libby remembered that this was her wedding night, and with a little help from Jess, managed to sit up. "The condo? They're staying there?"

"Yes. The couch makes out into a bed, and Cathy wants to be near the hospital."

Libby reached out, touched Jess's strong face. "I'm sorry," she said.

"About what?"

"About everything. Especially about tonight."

Jess's green eyes laughed at her, gentle, bright with understanding. "Don't worry about tonight, princess. There will be plenty of other nights."

"But—"

He stilled her protests with an index finger. "You are in no condition to consummate a marriage, Mrs. Barlowe. You need to sleep. So let's go home and get you tucked into bed—with a little luck, Stacey and Cathy won't keep us awake all night while they throw pots and pans at each other."

Jess's remark turned out to be remarkably apt, for when they reached the condo, Stacey and his wife were bellowing at each other and the floor was littered with sofa pillows and bric-a-brac.

"Don't mind us," Jess said with a companionable smile as he ushered his exhausted bride across the war-torn living room. "We're just mild-mannered honeymooners, passing through."

Jess and Libby might have been invisible, for all the notice they got.

"Maybe we should have stayed in a motel," Libby yawned as she snuggled into Jess's strong shoulder, minutes later, in the loft bed.

Something shattered downstairs, and Jess laughed. "And miss this? No chance."

Cathy and Stacey were yelling again, and Libby winced. "You don't think they'll hurt each other, do you?"

"They'll be all right, princess. Rest."

Too tired to discuss the matter further, Libby sighed and fell asleep, lulled by Jess's nearness and the soft sound of rain on the glass roof overhead. She awakened once, in the depths of the night, and heard the sounds of another kind of passion from the darkened living room. A smile curved her lips as she closed her eyes.

Cathy was blushing as she tried to neaten up the demolished living room and avoid Libby's gaze at the same time. Stacey, dead to the world, was sprawled out on the sofa bed, a silly smile shaping his mouth.

Libby made her way to the telephone in silence, called the hospital for a report on her father. He was still unconscious, the nurse on duty told her, but his vital signs were strong and stable.

Cathy was waiting, wide-eyed, when Libby turned away from the telephone.

Gently Libby repeated what the nurse had told her. After that, the two women went into the kitchen and began preparing a quick breakfast.

"I'm sorry about last night," Cathy said.

Standing at the stove, spatula in hand, Libby waited for her cousin to look at her and then asked, "Did you settle anything?"

Cathy's cheeks were a glorious shade of hot pink. "You heard!" she moaned.

Libby had been referring to the fight, not the lovemaking that had obviously followed, but there was no way she could clarify this without embarrassing her cousin further. She bit her lower lip and concentrated on the eggs she was scrambling.

"It was crazy," Cathy blurted, remembering. "I was *yelling* at Stacey! I wanted to hurt him, Libby—I really wanted to hurt him!"

Libby was putting slices of bread into the toaster and she offered no comment, knowing that Cathy needed to talk.

"I even threw things at him," confessed Cathy, taking orange juice from the refrigerator and putting it in the middle of the table. "I can't believe I acted like that, especially when Ken had just been hurt so badly."

Libby met her cousin's gaze and smiled. "I don't see what one thing has to do with the other, Cathy. You were angry with your husband— justifiably so, I'd say—and you couldn't hold it in any longer."

"I wasn't even worried about the way I sounded," Cathy reflected, shaking her head. "I suppose what happened to Ken triggered something inside me—I don't know."

"The important thing is that you stood up for yourself," Libby said, scraping the scrambled eggs out of the pan and onto a platter. "I was proud of you, Cathy."

"Proud? I acted like a fool!"

"You acted like an angry woman. How about calling those lazy husbands of ours to breakfast while I butter the toast?"

Cathy hesitated, wrestling with her old fear of being ridiculed, and then squared her shoulders and left the kitchen to do Libby's bidding.

Tears filled Libby's eyes at the sound of her cousin's voice. However ordinary the task was, it was a big step forward for Cathy.

The men came to the table, Stacey wearing only jeans and looking sheepish, Jess clad in slacks and a neatly pressed shirt, his green eyes full of mischief.

"Any word about Ken?" he asked.

Libby told him what the report had been and loved him the more for the relief in his face. He nodded and then executed a theatrical yawn.

Cathy blushed and looked down at her plate, while Stacey glared at his brother. "Didn't you sleep well, Jess?" he drawled.

Jess rolled his eyes.

Stacey looked like an angry little boy; Libby had forgotten how he hated to be teased. "I'll fight with my wife if I want to!" he snapped.

Both Libby and Jess laughed.

"Fight?" gibed Jess good-naturedly. "Was that what you two were doing? Fighting?"

"*Somebody* had to celebrate your wedding night," Stacey retorted, but then he gave in and laughed too.

When the meal was over, Cathy and Libby left the dirty dishes to their husbands and went off to get ready for the day.

They were allowed only a brief visit with Ken, and even though his doctor assured them that he was steadily gaining ground, they were both disheartened as they returned to the waiting room.

Senator Barlowe was there, with Jess and Stacey, looking as wan and worried as either of his daughters-in-law. Unaware of their approach, he was saying, "We've got every available man tracking that bear, plus hands from the Three Star and the Rocking C. All we've found so far is paw-prints and dead calves."

Libby was brought up short, not by the mention of the bear but by the look on Jess's face. He muttered something she couldn't hear.

Stacey sliced an ironic look in his brother's direction. "I suppose you think you can find that son of Satan when the hands from three of the biggest ranches in the state can't turn up a trace?"

"I know I can," Jess answered coldly.

"Dammit, we scoured the foothills, the ranges..."

Jess's voice was low, thick with contempt. "And when you had the chance to bring the bastard down, you let him trot away instead— wounded."

"What was I supposed to do? Ken was bleeding to death!"

"Somebody should have gone after the bear," Jess insisted relentlessly. "There were more than enough people around to see that Ken got to the hospital."

Stacey swore.

"Were you scared?" Jess taunted. "Did the big bad bear scare away our steak-house cowboy?"

At this, Stacey lunged toward Jess and Jess bolted out of his chair, clearly spoiling for a fight.

Again, as he had before, the senator averted disaster. "Stop it!" he hissed. "If you two have to brawl, kindly do it somewhere else!"

"You can bank on that," Jess said bitterly, his green gaze moving over Stacey and then dismissing him.

"What's gotten into the two of you?" Senator Barlowe rasped in quiet frustration. "This is a hospital! And have you forgotten that you're brothers?"

Libby cleared her throat discreetly, to let the men know that she and Cathy had returned. She was disturbed by the barely controlled hostility between Jess and his brother, but with Ken in the condition that he was, she had no inclination to pursue the issue.

It was later, in the Land Rover, when she and Jess were alone, that

Libby voiced a subject that had been bothering her. "You plan to go looking for that bear, don't you?"

Jess appeared to be concentrating on the traffic, but a muscle in his cheek twitched. "Yes."

"You're going back to the ranch and track him down," Libby went on woodenly.

"That's right."

She sank back against the seat and closed her eyes. "Let the others do it."

There was a short, ominous silence. "No way."

Libby swallowed the sickness and fear that roiled in her throat. God in heaven, wasn't it enough that she'd nearly lost her father to that vicious beast? Did she have to risk losing her husband too? "Why?" she whispered miserably. "Why do you want to do this?"

"It's my job," he answered flatly, and Libby knew that there was no point in trying to dissuade him.

She squeezed her eyes even more tightly shut, but the tears escaped anyway. When they reached the condo again, Stacey's car and Cleave's pulling in behind them, Jess turned to her, brushed the evidence of her fear from her cheeks with gentle thumbs and kissed her.

"I promise not to get killed," he said softly.

Libby stiffened in his arms, furious and full of terror. "That's comforting!"

He kissed the tip of her nose. "You can handle this alone, can't you? Going to the hospital, I mean?"

Libby bit her lower lip. Here was her chance. She could say that she needed Jess now, she could keep him from hunting that bear. She did need him, especially now, but in the end, she couldn't use weakness to hold him close. "I can handle it."

An hour later, when Stacey and the senator left for the ranch, Jess went with them. Libby was now keeping two vigils instead of one.

Understanding Libby's feelings but unable to help, Cathy built a fire in the fireplace, brewed cocoa, and tried to interest her cousin in a closed-caption movie on television.

Libby watched for a while, then got out her sketchbook and began to draw with furious, angry strokes: Jess on horseback, a rifle in the scabbard of his saddle; a full-grown grizzly, towering on its hind legs, ominous muscles rolling beneath its hide, teeth bared. Try though she did, Libby could not bring herself to put Jess and that bear in the same picture, either mentally or on paper.

That evening, when Libby and Cathy went to the hospital, Ken was awake. He managed a weak smile as they came to his bedside to bestow tearful kisses.

"Sorry about missin' the wedding," he said, and for all his obvious pain, there was mirth in his blue eyes.

Libby dashed away the mist from her own eyes and smiled a shaky smile, shrugging. "You've seen one, cowboy, you've seen them all."

Ken laughed and the sound was beautiful.

Chapter 12

Having assured herself that Ken was indeed recovering, Cathy slipped out to allow Libby a few minutes alone with her father.

"Thanks for scaring me half to death," she said.

Ken tried to shrug, winced instead. "You must have known I was too mean to go under," he answered. "Libby, did they get the bear?"

Libby stiffened. The bear, the bear—she was so damned sick of hearing about the bear! "No," she said after several moments, averting her eyes.

Ken sighed. He was pale and obviously tired. "Jess went after him, didn't he?"

Libby fought back tears of fear. Was Jess face to face with that creature even now? Was he suffering injuries like Ken's, or even worse? "Yes," she admitted.

"Jess will be all right, Libby."

"Like you were?" Libby retorted sharply, without thinking.

Ken studied her for a moment, managed a partial grin. "He's younger than I am. Tougher. No grizzly in his right mind would tangle with him."

"But this grizzly isn't in his right mind, is he?" Libby whispered, numb. "He's wounded, Dad."

"All the more reason to find him," Ken answered firmly. "That bear was dangerous before, Libby. He's deadly now."

Libby shuddered. "You'd think the beast would just crawl off and die somewhere."

"That would be real handy, but he won't do it, Lib. Grizzlies have nasty dispositions as it is—their eyesight is poor and their teeth hurt all the time. When they're wounded, they can rampage for days before they finally give out."

"The Barlowes can afford to lose a few cows!"

"Yes, but they can't afford to lose people, Lib, and that's what'll happen if that animal isn't found."

There was no arguing that; Ken was proof of how dangerous a beai could be. "The men from the Three Star and the Rocking C are helping with the hunt, anyway," Libby said, taking little if any consolation from the knowledge.

"That's good," Ken said, closing his eyes.

Libby bent, kissed his forehead and left the room.

Cathy was pacing the hallway, her lower lip caught in her teeth, her eyes wide. Libby chastised herself for not realizing that Stacey was probably hunting the bear too, and that her cousin was as worried as she was.

When Libby suggested a trip to the Circle Bar B, Cathy agreed immediately.

During the long drive, Libby made excuses to herself. She wasn't going just to check on Jess—she absolutely was not. She needed her drawing board, her pens and inks, jeans and blouses.

The fact that she could have bought any or all of these items in Kalispell was carefully ignored.

By the time Libby and Cathy drew the Corvette to a stop in the wide driveway of the main ranch house, the sun was starting to go down. There must have been fifty horsemen converging on the stables, all of them looking tired and discouraged.

Libby's heart wedged itself into her throat when she spotted Jess. He was dismounting, wrenching a high-powered rifle from the scabbard on his saddle.

She literally ran to him, but then she stopped short, her shoes encased in the thick, gooey mud Montanans call gumbo, her vocal cords no more mobile than her feet.

"Ken?" he asked in a hoarse whisper.

Libby was quick to reassure him. "Dad's doing very well."

"Then what are you doing here?"

Libby smiled, pried one of her feet out of the mud, only to have it succumb again when she set it down. "I had to see if you were all right," she admitted. "May I say that you look terrible?"

Jess chuckled, rubbed the stubble of beard on his chin, assessed the dirty clothes he wore in one downward glance. "You should have stayed in town."

Libby lifted her chin. "I'll go back in the morning," she said, daring him to argue.

Jess surrendered his horse to one of the ranch hands, but the rifle swung at his side as he started toward the big, well-lighted house. Libby slogged along at his side.

"Is that gun loaded?" she demanded.

"No," he replied. "Any more questions?"

"Yes. Did you see the bear?"

They had reached the spacious screened-in porch, where Mrs. Bradshaw had prudently laid out newspapers to accommodate dozens of mud-caked boots.

"No," Jess rasped, lifting his eyes to some distant thing that Libby could not see. "That sucker might as well be invisible."

Libby watched as Jess kicked off his boots, flung his sodden denim jacket aside, dispensed with his hat. "Maybe he's dead, Jess," she blurted out hopefully, resorting to the optimism her father had tacitly warned her against. "Maybe he collapsed somewhere—"

"Wrong," Jess bit out. "We found more cattle."

"Calves?"

"A bull and two heifers," Jess answered. "And the hell of it is, he didn't even kill them to eat. He just ripped them apart."

Libby shivered. "He must be enormous!"

"The men that were with Stacey and Ken said he stood over eight feet," Jess replied, and his green eyes moved wearily over Libby's face. "I don't suppose I need to say this, but I will. I don't like having you here, not now. For God's sake, don't go wandering off by yourself—not even to walk down to the mailboxes. The same goes for Cathy."

It seemed ludicrous that one beast could restrict the normal activities of human beings—in fact, the bear didn't seem real to Libby, even after what had happened to Ken. Instead, it was as though Jess was telling one of the delicious, scary stories he'd loved to terrify Libby with when they were children.

"That means, little one," he went on sternly, "that you don't go out to the barn and you don't go over to Ken's to sit and moon by that pond. Am I making myself clear?"

"Too clear," snapped Libby, following him as he carried the rifle through the kitchen, down a long hallway and into the massive billiard room where the gun cabinets were.

Jess locked the weapon away and turned to his wife. "I'm a little bit glad you're here," he confessed with a weary grin.

"Even tough cowboys need a little spoiling now and then," she replied, "so hie thyself to an upstairs bathroom, husband of mine, and get yourself a shower. I'll bring dinner to your room."

"And how do you know where my room is, Mrs. Barlowe?"

Libby colored a little. "I used to help Marion Bradshaw with the cleaning sometimes, remember?"

"I remember. I used to watch you bending over to tuck in sheets and smooth pillows and think what a great rear end you had."

She arched one eyebrow. "Had?"

Jess caught her bottom in strong hands, pressed her close to him. "Have," he clarified.

"Go take your shower!" Libby huffed, suddenly conscious of all the cowboys that would be gathering in the house for supper that night.

"Join me?" drawled Jess, persistent to the end.

"Absolutely not. You're exhausted." Libby broke away, headed toward the kitchen.

"Not *that* exhausted," Jess called after her.

Libby did not respond, but as she went in to prepare a dinner tray for her husband, she was smiling.

Minutes later, entering Jess's boyhood bedroom, she set the tray down on a long table under a line of windows. The door of the adjoining bathroom was open and steam billowed out like the mist in a spooky movie.

Presently Libby heard the shower shut off, the rustling sound of a towel being pulled from a rack. She sat down on the edge of Jess's bed and then bounded up again.

"Libby?"

She went cautiously to the doorway, looked in. Jess was peering into a steamy mirror, trying to shave. "Your dinner is getting cold," she said.

After flinging one devilish look at his wife, Jess grabbed the towel that had been wrapped around his hips and calmly used it to wipe the mirror. "I'll hurry," he replied.

Libby swallowed hard, as stunned by the splendor of his naked, muscle-corded frame as she had been on that first stormy night when they'd made love in the bedroom at Jess's house, the fevered motions of their bodies metered by the raging elements outside.

Jess finished shaving, rinsed his face, turned toward Libby like a proud savage. She could not look away, even though she wanted to. Her eyes were fixed on the rising, swelling shaft of his manhood.

Jess laughed. "I used to fantasize about this."

"What?" Libby croaked, her throat tight.

"Bringing the foreman's pretty daughter up here and having my way with her."

Libby's eyes were, at last, freed, and they shot upward to his face. "Oh, yeah?"

"Yeah."

"I thought you liked Cathy then."

He nodded. "I did. But even before she married Stacey, I thought of her as a sister."

"And what, pray tell, did you think of me as?"

"A hellion. But I wanted to be your lover, all the same. Since I didn't dare, I settled for making your life miserable."

"How very chivalrous of you!"

Jess was walking toward her now, holding her with the scorching assessment of those jade-green eyes even before his hands touched her. "Teenage boys are not chivalrous, Libby."

Libby closed her eyes as he reached her, drew her close. "Neither are men," she managed to say.

Her blouse was coming untucked from her jeans, rising until she felt the steamy air on her stomach and back. Finally it was bunched under her arms and Jess was tracing a brazen finger over the lines of her scanty lace bra. Beneath the fabric, her nipples sprang into full bloom, coy flowers offering their nectar.

"Y-your dinner," she reminded Jess, floating on the sensations he was stirring within her, too bedazzled even to open her eyes.

The bra slipped down, just on one side, freeing a hard-peaked, eager breast. "Yes," Jess breathed evilly, "my dinner."

"Not that. I mean—"

His mouth closed over the delicate morsel, drawing at it softly. With a pleased and somewhat triumphant chuckle, Jess drew back from the tender treat and Libby's eyes flew open as he began removing her blouse and then her bra, leaving her jeans as they were.

He led her slowly to the bed, but instead of laying her down there, as she had expected, Jess stretched out on his back and positioned her so that she was sitting up, astraddle of his hips.

Gripping her waist, he pulled her forward and lifted, so that her breasts were suspended within easy reach of his mouth.

"The age-old quandary," he breathed.

Libby was dazed. "What qu-quandary?"

"Which one," Jess mused. "How like nature to offer two when a man has only one mouth."

Libby blushed hotly as Jess nuzzled a knotted peak, a peak that ached to nourish him. "Oh, God, Jess," she whispered. "Take it...take it!"

He chuckled, flicked the nipple in question with an impertinent tongue. "I love it when you beg."

Both rage and passion moved inside Libby. "I'm...not...begging!" she gasped, but even as she spoke she was bracing herself with her hands, brushing her breast back and forth across Jess's lips, seeking admission.

"You will," he said, and then he caught the pulsing nipple between careful teeth, raking it to an almost unendurable state of wanting.

"Not on your wretched life!" moaned Libby.

"We'll see," he replied.

The opposite breast was found and thoroughly teased and Libby had to bite her lower lip to keep from giving in and pleading senselessly for the suckling Jess promised but would not give. He played with her, using his tongue and his lips, delighting in the rocking motion of her body and the soft whimpers that came from her throat.

The sweet torment became keener, and Libby both loved and hated Jess for being able to drive her to such lengths. "Make love to me...oh, Jess...make love...to me."

The concession elicited a hoarse growl from Jess, and Libby found herself spinning down to lie flat on the bed. Her remaining clothes were soon stripped away, her legs were parted.

Libby gasped and arched her back as he entered her in one ferocious, needing thrust. After gaining this warm and hidden place, Jess paused, his hard frame shuddering with restraint.

As bedazzled as she was, Libby saw her chance to set the pace, to take command, and she took it. Acting on an age-old instinct, she wrapped her legs around his hips in a fierce claiming and muttered, "Give me all of you, Jess—all of you."

He groaned in lusty surrender and plunged deep within her, seeking solace in the velvety heat of her womanhood. They were locked together for several glittering moments, each afraid to move. Soon enough, however, their bodies demanded more and began a desperate, swift rhythm.

Straining together, both moaning in fevered need, Libby and Jess reached their shattering pinnacle at the same moment, crying out as their two souls flared as one golden fire.

Twice after Jess lay still upon her, his broad back moist beneath her hands, Libby convulsed softly, whimpering.

"Some people are really greedy," he teased when, at last, her body had ceased its spasmodic clenching and unclenching.

Libby stretched, sated, cosseted in delicious appeasement. "More," she purred.

"What did I tell you?" Jess sighed. "The lady is greedy."

"Very."

He rolled, still joined with Libby, bringing her with him so that she once again sat astraddle of him. They talked, in hushed and gentle voices, of very ordinary things.

After some minutes had passed, however, Libby began to trace his nipples with feather-light fingertips. "I've always wanted to have my way with the boss's son," she crooned, teasing him as he had teased her earlier.

She bent forward, tasted those hardening nipples, each in turn, with only the merest flick of her tongue. Jess groaned and grew hard within her, by degrees, as she continued to torment him.

"How like nature," she gibed tenderly, "to offer two when a woman has only one mouth."

Jess grasped her hips in inescapable hands and thrust his own upward in a savage demand.

Libby's release came swiftly; it was soft and warm, rather than violent, and its passing left her free to bring Jess to exquisite heights. She set a slow pace for him, delighting in the look in his eyes, the back-and-forth motion of his head on the pillow, the obvious effort it took for him to lie still beneath her.

He pleaded for release, but Libby was impervious, guiding him gently, reveling in the sweet power she held over this man she so completely loved. "I'm going to love you in my own way," she told him. "And in my own time."

His head pressed back into the pillows in magnificent surrender, Jess closed his eyes and moaned. His control was awesome, but soon enough it slipped and he began to move beneath Libby, slowly at first and then quickly. Finally, his hands tangling in her hair, he cried out and his body spasmed as she purposely intensified his pleasure. His triumph seemed endless.

When Jess was still at last, his eyes closed, his body glistening with perspiration, Libby tenderly stroked a lock of hair back from his forehead and whispered, "Some people are really greedy."

Jess chuckled and was asleep before Libby withdrew from him to make her way into the bathroom for a shower of her own.

The dream was very sexy. In it, a blue-gray dawn was swelling at the bedroom windows and Libby's breast was full in Jess's hand, the nipple stroked to a pleading state.

She groaned as she felt his hard length upon her, his manhood seeking to sheathe itself in her warmth. Jess entered her, and his strokes were slow and gentle, evoking an immediate series of tremulous, velvet-smooth responses.

"Good," she sighed, giving herself up to the dream. "So good..."

The easy strokes became demanding thrusts. "Yes," said the dream Jess gruffly. "Good."

"Ooooooh," moaned Libby, as a sudden and piercing release rocked her, thrusting her into wakefulness.

And Jess was there, upon her, his face inches from her own. She watched in wonder and in love as his features grew taut and his splendid body flexed, more rapidly now. She thrust herself up to receive the fullness of his love.

Libby's hands clasped Jess's taut buttocks as he shuddered and delved deep, his manhood rippling powerfully within her, his rasping moan filling Libby's heart.

Minutes later, a languid, hazy sleep overtook Libby and she rolled over onto her stomach and settled back into her dreams. She stirred only slightly when Jess patted her derriere and left the bed.

Hours later, when she awakened fully, Libby was not entirely certain that she hadn't dreamed the whole gratifying episode. As she got out of bed, though, to take a bath and get dressed, Libby knew that Jess had loved her—the feeling of lush well-being she enjoyed was proof of that.

The pampered sensation was short-lived. When Libby went downstairs to search out a light breakfast, she found Monica Summers sitting in the kitchen, sipping coffee and reading a weekly newsmagazine.

Even though Monica smiled, her dark gray eyes betrayed her malice. "Hello...Mrs. Barlowe."

Libby nodded uneasily and opened the refrigerator to take out an apple and a carton of yogurt. "Good morning," she said.

"I was very sorry to hear about your father," Monica went on, the tone of her voice totally belying her expression. "Is he recovering?"

Libby got a spoon for her yogurt and sat down at the table. "Yes, thank you, he is."

"Will you be staying here with us, or going back to Kalispell?"

There was something annoyingly proprietary in the way Monica said the word "us," as though Libby were somehow invading territory where she didn't belong. She lifted her chin and met the woman's stormy-sky gaze directly. "I'll be going back to Kalispell," she said.

"You must hate leaving Jess."

The pit of Libby's stomach developed an unsettling twitch. She took a forceful bite from her apple and said nothing.

"Of course, I'll be happy to...look after him," sighed Monica, striking a flame to the fuse she had been uncoiling. "It's an old habit, you know."

Libby suppressed an unladylike urge to fly over the table, teeth bared, fists flying. "Sometimes old habits have to be broken," she said, sitting very still, reminding herself that she was a grown woman now, not the foreman's little brat. Furthermore, she was Jess's wife and she didn't have to take this kind of subtle abuse in any case.

Monica arched one perfect eyebrow. "Do they?"

Libby leaned forward. "Oh, yes. You see, Ms. Summers, if you mess with my husband, I'll not only break the habit for you, I'll break a few of your bones for good measure."

Monica paled, muttered something about country girls.

"I am not a girl," Libby pointed out. "I'm a woman, and you'd better remember it."

"Oh, I will," blustered Monica, recovering quickly. "But will Jess? That's the question, isn't it?"

If there was one thing in the world Libby had absolutely no doubts about, at that moment anyway, it was her ability to please her husband in the way Monica was referring to. "I don't see how he could possibly forget," she said, and then she finished her apple and her yogurt, dropped the remnants into the trash, and left the room.

Marion Bradshaw was sweeping away residual dried mud when Libby reached the screened porch, hoping for one glimpse of Jess before she had to go back to Kalispell.

He was nowhere in sight, of course—Libby had not really expected him to be.

"How's Ken getting on?" Marion asked.

Libby smiled. "He's doing very well."

The housekeeper sighed, leaning on her broom. "Thank the good Lord for that. Me and Ken Kincaid run this place, and I sure couldn't manage it alone!"

Libby laughed and asked if Cathy was around.

Sheer delight danced in Mrs. Bradshaw's eyes. "She's where she belongs—upstairs in her husband's bed."

Libby blushed. She had forgotten how much this astute woman knew about the goings-on on the ranch. Did she know, too, why Jess had never gotten around to eating his dinner the night before?

"No shame in loving your man," Mrs. Bradshaw twinkled.

Libby swallowed. "Do you know if Stacey went with the others this morning?"

"He did. You go ahead and wake Miss Cathy right now, if you want to."

Libby was grateful for an excuse to hurry away.

Finding Stacey's room from memory, in just the way she'd found Jess's, she knocked briskly at the closed door, realized the foolishness of that, and turned the knob.

Cathy was curled up like a kitten in the middle of a bed as mussed and tangled as the one Libby had shared with Jess.

Libby bent to give Cathy's bare shoulder a gentle shake. Her cousin sat up, mumbling, her face lost behind a glistening profusion of tangled hair. "Libby? What...?"

Libby laughed and signed, "I'm going back to town as soon as I pick up some of my things at the other house. Do you want to go with me?"

Cathy's full lips curved into a mischievous smile and she shook her head.

"Things are going well between you and Stacey, then?"

Cathy's hands moved in a scandalously explicit answer.

"I'm shocked!" Libby signed, beaming. And then she gave her cousin a quick kiss on the forehead, promised to call Mrs. Bradshaw if there was any sort of change in Ken's condition, and left the room.

In Jess's room she found paper and a pen, and probably because of the tempestuous night spent in his bed, dared to write, "Jess. I love you. Sorry I couldn't stay for a proper good-bye, but I've got to get back to Dad. Take care and come to me if you can. Smiles and sunshine, Libby."

On the way downstairs, Libby almost lost her courage and ran back to rip up the note. Telling Jess outright that she loved him! What if he laughed? What if he was derisive or, even worse, pitying?

Libby denied herself the cowardice of hiding her feelings any longer. It was time she took responsibility for her own emotions, wasn't it?

The weather was crisp and bright that day, and Libby hummed as she drove the relatively short distance to her father's house, parked her car behind his truck and went in to get the things she needed.

Fitting extra clothes and her special set of pens and inks into the back of the Corvette proved easy enough, but the drawing board was another matter. She turned it this way and that way and it just wouldn't fit.

Finally Libby took it back inside the house and left it there. She would just have to make do with the kitchen table at the condo for the time being.

Libby was just passing the passenger side of Ken's truck when she heard the sound; it was a sort of shifting rustle, coming from the direction of the lilac hedge on the far side of the yard. There followed a low, ominous grunt.

Instinctively Libby froze, the hair tingling on the nape of her neck. Dear God, it couldn't be... Not here—not when there were men with rifles searching every inch of the ranch...

She turned slowly, and her heart leapt into her throat and then spun back down into the pit of her stomach. The bear stood within ten feet of her, on its hind legs.

The beast growled and lolled its massive head to one side. Its mangy, lusterless hide seemed loose over the rolling muscles beneath, and on its flank was a bloodcrusted, seeping wound.

In that moment, it was as though Libby became two people, one hysterically afraid, one calm and in control. Fortunately, it was this second Libby that took command. Slowly, ever so slowly, she eased her hand back behind her, to the door handle, opened it. Just as the bear lunged toward her, making a sound more horrifying than she could ever have imagined, she leapt inside the truck and slammed the door after her.

The raging beast shook the whole vehicle as it flung its great bulk against its side, and Libby allowed herself the luxury of one high-pitched scream before reaching for Ken's CB radio under the dashboard.

Again and again, the furious bear pummeled the side of the truck, while Libby tried frantically to make the CB radio work. She knew that the cowboys would be carrying receivers, in order to communicate with each other, and they were her only hope.

Fingers trembling, Libby finally managed to lift the microphone to her mouth and press the button. Her mind skittered over a series of movies she'd seen, books she'd read. *Mayday,* she thought with triumphant terror. *Mayday!* But the magic word would not come past her tight throat.

Suddenly a giant claw thundered across the windshield, shattering it into a glittering cobweb of cracks. One more blow, just one, and the bear would reach her easily, even though she was now crouching on the floorboard.

At last she found her voice. "Cujo!" she screamed into the radio receiver. "Cujo!" She closed her eyes, gasping, tried to get a hold on herself. *This is not a Stephen King movie,* she reminded herself. *This is reality. And that bear out there is going to tear you apart if you don't do something!*

"Libby!" the radio squawked suddenly. "Libby, come in!"

The voice was Jess's. "Th-the bear," she croaked, remembering to hold in the button on the receiver when she talked. "Jess, the bear!"

"Where are you?"

Libby closed her eyes as the beast again threw itself against the truck. "My dad's house—in his truck."

"Hold on. Please, baby, hold on. We're not far away."

"Hurry!" Libby cried, as the bear battered the windshield again and tiny bits of glass rained down on her head.

Another voice came in over the radio, this one belonging to Stacey. "Libby," he said evenly, "honk the horn. Can you do that?"

Libby couldn't speak. There were tears pouring down her face and every muscle in her body seemed inert, but she did reach up to the center of the wheel and press the truck's horn.

The bear bellowed with rage, as though the sound had hurt him, but he stopped striking the truck and withdrew a little way. Libby knew he wasn't gone, for she could hear him lumbering nearby, growling in frustration.

Jess's men converged with Stacey's at the end of the rutted country road leading to Ken's house. When the pickup truck was in sight, they reined in their horses.

"He's mine," Jess breathed, reaching for the rifle in his scabbard, drawing it out, cocking it. He was conscious of the other men and their nervous, nickering horses, but only vaguely. Libby was inside that truck—his whole being seemed to focus on that one fact.

The bear rose up in full view suddenly, its enormous head visible even over the top of the pickup's cab. Even over the repeated honking of the truck's horn, the beast's hideous, echoing growl was audible.

"Sweet Jesus," Stacey whispered.

"Easy," said Jess, to himself more than the men around him, as he lifted the rifle, sighted in carefully, pulled back the trigger.

The thunderous shot struck the bear in the center of its nose, and the animal shrieked as it went down. The impact of its body was so solid that it seemed to shake the ground.

Instantly Jess was out of the saddle. "Make sure he's dead," he called over one shoulder as he ran toward the truck.

Stacey and several of his men reached the bear just as Jess wrenched open the door on the driver's side.

Libby scrambled out from under the steering wheel, her hair a wild, glass-spattered tangle, to fling herself, sobbing, into his arms. Jess cradled her in his arms, carried her away from the demolished truck and inside the house. His own knees suddenly weak, he fell into the first available chair and buried his face in Libby's neck.

"It's over, sweetheart," he said. "It's over."

Libby shuddered and wailed with terror.

When she was calmer, Jess caught her chin in his hand and lifted it. "What the hell did you mean, yelling 'Cujo! Cujo!'"

Libby sniffled, and the fight was back in her eyes, a glorious, snapping blue. "There was this book about a mad dog...and then there was a movie..."

Jess lifted his eyebrows and grinned.

"Oh, never mind!" hissed Libby.

Chapter 13

Libby froze in the doorway of Ken's room in the intensive-care unit, her mouth open, her heart racing as fast as it had earlier, when she'd been trapped by the bear.

"Where is he?" she finally managed to whisper. "Oh, Jess, where is my father?"

Standing behind Libby, Jess lifted his hands to her shoulders and gently ushered her back into the hallway, out of sight of the empty bed. "Don't panic," he said quietly.

Libby trembled, looked frantically toward the nurses' station. "Jess, what if he...?"

There was a gentle lecture forming in Jess's features, but before he could deliver it, an attractive red-headed nurse approached, trim in her uniform. "Mrs. Barlowe?"

Libby nodded, holding her breath.

"Your father is fine. We moved Mr. Kincaid to another floor earlier today, since he no longer needs such careful monitoring. If you will just come back to the desk with me, I'll be happy to find out which room he's in."

Libby's breath escaped in one long sigh. What with spending perilous minutes cowering inside a truck, with a rogue bear doing its best to get inside and tear her to bits, and then rushing to the hospital to find her father's bed empty, she had had more than enough stress for one day. "Thank you," she said, giving Jess a relieved look.

He got rather familiar during the elevator ride down to the second floor, but desisted when the doors opened again.

"You're incorrigible," Libby whispered, only half in anger.

"Snatching my wife from the jaws of death has that effect on me," he whispered back. "I keep thinking that I might never have gotten the chance to touch you like that again."

Libby paused, in the quest for Room 223, to search Jess's face. "Were you scared?"

"Scared? Sweet thing, I was *terrified*."

"You seemed so calm!"

He lifted one eyebrow. "Somebody had to be."

Libby considered that and then sighed. "I don't suppose we should tell Dad what actually happened. Not yet, at least."

Jess chuckled. "We'll tell a partial truth—that the bear is dead. The rest had better wait until he's stronger."

"Right," agreed Libby.

When they reached Ken's new room, another surprise was in store. A good-looking dark-haired woman was there plumping the patient's pillows, fussing with his covers. She wore well-cut jeans and a western shirt trimmed with a rippling snow-white fringe, and the way she laughed, low in her throat, said more about her relationship with Ken Kincaid than all her other attentions combined.

"Hello, Becky," said Jess, smiling.

Becky was one of those people, it seemed, who smile not just with the mouth but with the whole face. "Jess Barlowe," she crowed, "you black-hearted son-of-a-gun! Where ya been?"

Libby drew a deep breath and worked up a smile of her own. Was this the woman who had written that intriguing farewell on the condo's kitchen blackboard?

Deliberately she turned her attention on her father, who looked downright rakish as he favored his startled daughter with a slow grin and a wink.

"Who's this pretty little gal?" demanded Becky, giving Libby a friendly once-over.

For the first time, Ken spoke. "This is my daughter, Libby. Libby, Becky Stafford."

"I'll be!" cried Becky, clearly delighted. "Glad to meet ya!"

Libby found the woman's boisterous good nature appealing, and despite a few lingering twinges of surprise, she responded warmly.

"Did you get that bear?" Ken asked of Jess, once the women had made their exchange.

"Yes," Jess replied, after one glance at Libby.

Ken gave a hoot of delight and triumph. "Nail that son-of-a...nail that devil's hide to the barn door for me, will you?"

"Done," answered Jess with a grin.

A few minutes later, Jess and the energetic Becky left the room to have coffee in the hospital cafeteria. Libby lifted her hands to her hips, fixed her father with a loving glare and demanded, "Is there something you haven't told me?"

Ken laughed. "Maybe. But I'll wager that there are a few things you haven't told me, either, dumplin'."

"Who is Becky, exactly?"

Ken thought for a moment before speaking. "She's a good friend of mine, Libby. An old friend."

For some reason, Libby was determined to find something to dislike about Becky Stafford, difficult as it was. "Why does she dress like that? Is she a rodeo performer or something?"

"She's a cocktail waitress," Ken replied patiently.

"Oh," said Libby. And then she couldn't sustain her petty jealousy any longer, because Becky Stafford was a nice person and Ken had a right to like her. He was more than just her father, after all, more than just Senator Barlowe's general foreman. He was a man.

There was a brief silence, which Ken broke with a very direct question. "Do you like Becky, Lib?"

Like her? The warmth and humor of the woman still lingered in that otherwise dreary room, as did the earthy, unpretentious scent of her perfume. "Sure I do," said Libby. "Anybody with the perception to call Jess Barlowe a 'black-hearted son-of-a-gun' is okay in my book!"

Ken chuckled, but there was relief in his face, and his expression revealed that he knew how much Libby loved her husband. "How's Cathy?" he asked.

Remembering that morning's brief conversation with her cousin, Libby grinned. "She's doing fine, as far as I can tell. Bad as it was, your tussle with that bear seems to have brought Cathy and Stacey both to a point where they can open up to each other. Cathy actually talked to him."

Ken did not seem surprised by this last; perhaps he'd known all along that Cathy still had use of her voice. "I don't imagine it was peaceable," he observed dryly.

"Not in the least," confirmed Libby, "but they're communicating and...and, well, let's just say they're closer."

"That's good," answered Ken, smiling at his daughter's words. "That's real good."

Seeing that her father was getting very tired, Libby quickly kissed him and took her leave. When she reached the cafeteria, Becky was sitting alone at a table, staring sadly into her coffee cup.

Libby scanned the large room for Jess and failed to see him, but she wasn't worried. Probably he had gone back to Ken's room and missed seeing Libby on the way. Noticing the pensive look on Becky's face, she was glad for a few minutes alone with the woman her father obviously liked and perhaps even loved.

"May I sit down?" she asked, standing behind the chair that had probably been Jess's.

Becky looked up, smiled. "Sure," she said, and there was surprise in her dark eyes.

Libby sat down with a sigh. "I hate hospitals," she said, filled to aching with the memory of Jonathan's confinement.

"Me too," answered Becky, but her eyes were watchful. Hopeful, in a touchingly open way.

Libby swallowed. "My...my father has been very lonely, and I'm glad you're his friend."

Becky's smile was almost cosmic in scope. "That's good to hear," she answered. "Lordy, that man did scare the life out of me, going a round with that damned bear that way."

Libby thought of her own chance meeting with the creature and shivered. She hoped that she would never know that kind of numbing fear gain.

Becky's hand came to pat hers. "It's all right now, though, isn't it? That hairy booger is dead, thanks to Jess."

Libby laughed. Indeed, that "hairy booger" was dead, and she did have Jess to thank for her life. When she'd tried to voice her gratitude earlier, he had brushed away her words and said that she was his wife and, therefore, saving her from bears, fire-breathing dragons and the like was just part of the bargain.

As if conjured by her thoughts of him, Jess appeared to take Libby home.

The coming days were happy ones for Libby, if hectic. She visited her father morning and evening and worked on her cartoon strip and the panels for the book between times, her drawing board having been transported from the ranch by Jess and set up in the middle of the condo's living room.

Jess commuted between Kalispell and the ranch; many of Ken's duties had fallen to him. Instead of being exhausted by the crazy pace, however, he seemed to thrive on it and his reports on the stormy reconciliation taking place between Cathy and Stacey were encouraging. It appeared that, with the help of the marriage counselor they were seeing, their problems might be worked out.

The irrepressible Becky Stafford rapidly became Libby's friend. Vastly different, the two women nevertheless enjoyed each other—Libby found that Becky could draw her out when she became too burrowed down in her work, and just as quickly drive her back if she tried to neglect it.

"You did what?" Jess demanded archly one early-summer evening as he and Libby sat on the living-room floor consuming the take-out Chinese food they both loved.

Libby laughed with glee and a measure of pride. "I rode the mechanical bull at the bar where Becky works," she repeated.

Jess worked up an unconvincing scowl. "Hanging around bars these days, are you?" he demanded, waving a fortune cookie for emphasis.

Libby batted her eyelashes demurely. "Don't you worry one little bit," she said, feigning a musical southern drawl. "Becky guards mah virtue, y'all."

Jess's green eyes slipped to the V neck of Libby's white sweater, which left a generous portion of cleavage in full and enticing view. "Does she now? And where is she, at this very moment, when said virtue is in immediate peril?"

An anticipatory thrill gyrated in the pit of Libby's stomach and warmed her breasts, which were bare beneath her lightweight sweater. Jess had loved her often, and well, but he could still stir that sweet, needing tension with remarkable ease. "What sort of peril am I in, exactly?"

Jess grinned and hooked one finger in the V of her sweater, slid it downward into the warmth between her breasts. "Oh, the most scandalous sort, Mrs. Barlowe."

Libby's breath quickened, despite stubborn efforts to keep it even. "Your attentions are quite unseemly, Mr. Barlowe," she replied.

He moved the wanton finger up and down between the swelling softness that was Libby, and sharp responses ached in other parts of her. "Absolutely," he said. "I mean to do several unseemly things to you."

Libby tensed with delicious sensation as Jess's exploring finger slid aside, explored a still-hidden nipple.

"I want to see your breast, Libby. This breast. Show it to me."

The outrageous request made Libby color slightly, but she knew she would comply. She was a strong, independent person, but now, in this sweet, aching moment, she was Jess's woman. With one motion of her hand, she tugged the sweater's neckline down and to one side, so that it made a sort of sling for the breast that had been softly demanded.

Not touching the rounded pink-tipped treasure in any way, Jess admired it, rewarding it with an approving smile when the confectionlike peak tightened into an enticing point.

Libby was kneeling now, resting on her heels, the cartons littering the coffee table completely forgotten. She was at once too proud to plead for Jess's mouth and too needing of it to cover herself.

Knowing that, Jess chuckled hoarsely and bent to flick at the exposed nipple with just the tip of his tongue. Libby moaned and let her head fall back, making the captured breast even more vulnerable.

"Unseemly," breathed Jess, nibbling, drawing at the straining morsel with his lips.

Libby felt the universe sway in time with his tender plundering, but she bit down hard on the garbled pleas that were rising in her throat. They escaped through her parted lips, all the same, as small gasps.

Her heartbeat grew louder and louder as Jess finally took suckle; it muffled the sounds of his greed, of the cartons being swept from the surface of the coffee table in a motion of one of his arms.

The coolness of the air battled with the heat of Libby's flesh as she was stripped of her sweater, her white slacks, her panties. Gently he placed her on the coffee table.

Entranced, Libby allowed him to position her legs wide of each other, one on one side of the low table, one on the other. Beyond the glass roof, in the dark, dark sky, a million silvery stars surged toward her and then melted back into the folds of heaven, becoming pinpoints.

Jess found the silken nest of her passion and attended it lovingly, stroking, kissing, finding, losing. Libby's hips moved wildly, struggling even as she gave herself up.

And when she had to have this singular gratification or die, Jess understood and feasted unreservedly, his hands firm under her bottom, lifting her, the breadth of his shoulders making it impossible for her to deny him what he would have from her.

At last, when the tumult broke on a lusty cry of triumph from Libby, she saw the stars above plummet toward her—or had she risen to meet them?

"Of course you're going to the powwow!" cried Becky, folding her arms and leaning over the platter of french fries in front of her. "You can't miss that and call yourself a Barlowe!"

Libby shrank down a little in the benchlike steak-house seat. As this restaurant was a part of the Barlowe chain, the name drew immediate attention from all the waiters and a number of the other diners, too. "Becky," she began patiently, "even though Dad's getting out of the hospital this afternoon, he won't be up to something like that, and I wouldn't feel right about leaving him behind."

"Leaving Ken behind?" scoffed Becky in a more discreet tone of voice. "You just try keeping him away—he hasn't missed a powwow in fifteen years."

Libby's memories of the last Indian powwow and all-day rodeo she had attended were hardly conducive to nostalgia. She remembered the dust, the hot glare of the summer sun, the seemingly endless rodeo events, the drunks—Indian and white alike—draped over the hoods of parked cars and sprawled on the sidewalks. She sighed.

"Jess'll go," Becky prodded.

Libby had no doubt of that, and having spent so much time away from Jess of late, what with him running the ranch while she stayed in Kalispell, she was inclined to attend the powwow after all.

Becky saw that she had relented and beamed. "Wait'll you see those Sioux Indians doing their war dances," she enthused. "There'll be Blackfoot, too, and Flathead."

Libby consoled herself with the thought of Indians doing their dances and wearing their powwow finery of feathers and buckskin and beads. She could take her sketchbook along and draw, at least.

Becky wasn't through with her conversation. "Did you tell Jess how you rode that electric bull over at the Golden Buckle?"

Libby tried to look dignified in the wake of several molten memories. "I told him," she said shyly.

Her friend laughed. "If that wasn't a sight! I wish I woulda took your picture. Maybe you should enter some of the events at the powwow, Libby." Her face took on a disturbingly serious expression. "Maybe barrel racing, or women's calf roping—"

"Hold it," Libby interceded with a grin. "Riding a mechanical bull is one thing and calf roping is quite another. The only sport I'm going to take part in is stepping over drunks."

"Stepping over what?" inquired a third voice, masculine and amused, from the table side.

Libby looked and saw Stacey. "What are you doing here?"

He laughed, turning his expensive silver-banded cowboy hat in both hands. "I own the place, remember?"

"Where's Cathy?" Becky wanted to know. As she had become Libby's friend, she had also become Cathy's—she was even learning to sign.

Stacey slid into the bench seat beside Libby. "She's seeing the doctor," he said, and for all his smiling good manners, he seemed nervous.

Libby elbowed her brother-in-law lightly. "Why didn't you stay there and wait for her?"

"She wouldn't let me."

Just then Becky stood up, saying that she had to get to work. A moment later, eyes twinkling over some secret, she left.

Libby felt self-conscious with Stacey, though he hadn't made any more advances or disturbing comments. She wished that Becky had been able to stay a little longer. "What's going on? Is Cathy sick?"

"She's just having a checkup. Libby..."

Libby braced herself inwardly and moved a little closer to the wall of the enclosed booth, so that Stacey's thigh wasn't touching hers. "Yes?" she prompted when he hesitated to go on.

"I owe you an apology," he said, meeting her eyes. "I acted like a damned fool and I'm sorry."

Knowing that he was referring to the rumors he'd started about their friendship in New York, Libby chafed a little. "I accept your apology, Stacey, but I truly don't understand why you said what you did in the first place."

He sighed heavily. "I love Cathy very much, Libby," he said. "But we do have our problems. At that time, things were a lot worse, and I started thinking about the way you'd leaned on me when you were going through all that trouble in New York. I liked having somebody need me like that, and I guess I worked the whole thing up into more than it was."

Tentatively Libby touched his hand. "Cathy needs you, Stacey."

"No," he answered gruffly, looking at the flickering bowl candle in the center of the table. "She won't allow herself to need me. After some of the things I've put her through, I can't say I blame her."

"She'll trust you again, if you're worthy of it," Libby ventured. "Just be there for Cathy, Stace. The way you were there for me when my whole life seemed to be falling apart. I don't think I could have gotten through those days without you."

At that moment Jess appeared out of nowhere and slid into the seat Becky had occupied before. "Now, that," he drawled acidly, "is really touching."

Libby stared at him, stunned by his presence and by the angry set of his face. Then she realized that both she and Stacey were sitting on the same side of the booth and knew that it gave an impression of intimacy. "Jess..."

He looked down at his watch, a muscle dancing furiously in his jaw. "Are you going to pick your father up at the hospital, or do you have more interesting things to do?"

Stacey, who had been as shocked by his brother's arrival as Libby had, was suddenly, angrily vocal. The candle leapt a little when he slammed one fist down on the tabletop and hissed, "Dammit, Jess, you're deliberately misunderstanding this!"

"Am I?"

"Yes!" Libby put in, on the verge of tears. "Becky and I were having lunch and then Stacey came in and—"

"Stop it, Libby," Stacey broke in. "You didn't do anything wrong. Jess is the one who's out of line here."

The long muscle in Jess's neck corded, and his lips were edged with white, but his voice was still low, still controlled. "I came here, Libby, because I wanted to be with you when you brought Ken home," he said, and his green eyes, dark with passion only the night before, were coldly indifferent now. "Are we going to collect him or would you rather stay here and carry on?"

Libby was shaking. "Carry on? *Carry on?*"

Stacey groaned, probably considering the scandal a scene in this particular restaurant would cause. "Couldn't we settle this somewhere else?"

"We'll settle it, all right," Jess replied.

Stacey's jaw was rock-hard as he stood up to let a shaken Libby out of the booth. "I'll be on the ranch," he said.

"So will I," replied Jess, rising, taking a firm grip on Libby's arm. "See you there."

"Count on it."

Jess nodded and calmly propelled Libby out of the restaurant and into the bright sunlight, where her shiny Corvette was parked. Probably he had seen the car from the highway and known that she was inside the steak house.

Now, completely ignoring her protests, he dragged her past her car and thrust her into the Land Rover beside it.

"Jess—damn you—will you *listen* to me?"

Jess started the engine, shifted it into reverse with a swift motion of his hand. "I'm afraid storytime will have to wait," he informed her. "We've got to go and get Ken, and I don't want him upset."

"Do you think I do?"

Jess sliced one menacing look in her direction but said nothing.

Libby felt a need to reach him, even though, the way he was acting, he didn't deserve reassurances. "Jess, how can you...after last night, how could you..."

"Last night," he bit out. "Yes. Tell me, Libby, do you do that trick for everybody, or just a favored few?"

It took all her determination not to physically attack him. "Take me back to my car, Jess," she said evenly. "Right now. I'll pick Dad up myself, and we'll go back to his house—"

"Correction, Mrs. Barlowe. *He* will go to his house. You, my little vixen, will go to mine."

"I will not!"

"Oh, but you will. Despite your obvious attraction to my brother, you are still my wife."

"I am not attracted to your brother!"

They had reached the hospital parking lot, and the Land Rover lurched to a stop. Jess smiled insolently and patted Libby's cheek in a way so patronizing that it made her screaming mad. "That's the spirit, Mrs. Barlowe. Walk in there and show your daddy what a pillar of morality you are."

Going into that hospital and pretending that nothing was wrong was one of the hardest things Libby had ever had to do.

Preparations for Ken's return had obviously been going on for some time. As Libby pulled her reclaimed Corvette in behind Jess's Land Rover, she saw that the front lawn had been mowed and the truck had been repaired.

Ken, still not knowing the story of his daughter, his truck, and the bear, paused after stepping out of Jess's Land Rover, his arm still in a sling. He looked his own vehicle over quizzically. "Looks different," he reflected.

Jess rose to the occasion promptly, smoothly. "The boys washed and waxed it," he said.

To say the very least, thought Libby, who would never forget, try though she might, how that truck had looked before the repair people in Kalispell had fixed and painted it. She opened her mouth to tell her father what had happened, but Jess stopped her with a look and a shake of his head.

The inside of the house had been cleaned by Mrs. Bradshaw and her band of elves; every floor and stick of furniture had been either dusted or polished or both. The refrigerator had been stocked and a supply of the paperback westerns Ken loved to read had been laid in.

As if all this wasn't enough to make Libby's services completely superfluous, it turned out that Becky was there too. She had strung streamers and dozens of brightly colored balloons from the ceiling of Ken's bedroom.

Her father was obviously pleased, and Libby's last hopes of drumming up an excuse to stay the night, at least, were dashed. Becky, however, was delighted with her surprise.

"I thought you were working!" Libby accused.

"I lied," replied Becky, undaunted. "After I left you and Stacey at the steak house, I got a friend to bring me out here."

Libby shot a glance in Jess's direction, knew sweet triumph as she saw that Becky's words had registered with him. After only a moment's chagrin, however, he tightened his jaw and looked away.

While Becky was getting Ken settled in his room and generally spoiling him rotten, Libby edged over to her husband. "You heard her," she whispered tersely, "so where's my apology?"

"Apology?" Jess whispered back, and there was nothing in his face to indicate that he felt any remorse at all. "Why should I apologize?"

"Because I was obviously telling the truth! Becky said—"

"Becky said that she left you and Stacey at the steak house. It must have been a big relief when she did."

Heedless of everything but the brutal effect of Jess's unfair words, Libby raised one hand and slapped him, hard.

Stubbornly, he refused her the satisfaction of any response at all, beyond an imperious glare, which she returned.

"Hey, do you guys...?" Becky's voice fell away when she became aware of the charged atmosphere of the living room. She swallowed and began again. "I was going to ask if you wanted to stay for supper, but maybe that wouldn't be such a good idea."

"You can say that again," rasped Jess, catching Libby's arm in a grasp she couldn't have broken without making an even more embarrassing scene. "Make our excuses to Ken, will you, please?"

After a moment's hesitation and a concerned look at Libby, Becky nodded.

"You overbearing bastard!" Libby hissed as her husband squired her out of the house and toward his Land Rover.

Jess opened the door, helped her inside, met her fiery blue gaze with one of molten green. Neither spoke to the other, but the messages flashing between them were all too clear anyway.

Jess still believed that Libby had been either planning or carrying on a romantic tryst with Stacey, and Libby was too proud and too angry to try to convince him otherwise. She was also too smart to get out of his vehicle and make a run for hers.

Jess would never hurt her, she knew that. But he would not allow her a dramatic exit, either. And she couldn't risk a screaming fight in the driveway of her father's house.

Because she was helpless and she hated that, she began to cry.

Jess ignored her tears, but he too was considerate of Ken—he did not gun the Land Rover's engine or back out at a speed that would fling gravel in every direction, as he might have at another time.

When they passed his house, with its window walls, and started up a steep road leading into the foothills beyond, Libby was still not afraid. For all his fury, this man was too tender a lover to touch her in anger.

"Where are we going?" she demanded.

He ground the Land Rover into a low gear and left the road, now little more than a cow path, for the rugged hillside. "On our honeymoon, Mrs. Barlowe."

Libby swallowed, unnerved by his quiet rage and the jostling, jolting ascent of the Land Rover itself. "If you take me in anger, Jess Barlowe, I'll never forgive you. Never. That would be rape."

The word "rape" got through Jess's hard armor and stung him visibly. He paled as he stopped the Land Rover with a lurch and wrenched on the emergency brake. "Goddammit, you *know* I wouldn't do anything like that!"

"Do I?" They were parked at an almost vertical angle, it seemed to Libby. Didn't he realize that they were almost straight up and down? "You've been acting like a maniac all afternoon!"

Jess's face contorted and he raised his fists and brought them down hard on the steering wheel. "Dammit it all to hell," he raged, "you drive me crazy! Why the devil do I love you so much when *you drive me crazy?*"

Libby stared at him, almost unable to believe what she had heard. Not even in their wildest moments of passion had he said he loved her, and if he had found that note she'd left for him, betraying her own feelings, the day the bear was killed, he'd never mentioned it.

"What did you say?"

Jess sighed, tilted his head back, closed his eyes. "That you drive me crazy."

"Before that."

"I said I loved you," he breathed, as though there was nothing out of the ordinary in that.

"Do you?"

"Hell, yes." The muscles in his sun-browned neck corded as he swallowed, his head still back, his eyes still closed. "Isn't that a joke?"

The words tore at Libby's heart. "A joke?"

"Yes." The word came, raw, from deep within him, like a sob.

"You idiot!" yelled Libby, struggling with the door, climbing out of the Land Rover to stalk up the steep hillside. She trembled, and tears poured down her face, and for once she didn't care who saw them.

At the top of the rise, she sat down on a huge log, her vision too blurred to take in the breathtaking view of mountains and prairies and an endless, sweeping sky.

She sensed Jess's approach, tried to ignore him.

"Why am I an idiot, Libby?"

Though the day was warm, Libby shivered. "You're too stupid to know when a woman loves you, that's why!" she blurted out, sobbing now. "Damn! You've had me every way but hanging from a chandelier, and you still don't know!"

Jess straddled the log, drew Libby into his arms and held her. Suddenly he laughed, and the sound was a shout of joy.

Chapter 14

Drunken cowboys and Indians notwithstanding, the powwow of the Sioux, Flathead and Blackfoot was a spectacle to remember. Held annually in the same small and otherwise unremarkable town, the meeting of these three tribes was a tradition that reached back to days of mist and shadow, days recorded on no calendar but that of the red man's legends.

Now, on a hot July morning, the erstwhile cow pasture and ramshackle grandstands were churning with activity, and Libby Barlowe's fingers ached to make use of the sketchbook and pencils she carried.

Craning her neck to see the authentic tepees and their colorfully clad inhabitants, she could hardly stand still long enough for the plump woman at the admission gate to stamp her hand.

There was so much noise—laughter, the tinkle of change in the coin box, the neighing and nickering of horses that would be part of the rodeo. Underlying all this was the steady beat of tom-toms and guttural chants of Indian braves.

"Enjoy yourself now, honey," enjoined the woman tending the cashbox, and Libby jumped, realizing that she was holding up the line behind her. After one questioning look at the hat the woman wore, which consisted of panels cut from various beer cans and crocheted together, she hurried through the gate.

Jess chuckled at the absorbed expression on Libby's face. There was so much to see that a person didn't know where to look first.

"I think I see a fit of creativity coming on," he said.

Libby was already gravitating toward the tepees, plotting light angles and shading techniques as she went. In her heart was a dream, growing bigger with every beat of the tom-toms. "I want to see, Jess," she answered distractedly. "I've got to *see*."

There was love in the sound of Jess's laughter, but no disdain. "All right, all right—but at least let me get you a hat. This sun is too hot for you to go around bareheaded.''

"Get me a hat, get me a hat," babbled Libby, zeroing in on a group of small Indian children, who wore little more than loincloths and feathers as they sat watching fathers, uncles and elder brothers perform the ancient rites for rain or success in warfare or hunting.

Libby was taken with the flash of their coppery skin, the midnight black of their hair, the solemn, stalwart expressions in their dark eyes. Flipping open her sketchbook, she squatted in the lush summer grass and began to rough in the image of one particular little boy.

Her pencil flew, as did her mind. She was thinking in terms of oil paints—vivid, primitive shades that would do justice to the child's coloring and the peacock splendor of his headdress.

"Hello," she said when the dark eyes turned to her in dour question. "My name is Libby, what's yours?"

"Jimmy," the little boy responded, but then he must have remembered the majesty of his ancestry, for he squared his small shoulders and amended, "Jim Little Eagle."

Libby made a hasty note in the corner of his sketch. "I wish I had a name like that," she said.

"You'll have to settle for 'Barlowe,'" put in a familiar voice from behind her, and a lightweight hat landed on the top of her head.

Libby looked up into Jess's face and smiled. "I guess I can make do with that," she answered.

Jess dropped to his haunches, assessed the sketch she'd just finished with admiring eyes. "Wow," he said.

Libby laughed. "I love it when you're profound," she teased. And then she took off the hat he'd given her and inspected it thoroughly. It was a standard western hat, made of straw, and it boasted a trailing tangle of turquoise feathers and crystal beads.

Jess took the hat and put it firmly back on, then arranged the feathers so that they rested on her right shoulder, tickling the bare, sun-gilded flesh there in a pleasant way. "Did you wear that blouse to drive me insane, or are you trying to set a world record for blistering sunburns?" he asked unromantically.

Libby looked down at the brief white eyelet suntop and wondered if she shouldn't have worn a western shirt, the way Becky and Cathy had. The garment she had on had no shoulders or sleeves; it was just a series of broad ruffles falling from an elasticized band that fitted around her chest, just beneath her collarbone. Not even wanting to think about the tortures of a sunburn, she crinkled her nose and said, "I wore it to drive you insane, of course."

Jess was going to insist on being practical; she saw it in his face. "They're selling T-shirts on the fairway—buy one."

"Now?" complained Libby, not wanting to leave the splendors of the recreated Indian village even for a few minutes.

Jess looked down at his watch. "Within half an hour," he said flatly. "I'm going to find Ken and the others in the grandstands, Rembrandt. I'll see you later."

Libby squinted as he rose against the sun, towering and magnificent even in his ordinary jeans and worn cowboy shirt. "No kiss?"

Jess crouched again, kissed her. "Remember. Half an hour."

"Half an hour," promised Libby, turning to a fresh page in her sketchbook and pondering a little girl with coal-black braids and a fringed buckskin shift. She took a new pencil from the case inside her purse and began to draw again, her hand racing to keep up with the pace set by her heart.

When the sketch was finished, Libby thought about what she meant to do and how the syndicate that carried her cartoon strip would react. No doubt they would be furious.

"Portraits!" her agent would cry. "Libby, Libby, there is no *money* in portraits."

Libby sighed, biting her lower lip. Money wasn't a factor really, since she had plenty of that as it was, not only because she had married a wealthy man but also because of prior successes in her career.

She was tired of doing cartoons, yearning to delve into other mediums—especially oils. She wanted color, depth, nuance—she wanted and needed to grow.

"Where the hell is that T-shirt I asked you to buy?"

Libby started, but the dream was still glowing in her face when she looked up to meet Jess's gaze. "Still on the fairway, I would imagine," she said.

His mouth looked very stern, but Jess's eyes were dancing beneath the brim of his battered western hat. "I don't know why I let you out of my sight," he teased. And then he extended a hand. "Come on, woman. Let's get you properly dressed."

Libby allowed herself to be pulled through the crowd to one of the concession stands. Here there were such thrilling offerings as ashtrays shaped like the state of Montana and gaudy scarves commemorating the powwow itself.

"Your secret is out," she told Jess out of the corner of her mouth, gesturing toward a display of hats exactly like her own. The colors of their feather-and-bead plumage ranged from a pastel yellow to deep, rich purple. "This hat is not a designer original!"

Jess worked up an expression of horrified chagrin and then laughed and began rifling through a stack of colorful T-shirts. "What size do you wear?"

Libby stood on tiptoe, letting her breath fan against his ear, delighting as that appendage reddened visibly. "About the size of the palm of your hand, cowboy."

"Damn," Jess chuckled, and the red moved out from his ear to churn under his suntan. "Unless you want me to drag you off somewhere and make love to you right now, you'd better not make any more remarks like that."

Suddenly Libby was as pink as the T-shirt he was measuring against her chest. Coming from Jess, this was no idle threat—since their new understanding, reached several weeks before on the top of the hill behind his house, they had made love in some very unconventional places. It would be like him to take her to one of the small trailers brought by some of the cowboys from the Circle Bar B and follow through.

Having apparently deemed the pink T-shirt appropriate, Jess bought it and gripped Libby's hand, fairly dragging her across the sawdust-covered fairgrounds. From the grandstands came the deafening shouts and boot-stompings of more than a thousand excited rodeo fans.

Reaching the rest rooms, which were housed in a building of their own, Jess gave an exasperated sigh. There must have been a hundred women waiting to use the facilities, and he clearly didn't want to stand around in the sun just so Libby could exchange her suntop for a T-shirt.

Before she could offer to wait alone so that Jess could go back and watch the rodeo, he was hauling her toward the nest of Circle Bar B trailers at such a fast pace that she had to scramble to keep up with him.

Thrusting her inside the smallest, which was littered with boots, beer cans and dirty clothes, he ordered, "Put on the shirt."

Libby's color was so high that she was sure he could see it, even in the cool darkness of that camper-trailer. "This is Jake Peterson's camper, isn't it? What if he comes back?"

"He won't come back—he's entered in the bull-riding competition. Just change, will you?"

Libby knew only too well what would happen if she removed that suntop. "Jess..."

He closed the camper door, flipped the inadequate-looking lock. Then he reached out, collected her befeathered hat, her sketchbook, her purse. He laid all these items on a small, messy table and waited.

In the distance, over the loudspeaker system, the rodeo announcer exalted, "This cowboy, folks, has been riding bulls longer'n he's been tying his shoes."

There was a thunderous communal cry as the cowboy and his bull apparently came out of their chute, but it was strangely quiet in that tiny trailer where Jess and Libby stood staring at each other.

Finally, in one defiant motion of her hands, Libby wrenched the suntop off over the top of her head and stood still before her husband, her breasts high and proud and completely bare. "Are you satisfied?" she snapped.

"Not yet," Jess retorted.

He came to stand very close, his hands gentle on her breasts. "You were right," he said into her hair. "You just fit the palms of my hands."

"Oh," said Libby in sweet despair.

Jess's hands continued their tender work, lulling her. It was so cool inside that trailer, so intimate and shadowy.

Presently Libby felt the snap on her jeans, and then the zipper, give way. She was conscious of a shivering heat as the fabric glided downward. Protesting was quite beyond her powers now; she was bewitched.

Jess laid her on the narrow camper bed, joining her within moments. Stretched out upon her, he entered her with one deft thrust.

Their triumph was a simultaneous one, reached after they'd both traveled through a glittering mine field of physical and spiritual sensation, and it was of such dizzying scope that it seemed natural for the unknowing crowd in the grandstands to cheer.

Furiously Libby fastened her jeans and pulled on the T-shirt that had caused this situation in the first place. She gathered up her things, plopped her hat onto her head, and glared into Jess's amused face.

He dressed at a leisurely pace, as though they weren't trespassing.

"If Jake Peterson ever finds out about his, I'll die," Libby said, casting anxious, impatient looks at the locked door.

Jess pulled on one boot, then the other, ran a hand through his rumpled hair. His eyes smoldering with mischief and lingering pleasure, he stood up, pulled Libby into his arms and kissed her. "I love you," he said. "And your shameful secret is safe with me, Mrs. Barlowe."

Libby's natural good nature was overcoming her anger. "Sure," she retorted tartly. "All the same, I think you should know that every man who had ever compromised me in a ranch hand's trailer has said that selfsame thing."

Jess laughed, kissed her again, and then released her. "Go back to your Indians, you little hellion. I'll find you later."

"That's what I'm afraid of," Libby tossed back over one shoulder as she stepped out of the camper into the bright July sunshine. Almost before her eyes had adjusted to the change, she was sketching again.

Libby hardly noticed the passing of the hours, so intent was she on recording the scenes that so fascinated her: braves festooned with colorful feathers, doing their war and rain dances; squaws, plump in their worn buckskin dresses, demonstrating the grinding of corn or making their beaded belts and moccasins; children playing games that were almost as old as the distant mountains and the big sky.

Between the residual effects of that scandalous bout of lovemaking in the trailer and the feast of color and sound assaulting her now, Libby's senses were reeling. She was almost relieved when Cathy came and signed that it was time to leave.

As they walked back to find the others in the still-dense crowd, Libby studied her cousin out of the corner of her eye. Cathy and Stacey were living together again, but there was a wistfulness about Cathy that was disturbing.

There would be no chance to talk with her now—there were too many distractions for that—but Libby made a mental vow to get Cathy alone later, perhaps during the birthday party that was being held on the ranch for Senator Barlowe that evening, and find out what was bothering her.

As the group made plans to stop at a favorite café for an early supper, Libby grew more and more uneasy about Cathy. What was it about her that was different, besides her obviously downhearted mood?

Before Libby could even begin to work out that complex question, Ken and Becky were off to their truck, Stacey and Cathy to their car. Libby was still staring into space when Jess gently tugged at her hand.

She got into the Land Rover, feeling pensive, and laid her sketchbook and purse on the seat.

"Another fit of creativity?" Jess asked quietly, driving carefully through a maze of other cars, staggering cowboys and beleaguered sheriff's deputies.

"I was thinking about Cathy," Libby replied. "Have you noticed a change in her?"

He thought, shook his head. "Not really."

"She doesn't talk to me anymore, Jess."

"Did you have an argument?"

Libby sighed. "No. I've been so busy lately, what with finishing the book and everything, I haven't spent much time with her. I'm ashamed to say that I didn't even notice the change in her until just a little while ago."

Jess gave her a gentle look. "Don't start beating yourself up Libby. You're not responsible for Cathy's happiness or unhappiness."

Surprised, Libby stared at him. "That sounds strange, coming from you."

They were pulling out onto the main highway, which was narrow and almost as choked with cars as the parking area had been. "I'm beginning to think it was a mistake, our being so protective of Cathy. We all meant well, but I wonder sometimes if we didn't hurt her instead."

"Hurt her?"

One of Jess's shoulders lifted in a shrug. "In a lot of ways, Cathy's still a little girl. She's never had to be a grown-up, Libby, because one of us was always there to fight her battles for her. I think she uses her deafness as an excuse not to take risks."

Libby was silent, reflecting on Cathy's fear of being a mother.

As though he'd looked into her mind, Jess went on to say, "Both Cathy and Stacey want children—did you know that? But Cathy won't take the chance."

"I knew she was scared—she told me that. She's scared of so many things, Jess—especially of losing Stacey."

"She loves him."

"I know. I just wish she had something more—something of her own so that her security as a person wouldn't hinge entirely on what Stacey does."

"You mean the way your security doesn't hinge on what I do?" Jess ventured, his tone devoid of any challenge or rancor.

Libby turned, took off her hat and set it down between them with the other things. "I love you very, very much, Jess, but I could live without you. It would hurt unbearably, but I could do it."

He looked away from the traffic only long enough to flash her one devilish grin. "Who would take shameful liberties with your body, if it weren't for me?"

"I guess I would have to do without shameful liberties," she said primly.

"Thank you for sidestepping my delicate male ego," he replied, "but the fact of the matter is, there's no way a woman as beautiful and talented as you are would be alone for very long."

"Don't say that!"

Jess glanced at her in surprise. "Don't say what?"

It was his meaning that had concerned Libby, not his exact words. "I don't even want to think about another man touching me the way you do."

Jess's attention was firmly fixed on the road ahead. "If you're trying to make me feel secure, princess, it's working."

"I'm not trying to make you feel anything. Jess, before we made love that first time, when you said I was really a virgin, you were right. Even the books I've read couldn't have prepared me for the things I feel when you love me."

"It might interest you to know, Mrs. Barlowe, that my feelings toward you are quite similar. Before we made love, sex was just something my body demanded, like food or exercise. Now it's magic."

She stretched to plant a noisy kiss on her husband's cheek. "Magic, is it? Well, you're something of a sorcerer yourself, Jess Barlowe. You cast spells over me and make me behave like a wanton."

He gave an exaggerated evil chuckle. "I hope I can remember the hex that made you give in to me back there at the fairgrounds."

Libby moved the things that were between them into the backseat and slid closer, taking a mischievous nip at his earlobe. "I'm sure you can," she whispered.

Jess shuddered involuntarily and snapped, "Dammit, Libby, I'm driving."

She was exploring the sensitive place just beneath his ear with the tip of her tongue. "Umm. You like getting me into situations where I'm really vulnerable, don't you, Jess?'' she breathed, sliding one hand inside his shirt. "Like today, for instance."

"Libby..."

"Revenge is sweet."

And it was.

Shyly Libby extended the carefully wrapped package that contained her personal birthday gift to Senator Barlowe. She had not shown it to anyone else, not even Jess, and now she was uncertain. After all, Monica had given Cleave gold cufflinks and Stacey and Cathy planned to present him with a bottle of rare wine. By comparison, would her offering seem tacky and homemade?

With the gentle smile that had won him so many hearts and so many votes over the years, he took the parcel, which was revealingly large and flat, and turned it in his hands. "May I?" he asked softly, his kind eyes twinkling with affection.

"Please do," replied Libby.

It seemed to take Cleave forever to remove the ribbons and wrapping paper and lift the lid from the box inside, but there was genuine emotion in his face when he saw the framed pen-and-ink drawing Libby had been working on, in secret, for days. "My sons," he said.

"That's us, all right," commented Jess, who had appeared at the senator's side. "Personally, I think I'm considerably handsomer than that."

Cleave was examining the drawing closely. It showed Jess looking forward, Stacey in profile. When the senator looked up, Libby saw the love he bore his two sons in his eyes. "Thank you," he said. "This is one of the finest gifts I've ever received." He assessed the drawing again, and when his gaze came back to meet hers, it was full of mischief. "But where are my daughters? Where are you and Cathy?"

Libby smiled and kissed his cheek. "I guess you'll have to wait until your *next* birthday for that."

"In that case," rejoined the senator, "why not throw in a couple of grandchildren for good measure?"

Libby grinned. "I might be able to come up with one, but a couple?"

"Cathy will just have to do her part," came the immediate reply. "Now, if you'll excuse me, I want to take this picture around and show all my guests what a talented daughter-in-law I have."

Once his father had gone, Jess lifted his champagne glass and one eyebrow. "'Talented' is definitely the word," he said.

Libby knew that he was not referring to her artwork and hastily changed the subject. "You look so splendid in that tuxedo that I think I'd like to dance with you."

Jess worked one index finger under the tight collar of his formal shirt, obviously uncomfortable. "Dance?" he echoed dryly. "Lead me to the organ grinder and we're in business."

Laughing, Libby caught at his free hand and dragged him into the spacious living room, which had been prepared for dancing. There was a small string band to provide the music.

Libby took Jess's champagne glass and set it aside, then rested both hands on his elegant satin lapels. The other guests—and there were dozens—might not have existed at all.

"Dance with me," she said.

Jess took her into his arms, his eyes never leaving hers. "You know," he said softly, "you look so wonderful in that silvery dress that I'm tempted to take you home and make damned sure my father gets that grandchild he wants."

"When we start a baby," she replied seriously, "I want it to be for us."

Jess's mouth quirked into a grin and his eyes were alight with love. "I wasn't going to tape a bow to the little stinker's head and hand it over to him, Libby."

Libby giggled at the picture this prompted in her mind. "Babies are so funny," she dreamed aloud.

"I know," Jess replied. "I love that look of drunken wonder they get when you lift them up high and talk to them. About that time, they usually barf in your hair."

Before she could answer, Ken and Becky came into the magical mist that had heretofore surrounded Libby and Jess.

"All right if I cut in?" Ken asked.

"How soon do you want a grandchild?" Jess countered.

"Sooner the better," retorted Ken. "And, Jess?"

"What?" demanded his son-in-law, eyes still locked with Libby's.

"The music stopped."

Jess and Libby both came to a startled halt, and Becky was so delighted by their expressions that her laughter pealed through the large room.

When the band started playing again, Libby found herself dancing with her father, while Jess and Becky waltzed nearby.

"You look real pretty," Ken said, beaming down at her.

"You're pretty fancy yourself," Libby answered. "In fact, you look downright handsome in that tuxedo."

"She says that to everybody," put in Jess, who happened to be whirling past with Becky.

Ken's laugh was low and throaty. "He never gets too far away from you, does he?"

"About as far as white gets from rice. And I like it that way."

"That's what I figured. Libby..."

The serious, tentative way he'd said her name gave Libby pause. "Yes?"

"Becky and I are going to get married," he blurted out, without taking a single breath.

Libby felt her eyes fill. "You were afraid to tell me that? Afraid to tell me something wonderful?"

Ken stopped, his arms still around his daughter, his blue eyes bright with relief and delight. Then, with a raucous shout that was far more typical of him than tuxedos and fancy parties, her father lifted her so high that she was afraid she would fall out of the top of her dress.

"That was certainly rustic," remarked Monica, five minutes later, at the refreshment table.

Libby saw Jess approaching through the crowd of guests and smiled down at the buttery crab puff in her fingers. "Are you making fun of my father, Ms. Summers?"

Monica sighed in exasperation. "This *is* a formal party, after all—not a kegger at the Golden Buckle. I don't know why the senator insists on inviting the help to important affairs."

Slowly, and with great deliberation, Libby tucked her crab puff into Monica's artfully displayed cleavage. "Will you hold this, please?" she trilled, and then walked toward her husband.

"The foreman's brat strikes again," Jess chuckled, pulling her into another waltz.

Cathy was sitting alone in the dimly lit kitchen, her eyes fixed on something far in the distance. Libby was careful to let her cousin see her, rather than startle her with a touch.

"Hi," she said.

Cathy replied listlessly.

Libby took a chair opposite Cathy's and signed, "I'd like to help if I can."

Cathy's face crumbled suddenly and she gave a soft cry that tore at Libby's heart. Her hands flew as she replied, "Nobody can help me!"

"Don't I even get to try?"

A tendril of Cathy's hair fell from the soft knot at the back of her head and danced against a shoulder left bare by her Grecian evening gown. "I'm pregnant," she whispered. "Oh, Libby, I'm pregnant!"

Libby felt confusion and just a touch of envy. "Is that so terrible? I know you were scared before, but—"

"I'm still scared!" Cathy broke in, her voice unusually loud.

Libby drew a deep breath. "Why, Cathy? You're strong and healthy. And your deafness won't be the problem you think it will—you and Stacey can afford to hire help, if you feel it's necessary."

"All of that is so easy for you to say, Libby!" Cathy flared with sudden and startling anger. "You can hear! You're a whole person!"

Libby felt her own temper, always suppressed when dealing with her handicapped cousin, surge into life. "You know something?" she said furiously. "I'm sick of your 'Poor Cathy' number! A child is just about the best thing that can happen to a person and instead of rejoicing, you're standing here complaining!''

"I have a reason to complain!''

Libby's arms flew out from her side in a gesture of wild annoyance. "All right! You're deaf, you can't hear! Poor, poor Cathy! Now, can we get past singing your sad song? Dammit, Cathy, I know how hard it must be to live in silence, but can't you look on the positive side for once? You're married to a successful, gentle-hearted man who loves you very much. You have everything!''

"Said the woman who could hear!'' shouted Cathy.

Libby sighed and sat back in her chair. "We're all handicapped in some way—Jess told me that once, and I think it's true.''

Cathy was not going to be placated. "What's your handicap, Libby?'' she snapped. "Your short fingernails? The fact that you freckle in the summer instead of getting tan?''

The derisive sarcasm of her cousin's words stung Libby. "I'm as uncertain of myself at times as you are, Cathy,'' she said softly. "Aaron—''

"Aaron!'' spouted Cathy with contempt. "Don't hand me that, Libby! So he ran around a little—I had to stand by and watch my husband adore my own cousin for months! And I'll bet Jess has made any traumas you had about going to bed with a man all better!''

"Cathy, please...''

Cathy gave a guttural, furious cry of frustration. "I'm so damned tired of you, Libby, with your career and your loving father and your...''

Libby was mad again, and she bounded to her feet. "And my what?'' she cried. "I can't help that you don't have a father—Dad tried to make up for that and I think he did a damned good job! As for a career—don't you dare hassle me about that! I worked like a slave to get where I am! If you want a career, Cathy, get off your backside and start one!''

Cathy stared at her, stunned, and then burst into tears. And, of course, Jess chose exactly that moment to walk in.

Giving Libby one scalding, reproachful look, he gathered Cathy into his arms and held her.

Chapter 15

After one moment of feeling absolutely shattered, Libby lifted her chin and turned from Jess's annoyance and Cathy's veiled triumph to walk out of the kitchen with dignity.

She encountered a worried-looking Marion Bradshaw just on the other side of the door. "Libby...Mrs. Barlowe...that man is here!"

Libby drew a deep breath. "What man?" she managed to ask half-heartedly.

"Mr. Aaron Strand, that's who!" whispered Marion. "He had the nerve to walk right up and ring the bell..."

Libby was instantly alert, alive in every part of her being, like a creature being stalked in the wilds. "Where is he now?"

"He's in the senator's study," answered the flushed, quietly outraged housekeeper. "He says he won't leave till he talks with you, Libby. I didn't want a scene, what with all these people here, so I didn't argue."

Wearily Libby patted Marion's shoulder. Facing Aaron Strand, especially now, was the last thing in the world she wanted to do. But she knew that he would create an awful fuss if his request was denied, and besides, what real harm could he do with so many people in the house? "I'll talk to him," she said.

"I'll get Jess," mused Mrs. Bradshaw, "and your daddy, too."

Libby shook her head quickly, and warm color surged up over her face. Jess was busy lending a strong shoulder to Cathy, and she was damned if she was going to ask for his help now, even indirectly. And though Ken was almost fully recovered from his confrontation with the bear, Libby had no intention of subjecting him to the stress that could result from a verbal round with his former son-in-law. "I'll handle this myself," she said firmly, and then, without waiting for a reply, she started for the senator's study.

Aaron was there, tall and handsome in his formal clothes.

"At least when you crash a party, you dress for it," observed Libby dryly from the doorway.

Aaron set down the paperweight he had been examining and smiled. His eyes moved over her in a way that made her want to stride across the room and slap him with all her might. "That dress is classy, sugarplum," he said in acid tones. "You're definitely bunkhouse-calendar material."

Libby bit her lower lip, counted mentally until the urge to scream passed. "What do you want, Aaron?" she asked finally.

"Want?" he echoed, pretending pleasant confusion.

"Yes!" hissed Libby. "You flew two thousand miles—you must want something."

He sighed, leaned back against the senator's desk, folded his arms. "Are you happy?"

"Yes," answered Libby with a lift of her chin.

Again he assessed her shiny silver dress, the hint of cleavage it revealed. "I imagine the cowboy is pretty happy with you, too," he said. "Which Barlowe is it, Libby? The steak-house king or the lawyer?"

Libby's head began to ache; she sighed and closed her eyes for just a moment. "What do you want?" she asked again insistently.

His shoulders moved in a shrug. "A baby," he answered, as though he was asking for a cup of coffee or the time of day. "I know you're not going to give me that, so relax."

"Why did you come here, then?"

"I just wanted a look at this ranch. Pretty fancy spread, Lib. You do know how to land on your feet, don't you?"

"Get out, Aaron."

"Without meeting your husband? Your paragon of a father? I wouldn't think of it, Mrs. Barlowe."

Libby was off balance, trying to figure out what reason Aaron could have for coming all the way to Montana besides causing her added grief. Incredible as it seemed, he had apparently done just that. "You can't hurt me anymore, Aaron," she said. "I won't let you. Now, get out of here, please."

"Oh, no. I lost everything because of you—everything. And I'll have my pound of flesh, Libby—you can be sure of that."

"If your grandmother relieved you of your company responsibilities, Aaron, that's your fault, not mine. I should think you would be glad— now you won't have anything to keep you from your wine, women and song."

Aaron's face was tense. Gone was his easy, gentlemanly manner. "With the company went most of my money, Libby. And let's not pretend, sweetness—I can make your bright, shiny new life miserable, and we both know it."

"How?" asked Libby, poised to turn and walk out of the study.

"By generating shame and scandal, of course. Your father-in-law is a prominent United States senator, isn't he? I should think negative publicity could hurt him very badly—and you know how good I am at stirring that up."

Rage made Libby tremble. "You can't hurt Cleave Barlowe, Aaron. You can't hurt me. Now, get out before I have you thrown out!"

He crossed the room at an alarming speed, had a hold on Libby's upper arms before she could grasp what was happening. He thrust her back against the heavy door of the study and covered her mouth with his own.

Libby squirmed, shocked and repulsed. She tried to push Aaron away, but he had trapped her hands between his chest and her own. And the kiss went on, ugly and wet, obscene because it was forced upon her, because it was Aaron's.

Finally he drew back, smirking down at her, grasping her wrists in both hands when she tried to wriggle away from him. And suddenly Libby was oddly detached, calm even. Mrs. Bradshaw had been right when she'd wanted to let Jess know that Aaron was here, so very right.

Libby had demurred because of her pride, because she was mad at Jess; she'd thought she could handle Aaron Strand. Pride be damned, she thought, and then she threw back her head and gave a piercing, defiant scream.

Aaron chuckled. "Do you think I'm afraid of your husband, Libby?" he drawled. Incredibly, he was about to kiss her again, it appeared, when he was suddenly wrenched away.

Libby dared one look at Jess's green eyes and saw murder flashing there. She reached for his arm, but he shook her hand away.

"Strand," he said, his gaze fixed on a startled but affably recovering Aaron.

Aaron gave a mocking half-bow. It didn't seem to bother him that Jess was coldly furious, that half the guests at the senator's party, Ken Kincaid included, were jammed into the study doorway.

"Is this the part," Aaron drawled, "where we fight over the fair lady?"

"This is the part," Jess confirmed icily.

Aaron shrugged. "I feel honor-bound to warn you," he said smugly, "that I am a fifth-degree black belt."

Jess spared him an evil smile, but said nothing.

Libby was afraid; again she grasped at Jess's arm. "Jess, he really is a black belt."

Jess did not so much as look at Libby; he was out of her reach, and not just physically. She felt terror thick in her throat, and flung an appealing look at Ken, who was standing beside her, one arm around her waist.

Reading the plea in his daughter's eyes, he denied it with an almost imperceptible shake of his head.

Libby was frantic. As Jess and Aaron drew closer to each other, circling like powerful beasts, she struggled to free herself from her father's restraining arm. For all his weaknesses of character, Aaron Strand was agile and strong, and if he could hurt Jess, he would, without qualms of any kind.

"Jess, no!" she cried.

Jess turned toward her, his jaw tight with cold annoyance, and Aaron struck in that moment. His foot came up in a graceful arc and caught Jess in the side of the neck. Too sick to stand by herself or run away, Libby buried her face in Ken's tuxedo jacket in horror.

There were sounds—terrible sounds. Why didn't someone stop the fight? Why were they all standing around like Romans thrilling to the exploits of gladiators? Why?

When the sounds ceased and Libby dared to look, Jess was still standing. Aaron was sitting on the floor, groaning theatrically, one corner of his lip bleeding. It was obvious that he wasn't badly hurt, for all his carrying on.

Rage and relief mingled within Libby in one dizzying sweep. "Animals!" she screamed, and when she whirled to flee the ugliness, no one moved to stop her.

Libby sat on the couch in the condo's living room, her arms wrapped around her knees, stubbornly ignoring the ringing of the telephone. She couldn't help counting, though—that had become something of a game in the two days since she'd left the ranch to take refuge here. Twenty-six rings. It was a record.

She stood up shakily, made her way into the kitchen, where she had been trying to sketch out the panels for her cartoon strip. "Back to the old drawing board," she said to the empty room, and the stale joke fell flat because there was no one there to laugh.

The telephone rang again and, worn down, Libby reached out for the receiver affixed to the kitchen wall and snapped, "Hello!"

"Lib?" The voice belonged to her father, and it was full of concern. "Libby, are you all right?"

"No," she answered honestly, letting a sigh carry the word. "As a matter of fact, I'm not all right. How are you?"

"Never mind me—why did you run off like that?"

"You know why."

"Are you coming back to the ranch?"

"Why?" countered Libby, annoyed. "Am I missing some bloody spectacle?"

Ken gave a gruff sigh. "Dammit, Libby, do you love Jess Barlowe or not?"

Tears stung her eyes. Love him? These two days away from him had been hell, but she wasn't about to admit that. "What does it matter?"

she shot back. "He's probably so busy holding Cathy's hand that he hasn't even noticed I'm gone."

"That's it. Cathy. Standing up for her is a habit with Jess, Lib—you know that."

Libby did know; in two days she'd had plenty of time to come to the conclusion that she had overreacted in the kitchen the night of the party when Jess had seemed to take Cathy's part against her. She shouldn't have walked out that way. "There is still the fight—"

"You screamed, Libby. What would you have done, if you'd been in Jess's place?" Without waiting for an answer, her father went on, "You're just being stubborn, and so is Jess. Do you love him enough to make the first move, Lib? Do you have the gumption?"

Libby reached out for a kitchen chair, sank into it. "Where is he?"

There was a smile in her father's voice. "Up on that ridge behind your place," he answered. "He's got a camp up there."

Libby knew mild disappointment; if Jess was camping, he hadn't been calling. She had been ignoring the telephone for two days for nothing. "It's nice to know he misses me so much," she muttered petulantly.

Having said his piece, Ken was silent.

"He does miss me, doesn't he?" demanded Libby.

"He misses you," chuckled Ken. "He wouldn't be doing his hermit routine if he didn't."

Libby sighed. "The ridge, huh?"

"The ridge," confirmed Ken with amusement. And then he hung up.

I shouldn't be doing this in my condition, Libby complained to herself as she made her way up the steep hillside. *But since the mountain won't come to me...*

She stopped, looked up. The smoke from Jess's campfire was curling toward the sky; the sun was hot and bright. What the devil did he need with a fire, anyway? It was broad daylight, for heaven's sake.

Muttering, holding on to her waning courage tenaciously, Libby made her way up over the rise to the top of the ridge. Jess was standing with his back to her, looking in the opposite direction, but the stiffness of his shoulders revealed that he knew she was there.

And suddenly she was furious. Hadn't she climbed up this cursed mountain, her heart in her throat, her pride God-only-knew-where? Wasn't the current situation as much his fault as her own? Hadn't she found out, the very day after she'd left him, that she was going to have his baby?

"Damn you, Jess Barlowe," she hissed, "don't you dare ignore me!"

He turned very slowly to face her. "I'm sorry," he said stiffly and with annoying effort.

"For what?" pressed Libby. Damned if she was going to make it easy! Jess sighed, idly kicked dirt over his campfire with one booted foot.

There was a small tent pitched a few feet away, and a coffeepot sat on a fallen log, along with a paperback book and a half-eaten sandwich. "For assuming that the scene with Cathy was your fault," he said.

Libby huffed over to the log, which was a fair distance from Jess, and sat down, folding her arms. "Well, praise be!" she murmured. "What about that stupid fistfight in your father's study?"

His green eyes shot to her face. "You'll grow horns, lady, before you hear me apologize for that!"

Libby bit her lower lip. Fighting wasn't the ideal way to settle things, it was true, but she couldn't help recalling the pleasure she herself had taken in stuffing that crab puff down the front of Monica Summers' dress at the party. If Monica had made one move to retaliate, she would have gladly tangled with her. "Fair enough," she said.

There was an uncomfortable silence, which Libby finally felt compelled to break. "Why did you have a fire going in the middle of the day?"

Jess laughed. "I wanted to make damned sure you found my camp," he replied.

"Dad told you I was coming!"

He came to sit beside her on the log and even though he didn't touch her, she was conscious of his nearness in every fiber of her flesh and spirit. "Yeah," he admitted, and he looked so sad that Libby wanted to cry.

She eased closer to him. "Jess?"

"What?" he asked, looking her squarely in the eyes now.

"I'm sorry."

He said nothing.

Libby drew a deep breath. "I'm not only sorry," she went on bravely, "I'm pregnant, too."

He was quiet for so long that Libby feared she'd been wrong to tell him about their child—at least for now. It was possible that he wanted to ask for a separation or even a divorce, but he might stay with her out of duty now that he knew. To hold him in that manner would break Libby's heart.

"When did you find out?" he asked finally, and the lack of emotion in his face and in his voice made Libby feel bereft.

"Day before yesterday. After Cathy said she was pregnant, I got to thinking and realized that I had a few symptoms myself."

Jess was silent, looking out over the trees, the ranges, the far mountains. After what seemed like an eternity, he turned to her again, his green eyes full of pain. "You weren't going to tell me?"

"Of course I was going to tell you, Jess. But, well, the time didn't seem to be right."

"You're not going to leave, are you?"

"Would I have climbed a stupid mountain, for pity's sake, if I wanted to leave you?"

A slow grin spread across Jess's face, and then he gave a startling hoot of delight and shot to his feet, his hands gripping Libby's and pulling her with him. If he hadn't caught her in his arms and held her, she would probably have fallen into the lush summer grass.

"Is it safe to assume you're happy about this announcement?" Libby teased, looking up at him and loving him all the more because there were tears on his face.

He lifted her into his arms, kissed her deeply in reply.

"Excuse me, sir," she said when he drew back, "but I was wondering if you would mind making love to me. You see, I'd like to find out if I'm welcome here."

In answer, Jess carried her to the tent, set her on her feet. "My tent is your tent," he said.

Libby blushed a little and bent to go inside the small canvas shelter. Since there wasn't room enough to stand, she sat on the rumpled sleeping bag and waited as Jess joined her.

She was never sure exactly how it came about, but within moments they were both lying down, facing each other. The weight of his hand was bliss on her breast, and so were the hoarse words he said.

"I love you, Libby. I need you. No matter how mad I make you, please don't leave me again."

Libby traced the strong lines of his jaw with a fingertip. "I won't, Jess. I might scream and yell, but I won't leave. I love you too much to be away from you—if I learned anything in the last two days, it was that."

He was propped up on one elbow now, very close, and he was idly unbuttoning her blouse. "I want you."

Libby feigned shock. "In a tent, sir?"

"And other novel places." He paused, undid the front catch of her bra.

Libby sighed, then gasped as the warmth of his mouth closed over the straining peak of her breast. The sensation was exquisite, sweeping through her, pushing away the weariness and confusion and pain. She tangled her fingers in his rumpled hair, holding him close.

Jess finally left the breast he had so gently plundered to remove his clothes, and then, more slowly, Libby's. When she lay naked before him in the cool shadows of the tiny tent, he took in her waiting body with a look of rapt wonder. "Little enchantress," he breathed, "let me worship you.

Libby could not bear to be separate from him any longer. "Be close to me, Jess," she pleaded softly, "be part of me."

With a groan, he fell to her, his mouth moist and commanding upon hers. His tongue mated with Libby's and his manhood touched her with fire, prodding, taking only partial shelter inside her.

At last Jess broke the kiss and lifted his head, and Libby saw, through a shifting haze, that he was savoring her passion as well as his own. She was aware of every muscle in his body as he struggled to defy forces that do not brook the rebellion of mere mortals.

Finally these forces prevailed, and Jess was thrust, with a raspy cry, into Libby's depths. They moved together wildly, seeking and reaching and finally breaking through the barriers that divide this world from the glories of the next.

Cathy assessed the large oil painting of Jim Little Eagle, the Indian child Libby had seen at the powwow months before, her hands resting on her protruding stomach.

Libby, whose stomach was as large as Cathy's, was wiping her hands on a rag reserved for the purpose. The painting was a personal triumph, and she was proud of it. "What do you think?" she signed, after setting aside the cloth.

Cathy grinned. "What do I think?" she asked aloud, sitting down on the tall stool behind Libby's drawing board. "I'll tell you what I think. I think you should sell it to me instead of letting that gallery in Great Falls handle it. After all, they've got your pen-and-ink drawings and the other paintings you did."

Libby tried to look stern. "Are you asking for special favors, Cathy Barlowe?"

Cathy laughed. "Yes!" Her sparkling green eyes fell to the sketch affixed to Libby's drawing board and she exclaimed in delighted surprise. "This is great!"

Libby came to stand behind her, but her gaze touched only briefly on the drawing. Instead, she was looking out at the snow through the windows of her studio in Ken and Becky's house.

"What are you going to do with this?" Cathy demanded, tugging at Libby's arm.

Libby smiled, looking at the drawing. It showed her cartoon character, given over to the care of another artist now. Liberated Lizzie was in an advanced state of pregnancy, and the blurb read, "If it feels good, do it."

"I'm going to give it to Jess," she said with a slight blush. "It's a private joke."

Cathy laughed again, then assessed the spacious, well-equipped studio with happy eyes. "I'm surprised you work down here at your dad's place. Especially with Jess home almost every day, doing paperwork and things."

Libby's mouth quirked in a grin. "That's *why* I work down here. If I tried to paint there, I wouldn't get anything done."

"You're really happy, aren't you?"

"Completely."

Cathy enfolded her in a hug. "Me, too," she said. And when her eyes came to Libby's face, they were dancing with mischief. "Of course, you and Jess have to understand that you will never win the Race. Stacey and I are ahead by at least a nose."

Libby stood straight and tried to look imperious. "We will not concede defeat," she said.

Before Cathy could reply to this, Stacey came into the room, pretending to see only Libby. "Pardon me, pudgy person," he began, "but has my wife waddled by lately?"

"Is she kind of short, with long, pretty hair and big green eyes and a stomach shaped rather like a watermelon?"

Stacey snapped his fingers and a light seemed to go on in his face. "That's a pretty good description."

"Haven't seen her," said Libby.

Cathy gave her a delighted shove and flung herself at her husband, laughing. A moment later they were on their way out, loudly vowing to win what Jess and Stacey had dubbed the Great Barlowe Baby Race.

Through with her work for the day and eager to get home to Jess, Libby cleaned her brushes and put them away, washed her hands again, and went out to find her coat. The first pain struck just as she was getting into the car.

At home, Jess was standing pensively in the kitchen, staring out at the heavy layer of snow blanketing the hillside behind the house. Libby came up as close behind him as her stomach would allow and wrapped her arms around his lean waist.

"I've just had a pretty good tip on the Baby Race," she said.

The muscles beneath his bulky woolen sweater tightened, and he turned to look down at her, his jade eyes dark with wonder. "What did you say?"

"We're on the homestretch, Jess. I need to go to the hospital. Soon."

He paled, this man who had hunted wounded bears and fire-breathing dragons. "My God!" he yelled, and suddenly they were both caught up in a whirlwind of activity. Phone calls were made, suitcases were snatched from the coat-closet floor, and then Jess was dragging Libby toward his Land Rover.

"Wait, I'm sure we have time—"

"I'm not taking any chances!" barked Jess, hoisting her pear-shaped and unwieldy form into the car seat.

"Jess," Libby scolded, grasping at his arm. "You're panicking!"

"You're damned right I'm panicking!" he cried, and then they were driving over the snowy, rutted roads of the ranch at the fastest pace he dared.

When they reached the airstrip, the Cessna had been brought out of the small hangar where it was kept and fuel was being pumped into it. After wrestling Libby into the front passenger seat, Jess quickly checked the engine and the landing gear. These were tasks, she had learned, that he never trusted to anyone else.

"Jess, this is ridiculous!" she protested when he scrambled into the pilot's seat and began a preflight test there. "We have plenty of time to drive to the hospital."

Jess ignored her, and less than a minute later the plane was taxiing down the runway. Out of the corner of one eye Libby saw a flash of ice blue.

"Jess, wait!" she cried. "The Ferrari!"

The plane braked and Jess craned his neck to see around Libby. Sure enough, Stacey and Cathy were running toward them, if Cathy's peculiar gait could be called a run.

Stacey leapt up onto the wing and opened the door. "Going our way?" he quipped, but his eyes were wide and his face was white.

"Get in," replied Jess impatiently, but his eyes were gentle as they touched Cathy and then Libby. "The race is on," he added.

Cathy was the first to deliver, streaking over the finish line with a healthy baby girl, but Libby produced twin sons soon after. Following much discussion, the Great Barlowe Baby Race was declared a draw.

* * * * *

THE DREAM UNFOLDS

Barbara Delinsky

1

They were three men with a mission late on a September afternoon. Purposefully they climbed from their cars, slammed their doors in quick succession and fell into broad stride on the brick walk leading to Elizabeth Abbott's front door. Gordon Hale rang the doorbell. It had been decided, back in his office at the bank, that he would be the primary speaker. He was the senior member of the group, the one who had organized the Crosslyn Rise consortium, the one who posed the least threat to Elizabeth Abbott.

Carter Malloy posed a threat because he was a brilliant architect, a rising star in his hometown, with a project in the works that stood to bring big bucks to the town. But there was more to his threat than that. He had known Elizabeth Abbott when they'd been kids, when he'd been the bad boy of the lot. The bad boy no longer, his biggest mistake in recent years had been bedding the vengeful Ms. Abbott. It had only happened once, he swore, and years before, despite Elizabeth's continued interest. Now, though, Carter was in love and on the verge of marrying Jessica Crosslyn, and Elizabeth had her tool for revenge. As chairman of the zoning commission, she was denying Crosslyn Rise the building permit it needed to break ground on its project.

Gideon Lowe was the builder for that project, and he had lots riding on its success. For one thing, the conversion of Crosslyn Rise from a single mansion on acres of land to an elegant condominium community promised to be the most challenging project he'd ever worked on. For another, it was the most visible. A job well-done there would be like a gold star on his résumé. But there was another reason why he wanted the project to be a success. He was an investor in it. For the first time, he had money at stake, *big* money. He knew he was taking a gamble, risking so much of his personal savings, but if things went well, he would have established himself as a businessman, a man of brain, as well as brawn. That was what he wanted, a change of image. And that was why he'd allowed himself to be talked into trading a beer with the guys after work for this mission.

A butler opened the door. "Yes?"

Gordon drew his stocky body to its full five-foot-ten-inch height. "My name is Gordon Hale. These gentlemen are Carter Malloy and Gideon Lowe. We're here to see Miss Abbott. I believe she's expecting us."

"Yes, sir, she is," the butler answered, and stood back to gesture them into the house. "If you'll come this way," he said as soon as they were all in the spacious front hall with the door closed behind them.

Gideon followed the others through the hall, then the living room and into the parlor, all the while fighting the urge to either laugh or say something crude. He hated phoniness. He also hated formality. He was used to it, he supposed, just as he was used to wearing a shirt and tie when the occasion called for it, as this one did. Still he couldn't help but feel scorn for the woman who was now rising, like a queen receiving her court, from a chintz-covered wingback chair.

"Gordon," she said with a smile, and extended her hand, "how nice to see you."

Gordon took her hand in his. "The pleasure's mine, Elizabeth." He turned and said nonchalantly, "I believe you know Carter."

"Yes," she acknowledged, and Gideon had to hand it to her. For a woman who had once lain naked and hot under Carter, she was cool as a cucumber now. "How are you, Carter?"

Carter wasn't quite as cool. Losing himself to the opportunity, he said, "I'd have been better without this misunderstanding."

"Misunderstanding?" Elizabeth asked innocently. "Is there a misunderstanding here?" She looked at Gordon. "I thought we'd been quite clear."

Gordon cleared his throat. "About denying us the building permit, yes. About why you've denied it, no. That's why we requested this meeting. But before we start—" he gestured toward Gideon "—I don't believe you've met Gideon Lowe. He's both a member of the consortium and our general contractor."

Elizabeth turned the force of her impeccably made-up blue eyes on Gideon. She nodded, then seemed to look a second time and with interest, after which she extended her hand. "Gideon Lowe? Have I heard that name before?"

"I doubt it, ma'am," Gideon said. Her hand felt as cool as that cuke, and nearly as hard. He guessed she was made of steel and could understand why once had been enough for Carter. He knew then and there that he wasn't interested even in once, himself, but he had every intention of playing the game. "Most of my work has been out in the western counties. I'm new to these parts." If he sounded like a nice country boy, even a little Southern, that was fine for now. Women liked that. They found it sweet, even charming, particularly when the man was as tall as Gideon was, and—he only thought it because, after thirty-nine years of hearing people say it, he supposed he had the right—as handsome.

"Welcome, then," she said with a smile. "But how did you come to be associated with these two rogues?"

"That's a damn good question," he said, returning the smile, even putting a little extra shine in it. "Seems I might have been taken in by promises of smooth sailing. We builders are used to delays, but that doesn't mean we like them. I've got my trucks ready to roll and my men champing at the bit. You're one powerful lady to control a group of guys that way.''

Elizabeth did something with her mouth that said she loved the thought of that, though she said a bit demurely, "I'm afraid I can't take all the credit. I'm only one of a committee."

"But you're its chairman," Gordon put in, picking up the ball. "May we sit, Elizabeth?"

Elizabeth turned to him with a look of mild indignance. "Be my guest, though it won't do you much good. We've made our decision. As a courtesy, I've agreed to see you, but the committee's next formal meeting won't be until February. I thought I explained all that to Jessica."

At mention of Jessica's name, Carter stiffened. "You explained just enough on the phone to upset her. Why don't you go over it once more, face-to-face, with us."

"What Carter means," Gordon rushed to explain, "is that we're a little confused. Until yesterday afternoon, we'd been under the impression that everything was approved. I've been in close touch with Donald Swett, who assured me that all was well."

"Donald shouldn't have said that. I suppose he can be excused, since he's new to the committee this year, but all is never 'well,' as you put it, until the last of the information has been studied. As it turns out, we have serious doubts about the benefit of your project to this community."

"Are you kidding?" Carter asked.

Gordon held up a hand to him. To Elizabeth, he said, "The proposal we submitted to your committee went through the issue of community impact, point by point. The town has lots to gain, not the least of which is new tax revenue."

Elizabeth tipped her head. "We have lots to lose, too."

"Like what?" Carter asked, though a bit more civilly.

"Like crowding on the waterfront."

Gordon shook his head. "The marina will be limited in size and exclusive, at that. The price of the slips, alone, will discourage crowds."

"That price will discourage the local residents, too," Elizabeth argued, "who, I might add, also pay taxes to this town."

"Oh, my God," Carter muttered, "you're worried about the common folk. Since when, Elizabeth? You never used to give a damn about anyone or anything—"

"Carter—" Gordon interrupted, only to be interrupted in turn by Elizabeth, who was glaring at Carter.

"I've moved up in the hierarchy of this town. It's become my responsibility to think of everyone here." When Carter snorted in disbelief, she deliberately looked back at Gordon. "There's also the matter of your shops and their effect on those we already have. The town owes something to the shopkeepers who've been loyal to us all these years. So you see, it's not just a matter of money.''

"That's the most honest thing you've said so far," Carter fumed. "In fact, it doesn't have a damn *thing* to do with money. Or with crowding the waterfront or squeezing out shops. It has to do with you and me—''

Gordon interrupted. "I think we're losing it a little, here."

"Did you expect anything different?'' Elizabeth said in a superior way. "Some people never change. Carter certainly hasn't. He was a trouble-maker as a boy, and he's a troublemaker now. Maybe *that's* one of the reservations my committee has—''

Carter sliced a hand through the air. "Your 'committee' has no res-ervations. You're the only one who does. I'd venture to guess that your 'committee' was as surprised as we were by this sudden withholding of a permit. Face it, Lizzie. You're acting on a personal vendetta. I wonder what your 'committee' would say, or the townspeople, for that matter, if they were to learn that you and I—''

"Carter!'' Gordon snapped at the very same time that Gideon decided things had gone far enough.

"Whoa,'' Gideon said in a firm but slow and slightly raspy voice. "Let's take it easy here." He knew Carter. When the man felt passion-ately about something, there was no stopping him. It had been that way with Jessica, whom he had wooed doggedly for months until finally, just the day before, she agreed to marry him. It was that way with Crosslyn Rise, where he had spent part of his childhood. Apparently it was that way, albeit negatively, with Elizabeth Abbott. But Gideon knew Eliza-beth's type, too. Over the years, he had done enough work for people like her to know that the more she was pushed, the more she would dig in her heels. Reason had nothing to do with it; pride did.

But pride wouldn't get the consortium the building permit it needed, and the permit was all Gideon wanted. "I think,'' he went on in the same slow and raspy voice, "that we ought to cool it a second." He scratched his head. "Maybe we ought to cool it longer than that. It's late. I don't know about you guys, but I've been working all day. I'm tired. We're all tired.'' He looked beseechingly at Elizabeth. "Maybe this discussion would be better saved for tomorrow morning."

"I don't believe I can make it then,'' she said.

Gordon added, "Tomorrow morning's booked for me, too."

Carter scowled. "I have meetings in Springfield."

"Then dinner now,'' Gideon suggested. "I'm starved."

Again Gordon shook his head. "Mary's expecting me home. I'm al-ready late.''

Carter simply said, "Bad night."

Gideon slid a look at Elizabeth. "We could talk over dinner, you and I. I know as much about this project as these bozos. It'd be a hell of a lot more peaceful. And pleasant," he added more softly. "What do you say?"

Elizabeth was interested. He could see that. But she wasn't about to accept his invitation too quickly, lest she look eager. So she regarded him contemplatively for a minute, then looked at Gordon and at Carter, the latter in a dismissive way, before meeting Gideon's gaze again.

"I say that would be a refreshing change. You're right. It would be more peaceful. You seem like a reasonable man. We'll be able to talk." She glanced at the slender gold watch on her wrist. "But we ought to leave soon. I have an engagement at nine."

As announcements went, it was a bitchy one. But Gideon was glad she'd made it for several reasons. For one thing, he doubted it was true, which dented her credibility considerably, which made him feel less guilty for the sweet talking he was about to do. For another, it gave him an out. He was more than willing to wine and dine Elizabeth Abbott for the sake of the project, but he wasn't going beyond that. Hopefully, he'd have the concessions he wanted by the time dessert was done.

Actually he did even better than that. Around and between sexy smiles, the doling out of small tidbits of personal information and the withholding of enough else to make Elizabeth immensely curious, he got her to agree that though some of her reservations had merit, the pluses of the Crosslyn Rise conversion outweighed the minuses. In a golden twist of fate—not entirely bizarre, Gideon knew, since the restaurant they were at was the only place for fine evening dining in town—two other members of the zoning commission were eating there with their wives. Unable to resist showing Gideon how influential she was, Elizabeth insisted on threading her arm through his and leading him to their table, introducing him around, then announcing that she had decided not to veto the Crosslyn Rise conversion after all. The men from the commission seemed pleased. They vigorously shook hands with Gideon and welcomed him to their town, while their wives looked on with smiles. Gideon smiled as charmingly at the wives as he did at Elizabeth. He knew it would be hard for her to renege after she'd declared her intentions before so many witnesses.

Feeling proud of himself for handling things with such aplomb, he sent a wink to a waitress whose looks tickled his fancy, as he escorted Elizabeth from the restaurant. At her front door, he graciously thanked her for the pleasure of her company.

"Will we do it again?" she asked.

"By all means. Though I feel a little guilty."

"About what?"

"Seeing you, given our business dealings. There are some who would say we have a conflict of interest."

"They won't say it to me," Elizabeth claimed. "I do what I want."

"In this town, yes. But I work all over the state. I won't have you as my guardian angel other places."

Elizabeth frowned. "Are you saying that we shouldn't see each other until you're done with all of Crosslyn Rise? But that's ridiculous! The project could take years!"

In a soft, very gentle, slightly naughty voice, he said, "That's not what I'm saying at all. I'm just suggesting we wait until my work with the zoning commission is done."

Her frown vanished, replaced by a smug smile. "It's done. You'll have your permit by ten tomorrow morning." She tugged at his lapel. "Any more problems?"

He gave her his most lecherous grin and looked at her mouth. "None at all, ma'am. What say I call you later in the week. I'm busy this weekend, but I'm sure we'll be able to find another time when we're both free." He glanced at his watch. "Almost nine. Gotta run before I turn into a mouse." He winked. "See ya."

"So what was she like?" Johnny McCaffrey asked him the next afternoon after work.

They were at Sully's, where they went most days when Gideon was home in Worcester. Sully's was a diner when the sun shone and a bar at night, the watering spot for the local rednecks. Gideon's neck wasn't as red as some, but he'd grown up with these guys. They were his framers, his plasterers, his masons. They were his teammates—softball in the summer, basketball the rest of the year. They were also his friends.

Johnny was the closest of those and had been since they were eight and pinching apples from Drattles' orchard on the outskirts of town. Ugly as sin, Johnny had a heart of gold, which was probably why he had a terrific wife, Gideon mused. He was as loyal as loyal came, and every bit as trustworthy. That didn't mean he didn't live a little vicariously through Gideon.

"She was incredible," Gideon said now of Elizabeth, and it wasn't a compliment. "She has everything going for her—blond hair, blue eyes, nice bod, great legs—then she opens her mouth and the arrogance pours out. And dim-witted? Man, she's amazing. What woman in this day and age wouldn't have seen right through me? I mean, I wasn't subtle about wanting that permit—and wanting it before I touched her. Hell, I didn't even have to *kiss* her for it."

"Too bad."

"Nah. She didn't turn *me* on." He took a swig of his beer.

Johnny tipped his own mug and found it empty. "That type used to. You must be getting old, pal. Used to be you'd take most anything, and the more hoity-toity the better." He punctuated the statement with two raps of his mug on the bar.

Gideon drew himself straighter on his stool and said with a self-mocking grin, "That was before I got hoity-toity myself. I don't need other people's flash no more. I got my own."

"Watch out you don't start believing that," Johnny teased. "Give me another, Jinko," he told the bartender. To Gideon, he said, "I bumped into Sara Thayer today. She wanted to know how you've been. She'd love a call."

Gideon winced. "Come on, Johnny. She's a kid."

"She's twenty-one."

"I don't fool with kids."

"She doesn't look like a kid. She's got everything right where it's supposed to be. And she ain't gonna wait forever."

Sara Thayer was Johnny's wife's cousin. She'd developed a crush on Gideon at a Christmas party two years before, and Johnny, bless his soul, had been a would-be matchmaker ever since. Sara was a nice girl, Gideon thought. But she *was* far too young, and in ways beyond her age.

As though answering a call, the waitress chose that moment to come close and drape an arm around Gideon's shoulder. He slid his own around her waist and pulled her close. "Now this," he told Johnny, "is the kind of woman for me. Solid and mature. Dedicated. Appreciative." He turned to her. "What do you say, Cookie? Want to go for a ride, you and me?"

Cookie snapped her gum while she thought about it, then planted a kiss on his nose. "Not tonight, big guy. I gotta work till twelve, and you'll be sound asleep by then. Hear you landed a big new job."

"Yup."

"Hear it's on the coast."

"Yup."

"Now why'd you do that for, Gideon Lowe? Every time you sign up to build something off somewhere, we don't see you so much. How long is this one gonna take?"

"A while. But I'm commuting. I'll be around."

Cookie snorted. "You better be. If I've gotta look at this guy—" she hitched her chin toward Johnny "—sittin' here with the weight of all your other jobs on his shoulders for long, I'll go nuts."

"John can handle it," Gideon said with confidence. Johnny had been his foreman for years and had never once let him down. "You just be good to him, babe, and he'll smile. Right, John?"

"Right," Johnny said.

Cookie snapped her gum by way of punctuation, then said, "You guys hungry? I got some great hash out back. Whaddya say?"

"Not for me," Johnny said. "I'm headin' home in another five."

Gideon was heading home, too, but not to a woman waiting with dinner. He was heading toward a deskful of paperwork. The idea of putting that off for just a little longer was mighty appealing.

"Is it fresh, the hash?" he asked.

Cookie cuffed him on the head.

"I'll have some," he said. "Fast." He gave Cookie a pat on the rump and sent her off.

"So you're all set to get started up there now that the permit's through?" Johnny asked.

"Yup. We'll break ground on Monday, get the foundation poured the week after, then start framing. October can be a bitch of a month if we get rain, but I really want to get everything up and closed in before the snows come."

"Think you can?"

Gideon thought about that, thought about the complex designs of the condominium clusters and the fact that the crews he used would be commuting better than an hour each way, just like he would. He'd debated using local subs, but he really wanted his own men. He trusted his own men. They knew him, knew what he demanded, and, in turn, he knew they could produce. Of course, if the weather went bad, or they dug into ledge and had to blast, things would be delayed. But with the permit now in hand, they had a chance.

"We're sure as hell gonna try," he said.

They did just that. With Gideon supervising every move, dump trucks and trailers bearing bulldozers and backhoes moved as carefully as possible over the virgin soil of Crosslyn Rise toward the duck pond, which was the first of three areas on the property being developed. After a cluster of eight condominiums was built there, another eight would be built in the pine grove, then another eight in the meadow. The duck pond had the most charm, Gideon thought and was pleased it was being developed first. Done right, it would be a powerful selling tool. That fact was foremost in his mind as the large machines were unloaded and the work began.

Fortunately, he and Carter had paved the way by having things cited, measured and staked well before the heavy equipment arrived. Though they were both determined to remove the least number of trees, several did have to come down to make room for the housing. A separate specialty crew had already done the cutting and chipping, leaving only stumping for the bulldozers when they arrived.

Once the best of the topsoil had been scraped off the top of the land and piled to the side, the bulldozers began the actual digging. Carter came often to watch, sometimes with Jessica, though the marring of the land tore her apart. She had total faith in Carter's plans and even, thanks to Carter's conviction, in Gideon's ability to give those plans form. Still, she had lived on Crosslyn Rise all her life, as had her father before her. The duck pond was only one of the spots she found precious.

Gideon could understand her feelings for the Rise. From the first time he'd walked through the land, he'd been able to appreciate its rare beauty. Being intimately involved in the work process, though, he had enough on his mind to keep sentimentality in check.

Contrary to Jessica, the deeper the hole got, the more excited he was.

There was some rock that could be removed without blasting, some that couldn't but that could be circumvented by moving the entire cluster over just a bit and making a small section of one basement a bit more shallow. But they hadn't hit water, and water was what Gideon had feared. The tests had said they wouldn't, but he'd done tests before and been wrong; a test done in one spot didn't always reveal what was in another. They'd lucked out, which meant that the foundation could be sunk as deeply as originally planned, which meant less grading later and a far more aesthetically pleasing result.

The cellar hole was completed and the forms for the foundation set up. Then, as though things were going too smoothly, just when the cement was to be poured, the rains came. They lasted only three days, but they came with such force—and on a Monday, Tuesday and Wednesday—that it wasn't until the following Monday that Gideon felt the hole had dried out enough to pour the foundation.

He mightn't have minded the layoff, since there were plenty of other things to be done on plenty of other projects that his crews were involved in, had it not been for Elizabeth Abbott's calls.

"She wants to see me," he told Gordon the following Saturday at Jessica and Carter's wedding reception. He'd cornered the banker at one end of the long living room of the mansion at Crosslyn Rise. They were sipping champagne, which Gideon rather enjoyed. He wasn't particularly enjoying his tuxedo, though. He felt slightly strangled in it, but Jessica had insisted. She wanted her wedding to be elegant, and Carter, lovesick fool that he was, had gone right along with her. When Gideon got married—*if* he ever did—he intended to wear jeans.

At the moment, though, that wasn't his primary concern; Elizabeth Abbott was. "I've already put her off two or three times, but she keeps calling. I'm telling you, the woman is either stubborn or desperate. She doesn't take a hint."

"Maybe you have to be more blunt," Gordon suggested. He was pursing his lips in a way that told Gideon he found some humor in the situation.

Gideon didn't find any humor in it at all. He felt a little guilty about what he'd done, leading Elizabeth on. Granted, he'd gotten his permit, which had made the entire eight-member consortium, plus numerous on-call construction workers very happy. None of the others, though, were getting suggestive phone calls.

"Oh, I can be more blunt," he said. "The question is whether there's anything else she can do to slow us down from here on. She's a dangerous woman. She's already shown us that. I wouldn't want to do or say anything to jeopardize this project."

Gordon seemed to take that part a bit more seriously. He thought about it for a minute while he watched Carter lead Jessica in a graceful waltz to the accompaniment of a string quartet. "There's not much she can do now," he said finally. "We have written permits for each of the different phases of this project. She could decide to rescind one or the other, but I don't think she'd dare. Not after she pulled back last time, then changed her mind. I don't think she'd want people knowing that it was Carter last time and you this time."

"It *isn't* me," Gideon said quickly. "I haven't slept with her. I haven't even gone *out* with her, other than that first dinner, and that was business."

"Apparently not completely," Gordon remarked dryly.

"It was business. The rest was all innuendo." His eyes were glued to the bride and groom, moving so smoothly with just the occasional dip and twirl. "Where in the hell did Carter learn to do that? He was born on the same side of the tracks as me. The son of a bitch must've taken lessons."

Gordon chuckled. "Must've."

Gideon followed them a bit longer. "They look happy."

"I'd agree with that."

"He's a lucky guy. She's a sweetie."

"You bet."

"She got any sisters?"

"Sorry."

Gideon sighed. "Then I guess I'll have to mosey over and see if I can't charm that redheaded cutie in the sparkly dress into swaying a little with me. I'm great at swaying." He took a long sip of his champagne. After it had gone down, he put a finger under his collar to give him a moment's free breath, set his empty glass on a passing tray, cleared his throat and was off.

The redheaded cutie in the sparkly dress turned out to be a colleague of Jessica's at Harvard. She swayed with Gideon a whole lot that night, then saw him two subsequent times. Gideon liked her. She had a spark he wouldn't have imagined a professor of Russian history to have. She also had a tendency to lecture, and when she did that, he felt as though he were seventeen again and hanging on by his bare teeth, just trying to make it through to graduation so that he could start doing, full-time, what he'd always wanted, which was to build houses.

So he let their relationship, what of it there had been, die a very natural death. Elizabeth Abbott, though, wasn't so easy to dispose of. The first time she called after the wedding, he said that he had a previously arranged date. The second time, he said he was seeing the same woman and that they were getting pretty involved. The third time, he said he just couldn't date other women until he knew what was happening with this first.

"I'm not saying we have to *date*," Elizabeth had the gall to say in a slithery purr. "You could just drop over here one evening and we could let nature take its course."

He mustered a laugh. "I don't know, Elizabeth. Nature hasn't been real kind to me lately. First we had rain, now an early frost. Maybe we shouldn't push our luck."

The purr was suddenly gone, yielding to impatience. "You know, Gideon, this whole thing is beginning to smell. Have you been leading me on all this time?"

He figured she'd catch on at some point. Fortunately, he'd thought out his answer. "No. I really enjoyed the dinner we had. You're one pretty and sexy lady. It's just that I was madly in love with Marie for years before she up and married someone else. Now she's getting a divorce. I was sure there wouldn't be anything left between us, but I was wrong. So I could agree to go out with you, or drop in at your place some night, but that wouldn't be fair to you. You deserve more than a man with half a heart." *Half a heart.* Not bad, bucko.

Elizabeth wasn't at all impressed. "If she's married and divorced, she's a loser. Weak women make weak marriages. You're looking for trouble, Gideon."

"Maybe," he said, leaving allowance for that should the day come when Elizabeth found out there wasn't anyone special in his life after all, "but I have to see it through. If not, I'll be haunted forever. I have to know, once and for all, whether she and I have a chance."

She accepted his decision, though only temporarily. She continued to call every few nights to check on the status of his romance with Marie. Gideon wasn't naturally a liar and certainly didn't enjoy doing it over and over again, but Elizabeth pushed him into a corner. There were times when he thought he was taking the wrong tactic, when he half wanted to take her up on her invitation, show up at her house, then proceed to be the worst lover in the world. But he couldn't do it. He couldn't demean her—or himself—that way.

So she continued to call, and he continued to lie, all the while cursing himself for doing it, cursing Carter and Gordon for setting him up, cursing Elizabeth for being so goddamned persistent. He was fit to be tied, wondering where it would end, when suddenly, one day, at the very worst possible moment, she appeared at the site.

At least he thought it was her. The hair was blond, the clothes conservative, the figure shapely, the legs long. But it had rained the night before, and the air was heavy with mist, reducing most everything to blandly generic forms.

He was standing on the platform that would be the second floor of one of the houses in the cluster and had been hammering right along with his crew, getting an end piece ready to raise. The work was done. The men had positioned themselves. They were slowly hoisting the large, heavy piece when the creamy figure emerged from the mist.

"Jeez, what's that?" one of the men breathed, diverting the attention of a buddy. That diversion, fractional though it was, was enough to upset the alignment of the skeletal piece. It wobbled and swayed as they tried to right it.

"Easy," Gideon shouted, every muscle straining as he struggled to steady the wood. "Ea-sy." But the balance was lost, and, in the next instant, the piece toppled over the side of the house to the ground.

Gideon swore loudly, then did it again to be heard above the ducks on the pond. He made a quick check to assure himself that none of his men had gone over with the frame. He stalked to the edge of the platform and glared at the splintered piece. Then he raised his eyes and focused on the woman responsible.

2

She was dressed all in beige, but Gideon saw red. Whirling around, he stormed to the rough stairway, clattered down to the first floor, half walked, half ran out of the house and, amid fast-scattering ducks, around to where she stood. Elizabeth Abbott had been a pain in the butt for weeks, but she hadn't disturbed his work until now. He intended to make sure she didn't do it again.

The only thing was that when he came face-to-face with her, he saw that it wasn't Elizabeth. At first glance, though, it could have been her twin, the coloring was so similar. His anger was easily transferred. The fact was that *regardless* of who she was, she was standing where she didn't belong.

"What in the hell do you think you're doing, just popping up out of thin air like that?" he bellowed with his hands on his hips and fury in his voice. Disturbed by his tone, the ducks around the pond quacked louder. "In case you didn't see the sign out front, this is private property. That means that people don't just go wandering around—" he tossed an angry hand back toward the ruined framework "—and for good reason. Look what you've done. My men spent the better half of a day working on that piece, and it'll have to be done over now, which isn't real great, since we were racing to get it up before the rain started again this afternoon. And that's totally aside from the fact that someone could have been hurt in this little fiasco. I carry insurance, lady, but I don't count on people tempting fate. You could have been killed. *I* could have been killed. Any of my *men* could have been killed. A whole goddamned feast worth of *ducks* could have been killed. This is no place for tourists!"

It wasn't that he ran out of breath. He could have ranted on for a while, venting everything negative that he was feeling, only something stopped him, something to do with the woman herself and the way she looked.

Yes, her coloring was like Elizabeth's. She had fair skin, blue eyes, and blond hair that was pulled back into a neat knot. And to some extent, she was dressed as he imagined Elizabeth might have been, though he'd only seen her that one time, when she'd been wearing a dress. This woman was wearing a long pleated skirt of the same cream color as her scarf, which was knotted around the neck of a jacket that looked an awful lot like his old baseball jacket, but of a softer, finer fabric. The jacket was taupe, as were her boots. She wore large button earrings that could have been either ivory or plastic—he wasn't a good judge of things like that in the best of times, and this wasn't the best of times. He was still deeply shaken from what had happened. The look on her face, the way her eyes were wide and her hands were tucked tightly into her pockets, said that she was shaken, too.

"I'm not a tourist," she said quietly. "I know the owner of Crosslyn Rise."

"Well, if you were hoping to find her out here in the rain, you won't. She's working. If you were really a friend of hers, you'd know that."

"I know it. But I didn't come to see Jessica. I came to see what was happening here. She said I could. She was the one who suggested I do it."

If there was one thing Gideon hated, it was people who managed to hold it together when he was feeling strewn. This woman was doing just that, which didn't endear her to him in the least. "Well, she should have let me know first," he barked. "I'm the one in charge here, I ought to know what's going on. If we're having visitors to the site, I can alert my men. There's no reason why they should be shocked the way they were."

"You're right," she agreed. "What's wrong with them? Haven't they ever seen a woman before?"

She was totally innocent, totally direct and quite cutting with that last statement. Gideon shifted her closer in ilk to Elizabeth again. "Oh, they've seen women. They've seen lots of them, and in great and frequent intimacy, I'd wager. But what you just did was like a woman showing up in the men's john."

She had the gall to laugh, but it, too, had an innocent ring. "Cute analogy, though it's not quite appropriate. The sign out front says Private Way. It doesn't say No Women Allowed. Is it my fault if your men get so rattled by the sight of a woman that they become unglued? Face it. You should be yelling at them, not me."

She had a point, he supposed, but he wasn't about to admit it. She had a quiet confidence to her that didn't need stroking. "The fact is that your appearance here has messed us up."

"I'm sorry for that."

"Fine for you to be sorry, after the fact."

"It's better than nothing, which is what I'm getting from you. You could try an apology, too."

"For what?"

"Nearly killing me. If I'd been a little closer, or that piece had shattered and bounced, I'd be lying on the ground bleeding right now."

He gave her a once-over, then drawled, "That wouldn't do much for your outfit."

"It wouldn't do much for your future, unless you have a fondness for lawsuits."

"You don't have the basis for any lawsuit."

"I don't know about that. You and your men were clearly negligent in this case."

Gideon drew himself straighter, making the most of his six-foot-four-inch frame. "So you're judge and jury rolled into one?"

She drew herself straighter to match, though she didn't have more than five foot seven to work with. "Actually, I'm an interior designer. It may well be that I'll be working on this project."

"Not if I can help it," he said, because she was a little too sure of herself, he thought.

"Well, then," she turned to leave, "it's a good thing you're not anyone who counts. If I take this job, I'll be answerable to the Crosslyn Rise consortium, not to some job foreman who can't control his men." With a final direct look, she started off.

Gideon almost let her go. After all, they were far enough from the building that his men hadn't heard what she'd said, so he didn't have to think about saving face, at least, not before them. There was, of course, the matter of his own pride. For years he'd been fighting for respect, and he was doing it now, on several levels, with this project. The final barrier to fall would be with people like this one, who were educated and cultured and arrogant enough to choke a horse.

"You really think you're something, don't you?" he called.

She stopped but didn't turn. "No. Not really. I'm just stating the facts."

"You don't know the facts."

"I know that the consortium controls this project. It isn't some sort of workmen's cooperative."

"In some ways it is. Carter Malloy is in the consortium, and he's the architect of record. Nina Stone is in the consortium, and she'll be marketing us."

There was an expectancy to her quiet. "So?"

He savored the impending satisfaction. "So I'm not just 'some job foreman.' I'm the general contractor here. I also happen to be a member of that consortium."

For another minute, she didn't move. Then, very slowly she turned her head and looked at him, in a new light, he thought.

He touched a finger to the nonexistent visor of the wool cap perched on the top of his head. "Name's Gideon Lowe. See y'in the boardroom." With that, he turned back to his men, yelled, "Let's get this mess cleaned up," and set about doing just that with a definitive spring to his step.

Christine Gillette was appalled. She hadn't imagined that the man who'd blasted her so unfairly was a member of the consortium. Granted, he was better spoken than some of the laborers she'd met. But he'd been bullheaded and rough-hewn, not at all in keeping with the image she had of polished men sitting around a boardroom table with Jessica Crosslyn Malloy at its head.

Unsure as to what to say or do, she turned and left when he returned to his work. During the forty-minute drive back to her Belmont office, she replayed their conversation over and over in her mind and never failed to feel badly at its end. She wasn't normally the kind to cut down other people with words, though she did feel she'd had provocation. She also felt that she was right. She *had* apologized. What more could she do?

The fact remained, though, that in several weeks' time she'd be making a presentation to the Crosslyn Rise consortium. Gideon Lowe would be there, no doubt wearing a smug smile on his handsome face. She was sure he'd be the first to vote against her. Smug, handsome, physical men were like that, she knew. They defined the world in macho terms and were perfectly capable of acting on that principle alone. No way would he willingly allow her to work on his project.

She wished she could say that she didn't care, that Crosslyn Rise was just another project, that something else as good would come along. But Crosslyn Rise was special, not only in terms of the project itself but what it would mean to her. She'd been a designer for nearly ten years, working her way up from the most modest jobs—even freebies, at first—to jobs that were larger and more prestigious. This job, if she got it, would be the largest and most prestigious yet. From a designer's standpoint, given the possibilities between the condominium clusters and the mansion, it was exciting. In terms of her career, it was even more so.

Her mind was filled with these thoughts and others when she arrived at her office. Margie Dow, her secretary, greeted her with a wave, then an ominous, "Sybil Thompson's on the warpath. She's called three times in the last two hours. She says she *needs* to talk with you."

Chris rolled her eyes, took the other pink slips that Margie handed her and headed into her office. Knowing that waiting wouldn't make things any better, she dialed Sybil's number. "Hi, Sybil. It's Chris. I just this minute got back to the office. Margie tells me you have a problem."

"*I* have a problem?" Sybil asked, giving Chris a premonition of what was coming. "*You* have a problem. I just came from Stanley's. Your people put down the wrong rug."

Stanley was Sybil's husband and a lawyer, and the carpeting in question was for his new suite of offices. Chris had been hired as the decorator one short month before and had been quite blunt, when Stanley and his partners had said that they wanted the place looking great within the week, about saying that quality outfittings were hard to find off the rack. They'd agreed to the month, and she'd done her best, running back and forth with pictures and swatches and samples, placing rush orders on some items, calling around to locate others in less well-traveled outlets. Now Sybil was saying that one of those items wasn't right.

Propping a shoulder to the phone to hold it at her ear, Chris went around her desk to the file cabinet, opened it and thumbed through. "I was there yesterday afternoon when it was installed, Sybil. It's the one we ordered."

"But it's too dark. Every tiny little bit of lint shows. It'll look filthy all the time."

"No. It's elegant." She extracted a file. It held order forms, sales receipts and invoices relating to the Thompsons' account. "It goes perfectly with the rest of the decor." She began flipping through.

"It's too dark. It really is. I'm sure we chose something lighter. Check the order form and you'll see."

"That's what I'm doing right now. According to this," Chris studied the slip, "we ordered Bold Burgundy, and Bold Burgundy is the color we installed yesterday."

"It can't be."

"It is." She spoke gently, easily understanding Sybil's confusion. "Everything was done quickly. You looked at samples of carpeting, chose what you wanted, and I ordered it. When things move fast like that, with as much done at one time as you did, it's only natural to remember some things one way and some things another way. I'd do it myself, if I didn't write everything down." Of course, that wasn't the only reason she wrote everything down. The major reason was to protect herself from clients who ordered one thing, saw it installed, then decided that it wasn't what they wanted after all. She didn't know whether Sybil fell into that category or whether this was an innocent mix-up. But Chris did have the papers to back up her case.

"I suppose you're right," Sybil said. "Still, that carpet's going to look awful."

"It won't. The cleaning people come through to vacuum every night. Besides, you don't get half the lint in a lawyer's office as you get at home, especially when you're dealing with the upscale clientele that your husband is. Trust me. Bold Burgundy looks great."

Sybil was weakening. "You think so?"

"I know so. Just wait. Give it a few weeks and see what the clients say. They'll rave about it. I'm sure. That carpeting gives a rich look. They'll feel privileged to be there, without knowing why."

Sybil agreed to wait. Satisfied, Chris hung up the phone and returned the folder to the cabinet. Then she opened another drawer, removed a thick cardboard tube, slid out the blueprints for Crosslyn Rise and spread them on her desk.

Carter was brilliant. She had to hand it to him. What he'd done— taking the Georgian colonial theme from the mansion, modifying columns and balconies, elongating the roof and adding skylights to give just a hint of something more contemporary—was perfect. The housing clusters were subtle and elegant, nestling into the setting as though they'd been there forever.

She sighed. She wanted to work on this project in one regard that had nothing to do with either challenge, prestige or money. It had to do with Crosslyn Rise itself. She thought it was gorgeous, real dream material. If ever she pictured a place she would have liked to call home, it was the mansion on the rise. Doing the decorating for it was the next best thing to living there.

She wanted that job.

Picking up the phone, she dialed Jessica Malloy's Harvard office. Despite what she'd told Gideon, Jessica and she were less friends than acquaintances. They had a mutual friend, who was actually the one to suggest to Jessica that Chris do the work on the Rise. They had met after that and hit it off. Though Chris knew that other designers were being considered for the job, she was sure she could compete—unless Gideon Lowe blackballed her.

"Hi," she said to the secretary who answered, "this is Christine Gillette. I'm looking for Jessica. Has she come back from her honeymoon?"

"She certainly has," the woman said. "Hold on, please."

Less than a minute later, Jessica came on the phone. "Christine, how are you?"

"I'm fine, but, hey, congratulations on your marriage." Last time they'd talked, Jessica had been up to her ears in plans. Apparently the wedding had been something of a last-minute affair thanks to Carter, who had refused to wait once Jessica had finally agreed to marry him. "I take it everything went well?"

"Perfectly," Jessica said.

Chris could hear her smile and was envious. "And the trip to Paris?"

"Too short, but sweet."

And terribly romantic, Chris was sure. Paris was that way, or so she was told. She'd never been there herself. "I'm sure you'll get back some day. Maybe for your fiftieth anniversary?"

"Lord, we'll be doddering by then," Jessica said, laughing, and again Chris was envious. To have someone special, like Jessica had Carter, was precious. So was growing old with that someone special. She hoped Jessica knew how lucky she was.

"I wouldn't worry about doddering. You have years of happiness ahead. I wish you both all the best."

"Thanks, Chris. But enough about me. Tell me what's doing with you. You are getting a presentation ready for us, aren't you?"

"Definitely," Chris said and took a breath, "but I had a small problem this morning. I'm afraid I went out to the Rise to walk around, and I upset some of the men working there."

"You upset them? I'd have thought it'd be the other way around. What they're doing to my gorgeous land upsets me to no end."

"But the mess is only temporary. You know that."

"I know, and I'm really excited about Carter's plans and about what the Rise will be, and I know this was my only out, since I couldn't afford the upkeep, not to mention repairs and renovations—'' She caught her breath. "Still, I have such sentimental feelings for the place that it's hard for me when even the smallest tree is felled.''

"I can understand that," Chris said with a smile. She really liked Jessica, among other things for the fact that she wasn't a money grubber. In that sense, Chris identified with her. Yes, the conversion of Crosslyn Rise would be profitable, but it was a means to an end, the end being the preservation of the Rise, rather than the enhancement of Jessica's bank account. Likewise, Chris sought lucrative jobs like decorating Stanley Thompson's law firm, redecorating the Howard family compound on the Vineyard, and yes, doing Crosslyn Rise, for a greater cause than her own. Her personal needs were modest and had always been so.

"Tell me what happened to you, though," Jessica was saying, returning to the events of that morning.

Chris told her about appearing at the site and jinxing Gideon's crew. "It was an innocent mistake, Jessica. Honestly. I never dreamed I'd disturb them, or I never would have gone. I thought I was being unobtrusive. I just stood there, watching without saying a word, but one of the guys saw me and two others looked and then the damage was done. I really am sorry. I tried to tell your contractor that, but I'm not sure I got through."

"To Gideon? I'm sure you did. He's a sensible guy."

"Maybe when he's cool, but he was pretty hot under the collar when that framework fell, and I don't blame him. Someone could have been hurt, and then there's the time lost in having to redo the piece, and the rain that he was trying to beat. I, uh, think we may have gotten off on the wrong foot, Gideon and I. He was annoyed and said some things that irked me, so I said some irksome things back, and I may have sounded arrogant. I'm not usually like that."

"And now you're worried that he'll stand in the way of your getting this job."

"That, and that if I do get the job, he and I will have trouble working together. He's a macho type. I don't do well with macho types. I kind of pull in and get intimidated, so I guess I put up a wall, and then I come off sounding snotty. I'm sure that's what he thinks."

"He'll change his mind when he meets you in a more controlled setting."

"When there are other people, *civilized* people around, sure. But if we work together, it won't always be in that kind of controlled setting. There won't always be other people around. We'll be spending a lot of time at the site. His subs and their crews may be around, but if today was any indication, they won't be much help."

The telephone line was quiet for a minute before Jessica asked, "Are you saying that you don't want to try for the job?"

"Oh, no!" Chris cried. "Not at all! I *want* the job. I want it a *lot!*"

Jessica sounded genuinely relieved. "That's good, because I really like what I've seen of your work. It has a sensitivity that I haven't found in some of the others' things. I don't want the Rise to look done up, or glossy. I don't want a 'decorated' look. I want something different and special, something with feeling. Your work has that. *You* have that, I think."

"I hope so, at least as far as my work goes," and she was deeply gratified to hear Jessica say it. But that wasn't why she'd called. "As far as this business with Gideon Lowe goes—"

"Don't think twice about it, Chris. You may not believe it, but Gideon is really a pretty easygoing kind of guy."

"You're right. I don't believe it."

Jessica laughed. "He is. Really. But he takes his work very seriously. He may have overreacted this morning, in which case he's probably feeling like a heel, but he'll get over it. This project means a lot to him. He has money invested in it. He'd be the first one to say that when we pick people to do the work, we have to pick the best."

"Is that why he picked himself as the builder?" Chris couldn't resist tossing out. She barely had to close her eyes to picture his smug smile or the broad set of his shoulders or the tight-hipped way he'd walked away from her.

"He's good. I've seen his things. Carter has worked with him before, and *he* says he's good. Gideon's reputation's at stake here, along with his money. He wants the best. And if the best turns out to be you, once we hear all the presentations, he'll go along with it."

"Graciously?" Somehow Chris couldn't see it.

"Graciously. He's a professional."

Chris thought a lot about that in the days following. She figured Jessica might be right. Gideon was a professional. But a professional what? A professional builder? A professional businessman? A professional bruiser? A professional lover? No doubt he had a wife stashed away somewhere, waiting with the television warmed and the beer chilled for the time when he got home from work and collapsed into his vinyl recliner. Chris could picture it. He looked like that type. Large, brawny, physical, he'd be the king of whatever castle he stormed.

Then again, he was a member of the consortium. Somehow that didn't jibe with the image. To be a member of a consortium, one needed money and brains. Chris knew there was good money in building, at least for the savvy builder, and the savvy builder had to be bright. But there were brains, and there were brains. Some were limited to one narrow field, while others were broader. She didn't picture Gideon Lowe being broad in any respect but his shoulders.

That was one of the reasons why she grew more nervous as the day

of the presentation drew near. She burned the midnight oil doing drawings, then redoing them, trying to get them just right. She sat back and
rethought her concept, then altered the drawings yet again to accommodate even the slightest shift. She knew that, given Gideon's predisposi-
tion, she'd have to impress the others in the group in a big way if she
wanted the job.

The day of the meeting was a beautiful one, cool and clear as the best
of November days were along the North Atlantic shore. Gideon felt good.
The first roof section had gone up despite a last-minute glitch that had
kept Carter and him sweating over the plans the weekend before. But
things had finally fit, and if all went well, the second, third and fourth
roof sections would be up by the end of the week. Once that was done,
the snows could come and Gideon wouldn't give a hoot.

It had also been eight whole days since he'd last heard from Elizabeth
Abbott.

So he was in a plucky mood when the eight members of the consortium
held their weekly meeting at seven that evening in Gordon's office. It
occurred to Gideon as he greeted the others and took his place at the
table, that he was comfortable with the group. It hadn't been so at first.
He had felt self-conscious, almost like an imposter, as though he didn't
have any business being there and they all knew it. Over the weeks that
they'd been meeting, though, he'd found himself accepted as a peer. More
than that, his status as the general contractor actually gave him a boost
in their eyes. He was the one member of the group most closely aligned
with the reality of the project.

There were Carter and Jessica, sitting side by side, then the three men
Gordon had brought in from other areas—Bill Nolan, from the Nolan
Paper Mill family in Maine, Ben Heavey, a real estate developer well-
known in the East, and Zach Gould, a retired banker with time and money
on his hands, who visited the site often. Rounding out the group were
John Sawyer, a local bookseller, and Nina Stone, the realtor who would
one day market the project.

Being single, Gideon had taken notice of Nina at the start. They'd even
gone out to dinner once, but neither had wanted a follow-up, certainly
not as a prelude to something deeper. Nina was a tough cookie, an aggressive woman, almost driven. Petite and a little bizarre, she wasn't
Gideon's type at all. By mutual agreement, they were simply friends.

After calling the meeting to order, Gordon, who always sat in as an
advisor of sorts, gave them a rundown of the money situation, then
handed the meeting over to Carter, who called in, one by one, the interior
designers vying for the project.

The first was a woman who worked out of Boston and had done several
of the more notable condo projects there in recent years. Gideon thought
her plans were pretentious.

The second was a man who talked a blue streak about glass and marble and monotonic values. Gideon thought everything about him sounded sterile.

The third was Christine Gillette, and Gideon didn't take his eyes off her once. She was wearing beige again, a suit this time, with a tweedy blazer over a solid-colored blouse and skirt, and he had to admit that she looked elegant. She also looked slightly nervous, if the faint shimmer of her silk blouse was any indication of the thudding of her heart. But she was composed, and obviously well rehearsed. She made her presentation, exchanging one drawing for another with slender fingers as she talked about recreating the ambience that she believed made Crosslyn Rise special. Her voice was soft, but it held conviction. She clearly believed in what she was saying.

Quite against his wishes, Gideon was impressed. Her eyes had glanced across his from time to time, but if she was remembering their last encounter, she didn't let on. She was cool, but in a positive way. Not haughty, but self-assured. She didn't remind him at all of Elizabeth Abbott.

At the end of her presentation she left, sent home, as the others had been, with word that a decision would be made within the week. It was obvious, though, where the group's sentiment lay.

"Christine's plans were the warmest," John Sawyer said. "I like the feeling she captured."

Zach Gould agreed. "I liked her, too. She wasn't heavy-handed like the first, or slick like the second."

"Her estimates are high," Ben Heavey reminded them. He was the most conservative of the group.

"All three are high," Nina said, "but the fact is that if we want this done right, we'll have to shell out. I have a feeling that Christine, more than the others, will be able to get us the most for the least. She seems the most inventive, the least programmed."

"I want to know what Gideon thinks," Carter said, looking straight at him. "He'll be spending more time with the decorator than the rest of us. There are things like moldings, doors, flooring and deck work that I specified in my plans but that are fully changeable if something else fits better with the decor. So, Gideon, what are your thoughts?"

Gideon, who had been slouched with an elbow on the arm of his chair and his chin on his fist, wasn't sure *what* those thoughts were. Christine was the best of the three, without a doubt, but he wasn't sure he wanted to work with her. There was something about her that unsettled him, though he couldn't put his finger on what it was.

"She's the least experienced of the lot," he finally said, lowering the fist and sitting straighter. "What's the setup of her firm?"

Jessica answered. "She's something of a single practitioner. Her office is small. She has one full-time secretary and two part-time assistants, both with degrees in decorating, both with small children. They're job-sharing. It works out well for them, and from what she says, it works out well for Chris.''

"Job-sharing," John mused with a grin. "I like that." They all knew that he was a single parent, and that though he owned his bookstore, he only manned the cash register during those hours when he had a sitter for his son. He had a woman who sold books for him the rest of the time, so he was basically job-sharing, himself.

Job-sharing didn't mean a whole lot to Gideon. Men did the work in his field, and even if their bosses allowed it, which they didn't, they weren't the types to leave at one in the afternoon to take a toddler to gym-and-swim.

He wondered what the story was on Christine Gillette. The résumé she'd handed out said nothing whatsoever about her personal life. He hadn't seen a wedding band, though that didn't mean anything in this day and age. He wondered whether she had a husband at home, and was vaguely annoyed at the thought.

"Does *she* have little kids who she'll have to miss work for each time they get a cold?" he asked, looking slightly miffed.

"Whoa," said John. "Be compassionate, my friend."

But Gideon wasn't a father, and as for compassion, there seemed to be plenty in the room for Christine Gillette without his. "Carter's right. If we decide to use this woman, I'm the one who'll be working most closely with her. Job-sharing may be well and good in certain areas, but construction isn't one. If I have to order bathroom fixtures, and she's off taking the kid to Disney World over school vacation so she can't meet with me, we'll be held back." He thought the argument was completely valid and he was justified to raise it. Christine might be able to charm the pants off this consortium, but if she couldn't come through when *he* needed her, he didn't want her at all! "I keep things moving. That's the way I work. I need people who'll be there."

"Chris will be there," Jessica assured him. "There are no little ones at home. From what I've been told—and from more than one source—she puts in fifty-hour weeks."

"Still," he cautioned, "if she's a single practitioner—"

"With a secretary and assistants," Jessica put in.

"Okay, with a secretary and assistants, but she's the main mover. Both of the other candidates for this position have partners, full partners, people who could take over if something happened."

"What could happen?" Jessica asked. "Chris is in good health. She has a reputation for finishing jobs on time, if not ahead. She's efficient and effective. And she needs this job." She held up a hand before he could comment on that. "I know, I know. You're going to ask me why she's so desperate, and she's not. Not desperate. But this job could give her career a boost, and she wants that. She deserves it."

Gideon didn't want to think that Christine, with her fair-haired fresh-ness, her poise, and legs long enough to drive a man wild, deserved a thing. "Hey, this isn't a charity. We're not in the business of on-the-job training."

"Gideon," Jessica said with a mocking scowl, "I know that. More than *anyone* here, I know it. I've lived on Crosslyn Rise all my life. I'm the one who's being torn apart that I can't leave it the way it always was—" She stopped for a minute when Carter put a hand on her arm. She nodded, took a calming breath. "I want the Rise to be the best it can possibly be, and if Chris wasn't the best, I wouldn't be recommending her."

"She's a friend," Gideon accused, recalling what Chris had told him.

"She's a friend of a friend, but I have no personal interest in her getting this job. If anything, I was wary when my friend mentioned her to me, because I'm *not* in the business of doing favors. Then I looked at pictures of other jobs Chris has done. Now, looking at what she's come up with for us, I'm more convinced than ever that she's the right one." She stopped, had another thought, went on. "Besides, there's a definite ad-vantage to working with someone with a smaller client list. It's the old issue of being a small fish in a big pond, or vice versa. Personally, I'd rather be the big fish in Chris's pond, than a small fish in someone else's, particularly since no one else's ideas for this project are anywhere near as good as hers."

Gideon might have said more, but didn't. Clearly the others agreed with Jessica, as the vote they took several minutes later proved. Christine was approved as the decorator for Crosslyn Rise by a unanimous vote. Or a nearly unanimous one. Gideon abstained.

"Why did you do that?" Carter asked quietly after the meeting had adjourned and most of the others had left.

Gideon didn't have a ready answer. "I don't know. Maybe because she didn't need my vote. She had the rest of you wowed."

"But you like her ideas."

"Yes, I like her ideas."

"Think you can work with her?"

Gideon jammed his fists into his pockets and rocked back on his heels. "Work with her? I suppose."

"So what bothers you?"

"I don't know."

Carter was beginning to have his suspicions, if the look on Gideon's face went for anything. "She's pretty, and she's single."

"Single?" Somehow that made Gideon feel worse.

"Single. Available. Is that a threat?"

"Only if she's on the make. Is she looking for it?"

"Not that I know of." Carter leaned closer. "Word has it she lives like a monk."

Gideon glowered. "Is that supposed to impress me?"

"If you're worried about being attacked, it should."

"Attacked? Me? By *her*? That's the last thing I'm worried about. Listen, man, I've got plenty of women to call when I get the urge. Snap my fingers, there they are."

"Christine isn't likely to do that."

"Don't you know it. She's the kind to snap *her* fingers. Well, I don't come running so fast, and I don't give a damn *how* pretty she is. Long legs are a dime a dozen. So are breasts, bottoms and big blue eyes, and as far as that blond hair of hers goes, it's probably right out of a bottle." He paused only for the quickest breath. "I can work with her. As long as she produces, I can work with her. But if she starts playing games, acting high and mighty and superior, and botching things up so *my* work starts looking shabby, we'll be in trouble. Big trouble."

Actually Gideon was in big trouble already, but it wasn't until three weeks had passed, during which time he couldn't get Christine Gillette out of his mind for more than a few hours at a stretch, that he realized it. The realization was driven home when she called to make an appointment to see him and he hung up the phone with a pounding heart and a racing pulse.

3

Christine was having a few small physical problems of her own as she left Belmont early that Thursday morning and headed north toward Crosslyn Rise. Her stomach was jumpy. Tea hadn't helped. Nor had a dish of oatmeal. Worse, the jitters seemed to echo through her body, leaving a fine tremor in her hands.

It was excitement, she told herself. She'd been flying high since receiving the call from Jessica that she'd landed the Crosslyn Rise job. She'd also been working her tail off since then to get ahead on other projects so that she'd have plenty of time to devote to the Rise. So maybe, she speculated as she turned onto Route 128, the trembling was from fatigue.

Then again, maybe it was nervousness. She didn't like to think so, because she'd never felt nervous this way about her work, but she'd never worked with anyone like Gideon Lowe before. She'd always managed to keep her cool, at least outwardly, with even the most intimidating of clients, but Gideon was something else. He was large, though she'd worked with larger men. He was quick-tempered, though she'd worked with some even more so. He was chauvinistic, though heaven knows she'd met worse. But he got to her as the others hadn't. He stuck in her mind. She wasn't quite sure why.

As the car cruised northward on the highway, she pondered that, just as she had been doing practically every free minute since her interview at the bank three weeks before.

She'd been slightly stunned to see him there—not to see him, per se, but to see how he looked. At the site, he'd been a craftsman. His work boots had been crusted with dirt, his jeans faded and worn. He'd been wearing a down vest, open over a plaid flannel shirt, which was open over a gray T-shirt dotted with sweat in spite of the cold. His dark hair had stuck out in a mess around the wool cap he wore. He needed a shower and a shave.

When she saw him at the bank, he'd had both. His hair was neatly combed, still longer than that of the other men in the room, though cut well. His jaw was smooth and tanned. His shoulders looked every bit as broad under a camel hair blazer as under a down vest. He knew how to knot a tie, even how to pick one, if indeed he'd picked out the paisley one he wore. And in the quick look she'd had, when the men had briefly stood as she entered then left the room, his gray slacks had fit his lean hips nearly as nicely as had a pair of jeans.

He was an extremely good-looking man, she had to admit, though she refused to believe that had anything to do with her nervousness. After all, she'd already decided that he was married, and anyway, she wasn't on the lookout for a man. She had one, a very nice one named Anthony Haskell, who was even-tempered and kind and took her to a show or a movie or to dinner whenever she had the time, which wasn't often. She didn't see him more than two or three times a month. But he was pleasant. He was an amiable escort. That was all she asked, all she wanted from a man—light companionship from time to time as a break from the rest of her life.

So, Gideon Lowe wasn't any sort of threat to her in that regard. Still he was so *physical.* A woman couldn't be within arm's reach of him and not feel his force. Hell, she'd been farther away than that in the boardroom at the bank, and she'd felt it. It started with his eyes and was powerful.

So he was slightly intimidating, she admitted with a sigh, and that was why she was feeling shaky. Of course, she couldn't let him know that. She'd taken the bull by the horns and called him for an appointment, making sure to sound fully composed, for that reason. Gideon looked to be the predatory type. If he sensed weakness, he'd zoom right in for the kill.

Fortifying herself with the determination to do the very best job for Crosslyn Rise that she possibly could, she turned off the highway and followed the shore road. Actually she would have preferred meeting Gideon at the bank or at Carter's office, either of which were safer places, given what had happened on that last misty morning. But Gideon had said that they should see what they were discussing, and she supposed he had a point.

The good news was that the day was sunny and bright, not at all like that other misty one. The bad news was that it was well below freezing, as was perfectly normal for December. There had already been snow, though barely enough to shovel. She couldn't help but wonder how Gideon's men kept from freezing as they worked.

As for her, she'd dressed for the occasion. She was wearing wool tights under wool slacks, a heavy cowl-neck sweater and a long wool coat. Beside her on the seat were a pair of mittens and some earmuffs. It had occurred to her that Gideon was testing her mettle, deliberately subjecting her to adverse conditions, but if so, she wasn't going to come up short. She could handle subfreezing weather. She'd done it many times before.

Of course, that didn't mean that she was thrilled to be riding in her car dressed as heavily as she was. If it hadn't been for the seat belt, she'd have shrugged out of her coat. She'd long since turned down the heat, and even then, by the time she arrived at Crosslyn Rise, she felt a trickle of perspiration between her breasts.

She drove directly to the duck pond over the trail that the trucks had made, but when she reached it, it looked deserted. There wasn't a car or truck in sight. She sat for a minute, then glanced at her watch. They'd agreed on eight-thirty, which it was on the nose. Gideon had told her, a bit arrogantly, she thought, that his men started work an hour before that. But she didn't see a soul working on this cold, crisp morning. She opened her door and stepped out. The only noise came from the ducks, their soft, random quacks a far cry from the sharp sounds of construction.

Slipping back into the car, she turned it around and retraced the trail to the point where the main driveway led to the mansion. She followed it, parked and went up the brick walk, under the ivy-draped portico, to the door. Putting her face to the sidelight, she peered inside.

The place was empty. Jessica and Carter had finally finished clearing things out, putting some in storage, selling others in a huge estate sale held several weekends before. The idea was for Gideon's men to spend the worst of the winter months inside, working on the renovations that would eventually make the mansion into a central clubhouse, health center and restaurant for the condominium complex. Whether Jessica and Carter would buy one of the condo units was still undecided. For the time being, they were living in Carter's place in Boston.

Reaching into her pocket, Chris took out the key Jessica had given her and let herself into the mansion. Seconds later, she was standing in the middle of the rotundalike foyer. Ahead of her was the broad sweeping staircase that she found so breathtaking, to the right the spacious living room lit by knee-to-ceiling windows bare of drapes, to the left the similarly bright dining room.

That was the direction in which she walked, her footsteps echoing through the silent house. As she stood under the open arch, looking from window to window, chandelier to wall sconce, spot to spot where paintings had so recently hung, she imagined the long, carved mahogany table dominating the room once more. The last time it had been used was for the wedding, and though she hadn't been there, she could easily picture its surface covered with fine linen, then silver tray after silver tray of elegantly presented food. Giving herself up to a moment of fancy, she felt the excitement, heard the sounds of happiness. Then she blinked, and those happy sounds were replaced by the loud and repeated honking of a horn.

She hurried back to the front door in time to see Gideon climb from his truck. He was wearing his work clothes with nothing more than the same down vest, which surprised her, given the weather. So he was hot-blooded. She should have guessed that.

"I thought we agreed to meet down there," he said by way of greeting. He looked annoyed. "I've been waiting for ten minutes."

She checked her watch. "Not ten minutes, because I was there five minutes ago. When you didn't show, I thought I'd take a look around here. Where is everyone? It's a gorgeous day. I thought for sure there'd be work going on one place or the other."

"There will be," Gideon said, holding her gaze as he approached. Stopping a few feet away, he hooked his hands on his hips. "The men are picking up supplies. They'll be along." He smirked. "This works out really well, don't you think? We can talk about whatever it is you want to talk about, then you can be long gone by the time they get here, so they can work undisturbed."

His reference to what had happened the last time was barely veiled. The look in his eye took it a step further with the implication that she'd been the one at fault. That bothered her. "You deliberately planned it this way, I take it."

He scratched his head, which was hatless, though from the looks of his hair, he'd just tumbled out of bed, stuck on his clothes and come. The thought made her feel warmer than she already was.

"Actually," he said, "the guys had to pick up the stuff either today or tomorrow anyway. After you and I arranged to meet, today sounded real good."

"It's a shame. I was hoping they'd be here. They'll have to get used to seeing me around. I will be, more and more, once things get going."

His smirk deteriorated. "Yeah. Well..."

"They won't bother *me* if that's got you worried," she went on, gaining strength from her own reassuring tone. "I'm with workmen all the time. It's part of my job. Plumbers, plasterers, painters—you name it, I've seen it. They may not love having me poking around, but at least if they know I'll be wandering in from time to time, they won't be alarmed when it happens."

"My men weren't alarmed," Gideon argued, "just distracted at a very critical time."

"Because they weren't expecting me. They had no idea who I was. Maybe it would help if I met them."

"It wouldn't help at all! You don't have any business with them. You have business with *me*!" He eyed her with sudden suspicion. "You want them around for protection, I think. You don't like being alone with me. Is that it? Is that what this is about? Because if it is—" he held both hands up "—I can assure you, you're safe. I don't fool with the hired help. And I don't fool with blondes."

"I'm relieved to hear *that*," she said, deliberately ignoring the business about "hired help" because it was a potential firecracker. The other was easier to handle. "What's wrong with blondes?"

"They're phony."

"Like rednecks are crude?"

Gideon glared at her for a minute, looking as though there were a dozen other derogatory things he wanted to say. Before he could get any out, though, she relented and said, "Look, I'm sorry. I'm not here to fight. I have a job to do, just like you. Name-calling won't help."

He continued to glare. "*Do* I make you nervous?"

"Of course not. Why would you think that?"

"You were nervous at the meeting at the bank."

And she thought she'd looked so calm. So much for show. "There were eight people—nine, counting the banker—at that meeting. I was auditioning for a job I really wanted. I had a right to be nervous." She wondered how he'd known, whether they'd all seen it or whether those dark gray eyes were just more keen than most.

"Were you surprised when you got the job?" he asked innocently enough.

"In a way. The others have bigger names than I do."

Again, innocently, he asked, "Did you think that I'd vote against you?"

"That thought did cross my mind."

"I didn't."

"Thank you."

"I abstained."

"Oh." She felt strangely hurt, then annoyed. "Well. I appreciate your telling me that. I'm glad to know you think so highly of my work."

He didn't blink. "I think your work is just fine, but I don't relish the idea of working with you. We rub each other the wrong way, you and me. I don't know why, but we do."

That about said it all. There wasn't much she could add. So she stood with her hands buried deep in the pockets of her coat, wondering what he'd say next. He seemed bent on throwing darts at her. She imagined that if she let him do it enough, let him get every little gripe off his chest, they might finally be able to work together.

Unfortunately, the darts stung.

He stared at her for a long, silent time, just stared. Holding her chin steady and her spine straight, she stared right back.

"Nothing to say?" he asked finally.

"No."

He arched a brow. "Nothing at all?"

She shook her head.

"Then why are we here?"

Chris felt a sudden rush of color to her face. "Uh, we're here to discuss business," she said, and hurried to gather her thoughts. Something had happened. Gideon's eyes must have momentarily numbed her mind. "I want to see where you're at with the condos. I thought maybe I could get a bead on things like roofing materials, stairway styles and so on." She stopped, took a deep breath, recomposed herself. "But I told you all that when I called. You were the one who said we should walk through what you've done." She gestured in the direction of the duck pond. "Can we?"

He shrugged. "Sure." He turned back toward his truck. "Climb in. I'll drive you down."

"Thanks, but I'll follow in my car."

He stopped and turned back. "Climb *in*. I'll drive you back here when we're done."

"That's not necessary," she said, but there was a challenge in his look. She wasn't sure whether it had to do with the idea of their being alone in the cab of a pickup or the idea of her climbing into a pickup, period, but in either case she had a point to make. "Okay. Let me get my purse." Crossing the driveway to her car, she took the large leather satchel in which she carried pen and paper, along with other necessities of life such as a wallet, tissues, lip gloss and appointment book. Hitching the bag to her shoulder, she grabbed her earmuffs and mittens. Then, putting on a show of confidence, she walked to the passenger's side of the truck, opened the door and climbed up.

"That was smooth," Gideon remarked.

She settled herself as comfortably as she could, given that she felt rattled. "My father is an electrician. I've been riding around in trucks all my life." And she knew how intimate they could be. A truck was like a man's office, filled with personal belongings, small doodads, tokens of that man's life. It also had his scent. Gideon's was clean, vaguely leathery, distantly coffee flavored, thanks to a half-filled cup on the console, and overwhelmingly male. She felt surrounded by it, so much so that it was a struggle to concentrate on what he was saying.

"Funny, you don't look like the type."

She swallowed. "What type?"

"To have an electrician for a father. I'd have thought your old man would be the CEO of some multinational corporation. Not an electrician."

Another dart hit home. She bristled. "There's nothing wrong with being an electrician. My father is honest and hardworking. He takes pride in what he does. *I'm* proud of what he does. And who are *you* to say something like that?"

"You asked. I answered." He shrugged. "I still don't peg you as the type to be around trucks."

"You think I'm lying?"

"No. But I think you could."

"What's *that* supposed to mean?"

"That I'd more easily believe you if you said you've had a silver spoon in your mouth for most of your life, got bored with doing nothing, so decided to dabble around as a decorator. Real estate and interior decorating—those are the two fields women go into when they want people to think they're aggressive little workers."

That dart hurt more than the others, no doubt because she was already bruised. "You don't know what you're talking about," she said.

"If the shoe fits, wear it."

His smug look did it. Turning to face him head-on, she said, "Well, it doesn't. And, quite frankly, I resent your even suggesting it. I work hard, probably harder than you do, and so do most of the women I know in *either* of the fields you mentioned. We have to work twice as hard to get half the respect, thanks to people like you." She took a fast breath. "And as for 'types,' I didn't have a silver spoon in my mouth at birth or at any *other* time in my life. My parents couldn't afford silver, or silk, or velvet, but they gave me lots and lots of love, which is clearly something you know nothing about. I feel badly for your wife, or your woman, whoever the hell it is you go home to at night." She reached for the door. "I'll take my own car, after all. Being cooped up in a truck with you is oppressive." In a second, she was out the door and looking back at him. "Better still, I think maybe we'd better do this another time. I'm feeling a little sick to my stomach."

Slamming the door, she stalked back to her car. She was trembling, and though she doubted he could see, she wouldn't have cared. She felt pervasive anger and incredible hurt, neither of which abated much as she sped back to Belmont. By the time she was back in her office, sitting at her desk with the door closed on the rest of the world, she was also feeling humiliated.

He'd won. He'd badgered her and she'd crumbled. She couldn't believe she'd done that. She prided herself on being strong. Lord knows, she'd had to overcome adversity to get where she was. She'd faced critics far more personal and cutting than Gideon Lowe and survived. With him, though, she'd fallen apart.

She was ashamed of herself.

She was also frightened. She wanted, *needed* to do Crosslyn Rise. By running, she may well have blown her credibility. If she'd thought working with Gideon was going to be hard before, it could well be impossible now. He'd seen her weakness. He could take advantage of it.

He could also spread word among the consortium members about what had happened, but she doubted he'd do that. He wasn't exactly an innocent party. He wouldn't want the others to know of his part. He had an image to protect, too.

Then again, he could lie. He could tell them that she made appointments, showed up, then took off minutes later. He could say that she wasted his time. He could suggest that she was mentally unbalanced.

If he spread that kind of word around, she'd be in a serious fix. Crosslyn Rise was supposed to make her career, not break it!

What to do, what to do. She sat at her desk with her feet flat on the floor, her knees pressed together, her elbows on the glass surface, her clasped hands pressed to her mouth, and wondered about that. She could call Jessica, she supposed. But she'd done that once regarding Gideon. To do it again would be tattling. Worse, it would smack of cowardice. Jessica might well begin to wonder what kind of woman she'd hired.

Nor could she call Carter. Gideon was his friend.

And she certainly couldn't call Gideon. They'd only get into another fight.

But she had to do something. She'd committed herself to Crosslyn Rise. Her reputation, her future was on the line.

The phone rang. She watched the flashing light turn solid when Margie picked it up. Distractedly she glanced at the handful of pink slips on the desk, all telephone messages waiting to be answered. She shuffled them around. Nothing interesting caught her eye.

The intercom buzzed. "Chris, you have a call from a Gideon Lowe. Do you want to take it, or should I take a message?"

Gideon Lowe. Chris's pulse skittered, then shot ahead. She didn't want to talk with him now. She was still stinging from his last shots. And embarrassed. And confused. And feeling less sure of herself than she had in years and years.

Did she want to take the phone? *No!* But that was foolish.

Bolstering herself with a deep breath, she said to Margie, "I'll take it." But she didn't pick up Gideon's call immediately. It took a few deep breaths, plus several seconds with her eyes shut tight before she felt composed enough. Even then, her finger shook when she punched in the button.

"Yes, Gideon." She wanted to sound all business. To her own ear though, she sounded frightened, just as she was feeling inside. She waited for him to blast her about driving off, leaving their meeting almost before it had begun. But he didn't say a thing. She looked at the telephone, thinking that maybe they'd been cut off. "Hello?"

"I'm sorry," he said in as quiet a tone as she'd heard from him yet. "That was not very nice of me. I shouldn't have said those things. Any of them."

"Then why did you?" she cried, only then realizing how personally she'd taken his barbs. She didn't understand *why* they bothered her so, since she and Gideon weren't anything more to each other than two people temporarily working together. But the fact was that they did, and she was upset enough to lose the cool she'd struggled to gain in the moments before she'd picked up the phone.

"Do you have something special against me?" she asked. "Have I ever done anything to you that warrants what you've been doing? I mean, I wandered innocently onto the site one day and was standing there, minding my own business, when your men saw me and botched the work they were doing. Forget that it wasn't my fault. I apologized, but it didn't make any difference. You've had it in for me ever since. Am I missing something here? Do I remind you of someone else, maybe someone unpleasant, someone who hurt you once, or who let you down? Why do you *hate* me?''

She ran out of breath. In the silence that ensued, she heard all that she'd blurted out and was appalled. She'd blown professionalism to bits, but then, that was something she seemed to do a lot in Gideon's company. She was debating hanging up the phone and burying her head in the trash can when he spoke again. His voice was still low. He actually sounded troubled.

''I don't hate you. I just look at you and...something happens. I can't explain it. Believe me, I've been trying. I've worked with lots of people over the years, lots of women, and I've never been this way before. People usually think I'm easygoing.''

Chris recalled Jessica saying something to that extent. She hadn't believed it then, and she didn't believe it now. ''Easygoing, like an angry bull,'' she murmured.

''I heard that. But it's okay. I deserve it.''

In response to the confession, she softened a bit. ''If you've never been this way before, then it's me. What is it I'm doing wrong? I'm trying. Really I am. I'm trying to be agreeable. I felt we should talk, because that's part of my job, and when you wanted to meet at the site, I agreed, even though it wasn't my first choice. I try to overlook some of the things you say, but they hurt, you know. I'm not a shallow person. I haven't gotten anything in life for free. I work hard at what I do, and I'm proud of that. So why do I annoy you so much?''

He was a minute in answering, and then he didn't get out more than a word when he was cut off by the operator. ''All right, all right,'' he muttered. ''Hold on Chris.''

She was puzzled. ''Where are you?''

She heard the clink of coins, then, ''At a pay phone in town. The phones have been taken out at the Rise, and none of the ones on the street take credit cards. Can you believe that? We're building a complex that's state-of-the-art as far as living goes, in the middle of a town that's old-fashioned as hell. I'm probably gonna have to get a car phone before this project is done.''

''Truck phone.''

''Hmm?''

She sat back in her chair. ''You drive a truck. Wouldn't you call it a truck phone?''

''I don't know. Do they? The guys who make them?''

''Beats me.''

''You don't have a phone in your car?''

''No. They're expensive. Besides, I like silence when I drive. It gives me a chance to think.''

''Aren't you worried about making the most of every minute?'' he asked.

"I am. Making the most, that is. Thinking is important."

"Yeah, but all I hear from people is that I could be answering phone calls, communicating with clients, even getting new jobs if I had a phone in my car. Don't all those things apply to you?"

Chris had heard the arguments, too. "If someone is so desperate for my work that they can't wait until I get back into my office to talk with me, I don't want the job. You can bet it would be a nightmare. Even the most simple jobs run into snags. But one where the client wants instant satisfaction? I'll pass those up, thanks. I'm no miracle worker." She tacked on a quiet, "I wish I was."

"If you were, what would you do?"

She took another deep breath, a calmer one this time. She'd settled down, she realized. When he wasn't yelling at her, Gideon's deep voice was strangely soothing. "Wave my magic wand over you so that whatever it is that bugs you about me would disappear. I want to do a good job at Crosslyn Rise. I'm a perfectionist. But I'm also a pacifist. I can't work in an atmosphere of hostility."

"I'm not feeling hostile now."

She thought about the conversation they were having, thought about the civility that they'd somehow momentarily managed to achieve. Her heart started beating faster, in relief, she figured. "Neither am I."

"That's 'cause we're talking on the phone. We're not face-to-face."

"What is it about my *face* that bugs you, then?"

"Nothing. It's beautiful."

The unexpected compliment left Chris speechless. Before she had a chance to start stammering simply to fill in the silence, Gideon said, "You guessed right, though. That first time, I thought you were someone else. She'd been such a royal pain in the butt that I guess I took my frustration out on you." Elizabeth had called the week before; he told her he was still seeing Marie. "After that, I couldn't confuse you with her. You're different."

Chris didn't know whether that was a compliment or not. She was still basking in the first, though she felt foolish for that. What did it matter that Gideon thought she was beautiful? He was someone she'd be working with. By all rights, she should be furious that he was thinking of her in terms of looks rather than ability. He was as sexist as they came. And as deceitful, if indeed he was married.

"Uh, Chris?" He sounded hesitant.

"Yes."

"I think there's something we ought to get straight right about now. What you said before in the truck about me and a wife or a woman or whoever—"

Her heart was hammering again. "Yes?"

"There isn't any wife. I'm not married. I was once, for a real short time, years ago. But I liked having fun more than I liked being married. So it died."

Chris felt a heat in the area of her breasts that had nothing to do with her heavy cowl-neck sweater. She almost resented his saying what he'd said, though deep down she'd known he wasn't married. But they had actually been getting along. Now, having his availability open and confirmed threw a glitch into the works. "Why are you telling me this?"

"Because I think it's part of the problem. For me, at least. I'm single, and you're single. Every time I look at you I get a little bothered."

"Bothered?" If he meant what she thought he meant, they were in trouble. Suddenly she didn't want to know. "Listen, if you're worried about me, don't be. I won't accost you. I'm not in this business to pick up men."

"That's not what I meant—"

"In fact," she cut in, "I'm not looking for a man at all. There's someone I've been seeing for a while, and he's a really nice guy, but to tell you the truth, I don't even have much time for him. I spend all my free time working."

"What fun is *that*?" Gideon asked indignantly.

On the defensive again, she sat straighter. "It's plenty of fun. I enjoy my work—except for those times when I get cut to ribbons by builders who take pleasure in making other people miserable."

"I don't do it on purpose. That's what I'm trying to tell you."

"Well, try something else. Try changing. Don't assume things about me, or make value judgments. Just because I think or act differently from you, doesn't mean that I'm wrong. I don't tell you what to like. Don't tell *me* what to like."

"I'm not *doing* that," Gideon insisted. "I'm just expressing my opinion. So I express it in a way that you find offensive. Well, maybe you're too sensitive."

"Maybe I'm human! Maybe I like to get along with people. Maybe I like to please them. Maybe I like to have their respect every once in a while."

"How can you have my respect," he threw back, "if you don't hang around long enough for me to get to know you? You got upset by what I said, so instead of sticking around and fighting it out, you took off. That doesn't solve anything, Chris."

Her hand tightened on the phone. "Ah. I knew we'd get around to that sooner or later. Okay. Why don't you say what you think, just get it off your chest. I'm already feeling crushed. A little more won't hurt."

He didn't say a word.

"Go on, Gideon. Say something. I know you're dying to. Tell me that I'm a coward. Tell me that you were being overly optimistic when you abstained in that vote. Tell me that you seriously doubt whether I have the wherewithal to make it through the decorating of Crosslyn Rise." She paused, waiting. "Tell me I'm in the wrong field. Tell me I should be doing something like secretarial work. Or teaching. Or waitressing." She paused again. "Go ahead. Be my guest. I'm steeled for it." A third time, she paused. Then, cautiously she said, "Gideon?"

"Are you done?"

She was relieved that he hadn't hung up. "Yes."

"Want to meet me for lunch tomorrow?"

That wasn't what she'd expected to hear. She was taken totally off guard. "Uh, uh—"

"Maybe you were right. Maybe what we need is a neutral place to talk. So you choose it. Wherever you want to go, we'll go. I can drive down there, you can drive up here, we can meet somewhere in the middle. But we both have to eat lunch. We can even go dutch if you want. I'm perfectly willing to pay, but you women have a thing about a man treating you. Heaven forbid you might feel a little indebted to him."

"That's not why we do it. We do it because it's the professional thing to do."

"If that's so, why is it that when I go out for a business lunch with another guy, one of us usually pays, with the understanding that the other'll do it the next time? Sometimes it's easier just to charge it rather than split the bill in two. But modern women have to make things so hard."

"Then why do you bother with us?"

"I don't, usually. On my own time, I steer as far away from you as I can get. Give me the secretary or the teacher or the waitress any day. They're not hung up on proving themselves. They like it when a man opens the door for them, or helps them with their coat, or holds their chair. They like to be treated like women."

"So do I."

"Could've fooled me."

"You were the one who suggested we go dutch. If you want to pay for lunch, be my guest. You probably make a whole lot more money than I do, anyway."

"What makes you think that?" he asked.

"You've invested in Crosslyn Rise, haven't you?"

"Yeah. With every last cent I had to my name. As far as cash flow goes, I'm just about up the creek."

"Was that a wise thing to do?"

"Ask me that two years from now and I may have an answer. I've got a whole lot riding on—" The telephone clicked, cutting him off. He came back in ripe form. "Damn, I'm out of change. Look, Chris, will you meet me or not?"

"Uh, tomorrow?" She looked at her calendar. "I wouldn't be able to make it until two. My morning's wild."

The phone clicked again. "Two is fine," he said hurriedly. "Name the place."

"Joe's Grille. It's in Burlington. Right off the Middlesex Turnpike."

"Joe's Grille at two. See you then."

She wasn't sure whether he hung up the phone or the operator cut him off, but after a minute of silence, she heard a dial tone. As the seconds passed, it seemed to grow louder and more blaring, almost like an alarm, and well it might have been. She'd arranged to see Gideon again. Granted, the conditions were more to her liking this time, but still she felt uneasy.

He was a very, very confusing man, annoying her most of the time, then, in the strangest ways and when she least expected it, showing charm. Not that she was susceptible to the charm. She'd made it clear that she wasn't available, and it was true. Still, she wished he was married. She'd have felt safer that way.

But he wasn't. And the fact was that they'd be working together. It helped some to know how much Crosslyn Rise meant to him. If he was telling the truth about his financial involvement, he couldn't afford to have anything go wrong, which ruled out his sabotaging her work. And he hadn't suggested that she pull out of the project. She'd given him the chance, had all but put the words into his mouth, but he hadn't used them.

That was the up side of the situation. The downside was the lunch that she'd stupidly agreed to. A meeting at the bank would have been better. Being in a restaurant, having lunch with Gideon seemed so...personal.

But she was a professional with a job to do. So she'd meet him, and she'd be in full control, and she'd show him that she was done being bullied. She could stand up to him. It was all a matter of determination.

4

Gideon was looking forward to lunch. He felt really good after their phone conversation, as though they'd finally connected, and that mattered to him. Despite everything that he found wrong with Chris, she intrigued him. She wasn't what he'd first assumed her to be. He suspected she wasn't what, even now, he assumed her to be. She was a mystery, and he was challenged.

He was also excited in a way that had nothing to do with making progress on Crosslyn Rise and everything to do with having a date with an attractive woman. Because it was a date. Chris could call it a professional lunch, and it was, a little, but in his mind it was first and foremost a date. His motives were far from professional. He wanted to get to know Chris, wanted to start to unravel the mystery that she was. "Start" was the operative word, of course, because he envisioned this as only the first of many dates. She had already proclaimed that she wasn't looking for a man, so clearly she wasn't going to be rushed. But there'd be fun in that. Gideon was anticipating the slow, increasingly pleasant evolution of their relationship.

This first date was very important in that it would be laying the groundwork for those to come. For that reason, he was determined to be on his best, most civil and urbane behavior. He would have liked to add sophisticated or cultured to that, only he wasn't either of those things. Pretending might have worked with Elizabeth, but it wouldn't work with Chris. She'd see through him in a minute. She was sharp that way—knew damn well that he hadn't been waiting at the duck pond for ten minutes and caught him on it, though he'd only exaggerated a little. But he didn't want to be caught again, not when he wanted to impress. So he'd be himself, or that part of himself that would be most apt to please her.

For starters, he dressed for the occasion. Though he was at Crosslyn Rise at seven-thirty with the rest of his men and put in a full morning of work, he left them on their own at midday and drove all the way home to clean up. After showering and shaving, he put on a pair of gray slacks, a pink shirt, a sweater that picked up variations of those shades, and loafers. It was his yuppie outfit, the one he'd bought in Cambridge on the day he had decided to invest in Crosslyn Rise. He figured that he owed himself a small extravagance before the big splurge, and that he could use the clothes. He hated shopping. But he had to look the part of the intelligent investor, and so he'd bought the outfit, plus a blazer, two

ties and a blue shirt. But he liked the pink one, at least to wear for Chris.
She'd appreciate the touch.

After all, rednecks didn't wear pink.

He also put on the leather jacket that his mother had sent him several
birthdays ago. It was one of the few gifts she'd given him that he liked.
Most of the others were too prissy, reminding him of all she wanted him
to be that he wasn't. The leather jacket, though, was perfect. It was conservative in style and of the richest brown leather he'd ever seen. He
wore it a lot.

Leaving his truck in the yard, he took the Bronco, allowing plenty of
time for traffic, and headed for Burlington. The route was the same to
Crosslyn Rise. There were times when he felt he could do it in his sleep,
except that he liked driving. Chris used her road time to think; he used
his to relax, which was why he resisted getting a car phone, himself. A
phone would interfere with his music. With sophisticated stereo setups in
both of his vehicles, his idea of heaven was cruising along the highway
at the fastest speed the traffic would bear, listening to Hank Jr., Willie or
Waylon.

He didn't listen to anyone now, though, because he was too busy thinking about Chris. She really was a knockout, pretty in a soft-as-woman
kind of way, despite the air of professionalism she tried to maintain. She
turned him on. Oh, yeah. There was no mistaking the heat she generated.
He was old enough and experienced enough—and blunt enough—to call
a spade a spade. Sure, he was a little nervous to see her. Sure, it was
cold outside. Sure, he hadn't eaten since six that morning. But the tiny
tremors he felt inside weren't from any of those things. They were from
pure, unadulterated lust.

That was the last thing he wanted Chris to know. And since it got
worse the longer he thought about her—and since she was probably sharp
enough to see *that* first thing, if he didn't do something to cool off—he
opened the windows, turned on the music and began to sing at the top
of his lungs. By the time he turned off the Middlesex Turnpike into the
parking lot of Joe's Grille, his cheeks were red from the cold, his voice
faintly hoarse, and his hands, as they pushed a comb through his windblown hair, slightly unsteady. He pulled on his jacket, checked the rearview mirror one last time to make sure he looked all right, took a breath
and stepped out.

He was early. They were supposed to meet at two, and it was ten before
the hour. He went into the restaurant just to make sure she hadn't arrived,
gave his name to the hostess, along with a five for a good table and a
wink for good cheer, then entered the adjoining mall and, hands stashed
in his pockets, started walking around. With less than three weeks to go
before Christmas, the holiday season was in full bloom. One store window was more festive, more glittery, more creative than the next. Almost
as an escape from tinsel overload, he found himself gravitating toward

the center of the mall, where a huge tree stood, decorated not with the usual ornaments, but with live flowers.

He stood there for a while, looking at the tree, thinking how pretty it was and that he didn't think he'd ever seen one quite like it before.

"I'm sorry," someone gasped beside him. He looked quickly down to see Chris. Her cheeks were flushed, and she was trying to catch her breath, but there was the hint of a smile on her face, even as she pressed a hand to her chest. "I got here a few minutes early, so I thought I'd pick up a gift or two, only the salesperson messed things up at the register and didn't know how to correct it, so I had to stand around waiting while he got his supervisor. The store was at the other end of the mall. I had to race back." She barely paused. "Have you been here long?"

"Not long," he said. He wondered if she was babbling because she was nervous, and hoped it was a good sign. "I was just wandering around. Everything's so pretty." But Chris took the cake. She was wearing a navy sweater and slacks and a long beige coat with a wool scarf hanging down the lapels. She might have pulled off the business look if it hadn't been for her cheeks and her hair, a few wisps of which had escaped its knot and were curling around her face, and her mouth, which looked soft, and her eyes, which were blue as the sky on a clear summer's day.

It struck him that she was more beautiful than the tree, but he wasn't about to say it. She thought she was here on business, and business partners didn't drool over each other. So he looked back at the tree. "I've never seen one decorated this way. The flowers are pretty. How do they stay so fresh?"

He hadn't actually been expecting an answer, but Chris had one nonetheless. "The stem of each is in a little tube that holds enough water to keep the flowers alive. If they're cut at the right time, lilies last a while."

"Those are lilies?"

"Uh-huh. Stargazers. I use them a lot in silk arrangements for front foyers or buffets or dining room tables. They're elegant."

He eyed her guardedly. "You do silk arrangements?"

"No. Someone does them for me. She's the artist, but whenever I see an arrangement of fresh-cuts that I like, I make a note and tell her about it later."

"I hate silk arrangements. They look fake."

"Then you've never seen good ones. Good silks are hard to tell from the real thing."

"I can tell. I can always tell."

"You've seen that many?"

"Enough to know that it's a matter of moisture." His gaze fell to her mouth. "I don't care how good the silk is, it doesn't breathe the way a real flower does. It doesn't shine or sweat. A real flower is like human skin that way." He brushed her cheek with the pad of his thumb, feeling the smoothness, the warmth, the dewiness that her run down the mall had brought. He also felt his own body responding almost instantaneously, so he cleared his throat, stuck his hand back into his pocket and said, "Are you hungry?"

She nodded.

"Wanna get lunch?"

"Uh-huh." She sounded breathless still.

Gideon wasn't rushing to attribute that breathlessness to anything other than the most innocent of causes, but he hadn't missed the way her eyes had widened just a fraction when he'd touched her face or the fact that she seemed glued to the spot.

He hitched his chin toward the restaurant.

With an effort, it seemed, Chris nodded again, then looked down to make sure that she had her bundle safely tucked under her arm.

"Can I carry that for you?" he asked.

"Uh, no. It's okay."

They started off. "What did you buy, anyway? Or is it a secret, maybe something black and sexy for your mom?" He faltered, suddenly wondering whether he'd put his foot in his mouth. "Uh, she's still around, isn't she?"

Chris smiled. The affection she so clearly felt for her mother brought added warmth to her eyes. "Quite. She's an energetic fifty-five. But she'd be embarrassed out of her mind to get something black and sexy. She doesn't define herself that way. No, this is for another relative. Something totally different. As a matter of fact, I don't know *what* to get my mother."

"What does she do?" Gideon asked, hoping to get hints about Chris through this mother she cared for.

"She reads, but books are so impersonal."

"What else does she do?"

"Needlepoint, but she's already in the middle of three projects and doesn't need a fourth."

"What else?"

"She cleans and cooks—" this was offered facetiously "—but I don't think she'd appreciate either a bottle of window cleaner or a tin of garlic salt."

Gideon was picturing a delightful homebody, someone he'd feel comfortable with in a minute. "How about a clay pot?"

Chris drew in her chin. "Clay pot?"

He'd seen them advertised on the back of one of the dozens of unsolicited catalogues that came in the mail every week. Rolled tight, those catalogues were kindling for his fire. Once in a while, something registered while he was doing the rolling. "You know, the kind you cook a whole meal in, kind of like a Crockpot, but clay." They'd reached the restaurant. He held the door for her to go through first.

"How do you know about clay pots?" she asked, shooting him a curious glance as she passed.

He shrugged. With a light hand on her waist, he guided her toward the hostess, who promptly led them to the quietest table in the house. Unfortunately, that wasn't saying a whole lot. The restaurant was filled, even at two, with a cross of business types from nearby office buildings and shoppers with kids. The business types were no problem, but the kids and their mothers were loud. Noting that the table the hostess had given them—a table for four, at that—was set slightly apart from the others, Gideon felt his money had been well spent. Every little bit of privacy helped when a man was pursuing his cause.

"Would you like me to hang up your coat?" he asked just before Chris slid into her seat.

She glanced at the nearby hooks. "Uh, okay." Depositing her bag and purse on one of the free chairs, she started to slip the coat off. Gideon took it from her shoulders and hung it up, then put his own jacket beside it. When he returned to the table, she was already seated. He took the chair to the right of hers, which was where the hostess had set the second menu, but no sooner had he settled in than he wondered if he'd made a mistake. Chris was sitting back in the pine captain's chair with her hands folded in her lap, looking awkward.

"Is this where I'm supposed to sit for a business lunch?" he asked, making light of it. "Or should I be sitting across from you?"

"I think," she said, glancing out at the crowd, "that if you sit across from me, I won't be able to hear a word you say. I thought most of the kids would be gone by now, but I guess at Christmastime anything goes."

"I take it you've been here before."

"Uh-huh. My family comes a lot."

"Family," he prodded nonchalantly, "as in mother and father?"

"And the rest. I'm the oldest. The youngest is just fifteen. It's harder now than it used to be, but we still try to do things together whenever we can." She opened her menu, but rather than looking at it, she took a drink of water. "The club sandwiches are good here. So are the ribs. I usually go for one of the salads. There's a great Cobb salad, and a spinach one."

"I hate spinach."

The blunt statement brought her eyes finally to his. "Like you hate silk flowers?"

"Pretty much." He paused, held her gaze, watched her cheeks turn a little pink and her slender fingers tuck a wisp of hair behind her ear. Unable to help himself, he said, "I like your outfit. You look nice in navy." He paused again. "Or aren't I supposed to say that at a business lunch?"

She looked at him for another minute, then seemed to relax. "Technically, it is a sexist thing to say."

"It's a compliment."

"Would you give a compliment like that to one of your men?"

"Like that? Of course not. He'd think I was coming on to him."

She arched an eloquent brow.

"I'm not coming on to you," Gideon told her, and in one sense it was true. He'd complimented her because he really *did* like the way she looked, and he was used to saying what he thought. "I'm just telling you you look pretty. It's a fact. Besides, I do give my men compliments. Just not like that."

"Like what, then?"

"Like...hey, man, that's a wild shirt...or...cool hat, bucko."

"Ah," she said gravely. "Man talk." She lowered her eyes to his shirt, then his sweater, and the corner of her mouth twitched. "I'll bet they had choice words to say about what you're wearing now."

Feeling a stab of disappointment, he looked down at himself. "What's wrong with what I'm wearing?"

"Nothing. It's a gorgeous outfit. But it's way different from what I've seen you wearing at the Rise."

It's a gorgeous outfit. Did that ever make him feel good! "Thanks, but I wasn't working in this." He snickered. "You're right. The guys would have kidded me off the lot. No, I went home to change."

She was silent, almost deliberative, for a minute before asking, "Where's home?"

"Worcester."

Her eyes went wide. "Worcester? That's halfway across the state. You're not actually commuting from there to Crosslyn Rise every day, are you?"

He nodded. "I can do it in an hour and a quarter."

"Speeding."

He shrugged.

"And you drove all that way this morning, then drove home, then drove all the way back to meet me?"

"I couldn't very well meet you in my work clothes. You wouldn't have wanted to sit across from me, much less next to me. Besides, I didn't have to drive *all* the way back. Crosslyn Rise is still farther on up."

"But I would have picked some place even closer, if I'd known." Her voice grew softer. "I'm sorry."

"Hey," he said with a puzzled smile, "it's no big thing. I asked you to name the place, and you named it." He looked around. "This is a nice place."

"Hello," the waitress said, materializing between them as though on cue. "My name is Melissa, and I'll be serving you today. May I get you something from the bar?"

Gideon raised his brows toward Chris.

She shook her head. "Tea for me, please."

"And you, sir?"

He wanted a beer, but that wasn't part of the image. Then again, he couldn't see himself ordering wine. So he settled for a Coke. "And maybe something to munch on," he said, waving his fingers a little. "What do you have?"

Chris spoke before Melissa could. "We'll have an order of skins, please. Loaded."

The minute Melissa left, he asked, "How do you know I like skins?"

"Do you?"

"Sure."

"Loaded?"

"Sure."

There was satisfaction in her smile. "So do my father and brothers, and they're all big and physical like you."

Gideon was thinking that being like her father and brothers was a good thing, since she clearly liked them, when he had a different thought. "What about your boyfriend? Does he like them?"

"My boyfriend? Oh, you mean Anthony. Uh, actually, he doesn't."

"So what does he eat when he comes here?"

"He doesn't."

"Doesn't eat?"

"Doesn't come here. He lives in Boston. And he's really not my boyfriend. Just a friend. I don't have time for a boyfriend. I told you that. I'm not interested."

"A girlfriend then?" he asked before he could think to hold his tongue.

She scowled at him. "Why *are* you so offensive." It wasn't a question.

He held up a hand and said softly, "Hey, I'm sorry. It's just that I like to know what's going on. I mean, why is a woman as beautiful and talented as you are still single?"

She threw the ball right back at him. "You're still single. What's *your* excuse?"

"I told you. I blew marriage once."

"A long time ago, you said. But you haven't tried again."

"But I date. I date a whole lot. There's just no one I like well enough to want to wake up to in the morning." He let the suggestiveness of that sink in, along with all the sexy images it brought. He could picture Chris in his bed, could picture it easily, and wondered if she could picture it, too.

She didn't look to be panting. Nor did she speak right away. Finally, slowly she said, "Then you live alone?"

He fancied he detected interest and grabbed onto the thought. "That's right."

"In an apartment?"

"A house. That I built."

A small smile touched the edge of her mouth. "Mmm. I should have guessed." She paused, seemed deliberative again. He guessed that she wasn't sure how personal to get.

"Go on," he coaxed gently. "Ask. I'll answer."

Given permission, she didn't waste any time. "You live all alone in a big house?"

"It's not big. But it's nice. And it's all I need."

"And you take care of yourself—cook, clean, do laundry?"

"I cook. I have someone come in to do the rest." He didn't see anything wrong with that. She couldn't expect that he'd do everything for himself when he had important work to do every day.

"You really do cook?"

"Enough to stay alive." He wondered what she was getting at. "Why?"

"Because you know about clay pots," she mused, and seemed suddenly, seriously pleased. "That's not a bad idea. My mother doesn't have anything like it. It's really a *good* idea. Thank you."

Gideon grinned. "Glad to be of help." Then his eyes widened at the sight of the skins that suddenly appeared on the table. They looked incredible and he was famished.

"Are you ready to order the rest?" Melissa asked.

Chris looked inquiringly at Gideon, but he hadn't even opened his menu. "Some kind of sandwich," he said softly. "You choose. You know what's good."

She ordered a triple-decker turkey club for him and a Cobb salad for herself. Then she hesitated, seeming unsure for a minute.

"Sounds great," he assured her, and winked at Melissa, who blushed and left. When he looked back at Chris, she was reaching into her purse and pulling out a notebook. Tugging a pen from its spiral binding, she opened to a page marked by a clip.

"What are you doing?" Gideon asked. He was being the gentleman, waiting for her to help herself to a potato skin before he dug in.

"I have questions for you. I want to make notes."

"About me?"

"About Crosslyn Rise."

"Oh." He looked longingly at the skins. Taking the two large spoons resting beside them, he transferred one to Chris's plate.

She protested instantly. "Uh-uh. Those are for you."

"I can't eat them all."

"Then you'll have to take them home for supper. All I want is a salad."

"Aha," he breathed, "you're one of those women who's always on a diet." He shot a quick look at her hips. "I don't see any fat."

"It's there."

"Where?"

"There." She sat back in her chair and stared at him.

Fantasize all he might, but that stare told him she wasn't saying a word about her thighs or her bottom or her waist or her breasts, if those were the spots where she imagined there was fat. So he helped himself to a skin and said, "Okay, what are your questions?" He figured that while he was eating, they could take care of business, so that by the time he was done they could move on to more interesting topics.

He had to hand it to her. She was prepared. She knew exactly what she wanted to ask and went right to it. "Will you consider putting wood shingles on the roof?"

"No." He said. "Next question." He forked half a skin into his mouth.

"Why not?"

"Mmm. These are great."

"Why not wood shingles?" she repeated patiently.

"Because they're expensive and impractical."

"But they look so nice."

"Brick does, too, but it's expensive as hell."

She held his gaze without so much as a blink. "That was my next question. Couldn't we use brick in a few select areas?"

"That's not part of Carter's concept. He wants clapboard."

"What do you think?"

"I think you should talk with Carter."

"What do *you* think?"

"I think we can do very well without that expense, too. Next question." He took another skin, cut it in two, downed the half.

"Windows. What about some half-rounds?"

"What about them?"

"They'd look spectacular over the French doors in the back."

Gideon had to agree with her there, but he was a realist. "It's still a matter of cost," he said when he'd finished what was in his mouth. "I based my bid on the plans Carter gave me. Half-rounds are expensive. If I go over budget, it's money out of my pocket any way you see it."

"Maybe you won't have to go over budget," she said hopefully, "not if you get a good deal from a supplier."

"You know a supplier who'll give us that kind of deal?"

Her hope seemed to fade. "I thought you might."

He looked down at his plate as he cut another skin, arching little more than a brow in her direction. "You're the one with connections in the business. Me, I'm on my own." He popped the skin into his mouth.

"You don't have any relatives in construction?"

After a minute of chewing, he said, "None living. My dad was a housepainter. But he's been gone for ten years now."

She sobered. "Ten years. He must have been very young."

"Not so young overall, but too young to die. There was an accident on the job. He never recovered.'' Gideon sent her a pointed look. ''That's one of the reasons I go berserk when I see carelessness at my sites.''

After a minute's quiet, she said, ''I can understand that.'' She'd put down the notebook, had her elbows on the arms of the chair and was making no attempt to look anywhere but at him. ''Were you working with him at the time?''

''No. I worked with him when I was a kid, but I was already into construction when the accident happened. He did a lot of work for me in those last years, but when he fell, it was on another job. The scaffolding collapsed.''

''I'm sorry,'' she said, and sounded it. ''Were you two close?''

''Growing up, he was all I had.''

''Your mother?''

''Left when I was three.''

''Just left?'' Chris asked, looking appalled.

''She met someone else, someone with more promise. So she divorced my dad, married the other guy and moved to California.'' He put down his fork. ''She did well. I have to give her that. She's become a very nice society lady—with silk arrangements all over her house.''

''Ah, but not *good* silks, if you thought they looked fake.'' She smiled for a second, then sobered again. ''Do you see her often?''

''Once, maybe twice a year. She keeps in touch. She even wanted me to come live with her at one point, but I wasn't about to betray my dad that way. Then, after he died, I wasn't about to move. My roots are here. My business is here.'' He smirked. ''She isn't wild about what I do. Thinks it's a little pedestrian. But that's okay. California doesn't tempt me, anyway. I'm not the beach boy type.''

Chris mirrored his smirk. ''Not into surfing?''

''Not quite. Softball and basketball. That's it.''

''That's enough,'' she said with feeling.

''Your father and brothers, too?'' he guessed.

''Brothers,'' she answered. ''They're basketball fanatics.''

''How about you? Are you into exercise?''

''Uh-huh. I do ballet.''

Ballet. He might have known. He had about as much appreciation for ballet as he did for Godiva chocolates. He was a Hershey man all the way. ''Do you dance in shows?''

''Oh, no. Even if I were good enough, which I'm not, and even if I were young enough, which I'm not, I wouldn't have the time. I go to class twice a week, for the fun and the exercise of it. In a slow and controlled kind of way, it's a rigorous workout.'' She took a fast breath. ''So why did you move from painting to construction?''

He wanted to know more about her, but she kept turning the questions back at him, which bothered him, on the one hand, because he wasn't used to talking about himself so much, at least not on really personal matters. For instance, he didn't usually tell people about his mother. Then again, Chris seemed genuinely interested, which made it easy to talk. She wasn't critical. Just curious. As though he were a puzzle she wanted to figure out.

So he'd be her puzzle. Maybe she'd be as intrigued with him as he was with her.

"Painting to construction?" He thought back to the time he'd made the switch, which had been hard, given his father's preference. "Money was part of it. The construction business was booming, while painting just went along on the same even keel. I also had a thing for independence. I didn't want to be just my dad's son. But I guess most of it had to do with challenge." He narrowed an eye. "Ever spend day after day after day painting a house? When I first started, I thought it was great. I could stand up there on a ladder, goin' back and forth with a brush, listening to my music from morning to night. Then the monotony set in. I used to feel like I was dryin' up inside. I mean, I didn't have to *think*."

"You certainly have to do that now."

"Thank you."

"I mean it."

"I know. Believe me, I *know* how much I have to think every day. There are times when it's a major pain in the butt, but I wouldn't trade what I do for any other job."

Chris looked puzzled at that. "But you've invested in Crosslyn Rise. You're a member of the consortium. Isn't that like stepping over the line?"

"I'm kind of straddling it right now."

"Then it's not a permanent move into development?"

Gideon thought about it for a minute. A month before, he'd have had a ready answer, but he didn't have one now. "I invested in the Rise because I've never invested in a project before. It was a step up the ladder, something I wanted to try, something I *had* to try." He frowned down at his plate, nudging it back and forth by tiny degrees. "So I'm trying it, and I'm finding that I really want it to work, I mean, *really* want it to work, and there's pressure that goes with that." His eyes sought hers. "Do you know what I mean?"

She nodded, but he wasn't done. "The pressure isn't all fun. And then there's the thing about working in an office, versus working at a site. I like the meetings at the bank. I like being involved at that level. But when the meetings adjourn and we all shake hands, there isn't the feeling of accomplishment that I get at the end of a day when I stand back and see the progress that's been made on a house. Or the feeling," he said, coming alive just at the thought, "of standing back and seeing the finished product, seeing people move in, seeing them live in a place I've built and loving it. I could never give up building. I could never give up that kind of satisfaction."

He said back quietly in his chair, thinking about what he'd said, feeling sheepish. "Funny, I hadn't quite put all those thoughts into words before. You're a positive influence."

"No," she said softly. "You'd have said those things, or recognized that you felt them, sooner or later. I just happened to ask the question that triggered it, that's all."

"I'll bet you do that a lot for people. It takes a good listener to ask a good question. You're a good listener."

She shrugged, then looked quickly up and removed a hand from the table when Melissa delivered their lunches. When they were alone again, she said, "Listening is important in my line of work. If I don't hear what a client is saying, I can't deliver." She dunked her tea bag into the minicarafe of hot water. "Speaking of which, I have more questions about Crosslyn Rise."

"If they involve spending money—"

"Of course they involve spending money," she teased, her blue eyes simultaneously dead serious and mischievous.

"Then you might as well save your breath," he warned, but gently. "We're locked into our budget, says Ben Heavey. He's one of the men you met at the bank that night, and a tightwad? He gives new meaning to the word."

"But what if I can save money here—" she held out her right hand, then her left "—and use it there?"

He pointed his fork at her plate. "Eat your salad."

"Take the flooring. Carter's blueprints call for oak flooring throughout the place, but the fact is that in practically every home I've decorated, the people want carpeting in the bedrooms. If we were to do that, substituting underlayment for oak in the bedrooms, even just the upstairs bedrooms, with the money we'd save, we could pickle the oak downstairs. *That* would look *spectacular*."

"Pickled oak is a bitch to keep clean."

"Only if you have little kids—"

"*I'd* have trouble with it—"

"Or big kids who don't know how to wipe their feet, but how many of those will we attract at Crosslyn Rise? Think about it, Gideon. Or ask Nina Stone. She'll be the first one to tell you that we're aiming at a mature buyer. Not a retiree, exactly, but certainly not a young couple with a whole gang of kids."

"How many kids did you say were in your family?"

"I didn't. But there are six."

"Six kids." He grinned. "That's fun. From what to fifteen?"

She saw through the ruse at once and told him so with a look. "Thirty-three. I'm thirty-three. Is that supposed to have something to do with Crosslyn Rise?"

"Would you move there?"

"If I wanted to live on the North Shore, which I don't, because my business is in Belmont."

"Where do you live now?" Of the information he wanted, that was one vital piece.

She hesitated for just a minute before saying, "Belmont."

"To be near your family?"

She nodded slowly. "You could say that."

"Because you're all so close," he said quickly, so that she wouldn't think he was interested, *personally* interested, in where she lived. "Do you know how lucky you are about that? I've never had any brothers or sisters. Thanksgiving was my dad and me. Christmas was my dad and me. Fourth of July was my dad and me."

"Didn't you have any friends?"

"Sure, lots of them, and we were invited places and *went* places all the time. But that's different from being home for the holidays." He grew still, picked up his sandwich and took a bite.

Chris speared a piece of lettuce. For a minute she seemed lost in her thoughts. Then, quietly she said, "My family means the world to me. I don't know what I'd do without them."

"Is that why you haven't married?"

She raised her head. "I told you why. Marriage just isn't high on my list of priorities."

"Because you're too busy. But you made time to have lunch with me."

"This is business."

"It's also fun. At least, I think so. It's the most fun I've had at lunch in a while." It was true, he realized. He'd had more bawdy lunches, certainly wilder ones, but never one that excited him more. Even aside from the sexual attraction, he liked Chris. She was intelligent. Interesting.

Concentrating on her salad, she began to eat, first a piece of lettuce, then a slice of olive, then some chicken and a crumble of blue cheese. Gideon, too, ate in silence, but he was watching her all the while.

"Well?" he said when he couldn't stand it any longer.

She looked up. "Well what?"

"Are you enjoying yourself?"

"Right now, no. I'm feeling very awkward."

"Because I'm watching you eat?"

"Because you're waiting for me to say something that I don't want to say." With care, she set down her fork. "Gideon, I'm not looking for a relationship. I thought I made that clear."

"Well, you said it, but do I have to take it for gospel?"

"Yes."

"Come on, Chris. I like you."

"I'm glad. That'll make it easier for us to work together."

"What about after work? Can I see you?"

"No. I told you. I don't have the time or desire for something like that."

Sitting back in his chair, he gave her a long, hard look. "I think you're bluffing," he said, and to some extent he was himself. He wasn't a psychologist. He wasn't into analyzing people's motives. But he was trying to understand Chris, to understand why she wouldn't date him, when he had a gut feeling they'd be good together. "I think you're protecting yourself, because maybe, just maybe you're afraid of involvement. You've got your family, and that's great, and I imagine it's time-consuming to give a big family a hunk of yourself. But I think that if the right thing came along, you'd have all the time in the world for it—" he leaned close enough to breathe in the gentle floral scent that clung to her skin "—and more desire than a man could begin to hope for." He stayed close for a minute, because he just couldn't leave her so soon. Unable to resist, he planted a soft kiss on her cheek. Then he straightened and sat back.

"I'm not giving up, Chris." His voice was thick, vibrating in response to all he felt inside. "I'll wait as long as it takes. I've got all the time in the world, too—and more desire than you could ever want."

5

Chris never knew how she made it through the rest of lunch. She felt warm all over, her insides were humming, and even after Gideon took pity on her and changed the subject, she was shockingly aware of him— shockingly, because the things she kept noticing she hadn't noticed in any man, *any* man since she'd been eighteen years old, and even then, it was different.

Brant had been eighteen, too. He'd been big and brawny, a football player, far from the best on the team but good enough to earn a college scholarship. She remembered the nights they'd spent before graduation, parked in the shadowy grove behind the reservoir in his secondhand Chevy. She'd worshiped him then, had thought him the most beautiful creature on earth. With his sable hair and eyes, his strong neck and shoulders, and hands that knew just what to do with her breasts, he excited her beyond belief. Wanting only to please him, she let him open her blouse and bra to touch her naked flesh, and when that wasn't enough, she let him slip a hand inside her jeans, and when even that wasn't enough, she wore a skirt, so that all he had to do was take off her panties, unzip his pants and push inside her. It had hurt the first time, and she bled, but after that it was better, then better still.

Looking back, trying to remember how she could have been so taken in, she wondered if she wasn't half-turned-on by the illicitness of what they were doing. She hadn't ever been a rebel, but she was a senior in high school and feeling very grown-up in a houseful of far younger siblings. And then, yes, there was Brant. Looking back, she saw that he was a shallow cad, but at the time he was every cheerleader's dream with his thick hair, his flexing muscles, his tiny backside and his large, strong thighs.

Gideon Lowe put her memory of Brant Conway to shame. Gideon was mature, richly so, a freewheeling individual with a wealth of character, all of which was reflected in his physicality. The things she noticed about him—that stuck in her mind long after she left Joe's Grille—were the dark shadow of a mustache over his clean-shaven upper lip, the neat, narrow lobe of his ear and the way his hair swept vibrantly behind it, the length of his fingers and their strength, their newly scrubbed look, the scar on the smallest of them. She noticed the tan—albeit fading with the season—on his neck and his face, the crinkles radiating outward from the corners of his eyes, the small indentation on his cheek that should have been a dimple but wasn't. She remembered his size—not only his largeness, but the way he leaned close, making her feel enveloped and protected. And his scent, she remembered that with every breath she took. It was clean, very male and very enticing.

The problem, of course, was resisting the enticement, which she was determined to do above all else. She meant what she told him. She didn't have time for a serious man in her life. Her career was moving, and when she wasn't working, her time was happily filled with family. Thanksgiving had been larger—now that Jason was married, Evan engaged, and Mark and Steven bringing friends home from college—and more fun than ever. Christmas promised to be the same. She wanted to enjoy the holiday bustle. And then, there was work, which felt the Christmas crunch, too. Clients wanted everything delivered and looking great for the holidays. That meant extra phone calls on Chris's part, extra appointments, extra deliveries, extra installations. She *really* didn't have time for Gideon Lowe.

Of course, trying to explain that to Gideon was like beating her head against a brick wall. He called an hour after she returned to the office, on the day they met for lunch, to make sure she'd gotten back safely. He called two days later to say that, though he couldn't promise anything, he was getting estimates on half-round windows. He called three days after that to ask her to dinner.

Just hearing his voice sparked the heat in her veins. She couldn't possibly go to dinner with him. Couldn't *possibly*. "I'm sorry, Gideon, but I can't."

"Can't, or won't?"

"Can't. I have other plans." Fortunately, she did.

"Break them."

"I can't do that." The Christmas concert was being held at the high school that night. She wouldn't miss it for the world.

"Then tomorrow night. We could take in a movie or something."

She squeezed her eyes shut and said more softly, "No. I'm sorry."

He was silent for a minute. "You won't see me at all?"

"I don't think it would be a good idea. We work together. Let's leave it at that."

"But I'm lonely."

She cast a helpless glance at the ceiling. When he was blunt that way, there was something so endearing about the man that she wanted to strangle him. He was making things hard for her. "I thought you said you date. In fact, you said you date *a whole lot*." She remembered that quite clearly.

"I did, and I do, but those women are just friends. They're fine for fast fun, but they don't do anything for loneliness. They don't fill my senses the way you do."

"For *God's* sake, Gideon," she breathed. He was being corny as hell, but she liked it. It wasn't fair.

"Say you'll see me this weekend. Sometime. Anytime."

"I have a better idea," she said, trying to regain control of herself and the situation. "I'll talk with you on the phone again next week. There are questions that I didn't get around to asking you when we had lunch—" questions that she hadn't had the presence of mind to ask after he'd leaned close and kissed her "—and I've had other thoughts on the Rise since then. What do you say we talk a week from today?"

"A week!"

"This is an awful season for me. I'm up to my ears in promises and commitments. A week from today? Please?"

Mercifully her plea got through to him, because he did agree to call her the following Thursday. She was therefore unprepared when, on that Tuesday, between calls to a furniture factory in North Carolina, a ceramic tile importer in Delaware and an independent carpenter in Bangor, Maine, she heard an unmistakably familiar male voice coming from the outer office.

After listening to it for a minute, she knew just what was happening. She had told Margie that she needed an uninterrupted hour to make all her calls. So Margie was giving Gideon a hard time. But Gideon wasn't giving up.

Leaving her chair, Chris opened the office door, crossed her arms over her breasts and leaned against the jamb. "What are you doing here, Gideon?" she asked in as stern a voice as she could produce, given the way her heart was thudding at first sound, then sight of him. He was wearing jeans, a sweater and a hip-length parka. His hair was combed, but he hadn't shaved, which suggested that he'd come straight from work, with the benefit of only cursory repairs in the truck. The image of that unsettled her even more. But the worst was the way his eyes lit up when she appeared.

"Hey, Chris," he said, as though finding her here were a total surprise, "what's up?"

"What are you doing here?" she repeated, but she was having trouble keeping a straight face. For a big, burly, bullheaded guy, he looked adorably innocent.

Sticking his hands into the pockets of his jeans—knowingly or unknowingly pushing his parka in the process to reveal the faithful gloving of his lower limbs—he shrugged and said, "I was in the neighborhood and thought I'd drop in. How've you been?"

She steeled herself against his charm. "Just fine since we talked last week."

"Have a good weekend?"

"Uh-huh. And you?"

"Lonely. Very lonely. But I told you it would be." The look in his eye told her that if she didn't invite him into her office, he'd elaborate on that in front of Margie.

Chris didn't want even the slightest elaboration. She didn't trust where he'd stop, and it wasn't only Margie who'd hear, but Andrea, who was with a client in the second office and would no doubt be out before long. Then there would be comments and questions and suggestions the minute he left, and she couldn't bear that. No, the less attention drawn to Gideon, the better.

Dropping her arms, she nodded him into her office. The minute he was inside with the door closed, she sent him a baleful stare. "I told you I couldn't see you, and I mean it, Gideon. I have work to do. I'm *swamped.*" She shook a hand at her desk. "See that mess? That's what the Christmas rush is about. I don't have time to play." Her eyes widened. "What are you doing?"

"Taking off my jacket. It's warm in here."

Didn't she know it. Something about the two of them closed in the same room sent the temperature soaring. She felt the rise vividly, and it didn't help that he looked to be bare under his sweater, which fell over his pectorals with taunting grace.

"Put that jacket back on," she ordered, and would have helped him with it if she dared touch him, which she didn't. "You're not staying."

"I thought we could talk about the Rise."

"Baloney. You're not here about the Rise, and you know it," she scolded, but she seemed to have lost his attention. He was looking around her office, taking in the apricot, pale gray and chrome decor.

"Not bad," he decided. Crossing to the upholstered sofa, he pushed at one of the cushions with a testing hand, then turned and lowered his long frame onto the piece. He stretched out his arms, one across the back of the sofa, the other along its arm, and looked as though he'd be pleased to stay there a week.

Chris had her share of male clients, many of whom had been in her office, but none had ever looked as comfortable on that sofa as Gideon did. He was that kind of man, comfortable and unpretentious—neither of which helped her peace of mind any more than his sweater did, or his jeans. "I have to work, Gideon," she pleaded softly.

He gestured toward the desk. "Be my guest. I won't say a word."

"I can't work with you here."

"Why not?"

"You'll distract me."

"You don't have to look at me."

"I'll see you anyway."

"Ahh." He sighed. "A confession at last."

She blushed, then scowled in an attempt to hide it. "Gideon. Please."

Coming forward, he put his elbows on his spread thighs and linked his hands loosely between his knees. His voice went lower, his eyes more soulful. "It's been just over a week since I've seen you, but it feels like a month. You look so pretty."

Chris was wearing a burgundy jumper that she'd pulled from the closet, and a simple cream-colored blouse with a large pin at the throat. It was one of her oldest outfits. She didn't think she looked pretty at all and was embarrassed that he should say it. "Please, Gideon."

But he wasn't taking back the words. "I think about you a lot. I think about what you're doing and who you're with. I think about—wonder about—whether you're thinking of me."

She shut her eyes tight against the lure of his voice. "I told you. Things have been wild."

"But when you're home alone at night, do you think about me then?"

She pressed two fingers to her lips, where, just the night before, she'd dreamed he'd kissed her. From behind the fingers, she breathed a soft, "This isn't what I want."

"It's not what I want, either, but it's happening, and I can't ignore it. I feel an attraction to you the likes of which I haven't felt in years. I've tried to hold back, Chris. I tried not to come today because I know how you feel. But I'm not real good at waiting around. Call it impatient or domineering or macho, but I'm used to taking the lead. I want to see you again."

Anthony Haskell waited around, Chris realized. Anthony waited around all the time for her to beckon him on, but when she did, there was never any heat. There was heat now, with Gideon. She felt it running from her head to her toes, stalling and pooling at strategic spots in between.

Needing a buffer, she took refuge in the large chair behind the desk. "I thought we agreed to talk on Thursday," she said a little shakily.

"We did. And we can. But you're right. I didn't come to talk about the Rise. And I don't really want to talk about it on Thursday. There's nothing pressing there, certainly nothing that can't wait until the beginning of January, especially if you're as busy now as you say."

"I *am* busy."

"I believe you," he said genially. "But you have to take a break sometime. Why can't you take one with me?"

"I don't *want* to."

"Why not?"

She could think of dozens of answers, none of which she was ready to share.

Gideon didn't have that problem. "Don't you like me?"

She scowled. "Of course, I like you. If I didn't, I'd have already called the police to kick you out. You're interfering with my business."

"Do I still make you nervous?"

"Not nervous. Exasperated. Gideon," she begged, "I have to work."

"Do I excite you?"

"Yeah, to thoughts of mayhem." She glowered at him. "This isn't the time or place for a discussion like this."

"You're right. Let me take you to dinner tonight."

She shook her head.

"Tomorrow night, then. Come on, Chris, you have to eat."

"I do eat. With my family."

"Can't they spare you for one night?"

She shook her head.

"Then let me come eat with you." He seemed to warm to the idea once it was out. "I'd like that. I mean, I'd really like it. Big family dinners are something I always wanted but never had. I'll bring flowers for your mom. I'll bring cigars for your dad—"

"He doesn't smoke."

"Then beer."

"He doesn't drink."

"Then cashew nuts."

She shook her head. "Sorry. Doctor's orders."

Gideon looked appalled. "The poor guy. What does he *do* for the little joys in life?"

"He sneaks out to the kitchen when he thinks none of us is looking and steals kisses from my mom while she does the dishes."

That shut Gideon up. For a minute he just stared at her as though he couldn't grasp the image. Then his expression slid from soft to longing. "That's nice," he finally said, his voice a little thick. "I'm envious of you all."

Chris was beginning to feel like the worst kind of heel. If she was to believe Gideon's act, he was all alone in the world. But he dated, he dated *a lot*. And he had a mother in California. Maybe even a stepfamily. No doubt there would be numerous brightly wrapped gifts under his Christmas tree. So why did he look as though spending a little time with her family might be the best gift of all?

"Look," she said with a helpless sigh, "my parents have a Christmas open house every year." It would be packed. She could do her good deed, ease her conscience and be protected by sheer numbers. "It's this Sunday. If you want, you could come."

He brightened. "I'll come. Tell me where and when."

Taking a business card—deliberately, as a reminder of the nature of their relationship—she printed the address on the back. "It runs from three to seven, with the best of the food hitting the table at six."

"What should I wear?" he asked as he rose from the sofa to take the card.

"Something casual. Like what you wore to lunch last week."

He looked at the card, then stretched a little to slide it into the front pocket of his jeans. Chris was barely recovering from the way that stretch had lengthened his body when he turned, grabbed his coat and threw it on. For a split second his sweater rose high enough to uncover a sliver of skin just above his jeans. In the middle of that sliver, directly above the snap, was a belly button surrounded by whorls of dark hair.

She felt as though she'd been hit by a truck.

Oblivious to her turmoil, Gideon made for the door. Once there, he turned and gave her an ear-to-ear grin. "You've made my day. Made my *week*. Thanks, Chris. I'll see you Sunday." With a wink, he was gone.

Five days was far too soon to see him again, Chris decided on Sunday morning as she pulled on a sweatshirt and sweatpants and went to help her mother prepare for the party. He was still too fresh in her mind—or rather, the effect he had on her was too fresh. Every time she thought of him, her palms itched. Itched to touch. Itched to touch hair-spattered male flesh. And every time she thought of doing it, she burned.

She didn't know what was wrong with her. For fifteen years, she hadn't felt the least attraction to a man, and it hadn't been deliberate. She was with men when she worked. Her dad had men over. So did her brothers. But none had ever turned her on, it was as simple, as blunt as that.

What she felt for Gideon Lowe made up for all those chaste years, so much so that she was frightened. She sensed she'd need far more than crowds to lessen the impact he had on her. She only prayed he'd arrive late to coincide with the food. The less time he stayed, the better.

Gideon would have arrived at three on the nose if it hadn't been for his truck, which coughed and choked and balked at having to go out in the cold. He called it every name in the book as he worked under its hood, finally even threatened to trade it in for a sports car. That must have hit home, because the next time he tried it, the engine turned smoothly over and hummed nicely along while he went back into the house to scrub his hands clean.

It was three-thirty when he pulled into the closest spot he could find to the address Chris had written down. The street was pretty and tree lined, though the trees were bare, in a neighborhood that was old and well loved. Wood-frame houses stood, one after another, on scant quarter-acre lots. Their closeness gave a cozy feeling that was reinforced by wreaths decorating each and every door and Christmas lights shining from nearly every window. None of the houses was large, including Chris's parents', but that added to the coziness.

From the looks of things, the party was in full swing. The front door was open, there were people preceding him up the walk, and the side stoop was occupied by a group of college-age kids who seemed oblivious to the cold.

Leaving his truck, he followed the walk to the door, dodging two young girls who darted out of the house to join their friends. Once on the threshold, he felt a little unsure for the first time since he'd bulldozed the invitation from Chris. He'd gone to parties at the homes of people far more wealthy and influential, but none mattered more to him than this one.

He assumed that he was looking a little lost, because he barely had time to take more than two steps into the house when he was greeted by a tall gray-haired man. "Welcome," the man said in a voice loud enough to be heard above the din. "Come on in."

Gideon extended his hand. "Mr. Gillette?"

"That I am," the man said, giving him a hearty shake, "but probably not the one you want. I'm Peter. If you're looking for my brother Frank, he's mixing the eggnog, which is real serious business, so I'd advise you to leave him be. If he messes up, we all lose out, if you get my drift."

"Actually," Gideon said, searching for a blond head among those crowded into the living room, "I'm looking for Christine. I'm a friend of hers, Gideon Lowe."

"Even better," Peter said with a broad grin. "Tell you what. Why don't you hang your coat up in the closet while I go find her."

Gideon was already working his way out of the leather jacket. "That's okay. I'll go." Spotting a hook at the end of the closet, he freed himself of the jacket. "Which direction?"

Peter looked first toward the dining room on the left, then the living room on the right, then back toward the dining room. "The kitchen, I guess. If she's not helping Frank, she'll be helping Mellie." He pointed through the dining room. "That way."

With a nod, Gideon started off. The dining room was filled with people helping themselves to drinks and the small holiday cookies and cakes that covered plate after plate on the table. At one end was a huge punch bowl, into which a man Gideon assumed to be Frank was alternately pouring eggnog and brandy. He was a good-looking man, Gideon thought, tall and stocky, with salt-and-pepper hair and a ruddy complexion. Despite the good-natured coaxing and wheedling of several onlookers, he was concentrating solely on his work.

Gideon inched between two people here, three others there, until he'd made his way to the far end of the dining room and slipped through the door into a small pantry that led to the kitchen. There he saw Chris. She was standing at the counter by the sink with her back to him. Beside her was the woman who had to be her mother, if the similarity of height, build and coloring were any indication. They were slicing hot kielbasa, putting toothpicks in each slice, arranging the slices on a platter.

Coming up close behind Chris, he bent and put a gentle kiss beneath her ear.

She cried out and jumped a mile, then whirled on him in a fury. "Gideon! Don't *ever* do that again! My God—" she pressed her hand to her heart "—you've aged me fifteen years."

He gestured toward her mother, who was eyeing him curiously. "If this lovely lady is any indication of what you'll look like fifteen years from now, you've got it made.'' He extended his hand toward Mellie. ''Mrs. Gillette?'' There was no mistaking it. The eyes were the same, the hair, the mouth. Chris was slimmer and, wearing loose pants with a tunic top, more stylishly dressed, but they were very definitely mother and daughter.

''Gideon...?''

''Gideon Lowe, Mom. He's the builder for Crosslyn Rise and may well be the death of me before I even get to the project.'' She scolded him with her eyes, then her voice. ''I thought you were coming later.''

''You suggested six if I was starved. I figured I'd give myself a while to build up to that.'' He shook Mellie's hand warmly.

''It's nice to meet you, Mr. Lowe.''

''Gideon. Nice to meet you, too, ma'am.'' He let her take her hand back and return to her work. ''This is quite some party.'' He looked down at the platter. ''Can I help?''

''No,'' both women said at the same time.

Chris elaborated. ''Men don't cook in my mother's kitchen. My father does the eggnog, but not in here. Men are good for cleaning up. That's all.''

''And a few other things,'' Mellie added softly, almost under her breath. Then she looked straight at Gideon and spoke up, ''But I don't want you in here. You're a guest. Christine, leave these now. I'll finish up. Take Gideon out and introduce him around.''

Gideon thought Chris was going to argue, but even he could see that Mellie wasn't taking no for an answer. So she washed and dried her hands, then led him through another door into a hallway that led back to the front. This hallway, too, was crammed with people, giving Gideon ample excuse to stay close to Chris.

''You look fantastic,'' he murmured into her ear as they inched their way along.

''Thanks,'' she murmured back.

''You taste even better.''

''Oh, please,'' she whispered, but before he had a chance to come back with anything wickedly witty, she half turned, took his elbow and drew him alongside her. ''Gideon, this is my brother Steven. He's a junior at U. of Mass. Steven, meet Gideon Lowe, a builder I work with.''

Gideon shook hands with a blond-haired young man who also had the family features. ''You must be one of the basketball fanatics,'' he said, noting that Steven stood nearly as tall as he did.

Steven grinned. ''You got it. You, too?''

''You bet. If not for this gorgeous sister of yours, I'd be at the game right now.'' Leaning close, he asked out of the corner of his mouth, ''Any fix on the score?''

In every bit as low a tone, Steven answered, "Last time I checked, the Celts were up by eight. Game's on upstairs, if you want."

Gideon slapped his shoulder and straightened. "Thanks for the word. Maybe later."

"Don't you dare go up and watch that game," Chris warned, leading him on by the hand. "That would be very rude."

"Keep holding my hand," he whispered, "and I'll stay right by your side." He raised his voice. "Ah, here comes another brother."

Chris shot him an amused grin. "This is Jason. He works with Dad. His wife's over there—" She stood on tiptoe, looking around, "Jase, where's Cheryl?"

Jason shook hands with Gideon. "Upstairs nursing the baby."

"Gideon Lowe," Gideon said. "What baby?"

"A little boy," Chris explained. "He's their first."

"Hey, congratulations."

"Thanks," Jason said, but he had something else on his mind. "Chrissie, you seen Mark? He parked that rattletrap of his in the driveway in back of the Davissons and they have to leave."

"Try the front steps. Last I knew he was holding court out there." Jason promptly made for the door, but before Chris and Gideon could make any progress, a loud cheer came from the dining room. Seconds later, a grinning Frank Gillette emerged through a gauntlet of backslapping friends. When he caught sight of Chris, his eyes lit up even more.

"Go on in and try it, honey. They say it's better than ever."

"I will," Chris said. Her hand tightened on Gideon's. "Dad, I'd like you to meet Gideon Lowe. He and I work together."

"Nice to meet you," Frank said, "and glad you could come."

"It's kind of you all to welcome me."

"Any friend of Chrissie's, as they say. Hey, Evan," he called, "get over here." Seconds later, he was joined by another fair-haired son. "Evan, say hello to Gideon Lowe. Gideon, this is my second oldest son, and his fiancée, Tina."

Gideon smiled and nodded to them. Waving, they continued on into the living room. Gideon was beginning to wonder how Chris kept her brothers apart when yet another stole by. This one was younger and faster. He would have made it out the front door if Frank hadn't reached out and grabbed his arm. "Where you off to so fast?"

"I want to see Mark's friends. Steve says there're a couple'a cool girls out there."

Chris grinned up at Gideon. "That's Alex, the baby."

Alex looked instantly grieved. "Come on, Chris. That's not fair. I'm fifteen. Besides, I'm not the baby. Jill is."

"Jill?" Gideon asked. Chris had said there were six kids in the family. He was sure he'd already met ten. "There's another one?"

"Yeah," Alex said, "and there she is." He pointed to the girl coming down the stairs. While everyone looked that way, he escaped out the door.

"Come over here, girl," Frank said, but it was to Chris's side that the girl came.

Accordingly Chris was the one to make the introduction. "Say hi to Gideon," she told Jill. "He's the builder for Crosslyn Rise, but be careful what you say. He's also on the consortium."

Jill grinned. "Ah, he's the one?"

"He's the one."

Gideon couldn't take his eyes off Jill. With her long brown hair and her large brown eyes, she was different from every other Gillette he'd met. A beauty, she looked to be at least seventeen, yet Alex had called her the baby, and he was fifteen. Gideon wondered if they were twins, with Jill the younger of the two by mere minutes. She couldn't possibly be *fourteen*.

He stuck out his free hand. "Hi, Jill."

For a split second she seemed a little shy, and in that second he almost imagined she could be younger. Then she composed herself and gave him her hand, along with Chris's smile. "Nice to meet you."

"The pleasure's mine. It's not often that I get to hang around with *two* gorgeous women."

Chris arched a brow at Jill. "Didn't I tell you?"

Grinning back, Jill nodded.

"What?" Gideon asked.

"You know how to throw it around," Jill said.

Gideon looked at Frank. "Was that bull? Are these two women gorgeous, or are they gorgeous?"

"They're gorgeous," Frank confirmed, "but who'm I to judge. I got a vested interest in them."

Gideon considered that interest as he looked from Chris's face to Jill's and back. "All those blondes and one brunette," he said to no one in particular. To Jill he said, "How old are you?"

"Fifteen."

To Chris, he said, "I thought Alex was fifteen."

"He is."

"Then they're twins?"

"Not exactly."

"Irish twins?"

Chris slid an amused glance at Jill before saying, "No. Jill is five months younger."

"Five months?" He frowned. "No, that can't be—" He stopped when Chris and Jill burst out laughing, then looked questioningly at Frank, who was scowling at Chris.

"That's not real nice, Chris. I told you not to do it. It isn't fair to put people on the spot like that."

"Thank you," Gideon told him, and directed his gaze at Chris. It was Jill, though, who offered the explanation he sought.

"I'm not his," she said, tossing her dark head toward Frank. "I'm *hers*." Her head bobbed toward Chris.

Hers? For a long minute, Gideon didn't make the connection. When he did, he ruled it out as quickly as it had come.

Chris squeezed his hand, which she hadn't let go of once. She was looking up at him, her eyes surprisingly serious. "Say something."

Gideon said the first thing that came to mind. "You're too young, and she's too old."

"I was eighteen when she was born."

"You look like sisters."

"If she were my sister, she'd be blond."

"But she has the Gillette smile."

"That's my smile. She's my daughter."

Daughter. Somehow, the word did it—that, and the fact that with two witnesses, one of whom had originally made the claim and the other of whom wasn't opening his mouth to rebut it, Gideon figured it had to be true. "Wow," he breathed. "A daughter."

"Does that shock you?"

"Yeah," he said, then felt it worth repeating. "Yeah."

"Kind of throws things into a new light?" Chris asked, but before he could answer, she released his hand, said a soft, "Excuse me, I want to check on Mom," and escaped into the crowd.

"Chris—"

Frank put a tempering hand on his arm. "Let her go. She'll be back."

But Gideon's eyes continued to follow her blond head as it moved farther away. "She'll misinterpret what I just said. I know shc will. She'll think I don't want any part of her because she has a child, but that's not what I'm feeling at all. I'm feeling that, my God, she's done this wonderful thing in life, and I haven't ever done anything that even comes *close* in importance to it."

"This is getting heavy," Jill drawled.

Gideon's eyes flew to hers. He'd forgotten she was there, and was appalled. "Hey, I'm sorry. I didn't mean to offend you, too. I really like...your mom. If you're her daughter, I like you, too. Hell, I like the whole damned family. I don't have *any* family."

Jill's eyes widened. "None?"

But before he could answer, there was an uproar at the door. Frank turned around, then, wearing a broad grin, turned back and leaned close to Gideon. "See that bald-headed son of a bitch who just walked in? I haven't seen him in twenty years." To Jill, he said, "Take Gideon around, honey. If you run out of things to say, point him toward the game. He's a fan."

"Chris said I couldn't," Gideon told him.

Frank made a face. "Mellie says I can't, but do I listen?" Slapping his shoulder, he went off to greet his friend.

"You don't have *any* family?" Jill repeated, picking up right where she'd left off.

He shook his head. His hand felt empty without Chris's, so he slipped it into his pocket.

"No family."

"That's awful. Do you live all alone?"

"All alone."

"Wow, I don't think I could do that. I'd miss having people around and things happening."

Gideon was trying to think back to what Chris had said about herself. There wasn't a whole lot. She had evaded some questions and turned others right back to him. He didn't think she had ever lied to him, per se, but she'd obviously chosen every word with care.

When it came to where she lived, he had the distinct impression that she had her own place close to her family's. He suddenly wondered whether, there too, she'd stretched the words. "You don't live *here*, do you?"

"Oh, no. We're next-door. But we're here all the time."

"Next-door?" He was trying to remember what that house had looked like. "To the right or the left?"

"Behind. We're in the garage."

"The *garage*."

She nodded. "Uh-huh."

"You're stuck in the *garage*?"

She shot him a mischievous grin. "Want to see?"

"Yeah, I want to see." It occurred to him that Chris's daughter was a treasure trove of information on Chris, and that he wasn't adverse to getting what he could.

Jill led him around the crowd at the door, out and across the frozen lawn to the driveway. "My friends love my place," she said when he'd come up alongside her. "They keep bugging their parents to do something like it for them."

From what Gideon could see, the garage was like any other. Detached from the house, it was set far back at the end of a long driveway, with a single large door that would raise and lower to allow two cars inside. His builder's mind went to work imagining all the possibilities, but when Jill opened a side door and beckoned him inside, he wasn't prepared for what he found.

The garage had been elongated at the rear and converted into a small house, with an open living-room-kitchen-dining area, then a balcony above, off which two doors led, he assumed, to bedrooms. To compensate for a dearth of windows, there were indirect lights aplenty, as befitted the home of the daughter and granddaughter of an electrician. But what impressed Gideon even more than that was the decor. Nearly everything was white, and what wasn't white was a soft shade of blue. There was a light, bright, clean feel to the place. He couldn't believe he was in a garage.

"This is fantastic," he said.

Jill beamed. "Mom designed it, and Gramp's friends did it. I was just a baby and Mom was still in school, so it meant she could leave me with Gramma and Alex during the day, then have me to herself here at night."

Gideon was still looking around, taking in the small, sweet touches—like pictures of Jill at every imaginable age, in frames that were unique, one from the other—but he heard what she said. "So you grew up right alongside Alex?"

"Uh-huh. He's not bad for an uncle."

Gideon looked at her to find a very dry, very mature grin on her face. Narrowing an eye, he said, "You get a kick out of that, don't you?"

"Kinda." She dropped onto the arm of a nearby sofa with her legs planted straight to the floor. "People don't know what to think when they meet Alex and me. I mean, we're in the same grade and we have the same last name but we look so different. They don't believe it when we tell them the truth. They get the funniest looks on their faces—like you did before."

He wondered what explanation she gave for where her own father was. He wanted to ask about that himself, but figured it was something better asked of Chris. "Do you mind your mom working?"

Jill shrugged. "She has to earn a living."

"But you must miss her."

"Yes and no. I have Gramma. She's always around. And I have a house full of uncles. And then Mom comes home at night and tells me about everything she did at work that day."

"Everything?"

Jill nodded. "We're very close."

He had the odd feeling that it was a warning. Cautiously he asked, "What did she say about me?"

Without any hesitancy—as though she'd been wanting the question and he'd done nothing more than follow her lead—she said, "That you were a builder, that you were on the committee that interviewed her, and that you were a real jerk." When Gideon's face fell, she burst out laughing. "Just kidding. She didn't say that. She did say that you were very good-looking and very confident and that she wasn't sure how easy it'd be working with you." Jill paused, then added, "She likes you, I think."

"I know she likes me—"

"I mean, *likes* you."

Gideon studied her hesitantly. "Think so?" When she nodded, he said, "How do you know?"

"The way she ran off after we told you about me. She was nervous about what you'd think. She wouldn't have been if she didn't care. And then there was the thing with the hands.''

"What thing?"

"She was holding yours. Or letting you hold hers. She doesn't usually do that with men. She's very prim.''

"But you noticed the hands.''

"I sure did.''

Gideon ran a finger inside the collar of his shirt. "How old did you say you were?''

"It was only hands," she said in a long-suffering way. "And I *ought* to notice things like that. She's my mother. I care about what she does with her life.''

He could see that she did, and had the oddest sense of talking with Chris's parent rather than her child. "Would it bother you if I dated her?''

"No. She ought to have more fun. She works too hard.''

"What about Anthony?''

"Anthony is a total dweeb.''

"Oh.'' That about said it. "Okay. Then he isn't competition?''

"Are you kidding?" she said with a look of such absurdity on her face that he would have laughed if they'd been talking about anything else. But his future with Chris was no laughing matter.

"So we rule out Anthony. Are there any others I should know about?''

"Did she say there were?''

"No.''

Jill tipped her head. "There's your answer.''

"And you wouldn't mind it if I took her out sometimes?''

The head straightened and there was a return hint of absurdity in her expression. "Why would I mind?''

"If I took her out, it would be taking her away from time spent with you.''

Jill didn't have to consider that for long. "There are times when I want to do things with friends, but I feel so guilty going out and leaving Mom alone here. She can go over to the house and be with everyone there, but it's not the same. I mean, I love her and all, but my friends go shopping or to the movies on the weekends, and it's fun to do that. And then there's college. I want to go away. I've never *been* away. But how can I do that if it means leaving her alone?''

Gideon scratched his head. "Y'know, if I didn't know better, I'd wonder whether you're trying to marry her off.''

"I'm not," Jill protested, and came off the sofa. "I wouldn't be saying this to just anyone, but you like her, and she likes you, and what I'm saying is that you can't use me as an excuse for not taking her out. I'm a good kid. I don't drink or do drugs or smoke. I'll be gone in three years. I won't be in the way.''

Gideon hadn't had much experience with fifteen-year-old girls, but he knew without doubt that this one had a soft and sensitive side. She might be totally adjusted to the fact of her parentage; she might be far more mature than her years. But only in some respects. In others, she was still a girl wanting to please the adults in her life.

The fact that she considered him one of those adults touched him to the core. Crossing to where she stood, he tipped her chin up and said, "You could never be in the way, Jill. I don't know what'll happen between your mother and me. Our relationship has barely gotten off the ground. But believe me when I say that your existence is a plus. A big, big plus. I've been alone most of my life. I *like* the idea of being with someone who has family."

"Family can get in the way sometimes."

"You wouldn't say that if you've been without the way I have."

"Are you gonna tell Mom that?"

"As soon as I can get her alone long enough to talk."

"What's going on here?" Chris asked from the door.

Jill slipped away from his hand. "Whoops. Looks like you'll have that chance sooner'n you thought." She grinned. "Hi, Mom. I think I'll go back to the house and get something to drink. I'm parched." She was halfway past Chris when she said, "Invite him for Christmas dinner. He's nice." Before Chris could begin to scold, she was gone.

6

"Whose idea was it to come back here?" Chris asked. She wasn't quite angry, wasn't quite pleased. In fact, she wasn't quite sure *what* she was feeling, and hadn't been since she'd shocked Gideon with the fact of Jill.

"Uh, I'm not sure. I think it was kind of mutual."

"Uh-huh." Chris understood. "It was Jill's idea. You're protecting her."

Gideon held up a cautioning hand. "Look, she may have suggested it, but only after I started pestering her about where you two lived." Dropping the hand to his pocket, he looked around. "It's a super place, Chris. I like it a lot."

"So do I, but it's only a place. Jill's a person. She means more to me than anything else on earth. I don't want her hurt."

Gideon straightened. "You think I could *hurt* her?"

That was exactly what Chris thought. "You could get real close, then lose interest. When I said that she throws a new light on things, I meant it."

"Hold on a minute. I'm not romancing Jill. It's you—"

"But she's part of the package," Chris interrupted, feeling the urgency of the message. "That's what I'm trying to tell you. You say you want to date me. You hoodwinked me into inviting you here today. Well, okay, you're here, and I'll date you, but you have to know where my priorities lie. I'm not like some women who flit around wherever the mood takes them. I'm not an independent agent. I'm not a free spirit."

"I never thought you were," Gideon said soberly. "From the start, you've been serious and down-to-earth. You made it clear how much your family means to you."

"Jill is more than family. She's someone I created—"

"Not alone."

"Someone I *chose* to bring into this world. I have a responsibility to her."

"And you think you're unique?" Gideon challenged impulsively. "Doesn't every mother feel that responsibility? Doesn't every single mother feel it even more strongly, just like you do? For God's sake, Chris, I'm not trying to come between you and your daughter. Maybe I'm trying to add something to both of your lives. Ever thought of it that way? I sure as hell know I'm trying to add something to mine." He swore again, this time under his breath. "*Trying* is the operative word here. You get so goddamned prickly that I'm not making a helluva lot of headway." He stopped, then started right back up in the next breath. "And as far as Jill's existence throwing a new light on things, let me tell you that I find the fact that you have a daughter to be incredibly wonderful—which you would have known sooner if you hadn't run off so fast. You do that a lot, Chris. It's a bad habit. You run off before things can be settled."

"There's nothing to be settled here," Chris informed him, staunchly sticking to her guns, "since nothing's open for discussion. Jill is my daughter. For the past fifteen years, she's been the first thought on my mind when I wake up in the morning and the last thought before I fall asleep at night."

"Is that healthy?" Gideon asked innocently, but the words set her off.

"Healthy or not, that's the way it is," she snapped. "A woman with a child isn't the same as one without. You ought to think really hard about that before you do any more sweet-talking around here." She turned and made for the door, but Gideon was across the floor with lightning speed, catching her arm, drawing her back into the living room and shoving the door shut.

"Not so fast. Not this time. This time we talk."

"I can't talk now," she cried. "I have a house full of Christmas guests to entertain."

But Gideon was shaking his head. "Those guests entertain themselves, and besides, there are a dozen other hosts in that house." His voice softened, as did his hand on her arm, though he didn't release her. "Just for a minute, Chris. I won't keep you long, but I want to make something very clear."

She glanced up at him, and her heart lurched. The look in his eyes was gentle, almost exquisitely so.

"I like you," he said. "God only knows why, because you give me a hard time, but I like you a lot. You could've had *five* kids, with half of them in diapers, and I wouldn't care. Knowing about Jill now, I respect you even more for what you've done with your business, and you've obviously done something right with her, or she wouldn't be as nice a kid as she seems to be." He paused. "When I said I was shocked back there, it was because you never let on—I didn't expect it. You just didn't strike me as the type to—"

"Get knocked up?"

"Have a baby so young. Okay, yeah, maybe be with a guy so young." A tiny crease appeared between his brows. Quietly he asked, "Who was he?"

"It doesn't matter," Chris said, and tried to turn back toward the door only to have Gideon lock a grip on her other arm, too.

"Did you love him?" he asked, still quietly, even unsurely.

Chris had been prepared for criticism, which was what she'd gotten most often when she'd first become pregnant. *Didn't you know what you were doing? Didn't you use anything? Didn't you stop to consider the consequences?* Rarely had she been asked what Gideon just asked her. Looking up into his deep charcoal eyes, she almost imagined he was worried.

"I thought I did," she told him in a voice as quiet as his. "We were both seniors. He was handsome and popular, full of charm and fun. I was totally snowed. We didn't have anywhere to go, so we used to park up behind the reservoir. That's where Jill was conceived."

She thought Gideon started to wince, but he caught himself. "What happened after?"

"He didn't want me or the baby," she said bluntly. She'd long since passed the time when she blamed herself for that. She might have loved Brant at the time, or thought she did, but the only person Brant had loved was himself. "He denied it was his."

This time Gideon's wince was for real. "What kind of selfish bastard was he?"

Chris shrugged. "He was going to college on a scholarship and didn't want anyone or anything to slow him down."

"So he left you in the lurch. You must have been furious."

"Furious, hurt, frightened."

"I'd be angry still."

"Why? I got the better part of the deal. I got Jill."

Gideon seemed momentarily stunned, as though that idea had never occurred to him. Finally, in a hoarse whisper, he said, "That's what I think I like about you so much. You feel things. You love."

Chris too was stunned, nearly as much by his whispered awe as by the reverence in his eyes. Then she didn't have time to think of either, because he lowered his head to kiss her. At least, that was what she thought he was going to do. She felt the approach of his mouth, the warmth of his breath—then he pulled back and looked at her again, and in the look, something gave inside her.

"Do it," she whispered, suddenly wanting his kiss more than anything else.

His lips were smooth and firm. They touched hers lightly, rubbed them open in a back and forth caress, then, just as his hands left her arms and framed her face, came in more surely.

Chris was overwhelmed by the warmth of the kiss, its wetness, and by Gideon's fresh male scent that seemed to fill her and overflow. Needs that had lain dormant for better than fifteen years suddenly came to life, touching off an explosion of awareness inside her. Her limbs tingled, her heart pounded, her blood rushed hot through her veins. Feeling dizzy and hungry at the same time, she clasped fistfuls of sweater at his waist, gave a tiny moan and opened her mouth to his silent demand.

The demand went on and on, sometimes pressing, sometimes hovering, sometimes sucking so strongly that she was sure she'd never emerge whole again. When, with several last, lingering touches, the kiss ended, she felt bereft.

It was a minute before she realized exactly what had happened, and by that time, Gideon had his mouth pressed to her temple and his arms wrapped tightly around her. With her slow return to reality came the awareness of a fine tremor snaking through his large frame.

"Gideon?" she whispered, shaky herself.

"Shh," he whispered back. "Give me a minute."

She knew all too well why he needed the time. She could feel the reason pressing insistently against her thigh, and while the strength of it shocked her, it also excited her beyond belief. She wanted another kiss. She wanted some touching. She wanted something even harder, something to relieve the deep ache she was feeling.

"I knew it'd be like that," he whispered again.

"I didn't know it *could* be."

He made a low, longing sound and crushed her even closer.

"That's not helping," she whispered, but neither was breathing against his neck the way she was doing. His skin was firm and hot and smelled wonderfully of man.

"I know, but I need it. I can't let you go just yet."

"You'll have to soon. Someone's apt to come looking."

Raising his head, he caught her eyes. His voice remained little more than a ragged train of breath. "Know what I'd do if I had my way?" When she shook her head, he said, "I'd back you right up to that door and make love to you here and now."

She felt a searing heat deep in her belly and had to swallow before she could get a word out. "You can't."

"Yes, I can. I'm hard. Can't you feel?" Slipping his hands to her bottom, he manipulated her hips against his. His arousal was electrifying.

She had to close her eyes against its force. "Don't, Gideon," she cried, her breath coming in shallow gusts. She lowered her forehead to his throat.

His mouth touched her ear. "Right against that door. Then, after that, on your bed. You've never done it on a bed, have you?"

"No." She tugged at his sweater, which she was still clutching for dear life. "Don't talk."

"Why not?"

"Because you're making things harder."

"I'll say," he muttered with the nudge of his hips.

Moaning against the fire that small movement sparked, she slipped her arms around his neck, drawing herself up on tiptoe, and hung on tight. Her body felt foreign but wonderful. It knew what it wanted. Her mind wasn't so sure. "I have to get back to the house."

"You don't want to."

"I have to." But she moved against him, needing the friction to ease the knot between her legs.

"You want to stay here and make love with me."

"Oh, Gideon!" she cried.

"You do. I'd make it so good, baby, so good. I wouldn't rush you, wouldn't hurt you, and it'd be so incredibly good." He slipped a hand from her bottom to her thigh, then moved upward and inward.

"Don't," she begged, but the plea was empty. Between his words and his closeness, she was floating, then soaring, burning up from the inside out. When he touched her where she was most sensitive, she cried out, and when he began to caress her, she held on tighter to his neck.

"You're so hot here," he whispered.

"Gideon," she moaned. "Oh, no." She was arching into his hand, coming apart with no way to stop it.

His stroking grew bolder. "That's it, baby. That's it. Feel it. Let it come."

She was lost. In a moment of blinding bliss, she convulsed into an orgasm that left her gasping for air. She couldn't speak, could only make small, throaty sounds. Gradually they eased. The next sound she made was a humiliated sob. Twisting away from Gideon with such suddenness that he was taken off guard, she stumbled around the sofa and collapsed into its corner, pressing her knees together and huddling low over them.

"It's okay, sweetheart," Gideon said, reaching out to stroke her hair.

She felt his hand and would have pulled away if there was anywhere to pull to. "That shouldn't have happened," she cried. "I'm so embarrassed."

Barely removing his hand, Gideon came around the end of the sofa and squatted close before her. "Don't be," he said. "I'm not. I feel so *good.*"

"You can't feel good. You didn't...get anything."

"Wrong. Way wrong. I got a whole lot." His strong hands were framing her neck, and his voice, though hoarse, was astonishingly tender. He leaned forward so that his breath brushed her cheek. "Was that the first time since—"

She gave a sharp, quick nod against her knees.

"The first time since Jill's father?"

She repeated the same sharp nod.

"You've never done it yourself?"

She kicked his leg.

"Chris?" When she didn't answer, he said again, "Chris?"

Her voice was small. "What?"

"I think I'm falling in love with you."

"Don't *say* that."

"But it's true."

She pressed her hands to her ears and shook her head.

Forcibly removing her hands, he raised her head until she was sitting up, looking at him. "I won't say it again, if it makes you uncomfortable. It shakes me a little, too. We don't know each other much, do we?"

Unable to take her eyes from his, she gave a feeble shake of her head.

"But there's a remedy for that," he went on. "You can stop cooking up cockamamy excuses for why you can't see me."

Chris pulled back as much as his hands would allow. "They're not cockamamy excuses. This is the busiest time of the year for me. Between work and all the things I want to do with Jill—"

"Invite me along. We don't have to be alone all the time."

She made a disbelieving face. "What kind of man wants to put up with that?"

His voice went low and husky again. "The kind of man who knows his woman is made of fire. As long as I know it's coming, I can wait."

Chris felt her cheeks go red. "I won't ever live that down, will I?"

"Not if I can help it. It was the most beautiful, most sensual, most natural and spontaneous response I've ever experienced with a woman."

She had to look away. His eyes were too intense. Very softly she said, "You've been with lots of women, haven't you?"

"Over the years? Enough." He paused. "But if it's the health thing that's got you worried, don't be. I've always used a rubber. Always. For birth control, as much as anything. I'm clean, Chris."

Focusing on a cable twist in his sweater, she murmured. "I wasn't worried about that." She was actually worried about the issue of experience, because, other than with Brant, she was very much without.

"I don't want to use anything with you."

Her eyes shot to his. "You have to. I don't have—I'm not taking—"

His mouth cut off the words, kissing her gently, then less gently, before he regained control and drew up his head. "If you got pregnant by me, I wouldn't run away. I'd want you and the baby and Jill and your family. I'd marry you in a minute."

Chris was having trouble breathing again. "This conversation is very premature."

"Just so you know how I feel."

"How can you feel that way so soon?"

"Beats me, but I do."

"I think you're getting carried away on some kind of fantasy."

"No fantasy. Just you."

How was she supposed to answer *that*? She swallowed. "I have to get back to the house."

Gideon sat on his heels. "I'm staying till the party's over. Can we talk more then?"

"Maybe we shouldn't. Maybe we should let things cool off a little."

"It won't help. The fire's there, whether we're together or not. It's there even when I sleep. I had a wet dream last night—"

"Gideon, for goodness' sakes!"

"I did."

"But don't *tell* me."

"Why not?" he asked reasonably. "I know damned well you're going to think back on what happened here and be embarrassed, and I just want you to know that you're not the only one who loses control sometimes. You had far more reason to than I did, what with the way I was touching you—"

She pressed a hand to his mouth. "Please," she begged in a whisper, "don't say another word." She waited. He was silent. She moved her fingers very lightly over his lips. "I'm going to get up now and go back to the house. If you'd like, you can come, too. You can talk with people— Jessica and Carter may be here by now—or even watch the game if it isn't over."

"The Lakers come on next," he murmured against her fingers.

"Okay. The Lakers. My brothers will be watching. You can get something to eat and stay as long as you want, but I can't go out with you afterward. I want to help my mother clean up. Then I want to spend some time with Jill. Then I want to go to bed. Tomorrow's as busy as Mondays get." Her hand slid from his mouth to the shirt collar that rose above the crew neck of his sweater.

"What's on for tomorrow night?"

"I have deliveries to supervise until eight."

"So Jill will be here with your folks?"

"She has Driver Ed on Monday nights. I'll pick her up on my way home."

"What about supper?"

"I'll grab something when I get home."

"Why don't I pick up Chinese and stop by your office?"

"Because I won't be at my office."

"So I'll go where you are."

"You can't. Not with food. My clients would die."

"Okay. What about Tuesday night? No, forget Tuesday night. I have a game." His eyes lit up. "Come see me play."

For an instant, he was so eager that she actually wished she could. But the logistics wouldn't work. "In Worcester?"

"Too far, hmm?"

"And I have ballet."

"Okay. What's on for Wednesday night?"

"Jill's piano recital."

"I'll come."

"You will not. She's nervous enough at recitals without having to worry about her mother's new boyfriend showing up."

Gideon grinned. "New boyfriend. I like that. It's better than the builder.'' His grin vanished. ''But I won't make her nervous. She likes me.''

''She likes you here, now, today. That's because you're one of lots of people coming to party. She's apt to be threatened when she realizes something's going on between us.''

''She already does. And she won't be threatened. She *likes* me. Besides, she wants you to date. She told me so.''

''She told you?''

''Yes.''

Chris felt just the slightest bit betrayed. ''What else did she tell you?''

''Not much. You came along before she had a chance. But, damn it, Chris, we haven't settled anything here. When can I see you again? We're up to Thursday.''

''Thursday's no good. I have ballet again, and then we're going shopping.''

''I'll go with you.''

But she shook her head. Last-minute Christmas shopping was something that had become almost traditional with Jill and her. Chris wasn't ready to let someone else intrude.

''Okay,'' Gideon said, ''that brings us to the weekend, and to Christmas Eve. So are you inviting me over, or what?''

Chris didn't know what to do. Christmas Eve, then Christmas Day were every bit as personal and special and traditional for the whole family as last-minute shopping was for Jill and her alone.

''Jill said you should,'' he reminded her.

''Jill was out of line.''

''What are all your plans?''

''Dinner, caroling, then Midnight Mass on Christmas Eve, and a huge meal on Christmas Day.''

''Is it all just family?''

''No,'' Chris answered truthfully. ''Friends come, too.'' She sighed and sent him a beseeching look. ''But this is happening too fast, Gideon. Can't we slow it down?''

''Some things won't be slowed down—like what happened a little while ago.''

She squeezed her eyes shut.

''What are you afraid of, Chris? What's holding you back?''

She had asked herself the same question more than once in recent weeks. Slowly she opened her eyes and met his. ''Being hurt. I'm afraid of that. Jill may be the highlight of my life, but what Brant did hurt. I got over it. I came back and built a life, and I think I've been a great mother. Things are going smoothly. I don't want that to change.''

''Not even for the better?''

''I don't *need* things to be better.''

The look on Gideon's face contradicted her even before he spoke. 'I think you do. There's a closeness only a man can give that I think you crave. It's like the way you held my hand back at the house, and the way you came apart before, even the way you're touching me right now."

"I'm not—"

"You are. Look at your hand."

Chris did. Her hand was folded over his collar, her fingers against the warm skin on the inside. Very carefully she removed them and put her hand into her lap. "I didn't know I was doing that," she said meekly.

"Like I didn't know what was happening until I woke up panting this morning. There's something to be said for the subconscious. It's more honest than we are sometimes."

He had a point, she supposed. She could deny that she wanted him, deny that she wanted any kind of relationship, but it wouldn't be the truth. Still, despite his arguments, she meant what she'd said about slowing things down.

"New Year's Eve," she said, focusing on her lap. "You probably already have plans—"

"I don't, and I accept. What would you like to do? We can work around Jill's plans or your family's plans. Just tell me. I'm open."

Hesitantly she raised her eyes. "Jill is going to a party at a friend's house. I have to drop her there, then pick her up. She's bringing two other friends home for a sleep-over."

"A sleep-over? Wow, that'd be fun!"

"Gideon, you're not invited to the sleep-over."

"So what *do* I get?"

"Four hours, while she's at the party. We could go somewhere to eat, maybe dance. Or we could go to First Night."

"First Night is loud and cold and crowded. I vote for the other."

"We may have trouble getting reservations this late."

"I don't want reservations. I want to eat here."

She didn't know whether to laugh or cry. "I didn't *invite* you to eat here."

"But it makes sense, doesn't it?" he argued. "Go to a restaurant on New Year's Eve, and it's crowded and overpriced and slow. You'll be nervous about getting back in time, so you won't be able to relax. On the other hand, if we eat here, we can talk all we want. We really need to do that, Chris, just talk. Besides, if we go somewhere fancy, I'll have to go shopping. You've already seen the sum total of my fancy wardrobe, and I hate shopping. Don't make me do it, not until after Christmas at least."

"If you hate shopping, why did you offer to go with Jill and me?"

"Because that would be fun. It's shopping for *me* that I hate."

She was bemused. "Why?"

"Because it's so damned hard to get things that fit. I'm broad up here, and long down there, so things have to be tailored, which means having some salesclerk feel me up.''

She sputtered out a laugh. "That's terrific."

"No, it's sickening. Anybody feels me up, I want it to be you. So what do you say? Dinner here on New Year's Eve? Nice and quiet and relaxed? I'll bring some food if you want. Better still, give me a list and I'll pick up groceries so we can make dinner together. Now *that's* a good idea."

Chris had to admit that it was. She wasn't a big one for public New Year's Eves and had always spent hers quietly. The idea of being with Gideon for those few hours while Jill was at her party was appealing.

"Okay," she said.

He broke out into a smile. Standing, he tugged her to her feet and wrapped an arm around her waist as he started for the door. "What time should I come? Four? Five?"

"Try eight-thirty." Jill's party began at eight. That would give Chris time to come home, change, get things ready.

"No way am I waiting around until eight-thirty, when everything closes at midafternoon. Five-thirty. I'll come at five-thirty. Then I can talk with Jill before she leaves."

"Jill will be totally preoccupied with her hair."

"So I'll be here to tell her how great it looks."

"Come at seven-thirty. You can go with me when I drive her to the party."

"Six. We can have appetizers early."

"Seven, and that's the earliest, the absolute earliest you can come."

"Can I bring champagne?"

"Wine. I like it better. And wear your fancy outfit. Is that the one you were wearing that day at the bank?" She wanted to see it again. Even through her nervousness his handsomeness that day had registered.

"Yeah," he protested, "but that defeats the purpose of staying in."

She shook her head and said softly, "It's New Year's Eve. If we're having a nice dinner with wine, we have to dress the part. And don't say I've already seen it, because I don't work that way. You don't have to wear something different every time you see me. I'm not that shallow."

"I didn't say you were. But it's me. My pride."

"Your pride is misplaced if you're hung up on clothes. Wear the blazer and slacks."

"The blazer and slacks?"

"Yes."

He sighed, gave her a squeeze and opened the door. "Okay. The blazer and slacks it is." He inhaled a hearty breathful of the fast-falling winter's night. "Wow, do I feel good."

Chris was surprised to realize that she did, too.

The feeling persisted. On the one hand, she could say it was the Christmas spirit. Her family always made the holiday a happy time. Deep down, though, she knew there were other reasons this year. Jill was happy. The business was going well. And Gideon had come on the scene.

He didn't let her forget that last fact. He called her every night, usually around ten, when he knew she'd be home, and though he never kept her on the phone for long—just wanted to see how her day had been or tell her something about his—the calls were sweet.

Jill was aware of them. She was the one who sat by the phone doing her homework when the ring pierced the quiet night, or talking with a friend when the call-waiting clicked. Sometimes Chris took the call in the same room, sometimes in another room. Each time, Jill acknowledged it afterward.

Not that Chris would have tried to hide anything. She knew that if she wanted Jill to be open and communicative with her, she had to be the same way right back. Their relationship had always been honest that way. And besides, there wasn't anything to hide. Gideon liked her. So he was calling her.

Of course, Jill wanted to know more. "Do you like him?" she asked, wandering down to the kitchen after one of the calls.

In a burst of late-night energy, Chris was making wreath cookies, which required a minimum of brain and a modicum of brawn. She was vigorously stirring the butter and marshmallows that she'd unceremoniously dumped into a pot.

"He's nice," she answered. "I didn't expect him to be after what happened at the Rise that first day." She'd told Jill about that when it happened, albeit more philosophically than she'd felt at the moment of confrontation. "So I'm surprised. But I still don't know him very well."

"It sounds like he wants to change that."

"Uh-huh." Chris felt the same shimmer of excitement she always felt when she anticipated seeing Gideon again.

"Why isn't he coming for Christmas?"

Chris kept stirring. "Because I didn't invite him."

"Why not?"

"Because he's too new. Christmas is for people we're really close to. Our family is special. If you're not one of us, you have to *earn* a place at our table." She'd been trying for a little dry wit. It went right past Jill.

"But he's alone. He'll be sitting there in a lonely apartment all by himself. He probably doesn't even have a tree."

Chris felt a moment's unease, wondering just how thickly Gideon had poured it on. If there was one thing she wouldn't abide, it was his using Jill to get to her. "Did he mention a lonely apartment?"

"No, but he said he had no family."

"Okay, that's true. But he doesn't live in an apartment, to begin with. He lives in a house that he built himself—"

"So he's sitting in a lonely house."

"He is not. Jill, he has lots of friends. I'm sure he's doing something with them." She hadn't asked, exactly, but she assumed that was the case. He was a really friendly guy, and he said he dated, he dated *a lot.* Chris didn't believe that he'd left all of his holiday time free.

Of course, he would have come for Christmas if she'd invited him, and he jumped at her first mention of New Year's Eve, so apparently whatever plans he had weren't etched in stone. She didn't want to think a woman was involved, didn't want to think he would break a date and disappoint someone. Better, she decided, to imagine that if he wasn't with her, he'd be with a large group of friends.

Maybe some of his workmen.

Maybe his basketball teammates.

She wondered what he wore on the court and how he looked.

"Do you think you could like him?"

Brought back from a small distance, Chris stirred the melting marsh-mallows with greater force. The roughness of the wooden spoon against the bottom of the pot told her that there was some sticking, apt punishment for a wandering mind. "I do like him. I told you that."

"Love him?"

Though she couldn't help but remember what Gideon had said about falling in love with her, Chris shook her head. "Too soon. Way too soon. Ask me that in another year or two."

"That's not how love happens. It happens quickly."

"Says the authority. Sweetheart, I forgot to take out the food coloring. Can you get it for me? Green?"

Jill took the small vial from the baking supply shelf and removed its lid. "How many drops?" She held it poised.

"Start with four."

Jill squeezed. Chris stirred. Gradually the thick white stuff turned a faintly minty shade.

"A little more, I think."

Jill squeezed, she stirred, but if she had hoped Jill would let the matter of love go, she was mistaken.

"You loved my father when I was conceived."

"Uh-huh." They had discussed that at length several years before, when Chris had sat down with Jill and explained what getting a period was about. Given the slightest encouragement, Jill had asked questions about making babies and making love. She knew who her father was, that he had left Massachusetts before her birth, that he was selling real estate in Arizona. At that time, she had wanted to know about Chris's relationship with him.

Chris had been forthright in telling her about feeling love and the specialness of the moment. She never wanted Jill to feel unwanted, though in essence Brant had made it clear that she was. His whole family had moved away—conveniently, a job transfer had come through for his father—and, to Chris's knowledge, none of them had been back. Outside of family, few people knew who Jill's father was.

"But you'd only been dating him for two months."

"I was young. When you're young, you're more quickly taken with things like love. Another drop, maybe?"

Jill added it, while Chris kept stirring.

"Don't you think it's more romantic when it's fast? I mean, I think what happened to you was *really* romantic. You saw each other in English, started doing homework together, fell in love and did it. Do you think he's married now?"

"Probably."

"Do you think he ever wonders about me?"

Chris sent her an affectionate smile. "He must. You're that strong a being."

"Think he ever wants to see me?"

"I think he doesn't dare." She tried to keep it light. "Seeing you, he'll realize all he's missed. He'll hate himself."

Jill frowned. "But what kind of parent isn't curious about his own child?"

Chris had asked herself that question dozens of times, and in many of those times she'd thought the lowliest things about Brant. But she'd vowed many years ago not to bad-mouth him in front of Jill. "The kind who may not be able to forgive himself for leaving you behind. He knows you exist. I imagine—" it was a wild guess, giving Brant a big benefit of the doubt "—that knowledge has been with him a lot."

Jill thought about that, standing back while Chris dumped the premeasured cups of corn flakes into the pot with the melted marshmallows that were now a comfortable Christmas green. Finally Jill said, "Do you ever imagine that you might open the front door one day and find him there?"

"No." That was the last thing Chris wanted. She had no desire to see Brant, no desire to have Brant see Jill. Jill was *hers*. She felt vehemently about that. For Jill's sake alone, she tempered her feelings. "He's probably very involved with his own life. His family only lived here for three years. They were midwesterners to begin with. They have no ties here."

"That didn't mean he couldn't have married you if he loved you."

Chris had to work hard stirring the mess in the pot, but she appreciated the physical demand. It was a good outlet. "He had plans. He was going to college. He had a scholarship."

But Jill was insistent. "If he loved you, he could have married you."

Her petulance, far more than the words themselves, stopped Chris. Leaving the wooden spoon sticking straight up, she turned and took Jill's face in her hands. "Then I guess he didn't love me," she said softly, "at least, not as much as I thought. And in that sense, it's a good thing we didn't get married. The marriage wouldn't have been good. We'd have been unhappy together. And you would have suffered." She paused. "Do you miss having a father so much?"

"No. Not so much. You know that." They'd talked about it before. "There are times when I wonder, that's all. There are times when I think it would be nice to go places, just the three of us."

"So what would Gramma and Gramps do?" she teased. "And Alex? And the others?"

Jill thought about that for a minute, gave a small smile of concession and shrugged, at which point Chris planted a kiss in the middle of her forehead. She was about to turn back to the pot when Jill said, "I still think you should have invited Gideon for Christmas dinner."

"Uh-oh. We're on this again?"

"It was just a thought."

"Well, here's another one. I think that sticky stuff in the pot may have hardened. You gonna clean up the mess?"

In a blink, Jill was the picture of innocence. "Me? I still have homework to do." She slipped smoothly away and was up the stairs before Chris could think to scold. Not that she would have. All too soon, Jill would be slipping smoothly away to college, then beyond. Chris wasn't about to scold away their time together, not when it was so dear.

7

Come New Year's Eve, Chris wasn't thinking of spending time with Jill, but spending time without her. Christmas with the family had been wonderfully fun and absorbing—her mother had *loved* the clay pot—but in the week that followed, in all the little in-between moments when her mind might have been on something else but wasn't, Chris thought of Gideon. Each time, she felt a warm suffusion of desire.

He continued to call every night, "just to make sure you don't forget me," he teased, which was a laugh. She couldn't have forgotten him if she'd tried. He was like a string tied around her finger, a tightness around her insides, cinching deeply and pleasantly.

Had anyone read her mind during that week, she would have been mortified, so carnal were her thoughts. Rather than picturing Gideon in his blazer and slacks, she pictured him in every state of undress imaginable. It didn't help that she was haunted by glimpses of a sliver of skin, a whorl of dark hair and a belly button. When he called at night, she pictured him lying in bed wearing briefs, or nothing. She pictured his body, pictured the dark hair that would mat it, clustering more thickly at some places than others. She pictured him coming to her on New Year's Eve, unbuttoning his shirt, removing it, opening his pants, removing them, baring himself to her, a man at the height of his virility and proud of it.

At times, she wondered if there was something wrong with her, if she was so sex starved that anyone would do. But the courier, who stopped by the office several times that week and was very attractive, didn't turn her on. Nor did her hairdresser, who was surprisingly straight. Nor did Anthony Haskell, who called several times wanting to see her and whom she turned down as gently as she could.

She didn't remember ever feeling quite so alive in quite as feminine a way as she did with the approach of New Year's Eve. Like an alarm that kept going off every few minutes, the buzz of arousal in the pit of her stomach had her counting the minutes until Gideon arrived.

Seven, she had told him. Fortunately, she was ready early, because when the bell rang at six-forty-five, she had no doubt who it was. Pulling the door open, she sent him a chiding look.

He shrugged. "I left extra time in case there was traffic, but there wasn't."

How could she get angry when the mere sight of him took her breath away? He was wearing a topcoat with the collar up against the cold, and between the lapels she caught sight of his blazer and slacks, but he looked far more handsome than he had that day at the bank. No doubt, she decided, it had to do with the ruddy hue on his cheeks.

That hue bemused her. "You look like you've been out in the cold." But he'd been in a heated car.

"Had the windows open," he said, not taking his eyes from her. She looked bright, almost glowing, sophisticated, but young and fresh. He decided that the young part had to do with her hair. Rather than pinning it in its usual knot, she'd left it down. It was shiny and smooth, swept from a side part, its blunt-cut ends dancing on her shoulders. "It was the only way I could keep my mind on the road."

She didn't have to ask where his mind would have been otherwise. The hunger in his eyes answered that quite well. It made her glad that she'd splurged on a new dress, though the splurging hadn't been painful. Contrary to Gideon, she loved to shop. She kept herself on a budget, but she'd been due for a treat. His appreciation made the effort more than worth it.

"May I come in?" he asked.

She blushed. "Of course. I'm sorry. Here, let me take that." She reached for the grocery bag he held in one arm. They had agreed that he would bring fresh French bread and some kind of dessert, since there was a bakery not far from his house. But he held tight to the bag and, instead, handed her the two bottles of wine that he was grasping by the neck with the fingers of one hand. She peered suspiciously at the bag, which seemed filled and heavy. "What's in there?"

"I got carried away," he confessed, thinking about sweets for the sweet and other trite expressions, but loath to voice them lest she think him a jerk. Elbowing the door shut behind him, he headed for the kitchen. He set the bag on the counter, relieved her of the wine and stood it beside the bag, then gave her a slow up and down.

"You look great," he said in an understatement that he hoped his appreciative tone would correct.

Her temperature was up ten degrees, making her words breathy and warm. "Thanks. You, too." Feeling a dire urge to touch him, she laced her fingers together in the area of her lap. "Please, take your coat off." When he'd done so, she hung it in the closet, then turned to find him directly behind her.

"Where's Jill?" he whispered.

"Upstairs," she whispered back.

"Does she know I'm here?"

"She must have heard the bell."

"Do we have time for a kiss?"

"If it's a quick one."

"I don't know if I can make it quick. I've been dreaming about it for more than ten days." His whisper was growing progressively rough. He felt desperately in need. "What I had in mind was something slow and deep and wet—"

"Hey, you guys," came Jill's full voice from halfway down the stairs. She trotted down the rest, her steps muted by the carpet. "What're you whispering about?"

Chris felt she'd been caught in the act of doing something naughty. It was a minute before she could compose herself enough to realize that she hadn't—and that even if she had, she was the mother and had that right. "Gideon was saying things that *definitely* shouldn't be heard by tender ears such as yours," she drawled, and made for the kitchen. "Do me a favor, sweetie? Keep him company while I get these hors d'oeuvres?"

Gideon put his hands into the pockets of his blazer and angled them forward to hide his arousal from Jill. "Can I help?" he called after Chris. To Jill, he said, "You may think I'm one of those helpless males, but believe me, I'm not. I'm a very handy man to have around the house. I know how to crack eggs, whip cream and brew coffee."

"We could've used you around here earlier," Jill said. "Mom ruined two batches of stuffed mushrooms before she finally got one that was edible. They're supposed to be her specialty. So she thought she knew the ingredients by heart, only she blew it. That was the first time. The second time she burned the meat."

"Distracted, huh?" Gideon asked, pleased by the thought.

"You could say that." She took a step back. "How do I look?"

He checked her over. "Spectacular. Great jeans skirt. Great sweater. Great legs. Is this a boy-girl party you're going to?"

She tossed a glance at the ceiling. "Of course! I am old enough for that, y'know."

He knew all too well. Where he'd grown up, fifteen-year-old girls did far more than go to parties. Instinct told him, though, that Jill wasn't that way. Common sense told him that Chris wouldn't have stood for it. "You're gonna knock 'em dead," he told her, feeling a pride he had no right to feel. "And your hair looks great, too."

"I'm not done with my hair."

"But it looks perfect."

"It looks blah," she maintained, drawing up a thick side swath with two fingers. "I think I need a clasp or something. And some earrings. Mom—" she called, only to be interrupted when Chris approached.

"No need to yell. I'm right here." To Gideon she said apologetically, "They weren't hot enough. They'll be ready in a minute."

"I need something large and silver, Mom."

"For her hair and ears," Gideon prompted in a soft voice to Chris, who was looking a bit helplessly at Jill.

"The last time I lent you something silver," she said, thinking of a bangle bracelet that she hadn't seen in months, "I didn't get it back. You can borrow something *only* if it's returned in the morning."

"She's so fussy," Jill said to Gideon. Then she turned and went back up the stairs, leaving Gideon and Chris momentarily alone.

Gideon started whispering again. "How long do you think she'll stay up there?"

"Five seconds," Chris whispered back.

Jill yelled down, "Can I wear the enamel hair clip you bought at the Vineyard last summer?"

"I thought you wanted something silver," Chris called back.

"But the enamel one has earrings to match."

"It also," Chris murmured for Gideon's benefit, "cost an arm and a leg. She's been wanting to wear that set since I bought it. I think she's taking advantage of the company and the night."

"You can always tell her no," Gideon suggested.

Chris snorted softly, then called to Jill, "If you're very, very, *very* careful." She caught Gideon's eye. "Don't look at me that way."

"Are you always such a pushover?"

"No. But we're talking a hair clip and some earrings here. If she asked for a quart of gin, I'd say no. Same for cigarettes or dope, if I had either around the house, which I don't. The way I see it, you have to pick and chose your battles."

Gideon considered that, then nodded. "Sounds right." He shot a glance over her shoulder toward the stove. "Think your mushrooms are hot yet?"

"It's only been a minute since I last checked."

"Check again," he said, and ushered her to the farthest reaches of the kitchen. Once there, he backed her to the counter, lowered his head and captured her lips in what would have been a deep, devouring kiss had not Jill's call intruded.

"Mom?"

With a low groan, he wrenched his mouth away and stepped back.

Chris felt she was spinning around, twisting at the end of a long, spiraling line. She was hot, dizzy and frustrated. It was a minute before she could steady herself to answer. "Yes?"

"Where *is* the set?"

Chris made a small sound and closed her eyes for a minute. Then, shaking her head, she sent Gideon an apologetic look and pushed off from the counter. Jill was at the top of the stairs.

"Just tell me where it is," she called down.

But Chris didn't remember exactly where it was. "I'm coming," she said lightly. Once upstairs, it took several minutes of searching through drawers before she finally located the clip and earrings. She handed them over with a repeat of the warning, "You'll be very, very, *very* careful."

"I will. See?" She held the earrings in her hand. "They're perfect with what I'm wearing."

Chris knew that just about anything would go with a blue denim skirt. But Jill had a point. The swirls of blue-and-green enamel picked up the color of her sweater beautifully.

Rubbing her hands together, she took a deep breath. "Okay. Are you all set now? Anything else you need?"

"Nope. Thanks, Mom."

"If you're using my perfume—" which happened often "—remember, a little goes a long way. You don't want to hit the party smelling like a whorehouse."

"Okay."

"I'll be downstairs. Come on down when you're ready and have some hors d'oeuvres."

"If there are any left. Gideon looks hungry."

You should only know, Chris thought, then was grateful Jill didn't. Too soon, she'd be into serious dating. Too soon, she would know about hunger, about the urges that drove men and women together at times that weren't always the wisest. What Chris had done with Brant sixteen years before hadn't been smart at all, though she'd never had cause to regret having Jill. She meant what she'd told Gideon, that she was happy with her life.

Would she be happier with a man in the picture? She didn't know. She did know that she was drawn to Gideon in an elemental way that refused to be ignored. She was older and wiser. Still, she was drawn. Even now, returning to the kitchen to find that he'd opened the wine and was filling two glasses, she felt a flare of excitement. For a split second, she was at the end of that truncated kiss again, spinning on a spiral of desire, feeling the frustration.

"Is Jill all set?" he asked, handing her one of the glasses.

"Uh-huh."

"To us, then," he said, raising the other.

Chris touched her glass to his, then took a sip. "Mmm. This is nice." Focusing on the amber liquid, she whispered, "Sorry about before. The timing was unfortunate."

"Did I complain?" he whispered back, coming in close to her side. "It just lengthens the foreplay, that's all."

Chris felt a soft shuddering inside. "Uh, maybe we ought to sit down."

"Maybe we ought to have something to eat."

"Right." Setting her wine on the counter, she put on mitts and removed the tray of mushrooms from the oven. She arranged half of them on a dish that also held a wedge of cheese and some crackers, then put the rest back. "So they'll stay warm."

Gideon carried the dish to the low glass table in front of the living room sofa. When Chris joined him there, he popped a mushroom into his mouth. "Whoa," he drawled when it was gone, "that was worth two wasted batches."

Chris went red. "I wasn't paying attention to what I was doing."

"Like my men weren't that day at Crosslyn Rise?" he teased, because he couldn't resist, and leaned close. "Was I the cause of your distraction?"

She focused on his tie, which was silk and striped diagonally in blue, yellow and purple. "Of course not. I was thinking about work."

"I'm work, aren't I?"

"Not actively. Not yet."

"I got some half-rounds."

Her eyes flew to his, wide and pleased. "You did?"

He nodded. "Above the French doors, like you wanted. Put them in last week."

"All those phone calls, and you didn't tell me?"

"I wanted to surprise you." His gaze fell to her mouth and stuck there. "Thought if I saved it for a special time, it might win me a kiss." His voice was rough. "How about it?"

Without a moment's hesitancy, Chris reached up and put a soft kiss on his mouth. Then, because it had been so sweet and too short, she followed it with a second.

"You smell good," he whispered against her lips. "I'll bet you smell like this all over." When she caught in a small gasp, he sealed it in with the full pressure of his mouth, giving her the kind of hard, hungry kiss he craved.

Chris wanted the hardness and more. She opened to the sweep of his tongue, but he was barely done when he ended the kiss. She felt she was hanging in midair. "What's wrong?"

"Too fast," he whispered, breathing heavily. "Too hot." He shot a glance toward the stairs. "Too public." Pulling away from her, he bent over, propping his elbows on his knees. The low sounds that escaped his throat as he tried to steady his breathing told her of his discomfort.

Chris felt dismayed. In the moment when he'd kissed her, she'd forgotten that Jill was still upstairs. "I should have realized," she whispered.

"Not your fault alone. It takes two to tango."

It was a figure of speech, but she latched on to it as a diversion from desire. "Do you tango?"

"Nope. Can't dance much at all. But I make love real good."

She moaned, picturing that with far too great an ease. In desperation, she reached for the dish of mushrooms. "Here. Have another. And tell me what else is happening at the Rise."

With a slightly shaky but nonetheless deep breath, Gideon straightened. He ate another mushroom, then a third. "These are really good." He glanced back toward the kitchen. "And something else smells good." He frowned, trying to identify it.

"Rock Cornish Hens," she said. "It's the orange sauce that you smell." But she wasn't feeling at all hungry for that. "Tell me about the Rise," she repeated. She needed to think of something settling.

Gideon understood and agreed. He really hadn't intended to start things off hot and heavy. It had just happened. For both of them. But the civil thing was to talk and visit and eat first.

Casually crossing an ankle over his knee as he would have done if he'd been with the guys, he began to talk. He told Chris about the progress his crew had made, the few problems they'd run into, the solutions they'd found, that they'd moved inside. The diversion worked. When Jill joined them some fifteen minutes later, they were involved in a discussion of staircase options.

"You look great, honey," Chris told her with a smile.

"Better than great," Gideon added. "Those poor guys won't be able to keep their hands off you."

Chris shot him a dirty look. "They'd better." To Jill, she said, "One swift kick you know where."

Jill seemed embarrassed. She glanced at Gideon before sitting close to Chris and saying quietly, "My hair looks awful."

"Your hair looks great."

"I should have had it cut."

"If you had, you'd be tugging at the ends to make it longer."

"It never curls the way I want. I've been fiddling with it for an hour, and it's still twisting the wrong way."

"You're the only one who knows that. To everyone else, me included, it looks great."

"You're just saying that because you're my mother."

"I'm not your mother," Gideon said, "and I say it, too."

Jill eyed him warily. "You'd say anything to please Mom."

"No way," he argued. "If you'd been down sooner, you'd have heard me telling her that she could grovel all night if she wanted, but I was not putting in winding staircases at Crosslyn Rise."

"This man," Chris told Jill, "is a cheapskate. There's a huge winding staircase in the mansion. It would be *perfect* to have smaller versions in the condos. Don't you think so?"

Jill crinkled her nose. "Winding staircases are good for long, sweeping dresses, but modern people don't wear them."

"That's right," Gideon chimed in. "They spend their money on skylights and Jacuzzis and Sub-Zero refrigerators instead. Face it, Chris, you're outvoted."

But Chris shook her head. "I still think they'd be great, and I'm the decorator."

"Well, I'm the builder, and I say they're too expensive. We can't fit them into the budget. That's all there is to it."

"You won't even *try*?"

"We're talking *ten grand* per staircase! I just can't do it."

Chris sensed that she could argue until she was blue in the face and she wouldn't get anywhere. She arched a brow Jill's way. "So much for trying to please me."

Jill's gaze bounced from Chris to Gideon and back. "Did I cause that fight?"

"Of course not—"

"It wasn't a fight—"

"You both look pretty ticked off."

"I'm not ticked off—"

"I never get ticked off—"

"Maybe you shouldn't be talking work on New Year's Eve."

"I don't know—"

"Yeah, well—"

Jill looked at her watch. "Hey, can we leave now?"

"Have something to eat first," Chris told her, escaping into the role of mother with ease.

"They'll have food at the party."

"Uh-huh. Pizza, but not for a few hours, I'd wager."

"They'll have munchies," Jill argued, and rose to get her coat. "We're picking up Jenny and Laura on the way, so they can put their stuff right in the car." She grew hesitant, again looking back and forth. "Uh, whose car?"

"My Bronco," Gideon said, "if that's okay with you. And it's fine about the stuff. We'll bring it in when we get back here."

Chris hadn't known they were picking up the two other girls and sensed that it had been a last-minute deal. She wondered if it had anything to do with Gideon being there, or more specifically, with the fact that Chris was seeing him. None of Jill's friends had ever seen Chris with a man. Maybe Jill wanted her friends to know that her mother was human.

Oh, she was human, all right, human and female. Once in the truck, sitting in the front seat with Gideon, she was as keenly aware of him as she'd been back in the house. Each move he made seemed to register. Fortunately, he kept up a steady conversation with Jill, asking about the party, who was going, who of those going she was closest to. That led into a fast discussion about school, what she was taking, what she liked best and worst. By the time they reached Jenny's house, Chris had picked up several tidbits even she hadn't known.

Jill and Jenny talked softly in back from there. They were soon joined by Laura, who directed Gideon the short distance from her house to the one where the party was being held. When they arrived, and Jenny and Laura climbed out, Jill hung back for a minute.

"So, you guys are going back home for dinner?"

"Uh-huh," Chris said.

"You're not going out to a movie or anything later?"

Chris gave her cheek a reassuring touch. "We'll be home. If there's any problem, just call and we'll be right here. Otherwise, we'll be back to pick you up at twelve-thirty." She kissed her. "Have a super time, honey."

"You, too, Mom," Jill said softly, then raised her voice. "You, too, Gideon."

"Thanks, Jill. Have fun. We'll be back."

With the slam of the door, she was gone. She glanced back once on the way to join her friends, then disappeared with them into the house.

"Was that nervousness?" Gideon asked as he shifted into gear and started off.

"I'm not sure. I think so. She's so grown-up in some ways, then in others..."

He knew just what she meant. Jill was physically mature. She was personable and poised. But the look in her eye from time to time told the truth. "She's only fifteen. That's pretty young."

"Sometimes I forget. We're such good friends."

"She's a really nice girl." He reached for Chris's hand, needing her warmth. "Even if she did interrupt what was promising to be one of the best kisses of my life."

Chris closed her fingers around his, but she didn't say a word. Left hanging, of course, was the fact that they could resume that kiss the minute they got home without worry of interruption.

"What are your parents doing tonight?" he asked a drop too casually. He was thinking of interruptions, too, but it seemed crass to let on. Hadn't he decided that they should talk and eat first?

"They're having dinner with friends. There's a local group that's been spending their New Year's Eves together for years. It used to be Mom and Dad would make a point to be home before midnight to be with us— Jill and me and anyone else who was home—but everyone's out this year."

"Except you," he said softly.

"Except me." She held more tightly to his hand. When he gave a tug, she slid closer to him.

"Are *you* nervous?" he asked. He supposed it was a form of talk, though it was getting right to the point.

She studied his face. Muted in the dark, his expression was strangely dear. "A little."

He drove quietly for a time before saying, "Does it help to know I am, too?"

"You? Buy why?"

"Because you're special. I want to make things good for you."

A light tremor shimmered through her insides. Swallowing, she said, "I think you could do that with your eyes closed."

"I don't want them closed. There's too much to see."

Like frames of a movie, the images that had haunted her flicked one after another through her mind. "Uh, Gideon?" she whispered. "I think there's something you should know."

"Don't tell me you're a virgin."

"I'm not, but—"

"You've had a baby, Chris."

"I know that," she said quickly, quietly, putting her cheek against his arm, "but the sum total of my experience with a man took place in the back seat of a '72 Chevy."

He was amused by that. "The back seat, eh?"

"It was dark. I didn't see much."

"I never did it in a car." Most everywhere else when he'd been younger, but never in a car. He'd gotten too big too fast. "What was it like?"

"That's not the point."

"But I want to know." He flattened her hand on his thigh and held it there. "Wouldn't I have to be kind of crunched up?"

"Gideon—"

"I'm too tall for a car."

She sighed. "No, you're not. You could do it. It'd just take a little ingenuity."

He began moving her hand around. "Like with positions?"

She nodded, still against his arm. She was picturing the wildest things. "You'd have to be kind of half on, half off the seat."

"I'd be on top?"

That was the only position Chris had ever known, but she'd read of others. "Or under," she murmured.

"Would we be undressed?"

"Just...vaguely."

"Could I touch your breasts?"

She sucked in a breath. "If you wanted to."

"Bare? Could I open your bra?"

"It might be cold."

His low voice, angled into her hair, was like liquid fire, which was precisely what was searing his gut. "I'd want to do it anyway. I want to see what you look like all over, then I'd warm you up."

She pressed her face into his arm. "Gideon—"

He slid her hand upward, urging it back and forth at the very top of his thigh. "Heating up?"

"Oh, yes."

"It doesn't take much with us."

"I know. I don't understand it. All these years, and I haven't been attracted to any other man." But she could feel the heat in him searing her palm and curling right through her. Later, thinking back on it, she wouldn't know which of them moved first, but suddenly she was covering his sex, shaping her fingers to his arousal, cupping the heaviness beneath.

"Chris." He made a deep, choking sound. She started to take her hand away, but he held it fast. "It's okay, okay." He made another sound when he swallowed. "How much longer till we're home?"

Chris looked out the window. It was a minute before she could focus, a minute more before she could identify the street they were on. "Two more blocks." She glanced up at his face, where the tension was marked. A surge of feeling welled up from inside, propelling her mouth to his jaw. She kissed it once, moved an inch, kissed it again. Her voice was like down against his rough skin. "Can you make it?"

"Oh, yeah," he gritted, and released her hand. "Loosen my tie, Chris? I'm being strangled."

She loosened it and unbuttoned the top button. "Better?"

"Yes...listen, Chris, if you think there's even the slightest chance that you may get cold feet on me and want to call this off, better tell me now so I can run around the block a couple of times before we go inside." He didn't think they were going to get in much talking or visiting or eating. They'd already passed that point.

"I won't get cold feet," she said, and knew she wouldn't, couldn't. She was too hot.

"What about the food?"

"It'll hold." She took a shallow breath. "Gideon, what I said the other night about birth control? I still don't have anything. I was thinking I should see my doctor, then I didn't know whether we'd really, uh, get together, and I felt funny. Do you have something?"

Turning into her street, he nodded. In a gritty whisper, he said, "Will you help me put it on?"

Her insides grew swollen at the thought. "I don't know how."

"I'll show you."

"So we'll be sharing the responsibility?"

"I wasn't thinking of it that way."

"What were you thinking of?"

"The turn-on. Having you touch me—having you look at me—" He was torturing himself, unable to stop.

"Gideon, what I was trying to tell you before—"

"Jeez, I've never talked about making love this way. Does it sound calculated?" He turned onto the driveway.

"It sounds hot."

"I *feel* hot." He pulled as close to the garage as he could.

"Gideon, there's something I want to *tell* you." She rushed the words out, fearful of being cut off again. "I may have had a baby, but I'm pretty new at this. I haven't even—"

"Shh," he whispered, pressing his fingers to her mouth. Opening the door, he slid out, drawing her along in nearly the same motion. A supportive arm circled her shoulders and hugged her to him as he guided her quickly toward the door. Once inside, with the cold air and all of humanity locked out, he pressed her to the wall, ran his mouth from her forehead, down her nose to her lips. She smelled sweet, almost innocent, and was soft to match. That softness burned into him, from the spot, waist high, where their bodies met to the one at the knee where they parted. She was giving, yielding. Her chin tipped up under the light urging of his thumbs. Her mouth opened to his, welcoming him inside. Every move she made was untutored, purely instinctive, intensely feminine. Each one called to the man in him that craved her possession.

"The nice thing," he breathed against her forehead as he pushed away the shoulders of her coat, "would have been to wait on this until later, but I can't, Chris." The coat slipped to the floor. "If that makes me a not-nice man, I guess that's what I am, but I need you too much now." His fingers met at her throat, touched the collar of her dress and the top buttons, then separated and slid over silk to her breasts. It was the first time he'd touched her there. She was full and firm. Even through her dress and a bra, he could feel the tightness of her nipples.

The sensation of being touched and held was so charged, Chris thought she'd die—just explode. With a small sound, she covered his hands.

He was instantly concerned. As aroused as he was, he had promised to make it good for her, and if it killed him, he intended to do just that. "Hurt?"

"Not enough." She felt impatient and greedy. Transferring her hands from her chest to his, she ran her open palms over him while he worked at the buttons of her dress. When it was open to the waist, she felt him part the fabric, then release the center clasp of her bra. She was holding him at the hips by that time, needing an anchor, feeling momentarily shy when he peeled back the lace and cool air hit her breasts.

Gideon sensed her shyness, and it fueled his fire. In the past, he'd had the most experienced of women, but none sparked him as Chris did. Angling his upper body away, he took pleasure in what he'd unclothed. Her breasts were pale, strawberry at their crests, quivering with each shallow breath she took.

He was smitten. Never in his life had he seen anything as beautiful as Chris against that door with her fingers clutching his hips, her eyes lowered to his belt, her dress open and her breasts bare and waiting. Unable to resist, he ducked his head and put his mouth to one. He drew it in. His tongue raked its turgid tip.

She cried out, a frantic whisper of his name.

"I want you so badly," he moaned. Dragging himself from her breast, he straightened and tore off his blazer. Holding her gaze, which had risen with him, he tugged off his tie, unbuttoned his shirt and unfastened his pants. Then he slid his fingers into her hair, held her head still and took her mouth in a strong, sucking kiss.

Chris wanted more than that. "Upstairs," she gasped when he finally allowed her a breath. "I want you in my bed." She took his hand, but no leading was necessary. He was right beside her, half-running up the stairs, stopping midway for another deep kiss before continuing to the top.

Her room was shadowed, lit only from the hall, though neither of them seemed aware. They were kissing again within seconds, but this time their hands were at work, fumbling with buttons, zippers and sleeves. Their fingers tangled. They alternately laughed, moaned and gasped. She was sitting on the edge of the bed pulling the stockings from her feet when he came down beside her.

"Help me," he said, fiddling with a small foil pack.

For a minute, she couldn't breathe. He was stark naked and fully aroused. She'd known he would be, of course, still her startled eyes were drawn to the thickly thatched spot from which his arousal jutted so tall and straight.

At her utter stillness, Gideon raised his head. He didn't have to follow her gaze to know what she was looking at. The thought that she might be afraid gave him the control he wouldn't otherwise have had. "It won't hurt," he whispered, drawing her close. "You know that. You've done this before."

"But I've never seen it before," she whispered back. "That was what I've been trying to tell you. I have lots of brothers, but by the time they reached puberty, I was out of the house. And with Brant it was always so dark." Tremulously she touched his stomach. "I'm not afraid. You're very beautiful." From his navel, she brushed the back of her fingers down the thin, dark line to where the hair grew more dense, then on to his velvety strength. Satin on steel, it seemed to her. She explored it lightly, felt it flex and grow.

Gideon croaked out her name.

She looked up. "Too much?"

"Too little." He reached again for the foil pack, but no sooner had he removed the condom than she took it from him.

"Tell me how," she whispered.

He told her. With surprising ease, given her trembling and his hardness, she had the condom on. Then, feeling proud and excited and filled with something else that was nearly overwhelming, she slipped her arms around his neck and put her mouth to his. "Love me?"

"I do," he muttered, near the end of his tether. With an arm around her slender waist, he fell over onto the bed, sweeping her beneath him as he drew them both up toward the pillows.

That was when Chris felt the full force of his nakedness. He was man through and through, from the luxury of his weight to the friction of his limbs. His hands seemed everywhere, touching her in large sweeps from her breasts to her hips, then the hot spot between her legs. Suddenly without patience, she opened for him.

"Hurry!"

Taut and trembling, Gideon lifted himself, positioned himself and slowly, slowly sank into the tightest sheath that had ever encased him. "There. Ah. Chris, you're so small."

She felt it. Small, feminine and cherished. And she loved it.

"Am I hurting you?" he asked.

"Oh, no. You feel so new. So special. So big."

Gideon nearly came. He went very still for a minute, shut his eyes tight, gritted his teeth until he'd regained control. "What you do to me."

Chris was thinking the same thing about him, because the small pinching she'd first felt at his entry was gone, leaving only a yearning to be stroked. Grasping his hair, she looked up at him and said, "Make love to me now, Gideon. Do it."

He didn't need any more urging than that. Withdrawing nearly all the way, he surged back with a cry of triumph, then repeated the pattern in a rhythm that seemed to anticipate, then mirror her need. Chris surrendered to that need, letting it take her higher and higher until, closing her eyes and arching her back, she tumbled head-on into a mindless riot of sensation.

Somewhere at the tail end of the riot, a low light came on, but awareness was slow to return. When her breathing had finally slowed and she opened her eyes, she found Gideon propped above her, looking down with a smile. He'd managed to light the lamp beside the bed without leaving her; he was as rigid as ever inside her. But that didn't seem to be bothering him. Though the muscles of his upper arms were taut beneath her hands and his breathing was heavy, something pleased him immensely.

"What?" she whispered with a shy smile.

"You wouldn't ask that if you could see what I do," he replied. His voice was low and husky, as tight as his body, but he wasn't rushing toward his own release. There was too much pleasure to be gained just in looking at Chris, with her blond hair mussed, her cheeks pink, her skin aglow with a light sheen of sweat, her lips rosy and full. There was too much pleasure to be gained just in holding himself inside her, knowing that for a short time she was all his. He felt more loved than he ever had in his life. "Was it good?"

She nodded. "You touch me, and...poof!"

His grin broadened. "That's good. I want it like that."

"But you haven't come."

"I will." He took a deep, shuddering breath. "I do love you, y'know."

She felt a burst of heat in the area of her heart. "How can you tell?"

"Because of what I feel, like I could stay this way forever and be perfectly happy. Before, when we were downstairs and then in the car, I thought I'd die if I didn't get into you fast, and maybe I would have. But now that I'm here, there's no rush. What you looked like when you came—what that look did to me—was more satisfying than any climax I've ever had."

Chris felt tears pool in the outside corners of her eyes. "That's beautiful," she whispered. She touched his chest, running a finger by his small, dark nipple. "You're beautiful." Giving more freedom to her hands, she let them familiarize themselves with the wedge of fine hair beneath his collarbone, the muscular ridges of his shoulders, the tapering strength of his back. She was entranced by his perfection, his mix of hard and soft, ragged and smooth, flat and curved. "You *are* beautiful," she whispered again. Curving her hands to his backside, she arched her back and rose off the bed to put her mouth to his throat.

Gideon lost it then. In her slow, gentle way, she was driving him to distraction. Unable to wait any longer, he began to make love to her again. He tempered himself only at the end, when he felt her coming so close, and when her senses erupted for a second time, he gave in to his own powerful release.

Later, much later that night, after the New Year had been welcomed in with toasts and kisses, after Jill and her friends had been fetched and settled, after Gideon had left for the ride back to Worcester and Chris was in bed, she thought about all that had happened.

Gideon had been incredible. He'd made love to her yet another time in her bed, then once in the shower before they dressed. It wasn't the fact of his physical prowess that impressed her as much as the soft things he'd said, the adoring look in his eye and the cherished way he'd made her feel.

Brant had never done that.

More than once, as she lay in bed that night, then on subsequent nights after talking with Gideon on the phone, she wondered if she loved him. The thought was a sobering one. She didn't have faith in herself when it came to love. She'd misjudged once before, and had spent fifteen years trying to make up for it to Jill. If she loved Gideon now, if she became more deeply involved with him than she already was, Jill was bound to be affected. Worse, if the involvement deepened and Jill came to love him, too, and then something happened, Chris would never forgive herself.

The dilemma was whether to take the chance or leave things the way they were. The answer eluded her.

8

Of all the months of the year, Chris liked January the least. It was the coldest and most bleak, physically and emotionally, a necessary evil to be suffered through to reach February, which had a vacation, at least. And then March came with its lengthening days, and April with its promise of rebirth, and by then she had it made.

This year, January was fun. For one thing, she got down to serious work on Crosslyn Rise, poring over Carter's plans, visiting the site at least once a week to check on the progress, wading through swatches of wallpaper and carpeting, studying furniture and cabinetry designs, pondering electrical and bathroom fixtures, and kitchen appliances.

Though she would be working with buyers as they came along later that summer, the plan was to completely outfit a model apartment in one of the units for potential clients to see. Moreover, she would be decorating the entire mansion, once it was subdivided into a restaurant, a health club and a meeting place. For that, she would be calling in experts to help, but she was the coordinator.

There was lots to think about, but she loved it. She also loved spending time with Gideon, which was probably why she went to the Rise so often, given the season and the relatively slow rate of the work. They argued often, but within reason. Though she'd yielded on the issue of winding stairways, she wanted marble tiles in the bathrooms, Corian in the kitchens, and full walls of brick where the fireplaces would go. Invariably Gideon rebelled at the cost, just as inevitably he went out of his way to try to accommodate her. Sometimes he made it, sometimes he didn't. But he tried. She couldn't ask for more.

January was also bright because she saw him after work. She kept it to once a week, on the weekend when Jill might have other plans, but the anticipation of that one night, along with his regular phone calls, kept her feeling alive in ways she hadn't known she'd been missing.

Come February, he asked to stay the weekend at her place, but she was uncomfortable with that. "Jill will be in and out. I just can't."

They were lying face-to-face on a bed in a small motel off the highway not far from Crosslyn Rise. It was three o'clock on a Thursday afternoon. Working together at the Rise shortly before, they'd suffered a sharp desire attack. The motel had been Gideon's suggestion. Chris hadn't protested.

Now, in the afterglow of what had been more hot and exciting than ever, Gideon only knew that he needed more of her. "Jill knows what's going on."

"She doesn't know that we sleep together." They'd been careful about that, choosing their time together with care.

"She knows," he insisted. "She's a perceptive kid. She sees the way we look at each other, the way we touch. She was the one who noticed the hand-holding that first day. You think she doesn't suspect that there's more than hands involved now?"

"I don't know what she suspects," Chris replied, feeling unsettled because it was true. And it was her own fault. She didn't have the courage to ask. "But I think it would be awkward for her if you slept over. It's too soon."

Nothing could be too soon for Gideon, whose love for Chris kept growing. Although he sensed she wasn't really ready, he wanted to ask her to marry him, which was a *really* big step. He'd been footloose and fancy-free for a good long time. But he was willing to give it all up for Chris. He *had* given it all up. Since meeting her, he hadn't dated another woman. Footloose and fancy-free had lost its lure.

He did agree, though, that Jill was a concern. "Does she ask you questions about what we do?"

"Surface ones, like where we ate and what we had for dinner."

"Do you think she accepts me?" He knew that Jill liked him, and remembered all too clearly the permission she'd given him to date Chris. But that had been before he'd started doing it. Faced with the reality of having someone to compete with for her mother's time, she might have had second thoughts.

Chris moved her hand through the hair on his chest. "She accepts you as someone I have a good time with on the weekends."

"But not as my lover?"

"She doesn't know you are."

"You think."

After a minute, she admitted, "I think."

"Maybe you should tell her. You're young. You're healthy. You're an adult. You have every right to want to be with a man."

"I'm supposed to set an example for her."

The sound of that gave Gideon a chill. He drew her closer to ward it off. "You're not doing anything illegal or immoral. You're making love with a man you care deeply about." His voice lowered. "You do care that way, don't you?"

Her eyes were soft, as was her voice. "You know I do." For a minute, secure in his arms, enveloped by his scent and lost in his gaze, she was engulfed by a longing for forever. Then the minute passed and reality returned. "But you have to understand, Gideon. You're the first man I've dated, really dated, in Jill's memory, and we haven't been doing it for long. If I suddenly have you staying the night, she's apt to think that it's okay to do that after a couple of dates.''

''It is. Sometimes.''

''She's only fifteen!''

''And you're thirty-three. She's bright enough to see the difference. It's okay for you to be doing what we're doing, Chris. It's *right* for you to be doing it, given what you feel. You're a passionate woman.'' How well he knew. Each time they made love, she was more hungry, more aggressive. ''How you kept it locked away for so long is beyond me.''

''It wasn't any big thing. I never wanted another man the way I do you.''

''Not even Brant?'' he couldn't resist asking.

''Not even Brant,'' she said, and knew it was true. What she felt for Gideon, what she did with him, had nothing to do with growing up, experimenting, feeling her oats or rebelling. It had to do with mature desires and deep inner feelings. ''We were young. Too young. I don't want Jill doing what we did.''

''You can't put a chastity belt on her.''

''No, but I can teach her the importance of waiting.''

''Would you have her be a virgin at her wedding?''

''I wouldn't mind it.''

''That's unrealistic, Chris.''

''I know. But it's not unrealistic to encourage her to wait until someone important to her comes along. I've tried to teach her that lovemaking is special.''

''It is. So why can't you tell her that we do it?''

''I can't. She'll jump to conclusions.''

''So talk to her. Explain.''

But Chris wasn't ready for that. ''She's always come first in my life. She may get nervous.''

''So you'll talk to her more. You'll explain more. You two are close. You talk about everything else. Why not this?''

She wished she could make him understand. ''Because it's so *basic*.''

''You're right about that,'' Gideon drawled, then grew intense. ''Lord, Chris, do you know how much I want to sleep with you? Not make love. *Sleep.* Roll over with you tucked up against me. Wake up that way, too.''

''And then what would happen?'' she asked knowingly.

''We'd make love.''

''Right. With Jill in the next room, listening to the headboard bang rhythmically against the wall.''

''So we'll pull the bed out.''

''The *frame* squeaks.''

''I'm a handyman. I'll fix it.''

''You're missing the *point*.''

"So we won't make love. I'll just go through the rest of the day suffering silently—"

"Gideon," she pleaded softly, "I need time. That's all. I need time to get Jill accustomed to a man in my life. I owe it to her, don't you see?"

As he saw it, she owed things to herself, too. But, then, he'd never been a parent. He'd never felt the kind of responsibility for another human being that Chris felt so keenly for Jill. Loving Chris as he did, he had to respect her feelings.

"Okay," he said in surrender, "then we go to plan B."

"Plan B?"

"We go away together."

Chris was dumbfounded. "Did you hear *anything* I said?"

"All three of us. Jill has school vacation coming up in two weeks. So we'll make reservations and go somewhere together. That way, she'll be able to get used to the idea of our being together."

"But that'll be no different than having you over at the house! The same problem exists."

"Not if we book separate rooms." When Chris seemed to listen at that, he went on. "You and Jill room together. I'll have my own. We could either go north to ski or south to sun and swim."

Chris wanted to tell him he was crazy, except that idea wasn't bad. In fact, the more she thought of it, the more she liked it. "Do you ski?" she asked.

"Sure, I ski," he answered. "I mean, I may not do my turns as neatly as I do my lay-ups, but neither do I make a fool out of myself." He could see she was tempted. "Ever been to Stowe?"

She shook her head against his shoulder. "Only to Woodstock, and not for skiing. Stowe is farther north. I never wanted to drive that long."

"Would you want to with me?"

"I wouldn't mind it."

"What about Jill?"

"She'd be game. She's dying to go skiing."

"Does she know how?"

"Barely."

"No sweat. The instructors are good. Would you prefer a condo or an inn?"

"An inn."

"Separate rooms?"

She nodded.

"Would you visit me in mine?"

She grinned. "Maybe."

With a grin of his own, he slid an arm around her hips, which was where, by a stretch of the imagination, there was a touch of fullness. "Maybe?"

"If it isn't too hard."

"It'll definitely be hard."

"Is that a warning," she asked softly, "or a promise?"

Eyes smoldering, he rolled to his back and drew her on top. His large hands cupped her head, directing her down for his kiss. It was the only answer he gave.

When Chris told Jill that they were going skiing, her eyes lit up. When she told her that Gideon would be coming, the light faded a little. "I didn't know he skied," she said with reluctant interest.

"I didn't, either. But he does. And he's been to Stowe before, so he knows the good places to eat."

"Will we rent a condo?"

"I thought we'd go to an inn." She paused. "I thought you'd be more comfortable that way."

"Will I have my own room?"

"We'll share, you and me."

Jill seemed surprised by that, and relieved. "You're not rooming with Gideon?"

Chris shook her head. "I'm rooming with you."

"Won't he mind?"

"He knows that's the way it has to be."

Jill considered that. "Do you wish it was different?"

"In what sense?"

"That you two were going away alone?"

"Of course not. You're my best friend."

"And what's he?"

"He's a man I'm seeing, who I like a lot."

"Do you love him?"

"You've asked me that before. What did I tell you then?"

"That it was too soon to ask you, but you've seen him a lot since then. You must have some idea what you feel. Or what you think you can feel. If we're going skiing with him—"

"We're doing it because it sounds like fun."

"We could drive up there, you and me, just ourselves."

"But it was Gideon's idea." She gave Jill a funny look. "Weren't you the one who felt so badly that he had to spend Christmas all by himself in a lonely house?"

"Yeah, but this is different. This is purely voluntary. It's my vacation time. Not his."

Chris felt a stab of concern. "Would you rather he not go?"

"No. He can go."

"Such enthusiasm," she teased, trying to hide her unease. "I thought you liked him."

"I *do*. And I'm *glad* we're going skiing with him. I just want to know if you love him."

Chris thought about it for a minute before finally, truthfully, saying, "I don't know. There are times when I think I do, but then there are so many considerations—"

"Like what?"

"Like whether he's prepared to play second fiddle to you. You come first, Jill. You always have and always will."

"But that's not fair to you. Maybe you want to be with Gideon. Maybe you *should* be with him."

"How would you feel if I were?"

Jill was awhile in answering. The words were cautious when they came. "Happy for you. Happy for Gideon."

"And for you?"

"Happy, too, I guess."

"You don't sound convinced."

She looked at her hands. "I don't know. It just takes some getting used to. I mean, I'd really like it because then you'd have things to do, yourself, and I wouldn't feel badly leaving you home all alone."

Chris hadn't realized. "Do you do that?"

"Sometimes. But then I like knowing you're here. I like knowing you're waiting for me. Selfish, huh?"

Brushing a wisp of dark hair from Jill's cheek, Chris said, "Not selfish at all. Just a little worried. You've been used to one thing, and now you see the possibility of things changing. Don't you think the idea of change frightens me, too? Don't you think it comes into play when you ask if I love Gideon?"

"Does it?"

"Sure, it does. I'm used to my life, our life. I like it. I'm not sure I want anything to disturb it."

"But if you love Gideon—"

"I don't know for sure that I do, which is one of the reasons why I really want the three of us to go on this trip. If I'm going to love any man, you'll have to feel comfortable with him—and vice versa—because no matter what else happens, I'm your mother. Always. I'll be here for you even if I love *ten* guys."

Jill smirked. "Ten guys? Fat chance. You're such a prude."

"What is that supposed to mean?" Chris asked with an indignance that was only half-feigned.

"You haven't even gone to bed with Gideon! I mean, look at him. He's gorgeous. Jenny and Laura are *still* drooling over him. Why aren't you?"

"Why aren't I drooling?"

"Why aren't you sleeping with him?"

Chris swallowed. As openings went, it was perfect. Remembering the conversation she'd had such a short time before with Gideon, she knew he was right. She and Jill were close. She'd always prided herself on forthrightness. She could explain her feelings. They could talk. It was time.

"How do you know I'm not?" she asked gently.

While Jill didn't jump immediately at the suggestion, she grew more alert. "When do you have time?"

"You make time for what you want."

"I mean, when have you had the *chance*?"

"You find chances, if you want them."

Jill was quiet. After a minute, she blurted out, "So have you—or haven't you?"

"Is it important to you to know?"

She backed down. "Not if you don't want to tell me."

"I do. I want to tell you. I want to, because some of the things Gideon and I have shared have been very, very beautiful. I've always told you that. With the right person, making love is precious."

Jill seemed suddenly shy, as though this Chris was a new and different person from the one she'd known moments before. "So you have," she whispered.

Chris nodded. "He is...very special."

"Does he love you?"

"Yes."

"Do you think you'll marry him?"

Chris had taught her that lovemaking should be with someone special, that marriage should be with someone special. So Jill had made the connection, as the mother in Chris wanted her to. Now Chris was caught in the middle.

"I don't know, honey. If what I feel for him proves to be love, I might. But that would be a long way off."

"Why?"

"Because I wouldn't do anything until you went to college."

"Will a man like Gideon wait around that long?"

"If he loves me enough. Maybe that's the test."

"What if you get pregnant before that?"

"Pregnant. Jill, I've taught *you* about using birth control. Don't you think I practice it myself?" She'd seen her doctor right after New Year's.

"What do you use?"

"*Jill.*"

"I'm not supposed to ask that?"

Chris closed her eyes for a second, then reached for her daughter's hand. "Of course you can. This is new for me. That's all."

"Birth control is?"

"Telling you about *my* using it is."

"Wouldn't you want to know what I used?"

"Jill, you're not—"

"No! But if I were, wouldn't you want me to discuss it with you?"

"Definitely."

"So?"

Chris sighed. "I got a diaphragm."

"Do you like it?"

"Uh, well, uh, it's okay, I mean, it's safe and effective, and if you, uh, if you have to use something—"

Jill started to laugh.

"What's so funny?"

"You. You're all red."

"This is *embarrassing*."

"Why? You've told me so many other things without getting embarrassed."

"This is different." She searched for the words. "It's like you're my mother, but I've never had this kind of discussion with my mother."

"That's why I came along."

"And the very best thing you were. I've never, *never* regretted having you, though there are times when I wished my timing had been better. There are times when I wish I could have given you a family of your own, maybe brothers and sisters."

"You could have more babies."

"Hey, I just said I was using birth control."

"But you could stop. Any time you wanted to. You're young enough to have lots more kids. Does Gideon want them?"

"I don't know. We haven't gotten that far."

"Do you?"

"I don't know. You'd be a pretty hard act to follow."

"Naturally," Jill said with a grin.

Chris grinned right back. "Naturally." She took a breath. "So. What do you say? Want to go skiing?"

The inn was small and quaint, with six guest rooms on the second floor and two baths. If she'd wanted to be secretive, Chris would have stolen into Gideon's room, which was down the hall from hers and Jill's, when she was supposedly using the bathroom. But Jill would have known. Besides, she wanted more time.

So she and Gideon returned to his room shortly after Jill had joined an afternoon ski class. Knowing that it would be three hours before she was done, they felt they had all the time in the world.

Chris never failed to marvel at Gideon's body, and this time was no exception. Wearing ski garb—navy stretch pants that clung to him like static and a lime-green turtleneck sweater that matched his navy-and-green parka—he presented the kind of figure that was regularly photographed for the pages of *W*. When that garb came off, though, slowly revealing broad shoulders, a lean stomach and long, long legs, he was Chris's own very personal fantasy come to life.

Dropping her panties onto the floor by the rest of her things, she approached him. Her hands found his shoulders, then moved down and around and back. "When we're out on the slopes," she said in a sultry whisper, "women do double takes when you pass. Your moves may not be studied, but you have a natural grace." She moved closer, bringing her breasts, her belly, her thighs into contact with his. "You do this way, too," she said. Opening her mouth on his neck, she dragged her lips over that corded column. "You are an incredible male." Her palms chafed his thighs, moving slowly in to frame his sex.

Gideon was sure he'd died and gone to heaven. "You make me this way," he said. "It's all for you." Lowering his head, he caught her lips at the same time that he lifted her legs to his hips. He slid into her with the comfort and ease of an old lover and the excitement of a new one.

Familiarity gave them the confidence to be inventive, and a boundless hunger gave them the fuel. Gideon loved her standing up, then sitting on the edge of the bed, then, with Chris astride, on the sheets. He paused midway to love her with his tongue until she was wild with need, then shot back into her with a speed and force that she welcomed. The quiet in the room was broken by gasps and cries. By the time those finally eased, they were both sated, their bodies slick with sweat, tangled but limp.

"Marry me, Chris."

She was half-asleep. "Hmm?"

"I want to marry you."

"I know," she mumbled.

"Will you?"

Eyes closed, she kissed the smooth, soft spot just before his armpit. "Ask me later. Can't think now."

Gideon gave her ten minutes. Then he nudged her partly awake, tipped up her face with a finger and kissed her the rest of the way.

She grinned. "Hi."

"Hi, yourself." He looked at her, then looked some more. Never in a million years would he tire of seeing her after they made love, when she was warm and wet and sensual. He had never before had the stamina to make love three or four times in a night, but he had it with Chris. She inspired him to great heights. "Are you up?"

Sleepily she nodded. "This is so nice. I'm *so* glad we came here."

"Me, too." He paused, figuring he'd take a different, less direct tack this time. "Hard to believe the week's almost done. I could take this on a regular basis for the next thirty or forty years."

Even in her half-dreamy state, Chris knew what he meant. "There's something about ski country. The air is so clear. So cold. So invigorating. It's so warm coming inside."

"When I grow up," Gideon said, "I'm going to buy a place, maybe not as far north as this, but closer, so I can use it on weekends." He ran the pad of his thumb over her eyebrows, first one, then the other. "What do you think? Make any sense?"

Chris thought the idea sounded divine. "What kind of place?" she asked, dreaming wide awake now.

"Something old. With charm."

"A Victorian on the edge of a town green, with the white spire of a church at one end and the stone chimney of the local library at the other."

"You got it. I'd do the place over inside myself, so that it had every modern convenience. I'd break down walls so everything was open, and redo the fireplace so you could see the fire front and back. I'd put in lofts and skylights and spiral stairways and—"

"A Jacuzzi."

"You'd like one?"

"Definitely."

"We've never made love in a Jacuzzi."

"I know." Chris let herself imagine it. "I'd like to."

He was getting hard just thinking of it. "So would I."

"You should have put one in when you built your house."

"But I hadn't met you then. Real men don't soak in tubs unless there's a woman with them, and you're the only woman I've ever entertained at my house."

"The only one?"

"Only one. I love you."

She smiled helplessly. "I know."

"How 'bout you?"

"I'm workin' on it," she teased.

But he was serious. "How far have you come?"

"I'm at the point," she said, "of being happier with you than I've ever been before in my life." There were times when she felt delirious inside, so pleased and excited that she didn't know what to do with her excess energy.

"How far is that from being in love?"

"Pretty close, I guess."

"How long will it take to make 'pretty close' *there*?"

"I don't know." That was where things got hairy, because she knew what was coming next.

"I need you, Chris," he said in the slow, rumbling voice that she'd come to associate with Gideon at his most intense. "I want to be with you morning and night for the rest of my life. I want us to get married."

She'd heard him ask her before, of course, but in the afterglow of loving, she'd pushed it from her mind. She couldn't do that now. She looked up at him to answer, then was momentarily stunned by the look in his eyes. They were so filled with love—and desperation—that she had to fight for a breath.

Coming up over him, she kissed him softly. Her forearms, resting on his chest, held her in position to meet his gaze. "I never thought I'd say this, I really didn't, because marriage wasn't something I ever spent much time considering, but I could almost see myself marrying you, Gideon. I could. I feel so much for you that it overwhelms me sometimes."

"That's love."

"Maybe. But I have to be sure. For me, and for you, and for Jill. I have to know it'll last."

"It'll last."

"So says every couple when they exchange wedding vows, but look at the statistics. I thought I was in love once, and I wasn't."

"You were too young to know what love was about. You're older now."

"We're both older. Look at you. You're almost forty. You were married once, and it didn't work, and now you've been single for years. Is what you feel for me different from what you felt for your first wife?"

"Totally," he said with conviction. "I never wanted to spend all my time with her, not even at the beginning. She had a limited time and place in my life. I had my friends, my business, my games, and I didn't want her to have any part of them. With you, I'm passing up all those other things just to be with you."

"You shouldn't—"

"I *want* to. I'd much *rather* be with you than be with anyone else. I'd much rather be with you than be alone. My first marriage wasn't fun. Being with you is. Know what I want?" The look in his eyes was precious in its enthusiasm.

"What?"

"I want us to work together all the time. We'd be partners. I build, you decorate. Would you like that?"

She would, a whole lot, but her throat was so tight that she could only nod her answer.

He ran his finger over her lips. "I want to make you happy, Chris, and that's another thing that's different from the first time. I never thought about making Julie happy. I was almost defiant about going on with my life as though marriage didn't change it at all." He made a small sound. "I'm not even married to you yet, and my life has changed. Everything I do is geared to when I'll be seeing you again, and I love it that way." He gave her a lopsided grin. "Johnny thinks I'm sick. We were having a sandwich at the diner the other day and these two women came in. Ten, fifteen, twenty minutes went by and he started looking at me strangely."

"Why?"

"Because he thought they were real lookers and I wasn't even interested. I guess they were pretty, but that's all. Hell, I don't even wink at Cookie anymore!"

"Poor Cookie."

"Yeah, she was kinda hurt."

"You have my permission to wink. There's no harm in that."

"But winking is a kind of come-on. It's like me saying, 'I'm a man, and I think you're cute.' But I'm not thinking about anyone else being cute anymore. No one but you."

"Oh, Gideon."

"I've even thought about living arrangements. We could buy a piece of land halfway between Worcester and Belmont, something really pretty, big and wooded. There're lots of bedroom communities with good schools for Jill—"

"I can't change her."

"Why not?"

"Because she's in high school. She's with friends she's grown up with, and they're just getting to the fun years. It'd be cruel to take her away from that."

"Then we'll live in Belmont until she's done with high school, and in the meanwhile we can be building our dream house—"

She pressed a hand to his mouth. "Shh."

"What?"

"You're being too accommodating."

"That's the point. I love you, so I *want* to be accommodating."

"But I can't be accommodating back!" she cried. "Don't you see? You're right about love meaning that, but I'm not free to love that way. I have Jill. I want things to be so right for her in the next few years."

Gideon felt that they had circled around and were right back to the point where they'd been weeks before. It was frustrating, but he wasn't about to give up. "I want things right for her, too. My coming into your life doesn't have to change anything."

"But it will. It will. And then if something goes wrong—"

"What something?"

"With our relationship, and there'd be tension and upset. I don't want to subject Jill to that. She's been so good about not having a father."

"But that's *another* thing," he went on. "You could *give* her a father, if you wanted. Me."

"It's not the same."

Gideon let the words sink in, along with the look on Chris's face. The moment was enlightening. "You feel guilty about that, don't you?"

"Yes, I feel guilty."

Wrapping his arms around her, he hugged her. "After all you've given Jill, the last thing you should be feeling is guilty. My God, Chris, you've been a saint."

"Not quite," she murmured, though she liked hearing him say it.

"Jill has had more love than most kids with *two* parents get. She wouldn't be as well adjusted if that weren't so."

"I want her to stay well adjusted."

"So do I," he said, and let it go at that. He knew from experience that where Jill's welfare was concerned, Chris was unyielding. It was simply going to be up to him, over the next weeks and months, to show her that he'd be good for Jill, too.

9

Gideon had the best of intentions. When he took Chris to a movie, he suggested Jill bring a friend along. When a foot of snow fell and school was canceled, he drove in from Worcester with a toboggan and took them all sliding. When Jill wanted to buy a gift for Chris's birthday, he took her to not one mall, not two, but *three* before she found what she wanted. And he was thrilled to do it. He genuinely enjoyed Jill. And he thought she enjoyed him.

Chris did, too. Jill looked forward to seeing him. At other times, though, she was more quiet than usual. More than once, when she was at the kitchen table doing homework at night and Chris was nearby, talking softly on the phone to Gideon, she sensed Jill looking at her, sensed a pensiveness that had nothing to do with schoolwork. At times, she thought that pensiveness was brooding, but when she asked, Jill shook her head in denial.

March came, then April, and Chris began to worry in earnest. Jill just wasn't herself. She was doing fine in school, and her social life was as active as ever, but at home she was definitely distracted. She continued to deny there was a problem, and Chris could only push so far. She thought, though, that it might be wise for them to spend some time alone together. They hadn't done it much of late, what with Chris's work—she was up to her ears with orders both for the model condo at Crosslyn Rise and the mansion, itself—and Gideon's presence. So, over dinner at home one midweek night, she broached the topic.

"Any thoughts on vacation, Jill?" When Jill set down her fork, alert but silent, Chris said, "I was thinking that we could go down to New York for a few days."

"New York?"

"Uh-huh. Just the two of us. We could shop, eat out, maybe take in a show or two. Would you like that?"

Jill lifted her fork again and pushed a piece of chicken around the plate.

"Jill?"

The fork settled. Looking young and vulnerable, Jill met her gaze. "I was thinking I'd use that vacation for something else."

"What's that?"

"I want to meet my father."

Chris felt the blood leave her face. Of all the things she'd imagined Jill wanting to do, that wasn't one. "Your father?"

"He's out there. I want to meet him."

"Uh, uh, what—" she cleared her throat "—what brought this on?"

Jill shrugged. "I'm curious."

"Is this what's been getting you down lately?"

"Not getting me down. But I've been thinking about it a lot. I really want to know who he is. I want to see him."

Chris felt dizzy. She took a deep breath to steady herself. "Uh, honey, I don't know where he is."

"You said he was in Arizona," Jill shot back in an accusing tone.

Chris tried to be conciliatory. "He was, last time I heard, but that was second- or thirdhand, and years ago."

"Where in Arizona?"

"Phoenix."

"So I could start looking there."

"In *person*?"

"Of course not. I'd call Directory Assistance. How many Brant Conways can there be?"

"Lots."

"Okay. You said he sells real estate. There must be some state list of people who do that. If he was there even ten years ago, he must have worked with someone who's kept in touch with him. I could find all that out on the phone."

Chris realized that Jill had given the possibilities a certain amount of very adult thought. She wondered how far that adult thought had gone. "And then what?"

"Then I'll call him, then fly out to see him during vacation."

"What if he doesn't want that?"

"Then we'll arrange another time to meet."

"What if he doesn't want that, either?"

"Then we'll arrange something else. There has to be *some* way we can get together."

Chris studied the napkin she was clutching so tightly in her lap. "Has it occurred to you that he might not want to see you?"

Sounding defiant but subdued, Jill said, "Yes. And if he doesn't, I won't go."

"But you'll be hurt in the process. I don't want that, Jill. I've tried to protect you from hurt. You don't *need* Brant. Trust me. You have everything that's good for you here, without him."

"But he's my father."

"Biologically, yes. Beyond that, he's nothing to you."

"He may be a very nice man."

"He may be, but he has his own life and you have yours."

"I don't want to be *in* his life. I just want to *meet* him."

Chris had always recognized the possibility of that, but she had kept it a very distant thought. Suddenly it was real and near, and she wasn't prepared to handle it.

She felt betrayed. She knew it was wrong. But that was how she felt.

"Why now?" she asked, half to herself.

"I already told you that."

But she had a sudden, awful suspicion. "It has something to do with Gideon, doesn't it?"

"What could it have to do with him?"

"He's the first man I've been interested in. In the past few weeks, he's probably come as close as you've ever come to having a father around." She'd known it. Damn it, she'd *known* something would happen. "I'm right, aren't I?"

"I like Gideon. I like being with him."

"But he's made you think of your father."

"It's not *Gideon's* fault."

But Chris had known. She'd *known*. Bolting from the table, she started pacing the room. "I told him it was too much, too fast. I asked him to slow things down, but did he? No. *He* knew what was best."

"Mom—"

"Over and over, I asked him to be patient. I told him I didn't want anything upsetting you. I told him you needed time."

"Mom—"

"The big expert, sticking his nose into other people's business."

"*Mom.*" She was twisted around in her chair. When Chris looked at her, she said, "This is *not Gideon's fault*! I love Gideon. He loves you, and you love him."

"I don't—"

"You do! I see it every night. It's written all over your face when you talk to him on the phone. And I think it's great. I *want* you to love him. I *want* you to marry him. I think it'd be fun to be a family. That's something I could never have with my father, and I accept that. I don't want anything with him. I like what I have. I just want to meet the man, so that I'll know who he is and who I am. Then I can be a stepdaughter to Gideon."

There had been certain times over the years when Chris had found motherhood to be overwhelmingly emotional. One had been when she'd first been presented her gooey, scrunched-up baby girl, another when Jill had gone off on the school bus for the very first time, another when Jill had had the lead in the middle school's musical production of *Snow White and the Seven Dwarfs*. Intense pride always affected Chris.

Intense pride was what she felt at that moment, along with a bit of humility. Fighting back tears, she put her arm around Jill and gave her a tight hug. "You are incredible."

Jill hugged her back. "I do love you, Mom. I'll always love you. I don't think I could ever love *him*, but I want to know who he is."

Regaining a modicum of composure, Chris slid back into her chair. She wanted to think clearly, wanted Jill to do the same. "I don't really know much about him. If he has a slew of other children, how will you feel?"

"Okay."

"What if he's big and bald and fat?"

"Haven't you been the one to always tell me not to judge a book by its cover?"

"But this is your father. You may be fantasizing that he's some kind of god—"

"If he were that, he'd have come for me, not the other way around." She took a breath, seeming strong now that she'd aired what had clearly been weighing so heavily on her mind. "Mom, I'm not looking for someone to take your place, and I'm *not* looking for another place to live. I just want to meet my father. Once I've seen him, I'll know who he is and that he exists, and that he knows *I* exist. Then I can go on with my life."

The words were all correct. They were grown-up and sensible. Chris knew that, but the knowledge was small solace for the fear she felt. Jill had been her whole life, and vice versa, for so long, that the thought of Brant intruding in any way was upsetting. She sensed that, for the first time, there was a crack in her relationship with Jill—not a crack as in hostility, but one as in growing up and separating. That too was inevitable, but Chris wasn't ready for it.

Nor was she ready for Gideon when he called that night. "I'm really tired. Why don't we connect later in the week."

He was immediately concerned. "Aren't you feeling well?"

"I'm fine. Just tired."

When he called the next night, she didn't claim fatigue, but she was quiet, answering his questions as briefly as possible, not offering anything extra. "Is something wrong?" he finally asked after five minutes of trying to pull her usual enthusiasm from her.

"Of course not. What could be wrong?"

He didn't know. But he knew she wasn't herself, and he feared that what was upsetting her had to do with him. "You sound angry."

"Not angry. Just busy."

"At ten o'clock at night?"

"I'm trying to get some papers in order. I have a slew of deliveries coming for five different jobs, and if the invoices get messed up—"

"I thought Margie took care of paperwork like that."

"Margie isn't involved the way I am, and I want these things to be right. If there are screwups, I'll have to be cleaning them up at the same time that Crosslyn Rise is picking up—''

Gideon interrupted. "Chris, why are you working so hard?"

"Because I'm a professional. I have commitments."

"But you don't have to work *this* hard."

"I have bills to pay," she snapped. "In case you've forgotten, I have a teenage daughter to support."

"I haven't forgotten," Gideon said quietly. "I want to help you do that."

"You've done enough!"

A heavy silence stretched between them before he said, "What's that supposed to mean?"

"Nothing."

"*What*, Chris?"

She sighed and rubbed the back of her neck. "*Nothing*. Listen, I'm tired and short-tempered. You'd probably be best to avoid me for a little while."

He didn't like the sound of that at all. "A little while?"

"A few days."

"No way. We have a date for dinner tomorrow night."

"Look, maybe that's not such a good idea."

"I think it is." He paused. "You're angry. What have I done? Damn it, Chris, if you don't tell me, I won't know and I can't do a goddamned thing about remedying it. Come on. *Talk* to me."

"Not tonight," she said firmly. "I'll be back in the office sometime after three tomorrow. Call me then and we'll decide what to do about dinner."

Gideon didn't call. True to form, he was there, waiting in her office when she returned. She stopped at the door when she saw him, feeling an overwhelming rush of sensation. He could arouse that, whether she was annoyed with him or not, and it wasn't only physical. Her heart swelled at the sight of him, which was probably why she hadn't wanted to see him. Looking at him, feeling the warm embrace of his eyes and the love that was so clearly behind it, she was more confused than ever about the anger she felt.

"Hi, doll," he said with a gentle smile. He went to her and kissed her cheek, then leaned back. "Uh-oh. I'm still in the doghouse?"

She slipped past him to her desk, where she deposited her briefcase and the folders she carried.

"Chris." He drew her name out in a way that said he knew something was wrong and wanted to know what it was before he lost his patience.

Knowing that she wouldn't have a chance of keeping still with him right there—and realizing she didn't *want* to—she sat down at her desk, linked her hands tightly in her lap, and said, "Jill wants to contact her father."

Gideon hadn't been expecting that, but he wasn't surprised. "Ahh. And that upsets you."

To put it mildly. "Of course, it upsets me! She wants to go off and find a man who, for all intents and purposes, doesn't want her around."

"How do you know that?"

"Because she's fifteen, and he's never once made the slightest attempt to see her—" she held up both hands "—and that's okay by me, because she doesn't need him in her life, but she's suddenly decided that she wants to know who he is. She's going to be hurt. I know it." Her fingers knotted again. "*That's* what I don't want!"

Knowing Chris the way he did, knowing what she wanted in life for Jill, Gideon could understand why she was upset, though he didn't completely agree. "She doesn't have to be hurt. He may be cordial. He may even welcome her."

Chris felt deep, dark fears rush to the surface. "And if that happens, she may want to see him again and again, and that'll mess her up completely."

"Her, or you?"

"What?"

"Are you afraid for her," Gideon repeated patiently, "or for you?"

Chris was furious that he was so calm when she felt as if the bottom of her world were falling away. "For *me*?" Emotional stress brought her out of her chair. "You think I'm being selfish?"

"No, that's not—"

"How *dare* you suggest that!" she fumed. "I've spent the better half of my life doing and thinking and feeling for that child. I've sacrificed a whole lot, and I'd do the same thing again in a minute." Trembling, she steadied her fingertips on the chrome rim of her desk. "Selfish? Who in the *hell* are you to tell me I'm selfish? You've never sacrificed for a child. You've never sacrificed for anyone!"

Gideon was on the verge of coming to his own defense, when Chris raced on. She needed to air what she was feeling, he realized. He also realized that he wanted to know it all. He'd been a nervous wreck wondering what was wrong with her. So, much as it hurt him, he leaned back against the wall, arms folded on his chest, and listened.

"You've lived life for your own pleasure and enjoyment," she charged. "You wanted something, you took it, and that included me. But that wasn't enough, was it? It wasn't enough that we started dating, even though I didn't want to, or that we kept *on* dating, even though I didn't want to, or that we started sleeping together. That wasn't enough for you. You wanted marriage, and you wanted it fast. When I said I was worried about Jill, you said, 'No sweat, she loves me,' and maybe she does. But it's thinking about you and wondering about us and whether we're getting married that's now making her think about Brant!''

Gideon remained quiet, waiting. When she didn't say anything, simply glared at him—albeit with tears in her eyes now, and that tore through him—he said, ''Are you done?''

''If it hadn't been for you, pushing your way into our lives, it wouldn't have *occurred* to her to think of him!''

Again Gideon was quiet, though it was harder to remain so with each word she said. In the old days, he wouldn't have put up with a woman throwing unjust claims at him. He'd either have thrown them right back or walked out the door. So maybe he was sacrificing for Chris now. If so, he was more than happy to do it.

''Can I speak?'' he asked, but again his quiet words spurred her on.

''Everything was so good! We had our lives together, she was well adjusted and happy, not going for alcohol or drugs the way some of the kids at her school are, I was beginning to earn some real money. Then you came along—'' she caught her breath, a single trickle of tears escaping from each eye ''—then you came along and upset it all!''

It was the trickle of tears that did it. Unable to stand still any longer, he left the wall and went to her. ''Honey, I think you're confusing the issues,'' he said softly, but when he reached for her, she batted his hands away.

''I'm not! I've done nothing but go over and over every single aspect of this for the past two days.''

''You've lost perspective.''

''I have *not*!''

''Maybe if you'd shared it sooner, you would have seen—''

''Seen what?'' she cut in shakily. ''That you're the answer to my problems? That all I have to do is marry you and let you take me away from here, so Jill can find herself with her father?''

''Of course not!'' Gideon argued. ''Jill is part of our lives. It's you, me and her. It has been right from the start.''

''But it's *not* her,'' Chris cried, and her chin began to wobble. ''She's going off to Arizona to see Brant.'' Her breathing grew choppy. ''Things won't ever be the same again!''

Gideon had had enough. He pulled her into his arms, then held her tighter when she struggled. Within seconds, she went limp against him, and within seconds of that, clutching his sweater, she began to cry softly.

''Oh, baby,'' he said, crushed by the sound of her sobs. He stroked her blond hair, rubbed her slender back, held her as close as he could until her weeping began to abate. Then he sat against the edge of the desk and propped her between his thighs. Her head was still down, her cheek against his chest. Quietly he began to speak.

''You're right, Chris. Things won't ever be the same again. We've found each other, Jill's growing up, Crosslyn Rise has been gutted. That's growth. It's progress. And you're afraid, because for the first time in a long time things are changing in your life, and that makes you nervous. It would make me nervous, too, I suppose, but that's just a guess, because you're right, I haven't been in your shoes. I haven't had a child. I haven't raised that child and poured every bit of myself into it. So I don't know what it's really like when suddenly something appears to threaten that relationship."

"I'm so scared," Chris whimpered.

He tightened his arms around her "I know, baby, I know, but there are a couple of things you're not taking into consideration. First off, just because Jill wants to see Brant, that doesn't mean she'll have an ongoing relationship with him."

"She will. I know she will."

"How do you know?" he challenged. When she didn't answer, he gentled his voice again. "You don't know, because you don't know who Brant is now, and because you're underestimating Jill. She wouldn't do anything to hurt you."

"She wants to see him!"

"She *needs* to see him. It's part of growing up. It's part of forming her identity. She's been wondering about him for a long time, now she needs to finally see who he is, so that she can put the wondering aside and go on living."

The thoughts sounded strangely familiar. In a slow, suspicious voice, Chris asked, "Did you discuss this with her?" The idea that Jill would go to Gideon before she went to her own mother was cutting.

But Gideon was quick to deny it. "Are you kidding? She wouldn't open to me that way. At least, not yet."

"But she said nearly the same thing you just did."

"That's because it's what she's feeling."

Chris looked up. "How would you know what she's feeling?"

He brushed at tear tracks with the pads of his thumbs. "Because I felt those same things myself when I was a kid. I was younger than she is. I didn't understand it the way she probably does, but after the fact I could see it. My mother came to visit me when I was little, but it wasn't the same. I couldn't put her in any kind of context. I reached a point of wanting—no, *needing*—to go to her, to see where she lived and who she lived with." He arched a dark brow. "You think my dad was pleased? He was *furious*! Couldn't understand why I'd spend all that money to fly all the way across the country to see a woman who hadn't cared enough to hang around. He yelled and yelled and carried on for a good long time until it finally hit me that he was jealous."

"I'm not jealous," Chris claimed, but more quietly. Her mind had been so muddled since Jill had mentioned Brant that she hadn't realized— hadn't remembered—that Gideon had been in a situation not unlike the one Jill was in. "I'm just scared."

"Well, my dad was, too. He was scared that I'd take a look at her life and reject him the way she had. He was scared that I'd pick up and move out to California to live with her, and that he'd be left all alone. He didn't even have family, the way you do."

Needing the cushion, she returned her head to his chest. "That doesn't make it any easier."

"I know," he crooned against her hair, "I know. The loss of a child like that would be traumatic in any case. But the fact was that he didn't lose me. I saw where my mother lived, and sure, she had plenty of money and could have given me a hell of a lot if I'd gone out there to live with her, but the fact is that I wouldn't have traded my father's love for a penny of her money in a million years."

It was a minute before his words penetrated fully and sank deep into her soul. Moaning, she slipped her arms around his waist. He was so dear.

But he wasn't done talking. "Don't you think Jill knows what a good thing she has in you? Don't you think she knows how much she loves you?"

"Yes, but she doesn't know how much I love *her*. She doesn't know that I'd be destroyed if she ever decided to live with Brant. He was so horrible doing what he did to me—and to her. One part of me is absolutely infuriated that she even wants to *see* him."

His breath was warm against her forehead. "But you can't tell her that—or show her, because that's not the way you are—so you took your anger out on me. And that's okay, Chris. I'd rather you took it out on me than on her. But you owed me an explanation, at least. It's not fair to refuse to talk to me, like you've done for two nights on the phone. If you want to scream and yell at me, fine. That's what I'm here for. Screaming and yelling is sometimes the only way to get anger out of your system. Or fear. Or worry." His voice grew more fierce. "Just don't shut me out, damn it. Don't shut me out."

Slipping her arms higher on his back, Chris buried her face against his neck. "I'm sorry," she whispered. "I guess you were the only scapegoat around. I've just been so miserable since she brought it up. I keep thinking of all the possibilities—"

"Not all of them. Only the worst ones."

He was probably right, she knew. "I keep thinking that she'll find him and like him and want to stay, or that she'll hate him but he'll like her and want a part of her, even, God forbid, sue for visitation rights. I keep worrying that her going after Brant will open a whole can of worms. She's such a terrific kid. I don't want her messed up."

"She won't be messed up."

Chris raised her eyes to his. "Look at all the kids whose parents are divorced."

"What about them?"

"They're messed up."

"Not all of them. But your situation isn't the same."

"If there's suddenly a tug-of-war between Brant and me, it's the same."

"There won't be any tug-of-war. Jill won't want to live with him. She's happy here, with you and all the friends she's grown up with. You said that yourself when I suggested we build a house somewhere other than Belmont, and it made sense. She isn't about to want to pick up and relocate all of a sudden."

"What if Brant wants it?"

"He won't want it. Not at this late date."

"But what if he does?"

"You'll tell him no."

"What if he fights?"

"You mean, goes to court? He won't do that." He snorted. "Talk about cans of worms. If he goes to court, you can sue him for back child support. Think he'll pay up?"

"What if he does? What if he does, and then wants visitation rights?"

"He won't have much of a chance of getting them. He knew he had a child fifteen years ago. He chose to ignore her. He didn't give money, and he didn't give time. No court is going to feel terribly sympathetic toward him. Besides, Jill isn't a baby. She's old enough to express her feelings and to have them taken into account."

"In court. Oh, God. I don't want her dragged through anything like that."

"She *won't* be." He took her face in his hands and put conviction into his words. "The chances of anything like that happening are so remote that it's absurd to even be thinking of it now."

"It's not absurd to me. I'm her mother. I *care*."

"So do I, Chris," he stated fiercely, "but it won't do her any good if you're a basket case worrying about worst-case scenarios. Chances are she'll meet the man, and that'll be it."

For the first time, hearing his words and the confidence behind them, Chris let herself believe it might be true. "I'd give anything for that."

He kissed her nose. "She's a good, sensible young woman, her mother's daughter all the way. My guess is that if she ever knew how upset you've been, she'd cancel her plans."

"If she did that, she'd always wonder."

"Uh-huh."

Though she could have done without his agreement, she felt herself beginning to relax. The breath she took was only slightly shaky, a vague reminder of her recent crying jag. "You don't think I'll lose her?"

"No *way* could you lose her. She'll probably go see Brant and then come back and be her good old self." He frowned. "You say the guy's in Arizona?"

"He was in Phoenix last time I heard. I told Jill we'd make some calls this weekend."

"Then you'll help her."

"Of course. I wouldn't put her through this alone. I wouldn't trust *him* alone with her."

"And you'll go out there with her?"

Chris nodded.

"It'll be the first time you've seen him since—"

She nodded again.

"Think you'll feel anything?"

Even if she hadn't sensed his unsureness, she would have said the same thing. "I'll feel exactly what I felt when he told me he didn't know if the baby was his and walked away—anger, frustration and fear." She touched Gideon's lean cheek and said softly. "But you have nothing to worry about. He won't interest me in the least."

"Maybe I could come with you."

"That might put more pressure on Jill."

"Then maybe I can help you find him. I have a friend who lives out there—" He stopped when she shook her head. "Why not? It might speed things up."

"It might tell her you're trying to get rid of her."

Gideon couldn't believe his ears. "Are you kidding? She knows better than that!" But Chris was wearing a strange expression. "But maybe you don't." He swore against the anguish that shot through him. "When will you accept the fact that I want her with us?"

"Some men wouldn't."

"I'm not some men," he barked.

"You've been a bachelor for a long time. It's one thing to live with a woman, another to suddenly inherit her teenage daughter."

He was hurt. "Have I ever complained? Have I ever suggested, even in the slightest way, that I didn't want her around?"

"I remember a few very frustrating times—"

"Yeah, I remember them, too, and I'd have felt that frustration whether it was Jill we had to behave for or a child that you and I had ourselves, but that doesn't mean I don't want her. Or them. I want kids, Chris. We're using birth control because we're not married yet, and because we want you to have a choice this time, but I do want kids. I want them for us, and I want them for Jill. She'd love some brothers and sisters. She told me so."

"She did?"

He nodded. "When we were out shopping the other week. She said that you were a great mother, and that she hoped you'd have some children so you'd have someone to take care of when she went off to school."

Chris's face fell. "Off to school. College."

"She is going."

"I know. It's creeping up so fast." Closing her eyes, she made a small, helpless sound. "Why do things have to change?" It was the question she'd been asking herself over and over again.

Gideon had never pretended to be a philosopher. All he could do was to speak from the heart. "Because we grow. We move on to things that are even better. Hey, listen, I know it's scary. Change always is. But just think—if Jill goes to see Brant and gets him out of her system, you won't have to worry about that anymore. Then, if you and I get married and have a few kids who adore Jill so much that they raise holy hell when she goes off to college, you'll have something else to think about besides an empty nest."

"Empty nest—hah. From the sounds of it, you've got the nest so full, there may not be room for any of us to breathe!"

"Not to worry," was his smug response. "I'm a builder. I'll enlarge the nest." He doubted it was the time or place, still he couldn't resist pressing his point. "So, what do you think?"

"About what?"

"Having kids."

"What about my career?"

"You'll cut back a few hours. So will I. Between the two of us, we'll handle things." He paused, wanting to believe but afraid to. "Are you considering it?"

"Not now. All I can do now is to get through this thing with Jill and Brant."

"You'll get through it," he said. Ducking his head, he kissed her on the lips. When she didn't resist, he did it again, more persuasively this time, more deeply. Just as he felt the beginning of her response, he tore his mouth away. "Do you still blame me for Jill wanting to go?"

Closing her eyes against his chin, Chris whispered, "How can I blame you for anything when you kiss me that way?"

"Are you gonna shut me out again?"

"You'll only barge your way back in."

"How about dinner tonight?"

"Goin' for broke, hmm?"

"Damn right."

She opened her eyes and slowly met his. "Okay, but I have to be home early. Jill will be back from her friend's at nine, and I want to be there."

Understanding why, Gideon nodded.

Chris studied his face, feature by handsome feature, for another minute before wrapping her arms around his neck. "Thank you, Gideon."

"For what?"

"Being my friend."

"My pleasure."

She was silent for a minute, thinking about how very much she did love him and how, surprisingly, she was coming to depend on him. She hadn't wanted that at all, but just then, she wasn't sorry. Having someone to lean on was a luxury. Sure, she had her parents and brothers, but it wasn't the same. Gideon was a man. Her man. Holding on to him, being held in return, was the nicest thing that had happened to her in two whole days.

10

Gideon would have liked to have been there when Chris made the call to Brant Conway. He knew the call was, in some respects, a pivotal point in her life, and he wanted to be part of it. But he also knew how worried she was about Jill. He could appreciate how sensitive a time it was for her. The last thing he wanted was to complicate things with his presence.

That didn't mean he couldn't keep in close contact by phone. He wanted to give Chris support, to show her that he could listen and comfort, even absorb her anger and frustration.

Actually, there was far less anger and frustration than he expected. When she finally contacted Brant, then called to tell him about it, she was more tired than anything else.

"It was so easy," she said in a quiet voice, talking in the privacy of her bedroom after Jill had finally gone to sleep. "One call to Directory Assistance did it. He's still living in Phoenix, still selling real estate."

Gideon wanted to know everything. "Who talked, you or Jill?"

"Me," Chris said emphatically. "Jill wanted to do it, but I put my foot down. Can you imagine what she'd have felt if he'd denied he was her father?"

"Did he?"

"I didn't give him a chance. He was slightly stunned when I told him my name. He never expected to hear from me. So I had an advantage to start with, and I pressed it. I told him Jill was fifteen, that she looked just like him, and that she wanted to see him. I told him we'd be flying out during April vacation."

"What'd he say?"

"He stammered a little. Then he said that he had a wife and two little boys, and that Jill's showing up out of nowhere would upset them."

"The bastard," Gideon muttered.

"Uh-huh."

"So what'd you say?"

"I wanted to tell him that he was the scum of the earth and the last person I wanted my daughter to see, but Jill was sitting right there beside me, hanging on my every word. So I just repeated what I'd said, that she wanted to see him. I made it sound as if we were coming whether he liked it or not. I suggested that we would stay in a hotel and that he could visit with her there."

"Did he agree?"

"Reluctantly. He must have figured that he had no choice. We'd gotten his phone number. We could get his address. I doubt he wants us showing up at his house and surprising the wife and kids."

Gideon heard bitterness at the last. "Does it bother you—the idea that he has a family?"

"I kind of figured he did," Chris said. She didn't have to think long about her feelings on that score. "I'm not personally bothered in the least. I wouldn't want the creep if he was presented to me on a silver platter. What does bother me is that he's given legitimacy to two other children, while denying it to Jill."

"She's better off without him. You know that."

"I do." Chris sighed. "I just wish she did."

"She will. Give her time." His thoughts jumped ahead. "When will you go?"

"A week from Monday. We'll come back Wednesday. That leaves Tuesday to see Brant."

Gideon remembered the trips he'd made to see his mother, when he'd flown west, visited and flown home. Years later, he wished he'd taken greater advantage of the cross-country flight. "What about seeing the Southwest? I hear it's beautiful. Maybe you could kind of make it a treat for Jill. I mean, since you're going so far—"

"I thought of doing that, and one part of me would like to. The other part doesn't think it would be so good."

"Why not?"

"Two reasons." She really had thought it out. "First, I don't want her directly associating Brant with that part of the country. I'd rather she see it at a separate time."

"The second reason?"

"You," Chris said softly. "I'd rather not be away from here so long."

Gideon swore. "Damn it, Chris, how can you say something like that on the phone, when I can't hold you or kiss you or love you?" The mere thought of doing all that made his body tighten.

"You asked."

"Right." And since she was in an answering mode, he went for it all. "You do love me, don't you?"

She sighed. "Yes, Gideon, I do love you."

"Since when?"

"I don't know since when. I knew I was in trouble way back at the beginning when you bothered me so much. You kept zinging me with these little darts. I think they had some kind of potion on them."

"Will you marry me?"

"Uh-huh."

"When?"

"Someday."

"'Someday'? What's *that* supposed to mean?"

"I have to get this business with Jill straightened out first."

Gideon's mind started working fast. "Okay. This is April. The trip's comin' right up. Can we plan on a wedding in May?"

"We can't plan on *anything*. We'll have to take it day by day."

"But you will marry me?" He was so desperate for it he'd even wear a tux if she asked. "Marry me, Chris?"

"Yes." And she knew she would. With his enthusiasm, his sense of humor, adventure and compassion, his gentleness and his fire, he had become a vital part of her life. "I do love you," she said, knowing he wanted to hear the words again, knowing he deserved them.

"Ahh." He let out his breath and grinned. "You've just made me a very happy man, Christine Gillette. Horny, but happy."

Both feelings persisted through the next day, which was Saturday. The first was remedied that night, in the coziness of Chris's bed, while Jill was at a movie with friends. The second just grew.

Sunday night, though, Chris phoned him in a state of restrained panic. Her sentences were short and fast, her voice higher than usual. "Brant called a little while ago. Jill answered the phone. I was in the bath. You won't believe what he did, Gideon! I still can't believe it myself! He is such a snake," she hissed, "such a snake!"

"Shh." His heart was pounding, but he said, "Take it slow, honey. Tell me."

"Instead of waiting until I could get to the phone, he talked directly to her. He said that his parents want her to stay with them. Her. Not me. Just her. He said that I shouldn't even bother coming out, that he would meet the plane himself and then deliver Jill to her grandparents." She nearly choked on the words. "Her grandparents. Well, at least he acknowledges that she's his, but to call those people her grandparents when they haven't given any more of a damn than he has all these years—"

"Chris, shh, Chris. Maybe they didn't know."

She was trembling, though whether from anger or fear she didn't know. "That's beside the point. They don't have any right to her. *He* doesn't have any right to her. She's mine. He should have made his plans through *me*." She caught in a livid breath. "Can you believe the *audacity* of the man to go over my head that way?"

"You'll tell him no."

"That's what I told Jill, and she got really upset. She said that he sounded nice, that she was old enough to travel alone, and that that was what she'd been planning to do in the first place." Her voice dropped to a desperate whisper. Though she had her door shut, she didn't want to take the chance that Jill might hear. "But how can I *let* her, Gideon? How can I let her fly all that way alone, then face a man who—for all I know—is strange or sadistic? It's been more than fifteen years since I've seen him. We were kids ourselves. I have no idea what kind of person he's become.''

"Did you know his parents?"

"I met them once or twice, but that was all." She could barely picture what they looked like. "What should I do, Gideon? This is my *baby*."

Gideon was silent for a bit. She wanted his opinion, but he was still a fledgling, as parents went. Talk about trial by fire...

"Have you run this by your parents?"

"Not yet. I want to know what *you* think."

"I think," he said slowly, "that you need more information before you can make any kind of judgment."

"Sure, I do," she returned facetiously. "I need a complete dossier on the man, but there's no way I can get that without hiring an investigator, and I refuse to do that! I shouldn't have to pay the money, and we don't have the time."

"I have a friend in Phoenix," Gideon reminded her. "He's a builder there. If he hasn't run across Conway himself, he's bound to know people who have. Let me call him. He may be able to tell us something about what kind of person he is."

"What kind of person is your friend?"

"A trustworthy one."

Chris wasn't about to look a gift horse in the mouth. She agreed to let Gideon do it and was grateful for his offer. Late the next day, he called with the information his friend had provided.

"According to Paul, Brant Conway has made a good name for himself. He's successful in his field, has some dough, lives in a nice house in Scottsdale. He isn't exactly a fixture in high society but he's respected and liked. His parents live in Scottsdale, too. They all do well for themselves."

Chris had mixed feelings about that. She was pleased for Jill, not so pleased for herself. If the report had come back in any way negative, she might have been able to cancel the trip. It looked as though she didn't have any grounds for that.

"And your friend is reliable?" she asked.

"'Fraid so," Gideon answered.

She paused. "Do you think I should let her go?"

"I think that if you don't, Jill may resent it. The fact is that if she wants to go, she'll go anyway, whether it's now or later. It would be awful if your refusal put a wedge between you. I think you have to trust that you've raised her the right way, and that she'll be able to take care of herself and know to call if there's any problem."

That was pretty much what Chris's parents had said when she'd talked it over with them that morning. She had wanted to argue then, just as she wanted to argue now, but she knew that they were all right. Jill wasn't a small child. She would be met at the airport and cared for by her grandparents, who possibly felt far more for her than Brant. Most importantly, Jill had a sane head on her shoulders. If something went wrong, she would know to get herself to the nearest phone.

Heart in her mouth, Chris saw Jill off for Phoenix on the Monday of her school vacation. Brant had suggested that she stay until Friday—another suggestion that Chris resented but that she was helpless to deny.

She did deny Gideon the chance of going to the airport. "My folks want to drive us. Any more people and it'll be a major production." But he was on the phone with her as soon as she returned to the office, and when she got home that night, he was waiting with his overnight bag in the bedroom.

Deliberately that first night, he didn't make love to her. Sex wasn't the reason he'd come. He was there to be with her, to hold her, to talk through her unease and help her pass the time until she heard from Jill.

Jill called late Monday night to say that the flight was fine, that Brant's parents' house was pretty and that Brant had been nice. Chris would have been reassured if she felt that Jill had been making the call in private. She could tell from the conversation, though, that Jill wasn't alone.

"Do you think she's hiding something?" Chris asked Gideon fearfully the minute they'd hung up.

Gideon had no way of knowing that, but he felt he had a handle on Jill. "Your daughter is no wilting violet. If there's something she wanted to tell you but couldn't, she'll find another time to call."

"What if they won't let her?"

"She'll find a way." Taking her in his arms, he hugged her tightly. "Chris, don't expect the worst. You have no reason to believe that Brant's parents are anything but lovely people just discovering a very beautiful granddaughter. Jill sounded well. She's doing fine."

The call that came from Phoenix Tuesday night was like the first, sweet and correct. This one held news on the weather, which was warm, the desert, which was in bloom, and her grandparents' swimming pool, which was "radical."

"See?" Gideon said when they hung up the phone this time. "She's being treated very well." He said it as much for Chris's benefit as for his own. Living with Chris, being part of her daily life, anticipating what it would be like when they married, he was approaching things from a new angle. He missed Jill. In truth, though he kept telling himself there was no cause, he was worried, too. "If they took her on a Jeep tour of the desert, they're obviously making an effort to show her the sights."

"Brant's parents are," Chris conceded reluctantly. "She doesn't say much about Brant."

"Maybe that's just as well. If she's seen him, her curiosity is satisfied. If there's going to be any kind of continuing relationship, let it be with his parents."

Chris couldn't imagine going through the hell of that kind of visit several times a year, but she knew Gideon was right. Grandparents were often kinder than parents. She supposed, if she was looking to the positive, she should be grateful they were there.

Clinging to that thought, she calmed herself some, enough so that she didn't fall apart when Jill called on Wednesday night sounding like she wanted to cry.

"What's wrong, baby?" she said softly. She could recognize throat-tight talk when she heard it, particularly in the daughter she knew so well.

After an agonizing minute, Jill said, "I miss you."

Tears came to Chris's eyes. "Oh, sweetheart, sweetheart, I miss you, too." She clutched Gideon's hand, wishing Jill had one as strong to hold. "Aren't you having a good time?"

Jill's voice fell to a murmur. "It's okay. But they're strangers. I don't think they knew I existed at all until he told them, after you called. They don't know what to do with me." Her murmur caught. "I wish you were here. You were right. We should have both come. We could have stayed at a hotel. Then it wouldn't have been so awkward."

Chris swallowed her tears. "Day after tomorrow you'll be home."

"I wish I was now."

"Hang in there, sweetheart. We'll be at the airport Friday to pick you up."

"Gideon, too?"

"Yeah. He misses you."

"Mom?"

"What?"

The murmur dropped to a whisper. "I'm glad you didn't marry Brant. Gideon's so much better."

"Oh, honey." Pressing her hands to her lips, Chris looked at Gideon through a pool of tears.

"What?" he whispered. He'd about had it with sitting still, trying to catch the gist of the conversation from Chris's short words and now her tears. Clearly Jill was upset. He wanted to snatch the phone away and talk to her himself, only he didn't know how appropriate it was. Chris might think he was butting in where he didn't belong, and though *he* knew he belonged there, he didn't know if Chris saw that yet.

In place of an answer, Chris transferred her fingers from her lips to his. To Jill, she said a soft, "Thanks, honey. Maybe you'll tell him that when you get home."

"I sure will," Jill said, sounding better.

"Are you okay, now?"

"I think so."

"If you want to call again, just call."

"I will."

"Don't forget."

"I won't."

"Bye-bye, sweetheart. I love you."

"I love you, too, Mom. Bye."

Chris hung up the phone, all the while looking at Gideon with eyes still moist with tears. "She's special."

"Damn it, I know that," Gideon said crossly. He was feeling shut out. "What's wrong out there?"

"She's lonesome. They're not what she's used to. She wished I'd gone with her."

Gideon stared at her for another minute before snatching up the phone. By the time he was done with his call, he was feeling defiant. "That's what I should have done in the first place," he told Chris.

Her mouth was agape and had been since the start of his call. "You made reservations to fly to Phoenix?"

"For two." His finger wagged between them. "You and me. I can't take this sitting around, worrying about her. We're leaving at dawn to-morrow, we'll be there by noon, so we'll have the rest of the day to pack her up and take her off and decide what we want to do for the rest of the week. I vote for the Grand Canyon. I've never been there. Jill will love it. And there are some great places to see along the way. Then we can fly home on Sunday."

Chris couldn't believe what he'd done. More than that, she couldn't believe the feeling she saw in his eyes. "But—but you have work," was all she could manage to say.

"I have Johnny, and even if I didn't, work'll wait. We're right on schedule, even a little ahead at the Rise, which is the one project I've been worried about. I could use a vacation."

"You took one in February."

"So did most of my men, so it didn't matter then, and we're only talking two days here. I deserve it." Scowling, he stuck his hands on his hips. "I should have suggested this when the plans were first made. It would have made things a whole lot more enjoyable for all of us. But I was afraid to say anything, because Jill's not my daughter, she's yours, and I'm not even your husband. But damn it, if we're gonna be a family, we're gonna be a family. That means good times and bad. It means we stick together. It means we share things." He held up a hand and arched a brow in warning. "Now, if that's not what you want, I think you'd better tell me right away, because if it isn't, I'm not the guy for you. If it is, let's get married—now. I have no intention of sitting at home by myself for the next three years until Jill goes off to college and you decide you're lonesome. Either you want me or you don't. Either you love me, or you don't. I've waited almost forty years for a woman as warm and giving and bright and sweet and sexy as you, and I can't wait any longer.

I just can't." He took a deep breath. "So, what'll it be, Chris? Do we get married, or do we call the whole thing off?"

Chris eyed him askance. "You're giving me an ultimatum?"

"That's right," he said, returning his hand to his hip. "Not only that, but I want an answer now. And don't tell me that I'm rushing you or pressuring you, because you either feel it here—" he knocked a fist to his heart "—or you don't. If you love me, and you know I love you, we'll be able to handle anything that comes up with Jill." His face went beseeching. "Don't you see, it's the love that counts?"

At that moment, Chris would have had to be blind not to see, ignorant not to know, heartless not to feel. Gideon Lowe, master-builder, macho flirt, notorious bachelor, rabid Celtics fan, was also a man of sensitivity and insight. If she'd ever wanted a stepfather for Jill, she couldn't have asked for a better one. But Gideon was more, even than that. Far more. He was kind and caring and generous. Yes, he'd upset the applecart of her life, but in such a way that the apples would never taste as sweet without him. When she was with him, she felt the kind of wholeness she'd seen in her parents. If she'd ever wanted a lover, she couldn't have asked for a better one. And if she'd ever wanted a husband...

"Yes," she said softly, and went to him. "I see. I do see." She slipped her arms around his neck, leaning into him in such a way that their physical fit was as perfect as everything else. "The love's there. Let's do it."

Gideon's eyes lit up in the endearingly naughty way that she loved. "*Do* it?"

She grinned, feeling, with the commitment, suddenly happier and more light-headed than she ever had before. "Get married." She paused. Her grin tilted. "And the other, too."

He didn't need to hear any more. Scooping her up in his arms, he made for the stairs.

"Put me down, Gideon Lowe," she cried, laughing. "Put me down. I can walk. This is embarrassing."

He didn't miss a step. "Embarrassing? It's supposed to be romantic."

"It's totally tough and macho."

He did stop then, just shy of the top step, and met her gaze. "The irony of that is really too much."

"What irony?"

"Crosslyn Rise. I went into the project to shake the image."

"What image?"

"Brawn versus brain. And here I am, carting you off to bed like the best of my big-rig buddies." His grin grew wicked. "Know something?" When she shook her head, he said, "This is the *smartest* damn thing I've ever done in my life." Still grinning, he took the last step.

UNDER THE KNIFE

Tess Gerritsen

To my mother and father

Prologue

Dear God, how the past comes back to haunt us.

From his office window, Dr. Henry Tanaka stared out at the rain battering the parking lot and wondered why, after all these years, the death of one poor soul had come back to destroy him.

Outside, a nurse, her uniform spotty with rain, dashed to her car. Another one caught without an umbrella, he thought. That morning, like most Honolulu mornings, had dawned bright and sunny. But at three o'clock the clouds had slithered over the Koolau range and now, as the last clinic employees headed for home, the rain became a torrent, flooding the streets with a river of dirty water.

Tanaka turned and stared down at the letter on his desk. It had been mailed a week ago; but like so much of his correspondence, it had been lost in the piles of obstetrical journals and supply catalogs that always littered his office. When his receptionist had finally called it to his attention this morning, he'd been alarmed by the name on the return address: Joseph Kahanu, Attorney at Law.

He had opened it immediately.

Now he sank into his chair and read the letter once again.

Dear Dr. Tanaka,
As the attorney representing Mr. Charles Decker, I hereby request any and all medical records pertaining to the obstetrical care of Ms. Jennifer Brook, who was your patient at the time of her death....

Jennifer Brook. A name he'd hoped to forget.

A profound weariness came over him—the exhaustion of a man who has discovered he cannot outrun his own shadow. He tried to muster the energy to go home, to slog outside and climb into his car, but he could only sit and stare at the four walls of his office. His sanctuary. His gaze traveled past the framed diplomas, the medical certificates, the photographs. Everywhere there were snapshots of wrinkled newborns, of beaming mothers and fathers. How many babies had he brought into the world? He'd lost count years ago....

It was a sound in the outer office that finally drew him out of his chair: the click of a door shutting. He rose and went to peer out at the reception area. "Peggy? Are you still here?"

The waiting room was deserted. Slowly his gaze moved past the flowered couch and chairs, past the magazines neatly stacked on the coffee table, and finally settled on the outer door. It was unlocked.

Through the silence, he heard the muted clang of metal. It came from one of the exam rooms.

"Peggy?" Tanaka moved down the hall and glanced into the first room. Flicking on the light, he saw the hard gleam of the stainless-steel sink, the gynecologic table, the supply cabinet. He turned off the light and went to the next room. Again, everything was as it should be: the instruments lined up neatly on the counter, the sink wiped dry, the table stirrups folded up for the night.

Crossing the hall, he moved toward the third and last exam room. But just as he reached for the light switch, some instinct made him freeze: a sudden awareness of a presence—something malevolent—waiting for him in the darkness.

In terror, he backed out of the room. Only as he spun around to flee did he realize that the intruder was standing behind him.

A blade slashed across his neck.

Tanaka staggered backward into the exam room and toppled an instrument stand. Stumbling to the floor, he found the linoleum was already slick with his blood. Even as he felt his life drain away, a coldly rational pocket of his brain forced him to assess his own wound, to analyze his own chances. *Severed artery. Exsanguination within minutes. Have to stop the bleeding....* Numbness was already creeping up his legs.

So little time. On his hands and knees, he crawled toward the cabinet where the gauze was stored. To his half-senseless mind, the feeble light reflecting off those glass doors became his guiding beacon, his only hope of survival.

A shadow blotted out the glow from the hall. He knew the intruder was standing in the doorway, watching him. Still he kept moving.

In his last seconds of consciousness, Tanaka managed to drag himself to his feet and wrench open the cabinet door. Sterile packets rained down from the shelf. Blindly he ripped one apart, withdrew a wad of gauze and clamped it against his neck.

He didn't see the attacker's blade trace its final arc.

As it plunged deep into his back, Tanaka tried to scream but the only sound that issued from his throat was a sigh. It was the last breath he took before he slid quietly to the floor.

CHARLIE DECKER lay naked in his small hard bed and he was afraid.

Through the window he saw the blood-red glow of a neon sign: *The Victory Hotel.* Except the *t* was missing from *Hotel.* And what was left made him think of *Hole*, which is what the place really was: *The Victory Hole*, where every triumph, every joy, sank into some dark pit of no return.

He shut his eyes but the neon seemed to burrow its way through his lids. He turned away from the window and pulled the pillow over his head. The smell of the filthy linen was suffocating. Tossing the pillow aside, he rose and paced over to the window. There he stared down at the street. On the sidewalk below, a stringy-haired blonde in a miniskirt was dickering with a man in a Chevy. Somewhere in the night people laughed and a jukebox was playing "It Don't Matter Anymore." A stench rose from the alley, a peculiar mingling of rotting trash and frangipani: the smell of the back streets of paradise. It made him nauseated. But it was too hot to close the window, too hot to sleep, too hot even to breathe.

He went over to the card table and switched on the lamp. The same newspaper headline stared up at him.

Honolulu Physician Found Slain.

He felt the sweat trickle down his chest. He threw the newspaper on the floor. Then he sat down and let his head fall into his hands.

The music from the distant jukebox faded; the next song started, a thrusting of guitars and drums. A singer growled out: "I want it bad, oh yeah, baby, so bad, so bad...."

Slowly he raised his head and his gaze settled on the photograph of Jenny. She was smiling; as always, she was smiling. He touched the picture, trying to remember how her face had felt; but the years had dimmed his memory.

At last he opened his notebook. He turned to a blank page. He began to write.

This is what they told me:
"It takes time...
Time to heal, time to forget."
This is what I told them:
That healing lies not in forgetfulness
But in remembrance
Of you.
The smell of the sea on your skin;
The small and perfect footprints you leave in the sand.
In remembrance there are no endings.
And so you lie there, now and always, by the sea.
You open your eyes. You touch me.
The sun is in your fingertips.
And I am healed.
I am healed.

Chapter One

With a steady hand, Dr. Kate Chesne injected two hundred milligrams of sodium Pentothal into her patient's intravenous line. As the column of pale yellow liquid drifted lazily through the plastic tubing, Kate murmured, "You should start to feel sleepy soon, Ellen. Close your eyes. Let go...."

"I don't feel anything yet."

"It will take a minute or so." Kate squeezed Ellen's shoulder in a silent gesture of reassurance. The small things were what made a patient feel safe. A touch. A quiet voice. "Let yourself float," Kate whispered. "Think of the sky... clouds...."

Ellen gave her a calm and drowsy smile. Beneath the harsh operating-room lights, every freckle, every flaw stood out cruelly on her face. No one, not even Ellen O'Brien, was beautiful on the operating table. "Funny," she murmured. "I'm not afraid. Not in the least...."

"You don't have to be. I'll take care of everything."

"I know. I know you will." Ellen reached out for Kate's hand. It was only a touch, a brief mingling of fingers. The warmth of Ellen's skin against hers was one more reminder that not just a body, but a woman, a friend, was lying on this table.

The door swung open and the surgeon walked in. Dr. Guy Santini was as big as a bear and he looked faintly ridiculous in his flowered paper cap. "How we doing in here, Kate?"

"Pentothal's going in now."

Guy moved to the table and squeezed the patient's hand. "Still with us, Ellen?"

She smiled. "For better or worse. But on the whole, I'd rather be in Philadelphia."

Guy laughed. "You'll get there. But minus your gallbladder."

"I don't know.... I was getting kinda...fond of the thing...." Ellen's eyelids sagged. "Remember, Guy," she whispered. "You promised. No scar...."

"Did I?"

"Yes...you did....."

Guy winked at Kate. "Didn't I tell you? Nurses make the worst patients. Demanding broads!"

"Watch it, Doc!" one of the O.R. nurses snapped. "One of these days we'll get *you* up on that table."

"Now *that's* a terrifying thought," remarked Guy.

Kate watched as her patient's jaw at last fell slack. She called softly: "Ellen?" She brushed her finger across Ellen's eyelashes. There was no response. Kate nodded at Guy. "She's under."

"Ah, Katie, my darlin'," he said, "you do such good work for a—"

"For a *girl*. Yeah, yeah. I know."

"Well, let's get this show on the road," he said, heading out to scrub. "All her labs look okay?"

"Blood work's perfect."

"EKG?"

"I ran it last night. Normal."

Guy gave her an admiring salute from the doorway. "With you around, Kate, a man doesn't even have to think. Oh, and ladies?" He called to the two O.R. nurses who were laying out the instruments. "A word of warning. Our intern's a lefty."

The scrub nurse glanced up with sudden interest. "Is he cute?"

Guy winked. "A real dreamboat, Cindy. I'll tell him you asked." Laughing, he vanished out the door.

Cindy sighed. "How does his wife stand him, anyway?"

For the next ten minutes, everything proceeded like clockwork. Kate went about her tasks with her usual efficiency. She inserted the endotracheal tube and connected the respirator. She adjusted the flow of oxygen and added the proper proportions of forane and nitrous oxide. She was Ellen's lifeline. Each step, though automatic, required double-checking, even triple-checking. When the patient was someone she knew and liked, being sure of all her moves took on even more urgency. An anesthesiologist's job is often called ninety-nine percent boredom and one percent sheer terror; it was that one percent that Kate was always anticipating, always guarding against. When complications arose, they could happen in the blink of an eye.

But today she fully expected everything to go smoothly. Ellen O'Brien was only forty-one. Except for a gallstone, she was in perfect health.

Guy returned to the O.R., his freshly scrubbed arms dripping wet. He was followed by the "dreamboat" lefty intern, who appeared to be a staggering five-feet-six in his elevator shoes. They proceeded on to the ritual donning of sterile gowns and gloves, a ceremony punctuated by the brisk snap of latex.

As the team took its place around the operating table, Kate's gaze traveled the circle of masked faces. Except for the intern, they were all comfortably familiar. There was the circulating nurse, Ann Richter, with her ash blond hair tucked neatly beneath a blue surgical cap. She was a coolheaded professional who never mixed business with pleasure. Crack a joke in the O.R. and she was likely to flash you a look of disapproval.

Next there was Guy, homely and affable, his brown eyes distorted by thick bottle-lens glasses. It was hard to believe anyone so clumsy could be a surgeon. But put a scalpel in his hand and he could work miracles.

Opposite Guy stood the intern with the woeful misfortune of having been born left-handed.

And last there was Cindy, the scrub nurse, a dark-eyed nymph with an easy laugh. Today she was sporting a brilliant new eye shadow called Oriental Malachite, which gave her a look reminiscent of a tropical fish.

"Nice eye shadow, Cindy," noted Guy as he held his hand out for a scalpel.

"Why thank you, Dr. Santini," she replied, slapping the instrument into his palm.

"I like it a lot better than that other one, Spanish Slime."

"Spanish *Moss*."

"This one's really, really striking, don't you think?" he asked the intern who, wisely, said nothing. "Yeah," Guy continued. "Reminds me of my favorite color. I think it's called Comet cleanser."

The intern giggled. Cindy flashed him a dirty look. So much for the dreamboat's chances.

Guy made the first incision. As a line of scarlet oozed to the surface of the abdominal wall, the intern automatically dabbed away the blood with a sponge. Their hands worked automatically and in concert, like pianists playing a duet.

From her position at the patient's head, Kate followed their progress, her ear tuned the whole time to Ellen's heart rhythm. Everything was going well, with no crises on the horizon. This was when she enjoyed her work most—when she knew she had everything under control. In the midst of all this stainless steel, she felt right at home. For her, the whooshes of the ventilator and the beeps of the cardiac monitor were soothing background music to the performance now unfolding on the table.

Guy made a deeper incision, exposing the glistening layer of fat. "Muscles seem a little tight, Kate," he observed. "We're going to have trouble retracting."

"I'll see what I can do." Turning to her medication cart, she reached for the tiny drawer labeled Succinylcholine. Given intravenously, the drug would relax the muscles, allowing Guy easier access to the abdominal cavity. Glancing in the drawer, she frowned. "Ann? I'm down to one vial of Succinylcholine. Hunt me down some more, will you?"

"That's funny," said Cindy. "I'm sure I stocked that cart yesterday afternoon."

"Well, there's only one vial left." Kate drew up 5 cc's of the crystal-clear solution and injected it into Ellen's IV line. It would take a minute to work. She sat back and waited.

Guy's scalpel cleared the fat layer and he began to expose the abdominal muscle sheath. "Still pretty tight, Kate," he remarked.

She glanced up at the wall clock. "It's been three minutes. You should notice some effect by now."

"Not a thing."

"Okay. I'll push a little more." Kate drew up another 3 cc's and injected it into the IV line. "I'll need another vial soon, Ann," she warned. "This one's just about—"

A buzzer went off on the cardiac monitor. Kate glanced up sharply. What she saw on the screen made her jump to her feet in horror.

Ellen O'Brien's heart had stopped.

In the next instant the room was in a frenzy. Orders were shouted out, instrument trays shoved aside. The intern clambered onto a footstool and thrust his weight again and again on Ellen's chest.

This was the proverbial one percent, the moment of terror every anesthesiologist dreads.

It was also the worst moment in Kate Chesne's life.

As panic swirled around her, she fought to stay in control. She injected vial after vial of adrenaline, first into the IV lines and then directly into Ellen's heart. *I'm losing her,* she thought. *Dear God, I'm losing her.* Then she saw one brief fluttering across the oscilloscope. It was the only hint that some trace of life lingered.

"Let's cardiovert!" she called out. She glanced at Ann, who was standing by the defibrillator. "Two hundred watt seconds!"

Ann didn't move. She remained frozen, her face as white as alabaster.

"Ann?" Kate yelled. *"Two hundred watt seconds!"*

It was Cindy who darted around to the machine and hit the charge button. The needle shot up to two hundred. Guy grabbed the defibrillator paddles, slapped them on Ellen's chest and released the electrical charge.

Ellen's body jerked like a puppet whose strings have all been tugged at once.

The fluttering slowed to a ripple. It was the pattern of a dying heart.

Kate tried another drug, then still another in a desperate attempt to flog some life back into the heart. Nothing worked. Through a film of tears, she watched the tracing fade to a line meandering aimlessly across the oscilloscope.

"That's it," Guy said softly. He gave the signal to stop cardiac massage. The intern, his face dripping with sweat, backed away from the table.

"No," Kate insisted, planting her hands on Ellen's chest. "It's not over." She began to pump—fiercely, desperately. *"It's not over."* She threw herself against Ellen, pitting her weight against the stubborn shield of rib and muscles. The heart had to be massaged, the brain nourished.

She had to keep Ellen alive. Again and again she pumped, until her arms were weak and trembling. *Live, Ellen,* she commanded silently. *You have to live....*

"Kate." Guy touched her arm.

"We're not giving up. Not yet...."

"Kate." Gently, Guy tugged her away from the table. "It's over," he whispered.

Someone turned off the sound on the heart monitor. The whine of the alarm gave way to an eerie silence. Slowly, Kate turned and saw that everyone was watching her. She looked up at the oscilloscope.

The line was flat.

KATE FLINCHED as an orderly zipped the shroud over Ellen O'Brien's body. There was a cruel finality to that sound; it struck her as obscene, this convenient packaging of what had once been a living, breathing woman. As the body was wheeled off to the morgue, Kate turned away. Long after the squeak of the gurney wheels had faded down the hall, she was still standing there, alone in the O.R.

Fighting tears, she gazed around at the bloodied gauze and empty vials littering the floor. It was the same sad debris that lingered after every hospital death. Soon it would be swept up and incinerated and there'd be no clue to the tragedy that had just been played out. Nothing except a body in the morgue.

And questions. Oh, yes, there'd be questions. From Ellen's parents. From the hospital. Questions Kate didn't know how to answer.

Wearily she tugged off her surgical cap and felt a vague sense of relief as her brown hair tumbled free to her shoulders. She needed time alone— to think, to understand. She turned to leave.

Guy was standing in the doorway. The instant she saw his face, Kate knew something was wrong.

Silently he handed her Ellen O'Brien's chart.

"The electrocardiogram," he said. "You told me it was normal."

"It was."

"You'd better take another look."

Puzzled, she opened the chart to the EKG, the electrical tracing of Ellen's heart. The first detail she noted was her own initials, written at the top, signifying that she'd seen the page. Next she scanned the tracing. For a solid minute she stared at the series of twelve black squiggles, unable to believe what she was seeing. The pattern was unmistakable. Even a third-year medical student could have made the diagnosis.

"That's why she died, Kate," Guy said.

"But— This is impossible!" she blurted. "I couldn't have made a mistake like this!"

Guy didn't answer. He simply looked away—an act more telling than anything he could have said.

"Guy, you *know* me," she protested. "You know I wouldn't miss something like—"

"It's right there in black and white. For God's sake, your *initials* are on the damn thing!"

They stared at each other, both of them shocked by the harshness of his voice.

"I'm sorry," he apologized at last. Suddenly agitated, he turned and clawed his fingers through his hair. "Dear God. She'd had a heart attack. A *heart attack*. And we took her to surgery." He gave Kate a look of utter misery. "I guess that means we killed her."

"IT'S AN OBVIOUS CASE of malpractice."

Attorney David Ransom closed the file labeled O'Brien, Ellen, and looked across the broad teak desk at his clients. If he had to choose one word to describe Patrick and Mary O'Brien, it would be *gray*. Gray hair, gray faces, gray clothes. Patrick was wearing a dull tweed jacket that had long ago sagged into shapelessness. Mary wore a dress in a black-and-white print that seemed to blend together into a drab monochrome.

Patrick kept shaking his head. "She was our only girl, Mr. Ransom. Our only child. She was always so good, you know? Never complained. Even when she was a baby. She'd just lie there in her crib and smile. Like a little angel. Just like a darling little—" He suddenly stopped, his face crumpling.

"Mr. O'Brien," David said gently, "I know it's not much of a comfort to you now, but I promise you, I'll do everything I can."

Patrick shook his head. "It's not the money we're after. Sure, I can't work. My back, you know. But Ellie, she had a life insurance policy, and—"

"How much was the policy?"

"Fifty thousand," answered Mary. "That's the kind of girl she was. Always thinking of us." Her profile, caught in the window's light, had an edge of steel. Unlike her husband, Mary O'Brien was done with her crying. She sat very straight, her whole body a rigid testament to grief. David knew exactly what she was feeling. The pain. The anger. Especially the anger. It was there, burning coldly in her eyes.

Patrick was sniffling.

David took a box of tissues from his drawer and quietly placed it in front of his client. "Perhaps we should discuss the case some other time," he suggested. "When you both feel ready...."

Mary's chin lifted sharply. "We're ready, Mr. Ransom. Ask your questions."

David glanced at Patrick, who managed a feeble nod. "I'm afraid this may strike you as...cold-blooded, the things I have to ask. I'm sorry."

"Go on," prompted Mary.

"I'll proceed immediately to filing suit. But I'll need more information before we can make an estimate of damages. Part of that is lost wages—what your daughter would have earned had she lived. You say she was a nurse?''

"In obstetrics. Labor and delivery."

"Do you know her salary?"

"I'll have to check her pay stubs."

"What about dependants? Did she have any?"

"None."

"She was never married?"

Mary shook her head and sighed. "She was the perfect daughter, Mr. Ransom, in almost every way. Beautiful. And brilliant. But when it came to men, she made...mistakes."

He frowned. "Mistakes?"

Mary shrugged. "Oh, I suppose it's just the way things are these days. And when a woman gets to be a—a certain age, she feels, well, *lucky* to have any man at all...." She looked down at her tightly knotted hands and fell silent.

David sensed they'd strayed into hazardous waters. He wasn't interested in Ellen O'Brien's love life, anyway. It was irrelevant to the case.

"Let's turn to your daughter's medical history," he said smoothly, opening the medical chart. "The record states she was forty-one years old and in excellent health. To your knowledge, did she ever have any problems with her heart?"

"Never."

"She never complained of chest pain? Shortness of breath?"

"Ellie was a long-distance swimmer, Mr. Ransom. She could go all day and never get out of breath. That's why I don't believe this story about a—a heart attack."

"But the EKG was strongly diagnostic, Mrs. O'Brien. If there'd been an autopsy, we could have proved it. But I guess it's a bit late for that."

Mary glanced at her husband. "It's Patrick. He just couldn't stand the idea—"

"Haven't they cut her up enough already?" Patrick blurted out.

There was a long silence. Mary said softly, "We'll be taking her ashes out to sea. She loved the sea. Ever since she was a baby..."

It was a solemn parting. A few last words of condolence, and then the handshakes, the sealing of a pact. The O'Briens turned to leave. But in the doorway, Mary stopped.

"I want you to know it's not the money," she declared. "The truth is, I don't care if we see a dime. But they've ruined our lives, Mr. Ransom. They've taken our only baby away. And I hope to God they never forget it."

David nodded. "I'll see they never do."

After his clients had left, David turned to the window. He took a deep breath and slowly let it out, willing the emotions to drain from his body.

But a hard knot seemed to linger in his stomach. All that sadness, all that rage; it clouded his thinking.

Six days ago, a doctor had made a terrible mistake. Now, at the age of forty-one, Ellen O'Brien was dead.

She was only three years older than me.

He sat down at his desk and opened the O'Brien file. Skipping past the hospital record, he turned to the curricula vitae of the two physicians.

Dr. Guy Santini's record was outstanding. Forty-eight years old, a Harvard-trained surgeon, he was at the peak of his career. His list of publications went on for five pages. Most of his research dealt with hepatic physiology. He'd been sued once, eight years ago; he'd won. Bully for him. Santini wasn't the target anyway. David had his cross hairs on the anesthesiologist.

He flipped to the three-page summary of Dr. Katharine Chesne's career.

Her background was impressive. A B.Sc in chemistry from U.C., Berkeley, an M.D. from Johns Hopkins, anesthesia residency and intensive-care fellowship at U.C., San Francisco. Now only thirty years old, she'd already compiled a respectable list of published articles. She'd joined Mid Pac Hospital as a staff anesthesiologist less than a year ago. There was no photograph, but he had no trouble conjuring up a mental picture of the stereotypical female physician: frumpy hair, no figure, and a face like a horse—albeit an extremely intelligent horse.

David sat back, frowning. This was too good a record; it didn't match the profile of an incompetent physician. How could she have made such an elementary mistake?

He closed the file. Whatever her excuses, the facts were indisputable: Dr. Katharine Chesne had condemned her patient to die under the surgeon's knife. Now she'd have to face the consequences.

He'd make damn sure she did.

GEORGE BETTENCOURT despised doctors. It was a personal opinion that made his job as CEO of Mid Pac Hospital all the more difficult, since he had to work so closely with the medical staff. He had both an M.B.A. and a Masters in public health. In his ten years as CEO, he'd achieved what the old doctor-led administration had been unable to do: he'd turned Mid Pac from a comatose institution into a profitable business. Yet all he ever heard from those stupid little surrogate gods in their white coats was criticism. They turned their superior noses up at the very idea that their saintly work could be dictated by profit-and-loss graphs. The cold reality was that saving lives, like selling linoleum, was a business. Bettencourt knew it. The doctors didn't. They were fools, and fools gave him headaches.

And the two sitting across from him now were giving him a migraine headache the likes of which he hadn't felt in years.

Dr. Clarence Avery, the white-haired chief of anesthesia, wasn't the problem. The old man was too timid to stand up to his own shadow, much less to a controversial issue. Ever since his wife's stroke, Avery had shuffled through his duties like a sleepwalker. Yes, he could be persuaded to cooperate. Especially when the hospital's reputation was at stake.

No, it was the other one who worried Bettencourt: the woman. She was new to the staff and he didn't know her very well. But the minute she'd walked into his office, he'd smelled trouble. She had that look in her eye, that crusader's set of the jaw. She was a pretty enough woman, though her brown hair was in a wild state of anarchy and she probably hadn't held a tube of lipstick in months. But those intense green eyes of hers were enough to make a man overlook all the flaws of that face. She was, in fact, quite attractive.

Too bad she'd blown it. Now she was a liability. He hoped she wouldn't make things worse by being a bitch, as well.

KATE FLINCHED AS Bettencourt dropped the papers on the desk in front of her. "The letter arrived in our attorney's office this morning, Dr. Chesne," he said. "Hand delivered by personal messenger. I think you'd better read it."

She took one look at the letterhead and felt her stomach drop away: *Uehara and Ransom, Attorneys at Law.*

"One of the best firms in town," explained Bettencourt. Seeing her stunned expression, he went on impatiently, "You and the hospital are being sued, Dr. Chesne. For malpractice. And David Ransom is personally taking on the case."

Her throat had gone dry. Slowly she looked up. "But how—how can they—"

"All it takes is a lawyer. And a dead patient."

"I've explained what happened!" She turned to Avery. "Remember last week—I told you—"

"Clarence has gone over it with me," cut in Bettencourt. "That isn't the issue we're discussing here."

"What *is* the issue?"

He seemed startled by her directness. He let out a sharp breath. "The issue is this: we have what looks like a million-dollar lawsuit on our hands. As your employer, we're responsible for the damages. But it's not just the money that concerns us." He paused. "There's our reputation."

The tone of his voice struck her as ominous. She knew what was coming and found herself utterly voiceless. She could only sit there, her stomach roiling, her hands clenched in her lap, and wait for the blow to fall.

"This lawsuit reflects badly on the whole hospital," he said. "If the case goes to trial, there'll be publicity. People—patients—will read those newspapers and it'll scare them." He looked down at his desk. "I realize your record up till now has been acceptable—"

Her chin shot up. "Acceptable?" she repeated incredulously. She glanced at Avery. The chief of anesthesia knew her record. And it was flawless.

Avery squirmed in his chair, his watery blue eyes avoiding hers. "Well, actually," he mumbled, "Dr. Chesne's record has been—up till now, anyway—uh, more than acceptable. That is..."

For God's sake, man! she wanted to scream. *Stand up for me!*

"There've never been any complaints," Avery finished lamely.

"Nevertheless," continued Bettencourt, "you've put us in a touchy situation, Dr. Chesne. That's why we think it'd be best if your name was no longer associated with the hospital."

There was a long silence, punctuated only by the sound of Dr. Avery's nervous cough.

"We're asking for your resignation," stated Bettencourt.

So there it was. The blow. It washed over her like a giant wave, leaving her limp and exhausted. Quietly she asked, "And if I refuse to resign?"

"Believe me, Doctor, a resignation will look a lot better on your record than a—"

"Dismissal?"

He cocked his head. "We understand each other."

"No." She raised her head. Something about his eyes, their cold self-assurance, made her stiffen. She'd never liked Bettencourt. She liked him even less now. "You don't understand me at all."

"You're a bright woman. You can see the options. In any event, we can't let you back in the O.R."

"It's not right," Avery objected.

"Excuse me?" Bettencourt frowned at the old man.

"You can't just fire her. She's a physician. There are channels you have to go through. Committees—"

"I'm well acquainted with the proper channels, Clarence! I was hoping Dr. Chesne would grasp the situation and act appropriately." He looked at her. "It really is easier, you know. There'd be no blot on your record. Just a notation that you resigned. I can have a letter typed up within the hour. All it takes is your..." His voice trailed off as he saw the look in her eyes.

Kate seldom got angry. She usually managed to keep her emotions under tight control. So the fury she now felt churning to the surface was something new and unfamiliar and almost frightening. With deadly calm she said, "Save yourself the paper, Mr. Bettencourt."

His jaw clicked shut. "If that's your decision..." He glanced at Avery. "When is the next Quality Assurance meeting?"

"It's—uh, next Tuesday, but—"

"Put the O'Brien case on the agenda. We'll let Dr. Chesne present her record to committee." He looked at Kate. "A judgment by your peers. I'd say that's fair. Wouldn't you?"

She managed to swallow her retort. If she said anything else, if she let fly what she really thought of George Bettencourt, she'd ruin her chances of ever again working at Mid Pac. Or anywhere else, for that matter. All he had to do was slap her with the label Troublemaker; it would blacken her record for the rest of her life.

They parted civilly. For a woman who'd just had her career ripped to shreds, she managed a grand performance. She gave Bettencourt a level look, a cool handshake. She kept her composure all the way out the door and on the long walk down the carpeted hall. But as she rode the elevator down, something inside her seemed to snap. By the time the doors slid open again, she was shaking violently. As she walked blindly through the noise and bustle of the lobby, the realization hit her full force.

Dear God, I'm being sued. Less than a year in practice and I'm being sued....

She'd always thought that lawsuits, like all life's catastrophes, happened to other people. She'd never dreamed she'd be the one charged with incompetence. *Incompetence.*

Suddenly feeling sick, she swayed against the lobby telephones. As she struggled to calm her stomach, her gaze fell on the local directory, hanging by a chain from the shelf. *If only they knew the facts,* she thought. *If I could explain to them...*

It took only seconds to find the listing: *Uehara and Ransom, Attorneys at Law.* Their office was on Bishop Street.

She wrenched out the page. Then, driven by a new and desperate hope, she hurried out the door.

Chapter Two

"Mr. Ransom is unavailable."

The gray-haired receptionist had eyes of pure cast iron and a face straight out of *American Gothic*. All she needed was the pitchfork. Crossing her arms, she silently dared the intruder to try—just try—to talk her way in.

"But I have to see him!" Kate insisted. "It's about the case—"

"Of course it is," the woman said dryly.

"I only want to explain to him—"

"I've just told you, Doctor. He's in a meeting with the associates. He can't see you."

Kate's impatience was simmering close to the danger point. She leaned forward on the woman's desk and managed to say with polite fury, "Meetings don't last forever."

The receptionist smiled. "This one will."

Kate smiled back. "Then so can I."

"Doctor, you're wasting your time! Mr. Ransom *never* meets with defendants. Now, if you need an escort to find your way out, I'll be happy to—" She glanced around in annoyance as the telephone rang. Grabbing the receiver, she snapped, "Uehara and Ransom! Yes? Oh, yes, Mr. Matheson!" She pointedly turned her back on Kate. "Let's see, I have those files right here..."

In frustration, Kate glanced around at the waiting room, noting the leather couch, the Ikebana of willow and proteus, the Murashige print hanging on the wall. All exquisitely tasteful and undoubtedly expensive. Obviously, Uehara and Ransom was doing a booming business. All off the blood and sweat of doctors, she thought in disgust.

The sound of voices suddenly drew Kate's attention. She turned and saw, just down the hall, a small army of young men and women emerging from a conference room. Which one was Ransom? She scanned the faces but none of the men looked old enough to be a senior partner in the firm. She glanced back at the desk and saw that the receptionist still had her back turned. It was now or never.

It took Kate only a split-second to make her decision. Swiftly, deliberately, she moved toward the conference room. But in the doorway she came to a halt, her eyes suddenly dazzled by the light.

A long teak table stretched out before her. Along either side, a row of leather chairs stood like soldiers at attention. Blinding sunshine poured in through the southerly windows, spilling across the head and shoulders of a lone man seated at the far end of the table. The light streaked his fair hair with gold. He didn't notice her; all his attention was focused on a sheaf of papers lying in front of him. Except for the rustle of a page being turned, the room was absolutely silent.

Kate swallowed hard and drew herself up straight. "Mr. Ransom?"

The man looked up and regarded her with a neutral expression. "Yes? Who are you?"

"I'm—"

"I'm so sorry, Mr. Ransom!" cut in the receptionist's outraged voice. Hauling Kate by the arm, the woman muttered through her teeth, "I *told* you he was unavailable. Now if you'll come with me—"

"I only want to talk to him!"

"Do you want me to call security and have you thrown out?"

Kate wrenched her arm free. "Go ahead."

"Don't tempt me, you—"

"What the hell is going on here?" The roar of Ransom's voice echoed in the vast room, shocking both women into silence. He aimed a long and withering look at Kate. "Just who *are* you?"

"Kate—" She paused and dropped her voice to what she hoped was a more dignified tone. "*Doctor* Kate Chesne."

A pause. "I see." he looked right back down at his papers and said flatly, "Show her out, Mrs. Pierce."

"I just want to tell you the facts!" Kate persisted. She tried to hold her ground but the receptionist herded her toward the door with all the skill of a sheepdog. "Or would you rather *not* hear the facts, is that it? Is that how you lawyers operate?" He studiously ignored her. "You don't give a damn about the truth, do you? You don't want to hear what really happened to Ellen O'Brien!"

That made him look up sharply. His gaze fastened long and hard on her face. "Hold on, Mrs. Pierce. I've just changed my mind. Let Dr. Chesne stay."

Mrs. Pierce was incredulous. "But—she could be violent!"

David's gaze lingered a moment longer on Kate's flushed face. "I think I can handle her. You can leave us, Mrs. Pierce."

Mrs. Pierce muttered as she walked out. The door closed behind her. There was a very long silence.

"Well, Dr. Chesne," David said. "Now that you've managed the rather miraculous feat of getting past Mrs. Pierce, are you just going to stand there?" He gestured to a chair. "Have a seat. Unless you'd rather scream at me from across the room."

His cold flippancy, rather than easing her tension, made him seem all the more unapproachable. She forced herself to move toward him, feeling his gaze every step of the way. For a man with his highly regarded reputation, he was younger than she'd expected, not yet in his forties. *Establishment* was stamped all over his clothes, from his gray pinstripe suit to his Yale tie clip. But a tan that deep and hair that sun-streaked didn't go along with an Ivy League type. *He's just a surfer boy, grown up,* she thought derisively. He certainly had a surfer's build, with those long, ropy limbs and shoulders that were just broad enough to be called impressive. A slab of a nose and a blunt chin saved him from being pretty. But it was his eyes she found herself focusing on. They were a frigid, penetrating blue; the sort of eyes that missed absolutely nothing. Right now those eyes were boring straight through her and she felt an almost irresistible urge to cross her arms protectively across her chest.

"I'm here to tell you the facts, Mr. Ransom," she said.

"The facts as you see them?"

"The facts as they *are.*"

"Don't bother." Reaching into his briefcase, he pulled out Ellen O'Brien's file and slapped it down conclusively on the table. "I have all the facts right here. Everything I need." *Everything I need to hang you,* was what he meant.

"Not everything."

"And now *you're* going to supply me with the missing details. Right?" He smiled and she recognized immediately the unmistakable threat in his expression. He had such perfect, sharp white teeth. She had the distinct feeling she was staring into the jaws of a shark.

She leaned forward, planting her hands squarely on the table. "What I'm going to supply you with is the truth."

"Oh, naturally." He slouched back in his chair and regarded her with a look of terminal boredom. "Tell me something," he asked offhandedly. "Does your attorney know you're here?"

"Attorney? I—I haven't talked to any attorney—"

"Then you'd better get one on the phone. Fast. Because, Doctor, you're damn well going to need one."

"Not necessarily. This is nothing but a big misunderstanding, Mr. Ransom. If you'll just listen to the facts, I'm sure—"

"Hold on." He reached into his briefcase and pulled out a cassette recorder.

"Just what do you think you're doing?" she demanded.

He turned on the recorder and slid it in front of her. "I wouldn't want to miss some vital detail. Go on with your story. I'm all ears."

Furious, she reached over and flicked the Off button. "This isn't a deposition! Put the damn thing away!"

For a few tense seconds they sized each other up. She felt a distinct sense of triumph when he put the recorder back in his briefcase.

"Now, where were we?" he asked with extravagant politeness. "Oh, yes. You were about to tell me what *really* happened." He settled back, obviously expecting some grand entertainment.

She hesitated. Now that she finally had his full attention, she didn't know quite how to start.

"I'm a very...careful person, Mr. Ransom," she said at last. "I take my time with things. I may not be brilliant, but I'm thorough. And I don't make stupid mistakes."

His raised eyebrow told her exactly what he thought of that statement. She ignored his look and went on.

"The night Ellen O'Brien came into the hospital, Guy Santini admitted her. But I wrote the anesthesia orders. I checked the lab results. And I read her EKG. It was a Sunday night and the technician was busy somewhere so I even ran the strip myself. I wasn't rushed. I took all the time I needed. In fact, more than I needed, because Ellen was a member of our staff. She was one of *us*. She was also a friend. I remember sitting in her room, going over her lab tests. She wanted to know if everything was normal."

"And you told her everything was."

"Yes. Including the EKG."

"Then you obviously made a mistake."

"I just told you, Mr. Ransom. I don't make stupid mistakes. And I didn't make one that night."

"But the record shows—"

"The record's wrong."

"I have the tracing right here in black and white. And it plainly shows a heart attack."

"That's *not* the EKG I saw!"

He looked as if he hadn't heard her quite right.

"The EKG I saw that night was normal," she insisted.

"Then how did this abnormal one pop into the chart?"

"Someone put it there, of course."

"Who?"

"I don't know."

"I see." Turning away, he said under his breath: "I can't wait to see how this plays in court."

"Mr. Ransom, if I made a mistake, I'd be the first to admit it!"

"Then you'd be amazingly honest."

"Do you really think I'd make up a story as—as *stupid* as this?"

His response was an immediate burst of laughter that left her cheeks burning. "No," he answered. "I'm sure you'd come up with something much more believable." He gave her an inviting nod. In a voice thick with sarcasm, he jeered, "Please, I'm *dying* to know how this extraordinary mix-up happened. How did the wrong EKG get in the chart?"

"How should I know?"

"You must have a theory."

"I don't."

"Come on, Doctor, don't disappoint me."

"I said I don't."

"Then make a guess!"

"Maybe someone beamed it there from the *Starship Enterprise*!" she yelled in frustration.

"Nice theory," he said, deadpan. "But let's get back to reality. Which, in this case, happens to be a particular sheet of wood by-product, otherwise known as paper." He flipped the chart open to the damning EKG. "Explain *that* away."

"I told you, I can't! I've gone crazy trying to figure it out! We do dozens of EKGs every day at Mid Pac. It could have been a clerical error. A mislabeled tracing. Somehow, that page was filed in the wrong chart."

"But you've written your initials on this page."

"No, I didn't."

"Is there some other K.C., M.D.?"

"Those are my initials. But I didn't write them."

"What are you saying? That this is a forgery?"

"It—it has to be. I mean, yes, I guess it is...." Suddenly confused, she shoved back a rebellious strand of hair off her face. His utterly calm expression rattled her. Why didn't the man react, for God's sake? Why did he just sit there, regarding her with that infuriatingly bland expression?

"Well," he said at last.

"Well what?"

"How long have you had this little problem with people forging your name?"

"Don't make me sound paranoid!"

"I don't have to. You're doing fine on your own."

Now he was silently laughing at her; she could see it in his eyes. The worst part was that she couldn't blame him. Her story *did* sound like a lunatic's ravings.

"All right," he relented. "Let's assume for the moment you're telling the truth."

"Yes!" she snapped. "Please do!"

"I can think of only two explanations for why the EKG would be intentionally switched. Either someone's trying to destroy your career—"

"That's absurd. I don't have any enemies."

"Or someone's trying to cover up a murder."

At her stunned expression, he gave her a maddeningly superior smile. "Since the second explanation obviously strikes both of us as equally absurd, I have no choice but to conclude you're lying." He leaned forward and his voice was suddenly soft, almost intimate. The shark was getting chummy; that had to be dangerous. "Come on, Doctor," he prodded. "Level with me. Tell me what really happened in the O.R. Was there a slip of the knife? A mistake in anesthesia?"

"There was nothing of the kind!"

"Too much laughing gas and not enough oxygen?"

"I told you, there were *no* mistakes!"

"Then why is Ellen O'Brien dead?"

She stared at him, stunned by the violence in his voice. And the blueness of his eyes. A spark seemed to fly between them, ignited by something entirely unexpected. With a shock, she realized he was an attractive man. Too attractive. And that her response to him was dangerous. She could already feel the blush creeping into her face, could feel a flood of heat rising inside her.

"No answer?" he challenged smoothly. He settled back, obviously enjoying the advantage he held over her. "Then why don't I tell *you* what happened? On April 2, a Sunday night, Ellen O'Brien checked into Mid Pac Hospital for routine gallbladder surgery. As her anesthesiologist, you ordered routine pre-op tests, including an EKG, which you checked before leaving the hospital that night. Maybe you were rushed. Maybe you had a hot date waiting. Whatever the reason, you got careless and you made a fatal error. You missed those vital clues in the EKG: the elevated ST waves, the inverted T waves. You pronounced it normal and signed your initials. Then you left for the night—never realizing your patient had just had a heart attack."

"She never had any symptoms! No chest pain—"

"But it says right here in the nurses' notes—let me quote—" he flipped through the chart "—'Patient complaining of abdominal discomfort.'"

"That was her gallstone—"

"Or was it her heart? Anyway, the next events are indisputable. You and Dr. Santini took Ms. O'Brien to surgery. A few whiffs of anesthesia and the stress was too much for her weakened heart. So it stopped. And you couldn't restart it." He paused dramatically, his eyes as hard as diamonds. "There, Dr. Chesne. You've just lost your patient."

"That's not how it happened! I remember that EKG. It was *normal!*"

"Maybe you'd better review your textbook on EKGs."

"I don't need a textbook. I *know* what's normal!" She scarcely recognized her own voice, echoing shrilly through the vast room.

He looked unimpressed. Bored, even. "Really—" he sighed "—wouldn't it be easier just to admit you made a mistake?"

"Easier for whom?"

"For everyone involved. Consider an out-of-court settlement. It'd be fast, easy, and relatively painless."

"A settlement? But that's admitting a mistake I never made!"

What little patience he had left finally snapped. "You want to go to trial?" he shot back. "Fine. But let me tell you something about the way I work. When I try a case, I don't do it halfway. If I have to tear you apart in court, I'll do it. And when I'm finished, you'll wish you'd never turned this into some ridiculous fight for your honor. Because let's face it, Doctor. You don't have a snowball's chance in hell.''

She wanted to grab him by those pinstriped lapels. She wanted to scream out that in all this talk about settlements and courtrooms, her own anguish over Ellen O'Brien's death had been ignored. But suddenly all her rage, all her strength, seemed to drain away, leaving her exhausted. Wearily she slumped back in her chair. "I wish I *could* admit I made a mistake," she said quietly. "I wish I could just say, 'I know I'm guilty and I'll pay for it.' I wish to God I could say that. I've spent the last week wondering about my memory. Wondering how this could have happened. Ellen trusted me and I let her die. It makes me wish I'd never become a doctor, that I'd been a clerk or a waitress—anything else. I love my work. You have no idea how hard it's been—how much I've given up—just to get to where I am. And now it looks as if I'll lose my job...." She swallowed and her head drooped in defeat. "And I wonder if I'll ever be able to work again...."

David regarded her bowed head in silence and fought to ignore the emotions stirring inside him. He'd always considered himself a good judge of character. He could usually look a man in the eyes and tell if he was lying. All during Kate Chesne's little speech, he'd been watching her eyes, searching for some inconsistent blip, some betraying flicker that would tell him she was lying through her teeth.

But her eyes had been absolutely steady and forthright and as beautiful as a pair of emeralds.

The last thought startled him, popping out as it did, almost against his will. As much as he might try to suppress it, he was all at once aware that she *was* a beautiful woman. She was wearing a simple green dress, gathered loosely at the waist, and it took just one glance to see that there were feminine curves beneath that silky fabric. The face that went along with those very nice curves had its flaws. She had a prizefighter's square jaw. Her shoulder-length mahogany hair was a riot of waves, obviously untamable. The curly bangs softened a forehead that was far too prominent. No, it wasn't a classically beautiful face. But then he'd never been attracted to classically beautiful women.

Suddenly he was annoyed not only at himself but at her, at her effect on him. He wasn't a dumb kid fresh out of law school. He was too old and too smart to be entertaining the peculiarly male thoughts now dancing in his head.

In a deliberately rude gesture, he looked down at his watch. Then, snapping his briefcase shut, he stood up. "I have a deposition to take and I'm already late. So if you'll excuse me..."

He was halfway across the room when her voice called out to him softly: "Mr. Ransom?"

He glanced back at her in irritation. "What?"

"I know my story sounds crazy. And I guess there's no reason on earth you should believe me. But I swear to you: it's the truth."

He sensed her desperate need for validation. She was searching for a sign that she'd gotten through to him; that she'd penetrated his hard shell of skepticism. The fact was, he didn't *know* if he believed her, and it bothered the hell out of him that his usual instinct for the truth had gone haywire, and all because of a pair of emerald-green eyes.

"Whether I believe you or not is irrelevant," he said. "So don't waste your time on me, Doctor. Save it for the jury." The words came out colder than he'd intended and he saw, from the quick flinch of her head, that she'd been stung.

"Then there's nothing I can do, nothing I can say—"

"Not a thing."

"I thought you'd listen. I thought somehow I could change your mind—"

"Then you've got a lot to learn about lawyers. Good-day, Dr. Chesne." Turning, he headed briskly for the door. "I'll see you in court."

Chapter Three

You don't have a snowball's chance in hell.

That was the phrase Kate kept hearing over and over as she sat alone at a table in the hospital cafeteria. And just how long did it take for a snowball to melt, anyway? Or would it simply disintegrate in the heat of the flames?

How much heat could she take before she fell apart on the witness stand?

She'd always been so adept at dealing with matters of life and death. When a medical crisis arose, she didn't wring her hands over what needed to be done; she just did it, automatically. Inside the safe and sterile walls of the operating room, she was in control.

But a courtroom was a different world entirely. That was David Ransom's territory. He'd be the one in control; she'd be as vulnerable as a patient on the operating table. How could she possibly fend off an attack by the very man who'd built his reputation on the scorched careers of doctors?

She'd never felt threatened by men before. After all, she'd trained with them, worked with them. David Ransom was the first man who'd ever intimidated her, and he'd done it effortlessly. If only he was short or fat or bald. If only she could think of him as human and therefore vulnerable. But just the thought of facing those cold blue eyes in court made her stomach do a panicky flip-flop.

"Looks like you could use some company," said a familiar voice.

Glancing up, she saw Guy Santini, rumpled as always, peering down at her through those ridiculously thick glasses.

She gave him a listless nod. "Hi."

Clucking, he pulled up a chair and sat down. "How're you doing, Kate?"

"You mean except for being unemployed?" She managed a sour laugh. "Just terrific."

"I heard the old man pulled you out of the O.R. I'm sorry."

"I can't really blame it on old Avery. He was just following orders."

"Bettencourt's?"

"Who else? He's labeled me a financial *liability*."

Guy snorted. "That's what happens when the damned M.B.A.'s take over. All they can talk about is profits and losses! I swear, if George Bettencourt could make a buck selling the gold out of patients' teeth, he'd be roaming the wards with pliers."

"And then he'd send them a bill for oral surgery," Kate added morosely.

Neither of them laughed. The joke was too close to the truth to be funny.

"If it makes you feel any better, Kate, you'll have some company in the courtroom. I've been named, too."

She looked up sharply. "Oh, Guy! I'm sorry...."

He shrugged. "It's no big deal. I've been sued before. Believe me, it's that first time that really hurts."

"What happened?"

"Trauma case. Man came in with a ruptured spleen and I couldn't save him." He shook his head. "When I saw that letter from the attorney, I was so depressed I wanted to leap out the nearest window. Susan was ready to drag me off to the psych ward. But you know what? I survived. So will you, as long as you remember they're not attacking *you*. They're attacking the job you did."

"I don't see the difference."

"And *that's* your problem, Kate. You haven't learned to separate yourself from the job. We both know the hours you put in. Hell, sometimes I think you practically live here. I'm not saying dedication's a character flaw. But you can overdo it."

What really hurt was that she knew it was true. She did work long hours. Maybe she needed to; it kept her mind off the wasteland of her personal life.

"I'm not completely buried in my job," she said. "I've started dating again."

"It's about time. Who's the man?"

"Last week I went out with Elliot."

"That guy from computer programming?" He sighed. Elliot was six-foot-two and one hundred and twenty pounds, and he bore a distinct resemblance to Pee-Wee Herman. "I bet that was a barrel of laughs."

"Well it was sort of...fun. He asked me up to his apartment."

"He did?"

"So I went."

"You *did*?"

"He wanted to show me his latest electronic gear."

Guy leaned forward eagerly. "What happened?"

"We listened to his new CDs. Played a few computer games."

"And?"

She sighed. "After eight rounds of Zork I went home."

Groaning, Guy sank back in his chair. "Elliot Lafferty, last of the red-hot lovers. Kate, what you need is one of these dating services. Hey, I'll even write the ad for you. 'Bright, attractive female seeks—'"

"Daddy!" The happy squeal cut straight through the cafeteria's hubbub.

Guy turned as running feet pattered toward him. "There's my Will!" Laughing, he rose to his feet and scooped up his son. It took only a sweep of his arms to send the spindly five-year-old boy flying into the air. Little Will was so light he seemed to float for a moment like a frail bird. He fell to a very soft, very safe landing in his father's arms. "I've been waiting for you, kid," Guy said. "What took you so long?"

"Mommy came home late."

"Again?"

Will leaned forward and whispered confidentially. "Adele was *really* mad. Her boyfriend was s'posed to take her to the movies."

"Uh-oh. We *certainly* don't want Adele to be mad at us, do we?" Guy flashed an inquiring look at his wife Susan, who was threading her way toward them. "Hey, are we wearing out the nanny already?"

"I swear, it's that full moon!" Susan laughed and shoved back a frizzy strand of red hair. "All my patients have gone absolutely loony. I couldn't get them out of my office."

Guy muttered grumpily to Kate, "And she swore it'd be a part-time practice. Ha! Guess who gets called to the E.R. practically every night?"

"Oh, you just miss having your shirts ironed!" Susan reached up and gave her husband an affectionate pat on the cheek. It was the sort of maternal gesture one expected of Susan Santini. "My mother hen," Guy had once called his wife. He'd meant it as a term of endearment and it had fit. Susan's beauty wasn't in her face, which was plain and freckled, or in her figure, which was as stout as a farm wife's. Her beauty lay in that serenely patient smile that she was now beaming at her son.

"Daddy!" William was prancing like an elf around Guy's legs. "Make me fly again!"

"What am I, a launching pad?"

"Up! One more time!"

"Later, Will," said Susan. "We have to pick up Daddy's car before the garage closes."

"Please!"

"Did you hear that?" Guy gasped. "He said the magic word." With a lion's roar, Guy pounced on the shrieking boy and threw him into the air.

Susan gave Kate a long-suffering look. "Two children. That's what I have. And one of them weighs two hundred and forty pounds."

"I heard that." Guy reached over and slung a possessive arm around his wife. "Just for that, lady, you have to drive me home."

"Big bully. Feel like McDonald's?"

"Humph. I know someone who doesn't want to cook tonight."

Guy gave Kate a wave as he nudged his family toward the door. "So what'll it be, kid?" Kate heard him say to William. "Cheeseburger?"

"Ice cream."

"Ice cream. Now that's an alternative I hadn't thought of...."

Wistfully Kate watched the Santinis make their way across the cafeteria. She could picture how the rest of their evening would go. She imagined them sitting in McDonald's, the two parents teasing, coaxing another bite of food into Will's reluctant mouth. Then there'd be the drive home, the pajamas, the bedtime story. And finally, there'd be those skinny arms, curling around Daddy's neck for a kiss.

What do I have to go home to? she thought.

Guy turned and gave her one last wave. Then he and his family vanished out the door. Kate sighed enviously. *Lucky man.*

AFTER HE LEFT his office that afternoon, David drove up Nuuanu Avenue and turned onto the dirt lane that wound through the old cemetery. He parked his car in the shade of a banyan tree and walked across the freshly mown lawn, past the marble headstones with their grotesque angels, past the final resting places of the Doles and the Binghams and the Cookes. He came to a section where there were only bronze plaques set flush in the ground, a sad concession to modern graveskeeping. Beneath a monkeypod tree, he stopped and gazed down at the marker by his feet.

Noah Ransom

Seven Years Old

It was a fine spot, gently sloping, with a view of the city. Here a breeze was always blowing, sometimes from the sea, sometimes from the valley. If he closed his eyes, he could tell where the wind was coming from, just by its smell.

David hadn't chosen this spot. He couldn't remember who had decided the grave should be here. Perhaps it had simply been a matter of which plot was available at the time. When your only child dies, who cares about views or breezes or monkeypod trees?

Bending down, he gently brushed the leaves that had fallen on the plaque. Then, slowly, he rose to his feet and stood in silence beside his son. He scarcely registered the rustle of the long skirt or the sound of the cane thumping across the grass.

"So here you are, David," called a voice.

Turning, he saw the tall, silver-haired woman hobbling toward him. "You shouldn't be out here, Mother. Not with that sprained foot."

She pointed her cane at the white clapboard house sitting near the edge of the cemetery. "I saw you through my kitchen window. Thought I'd better come out and say hello. Can't wait around forever for you to come visit me.''

He kissed her on the cheek. "Sorry. I've been busy. But I really *was* on my way to see you.''

"Oh, naturally." Her blue eyes shifted and focused on the grave. It was one of the many things Jinx Ransom shared with her son, that peculiar shade of blue of her eyes. Even at sixty-eight, her gaze was piercing. "Some anniversaries are better left forgotten," she said softly.

He didn't answer.

"You know, David, Noah always wanted a brother. Maybe it's time you gave him one.''

David smiled faintly. "What are you suggesting, Mother?''

"Only what comes naturally to us all.''

"Maybe I should get married first?''

"Oh, of course, of course.'' She paused, then asked hopefully: "Anyone in mind?''

"Not a soul.''

Sighing, she laced her arm through his. "That's what I thought. Well, come along. Since there's no gorgeous female waiting for you, you might as well have a cup of coffee with your old mother.''

Together they crossed the lawn toward the house. The grass was uneven and Jinx moved slowly, stubbornly refusing to lean on her son's shoulder. She wasn't supposed to be on her feet at all, but she'd never been one to follow doctors' orders. A woman who'd sprained her ankle in a savage game of tennis certainly wouldn't sit around twiddling her thumbs.

They passed through a gap in the mock-orange hedge and climbed the steps to the kitchen porch. Gracie, Jinx's middle-aged companion, met them at the screen door.

"There you are!'' Gracie sighed. She turned her mouse-brown eyes to David. "I have absolutely *no* control over this woman. None at all.''

He shrugged. "Who does?''

Jinx and David settled down at the breakfast table. The kitchen was a dense jungle of hanging plants: asparagus fern and baby's tears and wandering Jew. Valley breezes swept in from the porch, and through the large window, there was a view of the cemetery.

"What a shame they've trimmed back the monkeypod," Jinx remarked, gazing out.

"They had to," said Gracie as she poured coffee. "Grass can't grow right in the shade.''

"But the view's just not the same.''

David batted away a stray fern. "I never cared for that view anyway. I don't see how you can look at a cemetery all day.''

"I like my view," Jinx declared. "When I look out, I see my old friends. Mrs. Goto, buried there by the hedge. Mr. Carvalho, by the shower tree. And on the slope, there's our Noah. I think of them all as sleeping.''

"Good Lord, Mother.''

"Your problem, David, is that you haven't resolved your fear of death. Until you do, you'll never come to terms with life.''

"What do you suggest?''

"Take another stab at immortality. Have another child.''

"I'm not getting married again, Mother. So let's just drop the subject.'' Jinx responded as she always did when her son made a ridiculous request. She ignored it. "There was that young woman you met in Maui last year. Whatever happened to her?''

"She got married. To someone else.''

"What a shame.''

"Yeah, the poor guy.''

"Oh, David!'' cried Jinx, exasperated. "When are you going to grow up?''

David smiled and took a sip of Gracie's tar-black coffee, on which he promptly gagged. Another reason he avoided these visits to his mother. Not only did Jinx stir up a lot of bad memories, she also forced him to drink Gracie's god-awful coffee.

"So how was *your* day, Mother?'' he asked politely.

"Getting worse by the minute.''

"More coffee, David?'' urged Gracie, tipping the pot threateningly toward his cup.

"No!'' David gasped, clapping his hand protectively over the cup. The women stared at him in surprise. "I mean, er, no, thank you, Gracie.''

"So touchy,'' observed Jinx. "Is something wrong? I mean, besides your sex life.''

"I'm just a little busier than usual. Hiro's still laid up with that bad back.''

"Humph. Well, you don't seem to like your work much anymore. I think you were much happier in the prosecutor's office. Now you take the job so damned seriously.''

"It's a serious business.''

"Suing doctors? Ha! It's just another way to make a fast buck.''

"My doctor was sued once,'' Gracie remarked. "I thought it was terrible, all those things they said about him. Such a saint...''

"Nobody's a saint, Gracie,'' David said darkly. "Least of all, doctors.'' His gaze wandered out the window and he suddenly thought of the O'Brien case. It had been on his mind all afternoon. Or rather, *she'd* been on his mind, that green-eyed, perjuring Kate Chesne. He'd finally decided she was lying. This case was going to be even easier than he'd thought. She'd be a sitting duck on that witness stand and he knew just how he'd handle her in court. First the easy questions: name, education, postgraduate training. He had a habit of pacing in the courtroom, stalking circles around the defendant. The tougher the questions, the tighter the circles. By the time he came in for the kill, they'd be face-to-face. He felt an unexpected thump of dread in his chest, knowing what he'd have to do to finish it. Expose her. Destroy her. That was his job, and he'd always prided himself on a job well done.

He forced down a last sip of coffee and rose to his feet. "I have to be going," he announced, ducking past a lethally placed hanging fern. "I'll call you later, Mother."

Jinx snorted. "When? Next year?"

He gave Gracie a sympathetic pat on the shoulder and muttered in her ear, "Good luck. Don't let her drive you nuts."

"*I?* Drive *her* nuts?" Jinx snorted. "Ha!"

Gracie followed him to the porch door where she stood and waved. "Goodbye, David!" she called sweetly.

FOR A MOMENT, Gracie paused in the doorway and watched David walk through the cemetery to his car. Then she turned sadly to Jinx.

"He's *so* unhappy!" she said. "If only he could forget."

"He won't forget." Jinx sighed. "David's just like his father that way. He'll carry it around inside him till the day he dies."

Chapter Four

Ten-knot winds were blowing in from the northeast as the launch bearing Ellen O'Brien's last remains headed out to sea. It was such a clean, such a natural resolution to life: the strewing of ashes into the sunset waters, the rejoining of flesh and blood with their elements. The minister tossed a lei of yellow flowers off the old pier. The blossoms drifted away on the current, a slow and symbolic parting that brought Patick O'Brien to tears.

The sound of his crying floated on the wind, over the crowded dock, to the distant spot where Kate was standing. Alone and ignored, she lingered by the row of tethered fishing boats and wondered why she was here. Was it some cruel and self-imposed form of penance? A feeble attempt to tell the world she was sorry? She only knew that some inner voice, begging for forgiveness, had compelled her to come.

There were others here from the hospital: a group of nurses, huddled in a quiet sisterhood of mourning; a pair of obstetricians, looking stiffly uneasy in their street clothes; Clarence Avery, his white hair blowing like dandelion fuzz in the wind. Even George Bettencourt had made an appearance. He stood apart, his face arranged in an impenetrable mask. For these people, a hospital was more than just a place of work; it was another home, another family. Doctors and nurses delivered each other's babies, presided over each other's deaths. Ellen O'Brien had helped bring many of their children into the world; now they were here to usher her out of it.

The far-off glint of sunlight on fair hair made Kate focus on the end of the pier where David Ransom stood, towering above the others. Carelessly he pushed a lock of windblown hair into place. He was dressed in appropriately mournful attire—a charcoal suit, a somber tie—but in the midst of all this grief, he displayed the emotions of a stone wall. She wondered if there was anything human about him. *Do you ever laugh or cry? Do you ever hurt? Do you ever make love?*

That last thought had careened into her mind without warning. Love? Yes, she could imagine how it would be to make love with David Ransom: not a sharing but a claiming. He'd demand total surrender, the way he demanded surrender in the courtroom. The fading sunlight seemed to knight him with a mantle of unconquerability. What chance did she stand against such a man?

Wind gusted in from the sea, whipping sailboat halyards against masts, drowning out the minister's final words. When at last it was over, Kate found she didn't have the strength to move. She watched the other mourners pass by. Clarence Avery stopped, started to say something, then awkwardly moved on. Mary and Patrick O'Brien didn't even look at her. As David approached, his eyes registered a flicker of recognition, which was just as quickly suppressed. Without breaking stride, he continued past her. She might have been invisible.

By the time she finally found the energy to move, the pier was empty. Sailboat masts stood out like a row of dead trees against the sunset. Her foosteps sounded hollow against the wooden planks. When she finally reached her car, she felt utterly weary, as though her legs had carried her for miles. She fumbled for her keys and felt a strange sense of inevitability as her purse slipped out of her grasp, scattering its contents across the pavement. She could only stand there, paralyzed by defeat, as the wind blew her tissues across the ground. She had the absurd image of herself standing here all night, all week, frozen to this spot. She wondered if anyone would notice.

David noticed. Even as he waved goodbye and watched his clients drive away, he was intensely aware that Kate Chesne was somewhere on the pier behind him. He'd been startled to see her here. He'd thought it a rather clever move on her part, this public display of penitence, obviously designed to impress the O'Briens. But as he turned and watched her solitary walk along the pier, he noticed the droop of her shoulders, the downcast face, and he realized how much courage it had taken for her to show up today.

Then he reminded himself that some doctors would do anything to head off a lawsuit.

Suddenly disinterested, he started toward his car. Halfway across the parking lot, he heard something clatter against the pavement and he saw that Kate had dropped her purse. For what seemed like forever, she just stood there, the car keys dangling from her hand, looking for all the world like a bewildered child. Then, slowly, wearily, she bent down and began to gather her belongings.

Almost against his will, he was drawn toward her. She didn't notice his approach. He crouched beside her, scooped a few errant pennies from the ground, and held them out to her. Suddenly she focused on his face and then froze.

"Looks like you need some help," he said.

"Oh."

"I think you've got everything now."

They both rose to their feet. He was still holding out the loose change, of which she seemed oblivious. Only after he'd deposited the money in her hand did she finally manage a weak "Thank you."

For a moment they stared at each other.

"I didn't expect to see you here," he remarked. "Why did you come?"

"It was—" she shrugged "—a mistake, I think."

"Did your lawyer suggest it?"

She looked puzzled. "Why would he?"

"To show the O'Briens you care."

Her cheeks suddenly flushed with anger. "Is that what you think? That this is some sort of—of *strategy*?"

"It's not unheard of."

"Why are *you* here, Mr. Ransom? Is this part of *your* strategy? To prove to your clients you care?"

"I do care."

"And you think I don't."

"I didn't say that."

"You implied it."

"Don't take everything I say personally."

"I take everything you say personally."

"You shouldn't. It's just a job to me."

Angrily, she shoved back a tangled lock of hair. "And what *is* your job? Hatchet man?"

"I don't attack people. I attack their mistakes. And even the best doctors make mistakes."

"You don't need to tell me that!" Turning, she looked off to sea, where Ellen O'Brien's ashes were newly drifting. "I live with it, Mr. Ransom. Every day in that O.R. I know that if I reach for the wrong vial or flip the wrong lever, it's someone's life. Oh, we find ways to deal with it. We have our black jokes, our gallows humor. It's terrible, the things we laugh about, and all in the name of survival. Emotional survival. You have no idea, you lawyers. You and your whole damned profession. You don't know what it's like when everything goes wrong. When we lose someone."

"I know what it's like for the family. Every time you make a mistake, someone suffers."

"I suppose *you* never make mistakes."

"Everyone does. The difference is, you bury yours."

"You'll never let me forget it, will you?"

She turned to him. Sunset had painted the sky orange, and the glow seemed to burn in her hair and in her cheeks. Suddenly he wondered how it would feel to run his fingers through those wind-tumbled strands, wondered what that face would feel like against his lips. The thought had popped out of nowhere and now that it was out, he couldn't get rid of it. Certainly it was the last thing he ought to be thinking. But she was standing so dangerously close that he'd either have to back away or kiss her.

He managed to hold his ground. Barely. "As I said, Dr. Chesne, I'm only doing my job."

She shook her head and her hair, that sun-streaked, mahogany hair, flew violently in the wind. "No, it's more than that. I think you have some sort of vendetta. You're out to hang the whole medical profession. Aren't you?"

David was taken aback by her accusation. Even as he started to deny it, he knew she'd hit too close to home. Somehow she'd found his old wound, had reopened it with the verbal equivalent of a surgeon's scalpel. "Out to hang the whole profession, am I?" he managed to say. "Well, let me tell you something, Doctor. It's incompetents like you that make my job so easy."

Rage flared in her eyes, as sudden and brilliant as two coals igniting. For an instant he thought she was going to slap him. Instead she whirled around, slid into her car and slammed the door. The Audi screeched out of the stall so sharply he had to flinch aside.

As he watched her car roar away, he couldn't help regretting those unnecessarily brutal words. But he'd said them in self-defense. That perverse attraction he'd felt to her had grown too compelling; he knew it had to be severed, right there and then.

As he turned to leave, something caught his eye, a thin shaft of reflected light. Glittering on the pavement was a silver pen; it had rolled under her car when she'd dropped her purse. He picked it up and studied the engraved name: Katharine Chesne, M.D.

For a moment he stood there, weighing the pen, thinking about its owner. Wondering if she, too, had no one to go home to. And it suddenly struck him, as he stood alone on the windy pier, just how empty he felt.

Once, he'd been grateful for the emptiness. It had meant the blessed absence of pain. Now he longed to feel something—anything—if only to reassure himself that he was alive. He knew the emotions were still there, locked up somewhere inside him. He'd felt them stirring faintly when he'd looked into Kate Chesne's burning eyes. Not a full-blown emotion, perhaps, but a flicker. A blip on the tracing of a terminally ill heart.

The patient wasn't dead. Not yet.

He felt himself smiling. He tossed the pen up in the air and caught it smartly. Then he slipped it into his breast pocket and walked to his car.

THE DOG WAS deeply anesthetized, its legs spread-eagled, its belly shaved and prepped with iodine. It was a German shepherd, obviously well-bred and just as obviously unloved.

Guy Santini hated to see such a handsome creature end up on his research table, but lab animals were scarce these days and he had to use whatever the supplier sent him. He consoled himself with the knowledge that the animals suffered no pain. They slept blissfully through the entire surgical procedure and when it was over, the ventilator was turned off and they were injected with a lethal dose of Pentothal. Death came peacefully; it was a far better end than the animals would have faced on the streets. And each sacrifice yielded data for his research, a few more dots on a graph, a few more clues to the mysteries of hepatic physiology.

He glanced at the instruments neatly laid out on the tray: the scalpel, the clamps, the catheters. Above the table, a pressure monitor awaited final hookup. Everything was ready. He reached for the scalpel.

The whine of the door swinging closed made him pause. Footsteps clipped toward him across the polished lab floor. Glancing across the table, he saw Ann Richter standing there. They looked at each other in silence.

"I see you didn't go to Ellen's services, either," he said.

"I wanted to. But I was afraid."

"Afraid?" He frowned. "Of what?"

"I'm sorry, Guy. I no longer have a choice." Silently, she held out a letter. "It's from Charlie Decker's lawyer. They're asking questions about Jenny Brook."

"What?" Guy stripped off his gloves and snatched the paper from her hand. What he read there made him look up at her in alarm. "You're not going to tell them, are you? Ann, you can't—"

"It's a subpoena, Guy."

"Lie to them, for God's sake!"

"Decker's out, Guy. You didn't know that, did you? He was released from the state hospital a month ago. He's been calling me. Leaving little notes at my apartment. Sometimes I even think he's following me...."

"He can't hurt you."

"Can't he?" She nodded at the paper he was holding. "Henry got one, just like it. So did Ellen. Just before she..." Ann stopped, as if voicing her worst fears somehow would turn them to reality. Only now did Guy notice how haggard she was. Dark circles shadowed her eyes, and the ash-blond hair, of which she'd always been so proud, looked as if it hadn't been combed in days. "It has to end, Guy," she said softly. "I can't spend the rest of my life looking over my shoulder for Charlie Decker."

He crumpled the paper in his fist. He began to pace back and forth, his agitation escalating to panic. "You could leave the islands—you could go away for a while—"

"How long, Guy? A month? A year?"

"As long as it takes for this to settle down. Look, I'll give you the money—" He fumbled for his wallet and took out fifty dollars, all the cash he had. "Here. I promise I'll send you more—"

"I'm not asking for your money."

"Go on, take it."

"I told you, I—"

"For God's sake, *take it*!" His voice, harsh with desperation, echoed off the stark white walls. "Please, Ann," he urged quietly. "I'm asking you, as a friend. Please."

She looked down at the money he was holding. Slowly, she reached out and took it. As her fingers closed around the bills she announced, "I'm leaving tonight. For San Francisco. I have a brother—"

"Call me when you get there. I'll send you all the money you need." She didn't seem to hear him. "Ann? You'll do this for me. Won't you?"

She looked off blankly at the far wall. He longed to reassure her, to tell her that nothing could possibly go wrong; but they'd both know it was a lie. He watched as she walked slowly to the door. Just before she left, he said, "Thank you, Ann."

She didn't turn around. She simply paused in the doorway. Then she gave a little shrug, just before she vanished out the door.

As ANN HEADED for the bus stop, she was still clutching the money Guy had given her. Fifty dollars! As if that was enough! A thousand, a million dollars wouldn't be enough.

She boarded the bus for Waikiki. From her window seat she stared out at a numbing succession of city blocks. At Kalakaua, she got off and began to walk quickly toward her apartment building. Buses roared past, choking her with fumes. Her hands turned clammy in the heat. Concrete buildings seemed to press in on all sides and tourists clotted the sidewalks. As she wove her way through them, she felt a growing sense of uneasiness.

She began to walk faster.

Two blocks north of Kalakaua, the crowd thinned out and she found herself at a corner, waiting for a stoplight to change. In that instant, as she stood alone and exposed in the fading sunlight, the feeling suddenly seized her: *someone is following me.*

She swung around and scanned the street behind her. An old man was shuffling down the sidewalk. A couple was pushing a baby in a stroller. Gaudy shirts fluttered on an outdoor clothing rack. Nothing out of the ordinary. Or so it seemed....

The light changed to green. She dashed across the street and didn't stop running until she'd reached her apartment.

She began to pack. As she threw her belongings into a suitcase, she was still debating her next move. The plane to San Francisco would take off at midnight; her brother would put her up for a while, no questions asked. He was good that way. He understood that everyone had a secret, everyone was running away from something.

It doesn't have to be this way, a stray voice whispered in her head. *You could go to the police....*

And tell them what? The truth about Jenny Brook? Do I tear apart an innocent life?

She began to pace the apartment, thinking, fretting. As she walked past the living-room mirror, she caught sight of her own reflection, her blond hair in disarray, her eyes smudged with mascara. She hardly recognized herself; fear had transformed her face into a stranger's.

It only takes a single phone call, a confession. A secret, once revealed, is no longer dangerous....

She reached for the telephone. With unsteady hands she dialed Kate Chesne's home phone number. Her heart sank when, after four rings, a recording answered, followed by the message beep.

She cleared the fear from her throat. "This is Ann Richter," she said. "Please, I have to talk to you. It's about Ellen. I know why she died."

Then she hung up and waited for the phone to ring.

IT WAS HOURS before Kate heard the message.

After she left the pier that afternoon, she drove aimlessly for a while, avoiding the inevitable return to her empty house. It was Friday night. T.G.I.F. She decided to treat herself to an evening out. So she had supper alone at a trendy little seaside grill where everyone but her seemed to be having a grand old time. The steak she ordered was utterly tasteless and the chocolate mousse so cloying she could barely force it down her throat. She left an extravagant tip, almost as an apology for her lack of appetite.

Next she tried a movie. She found herself wedged between a fidgety eight-year-old boy on one side and a young couple passionately making out on the other.

She walked out halfway through the film. She never did remember the title—only that it was a comedy, and she hadn't laughed once.

By the time she got home, it was ten o'clock. She was half undressed and sitting listlessly on her bed when she noticed that the telephone message light was blinking. She let the messages play back as she wandered over to the closet.

"Hello, Dr. Chesne, this is Four East calling to tell you Mr. Berg's blood sugar is ninety-eight.... Hello, this is June from Dr. Avery's office. Don't forget the Quality Assurance meeting on Tuesday at four.... Hi, this is Windward Realty. Give us a call back. We have a listing we think you'd like to see...."

She was hanging up her skirt when the last message played back.

"This is Ann Richter. Please, I have to talk to you. It's about Ellen. I know why she died...."

There was the click of the phone hanging up, and then a soft whir as the tape automatically rewound. Kate scrambled back to the recorder and pressed the replay button. Her heart was racing as she listened again to the agonizingly slow sequence of messages.

"It's about Ellen. I know why she died...."

Kate grabbed the phone book from her nightstand. Ann's address and phone number were listed; her line was busy. Again and again Kate dialed but she heard only the drone of the busy signal.

She slammed down the receiver and knew immediately what she had to do next.

She hurried back to the closet and yanked the skirt from its hanger. Quickly, feverishly, she began to dress.

THE TRAFFIC HEADING into Waikiki was bumper-to-bumper.

As usual, the streets were crowded with a bizarre mix of tourists and off-duty soldiers and street people, all of them moving in the surreal glow of city lights. Palm trees cast their spindly shadows against the buildings. An otherwise distinguished-looking gentleman was flaunting his white legs and Bermuda shorts. Waikiki was where one came to see the ridiculous, the outrageous. But tonight, Kate found the view through her car window frightening—all those faces, drained of color under the glow of streetlamps, and the soldiers, lounging drunkenly in nightclub doorways. A wild-eyed evangelist stood on the corner, waving a Bible as he shouted "The end of the world is near!"

As she pulled up at a red light, he turned and stared at her and for an instant she thought she saw, in his burning eyes, a message meant only for her. The light turned green. She sent the car lurching through the intersection. His shout faded away.

She was still jittery ten minutes later when she climbed the steps to Ann's apartment building. As she reached the door, a young couple exited, allowing Kate to slip into the lobby.

It took a moment for the elevator to arrive. Leaning back against the wall, she forced herself to breathe deeply and let the silence of the building calm her nerves. By the time she finally stepped into the elevator, her heart had stopped its wild hammering. The doors slid closed. The elevator whined upward. She felt a strange sense of unreality as she watched the lights flash in succession: three, four, five. Except for a faint hydraulic hum, the ride was silent.

On the seventh floor, the doors slid open.

The corridor was deserted. A dull green carpet stretched out before her. As she walked toward number 710, she had the strange sensation that she was moving in a dream, that none of this was real—not the flocked wallpaper or the door looming at the end of the corridor. Only as she reached it did she see it was slightly ajar. "Ann?" she called out.

There was no answer.

She gave the door a little shove. Slowly it swung open and she froze, taking in, but not immediately comprehending, the scene before her: the toppled chair, the scattered magazines, the bright red splatters on the wall. Then her gaze followed the trail of crimson as it zigzagged across the beige carpet, leading inexorably toward its source: Ann's body, lying facedown in a lake of blood.

Beeps issued faintly from a telephone receiver dangling off an end table. The cold, electronic tone was like an alarm, screaming at her to move, to take action. But she remained paralyzed; her whole body seemed stricken by some merciful numbness.

The first wave of dizziness swept over her. She crouched down, clutching the doorframe for support. All her medical training, all those years of working around blood, couldn't prevent this totally visceral response. Through the drumbeat of her own heart she became aware of another sound, harsh and irregular. Breathing. But it wasn't hers.

Someone else was in the room.

A flicker of movement drew her gaze across to the living-room mirror. Only then did she see the man's reflection. He was cowering behind a cabinet, not ten feet away.

They spotted each other in the mirror at the same instant. In that split second, as the reflection of his eyes met hers, she imagined she saw, in those hollows, the darkness beckoning to her. An abyss from which there was no escape.

He opened his mouth as if to speak but no words came out, only an unearthly hiss, like a viper's warning just before it strikes.

She lurched wildly to her feet. The room spun past her eyes with excruciating slowness as she turned to flee. The corridor stretched out endlessly before her. She heard her own scream echo off the walls; the sound was as unreal as the image of the hallway flying past.

The stairwell door lay at the other end. It was her only feasible escape route. There was no time to wait for elevators.

She hit the opening bar at a run and shoved the door into the concrete stairwell. One flight into her descent, she heard the door above spring open again and slam against the wall. Again she heard the hiss, as terrifying as a demon's whisper in her ear.

She stumbled to the sixth-floor landing and grappled at the door. It was locked tight. She screamed and pounded. Surely someone would hear her! Someone would answer her cry for help!

Footsteps thudded relentlessly down the stairs. She couldn't wait; she had to keep running.

She dashed down the next flight and hit the fifth floor landing too hard. Pain shot through her ankle. In tears, she wrenched and pounded at the door. It was locked.

He was right behind her.

She flew down the next flight and the next. Her purse flew off her shoulder but she couldn't stop to retrieve it. Her ankle was screaming with pain as she hurtled toward the third-floor landing. Was it locked, as well? Were they all locked? Her mind flew ahead to the ground floor, to what lay outside. A parking lot? An alley? Is that where they'd find her body in the morning?

Sheer panic made her wrench with superhuman strength at the next door. To her disbelief, it was unlocked. Stumbling through, she found herself in the parking garage. There was no time to think about her next move; she tore off blindly into the shadows. Just as the stairwell door flew open again, she ducked behind a van.

Crouching by the front wheel, she listened for footsteps but heard nothing except the torrent of her own blood racing in her ears. Seconds passed, then minutes. Where was he? Had he abandoned the chase? Her body was pressed so tightly against the van, the steel bit into her thigh. She felt no pain; every ounce of concentration was focused on survival.

A pebble clattered across the ground, echoing like a pistol shot in the concrete garage.

She tried in vain to locate the source but the explosions seemed to come from a dozen different directions at once. *Go away!* she wanted to scream. *Dear God, make him go away....*

The echoes faded, leaving total silence. But she sensed his presence, closing in. She could almost hear his voice whispering to her *I'm coming for you. I'm coming....*

She had to know where he was, if he was drawing close.

Clinging to the tire, she slowly inched her head around and peered beneath the van. What she saw made her reel back in horror.

He was on the other side of the van and moving toward the rear. Toward her.

She sprang to her feet and took off like a rabbit. Parked cars melted into one continuous blur. She plunged toward the exit ramp. Her legs, stiff from crouching, refused to move fast enough. She could hear the man right behind her. The ramp seemed endless, spiraling around and around, every curve threatening to send her sprawling to the pavement. His footsteps were gaining. Air rushed in and out of her lungs, burning her throat.

In a last, desperate burst of speed, she tore around the final curve. Too late, she saw the headlights of a car coming up the ramp toward her.

She caught a glimpse of two faces behind the windshield, a man and a woman, their mouths open wide. As she slammed into the hood, there was a brilliant flash of light, like stars exploding in her eyes. Then the light vanished and she saw nothing at all. Not even darkness.

Chapter Five

"Mango season," Sergeant Brophy said as he sneezed into a soggy hand-kerchief. "Worst time of year for my allergies." He blew his nose, then sniffed experimentally, as if checking for some new, as yet undetected obstruction to his nasal passages. He seemed completely unaware of his gruesome surroundings, as though dead bodies and blood-spattered walls and an army of crime-lab techs were always hanging about. When Brophy got into one of his sneezing jags, he was oblivious of everything but the sad state of his sinuses.

Lieutenant Francis "Pokie" Ah Ching had grown used to hearing the sniffles of his junior partner. At times, the habit was useful. He could always tell which room Brophy was in; all he had to do was follow the man's nose.

That nose, still bundled in a handkerchief, vanished into the dead woman's bedroom. Pokie refocused his attention on his spiral notebook, in which he was recording the data. He wrote quickly, in the peculiar shorthand he'd evolved over his twenty-six years as a cop, seventeen of them with homicide. Eight pages were filled with sketches of the various rooms in the apartment, four pages of the living room alone. His art was crude but to the point. Body there. Toppled furniture here. Blood all over.

The medical examiner, a boyish, freckle-faced woman known to every-one simply as M.J., was making her walkaround before she examined the body. She was wearing her usual blue jeans and tennis shoes—sloppy dress for a doctor, but in her specialty, the patients never complained. As she circled the room, she dictated into a cassette recorder.

"Arterial spray on three walls, pattern height about four to five feet.... Heavy pooling at east end of living room where body is located.... Victim is female, blond, age thirty to forty, found in prone position, right arm flexed under head, left arm extended.... No hand or arm lacerations noted." M.J. crouched down. "Marked dependent mottling. Hmm." Frowning, she touched the victim's bare arm. "Significant body cooling. Time is now 12:15 a.m." She flicked off the cassette and was silent for a moment.

"Somethin' wrong, M.J.?" Pokie asked.

"What?" She looked up. "Oh, just thinking."

"What's your prelim?"

"Let's see. Looks like a single deep slash to the left carotid, very sharp blade. And very fast work. The victim never got a chance to raise her arms in defense. I'll get a better look when we wash her down at the morgue." She stood up and Pokie saw her tennis shoes were smeared with blood. How many crime scenes had those shoes tramped through?

Not as many as mine, he thought.

"Slashed carotid," he said thoughtfully. "Does that remind you of somethin'?"

"First thing I thought of. What was that guy's name a few weeks back?"

"Tanaka. He had a slash to the left carotid."

"That's him. Just as bloody a mess as this one, too."

Pokie thought a moment. "Tanaka was a doctor," he remarked. "And this one..." He glanced down at the body. "This one's a nurse."

"Was a nurse."

"Makes you wonder."

M.J. snapped her lab kit closed. "There's lots of doctors and nurses in this town. Just because these two end up on my slab doesn't mean they knew each other."

A loud sneeze announced Brophy's emergence from the bedroom. "Found a plane ticket to San Francisco on her dresser. Midnight flight." He glanced at his watch. "Which she just missed."

A plane ticket. A packed suitcase. So Ann Richter was about to skip town. Why?

Mulling over that question, Pokie made another circuit of the apartment, going through the rooms one by one. In the bathroom, he found a lab tech microscopically peering down at the sink.

"Traces of blood in here, sir. Looks like your killer washed his hands."

"Yeah? Cool cat. Any prints?"

"A few here and there. Most of 'em old, probably the victim's. Plus one fresh set off the front doorknob. Could belong to your witness."

Pokie nodded and went back to the living room. That was their ace in the hole. The witness. Though dazed and in pain, she'd managed to alert the ambulance crew to the horrifying scene in apartment 710.

Thereby ruining a good night's sleep for Pokie.

He glanced at Brophy. "Have you found Dr. Chesne's purse yet?"

"It's not in the stairwell where she dropped it. Someone must've picked it up."

Pokie was silent a moment. He thought of all the things women carried in their purses: wallets, driver's licenses, house keys.

He slapped his notebook closed. "Sergeant?"

"Sir?"

"I want a twenty-four-hour guard placed on Dr. Chesne's hospital room. Effective immediately. I want a man in the lobby. And I want you to trace every call that comes in asking about her.''

Brophy looked dubious. "All that? For how long?"

"Just as long as she's in the hospital. Right now she's a sitting duck."

"You really think this guy'd go after her in the hospital?"

"I don't know." Pokie sighed. "I don't know what we're dealing with. But I've got two identical murders." Grimly he slid the notebook into his pocket. "And she's our only witness."

PHIL GLICKMAN was making a pest of himself as usual.

It was Saturday morning, the one day of the week David could work undisturbed, the one day he could catch up on all the paperwork that perpetually threatened to bury his desk. But today, instead of solitude, he'd found Glickman. While his young associate was smart, aggressive and witty, he was also utterly incapable of silence. David suspected the man talked in his sleep.

"So I said, 'Doctor, do you mean to tell me the posterior auricular artery comes off *before* the superficial temporal?' And the guy gets all flustered and says, 'Oh, did I say that? No, of course it's the other way around.' Which blew it right there for him." Glickman slammed his fist triumphantly into his palm. "Wham! He's dead meat and he knows it. We just got the offer to settle. Not bad, huh?" At David's lackluster nod, Glickman looked profoundly disappointed. Then he brightened and asked, "How's it going with the O'Brien case? They ready to yell uncle?"

David shook his head. "Not if I know Kate Chesne."

"What, is she dumb?"

"Stubborn. Self-righteous."

"So it goes with the white coat."

David tiredly dragged his fingers through his hair. "I hope this doesn't go to trial."

"It'll be like shooting rabbits in a cage. Easy."

"Too easy."

Glickman laughed as he turned to leave. "Never seemed to bother you before."

Why the hell does it bother me now? David wondered.

The O'Brien case was like an apple falling into his lap. All he had to do was file a few papers, issue a few threatening statements, and hold his hand out for the check. He should be breaking out the champagne. Instead, he was moping around on a gorgeous Saturday morning, feeling sleazy about the whole affair.

Yawning, he leaned back and rubbed his eyes. It'd been a lousy night, spent tossing and turning in bed. He'd been plagued by dreams—disturbing dreams; the kind he hadn't had in years.

There had been a woman. She'd stood very still, very quiet in the shadows, her face silhouetted against a window of hazy light. At first he'd thought she was his ex-wife, Linda. But there were things about her that weren't right, things that confused him. She'd stood motionless, like a deer pausing in the forest. Eagerly he'd reached out to undress her, but his hands had been impossibly clumsy and in his haste, he'd torn off one of her buttons. She had laughed, a deliciously throaty sound that reminded him of brandy.

That's when he knew she wasn't Linda. Looking up, he'd stared into the green eyes of Kate Chesne.

There were no words between them, only a look. And a touch: her fingers, sliding gently down his face.

He'd awakened, sweating with desire. He'd tried to fall back to sleep. Again and again the dream had returned. Even now, as he sank back in his chair and closed his eyes, he saw her face again and he felt that familiar ache.

Brutally wrenching his thoughts back to reality, he dragged himself over to the window. He was too old for this nonsense. Too old and too smart to even fantasize about an affair with the opposition.

Hell, attractive women walked into his office all the time. And every so often, one of them would give off the sort of signals any red-blooded man could recognize. It took only a certain tilt of the head, a provocative flash of thigh. He'd always been amused but never tempted; bedding down clients wasn't included in his list of services.

Kate Chesne had sent out no such signals. In fact she plainly despised lawyers as much as he despised doctors. So why, of all the women who'd walked through his door, was she the one he couldn't stop thinking about?

He reached into his breast pocket and pulled out the silver pen. It suddenly occurred to him that this wasn't the sort of item a woman would buy for herself. Was it a gift from a boyfriend? he wondered, and was startled by his instant twinge of jealousy.

He should return it.

The thought set his mind off and racing. Mid Pac Hospital was only a few blocks away. He could drop off the pen on his way home. Most doctors made Saturday-morning rounds, so there was a good chance she'd be there. At the prospect of seeing her again, he felt a strange mixture of anticipation and dread, the same churning in his stomach he used to feel as a teenager scrounging up the courage to ask a girl for a date. It was a very bad sign.

But he couldn't get the idea out of his mind.

The pen felt like a live wire. He shoved it back in his pocket and quickly began to stuff his papers into the briefcase.

Fifteen minutes later he walked into the hospital lobby and went to a house telephone. The operator answered.

"I'm trying to reach Dr. Kate Chesne," David said. "Is she in the building?"

"Dr. Chesne?" There was a pause. "Yes, I believe she's in the hospital. Who's calling?"

He started to give his name, then thought better of it. If Kate knew it was his page, she'd never answer it. "I'm a friend," he replied lamely.

"Please hold."

A recording of some insipid melody came on, the sort of music they probably played on elevators in hell. He caught himself drumming the booth impatiently. That's when it struck him just how eager he was to see her again.

I must be nuts, he thought, abruptly hanging up the phone. Or desperate for female companionship. Maybe both.

Disgusted with himself, he turned to leave, only to find that his exit was blocked by two very impressive-looking cops.

"Mind coming with us?" one of them asked.

"Actually," responded David, "I would."

"Then lemme put it a different way," said the cop, his meaning absolutely clear.

David couldn't help an incredulous laugh. "What did I do, guys? Double-park? Insult your mothers?"

He was grasped firmly by both arms and directed across the lobby, into the administrative wing.

"Is this an arrest or what?" he demanded. They didn't answer. "Hey, I think you're supposed to inform me of my rights." They didn't. "Okay," he amended. "Then maybe it's time *I* informed *you* of my rights." Still no answer. He shot out his weapon of last resort. "I'm an attorney!"

"Goody for you" was the dry response as he was led toward a conference room.

"You know damn well you can't arrest me without charges!"

They threw open the door. "We're just following orders."

"*Whose* orders?"

The answer was boomed out in a familiar voice. "*My* orders."

David turned and confronted a face he hadn't seen since his days with the prosecutor's office. Homicide Detective Pokie Ah Ching's features reflected a typical island mix of bloods: a hint of Chinese around the eyes, some Portuguese in the heavy jowls, a strong dose of dusky Polynesian coloring. Except for a hefty increase in girth, he had changed little in the eight years since they'd last worked together. He was even wearing the same old off-the-rack polyester suit, though it was obvious those front buttons hadn't closed in quite some time.

"If it isn't Davy Ransom," Pokie grunted. "I lay out my nets, and look what comes swimming in."

"Yeah," David muttered, jerking his arm free. "The wrong fish."

Pokie nodded at the two policemen. "This one's okay."

The officers retreated. The instant the door closed, David barked out: "What the hell's going on?"

In answer, Pokie moved forward and gave David a long, appraising look. "Private practice must be bringin' in the bucks. Got yourself a nice new suit. Expensive shoes. Humph. Italian. Doing well, huh, Davy?"

"I can't complain."

Pokie settled down on the edge of the table and crossed his arms. "So how's it, workin' out of a nice new office? Miss the ol' cockroaches?"

"Oh, sure."

"I made lieutenant a month after you left."

"Congratulations."

"But I'm still wearin' the same old suit. Driving the same old car. And the shoes?" He stuck out a foot. "Taiwan."

David's patience was just about shredded. "Are you going to tell me what's going on? Or am I supposed to guess?"

Pokie reached in his jacket for a cigarette, the same cheap brand he'd always smoked, and lit up. "You a friend of Kate Chesne's?"

David was startled by the abrupt shift of subject. "I know her."

"How well?"

"We've spoken a few times. I came to return her pen."

"So you didn't know she was brought to the E.R. last night? Trauma service."

"What?"

"Nothing serious," Pokie said quickly. "Mild concussion. Few bruises. She'll be discharged today."

David's throat had suddenly tightened beyond all hope of speech. He watched, stunned, as Pokie took a long, blissful drag on his cigarette.

"It's a funny thing," Pokie remarked, "how a case'll just sit around forever, picking up dust. No clues. No way of closing the file. Then, pow! We get lucky."

"What happened to her?" David asked in a hoarse voice.

"She was in the wrong place at the wrong time." He blew out a lungful of smoke. "Last night she walked in on a very bad scene."

"You mean...she's a witness? To what?"

Pokie's face was impassive through the haze drifting between them. "Murder."

THROUGH THE CLOSED DOOR of her hospital room, Kate could hear the sounds of a busy hospital: the paging system, crackling with static, the ringing telephones. All night long she'd strained to hear those sounds; they had reminded her she wasn't alone. Only now, as the sun spilled in across her bed and a profound exhaustion settled over her, did she finally drift toward sleep. She didn't hear the first knock, or the voice calling to her through the door. It was the gust of air sweeping into the room that warned her the door had swung open. She was vaguely aware that someone was approaching her bed. It took all her strength just to open her eyes. Through a blur of sleep, she saw David's face.

She felt a feeble sense of outrage struggle to the surface. He had no right to invade her privacy when she was so weak, so exposed. She knew what she *ought* to say to him, but exhaustion had sapped her last reserves of emotion and she couldn't dredge up a single word.

Neither could he. It seemed they'd both lost their voices.

"No fair, Mr. Ransom," she whispered. "Kicking a girl when she's down..." Turning away, she gazed down dully at the sheets. "You seem to have forgotten your handy tape recorder. Can't take a deposition without a tape recorder. Or are you hiding it in one of your—"

"Stop it, Kate. Please."

She fell instantly still. He'd called her by her first name. Some unspoken barrier between them had just fallen, and she didn't know why. What she did know was that he was here, that he was standing so close she could smell the scent of his after-shave, could almost feel the heat of his gaze.

"I'm not here to...kick you while you're down." Sighing, he added, "I guess I shouldn't be here at all. But when I heard what happened, all I could think of was..."

She looked up and found him staring at her mutely. For the first time, he didn't seem so forbidding. She had to remind herself that he *was* the enemy; that this visit, whatever its purpose, had changed nothing between them. But at that moment, what she felt wasn't threatened but protected. It was more than just his commanding physical presence, though she was very aware of that, too; he had a quiet aura of strength. Competence. If only he'd been *her* attorney; if only he'd been hired to defend, not prosecute her. She couldn't imagine losing any battle with David Ransom at her side.

"All you could think of was what?" she asked softly.

Shifting, he turned awkwardly toward the door. "I'm sorry. I should let you sleep."

"Why did you come?"

He halted and gave a sheepish laugh. "I almost forgot. I came to return this. You dropped it at the pier."

He placed the pen in her hand. She stared down in wonder, not at the pen, but at his hands. Large, strong hands. How would it feel, to have those fingers tangled in her hair?

"Thank you," she whispered.

"Sentimental value?"

"It was a gift. From a man I used to—" Clearing her throat, she looked away and repeated, "Thank you."

David knew this was his cue to walk out. He'd done his good deed for the day; now he should cut whatever threads of conversation were being spun between them. But some hidden force seemed to guide his hand toward a chair and he pulled it over to the bed and sat down.

Her hair lay tangled on the pillow and a bruise had turned one cheek an ugly shade of blue. He felt an instinctive flood of rage against the man who'd tried to hurt her. The emotion was entirely unexpected; it surprised him by its ferocity.

"How are you feeling?" he asked, for want of anything else to say.

She gave a feeble shrug. "Tired. Sore." She paused and added with a weak laugh, "Lucky to be alive."

His gaze shifted to the bruise on her cheek and she automatically reached up to hide what stood out so plainly on her face. Slowly she let her hand fall back to the bed. He found it a very sad gesture, as if she was ashamed of being the victim, of bearing that brutal mark of violence.

"I'm not exactly at my most stunning today," she said.

"You look fine, Kate. You really do." It was a stupid thing to say but he meant it. She looked beautiful; she was alive. "The bruise will fade. What matters is that you're safe."

"Am I?" She looked at the door. "There's been a guard sitting out there all night. I heard him, laughing with the nurses. I keep wondering why they put him there...."

"I'm sure it's just a precaution. So no one bothers you."

She frowned at him, suddenly puzzled. "How did *you* get past him?"

"I know Lt. Ah Ching. We worked together, years ago. When I was with the prosecutor's office."

"You?"

He smiled. "Yeah. I've done my civic duty. Got my education in sleaze. At slave wages."

"Then you've talked to Ah Ching? About what happened?"

"He said you're a witness. That your testimony's vital to his case."

"Did he tell you Ann Richter tried to call me? Just before she was killed. She left a message on my recorder."

"About what?"

"Ellen O'Brien."

He paused. "I didn't hear about this."

"She *knew* something, Mr. Ransom. Something about Ellen's death. Only she never got a chance to tell me."

"What was the message?"

"'I know why she died.' Those were her exact words."

David stared at her. Slowly, reluctantly, he found himself drawn deeper and deeper into the spell of those green eyes. "It may not mean anything. Maybe she just figured out what went wrong in surgery—"

"The word she used was *why*. 'I know *why* she died.' That implies there was a reason, a—a *purpose* for Ellen's death."

"Murder on the operating table?" He shook his head. "Come on."

She turned away. "I should have known you'd be skeptical. It would ruin your precious lawsuit, wouldn't it? To find out the patient was murdered.''

"What do the police think?"

"How would I know?" she shot back in frustration. Then, in a tired voice, she said, "Your friend Ah Ching never says much of anything. All he does is scribble in that notebook of his. Maybe he thinks it's irrelevant. Maybe he doesn't want to hear any confusing facts." Her gaze shifted to the door. "But then I think about that guard. And I wonder if there's something else going on. Something he won't tell me..."

There was a knock on the door. A nurse came in with the discharge papers. David watched as Kate sat up and obediently signed each one. The pen trembled in her hand. He could hardly believe this was the same woman who'd stormed into his office. That day he'd been impressed by her iron will, her determination.

Now he was just as impressed by her vulnerability.

The nurse left and Kate sank back against the pillows.

"Do you have somewhere to go?" he asked. "After you leave here?"

"My friends...they have this cottage they hardly ever use. I hear it's on the beach." She sighed and looked wistfully out the window. "I could use a beach right now."

"You'll be staying there alone? Is that safe?"

She didn't answer. She just kept looking out the window. It made him uneasy, thinking of her in that cottage, alone, unprotected. He had to remind himself that she wasn't his concern. That he'd be crazy to get involved with this woman. Let the police take care of her; after all, she was their responsibility.

He stood up to leave. She just sat there, huddled in the bed, her arms crossed over her chest in a pitiful gesture of self-protection. As he walked out of the room, he heard her say, softly, "I don't think I'll ever feel safe again."

Chapter Six

"It's just a little place," explained Susan Santini as she and Kate drove along the winding North Shore highway. "Nothing fancy. Just a couple of bedrooms. An absolutely ancient kitchen. Prehistoric, really. But it's cozy. And it's so nice to hear the waves ..." She turned off the highway onto a dirt road carved through the dense shrubbery of halekoa. Their tires threw up a cloud of rich red dust as they bounced toward the sea. "Seems like we hardly use the place these days, what with one of us always being on call. Sometimes Guy talks about selling. But I'd never dream of it. You just don't find bits of paradise like this anymore."

The tires crunched onto the gravel driveway. Beneath a towering stand of ironwood trees, the small plantation-era cottage looked like nothing more than a neglected dollhouse. Years of sun and wind had faded the planks to a weathered green. The roof seemed to sag beneath its burden of brown ironwood needles.

Kate got out and stood for a moment beneath the trees, listening to the waves hiss onto the sand. Under the midday sun, the sea shone a bright and startling blue.

"There they are," said Susan, pointing down the beach at her son William, who was dancing a joyous little jig in the sand. He moved like an elf, his long arms weaving delicately, his head bobbing back and forth as he laughed. The baggy swim trunks barely clung to his scrawny hips. Framed against the brilliance of the sky, he seemed like nothing more than a collection of twigs among the trees, a mythical creature who might vanish in the blink of an eye. Nearby, a young woman with a sparrowlike face was sitting on a towel and flipping listlessly through a magazine.

"That's Adele," Susan whispered. "It took us half a dozen ads and twenty-one interviews to find her. But I just don't think she's going to work out. What worries me is William's already getting attached to her."

William suddenly spotted them. He stopped in his tracks and waved. "Hi, Mommy!"

"Hello, darling!" Susan called. Then she touched Kate's arm. "We've aired out the cottage for you. And there should be a pot of coffee waiting."

They climbed the wooden steps to the kitchen porch. The screen door squealed open. Inside hung the musty smell of age. Sunlight slanted in through the window and gleamed dully on the yellowed linoleum floor. A small pot of African violets sat on the blue-tiled countertop. Taped haphazardly to the walls was a whimsical collection of drawings: blue and green dinosaurs, red stick men, animals of various colors and unidentifiable species, each labeled with the artist's name: William.

"We keep the line hooked up for emergencies," Susan informed her, pointing to the wall telephone. "I've already stocked the refrigerator. Just the basics, really. Guy said we can pick up your car tomorrow. That'll give you a chance to do some decent grocery shopping." She made a quick circuit of the kitchen, pointing out various cabinets, the pots and pans, the dishes. Then, beckoning to Kate, she led the way to the bedroom. There she went to the window and spread apart the white lace curtains. Her red hair glittered in the stream of sunlight. "Look, Kate. Here's that view I promised you." She gazed out lovingly at the sea. "You know, people wouldn't need psychiatrists if they just had this to look at every day. If they could lie in the sun, hear the waves, the birds." She turned and smiled at Kate. "What do you think?"

"I think…" Kate gazed around at the polished wood floor, the filmy curtains, the dusty gold light shimmering through the window. "I think I never want to leave," she replied with a smile.

Footsteps pattered on the porch. Susan looked around as the screen door slammed. "So endeth the peace and quiet." She sighed.

They returned to the kitchen and found little William singing tunelessly as he laid out a collection of twigs on the kitchen table. Adele, her bare shoulders glistening with suntan oil, was pouring him a cup of apple juice. On the counter lay a copy of *Vogue*, dusty with sand.

"Look, Mommy!" exclaimed William, pointing proudly to his newly gathered treasure.

"My goodness, what a collection," said Susan, appropriately awed. "What are you going to do with all those sticks?"

"They're not sticks. They're swords. To kill monsters."

"Monsters? But, darling, I've told you. There aren't any monsters."

"Yes, there are."

"Daddy put them all in jail, remember?"

"Not all of them." Meticulously, he lay another twig down on the table. "They're hiding in the bushes. I heard one last night."

"William," Susan said quietly. "What monsters?"

"In the bushes. I told you, last night."

"Oh." Susan flashed Kate a knowing smile. "That's why he crawled into our bed at two in the morning."

Adele placed the cup of juice beside the boy. "Here, William. Your.. " She frowned. "What's that in your pocket?"

"Nothing."

"I saw it move."

William ignored her and took a slurp of juice. His pocket twitched.

"William Santini, give it to me." Adele held out her hand.

William turned his pleading eyes to the court of last appeals: his mother. She shook her head sadly. Sighing, he reached into his pocket, scooped out the source of the twitching, and dropped it in Adele's hand.

Her shriek was startling, most of all to the lizard, which promptly flung itself to freedom, but only after dropping its writhing tail in Adele's hand.

"He's getting away!" wailed William.

There followed a mad scrambling on hands and knees by everyone in the room. By the time the hapless lizard had been recaptured and jailed in a teacup, they were all breathless and weak from laughter. Susan, her red hair in wild disarray, collapsed onto the kitchen floor, her legs sprawled out in front of her.

"I can't *believe* it," she gasped, falling back against the refigerator. "Three grown women against one itty-bitty lizard. Are we helpless or what?"

William wandered over to his mother and stared at the sunlight sparkling in her red hair. In silent fascination, he reached for a loose strand and watched it glide sensuously across his fingers. "My mommy," he whispered.

She smiled. Taking his face in her hands, she kissed him tenderly on the mouth. "My baby."

"YOU HAVEN'T TOLD ME the whole story," said David. "Now I want to know what you've left out."

Pokie Ah Ching took a mammoth bite of his Big Mac and chewed with the fierce concentration of a man too long denied his lunch. Swiping a glob of sauce from his chin, he grunted, "What makes you think I left something out?"

"You've thrown some heavy-duty manpower into this case. That guard outside her room. The lobby stakeout. You're fishing for something big."

"Yeah. A murderer." Pokie took a pickle slice out of his sandwich and tossed it disgustedly on a mound of napkins. "What's with all the questions, anyway? I thought you left the prosecutor's office."

"I didn't leave behind my curiosity."

"Curiosity? Is that all it is?"

"Kate happens to be a friend of mine—"

"Hogwash!" Pokie shot him an accusing look. "You think I don't ask questions? I'm a detective, Davy. And I happen to know she's no friend of yours. She's the defendant in one of your lawsuits." He snorted. "Since when're you getting chummy with the opposition?"

"Since I started believing her story about Ellen O'Brien. Two days ago, she came to me with a story so ridiculous I laughed her out of my office. She had no facts at all, nothing but a disjointed tale that sounded flat-out paranoid. Then this nurse, Ann Richter, gets her throat slashed. Now *I'm* beginning to wonder. Was Ellen O'Brien's death malpractice? Or murder?''

"Murder, huh?" Pokie shrugged and took another bite. "That'd make it my business, not yours."

"Look, I've filed a lawsuit that claims it was malpractice. It's going to be pretty damned embarrassing—not to mention a waste of my time— if this turns out to be murder. So before I get up in front of a jury and make a fool of myself, I want to hear the facts. Level with me, Pokie. For old times' sake."

"Don't pile on the sentimental garbage, Davy. You're the one who walked away from the job. Guess that fat paycheck was too hard to resist. Me? I'm still here." He shoved a drawer closed. "Along with this crap they call furniture."

"Let's get one thing straight. My leaving the job had nothing to do with money."

"So why did you leave?"

"It was personal."

"Yeah. With you it's always *personal*. Still tight as a clam, aren't you?"

"We were talking about the case."

Pokie sat back and studied him for a moment. Through the open door of his office came the sound of bedlam—loud voices and ringing telephones and clattering typewriters. A normal afternoon in the downtown police station. In disgust, Pokie got up and shoved his office door closed. "Okay." He sighed, returning to his chair. "What do you want to know?"

"Details."

"Gotta be specific."

"What's so important about Ann Richter's murder?"

Pokie answered by grabbing a folder from the chaotic pile of papers on his desk. He tossed it to David. "M.J.'s preliminary autopsy report. Take a look."

The report was three pages long and cold-bloodedly graphic. Even though David had served five years as deputy prosecutor, had read dozens of such reports, he couldn't help shuddering at the clinical details of the woman's death.

Left carotid artery severed cleanly...razor-sharp instrument.... Laceration on right temple probably due to incidental impact against coffee table.... Pattern of blood spatter on wall consistent with arterial spray....

"I see M.J. hasn't lost her touch for turning stomachs," David said flipping to the second page. What he read there made him frown. "Now this finding doesn't make sense. Is M.J. sure about the time of death?''

"You know M.J. She's always sure. She's backed up by mottling and core body temp.''

"Why the hell would the killer cut the woman's throat and then hang around for three hours? To enjoy the scenery?''

"To clean up. To case the apartment.''

"Was anything missing?''

Pokie sighed. "No. That's the problem. Money and jewelry were lying right out in the open. Killer didn't touch any of it.''

"Sexual assault?''

"No sign of it. Victim's clothes were intact. And the killing was too efficient. If he was out for thrills, you'd think he would've taken his time. Gotten a few more screams out of her.''

"So you've got a brutal murder and no motive. What else is new?''

"Take another look at that autopsy report. Read me what M.J. wrote about the wound.''

"'Severed left carotid artery. Razor-sharp instrument.''' He looked up. "So?''

"So those are the same words she used in another autopsy report two weeks ago. Except that victim was a man. An obstetrician named Henry Tanaka.''

"Ann Richter was a nurse.''

"Right. And here's the interesting part. Before she joined the O.R. staff, she used to moonlight in obstetrics. Chances are, she knew Henry Tanaka.''

David suddenly went very, very still. He thought of another nurse who'd worked in obstetrics. A nurse who, like Ann Richter, was now dead. "Tell me more about that obstetrician,'' he said.

Pokie fished out a pack of cigarettes and an ashtray. "Mind?''

"Not if you keep talking.''

"Been dying for one all morning,'' Pokie grunted. "Can't light up when Brophy's around, whining about his damned sinuses.'' He flicked off the lighter. "Okay.'' He sighed, gratefully expelling a cloud of smoke. "Here's the story. Henry Tanaka's office was over on Liliha. You know, that god-awful concrete building. Two weeks ago, after the rest of his staff had left, he stayed behind in the office. Said he had to catch up on some paperwork. His wife says he always got home late. But she implied it wasn't paperwork that was keeping him out at night.''

"Girlfriend?''

"What else?''

"Wife know any names?''

"No. She figured it was one of the nurses over at the hospital. Anyway, about seven o'clock that night, couple of janitors found the body in one of the exam rooms. At the time we thought it was just a case of some junkie after a fix. There were drugs missing from the cabinet.''

''Narcotics?''

''Naw, the good stuff was locked up in a back room. The killer went after worthless stuff, drugs that wouldn't bring you a dime on the streets. We figured he was either stoned or dumb. But he was smart enough not to leave prints. Anyway, with no other evidence, the case sort of hit a wall. The only lead we had was something one of the janitors saw. As he was coming into the building, he spotted a woman running across the parking lot. It was drizzling and almost dark, so he didn't get a good look. But he says she was definitely a blonde.''

''Was he positive it was a woman?''

''What, as opposed to a man in a wig?'' Pokie laughed. ''That's one I didn't think of. I guess it's possible.''

''So what came of your lead?''

''Nothing much. We asked around, didn't come up with any names. We were starting to think that mysterious blonde was a red herring. Then Ann Richter got killed.'' He paused. ''She was blond.'' He snuffed out his cigarette. ''Kate Chesne's our first big break. Now at least we know what our man looks like. The artist's sketch'll hit the papers Monday. Maybe we'll start pulling in some names.''

''What kind of protection are you giving Kate?''

''She's tucked away on the North Shore. I got a patrol car passing by every few hours.''

''That's all?''

''No one'll find her up there.''

''A professional could.''

''What am I supposed to do? Slap on a permanent guard?'' He nodded at the stack of papers on his desk. ''Look at those files, Davy! I'm up to my neck in stiffs. I call myself lucky if a night goes by without a corpse rolling in the door.''

''Professionals don't leave witnesses.''

''I'm not convinced he *is* a pro. Besides, you know how tight things are around here. Look at this junk.'' He kicked the desk. ''Twenty years old and full of termites. Don't even mention that screwy computer. I still gotta send fingerprints to California to get a fast ID!'' Frustrated, he flopped back in his twenty-year-old chair. ''Look, Davy. I'm reasonably sure she'll be okay. I'd like to guarantee it. But you know how it is.''

Yeah, David thought. *I know how it is.* Some things about police work never changed. Too many demands and not enough money in the budget. He tried to tell himself that his only interest in this case was as the plaintiff's attorney; it was his job to ask all these questions. He had to be certain his case wouldn't crumble in the light of new facts. But his thoughts kept returning to Kate, sitting so alone, so vulnerable, in that hospital bed.

David wanted to trust the man's judgment. He'd worked with Pokie Ah Ching long enough to know the man was, for the most part, a competent cop. But he also knew that even the best cops made mistakes. Unfortunately cops and doctors had something in common: they both buried their mistakes.

THE SUN SLANTED DOWN on Kate's back, its warmth lulling her into an uneasy sleep. She lay with her face nestled in her arms as the waves lapped at her feet and the wind riffled the pages of her paperback book. On this lonely stretch of beach, where the only disturbance was the birds bickering and thrashing in the trees, she had found the perfect place to hide away from the world. To be healed.

She sighed and the scent of coconut oil stirred in her nostrils. Little by little, she was tugged awake by the wind in her hair, by a vague hunger for food. She hadn't eaten since breakfast and already the afternoon had slipped toward evening.

Then another sensation wrenched her fully awake. It was the feeling that she was no longer alone. That she was being watched. It was so definite that when she rolled over and looked up she was not at all surprised to see David standing there.

He was wearing jeans and an old cotton shirt, the sleeves rolled up in the heat. His hair danced in the wind, sparkling like bits of fire in the late-afternoon sunlight. He didn't say a thing; he simply stood there, his hands thrust in his pockets, his gaze slowly taking her in. Though her swimsuit wasn't particularly revealing, something about his eyes—their boldness, their directness—seemed to strip her against the sand. Sudden warmth flooded her skin, a flush deeper and hotter than any the sun could ever produce.

"You're a hard lady to track down," he said.

"That's the whole idea of going into hiding. People aren't supposed to find you."

He glanced around, his gaze quickly surveying the lonely surroundings. "Doesn't seem like such a bright idea, lying out in the open."

"You're right." Grabbing her towel and book, she rose to her feet. "You never know who might be hanging around out here. Thieves. Murderers." Tossing the towel smartly over her shoulder, she turned and walked away. "Maybe even a lawyer or two."

"I have to talk to you, Kate."

"I have a lawyer. Why don't you talk to him?"

"It's about the O'Brien case—"

"Save it for the courtroom," she snapped over her shoulder. She stalked away, leaving him standing alone on the beach.

"I may not be seeing you in the courtroom," he yelled.

"What a pity."

He caught up to her as she reached the cottage, and was right on her heels as she skipped up the steps. She let the screen door swing shut in his face.

"Did you hear what I said?" he shouted from the porch.

In the middle of the kitchen she halted, suddenly struck by the implication of his words. Slowly she turned and stared at him through the screen. He'd planted his hands on either side of the doorframe and was watching her intently. "I may not be in court," he said.

"What does that mean?"

"I'm thinking of dropping out."

"Why?"

"Let me in and I'll tell you."

Still staring at him, she pushed the screen door open. "Come inside, Mr. Ransom. I think it's time we talked."

Silently he followed her into the kitchen and stood by the breakfast table, watching her. The fact that she was barefoot only emphasized the difference in their heights. She'd forgotten how tall he was, and how lanky, with legs that seemed to stretch out forever. She'd never seen him out of a suit before. She decided she definitely liked him better in blue jeans. All at once she was acutely aware of her own state of undress. It was unsettling, the way his gaze followed her around the kitchen. Unsettling, and at the same time, undeniably exciting. The way lighting a match next to a powder keg was exciting. Was David Ransom just as explosive?

She swallowed nervously. "I—I have to dress. Excuse me."

She fled into the bedroom and grabbed the first clean dress within reach, a flimsy white import from India. She almost ripped it in her haste to pull it on. Pausing by the door, she forced herself to count to ten but found her hands were still unsteady.

When she finally ventured back into the kitchen, she found him still standing by the table, idly thumbing through her book.

"A war novel," she explained. "It's not very good. But it kills the time. Which I seem to have a lot of these days." She waved vaguely toward a chair. "Sit down, Mr. Ransom. I—I'll make some coffee." It took all her concentration just to fill the kettle and set it on the stove. She found she was having trouble with even the simplest task. First she knocked the box of paper filters into the sink. Then she managed to dump coffee grounds all over the counter.

"Let me take care of that," he said, gently nudging her aside.

She watched, voiceless, as he wiped up the spilled coffee. Her awareness of his body, of its closeness, its strength, was suddenly overwhelming. Just as overwhelming was the unexpected wave of sexual longing. On unsteady legs, she moved to the table and sank into a chair.

"By the way," he asked over his shoulder, "can we cut out the 'Mr. Ransom' bit? My name's David."

"Oh. Yes. I know." She winced, hating the breathless sound of her own voice.

He settled into a chair across from her and their eyes met levelly over the kitchen table.

"Yesterday you wanted to hang me," she stated. "What made you change your mind?"

In answer, he pulled a piece of paper out of his shirt pocket. It was a photocopy of a local news article. "That story appeared about two weeks ago in the *Star-Bulletin*."

She frowned at the headline: Honolulu Physician Found Slashed To Death. "What does this have to do with anything?"

"Did you know the victim, Henry Tanaka?"

"He was on our O.B. staff. But I never worked with him."

"Look at the newspaper's description of his wounds."

Kate focused again on the article. "It says he died of wounds to the neck and back."

"Right. Wounds made by a very sharp instrument. The neck was slashed only once, severing the left carotid artery. Very efficient. Very fatal."

Kate tried to swallow and found her throat was parched. "That's how Ann—"

He nodded. "Same method. Identical results."

"How do you know all this?"

"Lt. Ah Ching saw the parallels almost immediately. That's why he slapped a guard on your hospital room. If these murders are connected, there's something systematic about all this, something rational—"

"*Rational?* The killing of a doctor? A nurse? If anything, it sounds more like the work of a psychotic!"

"It's a strange thing, murder. Sometimes it has no rhyme or reason to it. Sometimes the act makes perfect sense."

"There's no such thing as a *sensible* reason to kill someone!"

"It's done every day, by supposedly sane people. And all for the most mundane of reasons. Money. Power." He paused. "Then again," he said softly, "there's the crime of passion. It seems Henry Tanaka was having an affair with one of the nurses."

"Lots of doctors have affairs."

"So do lots of nurses."

"Which nurse are we talking about?"

"I was hoping you could tell me."

"I'm sorry, but I'm not up on the latest hospital gossip."

"Even if it involves your patients?"

"You mean Ellen? I—I wouldn't know. I don't usually delve into my patients' personal lives. Not unless it's relevant to their health."

"Ellen's personal life may have been very relevant to her health."

"Well, she was a beautiful woman. I'm sure there were...men in her life." Kate's gaze fell once again to the article. "What does this have to do with Ann Richter?"

"Maybe nothing. Maybe everything. In the last two weeks, three people on Mid Pac's staff have died. Two were murdered. One had an unexpected cardiac arrest on the operating table. Coincidence?"

"It's a big hospital. A big staff."

"But those three particular people knew each other. They even worked together."

"But Ann was a surgical nurse—"

"Who used to work in obstetrics."

"What?"

"Eight years ago, Ann Richter went through a very messy divorce. She ended up with a mile-high stack of credit-card bills. She needed extra cash, fast. So she did some moonlighting as an O.B. nurse. The night shift. That's the same shift Ellen O'Brien worked. They knew each other, all right. Tanaka, Richter, O'Brien. And now they're all dead."

The scream of the boiling kettle tore through the silence but she was too numb to move. David rose and took the kettle off the stove. She heard him set out the cups and pour the water. The smell of coffee wafted into her awareness.

"It's strange," she remarked. "I saw Ann almost every day in that O.R. We'd talk about books we'd read or movies we'd seen. But we never really talked about *ourselves*. And she was always so private. Almost unapproachable."

"How did she react to Ellen's death?"

Kate was silent for a moment, remembering how, when everything had gone wrong, when Ellen's life had hung in the balance, Ann had stood white-faced and frozen. "She seemed...paralyzed. But we were all upset. Afterward she went home sick. She didn't come back to work. That was the last time I saw her. Alive, I mean...." She looked down, dazed, as he slid a cup of coffee in front of her.

"You said it before. She must have known something. Something dangerous. Maybe they all did."

"But, David, they were just ordinary people who worked in a hospital—"

"All kinds of things can go on in hospitals. Narcotics theft. Insurance fraud. Illicit love affairs. Maybe even murder."

"If Ann knew something dangerous, why didn't she go to the police?"

"Maybe she couldn't. Maybe she was afraid of self-incrimination. Or she was protecting someone else."

A deadly secret, Kate thought. Had all three victims shared it? Softly she ventured, "Then you think Ellen was murdered."

"That's why I'm here. I want you to tell *me*."

She shook her head in bewilderment. "How can I?"

"You have the medical expertise. You were there in the O.R. when it happened. How could it be done?"

"I've already gone over it a thousand times—"

"Then do it again. Come on, Kate, *think*. Convince me it was murder. Convince me I *should* drop out of this case."

His blunt command seemed to leave her no alternative. She felt his eyes goading her to recall every detail, every event leading up to those frantic moments in the O.R. She remembered how everything had gone so smoothly, the induction of anesthesia, the placement of the endotracheal tube. She'd double-checked the tanks and the lines; she knew the oxygen had been properly hooked up.

"Well?" he prodded.

"I can't think of anything."

"Yes, you can."

"It was a completely routine case!"

"What about the surgery itself?"

"Faultless. Guy's the best surgeon on the staff. Anyway, he'd just started the operation. He was barely through the muscle layer when—" She stopped.

"When what?"

"He—he complained about the abdominal muscles being too tight. He was having trouble retracting them."

"So?"

"So I injected a dose of succinylcholine."

"That's pretty routine, isn't it?"

She nodded. "I give it all the time. But in Ellen, it didn't seem to work. I had to draw up a second dose. I remember asking Ann to fetch me another vial."

"You had only one vial?"

"I usually keep a few in my cart. But that morning there was only one in the drawer."

"What happened after you gave the second dose of succinylcholine?"

"A few seconds went by. Maybe it was ten. Fifteen. And then—" Slowly she looked up at him. "Her heart stopped."

They stared at each other. Through the window, the last light of day slanted in, knifelike, across the kitchen. He leaned forward, his eyes hard on hers. "If you could prove it—"

"But I can't! That empty vial went straight to the incinerator, with all the rest of the trash. And there's not even a body left to autopsy." She looked away, miserable. "Oh, he was smart, David. Whoever the killer was, he knew exactly what he was doing."

"Maybe he's too smart for his own good."

"What do you mean?"

"He's obviously sophisticated. He knew exactly which drugs you'd be likely to give in the O.R. And he managed to slip something deadly into one of those vials. Who has access to the anesthesia carts?''

''They're left in the operating rooms. I suppose anyone on the hospital staff could get to them. Doctors. Nurses. Maybe even the janitors. But there were always people around.''

''What about nights? Weekends?''

''If there's no surgery scheduled, I guess they just close the suite down. But there's always a surgical nurse on duty for emergencies.''

''Does she stay in the O.R. area?''

She shrugged helplessly. ''I'm only there if we have a case. I have no idea what happens on a quiet night.''

''If the suite's left unguarded, then anyone on the staff could've slipped in.''

''It's not someone on the staff. I *saw* the killer, David! That man in Ann's apartment was a stranger.''

''Who could have an associate. Someone in the hospital. Maybe even someone you know.''

''A conspiracy?''

''Look at the systematic way these murders are being carried out. As if our killer—or killers—has some sort of list. My question is: Who's next?''

The clatter of her cup dropping against the saucer made Kate jump. Glancing down, she saw that her hands were shaking. *I saw his face,* she thought. *If he has a list, then my name's on it.*

The afternoon had slid into dusk. Agitated, she rose and paced to the open doorway. There she stood, staring out at the sea. The wind, so steady just moments before, had died. There was a stillness in the air, as if evening were holding its breath.

''He's out there,'' she whispered. ''Looking for me. And I don't even know his name.'' The touch of David's hand on her shoulder made her tremble. He was standing behind her, so close she could feel his breath in her hair. ''I keep seeing his eyes, staring at me in the mirror. Black and sunken. Like one of those posters of starving children...''

''He can't hurt you, Kate. Not here.'' David's breath seared her neck. A shudder ran through her body—not one of fear but of arousal. Even without looking at him, she could sense his need, simmering to the surface.

Suddenly it was more than his breath scorching her flesh; it was his lips. His face burrowed through the thick strands of her hair to press hungrily against her neck. His fingers gripped her shoulders, as if he was afraid she'd pull away. But she didn't. She couldn't. Her whole body was aching for him.

His lips left a warm, moist trail as they glided to her shoulder, and then she felt the rasp of his jaw.

He swung her around to face him. The instant she turned, his mouth was on hers.

She felt herself falling under the force of his kiss, falling into some deep and bottomless well, until her back suddenly collided with the kitchen wall. With the whole hard length of his body he pinned her there, belly against belly, thigh against thigh. Her lips parted and his tongue raged in, claiming her mouth as his. There was no doubt in her mind he intended to claim the rest of her, as well.

The match had been struck; the powder keg was about to explode, and her with it. She willingly flung herself into the conflagration.

No words were spoken; there were only the low, aching moans of need. They were both breathing so hard, so fast, that her ears were filled with the sound. She scarcely heard the telephone ringing. Only when it had rung again and again did her feverish brain finally register what it was.

It took all her willpower to swim against the flood of desire. She struggled to pull away. "The—the telephone—"

"Let it ring." His mouth slid down to her throat.

But the sound continued, grating and relentless, nagging her with its sense of urgency.

"David. Please..."

Groaning, he wrenched away and she saw the astonishment in his eyes. For a moment they stared at each other, neither of them able to believe what had just happened between them. The phone rang again. Jarred to her senses at last, she forced herself across the kitchen and picked up the reciever. Clearing her throat, she managed a hoarse "Hello?"

She was so dazed it took her a few seconds to register the silence on the line. "Hello?" she repeated.

"Dr. Chesne?" a voice whispered, barely audible.

"Yes?"

"Are you alone?"

"No, I— Who is this?" Her voice suddenly froze as the first fingers of terror gripped her throat.

There was a pause, so long and empty she could hear her own heart pounding in her ears. *"Hello?"* she screamed. *"Who is this?"*

"Be careful, Kate Chesne. For death is all around us."

Chapter Seven

The receiver slipped from her grasp and clattered on the linoleum floor. She reeled back in terror against the counter. "It's him," she whispered. Then, in a voice tinged with hysteria she cried out: *"It's him!"*

David instantly scrabbled on the floor for the receiver. "Who is this? Hello? *Hello?*" Cursing, he slammed the receiver back in the cradle and turned to her. "What did he say? Kate!" He took her by the shoulders and gave her a shake. "What did he say?"

"He—he said to be careful—that death was all around...."

"Where's your suitcase?" he snapped.

"What?"

"Your suitcase!"

"In—in the bedroom closet."

He stalked into the bedroom. Automatically she followed him and watched as he dragged her Samsonite down from the shelf. "Get your things together. You can't stay here."

She didn't ask where they were going. She only knew that she had to escape; that every minute she remained in this place just added to the danger.

Suddenly driven by the need to get away, she began to pack. By the time they were ready to leave, her compulsion to escape was so strong she practically flew down the porch steps to his car.

As he thrust the key in the ignition, she was seized by a wild terror that the car wouldn't start; that like some unfortunate victim in a horror movie, she would be stranded here, doomed to meet her death.

But at the first turn of the key, the engine started. The ironwood trees lunged at them as David sent the BMW wheeling around. Branches slashed the windshield. She felt another stab of panic as their tires spun uselessly in the sand. Then the car leaped free. The headlights trembled as they bounced up the dirt lane.

"How did he find me?" she sobbed.

"That's what I'm wondering." David hit the gas pedal as the car swung onto paved road. The BMW responded instantly with a burst of power that sent them hurtling down the highway.

"No one knew I was here. Only the police."

"Then there's been a leak of information. Or—" he shot a quick look at the rearview mirror "—you were followed."

"*Followed?*" She whipped her head around but saw only a deserted highway, shimmering under the dim glow of street lamps.

"Who took you to the cottage?" he asked.

She turned and focused on his profile, gleaming faintly in the darkness. "My—my friend Susan drove me."

"Did you stop at your house?"

"No. We went straight to the cottage."

"What about your clothes? How'd you get them?"

"My landlady packed a suitcase and brought it to the hospital."

"He might have been watching the lobby entrance. Waiting for you to be discharged."

"But we didn't see anyone follow us."

"Of course you didn't. People almost never do. We normally focus our attention on what's ahead, on where we're going. As for your phone number, he could've looked it up in the book. The Santinis have their name on the mailbox."

"But it doesn't make sense," she cried. "If he wants to kill me, why not just do it and get it over with? Why threaten me with phone calls?"

"Who knows how he thinks? Maybe he gets a thrill out of scaring his victims. Maybe he just wants to keep you from cooperating with the police."

"I was alone. He could have done it right there...on the beach...." She tried desperately not to think of what could have happened, but she couldn't shut out the image of her own blood seeping into the sand.

High on the hillside, the lights of houses flashed by, each one an unreachable haven of safety. In all that darkness, was there a haven for her? She huddled against the car seat, wishing she never had to leave this small cocoon of safety.

Closing her eyes, she forced herself to concentrate on the hum of the engine, on the rhythm of the highway passing beneath their wheels— anything to banish the bloodstained image. BMW. The ultimate driving machine, she thought inanely. Wasn't that what the ads said? High-tech German engineering. Cool, crisp performance. Just the kind of car she'd expect David to own.

"...and there's plenty of room. So you can stay as long as you need to."

"What?" Bewildered, she turned and looked at him. His profile was a hard, clean shadow against the passing streetlights.

"I said you can stay as long as you need to. It's not the Ritz, but it'll be safer than a hotel."

She shook her head. "I don't understand. Where are we going?"

He glanced at her and the tone of his voice was strangely unemotional. "My house."

"HOME," SAID DAVID, pushing open the front door. It was dark inside. Through the huge living-room windows, moonlight spilled in, faintly illuminating a polished wood floor, the dark and hulking silhouettes of furniture. David guided her to a couch and gently sat her down. Then, sensing her desperate need for light, for warmth, he quickly walked around the room, turning on all the lamps. She was vaguely aware of the muted clink of a bottle, the sound of something being poured. Then he returned and put a glass in her hand.

"Drink it," he said.

"What—what is it?"

"Whiskey. Go on. I think you could use a stiff one."

She took a deep and automatic gulp; the fiery sting instantly brought tears to her eyes. "Wonderful stuff." She coughed.

"Yeah. Isn't it?" He turned to leave the room and she felt a sudden, irrational burst of panic that he was abandoning her.

"David?" she called.

He immediately sensed the terror in her voice. Turning back, he spoke quietly: "It's all right, Kate. I won't leave you. I'll be right next door, in the kitchen." He smiled and touched her face. "Finish that drink."

Fearfully she watched him vanish through the doorway. Then she heard his voice, talking to someone on the phone. The police. As if there was anything they could do now. Clutching the glass in both hands, she forced down another sip of whiskey. The room seemed to swim as her eyes flooded with tears. She blinked them away and slowly focused on her surroundings.

It was, somehow, every inch a man's house. The furniture was plain and practical, the oak floor unadorned by even a single throw rug. Huge windows were framed by stark white curtains and she could hear, just outside, waves crashing against the seawall. Nature's violence, so close, so frightening.

But not nearly as frightening as the violence of man.

AFTER DAVID HUNG UP, he paused in the kitchen, trying to scrape together some semblance of composure. The woman was already frightened enough; seeing his agitation would only make things worse. He quickly ran his fingers through his ruffled hair. Then, taking a deep breath, he pushed open the kitchen door and walked back into the living room.

She was still huddled pitifully on the couch, her hands clenched around the half-empty glass of whiskey. At least a trace of color had returned to her face, but it was barely enough to remind him of a frost-covered rose petal. A little more whiskey was what she needed. He took the glass, filled it to the brim and placed it back in her hands. Her skin was icy.

She looked so stunned, so vulnerable. If he could just take her hands in his, if he could warm her in his arms, maybe he could coax some life back into those frozen limbs. But he was afraid to give in to the impulse; he knew it could lead to far more compelling urges.

He turned and poured himself a tall one. What she needed from him right now was protection. Reassurance. She needed to know that she would be taken care of and that things were still right with the world, though the truth of the matter was, her world had just gone to hell in a hand basket.

He took a deep gulp of whiskey, then set it down. What she really needed was a sober host.

"I've called the police," he said over his shoulder.

Her response was almost toneless. "What did they say?"

He shrugged. "What could they say? Stay where you are. Don't go out alone." Frowning at his glass, he thought, What the hell, and recklessly downed the rest of the whiskey. Bottle in hand, he returned to the couch and set the whiskey down on the coffee table. They were sitting only a few feet apart but it felt like miles of emptiness between them.

She stirred and looked toward the kitchen. "My—my friends—they won't know where I am. I should call them."

"Don't worry about it. Pokie'll let them know you're safe." He watched her sink back listlessly on the couch. "You should eat something," he said.

"I'm not hungry."

"My housekeeper makes great spaghetti sauce."

She lifted one shoulder—only one, as if she hadn't the energy for a full-blown shrug.

"Yep," he continued with sudden enthusiasm. "Once a week Mrs. Feldman takes pity on a poor starving bachelor and she leaves me a pot of sauce. It's loaded with garlic. Fresh basil. Plus a healthy slug of wine."

There was no response.

"Every woman I've ever served it to swears it's a powerful aphrodisiac."

At last there was a smile, albeit a very small one. "How helpful of Mrs. Feldman," she remarked.

"She thinks I'm not eating right. Though I don't know why. Maybe it's all those frozen-dinner trays she finds in my trash can."

There was another smile. If he kept this up, he just might coax a laugh out of her by next week. Too bad he was such a lousy comedian. Anyway, the situation was too damned grim for jokes.

The clock on the bookshelf ticked loudly—a nagging reminder of how much silence had passed between them. Kate suddenly stiffened as a gust rattled the windows.

"It's just the wind," he said. "You'll get used to it. Sometimes, in a storm, the whole house shudders and it feels like the roof will blow off."

He gazed up affectionately at the beams. "It's thirty years old. Probably should have been torn down years ago. But when we bought it, all we could see were the possibilities."

"We?" she asked dully.

"I was married then."

"Oh." She stirred a little, as though trying to show some semblance of interest. "You're divorced."

He nodded. "We lasted a little over seven years—not bad, in this day and age." He gave a short, joyless laugh. "Contrary to the old cliché, it wasn't an itch that finished us. It was more like a...fading out. But—" he sighed "—Linda and I are still friendly. Which is more than most divorced couples can say. I even like her new husband. Great guy. Very devoted, caring. Something I guess I wasn't...." He looked away, uncomfortable. He hated talking about himself. It made him feel exposed. But at least all this small talk was doing the trick. It was bringing her back to life, nudging the fear from her mind. "Linda's in Portland now," he went on quickly. "I hear they've got a baby on the way."

"You didn't have any children?" It was a perfectly natural question. He wished she hadn't asked it.

He nodded shortly. "A son."

"Oh. How old is he?"

"He's dead." How flat his voice sounded. As if Noah's death were as casual a topic as the weather. He could already see the questions forming on her lips. And the words of sympathy. That was the last thing he wanted from her. He'd heard enough well-meaning words of sympathy to last him the rest of his life.

"So anyway," he said, shifting the subject, "I'm what you'd call a born-again bachelor. But I like it this way. Some men just aren't meant to be married, I guess. And it's great for my career. Nothing to distract me from the practice, which seems to be going big guns these days."

Damn. She was still looking at him with those questions in her eyes. He headed them off with another change of topic.

"What about you?" he asked quickly. "Were you ever married?"

"No." She looked down, as if contemplating the benefits of another slug of whiskey. "I lived with a man for a while. In fact, he's the reason I came to Honolulu. To be near him." She gave a bitter laugh. "Guess that'll teach me."

"What?"

"Not to go chasing after some stupid man."

"Sounds like a nasty breakup."

She hiccuped. "It was very...civil, actually. I'm not saying it didn't hurt. Because it did." Shrugging, she surrendered to another gulp of whiskey. "It's hard, you know. Trying to be everything at once. I guess I couldn't give him what he needed: dinner waiting on the table, my undivided attention."

"Is that what he expected?"

"Isn't that what every man expects?" she snorted angrily. "Well, I didn't need all that—that male crap. I had a job that required me to jump at every phone call. Rush in for every emergency. He didn't understand."

"Was it worth it?"

"Was what worth it?"

"Sacrificing your love life for your career?"

She didn't answer for a while. Then her head drooped. "I used to think so," she said quietly. "Now I think of all those hours I put in. All those ruined weekends. I thought I was indispensable to the hospital. And then I find out I'm just as dispensable as anyone else. All it took was a lawsuit. Hell of an eye-opener." She tipped her glass at him bitterly. "Thanks for the revelation, counselor."

"Why blame me? I was just hired to do a job."

"For a nice fat fee, I imagine."

"I took the case on contingency. I won't be seeing a cent."

"You gave up all that money? Just because you think I'm telling the truth?" She shook her head in amazement. "I'm surprised the truth means so much to you."

"You have a nice way of making me sound like scum. But yes, the truth does matter to me. A great deal, in fact."

"A lawyer with principles? I didn't know there was such a thing."

"We're a recognized subspecies." His gaze inadvertently slid to the neckline of her gauze dress. The memory of how that silky skin had felt under his exploring fingers suddenly hit him with such force that he quickly turned and reached for the whiskey. There was no glass handy so he took a swig straight from the bottle. *Right,* he thought. *Get yourself drunk. See how many stupid things you can say before morning.*

Actually, they were both getting thoroughly soused. But he figured she needed it. Twenty minutes ago she'd been in a state of shock. Now, at least, she was talking. In fact she'd just managed to insult him. That had to be a good sign.

She gazed fervently into her glass. "God, I hate whiskey!" she said with sudden passion and gulped down the rest of the drink.

"I can tell. Have some more."

She eyed him suspiciously. "I think you're trying to get me drunk."

"Whatever gave you that idea?" He laughed, shoving the bottle toward her.

She regarded it for a moment. Then, with a look of utter disgust, she refilled her glass. "Good old Jack Daniel's," she sighed. Her hand was unsteady as she recapped the bottle. "What a laugh."

"What's so funny?"

"It was Dad's favorite brand. He used to swear this stuff was medicinal. Absolutely *hated* all my hair-of-the-dog lectures. Boy, would he get a kick out of seeing me now.'' She took a swallow and winced. ''Maybe he's right. Anything that tastes this awful *has* to be medicinal.''

''I take it your father wasn't a doctor.''

''He wanted to be.'' She stared down moodily at her drink. ''Yeah, that was his dream. He planned on being a country doctor. You know, the kind of guy who'd deliver a baby in exchange for a few dozen eggs. But I guess things didn't work out. I came along and then they needed money and...'' She sighed. ''He had a repair shop in Sacramento. Oh, he was handy! I used to watch him putter around in that basement. Dad could fix anything you put in his hands. TVs. Washing machines. He even held seventeen patents, none of them worth a damn cent. Except maybe the Handy Dandy apple slicer.'' She glanced at him hopefully. ''Ever heard of it?''

''Sorry. No.''

She shrugged. ''Neither has anyone else.''

''What does it do, exactly?''

''One flick of the wrist and whack! Six perfect slices.'' At his silence she gave him a rueful smile. ''I can see you're terribly impressed.''

''But I am. I'm impressed that your father managed to invent you. He must've been happy you became a doctor.''

''He was. When I graduated from med school, he told me it was the very best day of his life.'' She stopped, her smile suddenly fading. ''I think that's sad, don't you? That out of all the years of his life, that was the one single day he was happiest....'' She cleared her throat. ''After he died, Mom sold the shop. She got married to some high-powered banker in San Francisco. What a snooty guy. We can't stand each other.'' She looked down at her glass and her voice dropped. ''I still think about that shop sometimes. I miss the old basement. I miss all those dumb, useless gadgets of his. I miss—''

He saw her lower lip tremble and he thought with sudden panic: *Oh, no. Now she's going to cry.* He could deal with sobbing clients. He knew exactly how to respond to their tears. Pull out the box of Kleenex. Pat them on the back. Tell them he'd do everything he could.

But this was different. This wasn't his office but his living room. And the woman on the verge of tears wasn't a client but someone he happened to like very much.

Just as he thought the dam would burst, she managed to drag herself together. He saw only the briefest glitter of tears in her eyes, then she blinked and they were gone. Thank God. If she started bawling now, he'd be utterly useless.

He took her glass and deliberately set it down on the table. ''I think you've had enough for tonight. Come on, doctor lady. It's time for bed. I'll show you the way.'' He reached for her hand but she reflexively pulled back. ''Something wrong?''

''No. It's just...''

"Don't tell me you're worried about how it looks? Your staying here, I mean."

"A little. Not much, actually. I mean, not under the circumstances." She gave an awkward laugh. "Fear does strange things to one's sense of propriety."

"Not to mention one's sense of legal ethics." At her puzzled look, he said, "I've never done this before."

"What? Brought a woman home for the night?"

"Well, I haven't done *that* in a while, either. What I meant was, I make it a point never to get involved with any of my clients. And certainly never with the opposition."

"Then I'm the exception?"

"Yes. You are definitely the exception. Believe it or not, I don't normally paw every female who walks into my office."

"Which ones do you paw?" she asked, a faint smile suddenly tracing her lips.

He moved toward her, drawn by invisible threads of desire. "Only the green-eyed ones," he murmured. Gently he touched her cheek. "Who happen to have a bruise here and there."

"That last part sounds suspiciously kinky," she whispered.

"No, it's not." The intimate tone of his voice made Kate suddenly fall very still. His finger left a scorching trail as it stroked down her face.

She knew the danger of this moment. This was the man who'd once vowed to ruin her. He could still ruin her. *Consorting with the enemy,* she thought in sudden panic as his face drew closer. But she couldn't seem to move. A sense of unreality swept over her; a feeling that none of this could be happening, that it was only some hot, drunken fantasy. Here she was, sharing a couch with the very man she'd once despised, and all she could think of was how much she wanted him to haul her into his arms and kiss her.

His lips were gentle. It was no more than a brushing of mouths, a cautious savoring of what they both knew might follow, but it was enough to touch off a thousand flames inside her. Jack Daniel's had never tasted so good!

"And what will the bar association say to that?" she murmured.

"They'll call it outrageous...."

"Unethical."

"And absolutely insane. Which it is." Drawing away, he studied her for a moment; and his struggle for control showed plainly in his face. To her disappointment, common sense won out. He rose from the couch and tugged her to her feet. "When you file your complaint with the state bar, don't forget to mention how apologetic I was."

"Will it make a difference?"

"Not to them. But I hope it does to you."

They stood before the window, staring at each other. The wind lashed the panes, a sound as relentless as the pounding of her own heartbeat in her ears.

"I think it's time to go to bed," he said hoarsely.

"What?"

He cleared his throat. "I mean it's time you went to your bed. And I went to mine."

"Oh."

"Unless..."

"Unless?"

"You don't want to."

"Want to what?"

"Go to bed."

They looked at each other uneasily. She swallowed. "I think maybe I'd better."

"Yeah." He turned away and agitatedly plowed his fingers through his hair. "I think so, too."

"David?"

He glanced over his shoulder. "Yes?"

"Is it really a violation of legal ethics? Letting me stay here?"

"Under the circumstances?" He shrugged. "I think I'm still on safe ground. Barely. As long as nothing happens between us." He scooped up the whiskey bottle. Matter-of-factly he slid it into the liquor cabinet and shut the door. "And nothing will."

"Of course not," she responded quickly. "I mean, I don't need that kind of complication in my life. Certainly not now."

"Neither do I. But for the moment, we seem to need each other. So I'll provide you with a safe place to stay. And you can help me figure out what really happened in that O.R. A convenient arrangement. I ask only one thing."

"What's that?"

"We keep this discreet. Not just now but also after you leave. This sort of thing can only hurt both our reputations."

"I understand. Perfectly."

They both took a simultaneous breath.

"So...I think I'll say good-night," she said. Turning, she started across the living room. Her whole body felt like rubber. She only prayed she wouldn't fall flat on her face.

"Kate?"

Her heart did a quick somersault as she spun around to face him. "Yes?"

"Your room's the second door on the right."

"Oh. Thanks." Her flip-flopping heart seemed to sink like a stone as she left him standing there in the living room. Her only consolation was that he looked every bit as miserable as she felt.

LONG AFTER KATE had gone to her room, David sat in the living room, thinking. Remembering how she had tasted, how she had trembled in his arms. And wondering how he'd gotten himself into this mess. It was bad enough, letting the woman sleep under his roof, but to practically seduce her on his couch—that was sheer stupidity. Though he'd wanted to. God, how he'd wanted to.

He could tell by the way she'd melted against him that she hadn't been kissed in a very long time. Terrific. Here they were, two normal, healthy, *deprived* adults, sleeping within ten feet of each other. You couldn't ask for a more explosive situation.

He didn't want to think about what his old ethics professor would say to this. Strictly speaking, he couldn't consider himself off the O'Brien case yet. Until he actually handed the file over to another firm, he still had to behave as their attorney and was bound by legal ethics to protect their interests. To think how scrupulous he'd always been about separating his personal from his professional life!

If he'd had his head screwed on straight, he would have avoided the whole mess by taking Kate to a hotel or a friend's house. Anywhere but here. The problem was, he'd been having trouble thinking straight since the day he met her. Tonight, after that phone call, he'd had only one thought in mind: to keep her safe and warm and protected. It was a fiercely primitive instinct over which he had no control; and he resented it. He also resented her for stirring up all these inconvenient male responses.

Annoyed at himself, he rose from the couch and circled the living room, turning off lights. He decided he wasn't interested in being any woman's white knight. Besides, Kate Chesne wasn't the kind of woman who needed a hero. Or any man, for that matter. Not that he didn't like independent women. He did like them.

He also liked *her*. A lot.

Maybe too much.

KATE LAY CURLED UP in bed, listening to David's restless pacing in the living room. She held her breath as his footsteps creaked up the hall past her door. Was it her imagination or did he pause there for a moment before continuing on to the next room? She could hear him moving around, opening and closing drawers, rattling hangers in the closet. *My God,* she thought. *He's sleeping right next door.*

Now the shower was running. She wondered if it was a cold shower. She tried not to think about what he'd look like, standing under the stream of water, but the image had already formed in her head, the soapsuds sliding down his shoulders, the gold hairs matted and damp on his chest.

Now stop it. Right now.

She bit her lip—bit it so hard the image wavered a little. Damn. So this was lust, pure and unadulterated. Well, maybe slightly adulterated—

by whiskey. Here she was, thirty years old, and she'd never wanted any man so badly. She wanted him on a level that was raw and wild and elemental.

She'd certainly never felt this way about Eric. Her relationship with Eric had been excruciatingly civilized; nothing as primitive as this—this animal heat. Even their parting had been civilized. They'd discussed their differences, decided they were irreconcilable, and had gone their separate ways. At the time she'd thought it devastating, but now she realized what had been hurt most by the breakup was her pride. All these months, she'd nursed the faint hope that Eric would come back to her. Now she could barely conjure up a picture of his face. It kept blurring into the image of a man in a shower.

She buried her head in the pillow, an act that made her feel about as brilliant as an ostrich. And she was supposed to be so bright, so level-headed. Why, it was even official, having been stated in her performance evaluation as a resident: *Dr. Chesne is a superbly competent, levelheaded physician.* Ha! Levelheaded? Try dim-witted. Besotted. Or just plain dumb—for lusting after the man who'd once threatened to ruin her in court.

She had so many important things to worry about; matters, literally, of life and death. She was losing her job. Her career was on the skids. A killer was searching for her.

And she was wondering how much hair David Ransom had on his chest.

SHE WAS RUNNING down hundreds of steps, plunging deeper and deeper into a pit of darkness. She didn't know what lay at the end; all she knew was that something was right behind her, something terrible; she didn't dare look back to see its face. There were no doors, no windows, no other avenue of escape. Her flight was noiseless, like the flickering reel of a movie with no sound. In this silence lay the worst terror of all: no one would hear her scream.

With a sob, Kate wrenched herself awake and found herself staring up wildly at an unfamiliar ceiling. Somewhere a telephone was ringing. Daylight glowed in the window and she heard waves lapping the seawall. The ringing telephone suddenly stopped; David's voice murmured in another room.

I'm safe, she told herself. *No one can hurt me. Not here. Not in this house.*

The knock on the door made her sit up sharply.

"Kate?" David called through the closed door.

"Yes?"

"You'd better get dressed. Pokie wants us down at the station."

"Right now?"

"Right now."

It was his low tone of urgency that alarmed her. She scrambled out of bed and opened the door. "Why? What is it?"

His gaze slid briefly to her nightgown, then focused, utterly neutral, on her face. "The killer. They know his name."

Chapter Eight

Pokie slid the book of mug shots toward Kate. "See anyone you know, Dr. Chesne?"

Kate scanned the photographs and immediately focused on one face. It was a cruel portrait; every wrinkle, every hollow had been brought into harsh clarity by the camera lights. Yet the man didn't squint. He gazed straight ahead with wide eyes. It was the look of a lost soul. Softly she said, "That's him."

"You positive?"

"I—I remember his eyes." Swallowing hard, she turned away. Both men were watching her intently. They were probably worried she'd faint or get hysterical or do something equally ridiculous. But she wasn't feeling much of anything. It was as if she were detached from her body and were floating somewhere near the ceiling, watching a stock scene from a police procedural: the witness unerringly pointing out the face of the killer.

"That's our man," Pokie said with grim satisfaction.

A wan sergeant in plainclothes brought her a cup of hot coffee. He seemed to have a cold; he was sniffling. Through the glass partition, she saw him return to his desk and take out a bottle of nose spray.

Her gaze returned to the photo. "Who is he?" she asked.

"A nut case," replied Pokie. "The name's Charles Decker. That photo was taken five years ago, right after his arrest."

"On what charge?"

"Assault and battery. He kicked down the door of a medical office. Tried to strangle the doctor right there in front of the whole staff."

"A doctor?" David's head came up. "Which one?"

Pokie sat back, his weight eliciting a squeal of protest from the old chair. "Guess."

"Henry Tanaka."

Pokie's answer was a satisfied display of nicotine-stained teeth. "One and the same. It took us a while, but the name finally popped up on a computer search."

"Arrest records?"

"Yeah. We should've picked it up earlier, but it kind of slipped by during the initial investigation. See, we asked Mrs. Tanaka if her husband had any enemies. You know, routine question. She gave us some names. We followed up on 'em but they all came up clean. Then she mentioned that five years back, some nut had attacked her husband. She didn't remember his name and as far as she knew, the man was still in the state hospital. We went to the files and finally pulled out an arrest report. It was Charlie Decker's. And this morning I got word from the lab. Remember that set of fingerprints on the Richter woman's doorknob?"

"Charlie Decker's?"

Pokie nodded. "And now—" he glanced at Kate "—our witness gives us a positive ID. I'd say we got our man."

"What was his motive?"

"I told you. He's crazy."

"So are thousands of other people. Why did this one turn killer?"

"Hey, I'm not the guy's shrink."

"But you have an answer, don't you?"

Pokie shrugged. "All I got is a theory."

"That man threatened my life, Lieutenant," said Kate. "I think I have the right to know more than just his name."

"She does, Pokie," agreed David quietly. "You won't find it in any of your police manuals. But I think she has the right to know who this Charles Decker is."

Sighing, Pokie fished a spiral notebook out of his desk. "Okay," he grunted, flipping through the pages. "Here's what I got so far. Understand, it's still gotta be confirmed. Decker, Charles Louis, white male born Cleveland thirty-nine years ago. Parents divorced. Brother killed in a gang fight at age fifteen. Great start. One married sister, living in Florida."

"You talked to her?"

"She's the one who gave us most of this info. Let's see. Joined the navy at twenty-two. Based in various ports. San Diego. Bremerton. Got shipped here to Pearl six years ago. Served as corpsman aboard the USS *Cimarron*—"

"Corpsman?" Kate questioned.

"Assistant to the ship's surgeon. According to his superior officers, Decker was kind of a loner. Pretty much kept to himself. No history of emotional problems." Here he let out a snort. "So much for the accuracy of military files." He flipped to the next page. "Had a decent service record, couple of commendations. Seemed to be moving up the ranks okay. And then, five years ago, it seems something snapped."

"Nervous breakdown?" asked David.

"Lot more than that. He went berserk. And it all had to do with a woman."

"You mean a girlfriend?"

"Yeah. Some gal he'd met here in the Islands. He put in for permission to get married. It was granted. But then he and his ship sailed for six months of classified maneuvers off Subic Bay. Sailor in the next bunk remembers Decker spent every spare minute writing poems for that girlfriend. Must've been nuts about her. Just nuts." Pokie shook his head and sighed. "Anyway, when the *Cimarron* returned to Pearl, the girlfriend wasn't waiting on the pier with all the other honeys. Here's the part where things get a little confused. All we know is Decker jumped ship without permission. Guess it didn't take long for him to find out what'd happened."

"She found another guy?" David guessed.

"No. She was dead."

There was a long silence. In the next office, a telephone was ringing and typewriters clattered incessantly.

Kate asked softly, "What happened to her?"

"Complications of childbirth," explained Pokie. "She had some kind of stroke in the delivery room. The baby girl died, too. Decker never even knew she was pregnant."

Slowly, Kate's gaze fell to the photograph of Charlie Decker. She thought of what he must have gone through, that day in Pearl Harbor. The ship pulling into the crowded dock. The smiling families. *How long did he search for her face?* she wondered. *How long before he realized she wasn't there? That she'd never be there?*

"That's when the man lost it," continued Pokie. "Somehow he found out Tanaka was his girlfriend's doctor. The arrest record says he showed up at the clinic and just about strangled the doctor on the spot. After a scuffle, the police were called. A day later, Decker got out on bail. He went and bought himself a Saturday-night special. But he didn't use it on the doctor. He put the barrel in his own mouth. Pulled the trigger." Pokie closed the notebook.

The ultimate act, thought Kate. *Buy a gun and blow your own head off.* He must have loved that woman. And what better way to prove it than to sacrifice himself on her altar?

But he wasn't dead. He was alive. And he was killing people.

Pokie saw her questioning look. "It was a very cheap gun. It misfired. Turned his mouth into bloody pulp. But he survived. After a few months in a rehab facility, he was transferred to the state hospital. The nuthouse. Their records show he regained function of just about everything but his speech."

"He's mute?" asked David.

"Not exactly. Vocal cords were ripped to shreds during the resuscitation. He can mouth words, but his voice is more like a—a hiss."

A hiss, thought Kate. The memory of that unearthly sound, echoing in Ann's stairwell, seemed to reach out from her worst nightmares. *The sound of a viper about to strike.*

Pokie continued. "About a month ago, Decker was discharged from the state hospital. He was supposed to be seeing some shrink by the name of Nemechek. But Decker never showed up for the first appointment."

"Have you talked to Nemechek?" asked Kate.

"Only on the phone. He's at a conference in L.A. Should be back on Tuesday. Swears up and down that his patient was harmless. But he's covering his butt. Looks pretty bad when the patient you just let out starts slashing throats."

"So that's the motive," said David. "Revenge. For a dead woman."

"That's the theory."

"Why was Ann Richter killed?"

"Remember that blond woman the janitors saw running through the parking lot?"

"You think that was her?"

"It seems she and Tanaka were—how do I put it?—very well acquainted."

"Does that mean what I think it means?"

"Let's just say Ann Richter's neighbors had no trouble recognizing Tanaka's photo. He was seen at her apartment more than once. The night he was killed, I think she went to pay her favorite doctor a little social call. Instead she found something that scared the hell out of her. Maybe she saw Decker. And he saw her."

"Then why didn't she go to the police?" asked Kate.

"Maybe she didn't want the world to know she was having an affair with a married man. Or maybe she was afraid she'd be accused of killing her lover. Who knows?"

"So she was just a witness," said Kate. "Like me."

Pokie looked at her. "There's one big difference between you and her. Decker can't get to *you*. Right now no one outside this office knows where you're staying. Let's keep it that way." He glanced at David. "There's no problem, keeping her at your house?"

David's face was unreadable. "She can stay."

"Good. And it's better if she doesn't use her own car."

"My car?" Kate frowned. "Why not?"

"Decker has your purse. And a set of your car keys. So he knows you drive an Audi. He'll be watching for one."

Watching for me, she thought with a shudder. "For how long?" she whispered.

"What?"

"How long before it's all over? Before I have my life back?"

Pokie sighed. "It might take a while to find him. But hang in there, Doc. The man can't hide forever."

Can't he? wondered Kate. She thought of all the places a man could hide on Oahu: the nooks and crannies of Chinatown where no one ever asks questions. The tin-roofed fishing shacks of Sand Island. The concrete alleys of Waikiki. Somewhere, in some secret place, Charlie Decker was quietly mourning for a dead woman.

They rose to leave and a question suddenly came to her mind. "Lieutenant," she asked. "What about Ellen O'Brien?"

Pokie, who was gathering a pile of papers into a folder, glanced up. "What about her?"

"Does she have some connection to all this?"

Pokie looked down one last time at Charlie Decker's photo. Then he shut the folder. "No," he answered. "No connection at all."

"BUT THERE *HAS* TO BE a connection!" Kate blurted as they walked out of the station into the midmorning heat. "Some piece of evidence he hasn't found—"

"Or won't tell us about," finished David.

She frowned at him. "Why wouldn't he? I thought you two were friends."

"I deserted the trenches, remember?"

"You make police work sound like jungle warfare."

"For some cops, the job *is* a war. A holy war. Pokie's got a wife and four kids. But you'd never know it, looking at all the hours he puts in."

"So you do think he's a good cop?"

David shrugged. "He's a plough horse. Solid but not brilliant. I've seen him screw up on occasion. He could be wrong this time, too. But right now I have to agree with him. I don't see how Ellen O'Brien fits into this case."

"But you heard what he said! Decker was a corpsman. Assistant to the ship's surgeon—"

"Decker's profile doesn't fit the pattern, Kate. A psycho who works like Jack the Ripper doesn't bother with drug vials and EKGs. That takes a totally different kind of mind."

She stared down the street in frustration. "The trouble is, I can't see any way to prove Ellen *was* murdered. I can't even be sure it's possible."

David paused on the sidewalk. "Okay." He sighed. "So we can't prove anything. But let's think about the logistics."

"You mean of murder?"

He nodded. "Let's take a man like Decker. An outsider. Someone who knows a little about medicine. And surgery. Tell me, step by step. How would he go about getting into the hospital and killing a patient?"

"I suppose he'd have to...to..." Her gaze wandered up the street. She frowned as her eyes focused on a paperboy, waving the morning edition to passing cars. "Today's Sunday," she said suddenly.

"So?"

"Ellen was admitted on a Sunday. I remember being in her room, talking to her. It was eight o'clock on a Sunday night." She glanced feverishly at her watch. "That's in ten hours. We could go through the steps...."

"Wait a minute. You've lost me. What, exactly, are we doing in ten hours?"

She turned to him. Softly she said, "Murder."

THE VISITOR PARKING LOT was nearly empty when David swung his BMW into the hospital driveway at ten o'clock that night. He parked in a stall near the lobby entrance, turned off the engine and looked at Kate. "This won't prove a thing. You know that, don't you?"

"I want to see if it's possible."

"Possibilities don't hold up in court."

"I don't care how it plays in court, David. As long as *I* know it's possible."

She glanced out at the distant red Emergency sign, glowing like a beacon in the darkness. An ambulance was parked at the loading dock. On a nearby bench, the driver sat idly smoking a cigarette and listening to the crackle of his dispatch radio.

A Sunday night, quiet as usual. Visiting hours were over. And in their rooms, patients would already be settling into the blissful sleep of the drugged.

David's face gleamed faintly in the shadows. "Okay." He sighed, shoving open his door. "Let's do it."

The lobby doors were locked. They walked in the E.R. entrance, through a waiting room where a baby screamed in the lap of its glassy-eyed mother, where an old man coughed noisily into a handkerchief and a teenage boy clutched an ice bag to his swollen face. The triage nurse was talking on the telephone; they walked right past her and headed for the elevators.

"We're in, just like that?" David asked.

"The E.R. nurse knows me."

"But she hardly looked at you."

"That's because she was too busy ogling *you*," Kate said dryly.

"Boy, have you got a wild imagination." He paused, glancing around the empty lobby. "Where's Security? Isn't there a guard around?"

"He's probably making rounds."

"You mean there's only one?"

"Hospitals are really pretty boring places, you know," she replied and punched the elevator button. "Besides, it's Sunday."

They rose up to the fourth floor and stepped off into the antiseptic-white corridor. Freshly waxed linoleum gleamed under bright lights. A row of gurneys sat lined up against the wall, as though awaiting a deluge of the wounded. Kate pointed to the double doors marked No Admittance.

"The O.R.'s through there."

"Can we get in?"

She took a few experimental steps forward. The doors automatically slid open. "No problem."

Inside, only a single dim light shone over the reception area. A cup, half filled with lukewarm coffee, sat abandoned on the front desk awaiting its owner's return. Kate pointed to a huge wallboard where the next day's surgery schedule was posted.

"All tomorrow's cases are listed right there," she explained. "One glance will tell you which O.R. the patient will be in, the procedure, the names of the surgeon and anesthesiologist."

"Where was Ellen?"

"The room's right around the corner."

She led him down an unlit hall and opened the door to O.R. 5. Through the shadows they saw the faint gleam of stainless steel. She flicked on the wall switch; the sudden flood of light was almost painful.

"The anesthesia cart's over there."

He went over to the cart and pulled open one of the steel drawers. Tiny glass vials tinkled in their compartments. "Are these drugs always left unlocked?"

"They're worthless on the street. No one would bother to steal any of those. As for the narcotics—" she pointed to a wall cabinet "—we keep them locked in there."

His gaze slowly moved around the room. "So this is where you work. Very impressive. Looks like a set for a sci-fi movie."

She grinned. "Funny. I've always felt right at home in here." She circled the room, affectionately patting the equipment as she moved. "I think it's because I'm the daughter of a tinkerer. Gadgets don't scare me. I actually like playing with all these buttons and dials. But I suppose some people do find it all pretty intimidating."

"And you've never been intimidated?"

She turned and found he was staring at her. Something about his gaze, about the intensity of those blue eyes, made her fall very still. "Not by the O.R.," she said softly.

It was so quiet she could almost hear her own heartbeat thudding in that stark chamber. For a long time they stared at each other, as though separated by some wide, unbreachable chasm. Then, abruptly, he shifted his attention to the anesthesia cart.

"How long would it take to tamper with one of these drug vials?" he asked. She had to admire his control. At least he could still speak; she was having trouble finding her own voice.

"He'd—he'd have to empty out the succinylcholine vials. It would probably take less than a minute."

"As easy as that?"

"As easy as that." Her gaze shifted reluctantly to the operating table. "They're so helpless, our patients. We have absolute control over their lives. I never saw it that way before. It's really rather frightening."

"So murder in the O.R. isn't that difficult."

"No," she conceded. "I guess it isn't."

"What about switching the EKG? How would our killer do that?"

"He'd have to get hold of the patient's chart. And they're all kept on the wards."

"That sounds tricky. The wards are crawling with nurses."

"True. But even in this day and age, nurses are still a little intimidated by a white coat. I bet if we put you in uniform, you'd be able to breeze your way right into the nurses' station, no questions asked."

He cocked his head. "Want to try it?"

"You mean right now?"

"Sure. Find me a white coat. I've always wanted to play doctor."

It took only a minute to locate a stray coat hanging in the surgeons' locker room. She knew it was Guy Santini's, just by the coffee stains on the front. The size 46 label only confirmed it.

"I didn't know King Kong was on your staff," David grunted, thrusting his arms into the huge sleeves. He buttoned up and stood straight. "What do you think? Are they going to fall down laughing?"

Stepping back, she gave him a critical look. The coat sagged on his shoulders. One side of the collar was turned up. But the truth was, he looked absolutely irresistible. And perversely untouchable. She smoothed down his collar. Just that brief contact, that brushing of her fingers against his neck, seemed to flood her whole arm with warmth.

"You'll do," she said.

"I look that bad?" He glanced down at the coffee stains. "I feel like a slob."

She laughed. "The owner of that particular coat *is* a slob. So don't worry about it. You'll fit right in." As they walked to the elevators, she added, "Just remember to think *doctor*. Get into the right mind-set. You know—brilliant, dedicated, compassionate."

"Don't forget *modest*."

She gave him a slap on the back. "Go get'em, Dr. Kildare."

He stepped into the elevator. "Look, don't vanish on me, okay? If they get suspicious, I'll need you to back me up."

"I'll be waiting in the O.R. Oh, David...one last bit of advice."

"What's that?"

"Don't commit malpractice, Doctor. You might have to sue yourself."

He let out a groan as the doors snapped shut between them. The elevator whined faintly as it descended to the third floor. Then there was silence.

It was a simple test. Even if David was stopped by Security, it would take only a word from Kate to set him free. Nothing could possibly go wrong. But as she headed up the hallway, her uneasiness grew.

Back in O.R. 5, she settled into her usual seat near the head of the table and thought of all the hours she'd spent anchored to this one spot. A very small world. A very safe world.

The sound of a door slapping shut made her glance up. Why was David back so soon? Had there been trouble? She hopped off the stool and pushed into the corridor. There she halted.

Just down the hall, a faint crack of light shone through the door to O.R. 7. She listened for a moment and heard the rattle of cabinets, the squeal of a drawer sliding open.

Someone was rummaging through the supplies. A nurse? Or someone else—someone who didn't belong?

She glanced toward the far end of the corridor—her only route of escape. The reception desk lay around that corner. If she could just get safely past O.R. 7, she could slip out and call Security. She had to decide now; whoever was going through O.R. 7 might proceed to the other rooms. If she didn't move now, she'd be trapped.

Noiselessly she headed down the hall. The slam of a cabinet told her she wouldn't make it. O.R. 7's door suddenly swung open. Panicked, she reeled backward to see Dr. Clarence Avery freeze in the doorway. Something slid out of his hand and the sound of shattering glass seemed to reverberate endlessly in the hall. She took one look at his bloodlessly white face, and her fear instantly turned to concern. For a terrifying moment she thought he'd keel over right then and there of a heart attack.

"Dr.—Dr. Chesne," he stammered weakly. "I—I didn't expect— I mean, I..." Slowly he stared down at his feet; that's when she noticed, through the shadows, the sparkle of glass lying on the floor. He shook his head helplessly. "What...what a mess I've made...."

"It's not that bad," she responded quickly. "Here, I'll help you clean it up."

She flicked on the corridor lights. He didn't move. He just stood there, blinking in the sudden glare. She had never seen him look so old, so frail; the white hair seemed to tremble on his head. She grabbed a handful of paper towels from the scrub sink dispenser and offered him a few sheets, but he still didn't move. So she crouched at his feet and began gathering up the broken glass. He was wearing one blue sock and one white sock. As she reached for one of the shards, she noticed a label was still affixed.

"It's for my dog," he said weakly.

"Excuse me?"

"The potassium chloride. It's for my dog. She's very sick."

Kate looked up at him blankly. "I'm sorry" was all she could think of saying.

He lowered his head. "She needs to be put to sleep. All morning, she's been whimpering. I can't stand listening to it anymore. And she's old, you know. Over ninety in dog years. But it—it seems cruel, taking her to the vet for that. A total stranger. It would terrify her."

Kate rose to her feet. Avery just stood there, clutching the paper towels as if not quite sure what to do with them.

"I'm sure the vet would be gentle," she replied. "You don't have to do it yourself."

"But it's so much better if I do, don't you think? If I'm the one to tell her goodbye?"

She nodded. Then she turned to the anesthesia cart and took out a vial of potassium chloride. "Here—" She offered quietly, placing it in his hand. "This should be enough, don't you think?"

He nodded. "She's not a very...big dog." He let out a shaky breath and turned to leave. Then he stopped and looked back at her. "I've always liked you, Kate. You're the only one who never seemed to be laughing behind my back. Or dropping hints that I'm too old, that I ought to retire." He sighed and shook his head. "But maybe they're right, after all." As he turned to leave, she heard him say, "I'll do what I can at your hearing."

His footsteps creaked off into the corridor. As the sound faded away, her gaze settled on the bits of broken glass in the trash can. The label KCL stared up at her. Potassium chloride, she thought with a frown. When pushed intravenously, it was a deadly poison, resulting in sudden cardiac arrest. And it occurred to her that the same poison that would kill a dog could just as easily be used to kill a human being.

THE CLERK ON ward 3B was hunched at her desk, clutching a paperback book. On the cover, a half-naked couple grappled beneath the blazing scarlet title: *His Wanton Bride.* She flipped a page. Her eyes widened. She didn't even notice David walk by. Only when he was standing right beside her in the nurses' station did she bother to glance up. Instantly flushing, she slapped down the book.

"Oh! Can I help you, Doctor...uh..."

"Smith," finished David and flashed her such a dazzling smile that she sank like melted jelly into her chair. *Wow,* he thought as he gazed into a pair of rapturous violet eyes. *This white coat really does the trick.* "I need to see one of your charts," he said.

"Which one?" she asked breathlessly.

"Room...er..." He glanced over at the chart rack. "Eight."

"A or B?"

"B."

"Mrs. Loomis?"

"Yes, that's the name. Loomis."

She seemed to float out of her chair. Swaying over to the chart rack, she struck a pose of slinky indifference. It took her an inordinately long time to locate Room 8B's chart, despite the fact it was staring her right in the face. David glanced down at the book cover and suddenly felt like laughing.

"Here it is," she chirped, holding it out to him in both hands, like some sort of sacred offering.

"Why, thank you, Ms...."

"Mann. Janet. Miss."

"Yes." He cleared his throat. Then, turning, he fled to a chair as far away as possible from Miss Janet Mann. He could almost hear her sigh of disappointment as she turned to answer a ringing telephone.

"Oh, all right." She sighed. "I'll bring them down right now." She grabbed a handful of red-stoppered blood tubes from the pickup tray and hurried out, leaving David alone in the station.

So that's all there is to it, he thought, flipping open the metal chart cover. The unfortunate Mrs. Loomis in room 8B was obviously a complicated case, judging by the thickness of her record and the interminable list of doctors on her case. Not only did she have a surgeon and anesthesiologist, there were numerous consultation notes by an internist, psychiatrist, dermatologist and gynecologist. He was reminded of the old saying about too many cooks. Like the proverbial broth, this poor lady didn't have a chance.

A nurse walked past, wheeling a medication cart. Another nurse slipped in for a moment to answer the ringing telephone then hurried out again. Neither woman paid him the slightest attention.

He flipped to the EKG, which was filed at the back of the chart. It would take maybe ten seconds to remove that one page and replace it with another. And with so many doctors passing through the ward—six for Mrs. Loomis alone—no one would notice a thing.

Murder, he decided, couldn't be easier. All it took was a white coat.

Chapter Nine

"I guess you proved your point tonight," said David as he set two glasses of hot milk on the kitchen table. "About murder in the O.R."

"No, we didn't." Kate looked down bleakly at the steaming glass. "We didn't prove a thing, David. Except that the chief of anesthesia's got a sick dog." She sighed. "Poor old Avery. I must have scared the wits out of him."

"Sounds like you scared the wits out of each other. By the way, does he have a dog?"

"He wouldn't lie to me."

"I'm just asking. I don't know the man." He took a sip of milk and it left a faint white mustache on his stubbled lip. He seemed dark and out of place in his gleaming kitchen. A faint beard shadowed his jaw, and his shirt, which had started out so crisp this morning, was now mapped with wrinkles. He'd undone his top button and she felt a peculiar sense of weightlessness as she caught a glimpse of dark gold hair matting his chest.

She looked down fiercely at her milk. "I'm pretty sure he does have a dog," she continued. "In fact, I remember seeing a picture on his desk."

"He keeps a picture of a dog on his desk?"

"It's of his wife, really. She's holding this sort of brownish terrier. She was really very beautiful."

"I take it you mean his wife."

"Yes. She had a stroke a few months ago. It devastated that poor man, to put her in a nursing home. He's been shuffling through his duties ever since." Mournfully she took a sip. "I bet he couldn't do it."

"Do what?"

"Kill his dog. Some people are incapable of hurting a fly."

"While others are perfectly capable of murder."

She looked at him. "You still think it *was* murder?"

He didn't answer for a moment, and his silence frightened her. Was her only ally slipping away? "I don't know what I think." He sighed.

"So far I've been going on instinct, not facts. And that won't hold up in a courtroom."

"Or a committee hearing," she added morosely.

"Your hearing's on Tuesday?"

"And I still haven't the faintest idea what to tell them."

"Can't you get a delay? I'll cancel my appointments tomorrow. Maybe we can pull together some evidence."

"I've already asked for a delay. It was turned down. Anyway, there doesn't seem to *be* any evidence. All we have is a pair of murders, with no obvious connection to Ellen's death."

He sat back, frowning at the table. "What if the police are barking up the wrong tree? What if Charlie Decker's just a wild card?"

"They found his fingerprints, David. And I saw him there."

"But you didn't actually see him kill anyone."

"No. But who else had a motive?"

"Let's think about this for a minute." Idly, David reached for the saltshaker and set it in the center of the table. "We know Henry Tanaka was a very busy man. And I'm not talking about his practice. He was having an affair—" David moved the pepper shaker next to the salt "—probably with Ann Richter."

"Okay. But where does Ellen fit in?"

"That's the million-dollar question." He reached over and tapped the sugar jar. "Where does Ellen O'Brien fit in?"

Kate frowned. "A love triangle?"

"Possible. But a man doesn't have to stop at one mistress. He could've had a dozen. And they each in turn could have had jealous lovers."

"Triangles within triangles? This sounds wilder by the minute. All this romping around in bedrooms! Doctors having affairs left and right! I just can't picture it."

"It happens. And not just in hospitals."

"Law offices too, hmm?"

"I'm not saying *I've* done it. But we're all human."

She couldn't help smiling. "It's funny. When we first met, I didn't think of you as being particularly human."

"No?"

"You were a threat. The enemy. Just another damn lawyer."

"Oh. Scum of the earth, you mean."

"You did play the part well."

He winced. "Thanks a lot."

"But it's not that way anymore," she said quickly. "I can't think of you as just another lawyer. Not since…"

Her voice faded as their eyes suddenly locked.

"Not since I kissed you," he finished softly.

Warmth flooded her cheeks. Abruptly she rose to her feet and carried the glass to the sink, all the time aware of his gaze on her back. "It's all gotten so complicated," she commented with a sigh.

"What? The fact I'm human?"

"The fact we're *both* human," she blurted out. Even without looking at him, she could sense the attraction, the electricity, crackling between them.

She washed the glass. Twice. Then, calmly, deliberately, she sat back down at the table. He was watching her, a wry look of amusement on his face.

"I'll be the first to admit it," he said, his eyes twinkling. "It *is* a hell of an inconvenience, being human. A slave to all those pesky biological urges."

Biological urges. What a hopelessly pale description of the hormonal storm now raging inside her. Avoiding his gaze, she focused on the salt-shaker, sitting at the center of the table. She thought suddenly of Henry Tanaka. Of triangles within triangles. Had all those deaths been a consequence of nothing more than lust and jealousy gone berserk?

"You're right," she agreed, thoughtfully touching the saltshaker. "Being human leads to all sorts of complications. Even murder."

She sensed his tension before he even spoke a word. His gaze fell on the table and all at once he went completely still. "I can't believe we didn't think of it."

"Of what?" she asked.

He shoved his empty glass toward the sugar jar. It gave the diagram a fourth corner. "We're not dealing with a triangle. It's a *square*."

There was a pause. "Your grasp of geometry is really quite amazing," she said politely.

"What if Tanaka *did* have a second girlfriend—Ellen O'Brien?"

"That's our old triangle."

"But we've left someone out. Someone very important." He tapped the empty milk glass.

Kate frowned at the four objects on the table. "My God," she whispered. "Mrs. Tanaka."

"Exactly."

"I never even thought of his wife."

He looked up. "Maybe it's time we did."

THE JAPANESE WOMAN who opened the clinic door was wearing fire-engine-red lipstick and face powder that was several shades too pale for her complexion. She looked like a fugitive from a geisha house. "Then you're not with the police?" she asked.

"Not exactly," replied David. "But we do have a few questions—"

"I'm not talking to any more reporters." She started to shut the door.

"We're not reporters, Mrs. Tanaka. I'm an attorney. And this is Dr. Kate Chesne."

"Well, what do you want, then?"

"We're trying to get information about another murder. It's related to your husband's death."

Sudden interest flickered in the woman's eyes. "You're talking about that nurse, aren't you? That Richter woman."

"Yes."

"What do you know about her?"

"We'll be glad to tell you everything we know. If you'll just let us come in."

She hesitated, curiosity and caution waging a battle in her eyes. Curiosity won. She opened the door and gestured for them to come into the waiting room. She was tall for a Japanese; taller, even, than Kate. She was wearing a simple blue dress and high heels and gold seashell earrings. Her hair was so black it might have looked artificial had there not been the single white strand tracing her right temple. Mari Tanaka was a remarkably beautiful woman.

"You'll have to excuse the mess," she apologized, pausing in the impeccably neat waiting room. "But there's been so much confusion. So many things to take care of." She gazed around at the deserted couches, as though wondering where all the patients had gone. Magazines were still arrayed on the coffee table and a box of children's toys sat in the corner, waiting to be played with. The only hint that tragedy had struck this office was the sympathy card and a vase of white lilies, sent by a grieving patient. Through a glass partition in front of the reception desk, two women could be seen in the adjoining office, surrounded by stacks of files.

"There are so many patients to be referred," said Mrs. Tanaka with a sigh. "And all those outstanding bills. I had no idea things would be so chaotic. I always let Henry take care of everything. And now that he's gone…" She sank tiredly onto the couch. "I take it you know about my husband and that—that woman."

David nodded. "Did you?"

"Yes. I mean, I didn't know her name. But I knew there had to be someone. Funny, isn't it? How they say the wife is always the last to know." She gazed at the two women behind the glass partition. "I'm sure *they* knew about her. And people at the hospital, they must have known, as well. I was the only one who didn't. The *stupid* wife." She looked up. "You said you'd tell me about this woman. Ann Richter. What do you know about her?"

"I worked with her," Kate began.

"Did you?" Mrs. Tanaka shifted her gaze to Kate. "I never even met her. What was she like? Was she pretty?"

Kate hesitated, knowing instinctively that the other woman was only searching for more information with which to torture herself. Mari Tanaka seemed consumed by some bizarre need for self-punishment. "Ann was...attractive, I suppose," she said.

"Intelligent?"

Kate nodded. "She was a good nurse."

"So was I." Mrs. Tanaka bit her lip and looked away. "She was a blonde, I hear. Henry liked blondes. Isn't that ironic? He liked the one thing I couldn't be." She glanced at David with sudden feminine hostility. "And I suppose *you* like Oriental women."

"A beautiful woman is a beautiful woman," he replied, unruffled. "I don't discriminate."

She blinked back a veil of tears. "Henry did."

"Have there been other women?" Kate asked gently.

"I suppose." She shrugged. "He was a man, wasn't he?"

"Did you ever hear the name Ellen O'Brien?"

"Did she have some...connection with my husband?"

"We were hoping you could tell us."

Mrs. Tanaka shook her head. "He never mentioned any names. But then, I never asked any questions."

Kate frowned. "Why not?"

"I didn't want him to lie to me." Somehow, by the way she said it, it made perfect sense.

"Have the police told you there's a suspect?" David asked.

"You mean Charles Decker?" Mrs. Tanaka's gaze shifted back to David. "Sergeant Brophy came to see me yesterday afternoon. He showed me the man's photograph."

"Did you recognize the face?"

"I never saw the man, Mr. Ransom. I didn't even know his name. All I knew was that my husband was attacked by some psychotic five years ago. And that the stupid police let the man go the very next day."

"But your husband refused to press charges," said David.

"He what?"

"That's why Decker was released so quickly. It seems your husband wanted the matter dropped."

"He never told me that."

"What did he tell you?"

"Almost nothing. But there were lots of things we never talked about. That's how we managed to stay together all these years. By not talking about certain things. It was almost an agreement. He didn't ask how I spent the money. I didn't ask about his women."

"Then you don't know anything more about Decker?"

"No. But maybe Peggy can help you."

"Peggy?"

She nodded toward the office. "Our receptionist. She was here when it happened."

Peggy was a blond, fortyish Amazon wearing white stretch pants.

Though invited to sit, she preferred to stand. Or maybe she simply preferred not to occupy the same couch as Mari Tanaka.

"Remember the man?" Peggy repeated. "I'll never forget him. I was cleaning up one of the exam rooms when I heard all this yelling. I came right out and that psychotic was here, in the waiting room. He had his hands around Henry's—the doctor's—neck and he kept screaming at him."

"You mean cursing him?"

"No, not cursing. He said something like 'What did you do with her?'"

"Those were his words? You're sure?"

"Pretty sure."

"And who was this 'her' he was referring to? One of the patients?"

"Yes. And the doctor felt just awful about that case. She was such a nice woman, and to have both her and the baby die. Well..."

"What was her name?"

"Jenny... Let me think. Jenny something. Brook. I think that was it. Jennifer Brook."

"What did you do after you saw the doctor being attacked?"

"Well, I pulled the man away, of course. What do you think I did? He was holding on tight, but I got him off. Women aren't completely helpless, you know."

"Yes, I'm quite aware of that."

"Anyway, he sort of collapsed then."

"The doctor?"

"No, the man. He crumpled in this little heap over there, by the coffee table and he just sat there, crying. He was still there when the police arrived. A few days later, we heard he'd shot himself. In the mouth." She paused and stared at the floor, as though seeing some ghostlike remnant of the man, still sitting there. "It's weird, but I couldn't help feeling sorry for him. He was crying like a baby. I think even Henry felt sorry...."

"Mrs. Tanaka?" The other clerk poked her head into the waiting room. "You have a phone call. It's your accountant. I'll transfer it to the back office."

Mrs. Tanaka rose. "There's really nothing more we can tell you," she said. "And we do have to get back to work." She shot Peggy a meaningful glance. Then, with only the barest nod of goodbye, she walked sleekly out of the waiting room.

"Two weeks' notice," Peggy muttered sullenly. "That's what she gave us. And then she expects us to get the whole damn office in order. No wonder Henry didn't want that witch hanging around." She turned to go back to her desk.

"Peggy?" asked Kate. "Just one more question, if you don't mind. When your patients die, how long do you keep the medical records?"

"Five years. Longer if it's an obstetrical death. You know, in case some malpractice suit gets filed."

"Then you still have Jenny Brook's chart?"

"I'm sure we do." She went into the office and pulled open the filing cabinet. She went through the B drawer twice. Then she checked the J's. In frustration, she slammed the drawer closed. "I can't understand it. It should be here."

David and Kate glanced at each other. "It's missing?" said Kate.

"Well, it's not here. And I'm very careful about these things. Let me tell you, I do not run a sloppy office." She turned and glared at the other clerk as though expecting a dissenting opinion. There was none.

"What are you saying?" said David. "That someone's removed it?"

"He must have," replied Peggy. "But I can't see why he would. It's barely been five years."

"Why *who* would?"

Peggy looked at him as if he was dim-witted. "Dr. Tanaka, of course."

"JENNIFER BROOK," said the hospital records clerk in a flat voice as she typed the name into the computer. "Is that with or without an *e* at the end?"

"I don't know," answered Kate.

"Middle initial?"

"I don't know."

"Date of birth?"

Kate and David looked at each other. "We don't know," replied Kate.

The clerk turned and peered at them over her horn-rimmed glasses. "I don't suppose you'd know the medical-record number?" she asked in a weary monotone.

They shook their heads.

"That's what I was afraid of." The clerk swiveled back to her terminal and punched in another command. After a few seconds, two names appeared on the screen, a Brooke and a Brook, both with the first name Jennifer. "Is it one of these?" she questioned.

A glance at the dates of birth told them one was fifty-seven years old, the other fifteen.

"No," said Kate.

"It figures." The clerk sighed and cleared the screen. "Dr. Chesne," she continued with excruciating patience, "why, exactly, do you need this particular record?"

"It's a research project," Kate said. "Dr. Jones and I—"

"Dr. Jones?" The clerk looked at David. "I don't remember a Dr. Jones on our staff."

Kate said quickly, "He's with the University—"

"Of Arizona," David finished with a smile.

"It's all been cleared through Avery's office. It's a paper on maternal death and—"

"Death?" The clerk blinked. "You mean this patient is deceased?"

"Yes."

"Well, no wonder. We keep those files in a totally different place." From her tone, their other file room might have been on Mars. She rose reluctantly from her chair. "This will take a while. You'll have to wait." Turning, she headed at a snail's pace toward a back door and vanished into what was no doubt the room for deceased persons' files.

"Why do I get the feeling we'll never see her again?" muttered David.

Kate sagged weakly against the counter. "Just be glad she didn't ask for your credentials. I could get in big trouble for this, you know. Showing hospital records to the enemy."

"Who, me?"

"You're a lawyer, aren't you?"

"I'm just poor old Dr. Jones from Arizona." He turned and glanced around the room. At a corner table, a doctor was yawning as he turned a page. An obviously bored clerk wheeled a cart up the aisle, collecting charts and slapping them onto an already precarious stack. "Lively place," he remarked. "When does the dancing start?"

They both turned at the sound of footsteps. The clerk with the horn-rimmed glasses reappeared, empty-handed.

"The chart's not there," she announced.

Kate and David stared at her in stunned silence.

"What do you mean, it's not there?" asked Kate.

"It should be. But it's not."

"Was it released from the hospital?" David snapped.

The clerk looked aridly over her glasses. "We don't release originals, Dr. Jones. People always lose them."

"Oh. Well, of course."

The clerk sank down in front of the computer and typed in a command. "See? There's the listing. It's supposed to be in the file room. All I can say is it must've been misplaced." She added, under her breath, "Which means we'll probably never see it again." She was about to clear the screen when David stopped her.

"Wait. What's that notation there?" he asked, pointing to a cryptic code.

"That's a chart copy request."

"You mean someone requested a copy?"

"Yes," the clerk sighed wearily. "That is what it means, Doctor."

"Who asked for it?"

She shifted the cursor and punched another button. A name and address appeared magically on the screen. "Joseph Kahanu, Attorney at Law, Alakea Street. Date of request: March 2."

David frowned. "That's only a month ago."

"Yes, Doctor, I do believe it is."

"An attorney. Why the hell would he be interested in a death that happened five years ago?"

The clerk turned and looked at him dryly over her horn-rimmed glasses. "You tell me."

THE PAINT IN THE HALL was chipping and thousands of footsteps had worn a path down the center of the threadbare carpet. Outside the office hung a sign:

Joseph Kahanu, Attorney at Law
Specialist in Divorce, Child Custody, Wills, Accidents, Insurance, Drunk Driving, and Personal Injury

"Great address," whispered David. "Rats must outnumber the clients." He knocked on the door.

It was answered by a huge Hawaiian man dressed in an ill-fitting suit. "You're David Ransom?" he asked gruffly.

David nodded. "And this is Dr. Chesne."

The man's silent gaze shifted for a moment to Kate's face. Then he stepped aside and gestured sullenly toward a pair of rickety chairs. "Yeah, come in."

The office was suffocating. A table fan creaked back and forth, churning the heat. A half-open window, opaque with dirt, looked out over an alley. In one glance, Kate recognized all the signs of a struggling law practice: the ancient typewriter, the cardboard boxes stuffed with client files, the secondhand furniture. There was scarcely enough room for the lone desk. Kahanu looked unbearably hot in his suit jacket; he'd probably pulled it on at the last minute, just for the benefit of his visitors.

"I haven't called the police yet," said Kahanu, settling into an unreliable-looking swivel chair.

"Why not?" asked David.

"I don't know how you run *your* practice, but I make it a point not to squeal on my clients."

"You're aware Decker's wanted for murder."

Kahanu shook his head. "It's a mistake."

"Did Decker tell you that?"

"I haven't been able to reach him."

"Maybe it's time the police found him for you."

"Look," Kahanu shot back. "We both know I'm not in your league, Ransom. I hear you got some big-shot office over on Bishop Street. Couple of dozen lapdog associates. Probably spend your weekends on the golf course, cozying up to some judge or other. Me?" He waved around at his office and laughed. "I got just a few clients. Most times they don't even remember to pay me. But they're my clients. And I don't like to go against 'em.''

"You know two people have been murdered."

"They got no proof he did it."

"The police say they do. They say Charlie Decker's a dangerous man. A sick man. He needs help.''

"That what they call a jail cell these days? Help?'' Disgusted, he fished out a handkerchief and mopped his brow, as though buying time to think. "Guess I got no choice now," he muttered. "One way or the other, police'll be banging on my door.'' Slowly he folded the handkerchief and tucked it back in his pocket. Then, reaching into his drawer, he pulled out a folder and tossed it on the battered desk. "There's the copy you asked for. Seems you're not the only who one wants it.''

David frowned as he reached for the folder. "Has someone else asked for it?''

"No. But someone broke into my office.''

David looked up sharply. "When?''

"Last week. Tore apart all my files. Didn't steal anything, and I even had fifty bucks in the cash box. I couldn't figure it out at the time. But this morning, after you told me about those missing records, I got to thinking. Wondering if that file's what he was after.''

"But he didn't get it.''

"The night he broke in, I had the papers at home.''

"Is this your only copy?''

"No. I ran off a few just now. Just to be safe.''

"May I take a look?'' Kate asked.

David hesitated, then handed her the chart. "You're the doctor. Go ahead.''

She stared for a moment at the name on the cover: Jennifer Brook. Then, flipping it open, she began to read.

Recorded on the first few pages was a routine obstetrical admission. The patient, a healthy twenty-eight-year-old woman at thirty-six weeks of pregnancy, had entered Mid Pac Hospital in the early stages of labor. The initial history and physical exam, performed by Dr. Tanaka, were unremarkable. The fetal heart tones were normal, as were all the blood tests. Kate turned to the delivery-room record.

Here things began to go wrong. Terribly wrong. The nurse's painstakingly neat handwriting broadened into a frantic scrawl. The entries became terse, erratic. A young woman's death was distilled down to a few coldly clinical phrases.

Generalized seizures... No response to Valium and Dilantin... Stat page to E.R. for assistance... Respirations now irregular... Respirations ceased... No pulse... Cardiac massage started... Fetal heart

tones audible but slowing... Still no pulse... Dr. Vaughn from E.R. to assist with stat C-section...
Live infant...

The record became a short series of blotted-out sentences, totally unreadable.
On the next page was the last entry, written in a calm hand.

Resuscitation stopped. Patient pronounced dead at 01:30.

"She died of a cerebral hemorrhage," Kahanu said. "She was only twenty-eight."
"And the baby?" Kate asked.
"A girl. She died an hour after the mother."
"Kate," David murmured, nudging her arm. "Look at the bottom of the page. The names of the personnel in attendance."
Kate's gaze dropped to the three names. As she took them in one by one, her hands went icy.

Henry Tanaka, M.D.
Ann Richter, RN
Ellen O'Brien, RN

"They left out a name," Kate pointed out. She looked up. "There was a Dr. Vaughn, from the E.R. He might be able to tell us—"
"He can't," said Kahanu. "You see, Dr. Vaughn had an accident a short time after Jennifer Brook died. His car was hit head-on."
"You mean he's dead?"
Kahanu nodded. "They're all dead."
The chart slid from her frozen fingers onto the desk. There was something dangerous about this document, something evil. She stared down, unwilling to touch it, for fear the contagion would rub off.
Kahanu turned his troubled gaze to the window. "Four weeks ago Charlie Decker came to my office. Who knows why he chose me? Maybe I was convenient. Maybe he couldn't afford anyone else. He wanted a legal opinion about a possible malpractice suit."
"On this case?" said David. "But Jenny Brook died five years ago. And Decker wasn't even a relative. You know as well as I do the lawsuit would've been tossed right out."
"He paid for my services, Mr. Ransom. In cash."
In cash. Those were magic words for a lawyer who was barely surviving.
"I did what he asked. I subpoenaed the chart for him. I contacted the doctor and the two nurses who'd cared for Jenny Brook. But they never answered my letters."

"They didn't live long enough," explained David. "Decker got to them first."

"Why should he?"

"Vengeance. They killed the woman he loved. So he killed them."

"My client didn't kill anyone."

"Your client had the motive, Kahanu. And you provided him with their names and addresses."

"You've never met Decker. I have. And he's not a violent man."

"You'd be surprised how ordinary a killer can seem. I used to face them in court—"

"And I *defend* them! I take on the scum no one else'll touch. I *know* a killer when I see one. There's something different about them, about their eyes. Something's missing. I don't know what it is. A soul, maybe. I tell you, Charlie Decker wasn't like that."

Kate leaned forward. "What was he like, Mr. Kahanu?" she asked quietly.

The Hawaiian paused, his gaze wandering out the dirty window to the alley below. "He was—he was real... ordinary. Not tall, but not too short, either. Mostly skin and bones, like he wasn't eating right. I felt sorry for him. He looked like a man who's had his insides kicked out. He didn't say much. But he wrote things down for me. I think it hurt him to use his voice. He's got something wrong with his throat and he couldn't talk much louder than a whisper. He was sitting right there in that chair where you are now, Dr. Chesne. Said he didn't have much money. Then he took out his wallet and counted out these twenty-dollar bills, one at a time. I could see, just by the way he handled them, real slow and careful, that it was everything he had." Kahanu shook his head. "I still don't see why he even bothered, you know? The woman's dead. The baby's dead. All this digging around in the past, it won't bring'em back."

"Do you know where to find him?" asked David.

"He has a P.O. box," said Kahanu. "I already checked. He hasn't picked up his mail in three days."

"Do you have his address? Phone number?"

"Never gave me one. Look, I don't know where he is. I'll leave it to the police to find him. That's their job, isn't it?" He pushed away from the desk. "That's all I know. If you want anything else, you'll have to get it from Decker."

"Who happens to be missing," said David.

To which Kahanu added darkly: "Or dead."

Chapter Ten

In his forty-eight years as cemetery groundskeeper, Ben Hoomalu had seen his share of peculiar happenings. His friends liked to say it was because he was tramping around dead people all day, but in fact it wasn't the dead who caused all the mischief but the living: the randy teenagers groping in the darkness among the gravestones; the widow scrawling obscenities on her husband's nice new marble tombstone; the old man caught trying to bury his beloved poodle next to his beloved wife. Strange goings-on—that's what a fellow saw around cemeteries.

And now here was that car, back again.

Every day for the past week Ben had seen the same gray Ford with the darkly tinted windows drive through the gates. Sometimes it'd show up early in the morning, other times late in the afternoon. It would park over by the Arch of Eternal Comfort and just sit there for an hour or two. The driver never got out; that was odd, too. If a person came all this way to visit a loved one, wouldn't you think he'd at least get out and take a look at the grave?

There was no figuring out some folks.

Ben picked up the hedge clippers and started trimming the hibiscus bush. He liked hearing the clack, clack of the blades in the afternoon stillness. He looked up as a beat-up old Chevy drove through the gate and parked. A spindly man emerged from the car and waved at Ben. Smiling, Ben waved back. The man was carrying a bunch of daisies as he headed toward the woman's grave. Ben paused and watched the man go about his ritual. First, he gathered up the wilted flowers left behind on his previous visit and meticulously collected all the dead leaves and twigs. Then, after laying his new offering beside the stone, he settled reverentially on the grass. Ben knew the man would sit there a long time; he always did. Every visit was exactly the same. That was part of the comfort.

By the time the man got up to leave, Ben had finished with the hibiscus and was working on the bougainvillea. He watched the man walk slowly back to the car and felt a twinge of sadness as the old Chevy wound along the road toward the cemetery gates. He didn't even know the man's name; he only knew that whoever lay buried in that grave was still very much loved. He dropped his hedge clippers and wandered over to where the fresh daisies lay bundled together in a pink ribbon. There was still a dent in the grass where the man had knelt.

The purr of another car starting up caught his attention and he saw the gray Ford pull away from the curb and slowly follow the Chevy out the cemetery gates.

And what did *that* mean? Funny goings-on, all right.

He looked down at the name on the stone: Jennifer Brook, 28 years old. Already a dead leaf had blown onto the grave and now lay trembling in the wind. He shook his head.

Such a young woman. Such a shame.

"YOU GOT A HAM ON RYE, hold the mayo, and a call on line four," said Sergeant Brophy, dropping a brown bag on the desk.

Pokie, faced with the choice between a sandwich and a blinking telephone, reached for the sandwich. After all, a man had to set his priorities, and he figured a growling stomach ranked somewhere near the top of anyone's priority list. He nodded at the phone. "Who's calling?"

"Ransom."

"Not again."

"He's demanding we open a file on the O'Brien case."

"Why the hell's he keep bugging us about that case, anyway?"

"I think he's got a thing for that—that—" Brophy's face suddenly screwed up as he teetered on the brink of a sneeze and he whipped out a handkerchief just in time to muffle the explosion "—doctor lady. You know. Hearts 'n' flowers."

"Davy?" Pokie laughed out a clump of ham sandwich. "Men like Davy don't go for hearts 'n' flowers. Think they're too damn smart for all that romantic crap."

"No man's that smart," Brophy said glumly.

There was a knock on the door and a uniformed officer poked his head into the office. "Lieutenant? You got a summons from on high."

"Chief?"

"He's stuck with an office full of reporters. They're askin' about that missing Sasaki girl. Wants ya up there like ten minutes ago."

Pokie looked down regretfully at his sandwich. Unfortunately, on that cosmic list of priorities, a summons from the chief ranked somewhere on a par with breathing. Sighing, he left the sandwich on his desk and pulled on his jacket.

"What about Ransom?" reminded Brophy, nodding at the blinking telephone.

"Tell him I'll call him back."

"When?"

"Next year," Pokie grunted as he headed for the door. He added under his breath, "If he's lucky."

DAVID MUTTERED AN OATH as he slid into the driver's seat and slammed the car door. "We just got the brush-off."

Kate stared at him. "But they've seen Jenny Brook's file. They've talked to Kahanu—"

"They say there's not enough evidence to open a murder investigation. As far as they're concerned, Ellen O'Brien died of malpractice. End of subject."

"Then we're on our own."

"Wrong. We're pulling out." Suddenly agitated, he started the engine and drove away from the curb. "Things are getting too dangerous."

"They've been dangerous from the start. Why are you getting cold feet now?"

"Okay, I admit it. Up till now I wasn't sure I believed you—"

"You thought I was *lying*?"

"There was always this—this nagging doubt in the back of my mind. But now we're hearing about stolen hospital charts. People breaking into lawyer's offices. There's something weird going on here, Kate. This isn't the work of a raging psychopath. It's too reasoned. Too methodical." He frowned at the road ahead. "And it all has to do with Jenny Brook. There's something dangerous about her hospital chart, something our killer wants to keep hidden."

"But we've gone over that thing a dozen times, David! It's just a medical record."

"Then we're overlooking something. And I'm counting on Charlie Decker to tell us what it is. I say we sit tight and wait for the police to find him."

Charlie Decker, she thought. Her doom or her salvation? She stared out at the late-afternoon traffic and tried to remember his face. Up till now, the image had been jelled in fear; every time she'd thought of his face in the mirror, she'd felt an automatic surge of terror. Now she tried to ignore the sweat forming on her palms, the racing of her pulse. She forced herself to think of that face with its tired, hollow eyes. Killer's eyes? She didn't know anymore. She looked down at Jenny Brook's chart, lying on her lap. Did it contain some vital clue to Decker's madness?

"I'll corner Pokie tomorrow," said David, weaving impatiently through traffic. "See if I can't change his mind about the O'Brien case."

"And if you can't convince him?"

"I'm very convincing."

"He'll want more evidence."

"Then let *him* find it. I think we've gone as far as we can on this. It's time for us to back off."

"I can't, David. I have a career at stake—"

"What about your life?"

"My career is my life."

"There's one helluva big difference."

She turned away. "I can't really expect you to understand. It's not your fight."

But he did understand. And it worried him, that note of stubbornness in her voice. She reminded him of one of those ancient warriors who'd rather fall on their swords than accept defeat.

"You're wrong," he told her. "About it not being my fight."

"You don't have anything at stake."

"Don't forget I pulled out of the case—a potentially lucrative case, I might add."

"Oh. Well, I'm sorry I cost you such a nice fee."

"You think I care about the money? I don't give a damn about the money. It's my reputation I put on the line. And all because I happened to believe that crazy story of yours. Murder on the operating table! I'm going to look like a fool if it can't be proved. So don't tell me I have nothing to lose!" By now he was yelling. He couldn't help it. She could accuse him of any number of things and he wouldn't bat an eye. But accusing him of not giving a damn was something he couldn't stand.

Gripping the steering wheel, he forced his gaze back to the road. "The worst part is," he muttered, "I'm a lousy liar. And I think the O'Briens can tell."

"You mean you didn't tell them the truth?"

"That I think their daughter was murdered? Hell, no. I took the easy way out. I told them I had a conflict of interest. A nice, noncommittal excuse. I figured they couldn't get too upset since I'm referring the case to a good firm."

"You're doing *what*?" She stared at him.

"I was their attorney, Kate. I have to protect their interests."

"Naturally."

"This hasn't been easy, you know," he went on. "I don't like to shortchange my clients. Any of them. They're dealing with enough tragedy in their lives. The least I can do is see they get a decent shot at justice. It bothers the hell out of me when I can't deliver what I promise. You understand that, don't you?"

"Yes. I understand perfectly well."

He knew by the hurt tone of her voice that she really didn't. And that annoyed him because he thought she should understand.

She sat motionless as he pulled into the driveway. He parked the car and turned off the engine but she made no move to get out. They lingered there in the shadowy heat of the garage as the silence between them stretched into minutes. When she finally spoke again, it was in the flat tones of a stranger.

"I've put you in a compromising position, haven't I?"

His answer was a curt nod.

"I'm sorry."

"Look, forget about it, okay?" He got out and opened her door. She was still sitting there, rigid as a statue. "Well?" he asked. "Are you coming inside?"

"Only to pack."

He felt an odd little thump of dismay in his chest, which he tried to ignore. "You're leaving?"

"I appreciate what you've done for me," she answered tightly. "You went out on a limb and you didn't have to. Maybe, at the start, we needed each other. But it's obvious this...arrangement is no longer in your best interests. Or mine, for that matter."

"I see," he said, though he didn't. In fact he thought she was acting childishly. "And just where do you plan to go?"

"I'll stay with friends."

"Oh, great. Spread the danger to them."

"Then I'll check into a hotel."

"Your purse was stolen, remember? You don't have any money, credit cards." He paused for dramatic effect. "No nothing."

"Not at the moment, but—"

"Or are you planning to ask me for a loan?"

"I don't need your help," she snapped. "I've never needed any man's help!"

He briefly considered the old-fashioned method of brute force, but knowing her sense of pride, he didn't think it would work. So he simply retorted, "Suit yourself," and stalked off to the house.

While she was packing, he paced back and forth in the kitchen, trying to ignore his growing sense of uneasiness. He grabbed a carton of milk out of the refrigerator and took a gulp straight from the container. *I should order her to stay,* he thought. *Yes, that's exactly what I should do.* He shoved the milk back in the refrigerator, slammed the door and stormed toward her bedroom.

But just as he got there, he pulled himself up short. Bad idea. He knew exactly how she'd react if he started shouting out orders. You just didn't push a woman like Kate Chesne around. Not if you were smart.

He hulked in the doorway and watched as she folded a dress and tucked it neatly into a suitcase. The fading daylight was glimmering behind her in the window. She swept back a stray lock of hair and a lead weight seemed to lodge in his throat as he glimpsed the bruised cheek. It reminded him how vulnerable she really was. Despite her pride and her so-called independence, she was really just a woman. And like any woman, she could be hurt.

She noticed him in the doorway and she paused, nightgown in hand. "I'm almost finished," she said, matter-of-factly tossing the nightgown on top of the other clothes. He couldn't help glancing twice at the mound of peach-colored silk. He felt that lead weight drop into his belly. "Have you called a cab yet?" she asked, turning back to the dresser.

"No, I haven't."

"Well, I shouldn't be a minute. Could you call one now?"

"I'm not going to."

She turned and frowned at him. "What?"

"I said I'm not going to call a cab."

His announcement seemed to leave her momentarily stunned. "Fine," she said calmly. "Then I'll call one myself." She started for the door. But as she walked past him, he caught her by the arm.

"Kate, don't." He pulled her around to face him. "I think you should stay."

"Why?"

"Because it's not safe out there."

"The world's never been safe. I've managed."

"Oh, yeah. What a tough broad you are. And what happens when Decker catches up?"

She yanked her arm away. "Don't you have better things to worry about?"

"Like what?"

"Your sense of ethics? After all, I wouldn't want to ruin your precious reputation."

"I can take care of my own reputation, thank you."

She threw her head back and glared straight up at him. "Then maybe it's time I took better care of mine!"

They were standing so close he could almost feel the heat mounting in waves between them. What happened next was as unexpected as a case of spontaneous combustion. Their gazes locked. Her eyes suddenly went wide with surprise. And need. Despite all her false bravado, he could see it brimming there in those deep, green pools.

"What the hell," he growled, his voice rough with desire. "I think both our reputations are already shot."

And then he gave in to the impulse that had been battering at his willpower all day. He hauled her close into his arms and kissed her. It was a long and savagely hungry kiss. She gave a weak murmur of protest, just before she sagged backward against the doorway. Almost immediately he felt her respond, her body molding itself against his. It was a perfect fit. Absolutely perfect. Her arms twined around his neck and as he urged her lips apart with his, the kiss became desperately urgent. Her moan sent a sweet agony of desire knifing through to his belly.

The same sweet fire was now engulfing Kate. She felt him fumbling for the buttons of her dress but his fingers seemed as clumsy as a teenager's exploring the unfamiliar territory of a woman's body. With a groan of frustration, he tugged the dress off her shoulders; it seemed to fall in slow motion, hissing down her hips to the floor. The lace bra magically melted away and his hand closed around her breast, branding her flesh with his fingers. Under his pleasuring stroke, her nipple hardened instantly and they both knew that this time there would be no retreat; only surrender.

Already she was groping at his shirt, her breath coming in hot, frantic little whimpers as she tried to work the buttons free. Damn. Damn. Now they were both yanking at the shirt. Together they stripped it off his shoulders and she immediately sought his chest, burying her fingers in the bristling gold hairs.

By the time they'd stumbled down the hall and into the evening glow of his bedroom, his shoes and socks were tossed to the four corners of the room, his pants were unzipped and his arousal was plainly evident.

The bed creaked in protest as he fell on top of her, his hands trapping her face beneath his. There were no preludes, no formalities. They couldn't wait. With his mouth covering hers and his hands buried in her hair, he thrust into her, so deeply that she cried out against his lips.

He froze, his whole body suddenly tense. "Did I hurt you?" he whispered.

"No...oh, no...."

It took only one look at her face to tell him it wasn't pain that had made her cry out, but pleasure—in him, in what he was doing to her. She tried to move; he held her still, his face taut as he struggled for control. Somehow, she'd always known he would claim her. Even when the voice of common sense had told her it was impossible, she'd known he would be the one.

She couldn't wait. She was moving in spite of him, matching agony for agony.

He let her take him to the very brink and then, when he knew it was inevitable, he surrendered himself to the fall. In a frenzy he took control and plunged them both over the cliff.

The drop was dizzying.

The landing left them weak and exhausted. An eternity passed, filled with the sounds of their breathing. Sweat trickled over his back and onto her naked belly. Outside, the waves roared against the seawall.

"Now I know what it's like to be devoured," she whispered as the glow of sunset faded in the window.

"Is that what I did?"

She sighed. "Completely."

He chuckled and his mouth glided warmly to her earlobe. "No, I think there's still something here to eat."

She closed her eyes, surrendering to the lovely ripples of pleasure his mouth inspired. "I never dreamed you'd be like this."

"Like what?"

"So...consuming."

"Just what did you expect?"

"Ice." She laughed. "Was I ever wrong!"

He took a strand of her hair and watched it drift like a cloud of silk through his fingers. "I guess I can seem pretty icy. It runs in my family. My father's side, anyway. Stern old New England stock. It must've been terrifying to face him in court."

"He was a lawyer, too?"

"Circuit-court judge. He died four years ago. Keeled over on the bench, right in the middle of sentencing. Just the way he would've wanted to go." He smiled. "Run-'em-in Ransom, they used to call him."

"Oh. The law-and-order type?"

"Absolutely. Unlike my mother, who thrives on anarchy."

She giggled. "It must have been an explosive combination."

"Oh, it was." He stroked his finger across her lips. "Almost as explosive as we are. I never did figure out their relationship. It didn't make sense to me. But you could almost see the chemistry working between them. The sparks. That's what I remember about my parents, all those sparks, flying around the house."

"So they were happy?"

"Oh, yeah. Exhausted, maybe. Frustrated, a lot. But they were definitely happy."

Twilight glowed dimly through the window. In silent awe, he ran his hand along the peaks and valleys of her body, a slow and leisurely exploration that left her skin tingling. "You're beautiful," he whispered. "I never thought..."

"What?"

"That I'd end up in bed with a lawyer-hating doctor. Talk about strange bedfellows."

She laughed softly. "And I feel like a mouse cozying up to the cat."

"Does that mean you're still afraid of me?"

"A little. A lot."

"Why?"

"I can't quite get over the feeling you're the enemy."

"If I'm the enemy," he said, his lips grazing her ear, "then I think one of us has just surrendered."

"Is this all you ever think about, counselor?"

"Since I met you, it is."

"And before you met me?"

"Life was very, very dull."

"I find that hard to believe."

"I'm not saying I've been celibate. But I'm a careful man. Maybe too careful. I find it hard to...get close to people."

"You seem to be doing a pretty good job tonight."

"I mean, emotionally close. It's just the way I am. Too many things can go wrong and I'm not very good at dealing with them."

By the evening glow, she studied his face hovering just above hers. "What did go wrong with your marriage, David?"

"Oh. My marriage." He rolled over on his back and sighed. "Nothing, really. Nothing I can put my finger on. I guess that just goes to show you what an insensitive clod I am. Linda used to complain I was lousy at expressing my feelings. That I was cold, just like my father. I told her that was a lot of bull. Now I think she was right."

"And I think it's just an act of yours. An icy mask you like to hide behind." She rolled onto her side, to look at him. "People show affection in different ways."

"Since when did you go into psychiatry?"

"Since I got involved with a very complex man."

Gently he tucked a strand of hair behind her ear. His gaze lingered on her cheek. "That bruise of yours is already fading. Every time I see it I get angry."

"You told me once it turned you on."

"What it really does is make me feel protective. Must be some ancient male instinct. From the days when we had to keep the other cavemen from roughing up our personal property."

"Oh, my. We're talking *that* ancient, are we?"

"As ancient as—" his hand slid possessively down the curve of her hip "—this."

"I'm not so sure 'protective' is what you're feeling right now," she murmured.

"You're right. It's not." He laughed and gave her an affectionate pat on the rump. "What I'm feeling is starved—for food. Why don't we heat up some of Mrs. Feldman's spaghetti sauce. Open a bottle of wine. And then..." He drew her toward him and his skin seemed to sear right into hers.

"And then?" she whispered.

"And then..." His lips lingered maddeningly close. "I'll do to you what lawyers have been doing to doctors for decades."

"David!" she squealed.

"Hey, just kidding!" He threw his arms up in self-defense as she swung at him. "But I think you get the general idea." He pulled her out of bed and into his arms. "Come on. And stop looking so luscious, or we'll never get out of the room. They'll find us sprawled on the bed, starved to death."

She gave him a slow, naughty look. "Oh," she murmured, "but what a way to go."

IT WAS THE SOUND of the waves slapping the seawall that finally tugged Kate awake. Drowsily she reached out for David but her hand met only an empty pillow, warmed by the morning sun. She opened her eyes and felt a sharp sense of abandonment when she discovered that she was alone in the wide, rumpled bed.

"David?" she called out. There was no answer. The house was achingly silent.

She swung her legs around and sat up on the side of the bed. Naked and dazed, she peered slowly around the sunlit room and felt the color rise in her cheeks as the night's events came back to her. The bottle of wine. The wicked whispers. The hopelessly twisted sheets. She noticed that the clothes they'd both tossed aside so recklessly had all been picked up from the floor. His pants were hanging on the closet door; her bra and underwear were now draped neatly across a chair. It made her flush even hotter to think of him gathering up all her intimate apparel. Giggling, she hugged the sheets and found they still bore his scent. But where was he?

"David?"

She rose and went into the bathroom; it was empty. A damp towel hung on the rack. Next she wandered out into the living room and marveled at the morning sun, slanting in gloriously through the windows. The empty wine bottle was still sitting on the coffee table, mute evidence of the night's intoxication. She still felt intoxicated. She poked her head into the kitchen; he wasn't there, either. Back in the living room, she paused in that brilliant flood of sunlight and called out his name. The whole house seemed to echo with loneliness.

Her sense of desolation grew as she headed back up the hall, searching, opening doors, peeking into rooms. She had the strange feeling that she was exploring an abandoned house, that this wasn't the home of a living, breathing human being, but a shell, a cave. An inexplicable impulse sent her to his closet where she stood and touched each one of those forbidding suits hanging inside. It brought him no closer to her. Back in the hallway, she opened the door to a book-lined office. The furniture was oak, the lamps brass, and everything was as neat as a pin. A room without a soul.

Kate moved down the hall, to the very last room. She was prying, she knew it. But she missed him and she longed for some palpable clue to his personality. As she opened the door, stale air puffed out, carrying the smell of a space shut away too long from the rest of the world. She saw it was a bedroom. A child's room.

A mobile of prisms trembled near the window, scattering tiny rainbows around the room. She stood there, transfixed, watching the lights dance across the wallpaper with its blue Swedish horses, across the sadly gaping toy shelves, across the tiny bed with the flowered coverlet. Almost against her will, she felt herself moving forward, as though some small, invisible hand were tugging her inside. Then, just as suddenly, the hand was gone and she was alone, so alone, in a room that ached with emptiness.

For a long time she stood there among the dancing rainbows, ashamed that she had disturbed the sanctity of this room. At last she wandered over to the dresser where a stack of books lay awaiting their owner's return. She opened one of the covers and stared at the name on the inside flap. Noah Ransom.

"I'm sorry," she whispered, tears stinging her eyes. "I'm sorry...."

She turned and fled the room, closing the door behind her.

Back in the kitchen, she huddled over a cup of coffee and read and reread the terse note she'd finally discovered, along with a set of keys, on the white-tiled counter.

Catching a ride with Glickman. The car's yours today. See you tonight.

Hardly a lover's note, she thought. No little words of endearment, not even a signature. It was cold and matter-of-fact, just like this kitchen, just like everything else about this house. So that was David. Man of ice, master of a soulless house. They had just shared a night of passionate lovemaking. She'd been swept off her feet. He left impersonal little notes on the kitchen counter.

She had to marvel at how he'd compartmentalized his life. He had walled off his emotions into nice, neat spaces, the way he'd walled off his son's room. But she couldn't do that. Already she missed him. Maybe she even loved him. It was crazy and illogical; and she wasn't used to doing crazy, illogical things.

Suddenly annoyed at herself, she stood up and furiously rinsed her coffee cup in the sink. Dammit, she had more important things to worry about. Her committee hearing was this afternoon; her career hung in the balance. It was a stupid time to be fretting over a man.

She turned and picked up Jenny Brook's hospital chart, which had been lying on the breakfast table. This sad, mysterious document. Slowly she flipped through it, wondering what could possibly be so dangerous about a few pages of medical notes. But something terrible had happened the night Jenny Brook gave birth—something that had reached like a claw through time to destroy every name mentioned on these pages. Mother and child. Doctors and nurses. They were all dead. Only Charlie Decker knew why. And he was a puzzle in himself, a puzzle with pieces that didn't fit.

A maniac, the police had called him. A monster who slashed throats.

A harmless man, Kahanu had said. A lost soul with his insides kicked out.

A man with two faces.

She closed the chart and found herself staring at the back cover. A chart with two sides.

A man with two faces.

She sat up straight, suddenly comprehending. Of course.

Jekyll and Hyde.

"THE MULTIPLE PERSONALITY is a rare phenomenon. But it's well described in psychiatric literature." Susan Santini swiveled around and reached for a book from the shelf behind her. Turning back to her desk, she perused the index for the relevant pages. Her red hair, usually so unruly, was tied back in a neat little knot. On the wall behind her hung an impressive collection of medical and psychiatric degrees, testimony to the fact Susan Santini was more than just Guy's wife; she was also a professional in her own right, and a well-respected one.

"Here it is," she said, leaning forward. "'From Eve to Sybil. A collection of case histories.' It's really a fascinating topic."

"Have you had any cases in your practice?" asked Kate.

"Wish I had. Oh, I thought I had one, when I was working with the courts. But that creep turned out to be just a great actor trying to beat a murder rap. I tell you, he could go from Caspar Milquetoast to Hulk Hogan in the blink of an eye. What a performance!"

"It is possible, though? For a man to have two completely different personalities?"

"The human psyche is made up of so many clashing parts. Call it id versus ego, impulse versus control. Look at violence, for example. Most of us manage to bury our savage tendencies. But some people can't. Who knows why? Childhood abuse? Some abnormality in brain chemistry? Whatever the reason, these people are walking time bombs. Push them too far and they lose all control. The scary part is, they're all around us. But we don't recognize them until something inside them, some inner dam, bursts. And then the violent side shows itself."

"Do you think Charlie Decker could be one of these walking time bombs?"

Susan leaned back in her leather chair and considered the possibility. "That's a hard question, Kate. You say he came from a broken home. And he was arrested for assault and battery five years ago. But there's no lifelong pattern of violence. And the one time he used a gun, he turned it on himself." She looked doubtful. "I suppose, if he had some precipitating stress, some crisis..."

"He did."

"You mean this?" Susan gestured to the copy of Jenny Brook's medical chart.

"The death of his fiancée. The police think it triggered some sort of homicidal rage. That he's been killing the people he thought were responsible."

"It sounds weird, but the most compelling reason for violence does seem to be love. Think of all those crimes of passion. All those jealous spouses. Spurned lovers."

"Love and violence," said Kate. "Two sides of the same coin."

"Exactly." Susan handed the medical record back to Kate. "But I'm just speculating. I'd have to talk to this man Decker before I can pass judgment. Are the police getting close?"

"I don't know. They won't tell me a thing. A lot of this information I had to dig up myself."

"You're kidding. Isn't it their job?"

Kate sighed. "That's the problem. For them it's nothing but a job, another file to be closed."

The intercom buzzed. "Dr. Santini?" said the receptionist. "Your three-o'clock appointment's waiting."

Kate glanced at her watch. "Oh, I'm sorry. I've been keeping you from your patients."

"You know I'm always glad to help out." Susan rose and walked with her to the door. There she touched Kate's arm. "This place you're staying—you're absolutely sure it's safe?"

Kate turned and saw the worry in Susan's eyes. "I think so. Why?"

Susan hesitated. "I hate to frighten you, but I think you ought to know. If you're correct, if Decker is a multiple personality, then you're dealing with a very unstable mind. Someone totally unpredictable. In the blink of an eye, he could change from a man to a monster. So, please, be very, very careful."

Kate's throat went dry. "You—you really think he's that dangerous?"

Susan nodded. "Extremely dangerous."

Chapter Eleven

It looked like a firing squad and she was the one who'd been handed the blindfold.

She was sitting before a long conference table. Arranged in a grim row in front of her were six men and a woman, all physicians, none of them smiling. Though he'd promised to attend, Dr. Clarence Avery, the chief of anesthesia, was not present. The one friendly face in the entire room was Guy Santini's, but he'd been called only as a witness. He was sitting off to the side and he looked every bit as nervous as she felt.

The committee members asked their questions politely but doggedly. They responded to her answers with impassive stares. Though the room was air-conditioned, her cheeks were on fire.

"And you personally examined the EKG, Dr. Chesne?"

"Yes, Dr. Newhouse."

"And then you filed it in the chart."

"That's correct."

"Did you show the tracing to any other physician?"

"No, sir."

"Not even to Dr. Santini?"

She glanced at Guy, who was hunched down in his chair, staring off unhappily. "Screening the EKG was my responsibility, not Dr. Santini's," she said evenly. "He trusted my judgment."

How many times do I have to repeat this story? she asked herself wearily. *How many times do I have to answer the same damn questions?*

"Dr. Santini? Any comment?"

Guy looked up reluctantly. "What Dr. Chesne says is true. I trusted her judgment." He paused, then added emphatically, "I still trust her judgment."

Thank you, Guy, she thought. Their eyes met and he gave her a faint smile.

"Let's return to the events during surgery, Dr. Chesne," continued Dr. Newhouse. "You say you performed routine induction with IV Pentothal...."

The nightmare was relived. Ellen O'Brien's death was dissected as thoroughly as a cadaver on the autopsy table.

When the questions were over, she was allowed a final statement. She delivered it in a quiet voice. "I know my story sounds bizarre. I also know I can't prove any of it—at least, not yet. But I know this much: I gave Ellen O'Brien the very best care I could. The record shows I made a mistake, a terrible one. And my patient died. But did I kill her? I don't think so. I really don't think so...." Her voice trailed off. There was nothing else to say. So she simply murmured, "Thank you." And then she left the room.

It took them twenty minutes to reach a decision. She was called back to her chair. As her gaze moved along the table, she noticed with distinct uneasiness that two new faces had joined the group. George Bettencourt and the hospital attorney were sitting at one end of the table. Bettencourt looked coldly satisfied. She knew, before a word was even spoken, what the decision would be.

Dr. Newhouse, the committee chairman, delivered the verdict. "We know your recall of the case is at odds with the record, Dr. Chesne. But I'm afraid the record is what we must go on. And the record shows, unquestionably, that your care of patient Ellen O'Brien was substandard." Kate winced at the last word, as though the worst insult imaginable had just been hurled at her. Dr. Newhouse sighed and removed his glasses—a tired gesture that seemed to carry all the weight of the world. "You're new to the staff, Dr. Chesne. You've been with us for less than a year. This sort of...mishap, after so short a time on the staff, concerns us very much. We regret this. We really do. But based on what we've heard, we're forced to refer the case to the Disciplinary Committee. They'll decide what action to take in regards to your position here at Mid Pac. Until then—" he glanced at Bettencourt "—we have no objection to the measures already taken by the hospital administration regarding your suspension."

So it's over, she thought. *I was stupid to hope for anything else.*

They allowed her a chance to respond but she'd lost her voice; it was all she could manage to remain calm and dry-eyed in front of these seven people who'd just torn her life apart.

As the committee filed out, she remained in her chair, unable to move or even to raise her head. "I'm sorry, Kate," Guy said softly. He lingered beside her for a moment, as though hunting for something else to say. Then he, too, drifted out of the room.

Her name was called twice before she finally looked up to see Bettencourt and the attorney standing in front of her.

"We think it's time to talk, Dr. Chesne," announced the attorney.

She frowned at them in bewilderment. "Talk? About what?"

"A settlement."

Her back stiffened. "Isn't this a little premature?"

"If anything, it's too late."

"I don't understand."

"A reporter was in my office a few hours ago. It appears the whole case is out in the open. Obviously the O'Briens took their story to the newspapers. I'm afraid you'll be tried—and convicted—in print."

"But the case was filed only last week."

"We have to get this out of the public eye. Now. And the best way to do it is a very fast, very quiet settlement. All we need is your agreement. I plan to start negotiations at around half a million, though we fully expect they'll push for more."

Half a million dollars, she thought. It struck her as obscene, placing a monetary value on a human life. "No," she said.

The attorney blinked. "Excuse me?"

"The evidence is still coming in. By the time this goes to trial, I'm sure I'll be able to prove—"

"It won't go to trial. This case *will* be settled, Doctor. With or without your permission."

Her mouth tightened. "Then I'll pay for my own attorney. One who'll represent me and not the hospital."

The two men glanced at each other. When the attorney spoke again, his tone was distinctly unpleasant. "I don't think you fully understand what it means to go to trial. Dr. Santini will, in all probability, be dropped from the case. Which means *you* will be the principal defendant. *You'll* be the one sweating on that stand. And it'll be *your* name in the newspapers. I know their attorney, David Ransom. I've seen him rip a defendant to shreds in the courtroom. Believe me, you don't want to go through that."

"Mr. Ransom is no longer on the case," she said.

"What?"

"He's withdrawn."

He snorted. "Where on earth did you hear that rumor?"

"He told me."

"Are you saying you talked to him?"

Not to mention went to bed with him, she reflected, flushing. "It happened last week. I went to his office. I told him about the EKGs—"

"Dear God." The attorney turned and threw his pencil in his briefcase. "Well, that's it, folks. We're in big trouble."

"Why?"

"He'll use that crazy story of yours to push for a higher settlement."

"But he believed me! That's why he's withdrawing—"

"He couldn't possibly believe you. I know the man."

I know him too! she wanted to yell.

But there was no point; she'd never be able to convince them. So she simply shook her head. "I won't settle."

The attorney snapped his briefcase shut and turned in frustration to Bettencourt. "George?"

Kate shifted her attention to the chief administrator. Bettencourt was watching her with an utterly smooth expression. No hostility. No anger. Just that quintessential poker player's gaze.

"I'm concerned about your future, Dr. Chesne," he said.

So am I, she felt like snapping back.

"There's a good chance, unfortunately, that the Disciplinary Committee will view your case harshly. If so, they'll probably recommend you be terminated. And that would be a shame, having that on your record. It would make it almost impossible for you to find another job. Anywhere." He paused, to let his words sink in. "That's why I'm offering you this alternative, Doctor. I think it's far preferable to an out-and-out firing."

She stared down at the sheet of paper he was holding out to her. It was a typed resignation, already dated, with a blank space awaiting her signature.

"That's all that'd appear in your file. A resignation. There'd be no damning conclusions from the Disciplinary Committee. No record of termination. Even with this lawsuit, you could probably find another job, though not in this town." He took out a pen and held it out to her. "Why don't you sign it? It really is for the best."

She kept staring at the paper. The whole process was so neat, so efficient. Here was this ready-made document. All it needed was her signature. Her capitulation.

"We're waiting, Dr. Chesne," challenged Bettencourt. "Sign it."

She rose to her feet. She took the resignation sheet. Looking him straight in the eye, she ripped the paper in half. "There's my resignation," she declared. Then she turned and walked out the door.

Only as she stalked away past the administrative suite did it occur to her what she'd just done. She'd burned her bridges. There was no going back now; her only course was to slog it out to the very end.

Halfway down the hall, her footsteps slowed and finally stopped. She wanted to cry but couldn't. She stood there, staring down the corridor, watching the last secretary straggle away toward the elevators. It was five-fifteen and only a janitor remained at the far end of the hall, listlessly shoving a vacuum cleaner across the carpet. He rounded the corner and the sound of the machine faded away, leaving only a heavy stillness. Farther down the hall, a light was shining through the open door of Clarence Avery's office. It didn't surprise her that he was still at work; he often stayed late. But she wondered why he hadn't attended the hearing as he'd promised. Now, more than ever, she needed his support.

She went to the office. Glancing inside, she was disappointed to find only his secretary, tidying up papers on the desk.

The woman glanced up. "Oh. Dr. Chesne."

"Is Dr. Avery still in the hospital?" Kate asked.

"Haven't you heard?"

"Heard what?"

The secretary looked down sadly at the photograph on the desk. "His wife died last night, at the nursing home. He hasn't been in the hospital all day."

Kate felt herself sag against the doorway. "His...wife?"

"Yes. It was all rather unexpected. A heart attack, they think, but— Are you all right?"

"What?"

"Are you all right? You don't look well."

"No, I'm—I'm fine." Kate backed into the hall. "I'm fine," she repeated, walking in a daze toward the elevators. As she rode down to the lobby, a memory came back to her, an image of shattered glass sparkling at the feet of Clarence Avery.

She needs to be put to sleep.... It's so much better if I do it, if I'm there to say goodbye. Don't you think?

The elevator doors hissed open. The instant she stepped out into the bright lights of the lobby, a sudden impulse seized her, the need to flee, to find safety. To find David. She walked outside into the parking lot and the urge became compelling. She couldn't wait; she had to see him now. If she hurried, she might catch him at his office.

Just the thought of seeing his face filled her with such irrational longing that she began to run. She ran all the way to the car.

Her route took her into the very heart of downtown. Late-afternoon sunlight slanted in through the picket shadows of steel-and-glass high rises. Rush-hour traffic clogged the streets; she felt like a fish struggling upstream. With every minute that passed, her hunger to see him grew. And with it grew a panic that she would be too late, that she'd find his office empty, his door locked. At that moment, as she fought through the traffic, it seemed that nothing in her life had ever been as important as reaching the safety of his arms.

Please be there, she prayed. *Please be there....*

"AN EXPLANATION, Mr. Ransom. That's all I'm asking for. A week ago you said our chances of winning were excellent. Now you've withdrawn from the case. I want to know why."

David gazed uneasily into Mary O'Brien's silver-gray eyes and wondered how to answer her. He wasn't about to tell her the truth—that he was having an affair with the opposition. But he did owe her some sort of explanation and he knew, from the look in her eye, that it had better be a good one.

He heard the agitated creaking of wood and leather and he glanced in irritation at Phil Glickman, who was squirming nervously in his chair. David shot him a warning look to cool it. If that was possible. Glickman already knew the truth. And damned if he didn't look ready to blurt it all out.

Mary O'Brien was still waiting.

David's answer was evasive but not entirely dishonest. "As I said earlier, Mrs. O'Brien, I've discovered a conflict of interest."

"I don't understand what that means," Mary O'Brien said impatiently. "This conflict of interest. Are you telling me you work for the hospital?"

"Not exactly."

"Then what does it mean?"

"It's…confidential. I really can't discuss it." Smoothly changing the subject, he continued, "I'm referring your case to Sullivan and March. It's an excellent firm. They'll be happy to take it from here, assuming you have no objections."

"You haven't answered my question." She leaned forward, her eyes glinting, her bony hands bunched tightly on his desk. Claws of vengeance, he thought.

"I'm sorry, Mrs. O'Brien. I just can't serve your needs objectively. I have no choice but to withdraw."

It was a very different parting from the last visit. A cold and businesslike handshake, a nod of the head. Then he and Glickman escorted her out of his office.

"I expect there'll be no delays because of this," she said.

"There shouldn't be. All the groundwork's been laid." He frowned as he saw the frantic expression of his secretary at the far end of the hall.

"You still think they'll try to settle?"

"It's impossible to second-guess…." He paused, distracted. His secretary now looked absolutely panicked.

"You told us before they'd want to settle."

"Hmm? Oh." Suddenly anxious to get rid of her, he guided her purposefully toward the reception room. "Look, don't worry about it, Mrs. O'Brien," he practically snapped out. "I can almost guarantee the other side's discussing a settlement right—" His feet froze in their tracks. He felt as though he were mired in concrete and would never move again.

Kate was standing in front of him. Slowly, her disbelieving gaze shifted to Mary O'Brien.

"Oh, my God," Glickman groaned.

It was a tableau taken straight out of some soap opera: the shocked parties, all staring at one another.

"I can explain everything," David blurted out.

"I doubt it," retorted Mary O'Brien.

Wordlessly Kate spun around and walked out of the suite. The slam of the door shook David out of his paralysis. Just before he rushed out into the hall he heard Mary O'Brien's outraged voice say: "Conflict of interest? Now I know what he meant by *interest*!"

Kate was stepping into an elevator.

He scrambled after her but before he could yank her out, the door snapped shut between them. "Dammit!" he yelled, slamming his fist against the wall.

The next elevator took forever to arrive. All the way down, twenty floors, he paced back and forth like a caged animal, muttering oaths he hadn't used in years. By the time he emerged on the ground floor, Kate was nowhere to be seen.

He ran out of the building and down the steps to the sidewalk. Scanning the street, he spotted, half a block away, a bus idling near the curb. Kate was walking toward it.

Shoving frantically through a knot of pedestrians, he managed to grab her arm and haul her back as she was about to step aboard the bus.

"Let me go!" she snapped.

"Where the hell do you think you're going?"

"Oh, sorry. I almost forgot!" Thrusting her hand in her skirt pocket, she pulled out his car keys and practically threw them at him. "I wouldn't want to be accused of stealing your precious BMW!"

She looked around in frustration as the bus roared off without her. Yanking her arm free, she stormed away. He was right behind her.

"Just give me a chance to explain."

"What did you tell your client, David? That she'll get her settlement now that you've got the dumb doctor eating out of your hand?"

"What happened between you and me has nothing to do with the case."

"It has everything to do with the case! You were hoping all along I'd settle."

"I only asked you to think about it."

"Ha!" She whirled on him. "Is this something they teach you in law school? When all else fails, get the opposition into bed?"

That was the last straw. He grabbed her arm and practically dragged her off the sidewalk and into a nearby pub. Inside, he plunged straight through the boisterous crowd that had gathered around the bar and hauled her through the swirling cigarette smoke to an empty booth at the back. There he plopped her down unceremoniously onto the wooden bench. Sliding into the seat across from her, he shot her a look that said she was damn well going to hear him out.

"First of all—" he started.

"Good evening," said a cheery voice.

"Now what?" he barked at the startled waitress who'd arrived to take their order.

The woman seemed to shrink back into her forest-green costume. "Did you...uh, want anything—"

"Just bring us a couple of beers," he snapped.

"Of course, sir." With a pitying look at Kate, the waitress turned ruffled skirts and fled.

For a solid minute, David and Kate stared at each other with unveiled hostility. Then David let out a sigh and clawed his fingers through his already unruly hair. "Okay," he said. "Let's try it again."

"Where do we start? Before or after your client popped out of your office?"

"Did anyone ever tell you you've got a lousy sense of timing?"

"Oh, you're wrong there, mister. My sense of timing happens to be just dandy. What did I hear you say to her? 'Don't worry, there's a settlement in the works'?"

"I was trying to get her out of my office!"

"So how did she react to your straddling both sides of the lawsuit?"

"I wasn't—" he looked pained "—straddling."

"Working for her and going to bed with me? I'd call that straddling."

"For an intelligent woman, you seem to have a little trouble comprehending one little fact: I'm off the case. Permanently. And voluntarily. Mary O'Brien came to my office demanding to know why I withdrew."

"Did you—did you tell her about us?"

"You think I'm nuts? You think I'd come out and announce I had a roll in the hay with the opposition?"

His words hit her like a slap across her face. Was that all it had meant to him? She'd imagined their lovemaking meant far more than just the simple clash of hormones. A joining of souls, perhaps. But for David, the affair had only meant complications. An angry client, a forced withdrawal from a case And now the humiliation of having to confess an illicit romance. That he'd tried so hard to conceal their affair gave it all a lurid glow. People only hid what they were ashamed of.

"A weekend fling," she said. "Is that what I was?"

"I didn't mean it that way!"

"Well, don't worry about it, David," she assured him with regal composure as she rose to her feet. "I won't embarrass you any more. This is one skeleton who'll gladly step back into the closet."

"*Sit down.*" It was nothing more than a low growl but it held enough threat to make her pause. "Please," he added. Then, in a whisper, he said it again. "Please."

Slowly, she sat back down.

They fell silent as the waitress returned and set down their beers. Only when they were alone again did David say, quietly, "You're not just a fling, Kate. And as for the O'Briens, it's none of their business what I do on my weekends. Or weekdays." He shook his head in amazement. "You know, I've withdrawn from other cases, but it was always for perfectly logical reasons. Reasons I could defend without getting red in the face. This time, though..." He let out a brittle laugh. "At my age, getting red in the face isn't supposed to happen anymore."

Kate stared down at her glass. She hated beer. She hated arguing. Most of all, she hated this chasm between them. "If I jumped to conclusions," she admitted grudgingly, "I'm sorry. I guess I never did trust lawyers."

He grunted. "Then we're even. I never did trust doctors."

"So we're an unlikely pair. What else is new?"

They suffered through another one of those terrible loaded silences.

"We really don't know each other very well, do we?" she finally said.

"Except in bed. Which isn't the best place to get acquainted." He paused. "Though we certainly tried."

She looked up and saw an odd little tilt to his mouth, the beginnings of a smile. A lock of hair had slipped down over his brow. His shirt collar gaped open and his tie had been yanked into a limp version of a hangman's noose. She'd never seen him look so wrenchingly attractive.

"Are you going to get in trouble, David? What if the O'Briens complain to the state bar?" she asked softly.

He shrugged. "I'm not worried. Hell, the worst they can do is disbar me. Throw me in jail. Maybe send me to the electric chair."

"David."

"Oh, you're right, I forgot. Hawaii doesn't have an electric chair." He noticed she wasn't laughing. "Okay, so it's a lousy joke." He lifted his mug and was about to take a gulp of beer when he focused on her morose expression. "Oh, I completely forgot. What happened at your hearing?"

"There were no surprises."

"It went against you?"

"To say the least." Miserable, she stared down at the table. "They said my work was substandard. I guess that's a polite way of calling me a lousy doctor."

His silence, more than anything he could have said, told her how much the news disturbed him. With a sense of wonder she watched his hand close gently around hers.

"It's funny," she remarked with an ironic laugh. "I never planned on being anything but a doctor. Now that I'm losing my job, I see how poorly qualified I am for anything else. I can't type. I can't take dictation. For God's sake, I can't even *cook*."

"Uh-oh. Now that's a serious deficiency. You may have to beg on street corners."

It was another lousy joke, but this time she managed a smile. A meager one. "Promise to drop a few quarters in my hat?"

"I'll do better than that. I'll buy you dinner."

She shook her head. "Thanks. But I'm not hungry."

"Better take me up on the offer," he urged, squeezing her hand. "You never know where you next meal's coming from."

She lifted her head and their gazes met across the table. The eyes she'd once thought so icy now held all the warmth of a summer's day. "All I want is to go home with you, David. I want you to hold me. And not necessarily in that order."

Slowly he moved around the table and slid next to her. Then he pulled her into his arms and held her long and close. It was what she needed, this silent embrace, not of a lover but a friend.

They both stiffened at the sound of the waitress clearing her throat. "I don't believe this woman's timing," David muttered as he pulled away.

"Anything else?" asked the waitress.

"Yes," David replied, smiling politely through clenched teeth. "*If* you don't mind."

"What's that, sir?"

"A little privacy."

KATE LET HIM TALK her into dinner. A full stomach and a few glasses of wine left her flushed and giddy as they walked the dark streets to the parking garage. The lamps spilled a hazy glow across their faces. She clung to his arm and felt like singing, like laughing.

She was going home with David.

She slid onto the leather seat of the BMW and the familiar feeling of security wrapped around her like a blanket. She was in a capsule where no one, nothing, could hurt her. The feeling lasted all the way down the Pali Highway, clung to her as they slipped into the tunnel through the Koolau Mountains, kept her warm on the steep and winding road down the other side of the ridge.

It shattered when David glanced in the rearview mirror and swore softly.

She glanced sideways and saw the faint glow of a car's headlights reflected on his face. "David?"

He didn't answer. She felt the rising hum of the engine as they accelerated.

"David, is something wrong?"

"That car. Behind us."

"What?"

He frowned at the mirror. "I think we're being followed."

Chapter Twelve

Kate whipped her head around and stared at the pair of headlights twinkling in the distance. "Are you sure?"

"I only noticed because it has a dead left parking light. I know it pulled out behind us when we left the garage. It's been on our tail ever since. All the way down the mountain."

"That doesn't mean he's following us!"

"Let's try a little experiment." He took his foot off the gas pedal.

She went rigid in alarm. "Why are you slowing down?"

"To see what he does."

As her heart accelerated wildly, Kate felt the BMW drift down to forty-five, then forty. Below the speed limit. She waited for the headlights to overtake them but they seemed to hang in the distance, as though some invisible force kept the cars apart.

"Smart guy," said David. "He's staying just far enough behind so I can't read his license "

"There's a turnoff! Oh, please, let's take it!"

He veered off the highway and shot onto a two-lane road cut through dense jungle. Vine-smothered trees whipped past, their overhanging branches splattering the windshield with water. She twisted around and saw, through the backdrop of jungle, the same pair of headlights, twinkling in the darkness. Phantom lights that refused to vanish.

"It's him," she whispered. She couldn't bring herself to say the name, as if, just by uttering it, she would unleash some terrible force.

"I should have known," he muttered. "Dammit, I should've known!"

"What?"

"He was watching the hospital. That's the only way he could've followed you—"

He must have been right behind me, she thought, suddenly sick with the realization of what could have happened. *And I never even knew he was there.*

"I'm going to lose him. Hold on."

She was thrown sideways by the violent lurch of the car. It was all she could do to hang on for dear life. The situation was out of her hands; this show was entirely David's.

Houses leaped past, a succession of brightly lit windows punctuated by the silhouettes of trees and shrubbery. The BMW weaved like a slalom skier through the darkness, rounding corners at a speed that made her claw the dashboard in terror.

Without warning, he swerved into a driveway. The seat belt sliced into her chest as they jerked to a sudden standstill in a pitch-dark garage. Instantly, David cut off the engine. The next thing she knew, he was pulling her down into his arms. There she lay, wedged between the gearshift and David's chest, listening, waiting. She could feel his heart hammering against her, could hear his harsh, uneven breaths. At least he was still able to breathe; she scarcely dared to.

With mounting terror, she watched a flicker of light slowly grow brighter and brighter in the rearview mirror. From the road came the faint growl of an engine. David's arms tensed around her. Already he had shifted his weight and now lay on top of her, shielding her body with his. For an eternity she lay crushed in his embrace, listening, waiting, as the sound of the engine faded away. Only when there was total silence did they finally creep up and peer through the rear window.

The road was dark. The car had vanished.

"What now?" she whispered.

"We get the hell out of here. While we still can." He turned the key; the engine's purr seemed deafening. With his headlights killed, he let the car creep slowly out of the garage.

As they wound their way out of the neighborhood, she kept glancing back, searching for the twin lights dancing beyond the trees. Only when they'd reached the highway did she allow herself a breath of relief. But to her alarm, David turned the car back toward Honolulu.

"Where are we going?"

"We can't go home. Not now."

"But we've lost him!"

"If he followed you from the hospital, then he trailed you straight to my office. To me. Unfortunately, I'm in the phone book. Address and all."

She sank back in shock and struggled to absorb this latest blow. They entered the Pali Tunnel. The succession of lights passing overhead was wildly disorienting, flash after flash that shocked her eyes.

Where do I go now? she wondered. *How long before he finds me? Will I have time to run? Time to scream?* She shuddered as they emerged from the tunnel and were plunged into sudden darkness.

"It's my last resort," David said. "But it's the only place I can think of. You won't be alone. And you'll be perfectly safe." He paused and added with an odd note of humor, "Just don't drink the coffee."

She turned and stared at him in bewilderment. "Where are we going?" His answer had a distinctly apologetic ring. "My mother's."

THE TINY GRAY-HAIRED woman who opened the door was wearing a ratty bathrobe and pink bunny slippers. For a moment she stood there, blinking like a surprised mouse at the unexpected visitors. Then she clapped her hands and squeaked: "My goodness, David! How nice you've come for a visit! Oh, but this is naughty of you, not to call. You've caught us in our pajamas, like two ol—"

"You're gorgeous, Gracie," cut in David as he tugged Kate into the house. Quickly he locked and bolted the door. Then, glancing out the curtained window, he demanded, "Is Mother awake?"

"Why, yes, she's...uh..." Gracie gestured vaguely at the foyer.

From another room, a querulous voice called out: "For heaven's sake, get rid of whoever it is and get in here! It's your turn! And you'd better come up with something good. I just got a triple word score!"

"She's beating me again." Gracie sighed mournfully.

"Then she's in a good mood?"

"I wouldn't know. I've never seen her in one."

"Get ready," David muttered to Kate as he guided her across the foyer. "Mother?" he called out pleasantly. *Too* pleasantly.

In a mauve and mahogany living room, a regal woman with blue-gray hair was sitting with her back turned to them. Her wrapped foot was propped up on a crushed velvet ottoman. On the tea table beside her lay a Scrabble board, crisscrossed with tiles. "I don't believe it," she announced to the wall. "It must be an auditory hallucination." She turned and squinted at him. "Why, my son has actually come for a visit! Is the world at an end?"

"Nice to see you, too, Mother," he responded dryly. He took a deep breath, like a man gathering up the nerve to yank out his own teeth. "We need your help."

The woman's eyes, as glitteringly sharp as crystals, suddenly focused on Kate. Then she noticed David's arm, which was wrapped protectively around Kate's shoulder. Slowly, knowingly, she smiled. With a grateful glance at the heavens she murmured fervently: "Glory hallelujah!"

"YOU NEVER TELL ME anything, David," Jinx Ransom complained as she sat with her son in the fern-infested kitchen an hour later.

They were huddled over cups of cocoa, a ritual they hadn't shared since he was a boy. *How little it takes to be transported back to childhood,* he reflected. One sip of chocolate, one disapproving look from his mother, and the pangs of filial guilt returned. Good old Jinx; she really knew how to make a guy feel young again. In fact, she made him feel about six years old.

"Here you have a woman in your life," said Jinx, "and you hide her from me. As if you're ashamed of her. Or ashamed of me. Or maybe you're ashamed of us both.''

"There's nothing to talk about. I haven't known her that long."

"You're just ashamed to admit you're human, aren't you?"

"Don't psychoanalyze me, Mother."

"I'm the one who diapered you. I'm the one who watched you skin your knees. I even saw you break your arm on that blasted skateboard. You almost never cried, David. You still don't cry. I don't think you can. It's some gene you inherited from your father. The Plymouth Rock curse. Oh, the emotions are in there somewhere, but you're not about to let them show. Even when Noah died—''

"I don't want to talk about Noah."

"You see? The boy's been gone eight years now and you still can't hear his name without getting all tight in the face."

"Get to the point, Mother."

"Kate."

"What about her?"

"You were holding her hand."

He shrugged. "She has a very nice hand."

"Have you gone to bed with her yet?"

David sputtered hot chocolate all over the table. "Mother!"

"Well it's nothing to be ashamed of. People do it all the time. It's what nature intended, though I sometimes think you imagine yourself immune to the whole blasted process. But tonight, I saw that look in your eye."

Swatting away a stray fern, he went to the sink for a paper towel and began dabbing the cocoa from his shirt.

"Am I right?" asked Jinx.

"Looks like I'll need a clean shirt for tomorrow," he muttered. "This one's shot."

"Use one of your father's shirts. So am I right?"

He looked up. "About what, Mother?" he asked blankly.

She raised her arm and made a throttling motion at the heavens. "I knew it was a mistake to have only one child!"

Upstairs there was a loud thud. David glanced up at the ceiling. "What the hell is Gracie doing up there, anyway?"

"Digging up some clothes for Kate."

David shuddered. Knowing Gracie's incomparable taste in clothes, Kate would come down swathed from head to toe in some nauseating shade of pink. With bunny slippers to match. The truth was, he didn't give a damn what she was wearing, if only she'd hurry downstairs. They'd been apart only fifteen minutes and already he missed her. It annoyed him, all these inconvenient emotions churning around inside him. It made him feel weak and helpless and all too...human.

He turned eagerly at hearing a creak on the stairs and saw it was only Gracie.

"Is that hot chocolate, Jinx?" Gracie demanded. "You know the milk upsets your stomach. You really should have tea instead."

"I don't want tea."

"Yes, you do."

"No, I don't."

"Where's Kate?" David called out bleakly.

"Oh, she's coming," said Gracie. "She's up in your room, looking at your old model airplanes." Giggling, she confided to Jinx, "I told her they were proof that David was once a child."

"He was never a child," grumbled Jinx. "He sprang from the womb a fully mature adult. Though smaller, of course. Perhaps he'll do it backward. Perhaps he'll get younger as the years go by. We'll see him loosen up and become a real child."

"Like you, Mother?"

Gracie put on the teakettle and sighed happily. "It's so nice to have company, isn't it?" She glanced around, startled, as the phone rang. "My goodness, it's after ten. Who on earth—"

David shot to his feet. "I'll get it." He grabbed the receiver and barked out: "Hello?"

Pokie's voice boomed triumphantly across the wires. "Have I got news for you."

"You've tracked down that car?"

"Forget the car. We got the man."

"Decker?"

"I'll need Dr. Chesne down here to identify him. Half an hour, okay?"

David glanced up to see Kate standing in the kitchen doorway. Her eyes were filled with questions. Grinning, he snapped her a victorious thumbs-up sign. "We'll be right over," he told Pokie. "Where you holding him? Downtown station?"

There was a pause. "No, not the station."

"Where, then?"

"The morgue."

"HOPE YOU HAVE strong stomachs." The medical examiner, a grotesquely chirpy woman named M.J., pulled open the stainless-steel drawer. It glided out noiselessly. Kate cringed against David as M.J. casually reached in and unzipped the plastic shroud.

Under the harsh morgue lights, the corpse's face looked artificial. This wasn't a man; it was some sort of waxen image, a mockery of life.

"Some yachtie found him this evening, floating facedown in the harbor," explained Pokie.

Kate felt David's arm tighten around her waist as she forced herself to study the dead man's bloated features. Distorted as he was, the open eyes were recognizable. Even in death they seemed haunted.

Nodding, Kate whispered, "That's him."

Pokie grinned, a response that struck her as surreal in that nightmarish room. "Bingo," he grunted.

M.J. ran her gloved hand over the dead man's scalp. "Feels like we got a depressed skull fracture here...." She whisked off the shroud, revealing the naked torso. "Looks like he's been in the water quite a while."

Suddenly nauseated, Kate turned and buried her face against David's shoulder. The scent of his after-shave muted the stench of formalin.

"For God's sake, M.J.," David muttered. "Cover him up, will you?"

M.J. zipped up the shroud and slid the drawer closed. "You've lost the old ironclad stomach, hey, Davy boy? If I remember right, you used to shrug off a lot worse."

"I don't hang around stiffs the way I used to." He guided Kate away from the body drawers. "Come on. Let's get the hell out of here."

The medical examiner's office was a purposefully cheerful room, complete with hanging plants and old movie posters, a bizarre setting for the gruesome business at hand. Pokie poured coffee from the automatic brewer and handed two cups to David and Kate. Then, sighing with satisfaction, he settled into a chair across from them. "So that's how it wraps up," he said. "No trial. No hassles. Just a convenient corpse. Too bad justice ain't always this easy."

Kate stared down at her coffee. "How did he die, Lieutenant?" she whispered.

Pokie shrugged. "Happens now and then. Get some guy who's had a little too much to drink. Falls off a pier, bashes his head on the rocks. Hell, we find floaters all the time. Boat bums, mostly." He glanced at M.J. "What do you think?"

"Can't rule out anything yet," mumbled M.J. She was hunched at her desk and wolfing down a late supper. A meat-loaf sandwich dripping with ketchup, Kate noted, her stomach threatening to turn inside out. "When a body's been in the water that long, anatomy gets distorted. I'll tell you after the autopsy."

"Just how long was he in the water?" asked David.

"A day. More or less."

"A *day*?" He looked at Pokie. "Then who the hell was following us tonight?"

Pokie grinned. "You just got yourself an active imagination."

"I'm telling you, there was a car!"

"Lot of cars out on the road. Lot of headlights look the same."

"Well, it sure wasn't my guy in the drawer," said M.J., crumpling up her sandwich wrappings. She chomped enthusiastically into a bright red apple. "Far as I know, dead men don't drive."

"When are you going to know the cause of death?" David snapped.

"Still need skull X rays. I'll open him up tonight, check the lungs for water. That'll tell us if he drowned." She took another bite of apple. "But that's *after* I finish my dinner. In the meantime—" swiveling around, she grabbed a cardboard box from a shelf and tossed it down on the desk "—his personal effects."

Methodically she took out the items, each one sealed in its own plastic bag. "Plastic comb, black, pocket-size... cigarettes, Winston, half empty...matchbook, unlabeled...man's wallet, brown vinyl, containing fourteen dollars...various ID cards..." She reached in for the last item. "And these." The set of keys clattered on the desk. Attached was a plastic tag with gaudy red lettering: The Victory Hotel.

Kate picked up the key ring. "The Victory Hotel," she murmured. "Is that where he was living?"

Pokie nodded. "We checked it out. What a dive. Rats crawling all over the place. We know he was there Saturday night. But that's the last time he was seen. Alive, anyway."

Slowly Kate lay the keys down and stared at the mockingly bright lettering. She thought about the face in the mirror, about the torment in those eyes. And as she gazed at the sad and meager pile of belongings, an unexpected wave of sorrow welled up in her, sorrow for a man's shattered dreams. *Who were you, Charlie Decker?* she wondered. *Madman? Murderer?* Here were the bits and pieces of his life, and they were all so ordinary.

Pokie gave her a grin. "Well, it's over, Doc. Our man's dead. Looks like you can go home."

She glanced at David, but he was staring off in another direction. "Yes," she said in a weary voice. "Now I can go home."

WHO WERE YOU, Charlie Decker?

That refrain played over and over in her head as she sat in the darkness of David's car and watched the streetlights flash by. *Who were you?* She thought of all the ways he'd suffered, all the pain he'd felt, that man without a voice. Like everyone else, he'd been a victim.

And now he was a convenient corpse.

"It's too easy, David," she said softly.

He glanced at her through the gloom of the car. "What is?"

"The way it's all turned out. Too simple, too neat..." She stared off into the darkness, remembering the reflection of Charlie Decker's face in the mirror. "My God. I saw it in his eyes," she whispered. "It was right there, staring at me, only I was too panicked to recognize it."

"What?"

"The fear. He was terrified. He must have known something, something awful. And it killed him. Just like it killed the others...."

"You're saying he was a victim? Then why did he threaten you? Why did he make that call to the cottage?"

"Maybe it wasn't a threat...." She looked up with sudden comprehension. "Maybe he was warning me. About someone else."

"But the evidence—"

"What evidence? A few fingerprints on a doorknob? A corpse with a psychiatric record?"

"And a witness. You saw him in Ann's apartment."

"What if he was the real witness? A man in the wrong place at the wrong time." She watched their headlights slash the darkness. "Four people, David. And the only thing that linked them together was a dead woman. If I only knew why Jenny Brook was so important."

"Unfortunately, dead men don't talk."

Maybe they do. "The Victory Hotel," she said suddenly. "Where is it?"

"Kate, the man's dead. The answers died with him. Let's just forget it."

"But there's still a chance—"

"You heard Pokie. The case is closed."

"Not for me, it isn't."

"Oh, for God's sake, Kate! Don't turn this into an obsession!" Gripping the steering wheel, he forced out an agitated breath. When he spoke again, his voice was quiet. "Look, I know how much it means to you, clearing your name. But in the long run, it may not be worth the fight. If vindication's what you're after, I'm afraid you won't get it. Not in the courtroom, anyway."

"You can't be sure what a jury will think."

"Second-guessing juries is part of my job. I've made a good living, cashing in on doctors' mistakes. And I've done it in a town where a lot of lawyers can barely pay their rent. I'm not any smarter than the other guy, I just pick my cases well. And when I do, I'm not afraid to get down and get dirty. By the time I'm finished, the defendant's scarred for life."

"Lovely profession you're in."

"I'm telling you this because I don't want it to happen to you. That's why I think you should settle out of court. Let the matter die quietly. Discreetly. Before your name gets dragged through the mud."

"Is that how they do it in the prosecutor's office? 'Plead guilty and we'll make you a *deal*'?"

"There's nothing wrong with a settlement."

"Would you settle? If you were me?"

There was a long pause. "Yes. I would."

"Then we must be very different." Stubbornly she gazed ahead at the highway. "Because I can't let this die. Not without a fight."

"Then you're going to lose." It was more than an opinion; it was a pronouncement, as final as the thud of a judge's gavel in the courtroom.

"And I suppose lawyers don't take on losing battles, do they?"

"Not this lawyer."

"Funny. Doctors take them on all the time. Try arguing with a stroke. Or cancer. We don't make bargains with the enemy."

"And that's exactly how I make my living," he retorted. "On the arrogance of doctors!"

It was a vicious blow; he regretted it the instant he said it. But she was headed for trouble, and he had to stop her before she got hurt. Still, he hadn't expected such brutal words to pop out. It was one more reminder of how high the barriers were between them.

They drove the rest of the way in silence. A cloud of gloom filled the space of the car. They both seemed to sense that things were coming to an end; he guessed it had been inevitable from the start. Already he could feel her pulling away.

Back at his house, they drifted toward the bedroom like a pair of strangers. When she pulled down her suitcase and started to pack, he said simply, "Leave it for the morning," and shoved it back in the closet. That was all. He couldn't bring himself to say he wanted her to stay, needed her to stay. He just shut the closet door.

Then he turned to her. Slowly he removed his jacket and tossed it on the chair. He went to her, took her face in his hands and kissed her. Her lips felt chilled. He took her in his arms and held her, warmed her.

They made love, of course. One last time. He was there and she was there and the bed was there. Love among the ruins. No, not love. Desire. Need. Something entirely different, all-consuming yet wholly unsatisfying.

And afterward he lay beside her in the darkness, listening to her breathing. She slept deeply, the unarousable slumber of exhaustion. He should be sleeping, too. But he couldn't. He was too busy thinking about all the reasons he shouldn't fall in love.

He didn't like being in love. It left him far too vulnerable. Since Noah's death, he'd avoided feeling much of anything. At times he'd felt like a robot. He'd functioned on automatic pilot, breathing and eating out of necessity, smiling only when it was expected. When Linda finally left him, he'd hardly noticed; their divorce was a mere drop in an ocean of pain. He guessed he'd loved her, but it wasn't the same total, unconditional love he'd felt for his son. For David, love was quantified by how much he suffered by its loss.

And now here was this woman, lying beside him. He studied the dark pool of her hair against the pillow, the glow of her face. He tried to think of the last time there'd been a woman in his bed. It had been a long time ago, a blonde. But he couldn't even dredge up her name. That's how little she'd meant to him.

But Kate? He'd remember her name, all right. He'd remember this moment, the way she slept, curled up like a tired kitten, the way her very presence seemed to warm the darkness. He'd remember.

He rose from the bed and wandered into the hall. Some strange yearning pulled him toward Noah's room. He went inside and stood for a moment, bathed in the window's moonlight. For so long he'd avoided this room. He'd hated the sight of that unoccupied bed. He'd always remembered how it used to be, tiptoeing in to watch his son sleep. Noah, by some strange instinct, always seemed to choose that moment to awaken. And in the darkness, they'd murmur their ritual conversation.

Is that you, Daddy?

Yes, Noah, it's me. Go back to sleep.

Hug first. Please.

Good night. Don't let the bedbugs bite.

David sat down on the bed, listening to the echoes of the past, remembering how much it had hurt to love.

At last he went back to Kate's bed, crawled in beside her and fell asleep.

He woke up before dawn. In the shower he purposefully washed off all traces of their lovemaking. He felt renewed. He dressed for work, donning each item of clothing as if it was a piece of armor to shield him from the world. Alone in the kitchen, he had a cup of coffee.

Now that Decker was dead, there was no reason for Kate to stay. David had done his moral duty; he'd played the white knight and kept her safe. It had been clear from the start that none of this was for keeps. He'd never led her on. His conscience was clear. Now it was time for her to go home; and they both knew it. Perhaps her leaving was all for the better. A few days, a few weeks apart, might give him a saner perspective. Maybe he'd decide this was all a case of temporary, hormonal madness.

Or maybe he was only kidding himself.

He worried about all the things that could happen to her if she kept on digging into Charlie Decker's past. He also knew she would keep on digging. Last night he hadn't told her the truth: that he thought she was right, that there was more to this case than a madman's vengeance. Four people were dead; he didn't want her to be the fifth.

He got up and rinsed his cup. Then he went back to the bedroom. There he sat at the foot of the bed—a safe distance—and watched her sleep. Such a beautiful, stubborn, maddeningly independent woman. He used to think he liked independent women. Now he wasn't so sure. He almost wished Decker was still alive, just so Kate would go on needing him. How incredibly selfish.

Then he decided she did still need him. They'd shared two nights of passion. For that he owed her one last favor.

He nudged her gently. "Kate?"

Slowly she opened her eyes and looked at him. Those sleepy green eyes. He wanted so badly to kiss her but decided it was better if he didn't. "The Victory Hotel," he said. "Do you still want to go?"

Chapter Thirteen

Mrs. Tubbs, the manager of the Victory Hotel, was a toadlike woman with two pale slits for eyes. Despite the heat, she was wearing a ratty gray sweater over her flowered dress. Through a hole in her sock poked an enormously swollen big toe. "Charlie?" she asked, cautiously peering at David and Kate through her half-open door. "Yeah, he lived here."

In the room behind her, a TV game show blared and a man yelled, "You retard! I coulda guessed that one!"

The woman turned and yelled: "Ebbie! Turn that thing down! Can't you see I'm talkin' to someone?" She looked back at David and Kate. "Charlie don't live here no more. Got hisself killed. Po-lice already come by."

"If it's all right, we'd like to see his room," said Kate.

"What for?"

"We're looking for information."

"You from the po-lice?"

"No, but—"

"Can't let you up there without a warrant. Po-lice give me too much trouble already. Gettin' everyone in the building all nervous. 'Sides, I got orders. No one goes up." Her tone implied that someone very high, perhaps even God Himself, had issued those orders. To emphasize the point, she started to close the door. She looked outraged when David stopped it with a well-placed hand.

"Seems to me you could use a new sweater, Mrs. Tubbs," David remarked quietly.

The door swung open a fraction of an inch. Mrs. Tubbs's pale eyes peered at him through the crack. "I could use a lot of new things," she grunted. From the apartment came a man's loud and enthusiastic burp. "New husband, mostly."

"Afraid I can't help you there."

"No one can, 'cept maybe the good Lord."

"Who works His magic in unexpected ways." David's smile was dazzling; Mrs. Tubbs stared, waiting for the proffered miracle to occur.

David produced it in the form of two twenty-dollar bills, which he slipped discreetly into her fat hands.

She looked down at the money. "Hotel owner'll kill me if he finds out."

"He won't."

"Don't pay me nearly enough to manage this here trash heap. Plus I'm s'posed to pay off the city inspector." David slipped her another twenty. "But you ain't no inspector, right?" She wadded up the bills and stuffed them into the dark and bottomless recess of her bosom. "No inspector I seen ever come dressed like you." Shuffling out into the hall, she closed the door on Ebbie and the TV. In her stockinged feet, she led David and Kate toward the staircase. It was a climb of only one flight, but for her each step seemed to be agony. By the time she reached the top, she was wheezing like an accordion. A brown carpet—or had it once been mustard yellow?—stretched out into the dim hallway. She stopped before room 203 and fumbled for the keys.

"Charlie was here 'bout a month," she gasped out, a few words at a time. "Real quiet. Caused no...no trouble, not like some...some of them others...."

At the other end of the hall, a door suddenly opened and two small faces peered out.

"Charlie come back?" the little girl called.

"I already told you," Mrs. Tubbs said. "Charlie gone and left for good."

"But when's he comin' back?"

"You kids deaf or somethin'? How come you ain't in school?"

"Gabe's sick," explained the girl. As if to confirm the fact, little Gabe swiped his hand across his snotty nose.

"Where's your ma?"

The girl shrugged. "Out workin'."

"Yeah. Leaves you two brats here to burn down the place."

The children shook their heads solemnly. "She took away our matches," replied Gabe.

Mrs. Tubbs got the door unlocked. "There y'are," she said and pushed it open.

As the room swung into view, something small and brown rustled across the floor and into the shadows. The mingled odors of cigarette smoke and grease hung in the gloom. Pinpoints of light glittered through a tattered curtain. Mrs. Tubbs went over and shoved the curtain aside. Sunshine splashed in through the grimy window.

"Go 'head, have a look 'round," she said, planting herself in a corner. "But don't take nothin'."

It was easy to see why a visit by the city inspector might cause her alarm. A baited rattrap, temporarily unoccupied, lay poised near a trash can. A single light bulb hung from the ceiling, its wires nakedly exposed.

On a one-burner hot plate sat a frying pan coated with a thick layer of congealed fat. Except for the one window, there was no ventilation and any cóoking would have made the air swirl with grease.

Kate's gaze took in the miserable surroundings: the rumpled bed, the ashtray overflowing with cigarette butts, the card table littered with loose scraps of paper. She frowned at one of the pages, covered with scribblings.

Eight was great
Nine was fine,
And now you're ten years old.
Happy Birthday, Jocelyn,
The best will yet unfold!

"Who's Jocelyn?" she asked.

"That brat in 210. Mother's never around to watch 'em. Always out workin'. Or so she calls it. Kids just 'bout burned the place down last month. Woulda throwed 'em all out, 'cept they always pay me in cash."

"Just how much is the rent?" David asked.

"Four hundred bucks."

"You've got to be kidding."

"Hey, we got us a good location. Close to the bus lines. Free water 'n 'lectricity." At that instant, a cockroach chose to scuttle across the floor. "And we take pets."

Kate looked up from the pile of papers. "What was he like, Mrs. Tubbs?"

"Charlie?" She shrugged. "What's to say? Kept to hisself. Never made no noise. Never blasted the radio like some of these no-accounts. Never complained 'bout nothin' far as I remember. Hell, we hardly knew he was here. Yeah, a real good tenant."

By those standards, the ideal tenant would have been a corpse.

Mrs. Tubbs settled into a chair and watched as they searched the room. Their inspection revealed a few wrinkled shirts hanging in the closet, a dozen cans of Campbell's soup neatly stacked in the cabinet under the sink, some laundered socks and men's underwear in the dresser drawer. It was a meager collection of belongings; they held few clues to the personality of their owner.

At last Kate wandered to the window and looked down at a glass-littered street. Beyond a chain-link fence there was a condemned building with walls that sagged outward, as though a giant had stepped on it. A grim view of the world, this panorama of broken bottles and abandoned cars and drunks lolling on the sidewalk. This was a dead end, the sort of place you landed when you could fall no farther.

No, that wasn't quite right. There was one place lower you could fall: the grave.

"Kate?" said David. He'd been rummaging in the nightstand. "Prescription pills," he said, holding up a bottle. "Haldol, prescribed by Dr. Nemechek. State hospital."

"That's his psychiatrist."

"And look. I also found this." He held out a small, framed photograph.

The instant Kate saw the face, she knew who the woman was. She took the picture and studied it by the window's light. It was only a snapshot in time, a single image captured on a sheet of photographic paper, but the young woman who'd smiled into the camera's lens had the glow of eternity in her eyes. They were rich brown eyes, full of laughter, narrowed slightly in the sunlight. Behind her, a brassy sky met the turquoise blue of the sea. A strand of dark hair had blown across her face and clung almost wistfully to the curve of her cheek. She was wearing a simple white bathing suit; and though she'd struck a purposely sexy pose, kneeling there in the sand, there was a sweet gawkiness about her, like a child playing grown-up in her mother's clothes.

Kate slipped the photo out of its frame. The edges were tattered, lovingly worn by years of handling. On the other side was a handwritten message: "Till you come back to me. Jenny."

"Jenny," Kate said softly.

For a long time she stood there, staring at those words, written by a woman long since dead. She thought about the emptiness of this room, about the soup cans, so carefully stacked, about the pile of socks and underwear in the drawer. Charlie Decker had owned so very little. The one possession he'd guarded through the years, the one thing he'd treasured, had been this fading photograph of a woman with eternity in her eyes. It was hard to believe that such a glow could ever be extinguished, even in the depths of a grave.

She turned to Mrs. Tubbs. "What will happen to his things? Now that he's dead?"

"Guess I'll have to sell it all off," replied Mrs. Tubbs. "Owed me a week's rent. Gotta get it somehow. Though there ain't much of value in here. 'Cept maybe what you're holding."

Kate looked down at the smiling face of Jenny Brook. "Yes. She's beautiful, isn't she?"

"Naw, I don't mean the picture."

Kate frowned. "What?"

"The frame." Mrs. Tubbs went to the window and snapped the curtain closed. "It's silver."

JOCELYN AND HER BROTHER were hanging like monkeys on the chain-link fence. As David and Kate came out of the Victory Hotel, the children dropped to the ground and watched expectantly as though something extraordinary was about to happen. The girl—if she was indeed ten—was small for her age. Toothpick legs stuck out from under her baggy dress.

Her bare feet were filthy. The little boy, about six and equally filthy, held a clump of his sister's skirt in his fist.

"He's dead, isn't he?" Jocelyn blurted out. Seeing Kate's sad nod, the girl slouched back against the fence and addressed one of the smudges on her bodice. "You see, I knew it. Stupid grown-ups. Don't ever tell us the truth, any of 'em."

"What did they tell you about Charlie?" asked Kate.

"They just said he went away. But he never even gave me my present."

"For your birthday?"

Jocelyn stared down at her nonexistent breasts. "I'm ten."

"And I'm seven," her brother said automatically, as if it was called for in the script.

"You and Charlie must have been good friends," David remarked.

The girl looked up, and seeing his smile—a smile that could melt the heart of any woman, much less that of a ten-year-old—immediately blushed. Looking back down, she coyly traced one brown toe along a crack in the sidewalk. "Charlie didn't have any friends. I don't, either. 'Cept Gabe here, but he's just my brother."

Little Gabe smiled and rubbed his slimy nose on his sister's dress.

"Did anyone else know Charlie very well?" David asked. "I mean, besides you."

Jocelyn chewed her lip thoughtfully. "Well...you could try over at Maloney's. Up the street."

"Who's Maloney?"

"Oh, he's nobody."

"If he's nobody, then how does he know Charlie?"

"He's not a him. He's a place. I mean, *it's* a place."

"Oh, of course," said David, looking down into Jocelyn's dazzled eyes. "How stupid of me."

"WHAT'RE YOU KIDS doing in here again? Go on. Get out before I lose my license!"

Jocelyn and Gabe skipped through the air-conditioned gloom, past the cocktail tables and up to the bar. They clambered onto two counter stools. "Some people here to see you, Sam," announced Jocelyn.

"There's a sign out there says you gotta be twenty-one to come in here. You kids twenty-one yet?"

"I'm seven," answered Gabe. "Can I have an olive?"

Grumbling, the bartender dipped his soapy hand in a glass jar and plopped half a dozen green olives on the counter. "Okay, now get going before someone sees you in—" His head jerked up as he noticed David and Kate approaching through the shadows. From his wary look, it was obvious Maloney's was seldom frequented by such well-heeled clientele.

He blurted out: "It's not my doing! These brats come runnin' in off the street. I was just gonna throw 'em out."

"They're not liquor inspectors," said Jocelyn with obvious disdain as she popped an olive in her mouth.

Apparently everyone in this part of town lived in fear of some dreaded inspector or another.

"We need information," said David. "About one of your customers. Charlie Decker."

Sam took a long and careful look at David's clothes, and his train of thought was clearly mirrored in his eyes. *Nice suit. Silk tie. Yessir, all very expensive.* "He's dead," the bartender grunted.

"We know that."

"I don't speak ill of the dead." There was a long, significant pause. "You gonna order something?"

David sighed and finally settled onto a bar stool. "Okay. Two beers."

"That's all?"

"And two pineapple juices," added Jocelyn.

"That'll be twelve bucks."

"Cheap drinks," said David, sliding a twenty-dollar bill across the counter.

"Plus tax."

The children dumped the remaining olives in their drinks and began slurping down the juice.

"Tell us about Charlie," Kate prodded.

"Well, he used to sit right over there." Sam nodded at a dark corner table.

David and Kate leaned forward, waiting for the next pearl of information. Silence. "And?" prompted David.

"So that's where he sat."

"Doing what?"

"Drinking. Whiskey, mostly. He liked it neat. Then sometimes, I'd make him up a Sour Sam. That's if the mood hit him for somethin' different. That's my invention, the Sour Sam. Yeah, he'd drink one of those 'bout once a week. But mostly it was whiskey. Neat."

There was another silence. The talking machine had run out of money and needed a refill.

"I'll try a Sour Sam," said Kate.

"Don't you want your beer?"

"You can have it."

"Thanks. But I never touch the stuff." He turned his attention to mixing up a bizarre concoction of gin, club soda, and the juice of half a lemon, which undoubtedly accounted for the drink's name.

"Five bucks," he announced, passing it to Kate. "So how do you like it?"

She took a sip and gasped. "Interesting."

"Yeah, that's what everyone tells me."

"We were talking about Charlie," David reminded him.

"Oh, yeah, Charlie." The talking machine was back in order. "Let's see, he came around just 'bout every night. Think he liked the company, though he couldn't talk much, what with that bad throat of his. He'd sit there and drink, oh, one or two."

"Whiskeys. Neat," David supplied.

"Yeah, that's right. Real moderate, you know. Never got out-and-out drunk. He was a regular for 'bout a month. Then, few days ago, he stopped comin'. Too bad, you know? Hate to lose a steady one like that."

"You have any idea why he stopped?"

"They say police were looking for him. Word was out he killed some people."

"What do you think?"

"Charlie?" Sam laughed. "Not a chance."

Jocelyn handed Sam her empty glass. "Can I have another pineapple juice?"

Sam poured out two more pineapple juices and slid them over to the kids. "Eight bucks." He looked at David, who resignedly reached for his wallet.

"You forgot the olives," said Gabe.

"Those are free." The man wasn't entirely heartless.

"Did Charlie ever mention the name Jenny Brook?" Kate asked.

"Like I said, he never talked much. Yeah, ol' Charlie, he'd just sit over at that table and write those ol' poems. He'd scribble and scribble for hours just to get one right. Then he'd get mad and toss it. There'd be all these wadded-up papers on the floor whenever he left."

Kate shook her head in wonder. "I never imagined he'd be a poet."

"Everyone's a poet these days. That Charlie, though, he was real serious about it. That last day he was here, didn't have no money to pay for his drink. So he tears out one of his poems and gives it to me. Says it'll be worth somethin' some day. Ha! I'm such a sucker." He picked up a dirty rag and began to give the counter an almost sensuous rubdown.

"Do you still have the poem?" asked Kate.

"That's it, tacked over on the wall there."

The cheap, lined paper hung by a few strips of Scotch tape. By the dim light of the bar, the words were barely readable.

This is what I told them:
That healing lies not in forgetfulness
But in remembrance
Of you.
The smell of the sea on your skin.
The small and perfect footprints you leave in the sand.
In remembrance there are no endings.

And so you lie there, now and always, by the sea.
You open your eyes. You touch me.
The sun is in your fingertips.
And I am healed.
I am healed.

"So," said Sam, "think it's any good?"
"Gotta be," said Jocelyn. "If Charlie wrote it."
Sam shrugged. "Don't mean nothin'."

"SEEMS LIKE WE'VE HIT a dead end," David commented as they walked out into the blinding sunshine.

He might as well have said it of their relationship. He was standing with his hands thrust deep in his pockets as he gazed down the street at a drunk slouched in a doorway. Shattered glass sparkled in the gutter. Across the street, lurid red letters spelled out the title *Victorian Secrets* on an X-rated movie marquee.

If only he'd give her a smile, a look, anything to indicate that things weren't drawing to a close between them. But he didn't. He just kept his hands in his pockets. And she knew, without him saying a word, that more than Charlie Decker had died.

They passed an alley, scattering shards of broken beer bottles as they walked.

"So many loose ends," she remarked. "I don't see how the police can close the case."

"When it comes to police work, there are always loose ends, nagging doubts."

"It's sad, isn't it?" She gazed back at the Victory Hotel. "When a man dies and he leaves nothing behind. No trace of who or what he was."

"You could say the same about all of us. Unless we write great books or put up buildings, what's left of us after we're gone? Nothing."

"Only children."

For a moment he was silent. Then he said, "That's if we're lucky."

"We do know one thing about him," she concluded softly. "He loved her. Jenny." Staring down at the cracked sidewalk, she thought of the face in the photograph. An unforgettable woman. Even five years after her death, Jenny Brook's magic had somehow affected the lives of four people: the one who had loved her and the three who'd watched her die. She was the one tragic thread weaving through the tapestry of their deaths.

What would it be like, she wondered, to be loved as fiercely as Jenny had been? What enchantment had she possessed? *Whatever it was, I certainly don't have it.*

She said, without conviction, "It'll be good to get home again."

"Will it?"

"I'm used to being on my own."

He shrugged. "So am I."

They'd both retreated to their separate emotional corners. So little time left, she thought with a sense of desolation. And here they were, mouthing words like a pair of strangers. This morning, she'd awakened to find him showered and shaved and dressed in his most forbidding suit. Over breakfast they'd discussed everything but the subject that was uppermost in her mind. He could have made the first move. The whole time she was packing, he'd had the chance to ask her to stay. And she would have.

But he didn't say a thing.

Thank God she'd always been so good at holding on to her dignity. Never any tears, any hysterics. Even Eric had said as much. You've always been so sensible about things, he'd told her as he'd walked out the door.

Well, she'd be sensible this time, too.

The drive was far too short. Glancing at his profile she remembered the day they'd met. An eternity ago. He looked just as forbidding, just as untouchable.

They pulled up at her house. He carried her suitcase briskly up the walkway; he had the stride of a man in a hurry.

"Would you like to come in for a cup of coffee?" she asked, already knowing what his answer would be.

"I can't. Not right now. But I'll call you."

Famous last words. She understood perfectly, of course. It was all part of the ritual.

He cast a furtive glance at his watch. *Time to move on,* she reflected. *For both of us.*

Automatically she thrust the key in the lock and gave the door a shove. It swung open. As the room came into view, she halted on the threshold, unable to believe what she was seeing.

Dear God, she thought. *Why is this happening? Why now?*

She felt David's steadying hand close around her arm as she swayed backward in horror. The room swam, just for an instant, and then her eyes refocused on the opposite wall.

On the flowered wallpaper the letters "MYOB" had been spray painted in bloodred. And below them was the hollow-eyed figure of a skull and crossbones.

Chapter Fourteen

"No dice, Davy. The case is closed."

Pokie Ah Ching splashed coffee from his foam cup as he weaved through the crammed police station, past the desk sergeant arguing into the phone, past clerks hurrying back and forth with files, past a foul-smelling drunk shouting epithets at two weary-looking officers. Through it all, he moved as serenely as a battleship gliding through stormy waters.

"Don't you see, it was a warning!"

"Probably left by Charlie Decker."

"Kate's neighbor checked the house Tuesday morning. That message was left sometime later, when Decker was already dead."

"So it's a kid's prank."

"Yeah? Why would some kid write MYOB? Mind your own business?"

"You understand kids? I don't. Hell, I can't even figure out my own kids." Pokie headed into his office and scooted around to his chair. "Like I said, Davy, I'm busy."

David leaned across the desk. "Last night I told you we were followed. You said it was all in my head."

"I still say so."

"Then Decker turns up in the morgue. A nice, convenient little accident."

"I'm starting to smell a conspiracy theory."

"Your sense of smell is amazing."

Pokie set his cup down, slopping coffee on his papers. "Okay." He sighed. "You got one minute to tell me your theory. Then I'm throwing you out."

David grabbed a chair and sat down. "Four deaths. Tanaka. Richter. Decker. And Ellen O'Brien—"

"Death on the operating table isn't in my jurisdiction."

"But murder is. There's a hidden player in this game, Pokie. Someone who's managed to get rid of four people in a matter of two weeks. Someone smart and quiet and medically sophisticated. And very, very scared."

"Of what?"

"Kate Chesne. Maybe Kate's been asking too many questions. Maybe she knows something and just doesn't realize it. She's made our killer nervous. Nervous enough to scrawl warnings all over that wall."

"Unseen player, huh? I suppose you already got me a list of suspects."

"Starting with the chief of anesthesia. You check out that story on his wife yet?"

"She died Tuesday night in the nursing home. Natural causes."

"Oh, sure. The night after he walks off with a bunch of lethal drugs, she kicks the bucket."

"Coincidence."

"The man lives alone. There's no one to track his comings and go-ings—"

"I can just see the old geezer now." Pokie laughed. "Geriatric Jack the Ripper."

"It doesn't take much strength to slit someone's throat."

"But what's the old guy's motive, huh? Why would he go after members of his own staff?"

David let out a frustrated sigh. "I don't know," he admitted. "But it's got something to do with Jenny Brook."

Ever since he'd laid eyes on her photograph, he'd been unable to get the woman out of his mind. Something about her death, about the cold details recorded in her medical chart kept coming back to him, like a piece of music being played over and over in his head.

Uncontrollable seizures.

An infant girl, born alive.

Mother and child, two soft sparks of humanity, extinguished in the glare of the operating room.

Why, after five years, did their deaths threaten Kate Chesne?

There was a knock on the door. Sergeant Brophy, red-eyed and snif-fling, dropped some papers on Pokie's desk. "Here's that report you been waiting for. Oh, and we got us another sighting of that Sasaki girl."

Pokie snorted. "Again? What does that make it? Forty-three?"

"Forty-four. This one's at Burger King."

"Geez. Why do they always spot 'em at fast-food chains?"

"Maybe she's sittin' there with Jimmy Hoffa and—and—" Brophy sneezed. "Elvis." He blew his nose three times. They were great loud honks that, in the wild, could have attracted geese. "Allergies," he said, as if that was a far more acceptable excuse than the common cold. He aimed a spiteful glance out the window at his nemesis: a mango tree, seething with blossoms. "Too many damn trees around here," he mut-tered, retreating from the office.

Pokie laughed. "Brophy's idea of paradise is an air-conditioned con-crete box." Reaching for the report, he sighed. "That's it, Davy. I got work to do."

"You going to reopen the case?"

"I'll think about it."

"What about Avery? If I were you, I'd—"

"I said I'll think about it." He flipped open the report, a rude gesture that said the meeting was definitely over.

David saw he might as well bang his head against a brick wall. He rose to leave. He was almost to the door when Pokie suddenly snapped out: "Hold it, Davy."

David halted, startled by the sharpness of Pokie's voice. "What?"

"Where's Kate right now?"

"I took her to my mother's. I didn't want to leave her alone."

"Then she is in a safe place."

"If you can call being around my mother safe. Why?"

Pokie waved the report he was holding. "This just came in from M.J.'s office. It's the autopsy on Decker. He didn't drown."

"What?" David moved over to the desk and snatched up the report. His gaze shot straight to the conclusions.

Skull X rays show compression fracture, probably caused by lethal blow to the head. Cause of death: epidural hematoma.

Pokie sank back wearily and spat out an epithet. "The man was dead hours before he hit the water."

"Vengeance?" said Jinx Ransom, biting neatly into a freshly baked gingersnap. "It's a perfectly reasonable motive for murder. If, that is, one accepts there is such a thing as a reasonable motive for murder."

She and Kate were sitting on the back porch, overlooking the cemetery. It was a windless afternoon. Nothing moved—not the leaves on the trees, not the low-lying clouds, not even the air, which hung listless over the valley. The only creature stirring was Gracie, who shuffled out of the kitchen with a tray of rattling coffee cups and teaspoons. Pausing outside, Gracie cocked her head up at the sky.

"It's going to rain," she announced with absolute confidence.

"Charlie Decker was a poet," said Kate. "He loved children. Even more important, children loved him. Don't you think they'd know? They'd sense it if he was dangerous?"

"Nonsense. Children are as stupid as all the rest of us. And as for his being a mild-mannered poet, that doesn't mean a thing. He had five years to brood about his loss. That's certainly long enough to turn an obsession into violence."

"But the people who knew him all agree he wasn't a violent man."

"We're all violent. Especially when it concerns the ones we love. They're intimately connected, love and hate."

"That's a pretty grim view of human nature."

"But a realistic one. My husband was a circuit-court judge. My son was once a prosecutor. Oh, I've heard all their stories and believe me, reality's much grimmer than we could ever imagine.''

Kate gazed out at the gently sloping lawn, at the flat bronze plaques marching out like footsteps across the grass. "Why did David leave the prosecutor's office?"

"Hasn't he told you?"

"He said something about slave wages. But I get the feeling money doesn't really mean much to him."

"Money doesn't mean diddly squat to David," Gracie interjected. She was looking down at a broken gingersnap, as if she wasn't quite sure whether to eat it or toss it to the birds.

"Then why did he leave?"

Jinx gave her one of those crystal-blue looks. "You were a surprise to me, Kate. It's rare enough for David to bring any woman to meet me. And then, when I heard you were a doctor...Well." She shook her head in amazement.

"David doesn't like doctors much," Gracie explained helpfully.

"It's a bit more than just dislike, dear."

"You're right," agreed Gracie after a few seconds' thought. "I suppose *loathe* is a better word."

Jinx reached for her cane and stood up. "Come, Kate," she beckoned. "There's something I think you should see."

It was a slow and solemn walk, through the feathery gap in the mock orange hedge, to a shady spot beneath the monkeypod tree. Insects drifted like motes in the windless air. At their feet, a small bunch of flowers lay wilting on a grave.

Noah Ransom
Seven years old.

"My grandson," said Jinx.

A leaf fluttered down from the tree and lay trembling on the grass.

"It must have been terrible for David," Kate murmured. "To lose his only child."

"Terrible for anyone. But especially for David." Jinx nudged the leaf aside with her cane. "Let me tell you about my son. He's very much like his father in one way: he doesn't love easily. He's like a miser, holding on to some priceless hoard of gold. But then, when he does release it, he gives it all and that's it. There's no turning back. That's why it was so hard on him, losing Noah. That boy was the most precious thing in his life and he still can't accept the fact he's gone. Maybe that's why he has so much trouble with you." She turned to Kate. "Do you know how the boy died?"

"He said it was a case of meningitis."

"Bacterial meningitis. Curable illness, right?"

"If it's caught early enough."

"*If.* That's the word that haunts David." She looked down sadly at the wilted flowers. "He was out of town—some convention in Chicago—when Noah got sick. At first, Linda didn't think much of it. You know how kids are, always coming down with colds. But the boy's fever wouldn't go away. And then Noah said he had a headache. His usual pediatrician was on vacation so Linda took the boy to another doctor, in the same building. For two hours they sat in the waiting room. After all that, the doctor spent only five minutes with Noah. And then he sent him home."

Kate stared down at the grave, knowing, fearing, what would come next.

"Linda called the doctor three times that night. She must have known something was wrong. But all she got from him was a scolding. He told her she was just an anxious mother. That she ought to know better than to turn a cold into a crisis. When she finally brought Noah into Emergency, he was delirious. He just kept mumbling, asking for his Daddy. The hospital doctors did what they could, but..." Jinx gave a little shrug. "It wasn't easy for either of them. Linda blamed herself. And David...he just withdrew. He shrank into his tight little shell and refused to come out, even for her. I'm not surprised she left him." Jinx looked off, toward the house. "It came out later, about the doctor. That he was an alcoholic. That he'd lost his license in California. That's when David turned it into his personal crusade. Oh, he ruined the man, all right. He did a very thorough job of it. But it took over his life, wrecked his marriage. That's when he left the prosecutor's office. He's made a lot of money since then, destroying doctors. But the money's not why he does it. Somewhere, in the back of his mind, he'll always be crucifying that one doctor. The one who killed Noah."

That's why we never had a chance, Kate thought. *I was always the enemy. The one he wanted to destroy.*

Jinx wandered slowly back to the house. For a long time, Kate stood alone in the shadow of the old tree, thinking about Noah Ransom, seven years old. About how powerful a force it was, this love for a child; as cruelly obsessive as anything between a man and a woman. Could she ever compete with the memory of a son? Or ever escape the blame for his death?

All these years, David had held on to that pain. He'd used it as some mystical source of power to fight the same battle over and over again. The way Charlie Decker had used his pain to sustain him through five long years in a mental hospital.

Five years in a hospital.

She frowned, suddenly remembering the bottle of pills in Decker's nightstand. Haldol. Pills for psychotics. Was he, in fact, crazy?

Turning, she looked back at the porch and saw it was empty. Jinx and

Gracie had gone into the house. The air was so heavy she could feel it weighing oppressively on her shoulders. A storm on the way, she thought.

If she left now, she might make it to the state hospital before the rain started.

DR. NEMECHEK was a thin, slouching man with tired eyes and a puckered mouth. His shirt was rumpled and his white coat hung in folds on his frail shoulders. He looked like a man who'd slept all night in his clothes.

They walked together on the hospital grounds. All around them, white-gowned patients wandered aimlessly like dandelion fluffs drifting about the lawn. Every so often, Dr. Nemechek would stop to pat a shoulder or murmur a few words of greeting. *How are you, Mrs. Solti? Just fine, Doctor. Why didn't you come to group therapy? Oh, it's my old trouble, you know. All those mealyworms in my feet. I see. I see. Well, good afternoon, Mrs. Solti. Good afternoon, Doctor.*

Dr. Nemechek paused on the grass and gazed around sadly at his kingdom of shattered minds. "Charlie Decker never belonged here," he remarked. "I told them from the beginning that he wasn't criminally insane. But the court had their so-called expert from the mainland. So he was committed." He shook his head. "That's the trouble with courts. All they look at is their evidence, whatever that means. I look at the man."

"And what did you see when you looked at Charlie?"

"He was withdrawn. Very depressed. At times, maybe, delusional."

"Then he was insane."

"But not criminally so." Nemechek turned to her as if he wanted to be absolutely certain she understood his point. "Insanity can be dangerous. Or it can be nothing more than a gentle affliction. A merciful shield against pain. That's what it was for Charlie: a shield. His delusion kept him alive. That's why I never tried to tamper with it. I felt that if I ever took away that shield, it would kill him."

"The police say he was a murderer."

"Ridiculous."

"Why?"

"He was a perfectly benign creature. He'd go out of his way to avoid stepping on a cricket."

"Maybe killing people was easier."

Nemechek gave a dismissive wave. "He had no reason to kill anyone."

"What about Jenny Brook? Wasn't she his reason?"

"Charlie's delusion wasn't about Jenny. He'd accepted her death as inevitable."

Kate frowned. "Then what was his delusion?"

"It was about their child. It was something one of the doctors told him, about the baby being born alive. Only Charlie got it twisted around in his head. That was his obsession, this missing daughter of his. Every August, he'd hold a little birthday celebration. He'd tell us, 'My girl's five years old today.' He wanted to find her. Wanted to raise her like a little princess, give her dresses and dolls and all the things girls are supposed to like. But I knew he'd never really try to find her. He was terrified of learning the truth: that the baby really was dead.''

A sprinkling of rain made them both glance up at the sky. Wind was gusting the clouds and on the lawn, nurses hurried about, coaxing patients out of the coming storm.

"Is there any possibility he was right?" she asked. "That the girl's still alive?"

"Not a chance." A curtain of drizzle had drifted between them, blotting out his gray face. "The baby's dead, Dr. Chesne. For the last five years, the only place that child existed was in Charlie Decker's mind."

THE BABY'S DEAD.

As Kate drove the mist-shrouded highway back to Jinx's house, Dr. Nemechek's words kept repeating in her head.

The baby's dead. The only place that child existed was in Charlie Decker's mind.

If the girl had lived, what would she be like now? Kate wondered. Would she have her father's dark hair? Would she have her mother's glow of eternity in her five-year-old eyes?

The face of Jenny Brook took shape in her mind, an impish smile framed by the blue sky of a summer day. At that instant, fog puffed across the road and Kate strained to see through the mist. As she did, the image of Jenny Brook wavered, dissolved; in its place was another face, a small one, framed by ironwood trees. There was a break in the clouds; suddenly, the mist vanished from the road. And as the sunlight broke through, so did the revelation. She almost slammed on the brakes.

Why the hell didn't I see it before?

Jenny Brook's child was still alive.

And he was five years old.

"WHERE THE HELL is she?" muttered David, slamming the telephone down. "Nemechek says she left the state hospital at five. She should be home by now." He glanced irritably across his desk at Phil Glickman, who was poking a pair of chopsticks into a carton of chow mein.

"You know," Glickman mumbled as he expertly shuttled noodles into his mouth, "this case gets more confusing every time I hear about it. You start off with a simple act of malpractice and you end up with murder. In plural. Where's it gonna lead next?"

"I wish I knew." David sighed. Swiveling around toward the window, he tried to ignore the tempting smells of Glickman's take-out supper. Outside, the clouds were darkening to a gunmetal gray. It reminded him of just how late it was. Ordinarily, he'd be packing up his briefcase for home. But he'd needed a chance to think, and this was where his mind seemed to work best—right here at this window.

"What a way to commit murder, slashing someone's throat," Glickman said. "I mean, think of all that blood! Takes a lot of nerve."

"Or desperation."

"And it can't be that easy. You'd have to get up pretty close to slice that neck artery." He slashed a chopstick through the air. "There are so many easier ways to do the job."

"Sounds like you've put some thought into the matter."

"Don't we all? Everyone has some dark fantasy. Cornering your wife's lover in the alley. Getting back at the punk who mugged you. We can all think of someone we'd really like to put away. And it can't be that hard, you know? Murder. If a guy's smart, he does it with subtlety." He slurped up a mouthful of noodles. "Poison, for instance. Something that kills fast and can't be traced. Now there's the perfect murder."

"Except for one thing."

"What's that?"

"Where's the satisfaction if your victim doesn't suffer?"

"A problem," Glickman conceded. "So you make 'em suffer through terror. Warnings. Threats."

David shifted uneasily, remembering the bloodred skull on Kate's wall. Through narrowed eyes, he watched the clouds hanging low on the horizon. With every passing minute, his sense of impending disaster grew stronger.

He rose to his feet and began throwing papers into his briefcase. It was useless, hanging around here; he could worry just as effectively at his mother's house.

"You know, there's one thing about this case that still bothers me," remarked Glickman, gulping the last of his supper.

"What's that?"

"That EKG. Tanaka and Richter were killed in just about the bloodiest way possible. Why should the murderer go out of his way to make Ellen O'Brien's death look like a heart attack?"

"The one thing I learned in the prosecutor's office," said David, snapping his briefcase shut, "is that murder doesn't have to make sense."

"Well, it seems to me our killer went to a lot of trouble just to shift the blame to Kate Chesne."

David was already at the door when he suddenly halted. "What did you say?"

"That he went to a lot of trouble to pin the blame—"

"No, the word you used was *shift*. He *shifted* the blame!"

"Maybe I did. So?"

"So who gets sued when a patient dies unexpectedly on the operating table?"

"The blame's usually shared by..." Glickman stopped. "Oh, my God. Why the hell didn't I think of that before?"

David was already reaching for the telephone. As he dialed the police, he cursed himself for being so blind. The killer had been there all along. Watching. Waiting. He must have known that Kate was hunting for answers, and that she was getting close. Now he was scared. Scared enough to scrawl a warning on Kate's wall. Scared enough to tail a car down a dark highway.

Maybe even scared enough to kill one more time.

IT WAS FIVE-THIRTY and most of the clerks in Medical Records had gone for the day. The lone clerk who remained grudgingly took Kate's request slip and went to the computer terminal to call up the chart location. As the data appeared, she frowned.

"This patient's deceased," she noted, pointing to the screen.

"I know," said Kate, wearily remembering the last time she'd tried to retrieve a chart from the Deceased Persons' room.

"So it's in the inactive files."

"I understand that. Could you please get me the chart?"

"It may take a while to track it down. Why don't you come back tomorrow?"

Kate resisted the urge to reach over and grab the clerk by her frilly dress. "I need the chart *now*." She felt like adding: *It's a matter of life and death.*

The clerk looked at her watch and tapped her pencil on the desk. With agonizing slowness, she rose to her feet and vanished into the file room.

Fifteen minutes passed before she returned with the record. Kate retreated to a corner table and stared down at the name on the cover: Brook, Baby Girl.

The child had never even had a name.

The chart contained pitifully few pages, only the hospital face sheet, death certificate, and a scrawled summary of the infant's short existence. Death had been pronounced August 17 at 2:00 a.m., an hour after birth. The cause of death was cerebral anoxia: the tiny brain had been starved of oxygen. The death certificate was signed by Dr. Henry Tanaka.

Kate next turned her attention to the copy of Jenny Brook's chart, which she'd brought with her. She'd read these pages so many times before; now she studied it line by line, pondering the significance of each sentence.

"...28-year-old female, G1P0, 36 weeks' gestation, admitted via E.R. in early labor..."

A routine report, she thought. There were no surprises, no warnings of the disaster to come. But at the bottom of the first page she stopped, her gaze focusing on a single statement: "Because of maternal family history of spina bifida, amniocentesis was performed at eighteen weeks of pregnancy and revealed no abnormalities.''

Amniocentesis. Early in her pregnancy, fluid had been withdrawn from Jenny Brook's womb for analysis. This would have identified any fetal malformations. It also would have identified the baby's sex.

The amniocentesis report was not included in the hospital chart. That didn't surprise her; the report had probably been filed away in Jenny Brook's outpatient record.

Which had conveniently vanished from Dr. Tanaka's office, she realized with a start.

Kate closed the chart. Suddenly feverish, she rose and returned to the file clerk. "I need another record," she said.

"Not another deceased patient, I hope."

"No, this one's still alive."

"Name?"

"William Santini."

It took only a minute for the clerk to find it. When Kate finally held it in her hands, she was almost afraid to open it, afraid to see what she already knew lay inside. She stood there beside the clerk's desk, wondering if she really wanted to know.

She opened the cover.

A copy of the birth certificate stared up at her.

Name: William Santini.
Date of Birth: August 17
Time: 03:00.

August 17, the same day. But not quite the same time. Exactly one hour after Baby Girl Brook had left the world, William Santini had entered it.

Two infants; one living, one dead. Had there ever been a better motive for murder?

"Don't tell me you still have charts to finish," remarked a shockingly familiar voice.

Kate's head whipped around. Guy Santini had just walked in the door. She slapped the chart closed but instantly realized the name was scrawled in bold black ink across the cover. In a panic, she hugged the chart to her chest as an automatic smile congealed on her face.

"I'm just...cleaning up some last paperwork." She swallowed and managed to add, conversationally, "You're here late."

"Stranded again. Car's back in the shop so Susan's picking me up." He glanced across the counter, searching for the clerk, who'd temporarily vanished. "Where's the help around here, anyway?"

"She was, uh, here just a minute ago," said Kate, inching toward the exit.

"I guess you heard the news. About Avery's wife. A blessing, really, considering her—" He looked at her and she froze, just two feet from the door.

He frowned. "Is something wrong?"

"No. I've just— Look, I've really got to go." She turned and was about to flee out the door when the file clerk yelled: "Dr. Chesne!"

"What?" Kate spun around to see the woman peering at her reproachfully from behind a shelf.

"The chart. You can't take it out of the department."

Kate looked down at the folder she was still holding to her chest and frantically debated her next move. She didn't dare return the chart while Guy was standing right beside the counter; he'd see the name. But she couldn't stand here like a half-wit, either.

They were both frowning at her, waiting for her to say something.

"Look, if you're not finished with it, I can hold it right here," the clerk offered, moving to the counter.

"No. I mean..."

Guy laughed. "What's in that thing, anyway? State secrets?"

Kate realized she was clutching the chart as though terrified it would be forcibly pried from her grasp. With her heart hammering, she willed her feet to move forward. Her hand was barely steady as she placed the chart facedown on the counter. "I'm not finished with it."

"Then I'll hold it for you." The clerk reached over and for one terrifying second seemed poised to expose the patient's name. Instead she merely scooped up the request list that Guy had just laid on the counter. "Why don't you sit down, Dr. Santini?" she suggested. "I'll bring your records over to you." Then she turned and vanished into the file room.

Time to get the hell out of here, thought Kate.

It took all her self-control not to bolt out the door. She felt Guy's eyes on her back as she moved slowly and deliberately toward the exit. Only when she'd actually made it into the hall, only when she heard the door thud shut behind her, did the impact of what she'd discovered hit her full force. Guy Santini was her colleague. Her friend.

He was also a murderer. And she was the only one who knew.

GUY STARED AT THE DOOR through which Kate had just retreated. He'd known Kate Chesne for almost a year now and he'd never seen her so jittery. Puzzled, he turned and headed to the corner table to wait. It was his favorite spot, this little nook; it gave him a sense of privacy in this vast, impersonal room. Someone else obviously favored it, as well. There were two charts still lying there, waiting to be refiled. He grabbed a chair and was about to nudge the folders aside when his gaze suddenly froze on the top cover. He felt his legs give away. Slowly he sank into the chair and stared at the name.

Brook, Baby Girl. Deceased.

Dear God, he thought. *It can't be the same Brook.*

He flipped it open and hunted for the mother's name on the death certificate. What he saw sent panic knifing through him.

Mother: Brook, Jennifer.

The same woman. The same baby. He had to think; he had to stay calm. Yes, he would stay calm. There was nothing to worry about. No one could connect him to Jenny Brook or the child. The four people involved with that tragedy of five years ago were now dead. There was no reason for anyone to be curious.

Or was there?

He shot to his feet and hurried back to the counter. The chart that Kate had so reluctantly parted with was still lying there, face down. He flipped it over. His own son's name stared up at him.

Kate Chesne knew. She *had* to know. And she had to be stopped.

"Here you are," said the file clerk, emerging from the shelves with an armload of charts. "I think I've got all—" She halted in amazement. "Where are you going? Dr. Santini!"

Guy didn't answer; he was too busy running out the door.

THE HOSPITAL LOBBY was reassuringly bright when Kate stepped off the elevator. A few visitors still lingered by the lobby doors, staring out at the storm. A security guard lounged at the information desk, chatting with a pretty volunteer. Kate hurried over to the public telephones. An out-of-order sign was taped to the first phone; a man was feeding a quarter into the other. She planted herself right behind him and waited. Wind rattled the lobby windows; outside, the parking lot was obscured by a heavy curtain of rain. She prayed that Lieutenant Ah Ching would be at his desk.

But at that moment it wasn't Ah Ching's voice she longed to hear most of all; it was David's.

The man was still talking on the phone. Glancing around, she was alarmed to see the security guard had vanished. The volunteer was already closing down the information desk. The place was emptying out too fast. She didn't want to be left alone—not here, not with what she knew.

She fled the hospital and headed out into the downpour.

She'd parked Jinx's car at the far end of the lot. The storm had become a fierce, tropical battering of wind and rain. By the time she'd dashed across to the car, her clothes were soaked. It took a few seconds to fumble through the unfamiliar set of keys, another few seconds to unlock the door. She was so intent on escaping the storm that she scarcely noticed the shadow moving toward her through the gloom. Just as she slid onto the driver's seat, the shadow closed in. A hand seized her arm.

She stared up to see Guy Santini towering over her.

Chapter Fifteen

"Move over," he said.

"Guy, my arm—"

"I said move over."

Desperate, she glanced around for some passerby who might hear her screams. But the lot was deserted and the only sound was the thudding of rain on the car's roof.

Escape was impossible. Guy was blocking the driver's exit and she'd never be able to scramble out the passenger door in time.

Before she could even plan her next move, Guy shoved her aside and slid onto the driver's seat. The door slammed shut. Through the window, the gray light of evening cast a watery glow on his face.

"Your keys, Kate," he demanded.

The keys had dropped beside her on the seat; she made no move to retrieve them.

"Give me the damn keys!" He suddenly spotted them in the dim light. Snatching them up, he shoved the key into the ignition. The second he did, she lashed out. Like a trapped animal, she clawed at his face but at the last instant, some inner revulsion at the viciousness of her attack made her hesitate. It was only a split second, but it was enough time for him to react.

Flinching aside, he seized her wrist and wrenched her sideways so hard she was thrown back against the seat.

"If I have to," he said in a deadly quiet voice, "I swear I'll break your arm." He threw the gear in reverse and the car jerked backward. Then, hitting the gas, he spun the car out of the parking lot and into the street.

"Where are you taking me?" she asked.

"Somewhere. Anywhere. I'm going to talk and you're going to listen."

"About—about what?"

"You know what the hell about!"

Her chin snapped up expectantly as they approached an intersection. If she could throw herself out—

But he'd already anticipated her move. Seizing her arm, he yanked her toward him and sped through the intersection just as the signal turned red.

That was the last stoplight before the freeway. The car accelerated. She watched in despair as the speedometer climbed to sixty. She'd missed her chance. If she tried to leap out now, she'd almost certainly break her neck.

He knew as well as she did that she'd never be so reckless. He released her arm. "It was none of your business, Kate," he said, his eyes shifting back to the road. "You had no right to pry. No right at all."

"Ellen was my patient—*our* patient—"

"That doesn't mean you can tear my life apart!"

"What about her life? And Ann's? They're dead, Guy!"

"And the past died with them! I say let it stay dead."

"My God, I thought I knew you. I thought we were friends—"

"I have to protect my son. And Susan. You think I'd stand back and let them be destroyed?"

"They'd never take the boy away from you! Not after five years! The courts are bound to give you custody—"

"You think all I'm worried about is custody? Oh, we'd keep William all right. There's no judge on earth who'd be able to take him away from me! Who'd hand him over to some lunatic like Decker! No. It's Susan I'm thinking of."

The highway was slick with rain, the road treacherous. Both his hands were fully occupied on the steering wheel. If she lunged at him now, the car would surely spin out of control, killing them both. She had to wait for another time, another chance to escape.

"I don't understand," she persisted, scanning the road ahead for a stalled car, a traffic jam, anything to slow them down. "What do you mean, it's Susan you're worried about?"

"She doesn't know." At Kate's incredulous look, he nodded. "She thinks William is hers."

"How can she not know?"

"I've kept it from her. For five years, it's been my little secret. She was under anesthesia when our baby was born. It was a nightmare, all that rush, all that panic to do an emergency C-section. That was our third baby, Kate. Our last chance. And she was born dead...." He paused and cleared his throat; when he spoke again, his voice was still thick with pain. "I didn't know what to do. What to tell Susan. There she was, sleeping. So peaceful, so happy. And there I was, holding our dead baby girl."

"You took Jenny Brook's baby as your own."

He hastily scraped the back of his hand across his face. "It was—it was an act of God. Can't you see that? *An act of God.* That's how it seemed to me at the time. The woman had just died. And there was her baby boy, this absolutely *perfect* baby boy, crying in the next room. No one to hold him. Or love him. No one knew a thing about the child's father. There didn't seem to be any relatives, anyone who cared. And there was Susan, already starting to wake up. Can't you understand? It would have killed her to find out. God *gave* us that boy! It was as if— as if He had planned it that way. We all felt it. Ann. Ellen. Only Tanaka—''

''He didn't agree?''

''Not at first. I argued with him. I practically begged him. It was only when Susan opened her eyes and asked for her baby that he finally gave in. So Ellen brought the boy to the room. She put him in Susan's arms. And my Susan—she just looked at him and then she—she started to cry....'' Guy wiped his sleeve across his face. ''That's when we knew we'd done the right thing.''

Yes, Kate could see the perfection of that moment. A decision as wise as Solomon's. What better proof of its rightness than the sight of a newborn baby curled up in his mother's arms?

But that same decision had led to the murder of four people.

Soon it would be five.

The car suddenly slowed; with a new burst of hope, she looked up. Traffic was growing heavier. Far ahead lay the Pali tunnel, curtained off by rain. She knew there was an emergency telephone somewhere near the entrance. If he would just slow down a little more, if she could shove the car door open, she might be able to fling herself out before he could stop her.

The chance never came. Instead of heading into the tunnel, Guy veered off onto a thickly wooded side road and roared past a sign labeled: Pali Lookout. The last stop, she thought. Set on a cliff high above the valley, this was the overhang where suicidal lovers sealed their pacts, where ancient warriors once were flung to their deaths. It was the perfect spot for murder.

A last flood of desperation made her claw for the door. Before she could get it open, he yanked her back. She turned and flew at him with both fists. Guy struggled to fight her off and lost control of the wheel. The car swerved off the road. By the erratic beams of their headlights, she caught glimpses of trees looming ahead. Branches thudded against the windshield but she was beyond caring whether they crashed; her only goal was escape.

It was Guy's overwhelming strength that decided the battle. He threw all his weight into shoving her back. Then, cursing, he grabbed the wheel and spun it wildly to the left. The right fender scraped trees as the car veered back onto the road. Kate, sprawled against the seat, could only watch in defeat as they weaved up the last hundred yards to the lookout.

Guy stopped the car and killed the engine. For a long time he sat in silence, as though summoning up the courage to get the job done. Outside, the rain had slowed to a drizzle and beyond the cliff's edge, mist swirled past, shrouding the fatal plunge from view.

"That was a damned crazy stunt you pulled," he said quietly. "Why the hell did you do it?"

Slowly she bowed her head; she felt a profound sense of weariness. Of inevitability. "Because you're going to kill me," she whispered. "The way you killed the others."

"I'm going to *what*?"

She looked up, searching his eyes for some trace of remorse. If only she could reach inside him and drag out some last scrap of humanity! "Was it easy?" she asked softly. "Cutting Ann's throat? Watching her bleed to death?"

"You mean— You really think I— Dear God!" He dropped his head in his hands. Suddenly he began to laugh. It was soft at first, then it grew louder and wilder until his whole body was racked by what sounded more like sobs than laughter. He didn't notice the new set of headlights, flickering like a beacon through the mist. She glanced around and saw that another car had wandered up the road. This was her chance to throw open the door, to run for help. But she didn't. In that instant she knew that Guy had never really meant to hurt her. That he was incapable of murder.

Without warning, he shoved his door open and stumbled out into the fog. At the edge of the lookout, he halted, his head and shoulders bowed as if in prayer.

Kate got out of the car and followed him. She didn't say a thing. She simply reached out and touched his arm. She could almost feel the pain, the confusion, coursing through his body.

"Then you didn't kill them," she said.

He looked up and slowly took in a deep breath of air. "I'd do almost anything to keep my son. But murder?" He shook his head. "No. God, no. Oh, I thought about killing Decker. Who would have missed him? He was nothing, just a—a scrap of human garbage. And it seemed like such an easy way out. Maybe the only way out. He wouldn't give up. He kept hounding people for answers. Demanding to know where the baby was."

"How did he know the baby was alive?"

"There was another doctor in the delivery room that night—"

"You mean Dr. Vaughn?"

"Decker talked to him. Learned just enough."

"And then Vaughn died in a car accident."

Guy nodded. "I thought it'd all be okay, then. I thought it was over. But then Decker got out of the state hospital. Sooner or later, someone would've talked. Tanaka was ready to. And Ann was scared out of her mind. I gave her some money, to leave the islands. But she never made it. Decker got to her first."

"That doesn't make sense, Guy. Why would he kill the only people who could give him the answers?"

"He was psychotic."

"Even psychotics have some sort of logic."

"He must have done it. There was no one else who—"

From somewhere in the mist came the hard click of metal. Kate and Guy froze as footsteps rapped slowly across the pavement. Out of the gathering darkness, a figure emerged, like vapor taking on substance until it stood before them. Even in the somber light of dusk, Susan Santini's red hair seemed to sparkle with fire. But it was the dull gray of the gun that held Kate's gaze.

"Move out of the way, Guy," Susan ordered softly.

Guy was too stunned to move or speak; he could only stare mutely at his wife.

"It was you," Kate murmured in astonishment. "All the time *you* were the one. Not Decker."

Slowly, Susan turned her unfocused gaze on Kate. Through the veil of mist drifting between them, her face was as vague and formless as a ghost's. "You don't understand, do you? But you've never had a baby, Kate. You've never been afraid of someone hurting it or taking it away. That's all a mother ever thinks about. Worries about. It's all *I* ever worried about."

A low groan escaped Guy's throat. "My God, Susan. Do you understand what you've done?"

"You wouldn't do it. So I had to. All those years, I never knew about William. You should have told me, Guy. You should have told me. I had to hear it from Tanaka."

"You killed four people, Susan!"

"Not four. Only three. I didn't kill Ellen." Susan looked at Kate. "She did."

Kate stared at her. "What do you mean?"

"That wasn't succinylcholine in the vial. It was potassium chloride. You gave Ellen a lethal dose." Her gaze shifted back to her husband. "I didn't want you to be blamed, darling. I couldn't stand to see you hurt, the way you were hurt by the last lawsuit. So I changed the EKG. I put *her* initials on it."

"And I got the blame," finished Kate.

Nodding, Susan raised the gun. "Yes, Kate. You got the blame. I'm sorry. Now please, Guy. Move away. It has to be done, for William's sake."

"No, Susan."

She frowned at him in disbelief. "They'll take him away from me. Don't you see? They'll take my baby away."

"I won't let them. I promise."

Susan shook her head. "It's too late, Guy. I've killed the others. She's the only one who knows."

"But *I* know!" Guy blurted out. "Are you going to kill me, too?"

"You won't tell. You're my husband."

"Susan, give me the gun." Guy moved slowly forward, his hand held out to her. His voice dropped, became gentle, intimate. "Please, darling. Nothing will happen. I'll take care of everything. Just give it to me."

She retreated a step and almost lost her balance on the uneven terrain. Guy froze as the barrel of the gun swayed for an instant in his direction.

"You're not going to hurt me, Susan."

"Please, Guy..."

He took a step forward. "Are you?"

"I love you," she moaned.

"Then give me the gun. Yes, darling. Give it to me...."

The distance between them slowly evaporated. Guy's hand stretched out to her, coaxing her with the promise of warmth and safety. She stared at it with longing, as though knowing in some deep part of her mind that it was forever beyond her reach. The gun was only inches from Guy's fingers and still she didn't move; she was paralyzed by the inevitability of defeat.

Guy, at last sensing he had won, quickly closed the gap between them. Seizing the gun by the barrel, he tried to tug it from her hands.

But she didn't surrender it. At that instant, something inside her, some last spark of resistance, seemed to flare up and she tried to wrench it back.

"Let go!" she screamed.

"Give it to me," Guy demanded, wrestling for control of the weapon. "Susan, give it to me!"

The gun's blast seemed to trap them in freeze-frame. They stared at each other in astonishment, neither of them willing to believe what had just happened. Then Guy stumbled backward, clutching his leg.

"No!" Susan's wail rose up and drifted, ghostlike, through the mist. Slowly she turned toward Kate. The glow of desperation was in her eyes. And she was still clutching the gun.

That's when Kate ran. Blindly, desperately, into the mist. She heard a pistol shot. A bullet whistled past and thudded into the dirt near her feet. There was no time to get her bearings, to circle back toward the road. She just kept running and prayed that the fog would shroud her from Susan.

The ground suddenly rose upward. Through fingers of mist, she saw the sheer face of the ridge, sparsely stubbled with brush. She spun around and realized instantly that the way back to the main road was blocked by Susan's approach. Her only escape route lay to the left, down the crumbling remains of the old Pali road. It was the original cliff pass. The road had long ago been abandoned to the elements. She had no idea how far it would take her; parts of it, she knew, had collapsed down the sheer slope.

The sound of footsteps closing in left her no choice. She scrambled over a low concrete wall and at once found herself sliding helplessly down a muddy bank. Clawing at branches and vines, she managed to break her fall until she landed, scratched and breathless, on a slab of pavement. The old Pali road.

Somewhere above, hidden among the clouds, bushes rustled. "There's nowhere to run, Kate!" Susan's disembodied voice seemed to come from everywhere at once. "The old road doesn't go very far. One wrong step and you'll be over the cliff. So you'd better be careful...."

Careful...careful... The shouted warning echoed off the ridge and shattered into terrifying fragments of sound. The rustling of bushes moved closer. Susan was closing in. She was taking her time, advancing slowly, steadily. Her victim was trapped. And she knew it.

But trapped wasn't the same as helpless.

Kate leaped to her feet and began to run. The old road was full of cracks and potholes. In places it had crumbled away entirely and young trees poked through, their roots rippling the asphalt. She strained to see through the fog but could make out no more than a few feet ahead. Darkness was falling fast; it would cut off the last of her visibility. But it would also be a cloak in which to hide.

But where could she hide? On her right, the ridge loomed steeply upward; on her left, the pavement broke off sharply at the cliff's edge. She had no choice; she had to keep running.

She stumbled over a loose boulder and sprawled onto the brutal asphalt. At once she was back on her feet, mindless of the pain searing her knees. Even as she ran, she forced herself to think ahead. Would there be a barrier at the road's end? Or would there simply be a straight drop to oblivion? In either case, there'd be no escape. There would only be a bullet, and then a plunge over the cliff. How long would it be before they found her body?

A gust of wind swept the road. For an instant, the mist cleared. She saw looming to her right the face of the ridge, covered by dense brush. Halfway up, almost hidden by the overgrowth, was the mouth of a cave. If she could reach it, if she could scramble up those bushes before Susan passed this way, she could hide until help arrived. If it arrived.

She threaded her way into the shrubbery and began clambering up the mountainside. Rain had muddied the slope; she had to claw for roots and branches to pull herself up. All the time, there was the danger of dislodging a boulder, of sending it thundering to the road. The crash would certainly alert Susan. And here she'd be, poised like a fly on the wall. One well-placed bullet would end it all.

The sound of footsteps made her freeze. Susan was approaching. Desperately, Kate hugged the mountain, willing herself to blend into the bushes.

The footsteps slowed, stopped. At that instant, the wind nudged the clouds against the ridge, draping Kate in silvery mist. The footsteps moved on, slowly clipping across the pavement. Only when the sound had faded did Kate dare continue her climb.

By the time she reached the cave's mouth, her hands had cramped into claws. In took her last ounce of strength to drag herself up into the muddy hollow. There she collapsed, fighting to catch her breath. Dampness trickled from the tree roots above and dripped onto her face. She heard, deep in the shadows, the rustle of movement and something scuttled across her arm. A beetle. She didn't have the energy to brush it off. Exhausted and shivering, she curled up like a tired puppy in the mud. The wind rose, sweeping the clouds from the pass. Already the mist was fading. If she could just hold out until nightfall. That was the most she could hope for: darkness.

Closing her eyes, she focused on a mental image of David. If only he could hear her silent plea for help. But he couldn't help her. No one could. She wondered how he'd react to her death. Would he feel any grief? Or would he simply shrug it off as a tragic end to a fading love affair? That was what hurt most—the thought of his indifference.

She cradled her face in her arms, and warm tears mingled with the icy water on her cheeks. She'd never felt so alone, so abandoned. Suddenly it didn't matter whether she lived or died; only that someone cared.

But I'm the only one who really cares.

A desperate new strength stirred inside her. Slowly she unfolded her limbs and looked out at the thin wisps of fog drifting past the cave. And she felt a new sense of fury that her life might be stolen from her and that the man she loved wasn't even here to help.

If I want to be saved, I have to do it myself.

It was the footsteps, moving slowly back along the road, that told her darkness would come too late to save her. Through the tangle of branches fringing the cave mouth, she saw against the sky's fading light the velvety green of a distant ridge. The mist had vanished; so had her invisibility.

"You're up there, aren't you?" Susan's voice floated up from the road, a sound so chilling Kate trembled. "I almost missed it. But there's one unfortunate thing about caves. Something I'm sure you've realized by now. They're dead ends."

Rocks rattled down the slope and slammed onto the road, their impact echoing like gunshot. *She's climbing the ridge,* Kate thought frantically. *She's coming for me....*

Her only escape route was back out through the cave mouth. Right into Susan's line of fire.

A twig snapped and more rocks slithered down the mountain. Susan was closing in. Kate had no choice left; either she bolted now or she'd be trapped like a rat.

Swiftly she groped around in the mud and came up with a fist-size rock. It wasn't much against a gun, but it was all she had. Cautiously, she eased her head out. To her horror, she saw that Susan was already halfway up the slope.

Their eyes met. In that instant, each recognized the other's desperation. One was fighting for her life, the other for her child. There could be no compromise, no surrender, except in death.

Susan took aim; the barrel swung up toward her prey's head.

Kate hurled the rock.

It skimmed the bushes and thudded against Susan's shoulder. Crying out, Susan slid a few feet down the mountainside before she managed to grab hold of a branch. There she clung for a moment, stunned.

Kate scrambled out of the cave and began clawing her way up the ridge. Even as she pulled herself up, branch by branch, some rational part of her brain was screaming that the ascent was impossible, that the cliff face was too steep, the bushes too straggly to support her weight. But her arms and legs seemed to move on their own, guided not by logic but by the instinct to survive. Her sleeves were shredded by thorns and her hands and arms were already scraped raw but she was too numbed by terror to feel pain.

A bullet ricocheted off a boulder. Kate cringed as shattered rock and earth spat out and stung her face. Susan's aim was wide; she couldn't cling to the mountain and shoot accurately at the same time.

Kate looked up to find herself staring at an overhanging rock, laced with vines. Was she strong enough to drag herself over the top? Would the vines hold her weight? The surface was impossibly steep and she was so tired, so very tired....

Another shot rang out; the bullet came so close she could feel it whistle past her cheek. Kate frantically grabbed a vine and began to drag herself up the rock face. Her shoes slid uselessly downward, then found a toe hold. She shimmied up a few precious inches, then a few more, her knees scraping the harsh volcanic boulder. High above, clouds raced across the sky, taunting her with the promise of freedom. How many bullets were left?

It only takes one....

Every inch became an agony. Her muscles screamed for rest. Even if a bullet found its mark, she doubted she'd feel the pain.

When at last she cleared the overhang, she was too exhausted to feel any sense of triumph. She hauled herself over the top and rolled onto a narrow ledge. It was nothing more than a flat boulder, turned slick with rain and lichen, but no bed had ever felt so wonderful. If only she could lie here forever. If she could close her eyes and sleep! But there was no time to rest, no time to allow the agony to ease from her body; Susan was right behind her.

She staggered to her feet, her legs trembling with exhaustion, her body buffeted by the whistling wind. One of her shoes had dropped off during the climb and with every step, thorns bit into her bare foot. But here the ascent was easier and she had only a few yards to go until she reached the top of the ridge.

She never made it.

A final gunshot rang out. What she felt wasn't pain, but surprise. There was the dull punch of the bullet slamming into her shoulder. The sky spun above her. For a moment she swayed, as unsteady as a reed in the wind. Then she felt herself fall backward. She was rolling, over and over, tumbling toward oblivion.

It was a halekoa bush—one of those tough stubborn weeds that clamp their roots deep into Hawaiian soil—that saved her life. It snagged her by the legs, slowing her fall just enough to keep her from plunging over the edge of the boulder. As she lay there, fighting to make sense of where she was, she became aware of a strange shrieking in the distance; to her confused brain, it sounded like an infant's wail, and it grew steadily louder.

The hallucination dragged her into consciousness. Groggily she opened her eyes to the dull monochrome of a cloudy sky. The infant's cry suddenly turned into the rhythmic wail of police sirens. The sound of help. Of salvation.

Then, across her field of vision, a shadow moved. She struggled to make out the figure standing over her. Against the sky's fading light, Susan Santini's face was nothing more than a black cutout with wind-lashed hair.

Susan said nothing as she slowly pointed her gun at Kate's head. For a moment she stood there, her skirt flapping in the wind, the pistol clutched in both hands. A gust whipped the narrow ledge, making her sway uneasily on the slippery rock.

The siren's cry suddenly cut off; men's shouts rose up from the valley.

Kate struggled to sit up. The barrel was staring her in the face. She managed to say, quietly, "There's no reason to kill me now, Susan. Is there?"

"You know about William."

"So will they." Kate nodded feebly toward the distant voices, which were already moving closer.

"They won't. Not unless you tell them."

"How do you know I haven't?"

The gun wavered. "No!" Susan cried, her voice tinged with the first trace of panic. "You couldn't have told them! You weren't certain—"

"You need help, Susan. I'll see you get it. All the help you need."

The barrel still hovered at her head. It would take only a twitch of the finger, the clap of the pistol hammer, to make Kate's whole world disintegrate. She gazed up into that black circle, wondering if she would feel the bullet. How strange, that she could face her own death with such calmness. She had fought to stay alive and she had lost. Now all she could do was wait for the end.

Then, through the wind's scream, she heard a voice calling her name. *Another hallucination,* she thought. *It must be....*

But there it was again: David's voice, shouting her name, over and over.

Suddenly she wanted to live! She wanted to tell him all the things she'd been too proud to say. That life was too precious to waste on hurts of the past. That if he just gave her the chance, she could help him forget all the pain he'd ever suffered.

"Please, Susan," she whispered. "Put it down."

Susan shifted but her hands were still gripping the pistol. She seemed to be listening to the voices, moving closer along the old Pali road.

"Can't you see?" cried Kate. "If you kill me, you'll destroy your only chance of keeping your son!"

Her words seemed to drain all the strength from Susan's arms. Slowly, almost imperceptibly, she let the gun drop. For a moment she stood motionless, her head bent in a silent gesture of mourning. Then she turned and gazed over the ledge, at the road far below. "It's too late now," she said in a voice so soft it was almost drowned in the wind. "I've already lost him."

A chorus of shouts from below told them they'd been spotted.

Susan, her hair whipping like flames, stared down at the gathering of men. "It's better this way," she insisted. "He'll have only good memories of me. That's the way childhood should be, you know. Only good memories..."

Perhaps it was a sudden gust that threw Susan off balance; Kate could never be certain. All she knew was that one instant Susan was poised on the edge of the rock and then, in the next instant, she was gone.

She fell soundlessly, without uttering a cry.

It was Kate who sobbed. She collapsed back against the cold and unforgiving bed of stone. As the world spun around her she cried, silently, for the woman who had just died, and for the four others who had lost their lives. So many deaths, so much suffering. And all in the name of love.

Chapter Sixteen

David was the first to reach her.

He found her seventy-five feet up the mountainside, unconscious and shivering on a bloodstained boulder. What he did next had nothing to do with logic; it was pure panic. He ripped off his jacket and threw it over her body, only one thought in his mind. *You can't die. I won't let you. Do you hear me, Kate? You can't die!*

He cradled her in his arms and as the warmth of her blood seeped through his shirt, he said her name over and over, as though he could somehow keep her soul from drifting forever beyond his reach. He scarcely heard the shouts of the rescue workers or the ambulance sirens; his attention was focused on the rhythm of her breathing and the beating of her heart against his chest.

She was so cold, so still. If only he could give her his warmth. He had made just such a wish once before, when his only child had lain dying in his arms. *Not this time,* he prayed, pulling her tightly against him. *Don't take her from me, too....*

That plea rang over and over in his head as they carried her down the mountain. The descent ended in mass confusion as ambulance workers crowded in to help. David was shunted to the sidelines, a helpless observer of a battle he wasn't trained to fight.

He watched the ambulance scream off into the darkness. He imagined the emergency room, the lights, the people in white. He couldn't bear to think of Kate, lying helplessly in all that chaos. But that's where she would be soon. It was her only chance.

A hand clapped him gently on the shoulder. "You okay, Davy?" Pokie asked.

"Yeah." He sighed deeply. "Yeah."

"She'll be all right. I got a crystal ball on these things." He turned at the sound of a sneeze.

Sergeant Brophy approached, his face half-buried in a handkerchief. "They've brought the body up," said Brophy. "Got tangled up in all that—that—" he blew his nose "—shrubbery. Broken neck. Wanna take a look before it goes to the morgue?"

"Never mind," Pokie grunted. "I'll take your word for it." As they walked to the car, he asked, "How did Dr. Santini handle the news?"

"That's the weird thing," replied Brophy. "When I told him about his wife, he sort of acted like—well, he'd expected it."

Pokie frowned at the covered body of Susan Santini, now being loaded into the ambulance. He sighed. "Maybe he did. Maybe he knew all along what was happening. But he didn't want to admit it. Even to himself."

Brophy opened the car door. "Where to, Lieutenant?"

"The hospital. And move it." Pokie nodded toward David. "This man's got some serious waiting to do."

IT WAS FOUR HOURS before David was allowed to see her. Four hours of pacing the fourth-floor waiting room. Four hours of walking back and forth past the same *National Enquirer* headline on the coffee table: Woman's Head Joined To Baboon's Body.

There was only one other person in the room, a mule-faced man who slouched beneath a No Smoking sign, puffing desperately on a cigarette. He stubbed out the butt and reached for another. "Getting late," the man commented. That was the extent of their conversation. Two words, uttered in a monotone. The man never said who he was waiting for. He never spoke of fear. It was there, plain in his eyes.

At eleven o'clock, the mule-faced man was called into the recovery room and David was left alone. He stood at the window, listening to the wail of an approaching ambulance. For the hundredth time, he looked at his watch. She'd been in surgery three hours. How long did it take to remove a bullet? Had something gone wrong?

At midnight, a nurse at last poked her head into the room. "Are you Mr. Ransom?"

He spun around, his heart instantly racing. "Yes!"

"I thought you'd want to know. Dr. Chesne's out of surgery."

"Then... She's all right?"

"Everything went just fine."

He let out a breath so heavy its release left him floating. *Thank you,* he thought. *Thank you.*

"If you'd like to go home, we'll call you when she—"

"I have to see her."

"She's still unconscious."

"I have to see her."

"I'm sorry, but we only allow immediate family into..." Her voice trailed off as she saw the dangerous look in his eyes. She cleared her throat. "Five minutes, Mr. Ransom. That's all. You understand?"

Oh, he understood, all right. And he didn't give a damn. He pushed past her, through the recovery-room doors.

He found her lying on the last gurney, her small, pale form drowning in bright lights and plastic tubes. There was only a limp white curtain separating her from the next patient. David hovered at the foot of her stretcher, afraid to move close, afraid to touch her for fear he might break one of those fragile limbs. He was reminded of a princess in a glass bell, lying in some deep forest: untouchable, unreachable. A cardiac monitor chirped overhead, marking the rhythm of her heart. Beautiful music. Good and strong and steady. Kate's heart. He stood there, immobile, as the nurses fussed with tubes, adjusted IV fluids and oxygen. A doctor came to examine Kate's lungs. David felt useless. He was like a great big boulder in everyone's path. He knew he should leave and let them do their job, but something kept him rooted to his spot. One of the nurses pointed to her watch and said sternly, "We really can't work around you. You'll have to leave now."

But he didn't. He wouldn't. Not until he knew everything would be all right.

"SHE'S WAKING UP."

The light of a dozen suns seemed to burn through her closed eyelids. She heard voices, vaguely familiar, murmuring in the void above her. Slowly, painfully, she opened her eyes.

What she saw first was the light, brilliant and inescapable, glaring down at her. Bit by bit, she made out the smiling face of a woman, someone she knew from some dim and distant past, though she couldn't quite remember why. She focused on the name tag: Julie Sanders, RN. Julie. Now she remembered.

"Can you hear me, Dr. Chesne?" Julie asked.

Kate made a feeble attempt to nod.

"You're in the recovery room. Are you in pain?"

Kate didn't know. Her senses were returning one by one, and pain had yet to reawaken. It took her a moment to register all the signals her brain was receiving. She felt the hiss of oxygen in her nostrils and heard the soft beep of a cardiac monitor somewhere over the bed. But pain? No. She felt only a terrible sense of emptiness. And exhaustion. She wanted to sleep....

More faces had gathered around the bed. Another nurse, a stethoscope draped around her neck. Dr. Tam, dour as always. And then she heard a voice, calling softly to her.

"Kate?"

She turned. Framed against the glare of lights, David's face was blackly haggard. In wonder, she reached up to touch him but found that her wrist was hopelessly tangled in what seemed like a multitude of plastic tubes. Too weak to struggle, she let her hand drop back to the bed.

That's when he took it. Gently, as if he were afraid he might break her.

"You're all right," he whispered, pressing his lips to her palm. "Thank God you're all right...."

"I don't remember...."

"You've been in surgery." He gave her a small, tense smile. "Three hours. It seemed like forever. But the bullet's out."

She remembered, then. The wind. The ridge. And Susan, quietly slipping away like a phantom. "She's dead?"

He nodded. "There was nothing anyone could do."

"And Guy?"

"He won't be able to walk for a while. I don't know how he made it to that phone. But he did."

For a moment she lay in silence, thinking of Guy, whose life was now as shattered as his leg. "He saved my life. And now he's lost everything...."

"Not everything. He still has his son."

Yes, she thought. *William will always be Guy's son.* Not by blood, but by something much stronger: by love. Out of all this tragedy, at least one thing would remain intact and good.

"Mr. Ransom, you really will have to leave," insisted Dr. Tam.

David nodded. Then he bent over and dutifully gave Kate a gruff and awkward kiss. If he had told her he loved her, if he had said anything at all, she might have found some joy in that dry touch of lips. But too quickly his hand melted away from hers.

Things seemed to move in a blur. Dr. Tam began asking questions she was too dazed to answer. The nurses bustled around her bed, changing IV bottles, disconnecting wires, tucking in sheets. She was given a pain shot. Within minutes, she felt herself sliding irresistibly toward sleep.

As they moved her out of the recovery room, she fought to stay awake. There was something important she had to say to David, something that couldn't wait. But there were so many people around and she lost track of his voice in the confusing buzz of conversation. She felt a burst of panic that this was her last chance to tell him she loved him. But even to the very edge of consciousness, some last wretched scrap of pride kept her silent. And so, in silence, she let herself be dragged once again into darkness.

DAVID STAYED in her hospital room until almost dawn. He sat by her bed, holding her hand, brushing the hair off her face. Every so often he would say her name, half hoping she would awaken. But whatever pain shot they'd given her was industrial strength; she scarcely stirred all night. If only once she'd called for him in her sleep, if she'd said even the first syllable of his name, it would have been enough. He would have known she needed him and then he would have told her he needed her. It wasn't the sort of thing a man could just come out and say to anyone. At least, *he* couldn't. In truth, he was worse off than poor mute Charlie Decker. At least Decker could express himself in a few lines of wretched poetry.

It was a long drive home.

As soon as he walked in the door, he called the hospital to check on her condition. "Stable." That was all they'd say but it was enough. He called a florist and ordered flowers delivered to Kate's room. Roses. Since he couldn't think of a message, he told the clerk to simply write "David." He fixed himself some coffee and toast and ate like a starved man, which he was, since he'd missed supper the night before. Then, dirty, unshaven, exhausted, he went into the living room and threw himself on the couch.

He thought about all the reasons he couldn't be in love. He'd carved out a nice, comfortable existence for himself. He looked around at the polished floor, the curtains, the books lined up in the glass cabinet. Then it struck him how sterile it all was. This wasn't the home of a living, breathing man. It was a shell, the way he was a shell.

What the hell, he thought. She probably wouldn't want him anyway. Their affair had been rooted in need. She'd been terrified and he, conveniently, had been there. Soon she'd be back on her feet, her career on track. You couldn't keep a woman like Kate down for long.

He admired her and he wanted her. But did he love her? He hoped not.

Because he, better than anyone else, knew that love was nothing more than a setup for grief.

DR. CLARENCE AVERY stood awkwardly in the doorway of Kate's hospital room and asked if he could come in. He was carrying a half dozen hideously tinted green carnations, which he waved at her as though he had no idea what one did with flowers. Tinted green ones, anyway. The stems were still wrapped in supermarket cellophane, price tag and all.

"These are for you," he said, just in case she wasn't quite certain about that point. "I hope... I hope you're not allergic to carnations. Or anything."

"I'm not. Thank you, Dr. Avery."

"It's nothing, really. I just..." His gaze wandered to the dozen long-stemmed red roses set in a porcelain vase on the nightstand. "Oh. But I see you've already gotten flowers. Roses." Sadly, he looked down at his green carnations the way one might study a dead animal.

"I prefer carnations," she replied. "Could you put them in water for me? I think I saw a vase under the sink."

"Certainly." He took the flowers over to the sink and as he bent down, she saw that, as usual, his pants were wrinkled and his socks didn't match. The carnations looked somehow touching, flopping about in the huge, watery vase. What mattered most was that they'd been delivered in person, which was more than could be said about the roses.

They had arrived while she was still sleeping. The card said simply, "David." He hadn't called or visited. She thought maybe he'd decided this was the time to make the break. All morning she'd alternated between wanting to tear the flowers to bits and wanting to gather them up and hug them. Now that was an apt analogy—hugging thorns to one's breast.

"Here," she said. "Put the carnations right next to me. Where I can smell them." She brusquely shoved the roses aside, an act that made her wince. The surgical incision had left her with dozens of stitches and it had taken a hefty dose of narcotics just to dull the pain. Carefully she eased back against the pillows.

Pleased that his offering was given such a place of honor, Dr. Avery took a moment of silence to admire the limp blossoms. Then he cleared his throat. "Dr. Chesne," he began, "I should tell you this isn't just a—a social visit."

"It's not?"

"No. It has to do with your position here at Mid Pac."

"Then there's been a decision," she said quietly.

"With all the new evidence that's come out, well..." He gave a little shrug. "I suppose I should have taken your side earlier. I'm sorry I didn't. I suppose I was... I'm just sorry." Shuffling, he looked down at his ink-stained lab coat. "I don't know why I've held on to this blasted chairmanship. It's never given me anything but ulcers. Anyway, I'm here to tell you we're offering you your old job back. There'll be nothing on your record. Just a notation that a lawsuit was filed against you and later dropped. Which it will be. At least, that's what I'm told."

"My old job," she murmured. "I don't know." Sighing, she turned and looked out the window. "I'm not even sure I want it back. You know, Dr. Avery, I've been thinking. About other places."

"You mean another hospital?"

"Another town." She smiled at him. "It's not so surprising, is it? I've had a lot of time to think these last few days. I've been wondering if I don't belong somewhere else. Away from all this—this ocean." *Away from David.*

"Oh, dear."

"You'll find a replacement. There must be hundreds of doctors begging to come to paradise."

"No, it's not that. I'm just surprised. After all the work Mr. Ransom put into this, I thought certainly you'd—"

"Mr. Ransom? What do you mean?"

"All those calls he made. To every member of the hospital board."

A parting gesture, she thought. *At least I should be grateful for that.*

"It was quite a turnaround, I must say. A plaintiff's attorney asking—demanding—we reinstate a doctor! But this morning, when he presented the police evidence and we heard Dr. Santini's statement, well, it took the board a full five minutes to make a decision." He frowned. "Mr. Ransom gave us the idea you wanted your job back."

"Maybe I did once," she replied, staring at the roses and wondering why she felt no sense of triumph. "But things change. Don't they?"

"I suppose they do." Avery cleared his throat and shuffled a little more. "Your job is there if you want it. And we'll certainly be needing you on staff. Especially with my retirement coming up."

She looked up in surprise. "You're retiring?"

"I'm sixty-four, you know. That's getting along. I've never seen much of the country. Never had the time. My wife and I, we used to talk about traveling after my retirement. Barb would've wanted me to enjoy myself. Don't you think?"

Kate smiled. "I'm sure she would have."

"Anyway..." He shot another glance at the drooping carnations. "They are rather pretty, aren't they?" He walked out of the room, chuckling. "Yes. Yes, much better than roses, I think. Much better."

Kate turned once again to the flowers. Red roses. Green carnations. What an absurd combination. Just like her and David.

IT WAS RAINING HARD when David came to see her late that afternoon. She was sitting alone in the solarium, gazing through the watery window at the courtyard below. The nurse had just washed and brushed her hair and it was drying as usual into those frizzy, little-girl waves she'd always hated. She didn't hear him as he walked into the room. Only when he said her name did she turn and see him standing there, his hair damp and windblown, his suit beaded with rain. He looked tired. Almost as tired as she felt. She wanted him to pull her close, to take her in his arms, but he didn't. He simply bent over and gave her an automatic kiss on the forehead and then he straightened again.

"Out of bed, I see. You must be feeling better," he remarked.

She managed a wan smile. "I guess I never was one for lying around all day."

"Oh. I brought you these." Almost as an afterthought, he handed her a small foil-wrapped box of chocolates. "I wasn't sure they'd let you eat anything yet. Maybe later."

She looked down at the box resting in her lap. "Thank you," she murmured. "And thank you for the roses." Then she turned and stared out at the rain.

There was a long silence, as if both of them had run out of things to say. The rain slid down the solarium windows, casting a watery rainbow of light on her folded hands.

"I just spoke with Avery," he finally said. "I hear you're getting your old job back."

"Yes. He told me. I guess that's something else I have to thank you for."

"What's that?"

"My job. Avery said you made a lot of phone calls."

"Just a few. Nothing, really." He took a deep breath and continued with forced cheerfulness, "So. You should be back at work in the O.R. in no time. With a big raise in pay, I hope. It must feel pretty good."

"I'm not sure I'm taking it—the job."

"What? Why on earth wouldn't you?"

She shrugged. "You know, I've been thinking about other possibilities. Other places."

"You mean besides Mid Pac?"

"I mean...besides Hawaii." He didn't say a thing, so she added, "There's really nothing keeping me here."

There was another long silence. Softly he said, "Isn't there?"

She didn't answer. He watched her, sitting so quiet, so still in her chair. And he knew he could wait around till doomsday and there she'd still be. *A fine pair we are,* he thought in disgust. They were two so-called intelligent people, and they couldn't hunt up a single word between them.

"Dr. Chesne?" A nurse appeared in the doorway. "Are you ready to go back to your room?"

"Yes," Kate answered. "I think I'd like to sleep."

"You do look tired." The nurse glanced at David. "Maybe it's time you left, sir."

"No," said David, suddenly drawing himself to his full height.

"Excuse me?"

"I'm not going to leave. Not yet." He looked long and hard at Kate. "Not until I've finished making a fool of myself. So could you leave us alone?"

"But, sir—"

"Please."

The nurse hesitated. Then, sensing that something momentous was looming in the balance, she retreated from the solarium.

Kate was watching him, her green eyes filled with uncertainty. And maybe fear. He reached down and gently touched her face.

"Tell me again what you just said," he murmured. "That you have nothing to keep you here."

"I don't. What I mean is—"

"Now tell me the real reason you want to leave."

She was silent. But he saw the answer in her eyes, those soft and needy eyes. What he read there made him suddenly shake his head in wonder. "My God," he muttered. "You're a bigger coward than I am."

"A coward?"

"That's right. So am I." He turned away and with his hands in his pockets began to wander restlessly around the room. "I didn't plan to say this. Not yet, anyway. But here you're talking about leaving. And it seems I don't have much of a choice." He stopped and looked out the window. Outside, the world had gone silvery. "Okay." He sighed. "Since you're not going to say it, I guess I will. It's not easy for me. It's never been easy. After Noah died, I thought I'd taught myself not to feel. I've managed it up till now. Then I met you and..." He shook his head and laughed. "God, I wish I had one of Charlie Decker's poems handy. Maybe I could quote a few lines. Anything to sound halfway intelligible. Poor old Charlie had that much over me: his eloquence. For that I envy him." He looked at her and a half smile was on his lips. "I still haven't said it, have I? But you get the general idea."

"Coward," she whispered.

Laughing, he went to her and tilted her face up to his. "All right, then. I love you. I love your stubbornness and your pride. And your independence. I didn't want to. I thought I was going along just fine on my own. But now that it's happened, I can't imagine ever not loving you." He pulled away, offering her a chance to retreat.

She didn't. She remained perfectly still. Her throat seemed to have swollen shut. She was still clutching the little box of candy, trying to convince herself it was real. That he was real.

"It won't be easy, you know," he said.

"What won't?"

"Living with me. There'll be days you'll want to wring my neck or scream at me, anything to make me say 'I love you.' But just because I don't say it doesn't mean I don't feel it. Because I do." He let out a long sigh. "So. I guess that's about it. I hope you were listening. Because I'm not sure I could come up with a repeat performance. And damned if this time I forgot to bring my tape recorder."

"I've been listening," she replied softly.

"And?" he asked, not daring to let his gaze leave her face. "Do I hear the verdict? Or is the jury still out?"

"The jury," she whispered, "is in a state of shock. And badly in need of mouth-to-mouth—"

If resuscitation was what he'd intended, his kiss did quite the opposite. He lowered his face to hers and she felt the room spin. Every muscle of her neck seemed to go limp at once and her head sagged back against the chair.

"Now, fellow coward," he murmured, his lips hovering close to hers. "Your turn."

"I love you," she said weakly.

"That's the verdict I was hoping for."

She thought he would kiss her again but he suddenly pulled away and frowned. "You're looking awfully pale. I think I should call the nurse. Maybe a little oxygen—"

She reached up and wound her arms around his neck. "Who needs oxygen?" she whispered, just before his mouth settled warmly on hers.

Epilogue

There was a brand-new baby visiting the house, a fact made apparent by the indignant squalls coming from the upstairs bedroom.

Jinx poked her head through the doorway. "What in heaven's name is the matter with Emma now?"

Gracie, her mouth clamped around a pale pink safety pin, looked up helplessly from the screaming infant. "It's all so new to me, Jinx. I'm afraid I've lost my touch."

"Your touch? When were you ever around babies?"

"Oh, you're right." Gracie sighed, tugging the pin out of her mouth. "I suppose I never did have the touch, did I? That explains why I'm doing such a shoddy job of it."

"Now, dear. Babies take practice, that's all. It's like the piano. All those scales, up and down, every day."

Gracie shook her head. "The piano's much easier." Resignedly, she stuffed the safety pin back between her lips. "And look at these impossible diapers! I just don't see how anyone could poke a pin through all that paper and plastic."

Jinx burst out in hoots of laughter, so loud that Gracie turned bright red with indignation. "And exactly what did I say that was so funny?" Gracie demanded.

"Darling, haven't you figured it out?" Jinx reached out and peeled open the adhesive flap. "You don't use pins. That's the whole *point* of disposable diapers." She looked down in astonishment as baby Emma suddenly let out a lusty howl.

"You see?" sniffed Gracie. "She didn't like your pun, either."

A LEAF DRIFTED DOWN from the monkeypod tree and settled beside the fresh gathering of daisies. Chips of sunlight dappled the grass and danced on David's fair hair. How many times had he grieved alone in the shade of this tree? How many times had he stood in silent communion with his son? All the other visits seemed to blend together in a gray and dismal remembrance of mourning.

But today he was smiling. And in his mind, he could hear the smile in Noah's voice, as well.

Is that you, Daddy?

Yes, Noah. It's me. You have a sister.

I've always wanted a sister.

She sucks the same two fingers you did....

Does she?

And she always smiles when I walk in her room.

So did I. Remember?

Yes, I remember.

And you'll never forget, will you, Daddy? Promise me, you'll never forget.

No, I'll never forget. I swear to you, Noah, I will never, ever forget....

David turned and through his tears he saw Kate, standing a few feet away. No words were needed between them. Only a look. And an outstretched hand.

Together they walked away from that sad little patch of grass. As they emerged from the shade of the tree, David suddenly stopped and pulled her into his arms.

She touched his face. He felt the warmth of the sun in her fingertips. And he was healed.

He was healed.

#1 *New York Times* bestselling author

NORA ROBERTS

Presents a brand-new book in the beloved MacGregor series:

THE WINNING HAND
(SSE#1202)

October 1998 in

Silhouette SPECIAL EDITION®

Innocent Darcy Wallace needs Mac Blade's protection in the high-stakes world she's entered. But who will protect Mac from the irresistible allure of this vulnerable beauty?

Coming in March, the much-anticipated novel,
THE MacGREGOR GROOMS
Also, watch for the MacGregor stories
where it all began!

December 1998:
THE MacGREGORS: Serena—Caine

February 1999:
THE MacGREGORS: Alan—Grant

April 1999:
THE MacGREGORS: Daniel—Ian

Available at your favorite retail outlet, only from

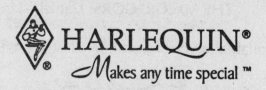

*The only way to be a bodyguard
is to stay as close as a lover...*

STAND
BY ME

The relationship between bodyguard and client is always close...sometimes too close for comfort. This September, join in the adventure as three bodyguards, protecting three very distracting and desirable charges, struggle not to cross the line between business and pleasure.

STRONG ARMS OF THE LAW
by Dallas SCHULZE

NOT WITHOUT LOVE
by Roberta LEIGH

SOMETIMES A LADY
by Linda Randall WISDOM

*Sometimes danger makes
a strange bedfellow!*

Available September 1998 wherever
Harlequin and Silhouette books are sold.

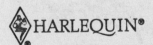 

WHEN THINGS START TO HEAT UP
HIRE A BODYGUARD...

YOUR BODY IS OUR BUSINESS

Discreet, professional
protection

1-800-555-HERO

AND THEN IT GETS HOTTER!

There's a bodyguard agency in San Francisco where you can always find a HERO FOR HIRE, and the man of your sexiest fantasies.... Five of your favorite Temptation authors have just been there:

JOANN ROSS *1-800-HERO*
August 1998
KATE HOFFMANN *A BODY TO DIE FOR*
September 1998
PATRICIA RYAN *IN HOT PURSUIT*
October 1998
MARGARET BROWNLEY *BODY LANGUAGE*
November 1998
RUTH JEAN DALE *A PRIVATE EYEFUL*
December 1998

HERO FOR HIRE
A blockbuster miniseries.

Available at your favorite retail outlet.

HARLEQUIN®

Temptation

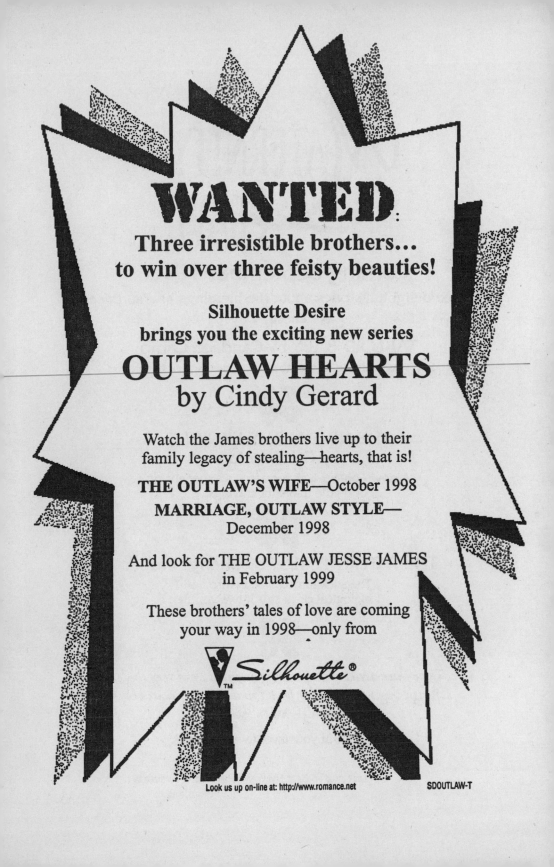

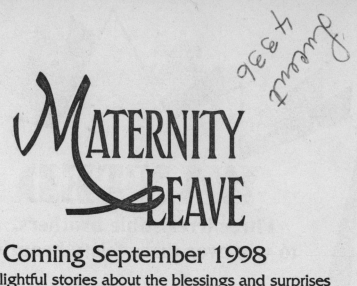